Short Stories *for Students*

National Advisory Board

Short Stories *for Students*

Presenting Analysis, Context, and Criticism on Commonly Studied Short Stories

Volume 23

Anne Marie Hacht, Project Editor

Foreword by Thomas E. Barden

Detroit • New York • San Francisco • San Diego • New Haven, Conn. • Waterville, Maine • London • Munich

Short Stories for Students, Volume 23

Project Editor
Anne Marie Hacht

Editorial
Sara Constantakis, Angela Doolin, Ira Mark Milne

Rights Acquisition and Management
Lisa Kincade, Jackie Jones, and Kim Smilay

Manufacturing
Drew Kalasky

Imaging and Multimedia
Lezlie Light, Mike Logusz, Kelly A. Quin

Product Design
Pamela A. E. Galbreath

Vendor Administration
Civie Green

Product Manager
Meggin Condino

For more information, contact
Thomson Gale
27500 Drake Rd.
Farmington Hills, MI 48331-3535
Or you can visit our Internet site at
http://www.gale.com

ISBN 0-7876-7031-6
ISSN 1092-7735

Printed in the United States of America
10 9 8 7 6 5 4 3 2 1

Table of Contents

Why Study Literature At All?

Short Stories for Students is designed to provide readers with information and discussion about a wide range of important contemporary and historical works of short fiction, and it does that job very well. However, I want to use this guest foreword to address a question that it does *not* take up. It is a fundamental question that is often ignored in high school and college English classes as well as research texts, and one that causes frustration among students at all levels, namely why study literature at all? Isn't it enough to read a story, enjoy it, and go about one's business? My answer (to be expected from a literary professional, I suppose) is no. It is not enough. It is a start; but it is not enough. Here's why.

First, literature is the only part of the educational curriculum that deals directly with the actual world of lived experience. The philosopher Edmund Husserl used the apt German term *die Lebenswelt*, "the living world," to denote this realm. All the other content areas of the modern American educational system avoid the subjective, present reality of everyday life. Science (both the natural and the social varieties) objectifies, the fine arts create and/or perform, history reconstructs. Only literary study persists in posing those questions we all asked before our schooling taught us to give up on them. Only literature gives credibility to personal perceptions, feelings, dreams, and the "stream of consciousness" that is our inner voice. Literature wonders about infinity, wonders why God permits evil, wonders what will happen to us after we die. Literature admits that we get our hearts broken, that people sometimes cheat and get away with it, that the world is a strange and probably incomprehensible place. Literature, in other words, takes on all the big and small issues of what it means to be human. So my first answer is that of the humanist: we should read literature and study it and take it seriously because it enriches us as human beings. We develop our moral imagination, our capacity to sympathize with other people, and our ability to understand our existence through the experience of fiction.

My second answer is more practical. By studying literature we can learn how to explore and analyze texts. Fiction may be about *die Lebenswelt*, but it is a construct of words put together in a certain order by an artist using the medium of language. By examining and studying those constructions, we can learn about language as a medium. We can become more sophisticated about word associations and connotations, about the manipulation of symbols, and about style and atmosphere. We can grasp how ambiguous language is and how important context and texture is to meaning. In our first encounter with a work of literature, of course, we are not supposed to catch all of these things. We are spellbound, just as the writer wanted us to be. It is as serious students of the writer's art that we begin to see how the tricks are done.

Seeing the tricks, which is another way of saying "developing analytical and close reading skills," is important above and beyond its intrinsic literary educational value. These skills transfer to other fields and enhance critical thinking of any kind. Understanding how language is used to construct texts is powerful knowledge. It makes engineers better problem solvers, lawyers better advocates and courtroom practitioners, politicians better rhetoricians, marketing and advertising agents better sellers, and citizens more aware consumers as well as better participants in democracy. This last point is especially important, because rhetorical skill works both ways when we learn how language is manipulated in the making of texts the result is that we become less susceptible when language is used to manipulate us.

My third reason is related to the second. When we begin to see literature as created artifacts of language, we become more sensitive to good writing in general. We get a stronger sense of the importance of individual words, even the sounds of words and word combinations. We begin to understand Mark Twain's delicious proverb "The difference between the right word and the almost right word is the difference between lightning and a lightning bug." Getting beyond the "enjoyment only" stage of literature gets us closer to becoming makers of word art ourselves. I am not saying that studying fiction will turn every student into a Faulkner or a Shakespeare. But it will make us more adaptable and effective writers, even if our art form ends up being the office memo or the corporate annual report.

Studying short stories, then, can help students become better readers, better writers, and even better human beings. But I want to close with a warning. If your study and exploration of the craft, history, context, symbolism, or anything else about a story starts to rob it of the magic you felt when you first read it, it is time to stop. Take a break, study another subject, shoot some hoops, or go for a run. Love of reading is too important to be ruined by school. The early twentieth century writer Willa Cather, in her novel *My Antonia*, has her narrator Jack Burden tell a story that he and Antonia heard from two old Russian immigrants when they were teenagers. These immigrants, Pavel and Peter, told about an incident from their youth back in Russia that the narrator could recall in vivid detail thirty years later. It was a harrowing story of a wedding party starting home in sleds and being chased by starving wolves. Hundreds of wolves attacked the group's sleds one by one as they sped across the snow trying to reach their village. In a horrible revelation, the old Russians revealed that the groom eventually threw his own bride to the wolves to save himself. There was even a hint that one of the old immigrants might have been the groom mentioned in the story. Cather has her narrator conclude with his feelings about the story. "We did not tell Pavel's secret to anyone, but guarded it jealously as if the wolves of the Ukraine had gathered that night long ago, and the wedding party had been sacrificed, just to give us a painful and peculiar pleasure." That feeling, that painful and peculiar pleasure, is the most important thing about literature. Study and research should enhance that feeling and never be allowed to overwhelm it.

Thomas E. Barden
Professor of English and
Director of Graduate English Studies
The University of Toledo

Introduction

Purpose of the Book

The purpose of *Short Stories for Students* (*SSfS*) is to provide readers with a guide to understanding, enjoying, and studying short stories by giving them easy access to information about the work. Part of Gale's "For Students" Literature line, *SSfS* is specifically designed to meet the curricular needs of high school and undergraduate college students and their teachers, as well as the interests of general readers and researchers considering specific short fiction. While each volume contains entries on "classic"stories frequently studied in classrooms, there are also entries containing hard-to-find information on contemporary stories, including works by multicultural, international, and women writers.

The information covered in each entry includes an introduction to the story and the story's author; a plot summary, to help readers unravel and understand the events in the work; descriptions of important characters, including explanation of a given character's role in the narrative as well as discussion about that character's relationship to other characters in the story; analysis of important themes in the story; and an explanation of important literary techniques and movements as they are demonstrated in the work.

In addition to this material, which helps the readers analyze the story itself, students are also provided with important information on the literary and historical background informing each work. This includes a historical context essay, a box comparing the time or place the story was written to modern Western culture, a critical overview essay, and excerpts from critical essays on the story or author. A unique feature of *SSfS* is a specially commissioned critical essay on each story, targeted toward the student reader.

To further aid the student in studying and enjoying each story, information on media adaptations is provided (if available), as well as reading suggestions for works of fiction and nonfiction on similar themes and topics. Classroom aids include ideas for research papers and lists of critical sources that provide additional material on the work.

Selection Criteria

The titles for each volume of *SSfS* were selected by surveying numerous sources on teaching literature and analyzing course curricula for various school districts. Some of the sources surveyed include: literature anthologies, *Reading Lists for College-Bound Students: The Books Most Recommended by America's Top Colleges*; *Teaching the Short Story: A Guide to Using Stories from around the World*, by the National Council of Teachers of English (NCTE); and "A Study of High School Literature Anthologies," conducted by Arthur Applebee at the Center for the Learning and Teaching of Literature and sponsored by the National Endowment for the Arts and the Office of Educational Research and Improvement.

Input was also solicited from our advisory board, as well as educators from various areas. From these discussions, it was determined that each volume should have a mix of "classic" stories (those works commonly taught in literature classes) and contemporary stories for which information is often hard to find. Because of the interest in expanding the canon of literature, an emphasis was also placed on including works by international, multicultural, and women authors. Our advisory board members—educational professionals—helped pare down the list for each volume. Works not selected for the present volume were noted as possibilities for future volumes. As always, the editor welcomes suggestions for titles to be included in future volumes.

How Each Entry Is Organized

Each entry, or chapter, in *SSfS* focuses on one story. Each entry heading lists the title of the story, the author's name, and the date of the story's publication. The following elements are contained in each entry:

- **Introduction:** a brief overview of the story which provides information about its first appearance, its literary standing, any controversies surrounding the work, and major conflicts or themes within the work.
- **Author Biography:** this section includes basic facts about the author's life, and focuses on events and times in the author's life that may have inspired the story in question.
- **Plot Summary:** a description of the events in the story. Lengthy summaries are broken down with subheads.
- **Characters:** an alphabetical listing of the characters who appear in the story. Each character name is followed by a brief to an extensive description of the character's role in the story, as well as discussion of the character's actions, relationships, and possible motivation.

  Characters are listed alphabetically by last name. If a character is unnamed—for instance, the narrator in "The Eatonville Anthology"—the character is listed as "The Narrator" and alphabetized as "Narrator." If a character's first name is the only one given, the name will appear alphabetically by that name.
- **Themes:** a thorough overview of how the topics, themes, and issues are addressed within the story. Each theme discussed appears in a separate subhead, and is easily accessed through the boldface entries in the Subject/Theme Index.
- **Style:** this section addresses important style elements of the story, such as setting, point of view, and narration; important literary devices used, such as imagery, foreshadowing, symbolism; and, if applicable, genres to which the work might have belonged, such as Gothicism or Romanticism. Literary terms are explained within the entry, but can also be found in the Glossary.
- **Historical Context:** this section outlines the social, political, and cultural climate *in which the author lived and the work was created.* This section may include descriptions of related historical events, pertinent aspects of daily life in the culture, and the artistic and literary sensibilities of the time in which the work was written. If the story is historical in nature, information regarding the time in which the story is set is also included. Long sections are broken down with helpful subheads.
- **Critical Overview:** this section provides background on the critical reputation of the author and the story, including bannings or any other public controversies surrounding the work. For older works, this section may include a history of how the story was first received and how perceptions of it may have changed over the years; for more recent works, direct quotes from early reviews may also be included.
- **Criticism:** an essay commissioned by *SSfS* which specifically deals with the story and is written specifically for the student audience, as well as excerpts from previously published criticism on the work (if available).
- **Sources:** an alphabetical list of critical material used in compiling the entry, with bibliographical information.
- **Further Reading:** an alphabetical list of other critical sources which may prove useful for the student. Includes full bibliographical information and a brief annotation.

In addition, each entry contains the following highlighted sections, set apart from the main text as sidebars:

- **Media Adaptations:** if available, a list of film and television adaptations of the story, including source information. The list also includes stage adaptations, audio recordings, musical adaptations, etc.
- **Topics for Further Study:** a list of potential study questions or research topics dealing with the story. This section includes questions related to other disciplines the student may be studying, such as American history, world history, science, math, government, business, geography, economics, psychology, etc.

- **Compare and Contrast:** an "at-a-glance" comparison of the cultural and historical differences between the author's time and culture and late twentieth century or early twenty-first century Western culture. This box includes pertinent parallels between the major scientific, political, and cultural movements of the time or place the story was written, the time or place the story was set (if a historical work), and modern Western culture. Works written after 1990 may not have this box.
- **What Do I Read Next?:** a list of works that might complement the featured story or serve as a contrast to it. This includes works by the same author and others, works of fiction and nonfiction, and works from various genres, cultures, and eras.

Other Features

SSfS includes "Why Study Literature At All?," a foreword by Thomas E. Barden, Professor of English and Director of Graduate English Studies at the University of Toledo. This essay provides a number of very fundamental reasons for studying literature and, therefore, reasons why a book such as *SSfS*, designed to facilitate the study of literture, is useful.

A Cumulative Author/Title Index lists the authors and titles covered in each volume of the *SSfS* series.

A Cumulative Nationality/Ethnicity Index breaks down the authors and titles covered in each volume of the *SSfS* series by nationality and ethnicity.

A Subject/Theme Index, specific to each volume, provides easy reference for users who may be studying a particular subject or theme rather than a single work. Significant subjects from events to broad themes are included, and the entries pointing to the specific theme discussions in each entry are indicated in **boldface**.

Each entry may include illustrations, including photo of the author, stills from film adaptations (if available), maps, and/or photos of key historical events.

Citing Short Stories for Students

When writing papers, students who quote directly from any volume of *SSfS* may use the following general forms to document their source. These examples are based on MLA style; teachers may request that students adhere to a different style, thus, the following examples may be adapted as needed.

When citing text from *SSfS* that is not attributed to a particular author (for example, the Themes, Style, Historical Context sections, etc.), the following format may be used:

> "The Celebrated Jumping Frog of Calavaras County." *Short Stories for Students*. Ed. Kathleen Wilson. Vol. 1. Detroit: Gale, 1997. 19–20.

When quoting the specially commissioned essay from *SSfS* (usually the first essay under the Criticism subhead), the following format may be used:

> Korb, Rena. Critical Essay on "Children of the Sea." *Short Stories for Students*. Ed. Kathleen Wilson. Vol. 1. Detroit: Gale, 1997. 39–42.

When quoting a journal or newspaper essay that is reprinted in a volume of *Short Stories for Students*, the following form may be used:

> Schmidt, Paul. "The Deadpan on Simon Wheeler." *Southwest Review* Vol. XLI, No. 3 (Summer, 1956), 270–77; excerpted and reprinted in *Short Stories for Students*, Vol. 1, ed. Kathleen Wilson (Detroit: Gale, 1997), pp. 29–31.

When quoting material from a book that is reprinted in a volume of *SSfS,* the following form may be used:

> Bell-Villada, Gene H. "The Master of Short Forms," in *García Márquez: The Man and His Work*. University of North Carolina Press, 1990, pp. 119–36; excerpted and reprinted in *Short Stories for Students*, Vol. 1, ed. Kathleen Wilson (Detroit: Gale, 1997), pp. 89–90.

We Welcome Your Suggestions

The editor of *Short Stories for Students* welcomes your comments and ideas. Readers who wish to suggest short stories to appear in future volumes, or who have other suggestions, are cordially invited to contact the editor. You may contact the editor via E-mail at: **ForStudentsEditors@thomson.com.** Or write to the editor at:

Editor, *Short Stories for Students*
Thomson Gale
27500 Drake Road
Farmington Hills, MI 48331-3535

Literary Chronology

1890: Katherine Anne Porter (Callie Russell Porter) is born on May 15 in Indian Creek, Texas.

1912: Mary Lavin is born in East Walpole, Massachusetts.

1922: José Saramago is born on November 16 in Azinhaga, Ribatejo, Portugal.

1922: James Hurst is born near Jacksonville, North Carolina.

1935: Annie Proulx is born in Norwich, Connecticut.

1938: Raymond Carver is born on May 25 in Clatskanie, Oregon.

1942: Stuart Dybek is born on April 10.

1943: James Alan McPherson is born in Savannah, Georgia.

1945: Thom Douglas Jones is born on January 26 in Aurora, Illinois.

1949: Haruki Murakami is born on January 12 in Ashiya City, Japan.

1960: Katherine Anne Porter's "Holiday" is published.

1960: James Hurst's "The Scarlet Ibis" is published.

1962: Carolyn Ferrell is born on April 29 in Brooklyn, New York.

1966: Katherine Anne Porter's *Collected Stories* wins the Pulitzer Prize for Fiction.

1968: Heidi Julavits is born in Portland, Maine.

1973: Julie Orringer is born on June 12 in Miami, Florida.

1977: James Alan McPherson's "Elbow Room" is published.

1979: James Alan McPherson's *Elbow Room* wins the Pulitzer Prize for Fiction.

1980: Katherine Anne Porter dies on September 18.

1983: Raymond Carver's "A Small, Good Thing" is published.

1984: Stuart Dybek's "Hot Ice" is published.

1984: Raymond Carver's *Cathedral* is nominated for the Pulitzer Prize for Fiction.

1988: Raymond Carver dies on August 2 of lung cancer at his home in Port Washington.

1991: Haruki Murakami's "The Elephant Vanishes" is published.

1993: Carolyn Ferrell's "Proper Library" is published.

1993: Thom Jones's "The Pugilist at Rest" is published.

1996: Mary Lavin dies in March in Dublin, Ireland.

1998: Annie Proulx's "Brokeback Mountain" is published.

1998: Mary Lavin's "In the Middle of the Fields" is published.

1998: Heidi Julavits's "Marry the One Who Gets There First" is published.

1998: José Saramago wins the Nobel Prize for Literature.

2000: Mary Swan's "The Deep" is published.

2003: Julie Orringer's "The Smoothest Way Is Full of Stones" is published.

2004: José Saramago's "The Centaur" is published.

Acknowledgments

The editors wish to thank the copyright holders of the excerpted criticism included in this volume and the permissions managers of many book and magazine publishing companies for assisting us in securing reproduction rights. We are also grateful to the staffs of the Detroit Public Library, the Library of Congress, the University of Detroit Mercy Library, Wayne State University Purdy/Kresge Library Complex, and the University of Michigan Libraries for making their resources available to us. Following is a list of the copyright holders who have granted us permission to reproduce material in this volume of ***Short Stories for Students (SSfS)***. Every effort has been made to trace copyright, but if omissions have been made, please let us know.

COPYRIGHTED MATERIALS IN *SSfS*, VOLUME 23, WERE REPRODUCED FROM THE FOLLOWING PERIODICALS:

Critique, v. 24, 1982. Copyright © 1982 by Helen Dwight Reid Educational Foundation. Reproduced with permission of the Helen Dwight Reid Educational Foundation, published by Heldref Publications, 1319 18th Street, NW, Washington, DC 20036-1802.—***Dissent***, v. 47, summer, 2000. Copyright © 2000 by Dissent Publishing Corporation. Reproduced by permission.—***Houston Chronicle***, November 14, 2003 for 'Dark Debut Skims Surface of Emotions,' by Harvey Grossinger. Reproduced by permission of the author.—***Los Angeles Times Book Review***, April 4, 1993. Reproduced by permission.—***MELUS***, v. 20, summer, 1995. Copyright MELUS: The Society for the Study of Multi-Ethnic Literature of the United States, 1995. Reproduced by permission.—***Missouri Review***, v. 22, 1999. Reproduced by permission.—***Nation***, v. 257, September 6, 1993. Copyright © 1993 by The Nation Magazine/The Nation Company, Inc. Reproduced by permission.—***New York Times***, September 25, 1977 for "White and Black and Everything Else," by Robie Macauley. Copyright © 1977 by The New York Times Company. Reproduced by permission of Pamela Painter, on behalf of Robie Macauley.—***Ploughshares***, v. 19, fall, 1993 for a review of "The Pugilist at Rest," by Kevin Miller. Reproduced by permission of the author.—***PN Review***, v. 16, 1989. Copyright © Poetry Nation Review, 1989. Reproduced by permission of Carcanet Press Limited.—***Portuguese Studies***, v. 15, 1999. Copyright © Modern Humanities Research Association 1999. Reproduced by permission of the publisher.—***Progressive***, September, 1999. Copyright © 1999 by The Progressive, Inc. Reproduced by permission of The Progressive, 409 East Main Street, Madison, WI 53703, www.progressive.org.—***Publishers Weekly***, v. 228, September 20, 1991; v. 250, November 3, 2003. Copyright © 1991, 2003 by Reed Publishing USA. All reproduced from *Publishers Weekly*, published by the Bowker Magazine Group of Cahners Publishing Co., a division of Reed Publishing USA., by permission—***Review of Contemporary Fiction***, v. 13, fall, 1993. Copyright © 1993 *The Review of Contemporary Fiction*. Reproduced by permission.—***Studies in Short Fiction***, v. 23, summer, 1986; v. 31, summer, 1994. Copyright © 1986, 1994 by Studies in Short Fiction. All reproduced by permission.—***Women's Studies***, v. 25, November, 1995. © 1995 by OPA (Oversees Publishers Association) Amsterdam B.V. All rights reserved. Reproduced by permission of Taylor & Francis Group, LLC, http://www.taylorandfrancis.com, and the author.—***World Literature Today***, v. 68, spring, 1994; v. 71, winter, 1997; v. 74, spring, 2000. Copyright © 1994, 1997, 2000 by *World Literature Today*. All reproduced by permission of the publisher.

COPYRIGHTED MATERIALS IN *SSfS*, VOLUME 23, WERE REPRODUCED FROM THE FOLLOWING BOOKS:

Saltzman, Arthur M., From ***Understanding Raymond Carver***, University of South Carolina Press, 1988. Copryight © University of South Carolina 1988. Reproduced by permission.

Contributors

Bryan Aubrey: Aubrey holds a Ph.D. in English and has published many articles on literature. Entries on *Marry the One Who Gets There First*, *The Pugilist at Rest*, *A Small, Good Thing*, and *The Smoothest Way Is Full of Stones*. Original essays on *Marry the One Who Gets There First*, *The Pugilist at Rest*, *A Small, Good Thing*, and *The Smoothest Way Is Full of Stones*.

Timothy Dunham: Dunham has a master's degree in communication and bachelor's degree in English. Original essay on *The Deep*.

Sheldon Goldfarb: Goldfarb has a Ph.D. in English and has published two books on the Victorian author William Makepeace Thackeray. Original essays on *Proper Library* and *The Scarlet Ibis*.

Anna Maria Hong: Hong is a published poet and an editor of the fiction and memoir anthology *Growing Up Asian American*. Entry on *The Centaur* and *The Elephant Vanishes*. Original essays on *The Centaur* and *The Elephant Vanishes*.

David Kelly: Kelly is an instructor of creative writing and literature. Entries on *Elbow Room* and *Hot Ice*. Original essays on *Elbow Room* and *Hot Ice*.

Melodie Monahan: Monahan has a Ph.D. in English and operates an editing service, The Inkwell Works. Original essay on *The Deep*.

Wendy Perkins: Perkins is a professor of American and English literature and film. Entries on *Brokeback Mountain* and *In the Middle of the Fields*. Original essays on *Brokeback Mountain* and *In the Middle of the Fields*.

Laura Pryor: Pryor has a bachelor of arts from the University of Michigan and twenty years experience in professional and creative writing. Entries on *Holiday* and *Proper Library*. Original essays on *Elbow Room*, *Holiday*, *Marry the One Who Gets There First*, and *Proper Library*.

David Remy: Remy is a freelance writer in Warrington, Florida. Original essays on *Proper Library* and *The Scarlet Ibis*.

Claire Robinson: Robinson is a writer and editor. Entry on *The Scarlet Ibis*. Original essay on *The Scarlet Ibis*.

Carol Ullmann: Ullmann is a freelance writer and editor. Entry on *The Deep*. Original essay on *The Deep*.

Bonnie Weinreich: Weinreich has a bachelor's degree in English and is a freelance writer and former reporter for a daily newspaper. Original essay on *Elbow Room* and *Marry the One Who Gets There First*.

Brokeback Mountain

Annie Proulx

1998

Annie Proulx's short story "Brokeback Mountain" gained a great deal of attention before it was collected into her *Close Range: Wyoming Stories* in 1999. It was first published in the *New Yorker* in 1998 and subsequently won the magazine's award for fiction that year. It also appeared in the 1998 edition of *The O. Henry Stories*. Recognizing that it was the strongest story in her collection, Proulx placed it at the end of the book. When the reviews of *Close Range* appeared, "Brokeback Mountain" was consistently singled out for its evocative detail and compelling narrative.

The story chronicles the relationship between Ennis del Mar and Jack Twist, two men who develop a deep love for each other but who are forced to live separate lives in an intolerant world. They meet as teenagers hired to herd sheep on Brokeback Mountain in Wyoming. Their quick friendship soon evolves into a strong sexual and emotional union—one that they fear may eventually cost them their lives. As Proulx traces the development of the love that grows between these two men and the forces that try to impede that love, she shapes the interplay of desire and denial into a heartbreaking story of loss and endurance.

Author Biography

Annie Proulx was born in Norwich, Connecticut, in 1935 to George and Lois Proulx. Her ancestors had lived in the area of Connecticut for over

Annie Proulx John Harding/Time Life Pictures/Getty Images

350 years as farmers, artists, and mill workers. During Annie's youth, her father worked in the textile industry, so the family moved all over the country as he advanced his career. Annie attended high school in North Carolina and Maine; the family also spent time in Vermont and Rhode Island.

After graduating high school, Proulx attended the University of Vermont, where she received her bachelor of arts in 1969. She then attended graduate school in Montreal at Sir George Williams University where she received her master of arts in 1973.

Proulx's mother, Lois, was an artist and had a strong family tradition of oral story-telling. Many of her inventive ancestors could tell a story using everyday objects. This tradition helped to spawn Annie's interest in telling stories of her own. Proulx began writing initially to support her three children. She wrote mostly informational books that covered topics ranging from canoeing to African beadwork. During this period, she somehow found time to write fiction as well, which eventually was collected into *Heart Songs and Other Stories* in 1988.

After the success of this collection, her publisher persuaded her to write a novel. Her first, *Postcards* (1992), is about the decline of the American farm family. *Postcards* won the PEN/Faulkner Award as well as rave reviews from publications such as the *New York Times*.

Proulx had another novel published the following year, *The Shipping News*, which won her even more critical acclaim as well as a Pulitzer Prize. This novel captured her love for Newfoundland's history, geography, and people. It illustrated the struggle between the harsh geography and climate of the region and its inhabitants.

Her next novel, *Accordion Crimes*, published in 1996, gained decent reviews, although not as strong as those for *The Shipping News* and *Postcards*. *Accordion Crimes* did, however, earn Proulx the Dos Passos Prize for literature.

After this novel, Proulx decided to go back to her first love, short-story writing. She prefers writing short stories to novels since she enjoys the challenges involved with making every word count. Her collection of short stories *Close Range: Wyoming Stories*, published in 1999, explores myths of the West, in which Proulx had been interested since she moved to Wyoming in 1995. The collection earned her overwhelmingly positive reviews. "Brokeback Mountain," the most critically acclaimed story in the collection, earned the *New Yorker* Award for fiction in 1998 and has been often anthologized, including in *The O. Henry Stories* published in 1998.

Plot Summary

Part 1

"Brokeback Mountain" begins in the present with Ennis Del Mar waking up in his trailer parked on the Wyoming ranch where he has been working. He thinks about finding a new job since the owner is ready to sell the ranch and acknowledges that he may have to live with his daughter for a while. This morning, though, he feels happy because he dreamed of Jack Twist the night before and of their time together on Brokeback Mountain.

At this point, the narrative shifts to 1983, when he and Jack were both teenagers during Ennis's first summer on the mountain where they worked as sheep herders. Day after day, Ennis tends the camp while Jack herds the sheep and sleeps out on the mountain with them. One day, when Jack complains about his "commutin four hours a day," he accepts Ennis's offer to switch jobs.

Every evening, they share supper by the campfire, "talking horses and rodeo, roughstock events, wrecks and injuries sustained," and other details of their hard lives in the West. Toward the end of the summer when they shift the camp, the distance Ennis has to ride out to the sheep grows longer and he begins to stay later at the camp at night. One evening, after the two sing drunken songs by the campfire, Ennis decides it is too late to go out to the sheep and so beds down at the campsite. After his shivering wakes Jack, the latter insists that Ennis share his bedroll. Soon after, the two have sex, something Ennis had never done before.

Their sexual activity becomes more frequent in the following days while they both insist that neither of them is "queer." One day the foreman, Joe Aguirre, watches them together through his binoculars. Toward the end of the summer, after Ennis spends an entire night with Jack, the sheep wander off and mix with another group of sheep. Ennis tries unsuccessfully to sort them out. When they come down off the mountain after the first snowfall, Aguirre notes with displeasure that the sheep count is low and the herd is mixed.

When Jack asks Ennis if he is coming back to the mountain the next summer, Ennis tells him that he will be getting married in December and then will try to find work on a ranch. Jack determines to go back home and then maybe to Texas, and the two say an awkward goodbye. As Ennis drives away, his gut wrenches and he retches along the side of the road. He feels "about as bad as he ever had," a feeling that stays with him for a long time.

Part 2

Ennis marries Alma and a year later their child is born. After the ranch where he was working folds, he reluctantly takes work on a road crew. When their second child is born, Alma convinces him to get a place in town so that she will not have to live on any more "lonesome ranches."

Four summers after their first on Brokeback Mountain, Jack visits Ennis. When Jack first arrives, he and Ennis share a passionate embrace, watched by Alma. When Jack meets Alma, he announces that he too is married and has one child. After a few awkward moments, Ennis and Jack leave, pick up a bottle of whiskey and head for a motel where they spend the night together.

They talk of how they missed each other and of Jack's career as a bull rider. Jack suggests that he married his wife, Lureen, because she came from a wealthy family. Ennis admits that he has been thinking about whether he is gay but insists that he is not. He explains that he does not enjoy sex with women, but he has not been with any other man. Jack declares the same. After the two express their passion for each other, Jack notes, "we got us a f—— situation here. Got a figure out what to do." Ennis determines that nothing can be done since they both have families and warns Jack that if they are seen together, they may be killed.

Jack informs Ennis that he thinks someone saw them together on the mountain, but does not tell him that it was Aguirre, who subsequently did not rehire Jack for the ranch. When Jack insists the two could get a ranch together, Ennis declares that he is stuck in his situation and cannot get out. He does not want to end up like a gay man in his hometown who was beaten to death by the locals. His father, who had taken him to see the corpse, would have, Ennis insists, done the same to him if he had walked into their motel room. The only future Ennis can see for the two of them is to get together once in a while, explaining "if you can't fix it you got to stand it." Despondent, Jack convinces Ennis to go with him for a few days into the mountains.

Part 3

Ennis and Alma grow apart as she begins to resent him for not finding a steady, well-paying job and for his occasional fishing trips with Jack. When she eventually divorces him, he returns to ranch work. He stays in touch with Alma, who has remarried, and with his children. One night when he visits them, Alma tells him that she knows that he and Jack never did any fishing on their trips together. When she voices her disgust over his relationship with Jack, Ennis physically threatens her and storms out to a bar where he picks a fight.

Media Adaptations

"Brokeback Mountain" was made into an award-winning film, starring Heath Ledger and Jake Gyllenhaal. Directed by Ang Lee, the film was released in 2005

During the following years, Ennis and Jack occasionally meet on different ranges throughout the West. One night, they catch each other up on their lives, both admitting affairs with women and problems with their own children. After complaining about the infrequency of their time together, Jack suggests that they move to Mexico, but Ennis declines, insisting that he has to stay and work. When Ennis expresses his pain over their separation, Jack reminds him that Ennis turned down a life together and declares that he can barely stand being apart from Ennis. Overwhelmed with emotion, Ennis drops to his knees. Later, Jack remembers a perfect moment of togetherness on Brokeback Mountain.

Part 4

Months later, when Ennis receives back a postcard he had sent to Jack marked "DECEASED," he calls Lureen, who informs him that Jack was killed when a tire blew up in his face. Ennis suspects, however, that he was murdered after he was caught with another man. He makes a trip to see Jack's parents and offers to take Jack's ashes up to Brokeback Mountain, where Jack had told Lureen that he wanted to be buried.

Jack's father admits that Jack had planned on bringing Ennis up to his family's ranch to work it with him. When Jack's father tells Ennis that not too long ago, Jack found another man that he wanted to bring to the ranch, Ennis realizes that Jack was murdered. As he notes Mr. Twist's coldness, Ennis remembers Jack telling him about a vicious beating he received from his father when he was a small child.

During the visit, Ennis goes up to Jack's room where he finds Jack's shirt, which is covered in Ennis's blood. He remembers Jack accidentally kneeing his nose during lovemaking on the mountain. Inside the shirt, he finds one of his own. Ennis then buries his face in Jack's shirt, hoping to be able to smell his scent, but there is nothing there. Before Ennis leaves, Mr. Twist informs him that Jack's ashes will be buried in the family plot, what Ennis calls that "grieving plain," instead of on the mountain.

The narrative then jumps back to the beginning of the story as Ennis orders a postcard of Brokeback Mountain in the local store. When it arrives, he pins it up in his trailer above the two shirts from Jack's room hung on a hanger. During that time, a young Jack appears in his dreams along with visions of their time at Brokeback Mountain, which would fill him sometimes with grief, sometimes with joy. The story ends with what has become Ennis's motto: "if you can't fix it you've got to stand it."

Characters

Joe Aguirre

Joe Aguirre, the foreman of the ranch that hires Ennis and Jack to herd sheep on Brokeback Mountain, considers the two to be a "[p]air of deuces going nowhere." He spies on them through binoculars, watching their lovemaking. His disgust over their homosexuality prompts him to refuse to rehire Jack the following summer. Joe's attitude foreshadows the prejudice the two will encounter as they continue their relationship.

Alma Del Mar

Alma Del Mar is present to show Ennis's failure to adopt a conventional heterosexual life. She adds to Ennis's sense of shame with "her misery voice" and her growing resentment over his relationship with Jack and his emotional distance from her and their children.

Ennis Del Mar

Nineteen-year-old Ennis Del Mar accepts a herding job on Brokeback Mountain in Wyoming so that he can earn enough money to marry Alma Beers. He was forced to drop out of high school after his parents died and now has no other prospects. He was brought up, though, "to hard work and privation," and "inured to the stoic life." This stoicism helps him endure the pain of Jack's death.

Up on the mountain, he begins a passionate yet limited relationship with Jack Twist. When Jack initiates their first sexual encounter, Ennis immediately responds since he "ran full-throttle on all roads whether fence mending or money spending." While on the mountain, Ennis feels that he and Jack "*owned the world and nothing seemed wrong*," yet he ultimately is unable to accept his homosexuality, insisting that he is "no queer." Ennis continually tries to deny his feelings, at one point telling Jack "I like doin it with women" and "I never had no thoughts a doin it with another guy." Yet the fact that he prefers anal sex with Alma suggests the true nature of his sexuality.

Ennis struggles to follow the conventional path, marrying Alma and raising a family, but he cannot completely repress his passion for Jack. He is unable to establish a sense of permanence with

Alma, continually choosing unfulfilling jobs and small apartments that "could be left at any time." Eventually, his emotional distance from Alma breaks up their marriage.

Ennis's shame over his sexual orientation makes it difficult for him to embrace Jack face to face. It also sometimes prompts violent outbursts. His father had taught him to solve problems with his fists when Ennis's older brother kept beating him up. This streak emerges when Alma voices her disgust over his relationship with Jack and in a jealous response to Jack's suggestion that he has been with other men in Mexico. Ennis warns him, "all them things I don't know could get you killed if I should come to know them."

Ennis's internalized homophobia and stoicism allow him to endure the long separations from Jack and Jack's death. He spends his final years alone, dreaming of his time with Jack on Brokeback Mountain.

Mr. Del Mar

Ennis's father, Mr. Del Mar, epitomizes the intolerant world that Ennis and Jack must face. Even though he never appears in the story, he has a strong impact on his son. His response to the murder of a homosexual man fills Ennis with shame and fear when his own homosexual longings emerge.

Jack Twist

Jack Twist comes to Brokeback Mountain because he is "crazy to be somewhere, anywhere else than Lightning Flat" where he grew up. Jack is able to express more freely his homosexuality, admitting that he never wanted a family. He engages in sexual relations with other men after he and Ennis leave Brokeback Mountain, which eventually gets him killed.

Since he conveys no sense of shame over his homosexuality, he has an easier time expressing his love for Ennis. He continually notes the magnitude of their feelings for each other, at one point insisting, "[t]his ain't no little thing that's happenin here." When Ennis refuses to spend more time with him, Jack becomes bitter and impatient. He recognizes the truth about their relationship in a way that Ennis cannot, noting that Ennis keeps him on a "short leash." Jack admits that his overwhelming, frustrated desire for Ennis has caused him to turn to other men. Yet Jack's deep love for him, which is not openly returned, causes him to declare to Ennis, "I wish I knew how to quit you."

Jack expresses the depth of his feeling for Ennis with his memory of a perfect moment they shared on the mountain. One day, Ennis had come up behind him and held him for a long time. That embrace became for him "the single moment of artless, charmed happiness in their separate and difficult lives." He longs to experience more of such moments with Ennis "in a way he could neither help nor understand."

Jack's lack of shame over his sexual orientation causes him to take too many chances in the intolerant world in which he lives. While his wife Lureen claims that Jack died when a tire he was fixing exploded in his face, Ennis understands that Jack was beaten to death, just like the homosexual man had been who lived in the town where Ennis grew up.

Lureen Twist

Jack marries Lureen because her family has money. She appears briefly in the story as a plot device in order to give Jack some financial options and to provide a conventional façade for him.

Mr. Twist

Mr. Twist is the embodiment of the masculine Western stereotype. Ennis recognizes his need to be "the stud duck in the pond" when he visits him after Jack's death. Mr. Twist displayed his cruelty when he beat Jack for his accidents in the bathroom and his insensitivity when he refuses to let Ennis take Jack's ashes to Brokeback Mountain.

Themes

Intolerance

The concept of masculinity in the American West does not include homosexuality. Western legends, in literature and film, glorify men who display courage in the face of overwhelming odds and who as pairs ride off together into the sunset or as individuals return to women waiting patiently in the schoolhouse or in the farmhouse. These mythic stereotypes reflect a predominantly conservative set of values in the American West that refuses to recognize as natural a sexual union between two men. Proulx placed her protagonists in this intolerant setting and traces the suffering they experience as a result.

From an early age both Ennis and Jack are taught harsh lessons on how to act like a man. Mr. Twist would not tolerate four-year-old Jack's

Topics for Further Study

- Read two other short stories in Proulx's *Close Range* and write an essay comparing and contrasting the main themes.
- Watch the film version of the story and prepare a classroom presentation using clips from the film that analyzes how the filmmaker translated the text to the screen.
- Investigate the measures being taken to combat hate crimes against homosexuals. Write an essay discussing the measures and their effectiveness.
- Write a short story or poem with the title "If You Can't Fix It You've Got to Stand It" that focuses on the subject of loss or on the internal dilemma one feels in enduring a situation which cannot be fixed.

accidents in the bathroom, especially one night when he flew into a rage and whipped him with his belt. The young Jack was forced to endure the abuse of his father urinating on him so that he would understand the proper way for a man to relieve himself.

Mr. Del Mar's hatred of homosexuals caused him to force his son to look at a man who had been beaten to death because he had dared to love another man. Ennis wonders whether his father was the murderer but is certain that if he ever discovered his son with Jack, he would kill him. Ennis and Jack understand that homosexuality "don't happen in Wyomin" and if it does, those involved soon flee or die.

The training Ennis and Jack received when they were children makes them wary of openly expressing their love for each other. Ennis is more wary than Jack, who takes too many chances and, as a result, ends up being beaten to death with a tire iron, much like the man Ennis had seen when he was young. Ennis's fear of a violent confrontation causes him to deny the intensity of his feelings for Jack and to reject Jack's offers to live together. Ennis's fears are reinforced by his wife's response to his relationship with Jack. While she tolerates her husband's homosexual tendencies for a while, she ultimately cannot cope with his emotional distance. She finally confronts him with her knowledge of what the two really did on their "fishing trips" together and calls him, "Jack Nasty."

Shame

Ennis's internalization of the belief that homosexuality is indecent and punishable by death causes him to be ashamed about the intensity of his feelings for Jack. At the beginning of their relationship on the mountain, he insists that he is not "queer," that their feelings for each other are not indicative of his sexual orientation.

His shame, coupled with his need to maintain the façade of his marriage in the face of public scrutiny, causes him to lie continually to Alma about his feelings for Jack, insisting that when she catches the two in a heated embrace, their actions are a result of their not having seen each other for four years. He also must deceive her each time he goes off with Jack, claiming that the two are on fishing trips. Alma discovers that he and Jack never actually fish on these trips when she tapes a note to his unused fishing rod.

His internalized homophobia makes him unable to accept himself or act congruently. This shame thus prevents him from escaping with Jack to a possibly more tolerant location, such as Mexico. Ennis needs to maintain the illusion of a conventional life, even if that life denies him the one person he desires most. Jack notes that as a result, all that they have left is their time on Brokeback Mountain, which Ennis thinks cast a spell on him, a belief that makes it easier for him to deal with his love for Jack.

Style

Setting as Symbol

Proulx uses setting details to heighten the the matic significance of the story. The most effective use of setting as symbol occurs when she juxtaposes harsh and beautiful images of the landscape's cruel beauty to suggest the difficult nature of Ennis's and Jack's relationship. Proulx presents this juxtaposition first when Ennis and Jack initially herd the sheep up to Brokeback Mountain. The narrator likens the sheep's movement up the trail to the flow of "dirty water through the timber and out above the tree line into the great flowery meadows and the coursing, endless wind." The contrast between the dirty sheep and the meadow flowers seems to foreshadow the love that will grow between the two men as well as the prejudice their relationship will inspire.

This foreshadowing is reinforced when Proulx juxtaposes the "sweetened" cold air of the mountain on their first morning with the phallic "rearing lodgepole pines . . . massed in slabs of somber malachite." When Ennis and Jack begin their sexual relationship, Proulx captures its harsh and exhilarating duality when she describes Jack and Ennis as "flying in the euphoric, bitter air" on the mountain.

After Jack dies, the landscape is filled with bleakness, containing no moments of beauty that can relieve Ennis's heartache. Then "the huge sadness of the northern plains rolled down on him" as he passes "desolate country" with "houses sitting blank-eyed in the weeds." Although he tries to convince Jack's father to let him take Jack's ashes up to Brokeback Mountain, the old man refuses, committing them instead to "the grieving plain" that echoes Ennis's suffering.

Historical Context

Stories of the American West

Stories about the American West gained attention in the mid-nineteenth century and remained a popular genre during the first part of the twentieth century. The early Westerns followed a formulaic, stereotypical pattern: the main characters were mythic heroes that represented the American spirit of self-reliance and courage. The world of the Western was dominated by men; women were relegated to lesser roles, either as titillating saloon prostitutes or virginal schoolmarms and motherly farm women. Settings were picturesque and plots melodramatic, with scenes of violence often interspersed with humor.

The most popular fiction focused on cowboys who emerged in dime novels at the end of the nineteenth century and stories in magazines such as *Atlantic*, *Harpers*, and *Scribner's*. Some of the most popular writers in this genre were Alfred Henry Lewis, Henry Wallace Phillips, William R. Lighton, Rex Beach, and O. Henry, who set some of his stories in Texas. Perhaps the most famous and acclaimed Western is Zane Grey's *Riders of the Purple Sage*, published in 1912.

Western stories lost popularity in the second half of the twentieth century when war heroes and hardboiled detectives took the cowboy's place. In the 1960s, writers began to break out of the confines of traditional subject and technique and gained new audiences who responded to narratives that focused on anti-heroes, such as those in Thomas Berger's *Little Big Man* (1964) and E. L. Doctorow's *Welcome to Hard Times* (1975), and minority cultures, as those found in the work of N. Scott Momaday, Maxine Hong Kingston, Simon Ortiz, and Leslie Silko.

Discrimination against Homosexuals

Although Congress has made it a crime to discriminate against anyone based on his/her race, religion, sex, or national origin, as of 2006 it has not recognized the same rights for homosexuals. Some states, however, including Connecticut, Hawaii, Massachusetts, New Jersey, and Wisconsin, have outlawed discrimination on the basis of sexual orientation. Sodomy statutes, which typically call for a three-month jail sentence and fine, are still on the books in many (predominantly southern) states.

Discrimination in the education system is supported in states such as Oklahoma and West Virginia where school boards are mandated by law to fire homosexual teachers. High school and college students in many states across the country find it difficult to organize gay and lesbian student organizations. Homosexuals have been blocked from participation in those occupations which involve children.

The government practices discrimination in the military and positions that require top secret security clearances. In 1993, President Clinton tried to end this discrimination with the "Don't Ask, Don't Tell, Don't Pursue" policy, which stated that military personnel would not be asked questions about their sexual orientation. Yet harassment and discrimination continue for anyone in the military who is openly gay or suspected of being so. The military has determined that homosexuals cannot have successful careers in any of its branches and so discharges approximately one hundred servicemen and women each year who have admitted to being gay. Security clearances are denied homosexuals under the presumption that they may become blackmail targets by ex-lovers.

In states that do not recognize the rights of homosexuals, housing can be refused by landlords and homeowners. While California, Connecticut,

Heath Ledger and Jake Gyllenhaal in a still from the movie Brokeback Mountain

Focus Features/The Kobal Collection

the District of Columbia, Hawaii, Maine, New Jersey, and Vermont do not as of 2006 recognize same-sex unions, they do grant beneficiary rights to partners in these long-term relationships. Same sex marriage, along with adoption rights, is recognized by several countries including Denmark, Sweden, and Canada.

Anti-gay attitudes in the United States have led to an increase in hate crimes against homosexuals. This issue attracted national attention after the murder of Matthew Shepard, a homosexual student at the University of Wyoming, in 1998.

Critical Overview

The response to *Close Range: Wyoming Stories* and especially "Brokeback Mountain" was overwhelmingly positive. Dean Bakopoulos, in *The Progressive*, considers *Close Range* a "well-crafted collection" claiming, "this is powerful fiction, and somehow Proulx manages to give each story the plot, depth of character, sense of setting, and thematic weight of an entire novel." Rita D. Jacobs in an article for *World Literature Today* praises the collection's "luscious prose" and "evocative descriptions" that make "a strong impression" on the reader.

A reviewer for *Publishers Weekly* considers the book a "breathtaking compilation of Proulx's short fiction" that contains "an amazing, exhilarating range of mood, atmosphere and theme. Every one boasts prose that is smart, lively and fused with laconic poetry" and "her dexterity with striking images creates delights on every page." The reviewer claims that her stories are "focused by an immaculate eye and ear" and "every detail rings true" and finds a "stringent authority in her meticulous descriptions." The "distinctive impact" of Proulx's stories, the reviewer claims, is created through her "empathetic observations of the harsh conditions of her characters' lives" and "her grim awareness of the deadly accidents that can strike like lightning in the midst of exhausting daily routine."

Bakopoulos finds fault, however, with the pace of some of the stories, arguing that "on occasion, she packs in too much detail" especially in her openings. He concludes that "while impressive, this background information often slows the stories down." Jacobs insists that the stories are "uneven, but when they work, they are wondrous, with characters so alive and touching that the reader feels the ache of loss as the final page is turned."

Reviewers' highest praise is reserved for "Brokeback Mountain," which Bakopoulos calls "a tender and heartbreaking love story." He claims that its "crushing last line . . . sums up all the loneliness and failed dreams that make *Close Range* such a moving and wise collection." The *Publishers Weekly* review also singles out the last line of the story, noting that in its "restrained but achingly tender narrative of forbidden love" Proulx merges "the matter-of-fact and the macabre, and her summary of life's pain in a terse closing sentence, will elicit gasps of pain and understanding." Jacobs argues that "Brokeback Mountain" is the collection's "most successful" story. She concludes, "In choosing such an unlikely setting for heartbreak and creating such strongly evocative settings and characters, Proulx proves her exquisite command of the story genre."

Criticism

Wendy Perkins

Perkins is a professor of American and English literature and film. In this essay, she examines the theme of desire and denial in the story.

"Ennis is determined to fight his desire for Jack because he cannot face the prejudice against such a union."

In an assessment of Annie Proulx's collection *Close Range*, a reviewer for *Publishers Weekly* notes "the mean, brutal pain-filled world" of her characters, "who need courage to sustain—much less find—a little dignity in the misery, futility and dread of daily existence on land plagued by drought and flood, sleet and scorching sun." "Brokeback Mountain," the most celebrated story in this collection, presents characters who suffer the bitter winds of Wyoming while they herd sheep in mountain pastures. Yet, in this tale, the land is not as harsh as the people on it, especially the violently intolerant ones who refuse to allow two men to openly love each other. This is the brutal world that Ennis Del Mar must find the courage to endure by juggling two competing impulses: desire and denial.

Ennis has never had a sexual relationship with a man before he goes up Brokeback Mountain to herd sheep with Jack Twist. On the day Ennis meets Jack, he is not yet twenty and plans to marry Alma Beers. These plans get complicated, however, when he crawls into Jack's bedroll one cold night on the mountain.

Ennis's desire for Jack stems from the combination of easy compatibility and sexual chemistry between the two. When they first arrive on the mountain, they spend many hours together and Ennis thinks "he'd never had such a good time." They talk about their past troubles and their future dreams, "respectful of each other's opinions, each glad to have a companion where none had been expected."

Their friendship eventually evolves into a sexual relationship that inspires feelings in Ennis that he occasionally tries to deny while the two are on the mountain. One night, he insists to Jack,

What Do I Read Next?

- *All the Pretty Horses* (1992), by Cormac McCarthy, focuses on the coming of age of its two protagonists in the Southwest and Mexico.
- Larry McMurtry's novel *Lonesome Dove* (1985) weaves together stories of cattle herding that portray the difficult lives men and women experienced in the American West at the end of the nineteenth century.
- Proulx's "The Half-Skinned Steer" (1998) appears in the same collection as "Brokeback Mountain" and focuses on the hard landscapes of the West and the troubled people who live there.
- *American West* (1994), by Dee Brown, explores the last half of the nineteenth century and the development of the enduring myths of the West.

"I'm not no queer" to which Jack responds, "me neither. A one-shot thing. Nobody's business but ours." However, when they eventually come down from the mountain, they cannot keep others from making it their business as well. The blatant homophobia that Ennis experiences causes him to deny his feelings for Jack and to try to adapt himself to the heterosexual culture.

On the mountain, they spend a "euphoric" summer—their relationship deepening into love for each other as they experience moments of sexual pleasure as well as a closeness that provides the satisfaction of a "shared and sexless hunger." They believe that they are alone on the mountain, but through his binoculars Joe Aguirre, the ranch foreman, has watched them acting out sexually. Aguirre, whose disgust over what he sees prompts him to refuse to rehire Jack the next summer, foreshadows the difficulties Ennis and Jack face when they try to express their love for each other after they come off of the mountain.

Ennis senses this approaching trouble when the sheep he and Jack are herding mix together with another herd. When he tries but fails to get them sorted out, he feels that "in a disquieting way everything seemed mixed." The landscape adds an air of danger when they prepare to leave the mountain before a blizzard approaches. As the clouds move in, the mountain appears to boil "with demonic energy" and the wind blows through the rock with a "bestial drone." As Ennis descends, he feels that he is traveling in a "slow motion, but headlong, irreversible fall."

This sense of impending danger causes Ennis to deny his feelings for Jack as much as he can. When the two part after they come down from the mountain, they say an awkward goodbye, knowing that there was "nothing to do but drive away in opposite directions." Yet the thought of not being with Jack sickens Ennis so intensely that he has to pull over to the side of the road and wretch, feeling "about as bad as he ever had and it [would take] a long time for the feeling to wear off."

Ennis tries to follow the rules of convention by marrying Alma and raising a family. Yet his propensity for anal sex, which Alma hates, suggests that although he is trying to suppress his homosexual desires, he does not succeed. When Jack arrives for a visit, four years after their time together on Brokeback Mountain, Ennis's passion for him becomes a "hot jolt" as the two lock together in a heated embrace and kiss on the lips, which Alma observes. He tries to excuse his display of feelings for Jack by explaining to her that the two had not seen each other for four years, but Alma "had seen what she had seen."

At this point, Ennis cannot check his desire for Jack, and so the two spend the night together in a motel bed after Ennis tells Alma they will be out "drinkin and talking" all night. They do talk that evening, about what they were going to do about their "situation." Ennis admits to Jack, "I shouldn't a let you out a my sights" when they came down Brokeback Mountain, but then tells him, "I doubt there's nothing now we can do."

Ennis is determined to fight his desire for Jack because he cannot face the prejudice against such a union. The dominant heterosexual society has taught him to believe that homosexuality is not "decent," and he knows that if the two are caught together in the wrong place, they could be killed. Ennis's conflicting emotions are so powerful that he admits, "it scares the piss out of [him]." This confusion of passion, shame, and violence had emerged on the mountain when after an intense sexual coupling, Ennis punched Jack so hard that he knocked him out.

When Jack talks about the two of them leaving their families and starting a ranch together, Ennis insists on following convention, telling Jack, "I'm stuck with what I got, caught in my own loop. Can't get out of it." He suggests that he would be ashamed to be openly homosexual when he notes, "I don't want a be like them guys you see around sometimes." He also recognizes the danger when he adds, "And I don't want a be dead."

Ennis illustrates the violent response that prejudice can inspire when he tells Jack about a homosexual man in his town who was beaten to death with a tire iron and then dragged through the streets for all to see. Ennis's father made sure that nine-year-old Ennis also saw the corpse as a warning that if he ever had a sexual relationship with a man, his father would come after him with a tire iron as well. With the acknowledgement that there would be many men out there waiting with tire irons, Ennis concludes that he and Jack can only see each other occasionally, and then "way the hell out in the back a nowhere."

The prejudice against homosexuality that he has witnessed causes Ennis to develop unconsciously an internalized homophobia, characterized by the same negative responses heterosexuals harbor toward gays and lesbians. Ennis struggles to align himself with the very culture that denies his right to exist because he cannot accept himself as the target of that culture's prejudice. His inability to identify himself as a homosexual and his need to be accepted by his straight community prompts him to reject Jack's suggestion that they find a more tolerant place to live where they might be able to enjoy a fulfilling relationship with each other.

Ennis's desire for Jack, however, refuses to be suppressed, which interferes with his determination to lead a conventional life. Even though he and Jack go off together infrequently, his marriage to Alma falls apart. Unable to check her resentment over his "fishing trips" with Jack, which she realizes do not involve fishing, and his emotional distance from her and their children, she divorces him. Ennis's conflicting emotions about his homosexuality again erupt in violence when one evening, Alma voices her disgust over his relationship with Jack. In response, he wrenches her wrist and threatens her as he storms out to a bar where he picks a "short dirty fight."

Even though Ennis is no longer married, his internalized homophobia prevents him from seeing Jack more than once or twice a year. His love for Jack, however, has not abated, which becomes evident during the tender moments they spend together. Yet "one thing never changed: the brilliant charge of their infrequent couplings was darkened by the sense of time flying, never enough time, never enough."

Ennis's fears about someone coming after him with a tire iron are realized not with him, but with Jack. After Mr. Frost tells him that Jack had planned to start a ranch first with Ennis, then with another man, Ennis understands that Jack's death was no accident. His intense sorrow over the loss of Jack becomes evident when he buries his face in Jack's shirt, hoping in vain to pick up his lover's scent.

In the years after Jack's death, Ennis finds a way to endure the pain through his dreams of their time together on Brokeback Mountain, from which "he would wake sometimes in grief, sometimes with the old sense of joy and release." In an effort to preserve his sense of dignity and to avoid a violent response to an open display of their love, Ennis could never allow himself to recognize the depth of his feelings for Jack, insisting "nothing could be done about it." In Ennis's final resolve that "if you can't fix it you've got to stand it," Proulx handles ironically Ennis's response to his difficult life without Jack. In one sense, Ennis has demonstrated the courage necessary to endure the sufferings of the human heart, but he also has revealed his inability to accept his homosexuality or act in any way to enlighten others about their prejudice. Through her portrayal of Ennis's struggle with desire and denial, Proulx reveals the subtle complexities inherent in the recognition and acceptance of self.

Source: Wendy Perkins, Critical Essay on "Brokeback Mountain," in *Short Stories for Students*, Thomson Gale, 2006.

Rita D. Jacobs

In the following review, Jacobs praises Proulx for her mastery of the short story form in "Brokeback Mountain."

Annie Proulx is perhaps best known for her Pulitzer Prize-winning novel *The Shipping News* and for her luscious prose, which is also in evidence in *Close Range* in evocative descriptions like the following: "It was her voice that drew you in, that low, twangy voice, wouldn't matter if she was saying the alphabet, what you heard was the rustle of hay. She could make you smell the smoke from an unlit fire."

These eleven stories are populated by images of unrequited longing, wide-open spaces, hardscrabble

"In choosing such an unlikely setting for heartbreak and creating such strongly evocative settings and characters, Proulx proves her exquisite command of the story genre."

lives, and characters with unlikely names: Ottaline Touhey, Sutton Muddyman, Car Scrope, Sweets Musgrove, to cite just a few. Two of the pieces, "The Blood Bay" and "55 Miles to the Gas Pump," are so short that they function more as anecdotes than stories, and the slightly longer "Job History" is just what the title indicates. In contrast to the often masterful longer stories, these pieces feel like filler.

The stories are uneven, but when they work, they are wondrous, with characters so alive and touching that the reader feels the ache of loss as the final page is turned. Most successful is the very last story in the volume, "Brokeback Mountain," the tale of two rough-and-tumble cowboys, Ennis del Mar and Jack Twist, who first meet and work together as sheepherder and camp tender on Brokeback Mountain in 1963 when they are young. Over a long summer alone together, the two men gradually fall in love. Needless to say, love is not acknowledged as love, and the story follows these men over the course of their years, as husbands and fathers who forge traditional lives. The story unfolds with a growing sense of Ennis's yearning for Twist, for the man whom he did love despite fate and ban and in a world where such a love cannot be recognized, often even by the people who are in love. In choosing such an unlikely setting for heartbreak and creating such strongly evocative settings and characters, Proulx proves her exquisite command of the story genre.

An almost equally notable work is "The Half-Skinned Steer," chosen by John Updike for inclusion in Houghton Mifflin's *Best American Stories of the Century*. This story chronicles a trip back home, back west, and back in time by an octogenarian in his Cadillac. Proulx indulges herself at times with sentences like the following:

> With the lapping subtlety of incoming tide the shape of the ranch began to gather in his mind; he could recall the intimate fences he'd made, caut wire and perfect corners, the draws and rock outcrops, the watercourse valley steepening, cliffs like bones with shreds of meat on them rising and rising, and the stream plunging suddenly underground, disappearing into subterranean darkness of blind fish, shooting out of the mountain ten miles west on a neighbor's place, but leaving their ranch some badland red country as dry as a cracker, steep canyons with high caves suited to lions.

Even for one who doesn't appreciate prose that calls attention to itself, these slightly purple flights suit Proulx's narrative.

Despite the unevenness of the stories, the volume makes a strong impression, seducing the reader into a modern romance, often verging on the Gothic, that is Proulx's vision of Wyoming.

Source: Rita D. Jacobs, "Review of *Close Range: Wyoming Stories*," in *World Literature Today*, Vol. 74, No. 2, Spring 2000, p. 369.

Dean Bakopoulos

In the following review, Bakopoulos calls "Brokeback Mountain" a "tender and heartbreaking love story" and Close Range *a "moving and wise collection."*

The American West has been a favorite setting for many of the heavy-weights of contemporary fiction: Cormac McCarthy, Rick Bass, Jim Harrison, Ivan Doig, and Richard Ford. Women who set their stories in Big Sky country (Wyoming, Montana, and Idaho) have not received the same critical acclaim and publishing hullabaloo as their male counterparts.

Enter Annie Proulx. She has only five books in print—including *Heart Songs and Other Stories* (1988), *Postcards* (1992), *The Shipping News* (1993), and *Accordion Crimes* (1996), all published by Scribner. Even so, Proulx has already won the Pen/Faulkner Award (for *Postcards*), as well as the National Book Award and the Pulitzer Prize (both for *The Shipping News*).

Her second collection of short stories, *Close Range: Wyoming Stories,* entertains the mythic legends of drunken cowboys, rodeo heroes, betrayed lovers, and aging ranchers, while exploring all the loneliness, blood, and dirt of the Western landscape.

The epigraph of *Close Range* is from a retired Wyoming rancher: "Reality's never been of much use out here." Most characters in these narratives veer between what is actually possible and what is dreamed, as many take on the complex "story-within-a-story" mode.

"The Half-Skinned Steer," which has been chosen for inclusion in John Updike's anthology *The Best American Short Stories of the Century* (Houghton Mifflin, 1999), is one of the highlights of this well-crafted collection. A retired rancher, Mero, in his eighties and with a mind full of flashbacks, makes his way across the country to the old family ranch for his brother Rollo's funeral. The ranch is now a tourist trap called "Down Under Wyoming," and the journey turns hellish because of winter storms and the old man's difficulty with driving. Here, Proulx sets up all the themes that dominate this volume: the struggle of hope against nature, mortality, and despair.

Some of the newer and less-heralded stories in this collection are even more impressive. "Job History" chronicles the economic woes of the West through the life of Leeland Lee, who moves from job to job and plan to plan with an unyielding hope that prosperity awaits over the next ridge: "Leeland quits truck driving. Lori [his wife] has saved a little money. Once more they decide to go into business for themselves. They lease the old gas station where Leeland had his first job and where they tried the ranch supply store. Now it is a gas station again, but also a convenience store. They try sure-fire gimmicks: plastic come-on banners that pop and tear in the wind, free ice cream cones with every fill-up, prize drawings. Leeland has been thinking of the glory days when a hundred cars stopped. Now Highway 36 seems the emptiest road in the country."

Through the sparse, understated chronology, Proulx depicts not only the difficult economic hurdles of the isolated region, but also the fierce emotional ones. This is powerful fiction, and somehow Proulx manages to give each story the plot, depth of character, sense of setting, and thematic weight of an entire novel.

But her talent is sometimes a flaw. On occasion, she packs in too much detail, particularly at the openings. She seems to be trying to show just how well she knows the geography, people, and history of Wyoming. While impressive, this background information often slows the stories down.

The final offering, "Brokeback Mountain," features two ranchers—hard-drinking, cussing, rough-and-tumble men. But here's a new perspective on the macho cowboy: These two men have an intense, erotic, exhausting relationship during a summer up on Brokeback Mountain. Afterward, they move off to opposite ends of the country, marry women, and have families. Four years later, their relationship resumes. It is a tender and heartbreaking love story.

The crushing last line of 'Brokeback Mountain' sums up all the loneliness and failed dreams that make *Close Range* such a moving and wise collection."

The crushing last line of "Brokeback Mountain" sums up all the loneliness and failed dreams that make *Close Range* such a moving and wise collection: "There was some open space between what he knew and what he tried to believe, but nothing could be done about it, and if you can't fix it you've got to stand it."

Source: Dean Bakopoulos, "Woes of the West," in *Progressive*, September 1999, pp. 43–44.

Annie Proulx

In the following interview conducted in May 1999, Proulx dicusses place and history in her works, and expounds on her exploration of the rural landscape and its inherent dangers in the stories in Close Range.

[*Missouri Review*]: *Your stories and novels cover a lot of ground, historically and geographically.* Accordion Crimes, *for example, is set all over the United States and spans much of the twentieth century.* Postcards *concerns World War II and post-World War II America. Can you talk about that?*

[*Proulx*]: Place and history are central to the fiction I write, both in the broad, general sense and in detailed particulars. Rural North America, regional cultures in critical economic flux, the images of an ideal and seemingly attainable world the

> "On a more intimate scale the stories explore human relationships and behavior, the individual caught in the whirlpool of change and chance."

characters cherish in their long views despite the rigid and difficult circumstances of their place and time. Those things interest me and are what I write about. I watch for the historical skew between what people have hoped for and who they thought they were and what befell them.

Even your novels and stories that aren't strictly historical all have a sense of history and place somehow going together and being at the center.

Much of what I write is set in contemporary North America, but the stories are informed by the past; I like stories with three generations visible. Geography, geology, climate, weather, the deep past, immediate events, shape the characters and partly determine what happens to them, although the random event counts for much, as it does in life. I long ago fell into the habit of seeing the world in terms of shifting circumstances overlaid upon natural surroundings. I try to define periods when regional society and culture, rooted in location and natural resources, start to experience the erosion of traditional ways, and attempt to master contemporary, large-world values. The characters in my novels pick their way through the chaos of change. The present is always pasted on layers of the past.

You studied history at the University of Vermont and Sir George Williams University, now Concordia University, in Montreal. Was there a particular approach to history that most interested you?

I was attracted to the French *Annales* school, which pioneered minute examination of the lives of ordinary people through account books, wills, marriage and death records, farming and crafts techniques, the development of technologies. My fiction reflects this attraction.

Had you already decided to write fiction during your university years?

No, while I was studying history I had no thought of writing fiction and no desire to do so.

Was there any pivotal moment that propelled you toward writing fiction?

The pivotal moment was not a moment but a slow, slow turning. I left graduate school and the study of history to live in Vermont's Northeast Kingdom with a friend. We were in a remote area with limited job possibilities; I started writing nonfiction, mostly magazine journalism and how-to books, for income. At the same time I began to write short fiction, mostly stories about hunting and fishing and rural life in northern New England, subjects that interested me intensely at the time. Almost all of these stories were published in *Gray's Sporting Journal,* then a new and strikingly beautiful quarterly concerned with the outdoor world in the same way Hemingway's Nick Adams stories are about the outdoor world—the primary weight on literature, not sport. There was an intense camaraderie and shared literary excitement among the writers whose fiction appeared in *Gray's,* something I have never encountered since. It may have been that the struggles to get paid by *Gray's* created a bond of shared adversity among the writers; it may have been the genuine pleasure in being part of this unusual publication that valued serious outdoor writing in contrast to the hook-and-bullet mags. It is hard to overestimate how important *Gray's* was for many of us. Without it I would probably never have tried to write fiction.

I continued writing short stories in a desultory way for the next five or six years. When my youngest son left home for school in the late 1980s, for the first time in my life I enjoyed long periods of unbroken time suited to concentrated work and began my first novel, *Postcards.*

In your latest book, Close Range: Wyoming Stories, *you have returned to the short story. Can you talk about the differences between that form and the novel?*

The construction of short stories calls for a markedly different set of mind than work on a novel, and for me short stories are at once more interesting and more difficult to write than longer work. The comparative brevity of the story dictates more economical and accurate use of words and images, a limited palette of events, fewer characters, tighter dialogue, strong title and punctuation that works to move the story forward. If the writer is trying to illustrate a particular period or place, a collection of short stories is a good way to take the reader inside a house of windows, each opening onto different but related views—a kind of flip book of place, time and manners.

Metaphors—a complex subject. What is involved in constructing them seems not so much a matter of seeking similitude or trying for explanation or description as multilevel word and image play. Metaphors set up echoes and reflections, not only of tone and color but of meaning in the story. The use of running metaphors in a piece—all related in some way to indigestion or water or loneliness or roller skates, or with a surrealistic or violent cast—will guide the reader in a particular direction as surely as stock can be herded.

For me, metaphors come in sheets of three or four at once, in floods, and so metaphor use often concerns selection rather than construction. There are private layers of meaning in metaphor that may be obscure to the reader but which have—beyond the general accepted meanings of the words—resonance for the writer through personal associations of language, ideas, impressions. So the writer may be using metaphor to guide the reader and deepen the story, for subtle effects but also for sheer personal pleasure in word play.

It sounds like it's a natural mode of thought for you.

I was very young, about three years old, when introduced to metaphor, and I remember the first sharp pleasure I felt in playing what seemed a kind of game. I was with my mother in the kitchen of our small house. Classical music came out of the radio, I have no idea what, some sweeping and lofty orchestral statement. I was not consciously listening until my mother, who was a skilled watercolorist, said, "What does this music make you think about, what do you *see?*" Immediately I translated the music I heard into an image. "A bishop running through the woods," I answered. I had no idea what a bishop was but liked the word for its conjunction of hiss and hiccup. What the music made me see in my mind's eye was a tall, glassy, salt-cellar figure—the bishop—gliding through a dark forest dappled with round spots of light. The connections of perception between the sounds of the music and the image of trees/slipping figure/broken light had been made. Thereafter, and forever more, I found myself constantly involved in metaphoric observation.

Do you have a standard operating procedure in the way you work? Do you start with place, or history, or character and story, or is it different with each book?

Where a story begins in the mind I am not sure—a memory of haystacks, maybe, or wheel ruts in the ruined stone, the ironies that fall out of the friction between past and present, some casual phrase overheard. But something kicks in, some powerful juxtaposition, and the whole book shapes itself up in the mind. I spend a year or two on the research and I begin with the place and what happened there *before* I fill notebooks with drawings and descriptions of rocks, water, people, names. I study photographs. From place come the characters, the way things happen, the story itself. For the sake of architecture, of balance, I write the ending first and then go to the beginning.

What's your approach to research?

The research is ongoing and my great pleasure. Since geography and climate are intensely interesting to me, much time goes into the close examination of specific regions—natural features of the landscape, human marks on it, earlier and prevailing economics based on raw materials, ethnic background of settlers.

Where do you go for that kind of information?

I read manuals of work and repair, books of manners, dictionaries of slang, city directories, lists of occupational titles, geology regional weather, botanists' plant guides, local histories, newspapers. I visit graveyards, collapsing cotton gins, photograph barns and houses, roadways. I listen to ordinary people speaking with one another in bars and stores, in laundromats. I read bulletin boards, scraps of paper I pick up from the ground. I paint landscapes because staring very hard at a place for twenty to thirty minutes and putting it on paper burns detail into the mind as no amount of scribbling can do.

Have you ever fallen in love with one of your characters?

I have never fallen in love with one of my characters. The notion is repugnant. Characters are made to carry a particular story; that is their work. The only reason one shapes a character to look as he or she does, behave and speak in a certain way, suffer particular events, is to move the story forward in a particular direction. I do not indulge characters nor give them their heads and "see where they go," and I don't understand writers who drift downriver in company with unformed characters. The character, who may seem to hold center stage in a novel, and in a limited sense does, actually exists to support the story. This is not to say that writing a character is like building a model airplane. The thoughtful and long work of inventing a believable and fictionally "true" person on paper is exhilarating, particularly as one knowingly skates near the thin ice of caricature.

I'm curious about Loyal Blood in Postcards. *What was his germ?*

The character Loyal Blood leaped complete and wholly formed from a 1930s Vermont state prison mug shot. A friend gave me a small stack of postcards sent out by the Windsor Prison warden's office in the 1930s to alert various sheriffs around the state to escapees. I knew nothing of the man on my postcard, but his face was arresting and the character jumped forward at once. The story's genesis was sparked by a small stack of state fire marshal's reports during the Depression. There were a number of dismal accounts of farmers burning down their houses and barns for the meager insurance money. They had nothing else. From this desperate arson, with its roots in the global economic slump, emerged the story.

Economic desperation is a common theme in your work.

The failure of the limited economic base for a region, often the very thing that gave the region its distinctive character and social ways, is interesting to me. I frequently focus on the period when everything—the traditional economic base, the culture, the family and the clan links—begins to unravel. I have taken a fictional look at this situation in northern New England, Newfoundland and Wyoming.

In *Heart Songs* I began to examine the decline of the small dairy farms that had been the backbone of northern New England's economy since the late eighteenth century, but which began to break down after the Second World War and finally collapsed in recent decades as moneyed outsiders poured into the state. *Postcards* continued and enlarged on this theme, taking as its landscape the sweep of country from New England to California. The character Loyal Blood denies his natural calling as a farmer. He picks up a dozen different regional occupations on his long journey westward, an ironic and miniature version of the American frontier expansion westward. There is a subtext on the tremendously important rural electrification program. The novel was concerned with what happens when a region has only one economic base and it goes under—the breakup and scattering of families, the subdivision of land, the outflow of old residents or the new position they adopt as service providers to the rich moving in. A population shift of moneyed second-home owners began to replace seventh-generation farm families.

We see a similar Concern in The Shipping News, *as well as in* Close Range.

If all you have is fishing and the fish stock begins to collapse from overfishing, destructive pressures, foreign and domestic policies, etc., what happens to the fishermen who have no other way to make a living? Relocation, government programs and the like. *The Shipping News* caught a Newfoundland fishing outport on the edge of the abyss. A few months after the novel was published, the Canadian government proclaimed a moratorium on cod fishing, and the traditional culture and economy quickly began to dissolve as thousands of out-of-work Newfoundlanders streamed onto the mainland, an exodus that continues.

In *Close Range,* a collection of short stories set in Wyoming, the focus was again on rural landscape, low population density, people who feel remote and isolated, cut off from the rest of the world, where accident and suicide rates are high and aggressive behavior not uncommon. Fifty percent of the University of Wyoming's graduation class must leave the state to find work. Again I was interested in looking at a limited economic structure—cattle ranching and extractive industries. What happens when the coal and oil run out, when the beef market falls away, when there are few chances outside the traditional ways of life? On a more intimate scale the stories explore human relationships and behavior, the individual caught in the whirlpool of change and chance.

In Accordion Crimes *you add another layer to the issue of economic struggle by focusing on the immigrant experience in particular.*

I was interested in the American character, unlike that of any other country—aggressive, protean, identity-shifting, mutable, restless and mobile. I wondered if the American penchant for self-invention was somehow related to the seminal immigrant experience, in which one had to renounce the past, give up the old culture, language, history, religion, even one's birth name, and replace the old self with American ideals, language, a new name and new ways. The novel looked at several generations of nine ethnic families through the medium of the immigrant's instrument, the accordion.

Do you believe that the ethnic variety of our nation—despite the "melting pot" history—is somehow forgotten or under-appreciated?

A major aim in writing *Accordion Crimes* was to show the powerful government and social pressures on foreigners that forced them into the so-called melting pot. The social pressures were enormous, and the cost of assimilation was staggering for the immigrants—their lives were often untimely truncated. They did not belong, they were ridiculed outsiders, they worked at the most miserable and dangerous jobs. They gave up personal identification and respect. The successes went to their children, the first generation of American-born. These American children commonly rejected the values, clothing, language, religion, food, music of their parents in their zeal to be 100 percent American. Hence the widespread disdain in America (nowhere else) for the accordion. Canada allowed its immigrants a large measure of cultural autonomy, and ethnic enclaves and settlements grew up in many regions, the so-called ethnic mosaic that contrasts with the melting-pot symbolism. Ironically, it is Canada that is plagued now by a separatist movement.

Does that imply that although the melting pot was responsible for suffering in the first generation of immigrants, it was the best thing for the nation?

My thinking does not sort out this way—"best," "worst," etc. The so-called melting pot is a vivid phrase that represented a dominant, narrow and forceful attitude in the United States in the late nineteenth and early twentieth centuries. That social and cultural attitude had no tolerance for ethnic, cultural or linguistic diversity. Immigrants had to become "American" in order to succeed here. Many of them did not and could not conform to the American ideal, and they lived their lives in sometimes dangerous backwaters. It isn't a question of whether or not it was the best thing for the nation or no. It was what it was, an expression of the American national character in that period. It was different in Canada—not better or worse, but different.

I can't resist asking you one question about your experience with Hollywood. I understand that your experience with making The Shipping News *into a movie has been a little frustrating.*

I sold the film rights to *The Shipping News* several years ago and so have no influence on, connection with or input into the fate of the novel in Hollywood's fumbling hands. It was important to me during the option negotiations to plead that the film be made in Newfoundland, and the studio signed a letter of intent to that end. The seesaw history of the work since then, the inaccurate reports, the gossip, the confusion, is best learned from other sources than me. I am out of the loop.

The film rights of the short story "Brokeback Mountain," the closing story in the new collection *Close Range,* were optioned by Larry McMurtry and Diana Ossana, who wrote an exceptionally fine screenplay. What happens next with it remains to be seen.

You have won numerous literary prizes, including the Pulitzer and the National Book Award. How has all the recognition affected your work?

I don't think prizes have affected me as much as they have my publisher. It is pleasant to have one's work recognized and praised, and prizes certainly have an effect on the way the body of work is perceived, and on one's income, but for me, when the manuscript of a story or novel is completed I am done with it and on to new work. I have a feeling of detachment for awards, perhaps because they come a year or more after publication, perhaps because it is difficult to believe that the work is considered prizeworthy. I am critical of my writing and tend to see the flaws and weaknesses. The best time for an award would be the instant one finally makes a stubborn paragraph or sentence lift its own weight off the page.

How important to you are the responses of your readers?

Response of readers . . . depends on which readers you mean. Readers come in a highly variable assortment—critics, other writers, old friends, fans, reading groups, adversaries, error-chasers, punctuation mavens, clever scholars, those who deeply understand the territory of the book or story, those who don't get any of it. Probably I value the response of fellow writers most highly because they understand the work of making fiction. But fine letters have come from every kind of reader, and I am grateful for them.

What, above all else, do you want your readers to take away with them after reading your works?

The novel should take us, as readers, to a vantage point from which we can confront our human condition, where we can glimpse something of what we are. A novel should somehow enlarge our capacity to see ourselves as living entities in the jammed and complex contemporary world.

You have been criticized by some for overemphasizing the bad luck and failure of you characters—for not finding the mitigating factor in their lives, if only in the way you frame their stories.

It is difficult to take this as a serious criticism. America is a violent, gun-handling country. Americans feed on a steady diet of bloody movies, television programs, murder mysteries. Road rage, highway killings, beatings and murder of those who are different abound; school shootings—almost all of them in rural areas—make headline news over and over. Most of the ends suffered by characters in my books are drawn from true accounts of public record: newspapers, accident reports, local histories, labor statistics for the period and place under examination. The point of writing in layers of bitter deaths and misadventures that befall characters is to illustrate American violence, which is real, deep and vast.

The rural farmers of Heart Songs, *the unlucky owners of the accordion in* Accordion Crimes, *the fatalistic westerners in* Close Range: *they're on the ragged edge, and often—too often, some critics would say—they fall off.*

Immigrants to this country suffered unbelievable damage, both psychological and physical. Rural life, too, is high in accident and, for many, suffused with a trapped feeling, a besetting sense of circumstances beyond individual control. Real rural life, enlivened with clear air, beautiful scenery, close-knit communities and cooperative neighbors, builds self-reliant, competent, fact-facing people; but it is also riddled with economic failure, natural disaster, poor health care, accidental death, few cultural opportunities, narrow world-views, a feeling of being separated from the larger society. Literary critics who live and work in urban and suburban milieus characterized by middle-class gentility and progressive liberalism are rarely familiar with the raw exigencies and pressures of rural life.

I am reminded of the uproar of disapproval over historian Michael Lesy's 1973 *Wisconsin Death Trip,* the author's gathering of newspaper accounts of nineteenth-century economic failure, madness, hoboes, suicide and murder in company with the extraordinary photographs by Charley Van Schaick. Real lives, real events, which displeased the many critics who denounced the book's darkness as distortion of history. One protesting group got out a rival collection of photographs entitled *Wisconsin Life Trip,* showing happy families, picnics, affection and peace. There is something in us that wants to believe in sweet harmony against all evidence.

Since I am often accused of writing darkly, I might add that although I am not immune to the flashes of humor and intense moments of joy that illuminate our lives, I am in deep sympathy with Paul Fussell when he describes seeing his first dead in *Doing Battle: The Making of a Skeptic,* ". . . and suddenly I knew that I was not and never would be in a world that was reasonable or just."

Do you think that serious fiction, by definition, ends unhappily?

No, of course not. I would like to get beyond this happy/unhappy-ending discussion, which seems to me to have more the character of trap than open door. It is very difficult to know what is "happy" or "unhappy." I wrote *The Shipping News* in direct response to the oft-repeated criticism that *Postcards* was "too dark." Ah, I said to myself, a happy ending is wanted, is it? Let us see what we can do. The "happy" ending of *Shipping News* is constructed on a negative definition—here happiness is simply the absence of pain, and so, the illusion of pleasure. I was quite surprised when readers and critics alike rejoiced in what they perceived as a joyful upbeat. The label "happy" is comparative, subjective, sometimes deliberately illusory, sometimes—as in *Shipping News*—ironic or not what it seems. In working endings for stories and novels I try simply for a natural cessation of story. Most of my writing focuses on a life or lives set against a particular time and place. This is the nature of things, and, though it sounds simplistic, this is what shapes my view of the past and present, both as related to my personal life and the lives of characters. One is born, one lives *in one's time,* one dies. I try to understand place and time through the events in a character's life, and the end is the end. The person, the character, is one speck of life among many, many. The ending, then, should reflect for the reader some element of value or importance in the telling of this ending among the possible myriad of stories that might have been told.

Source: Annie Proulx, "An Interview with Annie Proulx," in *Missouri Review*, Vol. 22, No. 2, 1999, pp. 79–90.

Sources

Bakopoulos, Dean, "Woes of the West," in the *Progressive* September 1999, pp. 43–44.

Jacobs, Rita D., Review of *Close Range: Wyoming Stories*, in *World Literature Today*, Vol. 74, No. 2, Spring 2000, p. 369.

Proulx, Annie, "Brokeback Mountain," in *Close Range: Wyoming Stories*, Scribner, 1999, pp. 255–85.

Review of *Close Range: Wyoming Stories*, in *Publishers Weekly*, March 29, 1999, p. 91.

Further Reading

Kowalewski, Michael, "Losing Our Place: A Review Essay," in *Michigan Quarterly Review*, Vol. 40, No. 1, Winter 2001, pp. 242–57.

This essay explores the sense of place in American fiction, including *Close Range*.

McGraw, Erin, "Brute Force: Violent Stories," in *Georgia Review*, Vol. 54, No. 2, Winter 2000, p. 351.

McGraw traces the theme of violence in American fiction and compares the stories in *Close Range* to that tradition.

McMurtry, Larry, ed., *Still Wild: Short Fiction of the American West 1950 to the Present*, Simon and Shuster, 2001.

This collection includes stories by Richard Ford, Raymond Carver, Leslie Marmon Silko, and Jack Kerouac.

Steinberg, Sybil, "E. Annie Proulx: An American Odyssey," in *Publishers Weekly*, June 3, 1996, pp. 57–58.

Steinberg focuses on Proulx's life and work in this overview.

The Centaur

José Saramago

2004

José Saramago's "The Centaur" was first published in English in the collection *Telling Tales*, edited by Nadine Gordimer and published by Picador in 2004. Giovanni Pontiero translated the story from Portuguese into English. The short story was published earlier in Portuguese in Saramago's short story collection *Objecto Quase* (Almost an Object) published by Editorial Caminho of Lisbon in 1978 and 1984.

Like other stories by the author, "The Centaur" involves a blending of the fantastical with the everyday or mundane. In the story, a centaur, who is the lone survivor of the mythical species, roams the Earth evading capture and persecution by human beings. As he travels toward his home country, which he has avoided returning to for millennia, he struggles to reconcile the opposite needs of his two halves: he possesses the mind and upper body of a man and the lower body of a horse. In this tale, Saramago explores the universal themes of alienation, loneliness, dualism, and the human fear and hatred of the unknown.

Author Biography

José Saramago was born on November 16, 1922, in Azinhaga, Ribatejo, Portugal. He is best known as a novelist, and in 1998 he became the first Portuguese writer to receive the Nobel Prize in Literature. Born into a family of rural workers, he grew

José Saramago AP Images

up in the city of Lisbon, often visiting relatives in the countryside, and attended a technical school to learn a trade. Before becoming a full-time professional writer, Saramago worked as a mechanic, a civil servant, a translator, a literary critic, a political commentator, and a journalist. In 1944, he married Ilda Reis, and they had a child named Violante in 1947.

Saramago published his first novel *Terra do pecado* in 1947. Almost thirty years later in 1976, Saramago published his next novel entitled *Manual de pintura e caligrafia* (Manual of Painting and Calligraphy). His third novel *Levantado do chao* (Raised from the Ground) was published in Portuguese in 1980. Following this novel, Saramago published several novels that were translated into English and which established his worldwide reputation as a novelist, including *Baltasar and Blimunda*, published in Portuguese in 1982 and in English in 1987, and *The Year of the Death of Ricardo Reis* published in Portuguese in 1984 and in English in 1991. In 1994, Saramago published two novels in English *The Stone Raft* and *The Gospel According to Jesus Christ*.

Saramago's other novels include *The History of the Siege of Lisbon* (published in English in 1996), *Blindness* (1997), *All the Names* (2000), *The Cave* (2002), and *The Double* (2004). Although primarily known as a novelist, Saramago has also written and published several collections of poetry, plays, non-fiction works, an opera libretto, and short stories. The short story "The Centaur" appears in the anthology *Telling Tales* (2004), a collection of stories by writers around the world, edited by Nadine Gordimer. The short story was translated into English by Giovanni Pontiero.

In addition to the Nobel Prize in Literature, Saramago has earned many awards, including Grinzane Cavour Prize, the Flaliano Prize, Premio Cidade de Lisboa (1980), Premio Vida Literaria (1993), and Premio Camoes (1995). In 1991, he received honorary doctorates from the University of Turin in Italy and the University of Seville in Spain.

Plot Summary

"The Centaur" opens with descriptions of a man and a horse moving over a riverbed and looking for a hiding place to sleep in as the day breaks. As the description continues, it quickly becomes obvious that the horse and the man are one mythical creature, the centaur, whose body consists of the head and chest of a man and the body and legs of a horse. After pausing to drink from a stream, the centaur finds a good spot to rest and sleep among some trees. As the centaur lies down to sleep, it struggles, since sustaining a comfortable position for both the man and the horse throughout the night is not possible.

Although the horse half falls asleep right away, the man lies awake for a while before falling asleep and beginning to dream. At this point in the story, the narrative shifts to the past tense: the narrator describes how the centaur became the lone survivor of his species. The narrator explains that after fighting in several battles, the centaurs were defeated by Heracles in an epic fight. The surviving centaur managed to escape somehow, after witnessing Heracles crush Nessos, the centaur leader, to death and drag his corpse along the ground. Since that battle, the surviving centaur—who remains unnamed throughout the story—has dreamed every day of fighting and killing Heracles as the gods watch and then recede into the heavens.

The narrator goes on to say how the centaur also roamed the Earth for thousands of years. At first, he was able to travel without fear during the day "as long as the world itself remained mysterious." During this age, people welcomed the centaur as a magical creature, giving him garlands of

Media Adaptations

- The Nobel Prize Internet Archive maintains an official Saramago page at http://www.nobelprizes.com/ which includes Saramago's Nobel lecture and features comprehensive information about the author, his books, and other media resources pertaining to him.
- The José Saramago page of the Nobel Prize website can be found at: http://nobelprize.org/literature/laureates/1998/index.html

flowers and entrusting their children to him. People at this time embraced him as a promoter of fertility, occasionally bringing him a mare with which to copulate.

The narrator explains, however, that at some point the world changed, and the centaur and other mythological creatures were persecuted and forced to hide from human beings. For several generations, the creatures, including unicorns, chimeras, werewolves, and other beings, lived together in the wilderness, but eventually they found they could not live there. They either disappeared from the world or found other ways to adapt to humans. The centaur alone remained, an obvious throwback to ancient times, roaming the Earth on his own. Although he traveled widely, he avoided going back to his native country, which is presumably Greece. He learned to sleep by day to avoid detection and to travel at night, sleeping only to dream.

At one point, during the millennia in which he travels alone, the centaur witnesses a man with a lance riding a scruffy horse fighting some windmills. After seeing the man tossed into the air, the centaur decides to avenge the thrown man. After leaving the windmills with broken blades, the centaur escapes pursuit by fleeing to the frontier of another country.

Following the recounting of this episode, the story returns to the present, with the centaur sleeping and waking to the smell of the sea. As night approaches, the centaur rises and starts to head south, because in his dream, Zeus had headed southward, after the centaur defeated Heracles as usual. Although he has not dared to travel during the daylight for many years, the man part of the centaur feels emboldened and excited and decides to take the risk.

After walking along a ditch and over a plain, the centaur hears a dog barking and starts galloping between two hills, still heading south. As he runs, the barking comes closer, and the centaur hears bells and a human voice. Next, the centaur finds himself among goats and a large dog. A shepherd screams and runs away. As the man part of the centaur grabs a branch to fight off the dog, the horse part kicks the dog and kills it, much to the shame of the human side of the centaur.

The sun goes down, and the centaur continues south. After encountering a wall and some houses, the centaur hears a shot, which hits the horse's flank. The people pursue and shoot at the centaur, but the centaur leaps over the wall and runs through the countryside. As the chase goes on, with dogs and people coming after the centaur, it begins to rain. The centaur manages to outrun the mob and reaches a place he recognizes as the frontier of his native country. The people and dogs stop pursuing the centaur at the border. As the rain becomes a torrential downpour, he crosses into the land.

The rain suddenly stops, and the sun comes out. The centaur proceeds down a mountainside and looks at a valley with three villages in it. He wonders if he can pass by the villages safely. Exhausted, he looks for a place to rest until dusk, so that he can recover some strength before continuing his journey to the sea. He finds the entrance to a cave and goes inside it to sleep. Although he sleeps, the man part of the centaur wakes up anguishing, because he has not dreamed for the first time in millennia. He wonders why he hasn't dreamed and gets up and goes out into the night.

He travels under a bright moon and reaches the valley. He sees a river and the largest of three villages across the way. After walking across the river to the other side, the centaur pauses and thinks about his route. He realizes that he cannot travel in daylight, since news of his existence has probably reached the land, and so he decides to walk along the riverbank underneath the trees. He continues south toward the sea.

The centaur suddenly hears the sound of lapping water, and as he pushes back branches to look at the river, he sees a naked woman emerging from the river after bathing. Having rarely seen women, the man part of the centaur impulsively picks up the woman in his arms as she screams in terror. As he runs with the woman in his arms, the centaur comes to a curve in the river. The woman stops screaming and cries instead. They hear other voices, and as the centaur rounds a bend, they encounter some houses and people. The centaur pulls the woman to his chest, as some people flee, while others retrieve rifles from their homes. The horse part of the centaur rears up, and the woman screams again.

A shot is fired into the air, and the centaur flees, successfully outrunning the villagers. Finding himself way ahead of the persecutors, the man part of the centaur pauses, holds the woman up in front of him, and tells her in his native tongue not to hate him. When he puts her gently on the ground, the woman does not run away, but instead recognizes him without fear, lies on the ground, and asks him to cover her. In frustration, the man part of the centaur looks at the woman longingly and then runs away bemoaning his fate. The villagers reach the woman and carry her away crying and wrapped in a blanket.

The whole country becomes aware of the centaur's existence, and people set out to capture him. The centaur travels south all night, and at daybreak he finds himself on top of a mountain with a view of the sea. After enjoying a moment of peace, the centaur hears a shot, and as men advance toward him with nets and other gear, the centaur rears up and slips on the edge of the slope, falling to his death. The centaur lands on a jutting edge of rock, which cuts through him exactly at the conjunction of his human and horse parts. As he lies dying, the man looks at the sky as if it were a sea and feels himself finally as a man and only a man. He sees the gods approaching and knows it is time to die.

Characters

The Centaur

An unnamed centaur is the protagonist of the story. Half-man and half-horse, he is the lone survivor of the mythical species, which according to the story existed in numbers, until Heracles defeated the centaurs in an epic battle thousands of years ago. This centaur managed to escape Heracles and has roamed the Earth ever since, evading capture or being killed by human beings. The centaur is a divided creature, with both human and horse parts, which are essentially at odds with one another. In the story, the narrator sometimes refers to just the man or the horse, as each part of the centaur has its own desires, needs, and wills. The horse embodies the animal part of the centaur, with bodily needs such as thirst and raw emotions such as fear. The man expresses more complex emotions and does all the thinking for the centaur. Lonely, exhausted from persecution, and perpetually frustrated, the centaur is the last of the mythical creatures to survive in the modern world.

The Mob

Two mobs of humans or villagers appear in the story, each time trying to kill the centaur out of hatred and fear.

The Woman

An unnamed woman appears toward the end of the story. The centaur happens upon her as she emerges from bathing in a river and grabs her much to her dismay. Although she screams and weeps at first, the woman seems to lose her fear of the centaur after he talks to her. She recognizes what he is and that he exists.

Themes

Dualism

One of the major themes of the story is the tension between the physical and the mental parts of the self. Throughout the story, Saramago underscores how these two sides of the character compete with one another for control, as the animal half expresses simple needs such as thirst, while the human half expresses more complex desires and thoughts. The author sometimes even refers to each part of the centaur separately as "the horse" and "the man," emphasizing how distinct they are. The human part of the centaur experiences great frustration as he is unable to fully realize his humanity until the very end of the story, after competing impulses in the centaur result in his falling to his death. A symbolic character, the centaur represents the human condition, as human beings continually struggle for reconciliation between the physical and mental parts of the self.

Loneliness and Isolation

The story's protagonist, the centaur, is an essentially lonely creature. The only survivor of his kind, he has been wandering the world alone for millennia, ever since Heracles killed the rest of his race. Although at one time the centaur had the

Topics For Further Study

- Choose another culture and read about creatures that are half-person and half-beast in that culture's mythology. Create an illustration or watercolor portraying that creature and describe it in a short paragraph. You may also invent a mythological creature that is half-human and half-animal. If you choose the latter option, tell what special powers the creature possesses.
- Research the history of the relations between human beings and horses. Find out how people learned to use horses to help with work and what roles horses play in the twenty-first century. Present your findings to the class.
- Read a psychology textbook or a similar source to research different theories of the divided self, such as Sigmund Freud's theory of the ego, id, and superego. With other students, write a scene in which different parts of the self interact. Perform the scene.
- Consult science magazines and the science section of the newspaper to find out about genetically modified food. Research how scientists have spliced animal genes with plant genes to create some of these genetically modified food-products. Present your findings using diagrams, charts, and other visual props.
- Find out which species are currently on the verge of extinction and research what people are doing that endangers the species and what others are doing to keep the species from dying out. Create a pamphlet describing the species and what factors threaten its existence, explaining what steps are being taken to preserve it.
- Read about ancient Greece in a history textbook or an encyclopedia. Then, imagine you are a citizen of one of the ancient Greek city-states and write a journal entry describing your day incorporating information you acquired in your research.

company of other mythological creatures, he has persisted alone for thousands of years, evading persecution by human beings who fear and hate him. He experiences this state of exile or extreme isolation, because of his difference and is doomed to travel in the dark alone until he dies. Thus, the story dramatizes how someone who is fundamentally different from the majority is excluded and isolated.

Wilderness

The wilderness is a safe haven for the centaur and other mythological beings. When they first experience persecution by humans, these creatures lived together in the wilderness. However, the narrator states that after a while, even the wilderness was encroached upon and the creatures had to disperse with some of them becoming extinct and the others adapting in order to live among people. The centaur alone managed to persist for millennia as a remnant from a more mysterious age. At the end of the story, as he stands on top of a mountain looking out toward the sea, the centaur imagines that he is once again in a world that appears "to be a wilderness waiting to be populated." He is wrong. The world has changed, and soon afterward, the centaur falls to his death. As a motif, the wilderness represents an earlier, less civilized world, in which the fantastical could exist peacefully.

Modern Times

Another theme of the story is how modern times exclude or disregard the fantastical. The narrator of the story points out that for ages, people welcomed the centaur as a special creature, promoting fertility and virility. Then the world changed, becoming less mysterious or rather intolerant and uninterested in the fantastical. When this happened, the centaur and other mythological creatures such as the unicorn and the chimera were banished and forced to flee from people. The events of the story take place in some time in the twentieth century, as the narrator mentions army helicopters preparing to hunt down the centaur at the end of the story. In modern times, the centaur experiences violence and hatred at the hands of human beings who do not understand him.

Style

Setting

The short story takes place in an unspecified land sometime in the twentieth century, after the invention of helicopters. The reader can guess that the native country the centaur returns to at the end of the story may be Greece, as the centaur's species was wiped out by Heracles, a hero in ancient Greek mythology. The mountainous land is close to the sea.

Point of View and Conflict

The story is told from the third-person point of view, with an unnamed narrator relating the events. The primary conflict in the story is internal, with the protagonist of the story, the centaur, struggling to reconcile his animal and human impulses. The human part of the centaur, in particular, strives to realize his humanity. The story's central conflict becomes resolved when the centaur falls to his death, landing on a rock and splitting into his distinct animal and human halves. As he lies dying, the half-man experiences relief, as he is finally separated from his animal side.

Allusion

Saramago alludes to the novel *Don Quixote*, when the narrator describes the centaur's greatest adventure as witnessing the fictional character of the same name fighting windmills. The reference is to the seventeenth-century work by Spanish author Miguel de Cervantes, *Don Quixote*, a forerunner of the modern novel which explores the tension between illusion and reality.

Motifs

Saramago uses the motifs of the sea and the sky to represent the centaur's goal or final destiny. (A motif is a recurring image or object that unifies a work.) After waking from a dream, the centaur hears the sound of the sea, which is a "vision of beating waves which his eyes have transformed into those sonorous waves which travel over the waters and climb up rocky gorges all the way to the sun and the blue sky which is also water." Here and elsewhere, Saramago conflates the images of sky and sea, so that they become one in the centaur's experience. The centaur's vision of sky and sea foreshadows his ultimate vision. Right before falling, he stands on a mountain from which he can see the sea. As he lies dying at the end of the story, the man-half looks up at the sky, which appears to be an "ever deepening sea overhead, a sea with tiny, motionless clouds that were islands, and immortal life." The sea toward which he had been moving suggests immortality.

Another type of body of water, the river, signals change in the story. The centaur walks along a riverbed several times in the story, and upon entering a river to cross it, he appears to be merely a man, as his horse-half is hidden underwater. The river moves the centaur toward humanity, and not too long after fording the river, the centaur sees a naked woman emerging from the same river. He notes that it is the first time he had seen a naked woman in his home country, and seeing her awakens human desires. Here again, the river serves to change the centaur momentarily, emboldening his human half.

Symbolism

The centaur can be considered a symbol, representing the dilemma of the human condition in which people struggle to reconcile their physical and mental or spiritual sides.

Historical Context

Saramago wrote and first published "The Centaur" in Portuguese in his short story collection *Objecto Quase* (Almost an Object) in 1978. At that time, Portugal had just emerged from nearly fifty years of fascist rule. On April 25, 1974, a triumphant revolution ended the dictatorships of António de Oliveira Salazar and his successor Marcelo Caetano. During the fascist rule of these dictators, Portuguese writers experienced repression and censorship and witnessed the effects of Portugal's colonial wars in Africa during the 1960s and early 1970s. The ill effects of those wars on Portuguese citizens led to the military coup of 1974 known as the Revolution of the Carnations, which resulted in democratic rule in Portugal and independence for Portugal's former African colonies.

Saramago wrote this story and most of his other works during this post-revolutionary period

Compare & Contrast

- **Portugal in the late 1970s:** Following the revolution to overthrow dictatorship, Portugal begins to make the transition to civilian rule. In April 1976, the nation approves a new constitution. The first free elections in fifty years soon follow.

  Portugal in the 1990s and early 2000s: A member of the European Union since 1986, the Portuguese economy enjoys a boom during the 1990s. In the early 2000s, Portugal faces complex socioeconomic challenges as one of the smaller members of the EU, even as the Portuguese population enjoys unprecedented expansion of civil liberties.

- **Portugal in the late 1970s:** Upon assuming control of the nation, President General António de Spínola promises decolonization. Portugal relinquishes control of former colonies, including Angola and East Timor, during the mid- to late-1970s.

  Portugal in the 1990s and early 2000s: In 1999, Portuguese citizens protest Indonesia's resistance to granting the power of self-determination in East Timor. Portuguese efforts to broker peace in Angola continue, as violent conflict persists in many of Portugal's former colonies.

in Portugal, which was initially marked by zealous revolutionary ideals and later characterized by more moderate Western European parliamentary methods. In his other writings, Saramago has often turned to Portuguese history as a source of inspiration, partly in order to reclaim and re-envision a history, which had become distorted by the official rhetoric of the ruling dictatorships. A committed Communist Party member and social activist, Saramago is the leading writer of Portugal's post-revolutionary generation.

"The Centaur" takes place in an indeterminate time, although one can conclude that the temporal setting is the twentieth century due to the references to army helicopters. Saramago may have chosen to make the time ambiguous to emphasize the setting as the modern age, as opposed to ancient times when the world appeared full of mystery. One of the themes of the story is how modern times exclude the possibility of the fantastical, with people misunderstanding and fearing the centaur. The author may have left the exact time of the story unspecified in order to highlight how people lost a sense of wonder long ago, much to the detriment of humankind. Although the story is not linked specifically to the time in which Saramago wrote it, the theme of an individual being persecuted for his difference resonates with the conditions Saramago worked under prior to the 1974 revolution.

Critical Overview

Because Saramago is mostly known as a novelist, the bulk of the criticism about his writings focuses on his many novels, which have been translated into over thirty languages and have been praised worldwide. Although the overtly political nature of some of his works has provoked censure from conservative critics who have denounced his writings as Communistic and anti-religious, many reviews of Saramago's work have been positive. According to the official Nobel Prize website, in awarding the author the Nobel Prize in 1998, the Swedish Academy lauded the author, "who with parables sustained by imagination, compassion and irony continually enables us once again to apprehend an elusory reality."

Many critics have noted Saramago's use of universal themes and his drive to portray common human experiences. Writing in *Portuguese Studies* Luis Rebelo de Sousa states, "Next to the innovatory character of Saramago's style—a style that keeps changing—lies the universal appeal of his work. He chooses for his fiction themes of universal appeal, dealing with questions of deep human resonance." Similarly, Saramago's translator Giovanni Pontiero, in his introduction to a section devoted to Saramago in a 1994 issue of the *Bulletin of Hispanic Studies*, emphasizes the author's

Antique vase illustration of Hercules fighting the centaur Chiron

ability to convey the full spectrum of human experience: "Convinced that the writer's task is to look behind the scenes, Saramago uncovers every facet of human experience. His novels instill a keen awareness of human aspirations and failures, for human destiny is the ultimate concern in each and every one of his books. Man, for Saramago, is a remarkable creature but he can only achieve his true potential in a climate of truth and freedom."

In his review of *Almost an Object* in the *Dictionary of Literary Biography*, José N. Ornelas also highlights Saramago's humanism: "The volume, which comprises six short stories mixing the fantastic and science fiction, focuses on themes that are valuable to the writer, such as the struggle against consumer society and totalitarian systems that have stripped individuals of their humanity and/or subjectivity and are the direct cause of their alienation." In a rare review of the short story *"The Centaur"* published in *Hispania*, Haydn Tiago Jones notes how Saramago begins to explore themes and devices in this story that later appear in his novels: "In the genre of short stories, José Saramago introduced the fantastical devices prevalent in his longer works. These devices include the introduction of figures usually associated with fairy tales, and the endowment of characters with quasi magical powers."

Criticism

Anna Maria Hong

Anna Maria Hong is a published poet and an editor of the fiction and memoir anthology Growing Up Asian American. In the following essay, Hong discusses how Saramago uses the mythical figure of the centaur to explore the themes of isolation and the tension between the physical and spiritual sides of humanity.

Like much of Saramago's fiction, "The Centaur" blends the fantastical with the actual to explore themes common to all humanity. One of the central themes of the story concerns how people struggle to reconcile their physical and spiritual needs, even as they grapple with external forces that threaten their survival. Saramago illustrates the internal conflict between parts of the self through the story's protagonist, an unnamed centaur, who literally embodies the split, as he possesses the mind and upper body of a man and the lower body of a horse.

> "In the modern age, people are intolerant of the fantastical, and in his depiction of the centaur's existence, Saramago underscores how violently people shun difference."

Throughout the story, the two halves of the centaur vie for dominance or control, and the centaur experiences his conflicting needs in a moment-to-moment kind of way. Saramago emphasizes how distinct the human and the horse parts of the centaur are by frequently referring to each part separately as "the man" and "the horse." Conflicts arise between the two halves, as they possess different kinds of desires. The animal half expresses physical needs such as wanting to quench thirst, while the human half experiences more complex longings such as the desire for revenge and love.

Sometimes, the needs of one half of the centaur are easily accommodated by the other half, as when the man half drinks from a stream to quench the horse half's thirst. Although the man does not feel thirsty, he can help the animal part without too much trouble. However, at other times, easy solutions evade the centaur. For example, the man finds himself perpetually fatigued, because finding a comfortable sleeping position for both the horse and the man is so difficult. The narrator states, "It was not a comfortable body. The man could never stretch out on the ground, rest his head on folded arms and remain there studying the ants or grains of earth, or contemplate the whiteness of a tender stalk sprouting from the dark soil." In descriptions such as this one, Saramago makes it clear that it is usually the human side of the centaur which suffers. The man half exists in a body that precludes comfort, but more than that, he is denied the pleasures of a full human, which would include being able to contemplate his surroundings in a leisurely way.

Perhaps the most frustrating thing for the human part of the centaur is his inability to connect with other creatures. The lone survivor of the once mighty race of centaurs, the centaur has been roaming the world alone for millennia, traveling by night to avoid detection by people. Saramago emphasizes that this state of extreme solitude was not always the centaur's lot, as he was once accepted and even embraced by human beings who regarded the centaur as a magical being with the power to promote fertility and virility. The centaur and other mythological creatures such as the unicorn and giant ants were free to travel openly and lived in harmony with people "so long as the world itself remained mysterious." The centaur's situation of perpetual exile occurred as a result of the world's losing its sense of mystery. The narrator notes that following this abrupt change, the centaur and other fantastical creatures of yore were persecuted and banished from the human world. Although they at first banded together, eventually only one centaur remained of his kind.

Saramago thus portrays the centaur's state of alienation as a direct result of humanity's transition into the modern age. The narrator stresses that at some point in the past few millennia, the centaur discovered that there was nowhere he could travel safely anymore. In his encounters with people, the centaur is consistently hunted by angry mobs with firearms and dogs. Rather than being recognized as a magical being, he is denigrated and loathed for his difference, and as he thinks about his situation, the centaur ruminates on "that incomprehensible hatred." In the modern age, people are intolerant of the fantastical, and in his depiction of the centaur's existence, Saramago underscores how violently people shun difference.

Ultimately, the centaur is unable to find fulfillment due to a combination of internal and external reasons. He is limited by his extraordinary body, which denies him full access to his own humanity. However, his state of internal conflict is severely complicated by the human world in which he lives. Long ago, people decimated his kind, leaving him to fend for himself for thousands of years. Over the millennia, as the expansion of human society encroached upon the wilderness where he could live safely, the centaur became increasingly marginalized, lonely, and exhausted.

The human part of the centaur's loneliness and longing for solace are depicted clearly when the centaur encounters a woman. Having never seen a woman before in his native land, to which he has just returned, the centaur grabs her and runs with her in his arms, inciting a chase by a mob of villagers. The woman is initially terrified, but after the centaur speaks to her and asks her not to hate him,

What Do I Read Next?

- Saramago's novel *Baltasar and Blimunda* (1982) is considered one of his great achievements. Set during the Inquisition in eighteenth-century Portugal, the book focuses on the attempts by two young characters, the disabled war veteran Baltasar and the visionary Blimunda, to transport themselves to the heavens. Like many of Saramago's works, this novel is praised as an innovative blending on the fantastical and the historical.
- Another highly lauded Saramago novel is *The Year of the Death of Ricardo Reis* (1984). The novel tells the story of Ricardo Reis, a poet-physician who returns to Portugal from Rio de Janeiro, his love interests, and the ghost of Portuguese poet Fernando Pessoa.
- Saramago's controversial novel *The Gospel According to Jesus Christ* (1991) imaginatively and idiosyncratically tells the story of Jesus' life, emphasizing the figure's humanity and portraying God as a bureaucratic character with questionable motives.
- *Poems of Fernando Pessoa* (1998), translated and edited by Edwin Honig and Susan M. Brown, collects the heteronymous poems of the great Portuguese modernist poet who wrote under the personas of Alberto Caeiro, Álvaro do Campos, and Ricardo Reis.
- A blend of non-fiction travelogue and novel, Saramago's book *Journey to Portugal: In Pursuit of Portugal's History and Culture*, published in English in 2001, recounts the author's travels across his country, as well as his reflections on Portuguese history and culture.
- *The Portuguese Empire, 1415–1808: A World on the Move* (1998), by A. J. R. Russell-Wood, traces the history of Portugal as the world's first colonial empire.

the woman speaks kindly to him. Seeming to recognize him as he is, the woman lies on the ground and asks him to cover her, but the centaur recognizes that connecting with her physically is impossible. After looking at her for a moment, he continues to run away from the mob, with the man part of the centaur lamenting his state of perpetual frustration and isolation.

Soon after his encounter with the woman, the centaur dies, falling to his death from a precipice and landing on a sharp rock, which cuts him in two exactly at the spot where the man and the horse are joined. Once again, in this final instance, Saramago makes it clear that the centaur's death results from both his internal and external struggles. Outwardly, he is being hunted by people who want to capture him with nets, ropes, nooses, and staffs. Having found love impossible for a final time, he falls to his death because he cannot resolve the battle for control between his two halves. As the narrator notes, "The horse reared into the air, shook its front hooves and swung round in a frenzy to face his enemies. The man tried to retreat. Both of them struggled, behind and in front." The struggle ends with the centaur falling into the abyss.

With this conclusion, Saramago emphasizes how the competing impulses of physical and mental or spiritual cannot be sustained. The conflict ends with a definite separation of the two sides, and with the man finally freed into his full humanity. As he lies dying, the severed man seems to have a transcendent moment, as he watches the sky, which appears to be the sea that he had been moving toward all along. The story ends with the man examining himself for the last time: "The man turned his head from one side to the other: nothing but endless sea, an interminable sky. Then he looked at his body. It was bleeding. Half a man. A man. And he saw the gods approaching. It was time to die."

As he leaves the body that has burdened him for so long, the man experiences relief as well as the contemplative peace that has previously eluded him. He is finally able to lie on his back and view his surroundings in a leisurely way, without having to run anymore. For the centaur, death is the only solution, as the modern world will not accommodate his particular struggle. He is reviled, not only as a strange remnant of a former time, but also perhaps as a thinking being that wants more than it can have.

As a symbolic character, the centaur dramatizes the human condition, as Saramago seems to indicate that the spiritual side of human beings is constantly under siege from both the demands of the physical body and the miscomprehension of others who leave little room for recognizing extraordinary phenomena such as the movement of clouds or the travails of a centaur. The centaur remains thoughtful, perceptive, and utterly alone to the very end.

Source: Anna Maria Hong, Critical Essay on "The Centaur," in *Short Stories for Students*, Thomson Gale, 2006.

Luis de Sousa Rebelo

In the following paper delivered on the occasion of the celebration for Saramago's Nobel Prize in December 1998, Rebelo surveys Saramago's novels, identifying the original stylistic and thematic elements that make him a great writer.

The success of Jose Saramago as a fiction writer has been built in less than two decades. It started with the publication of his novel, *Levantado do Chao,* in 1980, culminating in his apotheosis in Oslo last year, where he received the Nobel Prize for Literature.

As a novelist he started rather late in life or, to be more precise, in his early fifties. He began by reflecting on the problems of representation both in the plastic arts and literature, dealing with it not in a formal essay but within the boundaries of the novel itself. In *Manual de Pintura e Caligrafia,* an inauspicious title for a work of fiction, issued in 1977, he explores these questions and shows a deep interest in the commitment of the artist to a cause of social justice.

After the publication of this novel, Saramago seems to have solved the problems of artistic expression if we are to take his regular literary output (he published at the rate of one novel every two years) as a sign of the new way he had found for himself as a writer. Behind lay a solitary novel, forgotten for twenty years, which has now been rediscovered in the light of his current success.

In *Levantado do Chao* Saramago showed a command of form and style that signalled the period of great fiction that was to follow and captivated his public. The novel deals with the age old theme of oppression, the struggle of a family of labourers who try to eke out a living in Alentejo, a southern province of Portugal. It is a painful struggle seen through the eyes of three generations of working people with their joys and sadness. In order to research the book Saramago moved to Alentejo and lived there for a year, in this way finding his own roots, for he comes himself from the same humble origins. Naturally he understood the plight of this people, the people he was going to change into the characters of his novel, being able to share with them a common experience, living their hopes and frustrations. This is probably the reason why *Levantado do Chao* is such a moving book. Technically the author had to face some difficulties. Similar subjects had been treated more than once by the neorealists. By avoiding the tone and the literary conventions of the genre, Saramago succeeded in keeping his originality. He began by collecting individual reports on the life of the local peasants and on the basis of their accounts he started his creative work. As a narrator he adopts the voice of the old singer of tales, changing in this way the novel into a form of oral speech. These stylistic devices give him the status of an epic poet, making the story of these peasants a real saga. These qualifies would flourish later in the novels that firmly established his reputation, such as *Memorial do Convento* (1982) and *O Ano da Morte de Ricardo Reis* (1984). Trying to give the impression of recreating the oral tale through the written word, Saramago adopts in his prose the repetition of current speech. The anaphora enables him to develop the same idea in different ways. It attains a dramatic intensity that is persuasive and moving. The amplification of the narrative lends itself easily to the lyrical mode. The story flows as if it knew no ending, gaining the complicity of the reader for higher and higher flights of imagination, which seem so natural in the world described by the narrator. This style may perturb the reader unprepared for deep radical changes in the literary text and educated in a well-established tradition of literacy. The reader may also be confused by the pauses, the cadence, and the rhythm that follow the word delivery and alter the conventional system of punctuation. At one stage this system disappears, giving the reader the freedom to shape the text according to his own mood or inclination. The experiment had been tried before by the surrealists in their poetry, and to the same effect. Saramago himself had suggested that the difficulty would dissolve if the text were to be read aloud. More recently, in his latest novels, he has returned to the established conventions of punctuation.

The oral style, adapted to a written text, requires a special approach on the part of the author in relation to his subject matter and in his relationship with the reader. The narrator tries to give the impression of keeping on the same cultural level as that of his reader, sharing with him or her what seems to be a common knowledge, regaining in this way the reader's trust and complicity. There are strategic devices which enable the narrator to develop his story and make it move into new realms of meaning. If we choose the emphasis on words, we soon begin to relate the verbal structures we call literary to other verbal structures. We find there are no clearly marked boundaries, only centres of interest. There are many writers, ranging from Plato to Sartre, whom it is difficult to classify as literary or philosophical. Following this lead of Northrop Frye on the verbal attraction that makes up the nature of the text, it is easy to see how well Saramago's narrator fits in with the discursive categories that break all boundaries and nourish the illusions of the reader. The effect is a suspension of disbelief that opens the door to imaginary worlds, where magic and extraordinary events are accepted as plausible and as part of our own experience. Verbal attraction turns into a dialogue between different texts, which gives the opportunity to the narrator of sharing his encyclopaedic knowledge and his wisdom with his reader. In *O Ano da Morte de Ricardo Reis* the dialogic style shifts to an inner psychological space, where the exchanges between Ricardo Reis and Fernando Pessoa, between Reis and the dead man, who was his creator, sum up a philosophical recreation of the agonies of living, loving and dying.

The voice of Saramago's narrator, the voice of the author as he sometimes likes to emphasize it, is a friendly voice that has nothing of the neutral and impassive tone of the singer of tales of the *Odyssey*. His voice is warmer, moved by events, is full of wisdom and exudes a world weary experience, even a melancholy that brings him closer to his reader, creating that special relationship between the two that has so often been pointed out by critics.

Next to the innovatory character of Saramago's style—a style that keeps changing—lies the universal appeal of his work. He chooses for his fiction themes of universal appeal, dealing with questions of deep human resonance. These are for him metaphors of existence and of the world created by words to which all the credit must be given—illusions and nightmares that are not to be forgotten. History and historical discourse is the field where Saramago picks up his subjects and finds his centres of interest, trying to detect in its ambiguities the invisible side of reality.

"These are for him metaphors of existence and of the world created by words to which all the credit must be given--illusions and nightmares that are not to be forgotten."

By exploring the effects of a particular situation, he unveils what is hidden in human motivations. When Joao V was given an heir by his queen, he sees in the child the miracle that had been promised by her confessor, who was better informed than he of her pregnancy, being a confidant of the mysteries of her body and soul. He had promised the church to build a convent, and that he did. The novel, *Memorial do Convento* (*Baltasar and Blimunda*) reports the story of this prodigious project, shifting gradually to the adventures and vicissitudes of the ordinary people who built it, a baroque dream in an era of squalor and splendour fed by Brazilian gold. In the *Historia do Cerco de Lisboa* (1989), a proofreader inserts the word 'not,' the 'nao' in the text he is correcting, changing the course of historical narrative. The Crusaders, in his version, had not assisted Afonso Henriques, the first king of Portugal, in taking the Islamic town. This contrafactual, as some English historians would say now, had unforeseen consequences. Some of them not necessarily bad for the people involved in telling the story.

On the other hand, a moral or psychological problem may provide the novelist with the lead he needs for his narrative. The anxiety of former concentration camp inmates, who have survived the holocaust, is a well-known fact. Having lost their entire family and friends, they asked themselves why they were the only ones to be alive. Albert Camus noted this form of suffering as the tragic condition of modern man. The situation has its affinities with the drama of Joseph, the husband of Mary, as described by Jose Saramago in his novel,

O Evangelho Segundo Jesus Cristo (1991). Joseph is wracked by moral pain and cannot forgive himself for not passing to others the information he had received from the Roman soldiers regarding the imminent massacre of the innocents. Instead of doing what he ought to have done, he fled quietly in the night, taking with him Mary and the child, trying to allay any suspicion in the village with his movements. The premeditation of his actions, his silence, make him guilty and an accomplice to the massive killing. His choice, by keeping his secret, is an indictment of his behaviour. *O Evangelho Segundo Jesus Cristo* is a narrative that challenges accepted views and demands from us a constant meditation on the problems we face in our time considered in the context of Christian culture and civilization.

Subtle and ironic, Saramago explores in his fiction the complexity of the great choices we face at the end of the century. Vividly aware of the changes which are taking place in modern Europe and of their consequences for its future, in *A Jangada de Pedra* (1986) he stakes his claim to the vital importance of Iberia as a geographic, social and cultural entity. By describing a cataclysm that separates Iberia from the European continent the novelist shows in a powerful metaphor the destinies of a history that cannot be ignored with its many traditions, cultures and literatures: a stone raft adrift in the Atlantic between Africa and South America. The passion and suffering of men and women, caught up in the twists of history liberate in this story a poetic fantasy that runs across all literary boundaries to recreate dreams of love and hope.

Saramago's latest novels aim at an even wider and more universal appeal. The narrative is reduced to the bare bones of meaning, purged of all the literary conventions and accessories that make up the genre. In *Ensaio sobre a Cegueira* (1996), the characters are not named, being known only by their function in the story, which takes place nowhere and everywhere. The blindness that affects one individual and then spreads to a whole society, sparing only the sight of one woman who tells the tale, is not entirely physical, but mental and moral. Gradually that society sinks into self-destruction, undermined by selfishness, and is spared the ultimate abjection when people recover their sight as mysteriously as they had lost it. The point has been made. Love—and love is a saving and redeeming quality in all of Saramago's fiction—is at the centre of *Todos os Nomes* (1997). The bleak atmosphere of the Public Records Office, where the anonymous civil servant seeks the identity of a woman he has never known and comes to love, may not be unfamiliar to the reader of Kafka's work and Gogol's, but the meticulous description of his search, his obsessive investigation, his successes, and final frustration in a powerful and administrative machinery bear the stamp of a great writer. These are the parables and the allegories for which Saramago was awarded the Nobel Prize for Literature, 1998, by the Swedish Academy. Congratulations Jose Saramago.

Source: Luis de Sousa Rebelo, "A Tribute to Jose Saramago," in *Portugese Studies*, Vol. 15, 1999, pp. 178–81.

Giovanni Pontiero

In the following interview, Saramago discusses with Giovanni Pontiero his approach, his style, and the content of his writing.

[*Giovanni Pontiero:*] *Sr. Saramago, you started publishing your major novels late in life, at least relatively late for a writer of your stature and output. Were there sporadic publications before the appearance of your novel* Levantado do Chão [Raised From The Ground], *first published in 1980?*

[Jose Saramago:] Leaving aside my first book, a novel, which appeared in 1947 when I was only twenty-five years of age, and which I do not include nowadays in my list of works, my literary activity started in 1966 with the publication of a book of poems *Os Poemas Possíveis* [*Possible Poems*]. But by 1980 I had published nine more books (two books of poetry, two collections of chronicles, two collections of political essays, a novel, a collection of short stories and a play). It's true that I started to write late in life, but less late than you imagine if you start counting from the first of my more important novels.

How would you describe your initial development as a writer?

I was eighteen years of age when, during one of those conversations between adolescents which are one of life's greatest pleasures, I told the friends I was with that I should like to become a writer. By that time all I had written were sentimental and dramatic poems typical of the poetry young people wrote at that time. Probably the most important thing for my future as a writer was my love of reading from an early age.

Your major novels seem to take us back to the tradition of classical fiction in terms of scope, thematic richness, wealth of ideas and associations.

That might be claiming too much and I'm certainly not the best person to reply, since I'd have to be my own judge and advocate. It is true, however, that for me the novel is inseparable from a certain sense of breadth and comprehensiveness, rather like a tiny universe which expands and starts gathering and assimilating all the errant 'bodies' it encounters, sometimes contradictory, but finally capable of being harmonised. From this point of view, the novel, as I understand and practise it, should always tend towards the 'excessive.' Now then, 'excess,' at least in principle, should be incompatible with the 'classical' if the facts weren't there to prove otherwise: 'classical' novels are, as a general rule, 'excessive' . . .

While your books are vastly entertaining, they make real demands on the reader in terms of knowledge and curiosity.

It pleases me to know that my novels make the reader think. As for me, I thought a great deal while I was writing them. I thought as best I could and knew, and I should be disappointed if readers didn't find something more than the entertaining narrative I've also provided. If the entertainment has some value in itself, that value is greatly enhanced when the story becomes a passport to reflection.

You exercised various professions, mechanic, technical designer, literary editor and journalist before becoming a professional writer. Have these had any influence on your formation as a writer?

I don't think any of the various professional activities I have exercised have helped with my formation as a writer. They certainly helped to make me the man I am, along with many other factors, some perhaps identifiable, others of which I'm no longer aware. Who knows, perhaps simply by being a child sitting on a riverbank and watching the water flow past. That child will one day become a writer without ever knowing why.

At one point in A Jangada de Pedra [The Stone Raft] *you state that 'the objectivity of the narrator is a modern invention.' Could I ask you to comment on this concept, given your own clear preference for a non-objective stance?*

I shouldn't call it a concept, merely the formulation of the attitude adopted by the author when he identifies with the narrator and who, more often than not, deliberately takes his place. I'm opposed to a certain idea, which is fashionable nowadays, of an absent, impartial and objective narrator, who limits himself to registering impressions without reacting to them himself. Probably all this has to do with my inability (unpardonable from a theoretical point of view) to separate the narrator from the author himself.

"It pleases me to know that my novels make the reader think. As for me, I thought a great deal while I was writing them."

The writer and critic Irving Howe in his review of Memorial do Convento *(translated into English under the title* Baltasar and Blimunda*) described you as 'a connoisseur of ironies.' Undoubtedly, there is a strong vein of satire in your writing. I suspect that you enjoy being provocative especially where you refer to politicians and plutocrats.*

Irony, let's face it, is a poor safeguard against power and its abuses, whether that power be political, economic, or religious, just to give some examples. A great Portuguese novelist of the last century, Eça de Queiroz, once wrote that one way to overthrow an institution was to go round it three times with howls of laughter. I'm much less optimistic. Irony is like whistling as you walk through a cemetery at night: we think we can ignore death thanks to that tiny human sound which ill conceals fear. But it's also true that if we should lose the capacity of being ironic we should find ourselves completely disarmed.

How do you view the relationship between text and sub-text in your novels, with the frequent parentheses and cross-references?

That's a difficult question. As difficult as asking a tennis player, for example, how he executes a particular move. In reply, he would most likely repeat the move in slow motion before our eyes while explaining it step by step, breaking down, as it were, into fixed images what had previously been only one fluent and effective movement. The writer, I suppose, cannot observe himself as he is writing, nor do I believe that, once confronted with the written page, he is capable of analysing a relationship as complicated as the one your question raises. Molière, on bringing his 'bourgeois gentilhomme' to the conclusion that he was speaking prose without knowing it, wasn't merely presenting us with a situation, comic to the point of absurdity. There is more knowledge in the not-knowing than we imagine.

Your novels take us into a number of different worlds where we meet an impressive range of characters both real and fictitious. Your narratives are peopled by monarchs, poets, priests, artists, musicians, the professional classes, workers and peasants. Yet in the final analysis, for you, as for writers like Colombia's García Márquez and Russia's Solzhenitsyn 'the poor are the salt of the earth.' I refer to the 'poor in spirit' rather than those who are simply poor in material terms.

I don't think that the positions of García Márquez and Solzhenitsyn coincide on this point. I even believe they're referring to quite different things: whereas the Colombian writer would look for a primary and immutable innocence in his characters, the Russian, after establishing an implacable inventory of evils and crimes, would try to restore that innocence to those who had definitely lost it. As for me, who was born poor and am not rich, what drives me is to show that the worst waste is not that of consumer goods, but that of simple humanity: millions of human beings trampled underfoot by History, millions and millions of people who possessed nothing other than life itself, which was of such little use to them, yet much exploited by others, the clever, the strong, the powerful.

Your technique as a novelist is quite distinctive. On the one hand, you have a marked preference for austerity: punctuation limited to commas and full stops without any dashes, colons, semicolons, interrogation or exclamation marks. You rarely use the conjunctions and or but. On the other hand, you betray a penchant for baroque structures, circular oratory and ornate symmetrical patterns.

All the characteristics of my technique at present (I'd prefer to use the word style) stem from a basic principle whereby everything *said* is destined to be *heard.* What I am trying to say is that I see myself as an oral narrator when I write and that the words written by me are intended as much to be read as to be heard. Now, the oral narrator doesn't use punctuation, he speaks as if he were composing music and uses the same elements as the musician: sounds and pauses, high or low, some short, others long. Those tendencies which I acknowledge and endorse (baroque structures, circular oratory, symmetrical patterns), I suppose stem from a certain idea of an oral discourse accepted as music. I ask myself if there may not even be something more than a simple coincidence between the disorganized and fragmentary nature of spoken discourse today and the 'minimalist' expression of modern music.

Critics have commented on the amount of detail in your novels. How do you set about controlling so much detail as the narrative evolves?

I have no special method or discipline. Words emerge, one after another, in strict sequence, out of a kind of organic necessity, to put it loosely. But there is inside me a scale, a norm, which permits me to control, one might almost say intuitively, the 'economy' of detail. In principle, the logical *I* is open to all possibilities, but the intuitive *I* governs itself with its own laws which the other *I* has learnt to obey. All of this is clearly unscientific, unless as part of another involuntary and inherent science, impossible to define by someone like myself who simply practises the craft of writing.

Comparing the three major novels with which I have been closely involved as a translator, like all your readers I am impressed by your powers of invention. Memorial do Convento [Annals of the Convent], O Ano da Morte de Ricardo Reis [The Year of the Death of Ricardo Reis] *and* A Jangada de Pedra [The Stone Raft] *are all three vintage Saramago, yet each of these novels constitutes a fresh adventure, a new direction, a different perspective. Is there some point of unity here which you yourself judge to be important?*

It's generally said (and so many people say it that there must be some validity) that the author is the person least qualified to define what he has written, that the intentions which moved him to write are one thing and the final result another, where the so-called intentions (which the author nearly always insists on defending as being paramount in his work) end up by becoming secondary because of the emergence of the subconscious, the aleatory, the humoral, through which he has come to express his deep desire. It is in this domain of intentions (perhaps unfulfilled) that I should look for this point of unity: the attempt to reconcile two opposites—compassion and radical scepticism.

In A Jangada de Pedra, *in one of the most poetic and poignant passages in the entire novel, an anonymous voice reminds us that: 'Each of us sees the world with the eyes we possess, and our eyes see what they want to see.'*

The phrase would be more precise if written as follows: 'Each of us sees the world with the eyes we possess, and our eyes see what they can.' Wanting to, as we know, is not the same as being able to.

Could I ask you to comment on one recurring image, that of the journey—either in the form of a pilgrimage, exodus, migration or private journey in search of one's past?

Perhaps something of my own nature is expressed in this. In fact, as a person I'm really somewhat sedentary, and the proof of this is that for me to make a journey is rather like pursuing the path that will lead me back to the point of departure. On arriving at any place, I immediately begin to feel the need to get away from there. I'm convinced that the characters in my novels travel a lot because they want to return to where they were, that place where, in the final analysis, *they are.*

Your use of topography intrigues me. On the surface there are carefully researched locations, landmarks and itineraries. Beneath the surface these are unmistakably linked to states of mind and feeling.

If in the *Memorial do Convento* Blimunda kills the friar who tried to rape her, it was because in that part of the sierra the author found the ruins of a convent; if in *Jangada de Pedra* the lands of Orce are described in great detail, that's because the author travelled more than a thousand kilometres to see them with his own eyes. And there is also the fundamental question of names: of inhabited places, of rivers, of mountains. They are the names, the words, that clothe the world of the spirit.

Gabriel García Márquez once observed that every author, however prolific, in fact only writes one book. He then went on to say that his was the book of solitude. Would you agree? And how would you define your own books collectively?

I believe authors write because, to put it very simply, we do not want to die. Therefore I would say that the book we persist in writing, one in many or all in one, is the book of survival. Needless to say, we are fighting a lost battle: nothing survives.

Jorge Luis Borges has also left us a much-quoted maxim in which he states that: 'Any great and lasting book must be ambiguous.' I find a strong current of ambiguity running through your novels.

Key phrases uttered by famous authors always leave me somewhat cold. Taken out of context, isolated from the work as a whole, they become somewhat contentious and intimidating, and somehow paralyse our own thinking. Ambiguity in a book, if not a defect, should not be considered a virtue to the extent of making it a condition of lasting value. I see things as being much simpler: the ambiguity of authors is what makes the ambiguity of books. And most likely ambiguity is really something inherent in the act of writing. In which case we really ought to look for other factors before deciding whether a book is important or not.

Sex and religion are examined from every possible angle in your fiction. But I want to ask you more specifically about your interest in supernatural forces, in things prodigious and mysterious; one critic even speaks of mysticism in your work.

Things supernatural, prodigious, mysteries, are simply the things I ignore. One day the supernatural will become natural, the prodigious will be within everyone's grasp, the mystery will cease to exist. The problem is solely between me and the knowledge I possess, and, from this point of view, the computer on which I write my books strikes me as being every bit as enigmatic as life after death. I am not a mystic. If I speak so much about religion, it's because it exists, and above all, because it conditioned and still conditions my moral being. But, being an atheist, I always say that one needs a fair dose of religion in order to make a coherent atheist.

Looking at Portugal's fortunes from the days of mighty empire to dwindling power and influence, you would appear to regret not so much her loss of importance and influence in the political sphere as the danger of losing one's national identity.

The Europe of the Common Market is a holding company with large and small shareholders. Power is in the hands of the rich, the small countries have no choice other than to abide by and fulfil the policies which are, in fact, decided by the large countries, even if there is the appearance of democracy. Today, being in the right means having money. The recent gathering of the Seven Richest Countries In The World is, in my opinion, an obscenity, all the more flagrant insofar as it took place during the commemorative celebrations of a revolution which launched an ideal of liberty, equality and fraternity throughout the world, but which has now become nothing more than a tragic mockery. To give but one example, seventy per cent of the forestation area of my country will be used to plant eucalyptus, not because the Portuguese people want it, but because it has been decreed by the E.E.C.

Portugal looms large in your writing. Your country's history and destiny, her people and their aspirations are evoked with a degree of passion and genuine concern.

If I were North-American, Russian or British, or German or French, perhaps I'd feel proud of my country's power and wealth, even if I reaped no benefits or compensations from that wealth and power. As a Portuguese, I feel it would now be idle to take pride in the power and influence which Portugal once enjoyed. Our present is what confronts us: supranationality, limitation of sovereignty, diverse acculturation. I should like at least to preserve my difference, because, frankly, if the World and Europe are not interested in knowing who I am (I, Portuguese, We, Portuguese), I'm not particularly interested in being a citizen of the World or even a European.

In your essay published in the TLS *(December, 1988) under the title 'A Country Adrift,' there was one sentence which made a deep impression. I refer to those arresting words: 'Every manner of crime has been committed in the name of patriotism.' An accusation inevitably linked to your open distrust of Eurocentrism.*

I think these words are self-evident. When you send thousands or millions of people to their death with the pretext that the *Fatherland* is in danger—although what's really in danger are the individual interests of those who, directly or indirectly, hold power—that is a crime committed in the name of patriotism. People go to their deaths thinking they know why, and they are deceived to such an extent that they accuse of being unpatriotic anyone who tries to tell them the truth.

After absorbing your intimate portrait of Portugal and her people, I'm almost persuaded that 'small is truly beautiful.'

Small is not beautiful simply because it's small. It's beautiful if it enjoys justice and happiness. But small countries cannot, in fact, be as ambitious as big countries nearly always are. A small country, by dint of much effort, can only hope to get closer to achieving happiness and justice. The worst thing is that there are plenty of small countries in the world which are deprived of both justice and happiness.

At one point in A Jangada de Pedra *you write: 'Life itself enjoys cultivating a sense of the dramatic.' Does this account for your own keen sense of the dramatic in your writing, whether farcical or tragic?*

I don't have a dramatic concept of existence, or rather, I have it, but I de-dramatize it through irony. I try as hard as possible to avoid turning life into a Wailing Wall: to have to die is misfortune enough, but even that has its hour.

Have any of your own plays been performed on the stage?

Yes, I have written for the theatre, although I don't see myself as a playwright but rather as a novelist who occasionally writes for the theatre on request. I have written three plays to date, and all three have been performed on stage: *A Noite* [*The Night*] (where the action takes place in a newspaper office during the night of 24th to 25th April 1974), *Que Farei Com Este Livro? [What Shall I Do With This Book?]* (in which the protagonist is Luís de Camões after his return from India, when he was looking for a publisher for his epic poem) and *A Segunda Vida de Francisco de Assis* [*The Second Life of Francis of Assisi*] (the hero is, and is not, the saint).

In May, 1990, an opera entitled Blimunda, *based on your novel* Memorial do Convento, *will be given its première at La Scala, Milan. Can you tell me something about Azio Corghi, the composer of the opera?*

Azio Corghi is one of Italy's most prominent contemporary composers. He has mainly composed music for opera and ballet. His opera *Gargantua,* based on Rabelais and staged several years ago, caused quite a stir in musical circles.

Have you been involved in the preparation of the libretto?

The libretto of *Blimunda* was prepared by Azio Corghi and based on the Italian translation of *Memorial do Convento.* Any intervention on my part was limited to a general exchange of ideas and helping to find solutions for the dramatic expression of certain situations in the novel once adapted for the opera.

Who would you cite as important influences on your work?

Although this statement might sound absurdly pretentious, I don't recognise any significant influences on my work, except perhaps of certain affinities with Portuguese writers of the seventeenth century.

Who are the writers with whom you feel a certain affinity of temperament and outlook?

Gogol, Montaigne, Cervantes, all of them pessimists, and Padre António Vieira, who was a practical Utopian.

In your contribution to the B.B.C. television series of programmes about Portugal and the Portuguese, you expressed certain fears about literacy and culture. Could I ask you to elaborate on the crisis as you see it?

I suspect that this concern is not confined to Portugal. The number of illiterates in the world is growing. And in this day and age, there exists a very large number of people who have been taught to read and write but who, because of lack of continuity in reading and writing, effectively end up with the illiterate majority. This state of affairs probably suits the super-powers wherever they may be, for all they require to maintain and extend their predominance is to rely on the services of highly specialized minorities who monopolise the skills and means which permit a global vision, without which tactics cannot be defined, let alone strategies.

In recent years, a considerable number of talented Portuguese writers have come to the fore. Worldwide interest in the centenary celebrations to mark the birth of your great poet Fernando Pessoa may have helped to focus greater attention on Portuguese literature in recent years. But perhaps there are other reasons for this sudden interest abroad?

One cannot deny the influence Fernando Pessoa has exerted and continues to exert in the recent projection of Portuguese literature abroad, but it would be a mistake to imagine everything begins and ends with Pessoa. What is interesting to note, within proper limits, is that the Portuguese writers who came after Pessoa have matched up to the expectations aroused by Pessoa's writing. In other words, while no contemporary Portuguese writer aspires to the greatness of a Pessoa, their works nevertheless appear to the outside world as being worthy of attention. It's also possible that a certain crisis in creative writing in some countries has also contributed to this tiny discovery of a peripheral literature: the principle of communicating vessels is not the exclusive domain of physics.

I suspect that even you must be surprised at the ever increasing interest in your fiction abroad. Your novel Memorial do Convento, *for example, soon to be appearing in as many as twenty-five different languages.*

Frankly, I don't know. One day, conversing with my German publisher, I asked him why he had become interested in the books of an author hitherto unknown in the Federal Republic of Germany, an author originating from a small, remote country with a literature virtually ignored by the rest of Europe. He replied by explaining that he was looking for unconventional novels to publish and that he had found them in my work. I can only offer you this explanation for what it's worth and which isn't mine.

Your latest novel O Cerco de Lisboa [The Siege of Lisbon] *looks like equalling the success of your other novels. Is there any other novel on the way?*

The title of my next novel will be *O Evangelho Segundo Jesus Cristo [The Gospel According to Jesus Christ].* I leave the rest to the reader's imagination.

Source: Giovanni Pontiero, "Interview with Jose Saramago," in *PN Review*, Vol. 16, No. 4, 1989, pp. 38–42.

Sources

De Sousa, Luis Rebelo, "A Tribute to José Saramago," in *Portuguese Studies*, Vol. 15, 1999, pp. 178–81.

Jones, Haydn Tiago, Review of "Centauro," in *Objecto Quase*, in *Hispania*, Vol. 82, No. 1, March 1999, pp. 5–6.

Ornelas, José N., "José Saramago," in *Dictionary of Literary Biography*, Vol. 287: *Portuguese Writers*, edited by Monica Rector and Fred M. Clark, Thomson Gale, 2004, pp. 280–97.

Pontiero, Giovanni, "José Saramago: An Introduction," in *Bulletin of Hispanic Studies*, Vol. LXXI, No. 1, January 1994, pp. 115–17.

Saramago, José, "The Centaur," in *Telling Tales*, edited by Nadine Gordimer, Picador, 2004, pp. 15–34.

Tesser, Carmen Chaves, ed., "Introduction" to "A Tribute to José Saramago, 1998 Nobel Literature Laureate," in *Hispania*, Vol. 82, No. 1, March 1999, p. 1.

Further Reading

Bloom, Harold, ed., *José Saramago*, Chelsea House Publishers, 2005.

This collection contains an introduction by literary critic Harold Bloom and several scholarly essays by various critics on the author's works, focusing mostly on the major novels.

Bulfinch, Thomas, *Bulfinch's Mythology*, Modern Library, 1998.

During the nineteenth century, Bulfinch studied and retold the myths of Greek, Roman, and other cultures in several volumes, three of which have been collected in this useful book, which provides a handy reference to ancient myths, including those of the centaurs.

Cervantes, Miguel de, *Don Quixote*, Ecco, 2003.

Translated from the Spanish by Edith Grossman, this classic novel tells the adventures of Don Quixote, a romantic and idealistic knight, and his loyal squire Sancho Panza.

Gordimer, Nadine, ed., *Telling Tales*, Picador, 2004.

Edited by South African Nobel laureate Gordimer, this anthology comprises short stories by a diverse array of writers from around the world, including Salman Rushdie, Margaret Atwood, Chinua Achebe, Susan Sontag, and Kenzaburo Oe. The book's publishers donate the proceeds to HIV/AIDS preventive education and medical treatment for people suffering from the disease. "*The Centaur*" appears in this collection.

Hamilton, Edith, *Mythology*, Little, Brown, 1942.

Hamilton retells Greek, Roman, and Norse myths in this lively and comprehensive book, which includes sections on centaurs and the battle of Lapithae mentioned in Saramago's story.

Tamen, Miguel, and Helena Carvalhao Buescu, eds., *A Revisionary History of Portuguese Literature*, Garland Publishing, 1998.

This collection of essays explores the history of Portuguese literature from medieval times through the present, providing insight into the development of this literature.

The Deep

Mary Swan

2000

"The Deep," a novella by Canadian writer Mary Swan, was first published in the Canadian literary journal *The Malahat Review* in 2000. This story won the 2001 O. Henry Award for short fiction. "The Deep" has been republished in several books, including a collection of Swan's short fiction, *The Deep and Other Stories* (2004).

"The Deep" is a haunting tale about the life and death of twin sisters during World War I. The story is a complex weave of historical themes such as women's involvement in the war effort and more universal themes such as dysfunctional families. This story also explores the unique bond between identical twins. Swan has been writing and publishing short stories in the United States and Canada since the 1980s; "The Deep" is her most widely read and best-received work as of 2005.

Author Biography

Mary Swan is a very private person, and not much is known about her life. It is known that she graduated from York University and the University of Guelph, both in Ontario, Canada. As of 2005, she lives in Guelph, which is near Toronto, with her husband and daughter. She works at the University of Guelph library. Swan has traveled all over Europe.

As of 2005 Swan had been writing for over twenty years, ten of which were spent sporadically

Mary Swan © Alex Porter. Reproduced by permission

working on "The Deep." Her short stories have been published in numerous literary magazines, including *The Malahat Review*, *Harpers*, and the *Ontario Review*. Her work has also been anthologized in *Emergent Voices*, *Best Canadian Stories 92*, and *Coming Attractions*.

Swan came to popular attention when her short story "The Deep" won the 2001 O. Henry Award. "The Deep" was published as a novella chapbook in 2002 and then in a collection of Swan's short stories, *The Deep and Other Stories*, in 2004. Swan's other volume of short stories, *Emma's Hands*, was published by Porcupine Press in 2003.

Plot Summary

After

"The Deep" begins with the description of a room with tall windows and gauzy curtains. This first section is short, ending with a memory of a story about a queen's funeral.

How to Begin

An unnamed narrator describes what it is like to wake up uncertain of who and where one is. While the narrator is asleep, it may be 1918 France.

Survival Suit

The unnamed narrators, twins, are preparing to leave on a journey requiring camp equipment and vaccinations. They have lunch with Miss Reilly, who gives them each a pen so they will write her letters. The twins spend the next day with their father. He is terrified about their boat passage and insists on buying them survival suits. The twins are reminded of their doll Ophelia whom they tried unsuccessfully to float in a stream.

The Castle

The twins remember their mother as a sad woman and matter-of-factly state that they killed her—by being born. Their mother was distant from them, always resting. There is an implication that she suffered from postpartum depression. The twins' older brothers despised them for making their mother ill.

When the twins were young they went crawling through the kitchen garden, pretending to be an imprisoned princess. A fair-haired, blue-eyed prince riding a white horse would come to the rescue. He looked just like their father did as a young man. Their father smelled of the city: "cigars and dust and ashes." They thought he did not care about them but when they were older they realize he probably just does not know what to do with daughters.

The Corporal Remembers

Corporal Easton describes the twin girls as "skittish white horses."

The Fountain

The twins recall two portraits of their mother, one a formal painting, the other a sketch. In the sketch their mother wears a yellow dress and sits by a fountain with her sons, Marcus and James. The painting entrances the twins, "like a window to another world, and it seemed quite possible that by staring hard enough, we could step right through." When they are old enough to figure it out, the date on this painting indicates that their mother was pregnant with them when she posed for the artist. They realize, "we were already growing beneath that yellow dress, getting ready to smash that world to pieces."

The twins recall how the fountain was demolished and replaced by a flower bed. When they were very young the girl watching them fell asleep. As the twins remember it, unsupervised they played under the water, finding "absolute silence and peace" there. The final image is of two people carrying two bodies dripping wet and laying them on a stone. This image of the girls drowned foreshadows (or anticipates) their later double suicide.

Mrs. Moore

Mrs. Moore remembers the twins, Ruth and Esther, as serious-natured. She says they hung out with a young man who was handsome and funny. Mrs. Moore implies that he was being treated for a sexually transmitted disease. After he left the interim camp he would stop by to visit the twins, to work "that charm of his" on them. She recalls how strangely identical the sisters were, even individually referring to themselves as "we." Mrs. Moore speculates that maybe they both fell for that young man.

The Headmistress—1

The headmistress, Miss Reilly, recalls a meeting with the twins' father in which he implores her to convince his daughters not to go abroad. She refuses on the grounds that the twins are adults. But inwardly she feels some guilt. The headmistress and the father first met fifteen years earlier when he enrolled his daughters as pupils. He and the headmistress felt an immediate connection.

She considers something that has recently happened to be her fault. She remembers the letters she wrote to the twins, reassuring them in their work abroad but feels that she missed seeing something in their letters. Lastly the headmistress remembers a young lover who went to Africa after she refused to marry him. He died of a fever there. She would not marry him because she thought she needed an education and that marriage would deter her from that path.

Sailing

The twins stand on board, watching their father wave goodbye. His frantic waving makes them think they are seeing his real self. He has always moved slowly but now he is frenetic, just as he was the day their mother died and he raced up the stairs. The twins watch their father grow smaller as the ship sails away. They wonder why this departure should be such a big deal since they've been to Europe before.

On the ship the twins meet Elizabeth. She readily talks about herself, telling the twins that she volunteered so that she could look for her brother Arthur, who drives ambulances. His family has not heard from him in over six months. The twins are struck by how different their own family is. Their brother Marcus was too busy to come to the dock and their brother James was killed in action already. They remember James coming home to get some things after he enlisted. James was full of bravado but when he put another log on the fire, he burned his finger. The twins saw his tears and asked if he was afraid and he said that he was. Their sadness over his death is not for love but for the lack of it.

Life is different in camp, running the canteen. Everything they are occupied with is much more concrete—headaches, food shortages, sore feet, missing soldiers.

The Headmistress—2

Miss Reilly recalls first meeting the twins when they interviewed to attend her school: "[T]here was no hesitation, no collision, conversation flowing easily from one or the other so that the effect was of talking to a single person." She refers to news about the twins, mentions a memorial service. She looks at an old portrait of them taken a couple years after they started school. The photographer, Mr. Jones, failed to capture the essence of the twins in separate portraits and had to pose them together.

Letter

The letter is from the twins to their father. They thank him for sending gifts and tell him that they are close to the front, staffing a canteen at an interim camp. They describe their daily routine and the people they work with—primarily Mrs. Moore and Berthe. Although the work is hard, they feel it is important. On their free day they go to nearby hospitals and volunteer.

Stain

The twins remember their mother died on a Sunday morning in early June. Someone cried out and everyone went running to her room. Their father dropped his ink pen as he dashed up the stairs and Mrs. B picked it up. The pen made a stain in her apron pocket that spread as if "slowly to cover [the twins'] whole lives."

Marcus

Marcus remembers, on the day the girls were born, being called home from school because his mother was dying. He and his brother James tried killing the twins a few times. The twins seemed distant, almost foreign to him. The day of their mother's funeral the twins sliced themselves with glass. Marcus and James were glad to hear them cry.

The War Book

The twins conceive of a book they call *The War Book* in which they would record all the individual moments, questions, answers, and observations that people experience during the war. "And that would be the only way to communicate it, to give someone an idea of how it was."

The twins remember Hugh's story about his childhood friend Tom. Hugh and Tom signed up for the war together, and one quiet morning Tom was killed by a sniper while Hugh was bent over looking at something on the ground. Hugh became obsessed with trying to figure out if there were a way it could have been avoided and Tom's life saved.

Rain

The twins think about the rain that falls at the end of a tiring day. They think about how the rain is falling all across the country, straight to the Atlantic Ocean where beneath the surface everything is still and quiet. They think about their empty bedroom in England and declare that it is impossible for them to be there now.

In His Study the Father Closes His Eyes

The father feels the absence of his children in the house. He has decided to sell his house now that his wife and three of his children are dead. He mourns for the twins, recalling how he waved madly to them from the dock in the hopes that it would help them remember where to return.

His second son Marcus is still alive, living in the city. The father wonders if he will marry and have children of his own. Marcus is a successful businessman. The war has been good for business and that carries its own kind of guilt.

The twins' father remembers Anne Reilly, the headmistress. He acknowledges that there was always a possibility of a relationship with her. He remembers their first meeting, how he opened up to her. He kept on guard around her after that.

Soldiers—1

The twins recall a story Hugh told them. A soldier named Baker survived an assault and appeared to be fine. About two weeks later he began to cry and could not stop except when he was sleeping. Baker swore he was happy but he was so busy constantly clearing tears from his vision that his company had to send him back to civilian life.

Soldiers—2

Smythe, a soldier at the interim camp, was a "pig of a man" with little eyes. He offered to help the twins with a heavy pot and grabbed one of them around the waist. Hugh intervened, sending Smythe away. This was the first time the twins met Hugh.

Soldiers—3

The twins recall seeing a woman in a car in front of them while they were in Paris. She was with an officer and they knew she was a hired escort and hoped she would be treated well. But even as they thought it the officer grabbed her head and forced it down.

They also remember at a café sitting next to a table where two soldiers were filling an eleven-year-old boy with wine, chocolate, and friendly words. The twins see these bullies, cowards, and liars are also fighting for their country but their deaths in the trenches seem less of a tragedy.

Thinking about Home

Home was a remembered context that sustained people during the war, a reminder of a normal life; however, people superstitiously did not talk about going home. The twins recall standing in a smelly, smoky train station and seeing a mud- and blood-stained ten-year-old girl carrying a baby. They go to her, take the baby, and guide her toward those who can help.

Mrs. Moore misses her daughter, who is about to have a baby. The soldiers all have letters about home, even Smythe. "So even if they don't speak about *after*, it's always there, and home is something to go back to." At the hospital the twins help a boy whose hands had been blown off. They suggest he cut his thick, curly hair but he says he will not because his girlfriend at home loves to push back his hair. Another boy at the hospital is very ill and heavily drugged. He endlessly repeats a list, and people eventually deduce that it is a list of street names. No one knows him or where he is from so people guess that it is a route he imagines using to walk back home.

The twins think about their life back in England and feel distanced from it. They cannot remember ever being apart. Their experiences are thoroughly intertwined.

Interview

The twins tell a journalist—in response to a question about what it is like near the front—about walking along and finding an amputated child's hand.

Nan

Nan was originally caretaker to the twins' mother, Alice, and planned to retire to her sister's seaside cottage after the twins were born. She stayed on after the birth of the twins left Alice weak. Nan remembers the twins were serious as children but still normal. They had a secret language when they were five years old. They never really had close friends in school—just each other. Nan, like the twins' father, blames Miss Reilly for using her influence on the girls to get them to help out with the war effort. Nan remembers that "[t]alking to them was like talking to one person." She could not imagine them as married, normal adults. They came to visit her before they left for France. She tried to convince them not to go but they were determined. She knew she would not see them again.

In the Cellar

The twins run into Elizabeth in the cellar of a Parisian hotel during an air raid alert. She is very thin from being ill with the flu. Her family got word that Art died, and now Elizabeth is trying to find his burial place and take a picture of it. She confides in the twins that she feels broken and does not know how to go home. The twins comfort her and assure her that it will be all right, but they feel hypocritical.

The Sea King

The twins remember Nan's stories about the Sea King, an angry, wrathful figure. They wonder if he is not mad but sad because he has lost his children to the world of men. They see themselves as the Sea King's lost daughters.

Classmates

This section is told from the point of view of an old classmate, Jane. The twins run into Jane and Marjorie at a café in Paris. They are helping refugees but envy the twins for being so close to the front lines. The classmates' remembrances of the war are much lighter, and they do not appear to be emotionally damaged the way the twins and Elizabeth are.

Yellow Leaves

The twins remember how they were surprised by the noisiness of camp when they first arrived. During their last morning at home they sat outside and listened to leaves falling as the sun warmed the ice that encased them. Now they hear the horses, cars, feet, planes, and other sounds of the world mashed together: "This is the sound of the modern world, the world we are fighting for."

Letter

In a letter address to Miss Reilly, the twins express unhappiness that their father is making so much money off the war. They tell her how Paris is changed by the war, with taped up windows, sandbags, and soldiers. They write about their old classmates, remarking that she must be proud that so many of her students have joined the war effort. The twins wonder whether they could be of more use working with refugees or helping in a hospital. But their work at the canteen is also important.

They write about a dance they have to attend that night. They do not like the dances because the men vastly outnumber the women and the room is hot and crowded. They change partners every two minutes and sometimes there are fights.

The twins report seeing their first Germans recently; they noted how they were no different than their own men. "Oh, sometimes this war seems like a terrible machine, carried along by its own momentum. Chewing up lives and spitting them out." They wonder whether it was right to get involved with the war.

Sainte Germaine

The twins ask Hugh what it is like to fight in the war. He says it is mostly boring and that it has its own kind of logic. The three of them take an outing to Bar sur Aube and sit watching a well in the town square. They see one woman subtly ostracized by the others and make the connection between this scene and what Hugh is saying about war having its own logic.

They leave town to go swimming in a river. The twins admire Hugh for not bothering to try and tell them apart like most people do. "As if together we were too much for them, as if the only way they could deal with us was to divide, diminish us." The twins enjoy the swim in the river until they hit a cold patch in the water, panic, and quickly get out. Hugh asks them about the scars on their legs, and they tell him about their mother's death and how they acted out by drawing these lines on their legs with glass.

Hugh asks what it is like to be a twin. They tell him that it is safe because twins are never alone. He tells them about being raised by his widowed aunt—his parents are supposedly dead but he does not completely believe it. He tells them about his life-long friend Tom who shared his family with Hugh.

They retire to a nearby inn which is on a cliff. Hugh says it is the cliff of Sainte Germaine. Attila was camped on this cliff and demanded the town of Bar send up a pretty girl. They sent Germaine who, when she reached the top, ran off the edge of the cliff. Hugh argues that living is still the better choice.

On the drive back, Ruth wakes to hear Esther laughing with Hugh in the dark car.

Hugh

Hugh wants a quiet place to retire. When he first saw the twins and their twinned movements in the canteen, he found that quiet place inside himself. He would stay after the canteen closed and help clean up, then the three of them would talk. He saved things he saw to tell them; he liked to make them laugh. He learned about their deaths from an old newspaper while he was in Germany after the war.

About the Sentry

The sentry saw something that changed him imperceptibly and irrevocably. He blamed himself for what happened, but it is not clear yet what has occurred.

Near the Field of Crosses

Ruth thinks about how lives are made up of memories and moments strung together. She notes that each cross marks a life lived. Once she and Esther shared all their experiences, but then Ruth had a private and separate memory of waking in a dark car and hearing her sister and Hugh laughing.

In the Evening

Esther remembers the drive back from Bar sur Aube. Esther and Hugh talked while Ruth was asleep in the backseat, and Esther was overwhelmed by the sense that Hugh was talking only to her. One night she waits until Ruth is busy writing a letter. She takes a walk, hoping to intercept Hugh but he never comes. She is late arriving at the canteen and lies about why to Ruth. Hugh does not come to the canteen that night and the next day they see him as he is leaving with other soldiers. He went to a bar the night before and looks beaten up. Esther feels the chasm between her and her sister begin to widen.

Armistice

When the gunfire ceases for good, Berthe weeps. Everyone goes into town to celebrate, but the revelry is so frenzied and drunken that the twins return to camp. They hoped to sleep well, but instead they dream of dead men.

Teacup

The twins receive papers releasing them from duty. They miss their original camp, seeing now strange faces and fighting among restless men ready to go home. But also a new distance exists between the twins which has been developing since the night Esther lied to her sister. Their disconnection makes Esther think of Nan's teacup, which broke. Even though Nan fixed it and it still held liquid, one could see the place where it split.

Journey

The twins board a crowded train. The other people are happy, but the twins feel trapped. They remember the pleasure of sitting at a window on a rainy day, reading, imagining a hero appearing: "On the train we understood that there were no heroes, that such a life could not possibly be ours." They traveled for two days on the train, watching the passing scenery of blasted villages and people on foot. Their heads hurt. They eventually arrive in Bordeaux where they are swept along again, almost helplessly, up onto the ship to cross the English Channel.

Dr. Maitland

Dr. Maitland, a medical doctor aboard the ship, goes to see the twins in their cabin before the ship sails. One is pacing and the other is sitting at a desk, writing. They tell the doctor that they have not slept in two days and their heads hurt a lot. She gives them a sedative and promises to return in the morning. In retrospect, after the twins die, the doctor wonders how she could have prevented their double suicide. She understands that the war has been stressful and returning to a normal life is incomprehensible.

The Deep

The twins feel separated from each other, in pieces, grating against each other. Their heads hurt. They realize they are the same age their mother was when they were born. Their ills are beyond the help of the sedatives the doctor gives them. They finally decide what they have to do when the beam from the lighthouse cuts through their cabin.

Testimony of the Sentry

The sentry, Walter Allingham, saw two young women walking on deck around seven o'clock. They stopped at the bow and first one then the other quickly climbed the rail and jumped into the water.

After

Muffled sounds come through two tall windows draped in thin, white curtains. The twins wonder if someone has died.

Characters

Mr. A

See Father

Alice

See Mother

Walter Allingham

See Sentry

Mrs. B

Mrs. B is the housekeeper for the twins' family.

Baker

Baker is a soldier who survives an attack only to later be afflicted with tear ducts that run constantly, rendering him incapable of serving in combat. His story is ironic because he was a comedian before the war and now he cannot stop crying.

Berthe

Berthe is a French woman from a nearby town who works with the twins and Mrs. Moore at the canteen. She only speaks French but the twins translate for her. When the guns stop firing on Armistice Day, she weeps.

Corporal Easton

Corporal Easton drives the twins and others into town to celebrate on Armistice Day. He describes the twins as skittish white horses.

Elizabeth

Elizabeth is a British girl whom the twins meet on their crossing to France. She has light-colored hair, blue eyes, and is about twenty-two years old. She is very open about herself, telling the twins that she has signed up as a nurse so that she can come to France and look for her younger brother, Arthur, who drives ambulances. Their family has not heard from him in six months and is very worried. She has four other younger siblings, and their father is very ill so they do not have a lot of money.

When next the twins meet Elizabeth, after the Armistice, she is broken inside like they are, unsure of how to return home. She is very thin from a bout with influenza. She has learned her brother died shortly after arriving and has spent her time trying to find his burial place and take a photograph of it.

Esther

Esther is Ruth's identical twin and one of the central characters in this story. The father of the twins tells the two apart because he notes that Esther has a higher arch to her eyebrows. The twins are calm and serious, always referring to themselves as "we." Their mother became gravely ill from their birth and she died a few years later. Their two older brothers hate them for being born and taking their mother's vitality. Their father is remote but not unkind, and the twins suspect this is because he does not know what to do with daughters.

When the twins are eleven their father sends them to a nearby school. When they are twenty-six years old, under the influence of their former headmistress Miss Reilly, they decide to sign up to help with the war. They are given short notice to prepare to leave. Their father becomes very worried and attentive.

They are assigned to work at a canteen in an interim camp near the front lines in eastern France. They give out cigarettes, coffee, cocoa, sandwiches, and cakes. They help the soldiers with small tasks such as writing letters and mending clothes. They befriend a particular soldier, Hugh, who has a profound impact on their lives. On the return drive from a vacation in a nearby town, Esther and Hugh stay up talking and laughing while Ruth falls asleep. Esther later tries to intercept Hugh alone but he is elsewhere. A rift begins between her and her sister.

The war ends soon thereafter and their heads pound as they numbly go through the motions of returning home. Shortly after their ship sails for England, they jump overboard, committing suicide.

Father

Mr. A is father to James, Marcus, Ruth, and Esther. He is a grey-haired, successful businessman who appears to have had all the trappings of a happy life at one point. But his wife was very weak after their twin daughters were born and a few years later she died. His sons are sent away to boarding school because they threaten the lives of the twins. When the twins are eleven their father sends them to a nearby school as day pupils. He and the headmistress Anne Reilly have a spark between them, but she is confused by it and he chooses to ignore it because she makes him feel so vulnerable.

His eldest son James died in the war as a soldier. When Ruth and Esther sign up to help in the war abroad, their father tries to get them to stay home and, failing that, buys them rubber and cork survival suits to take on their boat crossing. He writes them letters and feels guilty for making profit off the war.

After his daughters commit suicide, he decides he must sell his empty house. His only remaining child, Marcus, lives in the city and has a career as a businessman. The father wonders if Marcus will marry, have children, and lead a normal life.

Hugh

Hugh is a British soldier in France. He smokes a pipe and wears worn smoke-colored sweaters and socks made for him by a girl back home. Hugh was raised by his aunt because his parents are either missing or dead. He and his childhood friend Tom enlisted in the war together; Tom is killed one quiet morning by sniper fire that could have just as easily killed Hugh, who was right next to him.

Hugh meets the twins at an interim camp near the front lines. For Hugh, the twins fulfill a need for peacefulness. The three quickly become friends, taking trips together on their days off. Returning from one of these trips, Esther becomes romantically interested in Hugh while her sister Ruth is asleep. Before a relationship can develop, Hugh is sent back to the trenches. After the war ends, Hugh is sent to Germany, and it is there, in an old newspaper, that he learns of the twins' suicide.

James

James is the twins' older brother and the eldest child of the four. He is described as stocky, with pale eyes and a square chin. He takes after his father. James is arrogant and despises his younger sisters for causing his mother to become ill and eventually die. He and his brother Marcus, as children, try to kill the twins. The boys are sent away to boarding school. When World War I breaks out, James enlists and dies very soon after he is sent off to fight.

Jane

Jane is an old classmate of the twins' from Miss Reilly's school. She lives in Paris with former classmate, Marjorie. They work with war refugees, but Jane is jealous of the twins because the twins work close to the front lines.

Mr. Jones

Mr. Jones is a young photographer who is hired in 1905 by Miss Reilly to take portraits of the students and staff of her school. He is very serious about his art, retaking portraits whenever they do not meet his artistic standard. He is never satisfied with his photographs of the twins until he poses them together. They are about thirteen years old at the time.

Dr. Maitland

Dr. Maitland is a medical doctor on the ship departing France for England at the end of the war. She visits the twins in their room on the ship after they complain of headaches and insomnia. She gives them a sedative. When their suicide is later reported, she states that there was no way she could have known that they posed this risk to themselves.

Marcus

Marcus is the twins' brother. He is older than the twins and younger than James. Like James, he is pale, but unlike James, he is tall. As children he follows James's lead, participating in attempts to murder their younger sisters. As an adult, he becomes a successful businessman like his father and lives in the city. He is the only child left alive at the end of the story, and his father wonders if Marcus will marry and have children.

Marjorie

Marjorie, an old classmate of the twins, is Jane's roommate in Paris where they work with war refugees.

Mrs. Moore

Mrs. Moore is the woman in charge of the interim camp canteen to which the twins are assigned during the war. She dates Dr. Thomas until he is sent home and then she dates Colonel MacAndrew. She has a daughter back home who is about to have her first baby.

Mother

Ruth and Esther's mother, Alice, loses her health after the birth of her twin daughters. Her condition is never specified but may be postpartum depression. She lingers on for several years, resting all the time and rarely interacting with her children. For this condition, the twins are resented by their brothers.

Nan

Nan is the twins' Irish nanny. She was the nanny for their mother Alice before they were born. Nan planned on retiring to her sister's seaside cottage but stayed with Alice after the twins were born because Alice was so weak from the birth. Nan grew up on an island and misses the seashore. She never does make it to her sister's cottage because her sister dies before Nan can retire.

Miss Anne Reilly

Miss Reilly is the headmistress for a girls' boarding school. Ruth and Esther attend her school as day pupils. Attractive and intelligent, she has focused on her education and career rather than pursuing romance. She was raised by her aunt and uncle after her parents died and it was an unpleasant situation. When she was young, she turned down a young man's offer of marriage because she felt she needed to get an education rather than be a wife. He shortly thereafter went to Africa and died of a fever. There is a spark of interest between Miss Reilly and the twins' widowed father, but neither does anything about it.

Miss Reilly feels guilty for not having better prepared Ruth and Esther to deal emotionally with the war, thus possibly saving them from suicide. Other people—the twins' father and Nan—also feel Miss Reilly bears responsibility for what happens to the twins.

Ruth

Ruth is Ether's identical twin sister. The twins are extremely close, to the point that they seamlessly complete each others' sentences and refer to themselves as "we." They consider themselves responsible for their mother's death simply by being born. They never get along with their two brothers, who hate them for making their mother so ill. Their father is not a warm man, although he does care about them.

Ruth and her sister sign up to aid in the war effort abroad, inspired by the confidence of their former headmistress, Miss Anne Reilly. They believe what she says, that women can change the world. They are assigned to work in an interim camp canteen in France near the front lines. While there they become friends with a soldier named Hugh. On a night drive home from a short holiday, Ruth falls asleep in the backseat of the car. She wakes up to hear Esther laughing with Hugh. Later she is struck that up until then her experiences and Esther's have been exactly the same. Esther falls for Hugh. Nothing happens between them, but the close relationship between the sisters is changed forever. Without the stability of that relationship, broken and hurting from what they see and experience of the war, Ruth and her sister Esther commit suicide by jumping off the bow of the ship bound for home.

Sentry

The sentry, Walter Allingham, of the 339th Field Artillery, is stationed on deck the Sunday night the twins take their lives. He sees them walk past him and then they climb the rail and jump before he can stop them.

Smythe

Smythe, who has a wife and three children back home, is a creepy soldier with small eyes. He makes the twins uncomfortable, getting too close physically after he offers to help them clean the canteen one night. Hugh intervenes and Smythe leaves.

Tom

Tom is Hugh's childhood friend. Tom and his family befriend Hugh when he is left to be raised by his aunt after his parents die. Tom and Hugh enlist in the war together. Tom is killed by sniper fire one quiet morning while Hugh is bent over looking at something on the ground. Hugh is devastated by the death of his friend but manages to carry on.

Themes

Dysfunctional Relationships

Relationships are highlighted in this story because of how the story is told. Half the story is told from the twins' point of view and the other half is told from that of people who knew the twins with varying levels of intimacy. The twins are not very close to anyone except each other, and in fact, their closeness seems to exclude others.

They never have much of a relationship with their mother whose health is fragile. She is always removed from them, resting up in her room or on the verandah, watching them from a distance. She dies while the twins are very young, depriving them of an important relationship in their formative years.

The ruined relationship between the twins and their older brothers is a direct result of the twins' birth and, later, their mother's death. James and Marcus resent and hate the twins because they hold the twins responsible for their mother's ill health. Marcus and Nan both refer to attempts by the boys to kill their sisters. In order to protect the twins, the boys are sent away to school.

Their father is a successful businessman who had a perfect life—with wife, house, and sons—before the twins are born. He does not appear to ever be upset with his daughters or even blame them for the role they played in altering his apparently perfect family life. The twins suspect, however, that he does not know what to do with them because they are girls. Their impulse is both

Topics For Further Study

- During World War I (1914–1919) women had to take on many roles traditionally held by men, such as mechanics, bus drivers, and assembly line workers. Research women' work during this period and make a list of five to ten of these roles. How many of these roles are apparent in Swan's story? Do you think there are roles today that are only open to men or only open to women simply because of tradition? Prepare a short presentation, with visual aids, about women during the Great War, focusing on the role you selected.
- O. Henry is a well-known, American short story writer. Read a biography of O. Henry and then three of his short stories. Write a paper about O. Henry's life and how it may have shaped both his stories and those of writers who followed him. When possible use the three stories you used by way of examples.
- Research the psychology and biology of identical and fraternal twins. Write a short story or poem about what you think it is like to be a twin or about observing twins using information found in your research.
- Classical and folk music were popular in Europe during World War I, while jazz and folk were popular in the United States. Research one of these music styles in the time of the first world war and prepare a musical presentation comparing songs from then and today (in the same genre). Create a CD or cassette tape mix of these songs to share with your classmates as part of the presentation.
- Who is your favorite relative and why? How long have you known each other? What do you like to do together when you see each other? Create a visual representation—for example, a painting, diorama, or movie—celebrating this person's strengths and the positive influence he or she has had in your life.

to act out against him and show off to make him proud.

Hugh has the most complex effect on the twins of all the people they meet during the war. The three of them are drawn together, as if they are kindred spirits, but Hugh unwittingly comes between the two women, affecting them in a way that no one else ever has. Esther is drawn to Hugh and to the sense of individuality that she feels when talking to him while her sister is asleep. This small event initiates a wedge between the sisters, which gives them separate experiences and suggests to them that heroes will not come to them. This awareness co-occurs with the end of the war.

In the end the most dysfunctional relationship in this story is the one between the twins because it is so close that the exclusion of others is an increasing strain as they get older. Any small intrusion is catastrophic to their balance because they are unused to individuality and to sharing each other with other people.

Roles of Women

"The Deep" examines the roles of women in Europe during the early 1900s. The twins fulfill many traditional roles such as daughter, sister, student, and domestic help. As students of Miss Reilly, they are encouraged to act out their nurturance and charity for others. So when World War I begins, the twins sign up to help the war effort. They are sent to eastern France, near the front lines. There they work in a canteen in an interim camp, supplying soldiers with hot drinks, food, cigarettes, and a place to sit and relax. On their days off, the twins help out the overburdened staff at nearby hospitals. Whenever there is a dance, they have to go because the women are extremely outnumbered by the men. They loathe this duty because even though it is deemed important for morale, there is nothing romantic or graceful about these dances. They are just female bodies for entertaining or comforting the soldiers.

Survival

The story of the twins' life is one of survival. They are born to a mother who barely lives through the birth, and because of the threat they posed to her life, they immediately come under threat from their own brothers. When their mother finally dies, they cut their legs with glass found in the kitchen garden but are luckily found and cleaned up before anything worse happens.

As adults, the twins resolve to help in the war effort. Then faced with the horrors of war, like the soldiers, they struggle to find a way to return to normal life. Although their life never was normal, they cannot return to what they knew before the war. Onboard the ship to return home, their relationship with each other in tatters, the twins realize they cannot survive this world any longer as they are. They take their lives by jumping overboard and drowning, thereby erasing their need to understand what has happened and find a way to continue living.

Hugh, by contrast, survives the loss of his best and oldest friend, Tom. He feels incredible guilt that it was Tom's life taken by the sniper's bullet and not his. Hugh searches for answers as to why Tom died but eventually comes to accept that there is no rational answer. He also survives his friendship with the twins, which became subtly volatile when one sister yearned for his separate attention. There is an implication that Hugh understood what was going on because on his last night at the interim camp, he went to a bar rather than to the canteen as was his habit. Thus he avoided meeting up with Esther alone. Unfortunately, irreparable damage had already been done to the twins' relationship.

Style

Non-Linear Narrative

The plot is told in a non-linear form, meaning that it is not chronological but jumps around in time. Half of the story pieces are told by the twins and generally are presented chronologically from their departure from England for France to the moment when they commit suicide in the English Channel on the return trip. Their narrations are filled with flashbacks.

The other narrative sections are told by people who are acquainted with the twins. These include everyone from their father to the woman in charge of the canteen where they work during the war. All of these sections are told from a time after the twins have died and some read as if the person speaking is being interviewed about his or her experiences with the twins.

Characterization

Characterization involves delineating details regarding physical attributes, personality, and history. Characterization is achieved by showing (rather than telling) the reader what a character thinks, what a character says and does, and what others say about the character. The many characters are dramatized in separate sections in which they have their separate opportunities to give their perceptions regarding the twins. Those who knew the twins focus on their memories of them; even minor characters give their remembrances of the twins. In this way they serve as witnesses, helping to explain the past and perhaps in part explaining the double suicide. For example, the head mistress is guilt-ridden for having encouraged the girls to volunteer; forlorn Elizabeth testifies to the effect war has on civilians who for whatever reasons went to war-torn France, the twins' sad and lonely father expresses how a man feels who outlives his children. Such a large number of characters in a short story can have the negative effect of complicating the storyline, but Swan expertly focuses their separate perceptions of the twins. Through their perspectives, Swan provides a fuller context in which to analyze what exactly happened to the twins that may account for their double suicide.

Historical Context

World War I

World War I (1914–1918), also known as the Great War, was the largest war known in history up to that point. The catalyst for the war was the assassination of Franz Ferdinand, the heir to the Austro-Hungarian Empire, by a Serbian rebel. The reasons for the outbreak of war are still debated although many agree that rising nationalism across Europe and western Asia as well as a heated arms race had much to do with the quick actions countries such as Russia and Austria-Hungary took over what initially appeared to be a minor conflict.

The Allied Powers of World War I were Britain, Russia, and France. The Central Powers were Germany and Austria-Hungary. Many other nations were involved in the war, whether willingly or not, such as Serbia, Belgium, Italy, Japan, the Ottoman Empire, Greece, China, Brazil, and the

United States. This war is infamous for its trench warfare, chemical warfare, and air bombings. More than 9 million people died as a result of World War I; over 23 million were wounded.

World War I ended with a series of armistices, or cease-fire agreements, the final one being signed by Germany on November 11, 1918. The Treaty of Versailles, signed on June 28, 1919, marked the official end of the war and assigned much of the blame and reparation responsibility to Germany. During the Great War, four empires fell—German, Austro-Hungarian, Ottoman, and Russian—leaving the map of Europe and Western Asia dramatically changed. The war also redefined how conflicts were fought between modern nations.

Women's Suffrage

Suffrage is defined as the civil right to vote. Women's suffrage was an important social and political issue that surfaced in the nineteenth century and was heatedly debated in the first two decades of the twentieth century. In the United States women won the right to vote in 1920. It took five years of debate in Congress and the Senate to pass the Nineteenth Amendment to the Constitution, which states, "The right of citizens of the United States to vote shall not be denied or abridged by the United States or by any State on account of sex."

In the United Kingdom, a series of laws permitting women of specific ages, marital statuses, and classes to vote were passed between 1869 and 1918. In 1928 a woman's right to vote was made equal to that of a man's in the United Kingdom. Women did not have the right to vote in France until 1945, after World War II.

World War I aided women's suffrage in all countries. Many men were either off fighting or dead, so women had to step into roles men traditionally held at home and in the workplace and to earn money for their families. This drove many women to seek an equal voice in political representation.

WWI soldiers in the trenches The Library of Congress

Critical Overview

Swan's work has received limited critical attention. Swan published about a dozen stories in various literary magazines across North America and had no books published before she won the 2001 O. Henry Award with her story "The Deep." Some journals in which her work was published are high caliber publications, such as *Harpers* and the *Ontario Review*. "The Deep" was republished in Swan's first book, a collection of short stories, *The Deep and Other Stories*. This collection was short-listed for the 2003 Commonwealth Writer's Prize "Best First Book" category.

In her introduction to Swan's story in the official O. Henry award volume, Mary Gordon, one of the judges for the 2001 O. Henry Award, commended Swan and "The Deep":

> I chose this story as first among so many strong others because of its utter originality, its daring to assert the primacy of complexity and mystery, its avoidance of the current appetite for ironic anomie and thinness.

Reviews of the "The Deep" have mostly been praiseworthy. Harvey Grossinger, writing for the *Houston Chronicle*, considers Swan's win to be "deserving." Charles May, writing for the *Milwaukee Journal Sentinel* in a broader article about judging "best" stories, says that Swan's story "nicely embodies all three of the criteria of poetry, mystery, and large truths urged by short fiction writers over the years."

However, an anonymous reviewer for *M2 Best Books* is less taken with "The Deep" than most people, describing the story as beautiful but too distant for readers to sympathize with the characters. Yet a *Publishers Weekly* anonymous review describes *The*

Deep and Other Stories as "an intense, accomplished first collection." A review in *Kirkus Reviews* states that the collection is "wonderful." Prudence Peiffer for *Library Journal* also celebrates Swan's rich prose, writing that Swan has a "strong command of metaphorical language." Marta Segal for *Booklist* describes Swan's collection as "graceful" and concludes that "Swan has a calm, almost resigned voice."

Unfortunately, Swan's other work has not received the same admiration as her award-winning story. Grossinger acknowledges this disappointment, stating that none of the other stories in her collection *The Deep and Other Stories* "displays either the mastery of craft or the intellectual reach of 'The Deep.'" Reviews of Swan's second collection *Emma's Hands* are mixed at best.

Criticism

Carol Ullmann

Carol Ullmann is a freelance writer and editor. In the following essay, Ullmann examines the complexity of relationships in Swan's short story "The Deep."

Mary Swan's "The Deep" is a novella rich with characters. The twins Ruth and Esther are at the axis of the interconnections between characters—each has relevance to the narrative because of his or her relationship to the twins. This story tells the life and death of the twins through the people they have known. Half of the story is told through their own eyes and from their memories and half is from the perspective and memory of people the twins have known. The twins have affected them all.

Ruth and Esther's family relationships are at once sad, strange, and yet familiar in the sense that no one's family is perfect. All families suffer unhappy times, anger, grief, distance, dysfuntionality, discord, regret, aggression, and other skeletons. While the reader experiences the twins' family traumas and tensions firsthand from many of the family members involved, it is actually the twins' friendship with Elizabeth that exposes how odd Ruth and Esther feel about their family. They see Elizabeth's family as loving while their own is cold and haunted. They do not feel they can expose the environment they come from to her for fear that she will not understand—or else understand too well and have it reflect badly upon them.

The twins' dead mother, Alice, and their alienated older brothers, James and Marcus, seem more standard fare for the dysfunctional family. Their mother's condition is only alluded to but she appears to suffer from debilitating postpartum depression following the birth of the twins. If she was depressed, she may have died by committing suicide—but the author gives no clues about this. James and Marcus grow up hating the twins for what they see as taking their mother from them. The reason for this emotion is understandable on the one hand and terrible on the other. Marcus explains, "James thought we should kill them, and we tried a few times. I don't remember how, childish things I'm sure, but someone always stopped us."

Their father, Mr. A, is much more complex than the other family members. He is a man who is simultaneously successful and a failure. He has done very well as a businessman and even in his personal life once performed well by securing the beautiful wife, the charming country estate, and not one son, but two. In his twin daughters he has both his future and the end of his earlier successful era. Although business continues to thrive—even flourish magnificently, disgustingly—during the war, the father pays on the personal front. His wife's health declines after the birth of their twin daughters; his sons hate their younger sisters and try to kill them; his wife dies; and the twins grow up strange, remote, and serious. They are normal enough as children, despite their seriousness, but Nan had her doubts for their future: "I used to wonder how they would ever get married and have a normal life. It was impossible to imagine them separated like that."

The twins' father seems to first realize, or perhaps first express, the importance of what he has in his daughters when they prepare to leave. Since they are female he perhaps never conceived that they too would leave for war. For a man who has already lost a wife and a son, he seems to feel the loss of his daughters at the mere suggestion of their assignment abroad. Failing to convince them to stay and failing to convince their former headmistress, Miss Reilly, to talk them into staying, he does the only thing he can think of to keep them safe short of going with them. He insists on buying them survival suits: rubber suits lined with cork designed to keep a person afloat and alive for 48 hours should their ship go down. The twins think it is silly but they go along with the purchase of the suits to appease their father in this small way. "Father seemed quite relieved that he had been able to purchase what was required to keep us safe." It is ironic that they later die by drowning. "Someone had told him that the crossing was more dangerous than anything

> "The broken feeling the war has left the twins with becomes a throb in their heads that will not quit."

we'd be close to in France. . . ." This is both true and not true—the twins commit suicide on the return crossing but the damage is done to them while they are in France.

The purchase of the survival suits is the father's hopeless gesture against fate. In one way or another, his daughters' lives had been under threat since they were born. He has done what he must to keep them safe (such as sending his sons to boarding school) but he has never been warm and affectionate with his daughters, which may be underlined by his own ambivalence about their presence in his life, a presence that heralded family hardship. If he blames them at all for the death of their mother, though, it is never apparent. Instead they appear to slip from his grasp as surely as their mother did.

Miss Anne Reilly, the twins' headmistress, inspires the twins with her talk of the capabilities of women and how women can do their part in the war effort. The twins and other classmates of theirs decide to sign up to help out after they graduate from school when the war breaks out. Miss Reilly, faced with the outcome of her influence—the suicide of the twins—and the twins' father asking her to intervene so they won't leave in the first place, begins to realize what her power is. "It comes to me that all the things I've said and done, all the battles fought, have been from this position of warmth and comfort." She wonders if she has used her power correctly and if she has properly prepared her students. "Perhaps I should have given them armor. Taught them to think but not to feel, taught them to save themselves."

Miss Reilly sends the twins off with her best intentions, her righteous conviction. She gives them pens and keeps up a correspondence. She is mentor and friend to them, but ultimately feels she has failed to support them as a mentor or friend would. She does not listen to what they say in their letters, only hearing what she wants to hear. The twins did not know how to process the horrors and pains they had experienced and then return to what they had once known at home. No normal future existed for them because of their upbringing, their unusual closeness as sisters, their lack of close friends, and their alienation from their family.

Miss Reilly herself has always chosen the practical over the romantic—an education over a potential husband and later she chooses pride over Mr. A, understanding him as a shrewd businessman rather than a grieving widower. The romantic interest between Miss Reilly and the twins' father is undeclared and unexplored. Neither is therefore able to provide the twins with a role model for a healthy romantic relationship.

The one apparent romantic interest for the twins was Hugh. He was a fast and true friend to them both, finding an elusive inner peace he long sought after meeting the twins, in their strange and perfect synchronicity. It is ironic, then, that Hugh is the catalyst for the discord that develops and quickly destroys Ruth and Esther. Esther's interest in Hugh—the simple first infatuation of youth—develops from a nighttime car ride where she finds herself talking to him alone while Ruth sleeps. She relishes the feeling that he is focused on *her* and this sense of individuality strengthens her but at the expense of her sister's strength.

Overcome with awkwardness concerning the trip home, unsure how they can reconcile their wartime experiences with the life that was and will be, the twins are emotionally unstable. This is not an unusual condition for those who experienced and survived the war, whether they were soldiers or not. Elizabeth suffers the same reluctance to go home and appeals to the twins: "'Something is broken in me. It's all just a horrible mess, and there's no meaning in any of it.'" Dr. Maitland also refers to the difficulties many people have returning to a normal life after the war: "You can't imagine what it was like, the stress we'd all been living under."

Hugh tips the scale. Although he has found his inner peace in the existence of these twins, he unwittingly robs them of their peace. The broken feeling the war has left the twins with becomes a throb in their heads that will not quit. Without each other they are groundless and without purchase. Their home was actually always in each other—and they lose that before they leave France.

The relationship between twins has long been a mystery of human nature. Swan's story takes this inexplicable, almost supernatural relationship to an extreme to illustrate her tale about women during the Great War. The twining of relationships throughout this story makes the net that holds the narrative together as it loops back and forth through the lives of Ruth and Esther.

Source: Carol Ullmann, Critical Essay on "The Deep," in *Short Stories for Students*, Thomson Gale, 2006.

Melodie Monahan

Monahan has a Ph.D. in English and operates an editing service, The Inkwell Works. In the following essay, Monahan examines various ways in which Mary Swan explores the concept of identity in the case of identical twins.

Mary Swan's story "The Deep" explores the concept of identity by tracing the complicated psychological development of identical twin sisters, whose sexual maturation ends their exclusive childhood relationship and contributes to their double suicide. The natural process of differentiation is stalled in the case of Esther and Ruth by their inability to relinquish their initial relationship to each other in the face of attachment to a sexual partner. Partly they are unable because of their distorted relationship to their mother, their alleged role in her death, and the way their births supposedly destroyed the world of the family that existed before them. Feeling guilty for having been born and facing early on the death of their soldier brother James, the twins volunteer to serve behind the Western Front. This work submerges them in the surreal social disruption and trauma of war at the same time that it exposes them to adult sexual interaction. The narrative comes piecemeal, through the twins' statements as they go through their experiences and by others who reflect about them after the fact of their deaths. In this multiple handling of point of view, Swan gives readers a chance to see the twins from their own perspective and from the perspective of witnesses who seek to understand what happened to them. One important message in the story is that in the case of Esther and Ruth sexual attachment to a partner corrodes their conjoined identity and paradoxically in order to save this sense of self they elect to kill themselves.

Awareness of separate identity is a developmental process: the fetus in utero probably does not distinguish itself from its mother. After birth, the baby begins to sense that its mother is separate from itself and indeed that the self exists even when the mother is absent. (Peek-a-boo games illustrate this discovery of the separate self and the pleasure of reconnection with the returning other who is not the self.) However, in the case of identical twins this process of differentiation is likely to be complicated by the very fact that the world of each twin presents a carbon copy of the self. For each sister, to be in the world with the identical sibling is to experience the self as both subject and object; the self and also its focal point or mirror image. In Swan's story, the protagonists are unable to adapt and evolve separately, and facing debilitating psychic fragmentation, they choose suicide, jumping overboard into the salt sea, which suggests a return to the amniotic fluid in which they began. In this case in which identity is established through exclusive identification with the twin, one sibling's nascent sexual attachment to a soldier heralds the siblings' destruction.

> "In this case in which identity is established through exclusive identification with the twin, one sibling's nascent sexual attachment to a soldier heralds the siblings' destruction."

From early on Esther and Ruth see themselves as one (they speak of "our headache," "our skin"). The two are inseparable and speak in unison, generally using the first-person plural, "we," instead of the first-person singular, "I." Miss Riley reports that speaking to them had "the effect . . . of talking to a single person." They share the same experience and the same relationship with parents who do not seem pressed to distinguish them from each other. Their mother calls each of them, "my darling." When she dies after a long siege of postpartum depression, their older brothers accuse the twins of murdering her, and the twins accept that accusation as a fait accompli (completed act): "We killed her, of course; everyone knew that." Esther and Ruth turn inward perhaps all the more for being born into a family in which the mother dies early on and the father (who is a surviving twin

What Do I Read Next?

- *Hateship, Friendship, Courtship, Loveship, Marriage: Stories* (2002), by Alice Munro, is a collection of short stories by an acclaimed Canadian writer. Munro often focuses on female protagonists and themes that appeal to women.
- *Emma's Hands* (2003) is Mary Swan's second collection of short stories. These stories range all over the world and across time. Swan's elegant and poetic style continues with the stories in this collection.
- *Prize Stories 2001: The O. Henry Awards* (2001), edited by Larry Dark, contains seventeen stories judged by Dark to be the best published in U.S. and Canadian periodicals during 2000. Swan's first-place story appears in this collection.
- *We Were the Mulvaneys* (1996), by Joyce Carol Oates, is the story of a family that seems to have it all, until things take a turn for the worse. Oates is one of the most prolific and respected of U.S. novelists writing in the early 2000s.
- *Forgotten Voices of the Great War: A History of World War I in the Words of the Men and Women Who Were There* (2004), by Max Arthur, tells the true story of what World War I was like for the people who lived through it. This book arose out of a thirty-year project by the British Imperial War Museum to collect firsthand accounts of World War I experiences from soldiers of many nationalities.

---

himself) absents himself psychologically, in which older male sibs blame them for destroying a perfect family by being born into it. In part children look to their parents and older siblings for clues about their own identity, for familial characteristics, shared attitudes and beliefs, a common lifestyle. But in this case, the twins are oddly unable to identify with their birth family; they are more alike between themselves than they are like any other member of the family. As their nurse Nan says, "they only had each other." Away in Europe the twins think of home, but not as "something to go back to" but rather as "something to figure out, to understand." By contrast to the problem home presents to them, they are pleased with being twins: "It's safe," they tell Hugh.

The narrow world of family home and property and the wider world of school and later volunteer service in Europe penetrate that twins' safety by increasing increments and finally erode it. As children, the sisters remain quite insulated at home while their brothers, Marcus and James, are sent away to boarding school. The twins stare at portraits of their mother, calculating by the date of one that she was pregnant with them when it was painted, scrutinizing the scene for evidence of the familial world which their births transformed. Moreover, their private play at home shows their assimilation of literature and fairy tale, and unbeknownst to them it foreshadows their adult experience.

An initial literary detail occurs in their comments about their doll, which they call Ophelia, and which when they want it to float down stream does so only "facedown." This literary allusion (or reference) is to Shakespeare's play *Hamlet* in which Ophelia is frustrated in her love for Prince Hamlet and when he scorns her decides to drown herself in a river. The play involves a problematic relationship between mother and child and the apparent or feigned madness of both Hamlet and Ophelia, so it is a rich reference point for Swan's story. A second reference is to the fairy tale of Sleeping Beauty. As children the twins imagine themselves "under a spell"; they crawl "through the tangled vines in the kitchen garden" and fantasize that the vines twine all over the house sealing it. They imagine a prince (who looks surprisingly like a younger version of their father) who carves his way through, leaving "his horse grazing in the hallway while he rescue[s] the sleeping princess." For the following feast, the princess "would wear a sea-green gown . . . and dance with the prince until morning." Important works of literature and fairy tales convey paradigmatic relationships and values: the twins' appropriation of the Sleeping Beauty tale delivers wish-fulfillment, vindication, and prophecy. First, the tale rewinds the withdrawal and death of their mother and reunites her with an earlier form of their father, thus reestablishing the world the twins' birth is said to have destroyed. Then too the tale of sexual awakening from a hundred-year-long virginal sleep predicts the female's life in adult sexual relationship with the male. In this second meaning, the story foreshadows (or anticipates) trouble for the twins when their sexual maturity comes face to face with a suitable male and dispels their obsessive fixation on one another. The sexually awakened female finds a new component in her own identity and turns to her partner, defining herself in relationship to this new and different other, thus demoting sibling and birth family to roles of lesser significance.

When the twins' father seeks a local school to which the twins can attend as day students, the girls come under the supervision of Miss Riley, a feminist who has chosen education and work over marriage and motherhood and yet who longs for the wider public sphere of action. Pursuing education, developing abilities, preparing oneself for the adult world of work and social roles, all serve as a bridge for the twins in their movement from the private sphere of home to the public one of action. As the twins volunteer to serve behind the Western Front, Miss Riley envies them the opportunity they have for adventure. After their deaths and now in retrospect, Miss Riley feels responsible in part for their decision to go to Europe, guilty for having encouraged them. In their going perhaps she saw an extension of her hopes for a life that mattered in the world, one that proved "women's capabilities." In their deaths, she is called to remember the suitor she refused who went off into the world and died.

The twins' work in camps behind the lines combines several typical female roles: they serve food and wash dishes, and at dances they partner soldiers for two-minute intervals of music. On their off days they assist in nearby hospitals, running errands and writing letters for injured soldiers. Inevitably they attract male attention, and this is how they meet Hugh. Initially, Hugh is different because in becoming their friend he does not try to tell them apart. In fact, when he first sees them, their synchronized gesture of brushing their hair from their eyes communicates a wholeness or oneness to Hugh which he finds comforting. In grief over the arbitrary and senseless death of his longtime friend with whom he enlisted, Hugh sees in Esther and Ruth's partnership a soothing image of connection. Yet he disrupts that connection, unwittingly creating an irreversible fissure. En route back from the threesome's all-day outing, Ruth awakens in the car to Hugh laughing with Esther over something Ruth did not hear. Suddenly a palpable space erupts between the twins; Esther explains, inserting a new "We" and a new "I" as she does so: "We were talking, Hugh and I, . . . and suddenly I felt such a great opening up. And I realized . . . it was because Hugh was talking to *me*." The next day Esther lies to Ruth, claiming to go out for a stroll when she hopes to meet Hugh. The meeting does not occur; Hugh leaves camp with other soldiers, "leaving me," Esther laments, "with a broken thing to try to put together." Given earlier references to Sleeping Beauty, Hugh's role here is plain. He awakens the one sister to her single identity and her response to him disconnects her from her still-sleeping twin. A permanent breach has occurred between the siblings which corrupts their mental health.

When the Armistice takes place, the twins feel "spun loose," aimless without their work and suffering "a strangeness" between them which was "the worse part." Esther explains that it was like they had suffered a stroke, "a severing in the brain," and with it, "a terrible thrumming panic." Having identified themselves in terms of one another and in terms of their closed and exclusive relationship, they are now traumatized by the disconnection which sexual awakening brings. As soon as Esther defines herself in relation to Hugh, she no longer mirrors Ruth. Esther explains the rift between her and Ruth as "a terrible pounding in our heads." By the time the twins are onboard for their return Atlantic crossing, they are acting separately. The doctor who checks on them later reports that when she entered their cabin one was sitting at a desk "scribbling on pieces of paper that fell to the floor" and the other was "pacing back and forth, her hands in her hair."

The twins regress in the face of this chaos: then in a psychotic fusing the "we" resumes in the penultimate section of the story: They say, "Without each other we are in pieces . . . we have to find a way back." The sentry on deck later reports how directly the twins climbed over the railing and jumped into the sea. He blames himself for not acting quickly to stop them. In psychological terms, in mythical terms, the double suicide is the snap return to the absolute oneness of their beginning. They return to the sea, to the amniotic connection of one undivided child bathed in the maternal womb. Having witnessed the fragmentation, loneliness, and widespread destruction of war, having felt the separateness that comes with individual sexual awakening, they recoil, seeking in death what they believe was theirs before their birth. In "The Deep" Mary Swan provides readers with a way of understanding how an arrested, rigid sense of identity blocks autonomous development and adult sexual bonding in the case of identical twins and effects their ultimate regression, which is suicide.

Source: Melodie Monahan, Critical Essay on "The Deep," in *Short Stories for Students*, Thomson Gale, 2006.

Timothy Dunham

Timothy Dunham has a master's degree in communication and bachelor's degree in English. In the following essay, Dunham considers how 1 Corinthians 13:12 casts some light on "The Deep," providing insight into the actions of the protagonists Esther and Ruth.

"For now we see through a glass, darkly; but then face to face: now I know in part; but then shall I know even as also I am known" (1 Cor. 13:12). These frequently quoted words of Saint Paul from I Corinthians, in the Authorized (King James) Version, have served as inspiration to philosophers and poets throughout the centuries and are at the heart of Mary Swan's novella, "The Deep," a haunting tale of twin sisters Esther and Ruth who abandon a life of privilege in Canada and set sail for France to play a part in the horrific drama that is World War I. Employing a unique narrative technique, Swan recounts the story of the twins by weaving a tapestry of vignettes in different voices: memories of the twins and of those who knew them, letters they wrote to their father and their former headmistress, family members' impressions of them, and even snatches of memory from soldiers who crossed paths with them. The reader is carried along with the twins on an unnerving, yet oddly hopeful journey from a world of quiet certitude into a world of chaos and ambiguity where Saint Paul's words become starkly real.

The mirror metaphor as Paul uses it to explain limited human knowledge was often echoed by writers of the English Renaissance. Defining the "Idols of the Tribe" in his *Aphorisms* (1625), Francis Bacon says, for example, that it is difficult to get at truth because much of what people see in the world is based on personal perception of it: "The human understanding is like a false mirror, which, receiving rays irregularly, distorts and discolours the nature of things by mingling its own nature with it." In "A Sermon Preached at St. Paul's for Easter-Day, 1628," John Donne expounds on the apostle's words, saying that before coming to a knowledge of God, human understanding of the world is blurred, "an obscure riddle, a representation, darkly, and in part, as we translate it." It may be argued that Swan seems to have had this metaphor in mind as she composed "The Deep," a metaphor she develops with specific imagery, both visual and aural, that lucidly reflects the world in which the twins are submerged: a world filled with ambiguity, where everything the twins know and believe is called into question and all is an obscure riddle.

The first image, in Baconian terms, is one of a false mirror. It appears at those moments (all in France) when the twins reflect back on their childhood and question whether things really happened as they remember. In the vignette, "The Fountain," the twins recall the time when they, hand-in-hand, climbed into the fountain in their yard and immersed themselves. Their recollection is vivid, even to the point of relating sensory details: "And we remember the magic of underwater, the absolute silence and peace. It's not likely there were fish in that fountain, but we remember the color, the darting streaks of light." But they are not sure what happened after that. They have two equally clear memories, one of helping each other out of the fountain on a bright day and walking toward the house where a door was opening and a white shape was running, the other of being carried from the fountain by two dark figures on a dismal, rainy day, "held forward in their arms like an offering about to be deposited on a stone." What is unclear is which, or if either, memory is accurate.

Furthermore, in the vignette, "Thinking about Home," the twins share many memories that they both remember exactly the same way, right down to the sound, feel, and taste. Before coming to France they would not have thought it strange to have identical memories; it would not have been questioned, not even considered, because that is just how it was. Life on the war-ravaged landscape of France, however, changes this unison. Their eyes are opened to the dark reality that things are not always what they appear to be, and they begin to have reservations and doubts, wondering what they experienced separately that they chose to forget:

> So many things seemed strange, there in France. It did not seem possible that our life was as we remembered it. But we both remembered it, so wasn't that some kind of proof? We were not together every minute of our childhood, every minute

> of our lives, although most, perhaps. But there must have been times when one of us was in a room but not the other. When only one of saw something, heard something, was spoken to. But we don't remember anything like that.

The next image Swan uses is a dominant one that permeates the entire story: the aural image of muddled sound, suggestive of E. M. Forster's "ou-boum" (the same monotonous echo produced by every sound, no matter if it is the blowing of a nose or the squeak of a boot) in the Marabar Caves in *A Passage to India* (1924). Coming from the quiet and peaceful environs of their home in Canada, the twins are unprepared for the noise of war, not the sounds of battle, but the "constant ruckus" that comes with living in a large group of people: "The shouting in the camp, the singing and sounds of hammering. Horses and motors and airplanes if they're near. The racket in the canteen or mess hall, always something."

In a world such as this, where nothing can be seen except 'through a glass, darkly,' the twins decide to complete their journey the only way they know how."

In the midst of all this commotion, the twins are reminded of a sound they heard right before they left for France: they were sitting on their kitchen porch when the silence was shattered by the snap and clatter of frosted yellow maple leaves thawing in the sun and falling to the ground. In one sense, the sound of falling leaves raises a specter of doubt as to whether life back home was really as quiet as they remember. More significantly, though, it serves as the twins' initiation into a world of constant noise. Like the "ou-boum" in a Marabar Cave, the sound of the modern world in "The Deep" is just one collective racket that saturates and unsettles the twins' lives: "There's no place for contemplation, no space for it, every waking moment, and even sleeping ones, filled with sound." And like "ou-boum," "racket" is devoid of real meaning; it is a collection of sounds comprising one distinct ambiguous sound, an apt symbol for a world the twins refer to as "the world of foggy air."

Swan makes use of the same image but handles it a little differently, in the bookend vignette, "After." Here, the twins describe the muddled sound of the street coming in through the windows of their house; but it is not a racket, it is muffled. The image neatly operates as a metaphor for ambiguity while setting up the dread revelation that in the twins' minds ambiguity is tantamount to death:

> Sounds reach us from the street, wheels turning and hard shoes and sometimes a voice raised, calling out something, and they are muffled, all these sounds. Distant. Father told us once about the Queen's funeral, straw laid in the street to mute the sound. It is like that, and we wonder if someone has died.

Consequently, this image of muddled sound foreshadows the closing moments of the twins' lives when they take their lives, making the plunge from the world of foggy air into the next.

The last image is a visual one that also serves as the story's primary symbol: a broken teacup. The twins tell a story of how their housekeeper, Nan, once broke her favorite teacup and spent the entire evening carefully gluing it back together. After that it still held tea, but the crack was always visible. While in France, the twins learn they are living in a world, which, like Nan's teacup, is fragile, broken, and can never be restored to the world they once knew (or thought they knew). Symbolically, the broken teacup points to the brokenness people experience in wartime.

The twins encounter three forms of brokenness. The first form is a broken spirit, a result of the senseless tragedy of war. During an air-raid alert one night in Paris, the twins bump into Elizabeth, a friend they met on the Atlantic crossing. Elizabeth came to France to look for her brother who, as it turns out, was killed in battle. As they wait out the alert in the hotel cellar, Elizabeth tells the twins that the war experience has broken her in such a way that she does know how she can go home again. She is a different person than she was when she arrived, and the world is now an ambiguous place: "'Something is broken in me. It's all just a horrible mess, and there's no meaning in any of it.'" All the twins can do is hold Elizabeth's hands and tell her that, in the end, the world will be a better place. It's a lie, of course. In the vignette "Thinking about Home," the twins' sentiments about home are the same as Elizabeth's: Home is not something they can go back to. The war has broken their spirits too.

The second form of brokenness is broken relationship. It comes as a result of the twins' friendship with the soldier Hugh and is set in motion one night while the three of them are driving back to camp from an outing. Ruth falls asleep in the back seat and wakes to find her sister and Hugh laughing. The unity of the twins' relationship is instantly breached. For the first time the twins can remember, memories are created that they do not share. (In Ruth's case, it is the memory of suddenly waking in the dark car to find Esther and Hugh laughing, while, for Esther, it is talking with Hugh while Esther sleeps in the back seat.) For the first time, the pronoun "I" must be used to refer to each of them. After a lifetime of using the pronoun "we," "I" sounds very lonely indeed.

It is the lie, however, that causes the permanent break. Esther is so overcome with emotion from the brand new experience of a having a man speak solely to her that she decides to meet Hugh, alone. Hoping to meet him on one of his evening walks, Esther tells Ruth she is going out for a stroll. She leaves Ruth to her letter writing and goes to wait for Hugh on the path. He never comes. Esther returns late with the excuse, "Sorry, I lost track of time." From this moment forward nothing can ever be the same. No matter how they try to mend their relationship the crack will remain, and this is something the twins cannot live with. The crack represents a break with the past, a past of unison and total shared existence, and it indicates an uncertain future, a future the twins are unequipped to handle. On the train ride back to the Atlantic they look at their reflections in the carriage window and whisper, "What can we do? What can we ever do?"

In a sense, these two forms of brokenness comprise the third form: a broken world. It is beautifully illustrated in the vignette, "Saint Germaine," which describes the outing Hugh and the twins take to the French town of Bar-Sur-Aube. While relaxing at a table, they observe some women chatting at the ancient well in the town square, a peaceful picture of life as it has been for centuries. Hugh picks up on this, saying, "'This should be what's real . . . What's been forever, what will go on, long after we're gone.'" No sooner does he say this than another woman, dressed the same way and about the same age as the others, approaches the well to draw water. For no apparent reason, the group does not look at her, does not as much as acknowledge her presence. They continue chatting as if she were not there. The woman's face reveals nothing, but her body language as she walks away shows she is not oblivious to the situation. Immediately, the twins realize that the words Hugh just spoke apply to this, too. The world is not, never has been, and never will be a perfect place. It is a world of ostracism and hate, of sadness and despair, of destruction and death. Taken altogether, these things amount to one deep "ouboum" in the twins' ears, and it is the sound of ambiguity, the sound of death. In a world such as this, where nothing can be seen except "through a glass, darkly," the twins decide to complete their journey the only way they know how.

The final stage of their journey may seem bleak or depressing to some readers; after all, the twins commit suicide at the end. However, within the framework of the I Corinthians 13:12 metaphor, it may be understood paradoxically as hopeful. The vignette, "The Sea King," which is the heart of the story and its spiritual foundation, supports this reading. In it, the twins reflect on a tale Nan told them when they were young about the Sea King, a violent and merciless creator of storms and destroyer of ships. The Sea King lived in a palace at the bottom of the ocean and wreaked havoc on passing ships, causing them to sink so he could steal their treasure. He used the bones of the dead sailors to build his gates and their skulls to guard his treasure room. In light of the twins' experiences in France, one might expect that reflecting on such a tale of mayhem and destruction would have a negative effect on their psyches, but it does not. In fact, the effect is just the opposite.

First of all, the tale of the Sea King helps the twins to believe in pure possibility. More specifically, it offers a belief that there is something more out there than what this broken world presents: something supernatural, something spiritual, something magical, something that cannot be proved wrong, something like the Sea King. In a world such as this, according to the twins, why can't the Sea King exist? They explain:

> We know, of course we know, that it's just a story Nan told. Spun out of her Irish dreams and taking hold in ours. . . . But we live in a world where everything we know has been proved wrong, a world gone completely mad. If this world can exist, then anything is possible.

The tale of the Sea King gives the twins hope. They reason that, if anything is possible in this world, then it is possible the tale was wrong. Perhaps the Sea King was not the angry dealer of death and destruction Nan portrayed him to be. "Perhaps," they say, "his kingdom was a beautiful, gentle place, his wrath really sorrow, pining for lost children who had disappeared into the world of men." Perhaps they are these lost children, "the Sea King's beautiful daughters . . . wandering ill at ease through the world of foggy air." If anything is possible, then there is hope that, somewhere out there, a better world awaits.

Perhaps this hope is what motivates the twins when they leap from the bow of the ship. Knowing they will never find peace in this world, they seek for it the only way they know how: by going underwater. Underwater is the place of their childhood fountain, a world of color and quietness. Underwater is the realm of the Sea King, a world of gentleness and peace. Underwater is the world of light, where the twins no longer see though a glass darkly, but face to face with the Father, no longer lost but found.

Source: Timothy Dunham, Critical Essay on "The Deep," in *Short Stories for Students*, Thomson Gale, 2006.

Harvey Grossinger

In the following review, Grossinger praises the "mastery of craft" and "intellectual reach" found in "The Deep."

"The Deep," the labyrinthine centerpiece of Canadian writer Mary Swan's first collection, instantly plunges the reader into dark and diverting Faulknerian waters. The deserving first-prize winner of the O. Henry Award in 2001, "The Deep" is the elaborate and perplexing story of Esther and Ruth, starry-eyed identical twin sisters working as volunteers in France during the wrenching meatgrinder that was trench warfare during World War I. Much of the sustaining power of this remarkable story evolves from Swan's accretion of subtle psychological and contextualized details, and the aesthetic equipoise that emerges from a narrative tone both illusion-free and devoid of histrionics.

Swan writes supple, wry and exacting narratives. Her stories convey trenchant images not only of individual lives but also of the atmospherics of a specific time, a culture, even a particular way of life. Her best stories are situated in the shifting territory where history and myth interact, and in that way they can be seen as background Rorschach blots, capable of evoking individual feelings and memories as well as the characteristic political and social disjunctions that marked a precise point in modern history.

"The Deep" is as allusive as a poem. It weaves back and forth in time. Individual and collective memory seem to inhere symbiotically, as if the past weren't even past, instead cleaving in a kind of biological synchronicity with the present. A mood of lugubrious fatalism—not hardboiled cynicism—permeates the story, as if the destinies of Esther and Ruth, as well as the fates of the warring nations, were inexorable.

"'The Deep' is as allusive as a poem. It weaves back and forth in time. Individual and collective memory seem to inhere symbiotically."

Since the premature death of their mother, who suffered from a pernicious postpartum depression, Esther and Ruth (note the biblical names, the only females to have their own books in the Old Testament) have been tucked away in an isolated English country house by their aloof, still-grieving father, who makes his fortune in the city.

The twins doubt he could have told them apart when they were little girls. They have only superficial relationships with their much older brothers. As a corollary to their sequestration, the sisters have developed a kind of incantatory and interchangeable speech, often speaking in unison.

This is depicted as more than just knowing each other's thoughts; they speak, and think, in a sometimes disconcerting merged voice, most often employing the plural "we" rather than the singular "I" when talking:

> When we heard that James had been killed we were sad, but in a strangely abstract way. Like hearing about the brother of someone you went to school with or met at a dance, . . . Our brother James was not particularly likable, meant little to us, nor we to him. Our sadness when he died was more because that was so. A moment in a rainy room, just one of the things we remember, should we happen to think of him.

In France the sisters are assigned to the canteen stations that service the combat infantrymen near the front, their repetitious work mostly about washing cups and dishes and brewing and pouring tea. Their real function is to provide feminine comfort and attentiveness to the beleaguered soldiers.

After weeks of listening to the men talk about what they've seen and done, the seemingly senseless death and destruction, the sisters start to break down emotionally. They themselves have become casualties of war and are in desperate need of solace. Eventually an empathic soldier named Hugh offers what consolation he is capable of giving, and it appears unavoidable that one of the sisters will become closer to him than the other, a state of affairs—a palpable crisis—that threatens to eviscerate their arcane union.

What drives the narrative besides the twins' twin voices are the fractured testimonies of those who have known them all their lives, including their Nan and headmistress and a doctor who treats them and one of their brothers. Their function is to forge the portraits of these two seemingly identical young women. But the result is counterintuitive. The doubling and tripling of perspectives doesn't clarify or amplify as much as reinforce the impression that the internal truth of any single life remains, ultimately, indecipherable.

Speakers are obsessively looking into the past to make the disharmonious present intelligible, and they are themselves caught between worlds they cannot fully comprehend. To Swan's credit, she deftly skirts sentimentality; there is plenty of sentiment, but no bathos. By focusing on the private griefs and losses of the sisters against the backdrop of wider historical dislocation, Swan has found a credible way to render tangible the shocking losses brought about by an unprecedented universal catastrophe. Each and every one of these varied intermingled voices—including the sisters'—sounds displaced and perhaps even abstract. All states of being are limited, all relocations temporary.

Yet there's something shopworn and superficial about all this, despite the mastery of Swan's prose and the undeniable power of her storytelling. A coldness and artificiality hover at the center of "The Deep," a detachment from deep human feeling that I find both distracting and disingenuous. The luminous beauty of the writing cannot, finally, disguise the fundamental emptiness at the heart of this story, a distancing from the rawness and brutality of its subject. It's analogous to the translucent carapace of an insect, the living thing gone from within.

None of the remaining stories in this collection displays either the mastery of craft or the intellectual reach of "The Deep." Still, there are some very good stories to savor here, including one titled 1917. Swan makes good use of her multiple-voice technique in this story, which is narrated by a cycle of women—telephone operators, nurses, canteen workers—in France during World War I. She begins each paragraph with "In those days," a device that might come across as affected or trite. The bigger issue is that "1917" reads like either a soft-focus prelude or a rehashed coda to "The Deep," and as such it is swamped by the structural and tonal complexity of the former.

In most of these stories, concrete social landscapes are filtered through a medley of dissimilar individuals so that a multidimensional image of a particular time and place emerges. Swan often telescopes on particular things or images and how they randomly summon forth whole histories that have been forgotten.

In stories such as "Hour of Lead" and "Peach," Swan draws connections with "The Deep" by weaving together disparate strands of memory and history to explore the hidden conjunctions between lives separated by geography and by the ineluctable passage of time. "On the Border," the story of a grief-stricken older woman living on a kibbutz and spiraling into dementia, conjoins individual confusion and dissolution to the moral and psychological fragmentation brought about by the Holocaust; what remains is the pervasive shadow of personal disorder and private sorrow that disfigures the buried self.

In her strongest stories, Swan eschews any illusory platitudes about the redemptive power of suffering or loss. In this way, she is able to convey the essential frailty and malleability of her characters.

Source: Harvey Grossinger, "Dark Debut Skims Surface of Emotions," in *Houston Chronicle*, November 14, 2003.

Sources

Bacon, Francis, *Aphorisms*, in *The Literature of Renaissance England*, Oxford University Press, 1973, p. 946.

Donne, John, "A Sermon Preached at St. Paul's for Easter-Day, 1628," in *The Literature of Renaissance England*, Oxford University Press, 1973, p. 563.

Forster, E. M., *A Passage to India*, Harcourt Brace Jovanovich, 1924, p. 141.

Gordon, Mary, Introduction to "The Deep," in *Prize Stories 2001: The O. Henry Awards*, edited by Larry Dark, Anchor Books, 2001, p. 3.

Grossinger, Harvey, "Dark Debut Skims Surface of Emotions," in the *Houston Chronicle*, November 16, 2003, Section ZEST, p. 19.

May Charles, "Judging 'Best' Short Stories by Mystery, Truths, Poetry," in the *Milwaukee Journal Sentinel*, December 9, 2001, Section Arts & Entertainment, p. 8.

Peiffer, Prudence, Review of *The Deep and Other Stories*, in *Library Journal*, Vol. 128, No. 8, May 1, 2003, p. 158.

Review of *The Deep and Other Stories*, in *Kirkus Reviews*, Vol. 71, No. 5, March 1, 2003, p. 345.

Review of *The Deep and Other Stories*, in *M2 Best Books*, November 13, 2003.

Review of *The Deep and Other Stories*, in *Publishers Weekly*, Vol. 250, No. 14, April 7, 2003, p. 48.

Segal, Marta, Review of *The Deep and Other Stories*, in *Booklist*, Vol. 99, No. 15, April 1, 2003, p. 1380.

Swan, Mary, "The Deep," in *The Deep and Other Stories*, Random House, 2003, pp. 3–71.

Further Reading

Allen, Hervey, *Toward the Flame: A Memoir of World War I*, illustrated by Lyle Justis, Bison Books, 2003.

Allen's memoir is about his service as a soldier during World War I. He recounts a march across the beautiful French countryside toward a battle that results in the destruction of his unit.

Howells, Coral Ann, *Contemporary Canadian Women's Fiction: Refiguring Identities*, Palgrave Macmillan, 2003.

In a series of essays, Howells examines the theme of changing cultural and national identities through Canadian fiction by women writers since the mid-1990s. She explores works by Margaret Atwood, Alice Munro, Carol Shields, among others.

Mayle, Peter, *A Year in Provence*, Vintage, 1991.

Mayle, a British travel writer, spent a year in the south of France and writes with candor and humor about his experiences in this memoir-travelogue.

Smith, C. Alphonse, *O. Henry*, University Press of the Pacific, 2003.

William Sidney Porter, whose pseudonym was O. Henry, was one of the most famous American short story writers, with over six hundred tales to his name. This comprehensive biography based on Porter's letters and other original sources, was first published in 1916.

Elbow Room

James Alan McPherson

1977

James Alan McPherson's story "Elbow Room" explores race relations in the United States during the 1960s and 1970s, soon after collapse of the rigid social standards that had been in place since the end of the Civil War, a century earlier. At the center of the story is a young couple: Virginia, a black woman whose travels across the world have opened her eyes to the ways in which American culture can be narrow-minded, and Paul, a white man who has opted out of the Vietnam War as a conscientious objector and is on his own personal search for truth. When they fall in love and marry, a friend of theirs, the story's narrator, predicts that they will find the challenges of being an interracial couple to be more than their youthful idealism has led them to expect. The biggest test comes from Paul's father, who rejects Virginia and the whole idea of the marriage, leading Paul to face life as an outsider. Throughout the telling of the story, McPherson weaves dialogues between the narrator and his editor. The editor, a cold and mechanical voice, insists that the story ought to contain a traditional narrative form and elements, but the narrator explains that the subject of race in the United States is too complex to be approached directly.

This story is a part of a short story collection also called *Elbow Room*, which won the Pulitzer Prize for Fiction in 1979.

James Alan McPherson © Bettmann/Corbis

Author Biography

James Alan McPherson was born in Savannah, Georgia, in 1943, and raised there. His background was lower-middle class, and he grew up at a time when Georgia's public schools were still segregated. He enrolled in Morgan State University in 1963 and earned his bachelor's degree from Morris Brown College in 1965. During the summers of his college years, he was a waiter in the dining cars of the Great Northern Railroad, an experience that allowed him to see what the world was like beyond the segregated South, influencing his sense of social justice and providing the breadth of experience from which he has drawn to craft his fiction.

After college, McPherson attended Harvard Law School, receiving his law degree in 1968. While still in law school, he began writing fiction. His story "Gold Coast" won a contest in the *Atlantic* magazine, which gave him encouragement to abandon his law career. McPherson's first short story collection, *Hue and Cry*, was published in 1969 by the *Atlantic*. He taught at the University of California at Santa Cruz in the 1969–1970 year while enrolled at the University of Iowa, where he received a master of fine arts degree from the famed Writers' Workshop program in 1971.

After 1969, McPherson worked as a contributing editor of the *Atlantic*. His collection *Elbow Room*, which contains this story, was published to critical acclaim in 1977 and was awarded the Pulitzer Prize for Fiction the following year. McPherson has been on the fiction writing faculty of the Iowa Writers Workshop since 1981 and has been a Behavioral Studies fellow at the University of California, Stanford, since 1997. In 1981 he won a MacArthur Foundation grant. He has contributed essays to numerous magazines throughout the years. In 1998 he published *Crabcakes: A Memoir*, his first book-length publication in over twenty years. His essays are collected in *A Region Not Home: Reflections from Exile*, which was published in 2000.

Plot Summary

Prologue

The brief, italicized section that precedes Section 1 is narrated by an unnamed editor, describing the author of the story that is to follow as "unmanageable." He or she talks about taking measures to make the author clarify what is said in the story. The editor wants to make the relationship between the reader and the writer more direct, describing this push toward clarity as a moral issue. The assumption here is that the narrator/writer in the story is one and the same with McPherson himself; certainly the two have similar characteristics. However, other readers may see the narrator/writer in the story as a character separate from and created by the author James Alan McPherson.

Section 1

The first section of the story describes the background of Paul Frost, referring to the time period of the story, presumably the 1960s, as "back during that time," as if it is telling a legend or fairy tale. Frost comes from a small town in Kansas. He went to college in Chicago, where he determined to stay out of the Vietnam War. Eventually, he was forced to go before the draft board back home, where he refused to participate in the army and was given alternative service as a conscientious objector. He was assigned to work in a mental hospital in Chicago. There, he observed the patients and decided that they did not seem any less sane than he did, which made him worry about his own sanity. After a year, he transferred to a hospital in Oakland, California.

Media Adaptations

- McPherson can be heard reading his own story "Gold Coast" on *The Best American Short Stories of the Century*, a compact disc collection released by Houghton Mifflin in 1999.
- McPherson talked about the frustrations and pleasures of writing on a segment of Public Broadcasting System's program *Writers' Workshop*. Filmed in 1980, it is available as of 2005 on videotape from PBS Video.

Section 1 ends with the note that while in California Paul met and married Virginia Valentine, a black woman from Tennessee, in what McPherson refers to as "his last act as a madman."

Section 2

Section 2 gives the background of Virginia Valentine. Born and raised in a country town outside Knoxville, Tennessee, Virginia realized, in the early 1960s, a degree of freedom that American blacks had not known before. She traveled the world, first as a member of the Peace Corps and then independently. The story mentions her exploits as she drifted through India, Kenya, Egypt, and Israel. Returning to the United States at age twenty-two, she continued to travel through the North. She made friends, finding many people like her, but after a while racial divisions made it difficult for people in her social crowd to really understand each other. At the end of this section, she moves to California to find "some soft, personal space to cushion the impact of her grounding."

Section 3

The third section of this story begins with an introduction of the narrator, a writer. The narrator feels that he has heard all of the stories in the East, where stories are not being taken seriously any more, and so he has moved to California, where he meets Virginia and, through her, Paul. After a few pages of his explaining about himself, the editor from the story's prologue interrupts, questioning why this information about the narrator's background and motives should be included, and the narrator defends his decisions.

The story continues with Virginia and Paul's decision to be married. The narrator, who knows Virginia well, feels that she might be rushing into a situation, an interracial marriage that she does not fully understand. At the same time, though, he knows that she has a sensitive, nurturing side that she hides from the outside world, and he thinks she needs someone like Paul to care for. Paul's parents from Kansas oppose the wedding, and they do not attend. Virginia's parents, from Tennessee, attend, even though their real wish is that she would have come back home. At the wedding, her father, Mr. Daniel Valentine, talks with the narrator, stating his objections but admitting begrudgingly that Paul and Virginia make a good couple.

As Paul and Virginia settle into their life together, his father presses him to forsake his marriage, offering to support him if he were to divorce. They have the narrator over to dinner, and he tries to explain how Paul's father might feel by pointing out the different attitudes that people living in different regions of the country have about certain subjects, indicating that the attitudes that his family has about racial issues might surface in Paul. He asks Paul to think about a traditional African mask that is hanging in the dining room, having him consider how he could make people realize that it is not just interesting, but actually beautiful. When he realizes that the narrator is making a veiled reference to his marriage, Paul becomes infuriated and tells him to leave.

Soon after, Virginia phones the narrator and invites him to attend New Year's Eve mass with her and Paul. At the mass, Virginia wears a man's hat, the same hat that she has always worn—in the Episcopal church, men are not allowed to wear hats but women are. An old man in the row behind her, assuming she is a man, tells her to remove it, but she just ignores him. Paul, however, turns around and raises his voice in anger at the man.

In the coming months, Paul experiences being called "nigger" while walking with his wife. He asks the narrator to explain what this word means to him and is told it is "an expression of the highest form of freedom." Virginia becomes pregnant, and her memories of her exotic travels begin to fade as she focuses more on her family. Paul realizes his own loneliness and begins reading philosophical and religious texts, in a search for understanding selfhood.

Paul's parents make gestures of friendliness. His father mentions that he supported the hiring of a black employee where he works, which Paul recognizes as a very slight way of bending toward acceptance. Thinking it over, his father tells Paul that Virginia will be welcomed in their house, but this time Virginia finds the gesture too weak. She explains to the narrator that being accepted under such circumstances would make her baby an "honorary white." They discuss how the world pushes one to be either white or black, and she reminisces about a time when she was able to travel comfortably in both worlds.

Paul and the narrator meet and walk through the city, discussing various matters of identity. Again, Paul asks the narrator about the meaning of "nigger." The narrator points out different types of people, but when he asks about the attitude Paul or his father would have about a well-dressed black man Paul bristles: he thinks that, by associating him with his father, the narrator is calling him a racist. He finishes his walk brusquely, turning before going into his house to defend himself once more as someone who has fought for racial justice.

The narrator never sees them again. He moves back east and receives a birth announcement sent from Kansas, with pictures of their child and with Paul's father, who seems, from his stiff posture, to have grudgingly accepted his daughter-in-law and grandchild. Virginia has written on the back of one picture, "He will be a *classic* kind of nigger."

The editor asks the narrator to explain Virginia's statement, but he cannot. He expresses his faith in the child's future, given the parents' personalities, noting that he found out that they left Kansas soon after to live in isolation in the backwoods of Tennessee.

Characters

The Editor

In this story, an anonymous editor, who speaks in a first-person, officious voice, interjects every once in a while. The voice is only formal, with no sense of personality: it is never clear whether this character is old or young, male or female. In the opening segment, the editor seems to be concerned that the narrator is trying to get out of performing his moral responsibility as a writer. The editor carries on a dialogue with the narrator, attempting to convince the narrator to steer the story down a more traditional, narrative path. For every objection that the editor raises, the narrator has a counterargument, which expresses why he feels that the story must be presented in the way that he has written it. The story ends with the editor still calling out for further explanation, showing that this story consciously does not meet standard editorial criteria for directness.

Paul Frost

Paul is an earnest young white man. During the Vietnam War, he refuses to join the army, and the Selective Service board in his Kansas home town gives him alternative duty to serve in a mental hospital in Chicago. Over the course of a year, he keeps to himself, and as he associates with mental patients doubts creep into his mind about his own sanity. He transfers to a hospital in Oakland, where he meets and marries Virginia Valentine, who is black.

Paul's greatest struggle in this story is with his parents, who disapprove of his relationship with Virginia. His father is so opposed to their relationship that he offers to support Paul financially if he would break off his marriage, and neither Paul's mother nor his father attends Paul's wedding. Their opposition makes Paul angry at intolerance, which makes him defensive: while the black characters in the story, the narrator and Virginia, take a philosophical view of small-minded people, Paul turns angry. This is particularly evident when it is he, not Virginia, who shouts at a man in church who sees Virginia from behind and thinks that she is a man who has neglected to take his hat off: Virginia ignores him when he says, "Young man, if you're too *dumb* to take your hat off in church, get out!" but Paul turns on him in full fury.

The narrator respects Paul for his eagerness to learn, but he also sees that Paul will never fully understand the social problems that concern Virginia. The narrator worries that the views of Paul's father and the society in which he grew up will have the most influence on Paul, but Paul does stay with Virginia through the end of the story.

Virginia Frost

See Virginia Valentine

The Narrator

Though he never gives his name in this story, the narrator is central to all of the action. He is a friend of Paul and Virginia Frost, interacting with them at several social functions over the course of years. He also acknowledges himself as the author of this short story, interacting with his editor in asides, explaining why he chose to include some particular details and why he decided to develop the story as he has. He is defensive of his method, believing that the story must be told the way he tells it even if it does not seem to follow a traditional narrative pattern.

The narrator, a black man of undetermined age, is interested in telling the stories of the times around him. When he feels that the stories he is hearing in the East are too familiar and that he is missing a fresh perspective on them, he goes to California. It is there that he becomes acquainted with Virginia and Paul. He becomes closer to Virginia, feeling that he understands her well, possibly even better than she understands herself. His relationship with Paul is uneven: they are friends, but the narrator sometimes says things that make Paul feel that he is being accused of racism.

The conversations between the narrator and his editor are formal, as if he is responding to the notes that the editor has written on a printed copy of his story. In these dialogues, the editor repeatedly calls for the story to follow a more orderly progression, accusing the narrator of wandering into irrelevancy. In defense, the narrator explains that the story he is telling and especially the racial implications of it are so complex and nuanced that it is at times necessary to approach the facts indirectly and to include details that might not seem relevant at first glance.

Mr. Daniel Valentine

The narrator meets Virginia Valentine's father at the wedding of Virginia and Paul. Daniel Valentine is disappointed that his daughter is marrying a white man because he had always assumed that racial separation was one of the few undeniable circumstances of the world. He accepts the marriage, though, and he and his wife show up at the wedding in San Francisco bearing gifts. After the ceremony, Mr. Valentine hands out congratulatory cigars to those in attendance. He explains to the narrator that he has no particular dislike for Paul but that he has threatened him if he ever makes Virginia unhappy.

Virginia Valentine

The narrator clearly respects Virginia as a strong, proud woman. She is a black woman from Tennessee who left home at a young age to travel the world, first as a member of the Peace Corps and then on her own, getting to know people and customs of different countries. She has ended her world travels among the disaffected youth of the United States of the late 1960s, living in different cities before ending up in the San Francisco area, where she met Paul. Although their courtship is viewed with skepticism by her parents and is openly opposed by his, she remains committed to him.

Throughout the story, Virginia is proven to be a person who understands the world and has seen the damages of racism. She does not enter into an interracial marriage lightly, but with the full knowledge of the sort of opposition that she and Paul can expect. The narrator reads Virginia's tough exterior demeanor as a mask, hiding an inner fear of being hurt. The refrain that he thinks of when he sees her is "Don't hurt my baby!" In the earlier sections of the story, this protectiveness is directed toward her husband Paul, who is shown as being unaware of the ways of the world. At the end, though, Virginia gives birth to a son, Daniel, who gives her something real to worry about.

Themes

Race

Race is the most important theme explored in "Elbow Room," though the story's view of U.S. racial divisions lacks the kind of heated rhetoric or violent extremism that often surrounds the subject in literature. For the most part, the opposition to Virginia and Paul's interracial marriage comes in subtle ways. The narrator does mention strangers, children, who shout offensive racial slurs at Paul, but this is handled in a dispassionate way: the characters who are black and are used to being pelted with such insults hardly notice the word that Paul is called, just his reaction to it.

The most constant and direct complication due to race comes from Paul's father. He refuses to acknowledge that his son has married a black woman and even tries to break up their marriage. In the end, though, the couple stays at the father's house, briefly, after the birth of their child. His opposition to interracial marriage is not absolute.

This story shows that racism in the United States can be overcome on an individual basis, but that racism is ingrained in U.S. culture. Even the most open relationships are tinged by its shadow. There is no doubt about Paul and Virginia's love, and they are clearly intelligent people who should be as capable as anyone of holding off against societal pressures; what is in doubt, however, is whether even the best equipped couple can hold up

Topics For Further Study

- Did race relations in the United States change much between 1975 and 2005? Read an article about the subject by a black scholar and an article by a white scholar, and write a report in which you evaluate their findings.
- In the story, Virginia wears a hat that was popular for men thirty or forty years earlier. Find some contemporary fashion style that was originally used for the other gender, and make a chart that traces its development over time.
- Research the significance of the Japanese tea ceremony and explain why McPherson may have decided to have the final scene between the narrator and Virginia in such a setting.
- Interracial dating and marriage are more common in the early 2000s than previously. Find out which states have had the most recent laws restricting interracial dating, as well as other organizations such as schools and clubs that have similar restrictions. Prepare a questionnaire for class members to answer in which they distinguish between actual rules and ones that you made up.
- In this story, Paul's experience as a conscientious objector from the draft gives him experiences that he never would have had. Read the interviews with conscientious objectors in Gerald R. Gioglio's *Days of Decision: An Oral History of Conscientious Objectors in the Military During the Vietnam War*, and report on what tendencies the men in the book have in common, and what characteristics distinguish Paul from them.

against the hostility between races that has been deeply ingrained over the course of generations. In the end, Virginia tells the narrator that she had thought that she could bridge the gap, move freely between black and white society, but the pull of tradition is just too strong.

Language and Meaning

The story of Paul and Virginia is woven together with the subplot about the narrator of the piece trying to convince his editor to let him tell the story in his own way. The very first words in the story are written from the perspective of the editor, who notes right from the start, "*Narrator is unmanageable*." After that, the editor interjects several times to tell the narrator that he is straying from the main story, and the narrator frequently defends his decision to include facts that are not directly related to what happens to Paul and Virginia.

The narrator insists the traditional narrative structure is unable to capture the complexity of the U.S. racial structure. He discusses his search for new stories, and he relates events, such as his effort to make Paul explain the beauty of an African mask, without explaining their meaning to the overall story. This leads the editor to charge the narrator with a failure to be clear, which he counters by stating that he is being as clear as he can be. He does not explain why the story must include the details it contains, suggesting that such explanations would convey his meaning less effectively than the way he chooses to use. The story tries to get past language's shortcomings by presenting ideas and incidents that readers have to figure out on their own.

Geographic Location

McPherson uses U.S. geography throughout this story to indicate the connection between place and attitude. Virginia comes from Tennessee, a southern state. Southern states have a tradition of institutionalized racial separation, from slavery before the Civil War and segregation after it. They also have a tradition of racial interaction, with poor whites and poor blacks living in close proximity. Paul comes from Kansas, a Midwestern state that is overwhelmingly white. The opposition that Paul's father has to his marriage indicates a fear based on unfamiliarity.

The narrator also distinguishes between attitudes on the East Coast and the West Coast. He identifies the East as a place where ideas are stagnant, calcified, frozen into place. As a storyteller, he cannot find any new stories in the East because the people there have lost their faith in telling stories. To find the sort of enthusiasm about life that once prevailed in the East, he goes to the West Coast, which he calls "the territory," a nod to the time in the eighteenth and nineteenth centuries when the United States was only established in the eastern half of the continent.

The decision to go west may also hide a subtle allusion to the final paragraph of *The Adventures of Huckleberry Finn* (1884), in which Huck says he must "light out for the territory." It seems relevant given what Huck himself has risked befriending the black slave, Jim. Moreover, in writing this story of his adventures, Huck in this paragraph laments that if he had known "what a trouble it was to make a book" he would not have tackled the project. This comment presents another parallel to McPherson's work, since the narrator in this story struggles with its writing in light of frequent criticism he receives from his editor.

On the West Coast, the narrator seeks other idealists who have left the East, such as Virginia, whose view of American attitudes toward race has been affected by her travels in Asia and Africa. Eventually, though, the narrator finds that the people who have moved to California are becoming just as jaded as their Eastern counterparts.

Innocence

"I am sure he was unaware of his innocence," the narrator says of Paul, who is searching to understand his own identity. He sees this search as one of the central attractions Paul has for Virginia. She is a strong woman, in search of someone whom she can support with that strength and concerned about innocent people who can be hurt by a world that she understands, from her life-long experience with racism, can be cruel. Even when Paul loses his temper, he is not seen as an angry man, but instead as an overgrown hurt child.

Virginia's concern for innocence is a defining part of her character, one that is not obvious to all who meet her, but is clear to the narrator. From the start, he reads in her eyes the plea, "*Don't hurt my baby*!" In the early part of their marriage, Paul, who is innocent about the complexity of race relations, is the "baby" she is protecting, but when she becomes pregnant her focus shifts to the actual baby she is carrying. In the end, she compromises her resistance to his parents and to hers in the name of raising their son so he can function in the American racial environment.

Style

First Person Narrator

Though McPherson focuses attention on Paul and Virginia throughout "Elbow Room," he also makes it clear that the first-person narrator has a life independent of them. This fact is established early with the editor's initial assessment of the story that is to come, in which he or she muses that the narrator has a defiant attitude. Throughout the story, readers are given brief dialogues between the editor and the narrator that interrupt the focus on Paul and Virginia. Though the narrator is a friend of the central couple and interacts with them frequently, readers are never allowed to forget that the narrator's access to their story is limited by social conventions. Readers do not really know what they think, only what the narrator thinks they think.

The nature of this narrator is complicated by the fact that he shows awareness of the fact that he is telling a story in those passages that relate his exchanges with his editor. McPherson uses these sections to draw readers' attention to the ways in which real life is captured and/or created in fiction. Readers are often meant to believe the events that are told by a first-person narrator, even after accounting for the fact that such narrators are not entirely reliable, but the speaker of this story serves to raise awareness of the writing and publishing process. Putting the narrator into the story as a first-person speaker often invites readers to reflect on the process of changing experiences into fiction: here, McPherson goes one step further, drawing attention to the ways in which the fiction an author imagines can be changed by the editorial process. The story may also be considered an example of what is called metafiction, that kind of fiction which in some way draws attention to itself as a work of fiction.

Subplot

Aside from the main plot of how Virginia and Paul will cope with the tradition that frowns on their relationship, this story provides a subplot about the narrator's search for a good story worth telling. As is the case with most subplots, the story is sufficient to stand alone without these added details, but it would not be as rich.

The narrator's interplay with his editor is a part of his separate subplot, identifying the narrator as a writer who is concerned with his craft. More relevant, though, are the passages in which he tells about times away from the Frosts, when he explains his actions as being driven by the search for stories. He tells readers that he came to the West Coast (or "the territory") to find stories, having realized that the people of the East were not telling him anything new. At one point he even diverts his focus to an entirely new character, a man who was paroled from prison after fifty years, leaving the Frosts out of "Elbow Room" for almost a page and showing this new character in a scene that has nothing to do with them, an indicator that the focus of this story is not strictly on Paul and Virginia's situation.

Though the editor complains that this section, as well as the other sections where the narrator discusses his interest in gathering stories, should be cut, it is this subplot that helps define what "Elbow Room" is about. The main story alone is about coping with love within a segregated and prejudiced culture, but these asides put the young couple's story in perspective: readers are not just asked to examine their story, but how their act of defiance can be framed and given meaning in a larger context.

Denouement

In story telling, the denouement is the resolution that comes after the climax. The word comes from the French word meaning "unraveling." Here, the denouement occurs after the narrator has lost touch with the Frosts, before the birth of their child: he discovers some facts about them from postcards that are sent from various places around the country and forwarded months later, but the information conveyed through such a method does not tell him much about their actual states of mind. The story reaches its climax with the narrator's last two one-on-one meetings with the couple: he has tea with Virginia in the park and they talk about the difficulties of thriving in a world dominated by the white perspective, and then he walks through the city with Paul, who is defensive about his struggle to understand the black perspective. These two discussions represent the turning point in the narrator's understanding of the situation: the events that follow are just the story's way of addressing curiosity about the plot.

Historical Context

Post Civil Rights

During the 1960s and 1970s, race relations in the United States changed more rapidly than they had since slavery was abolished during the Civil War. For the hundred years after President Lincoln signed the Emancipation Proclamation in 1863, the situation was firmly established particularly in the South to keep black Americans in conditions that were not much better than slavery had provided. In many southern states particularly, blacks were legally taken advantage of by a series of laws that have been dubbed collectively as the "Jim Crow laws," after an offensive comic character in minstrel shows. These laws divided public amenities and services between those for blacks and those for whites. From neighborhoods, jobs, and schools to railroad cars, hotels, and drinking fountains, there were certain accommodations for white citizens and inferior ones for black citizens. The legal theory, established in the 1896 Supreme Court finding in the case of *Plessey v. Ferguson*, was that the two races would be offered segregated yet comparable amenities: the "separate but equal" doctrine. In actuality, though, black Americans were restricted to inferior conditions in each case.

This prejudicial and immoral situation was not really addressed until after the Second World War. During the early 1950s, the civil rights movement took advantage of the post-war spread of television to make people around the country aware of the injustices perpetrated under Jim Crow laws. In 1954, Rosa Parks (1913–2005) made international news when she was arrested on a bus in Birmingham, Alabama, for refusing to give up her seat to a white man; also in 1954 the Supreme Court found that separate facilities were inherently unequal in *Brown v. Board of Education of Topeka, Kansas*. Throughout the decade, Reverend Martin Luther King Jr. and other civil rights leaders held public protests to show the world how, even when segregationist laws were struck down, communities often still fought against granting equal rights to African Americans. They often were faced with threats and intimidating terror tactics, but they also gained increasing support from whites, including northern students who traveled to the South to show their support to the fight against injustice. When state governors refused to enforce laws that mandated racial equality, the federal government passed the Civil Rights Act of 1964, explicitly banning segregation.

Compare & Contrast

- **1970s:** Kansas, where Paul's parents live, is one of the less racially diverse states in the nation. Ninety-two percent of the population of Kansas is white.

  Today: Kansas is still overwhelmingly white. In a period when non-white populations have grown steadily across the United States, Kansas still has an eighty-five percent white population.

- **1970s:** The San Francisco area is a bastion for holdouts from the hippie era of the late 1960s and early 1970s. The people that McPherson describes, coming to the area to "find themselves," move about freely, focused on personal experience.

  Today: San Francisco is considered one of the most expensive housing markets in the country. While reminders of its association with the hippie era exist, much of the area is associated with economic growth.

- **1970s:** Young women like Virginia Valentine travel freely through Africa and the Middle East, exploring new cultures and learning about different approaches to life.

  Today: Since the terror attacks of September 11, 2001, Americans have been more wary of the dangers involved in international travel.

- **1970s:** Young men who are conscientious objectors to war are able to work in service jobs in the States rather than going to fight in Vietnam.

  Today: The United States has a volunteer military force. Those who do not want to fight do not have to, although military recruiters work diligently to find those who might be interested.

- **1970s:** Romantic relationships between black and white Americans are uncommon and are frowned upon by society.

  Today: Americans are, for the most part, comfortable with interracial couples and make media heroes of biracial celebrities, such as Tiger Woods, Halle Barry, and Lenny Kravitz, to name just a few.

After the Civil Rights Act, it became possible for African Americans to sue in federal court against those who tried to prohibit their equal participation. In the aftermath, many facilities that had previously been closed to blacks became open. Racism was no longer permitted in the United States—at least, not legally. But the racist and separatist attitudes of the past lingered on. Covert or implied racism became more common. A business might, for instance, not explicitly deny an applicant employment due to race, but it might claim that all white applicants just happened to fit their needs more closely than any black applicant. Parents fought school integration that would take their children too far from their segregated neighborhoods, and social organizations fought for the right to associate with whomever they chose. In the 1960s and 1970s, the racial tensions that had once been written into law were expressed in subtle, frequently nonverbal ways.

Critical Overview

"Elbow Room" is the title story of James Alan McPherson's second short story collection. His first collection, *Hue and Cry*, established McPherson as a major literary voice when it was published in 1969; it included the story "Gold Coast" which was eventually included in the compilation *The Best American Short Stories of the Century* (1999), selected by John Updike. By the time *Elbow Room* was published in 1977, critics were looking forward to more of McPherson's fiction.

In *Newsweek*, Margo Jefferson credits McPherson with being "an astute realist who knows how to turn the conflicts between individual personalities and the surrounding culture into artful and highly serious comedies of manners." She notes his growth as an artist since *Hue and Cry*, explaining that over the eight intervening years he had "extended his ability to be tender but unsentimental—and sharpened his theatrical sense as well." The stories are so wise about human interaction that she concludes by wondering if he could also be "an intelligent, perceptive playwright."

In his review of *Elbow Room* in the *New York Times*, Robie Macauley, like most reviewers, brims with praise for McPherson: "A fine control of language and story, a depth in his characters, humane values," he writes in summary, "these are a few of the virtues James Alan McPherson displays in this fine collection of stories." Focusing particularly on the story "Elbow Room," Macauley notes that it presents "a ruinous struggle for a kind of psychological synthesis," observing that one of McPherson's recurring themes is that such syntheses never truly take place.

While negative criticism of this story and its namesake book are scarce, critics do point out its weaknesses. For instance, an unsigned review in the *New Yorker* in November of 1977 is generally positive but also makes the point that "Elbow Room" and several other stories in the collection "tell the reader a bit less than he wants to know about the characters' lives and a bit more than he wants to know about the ideological or artistic problems that confronted the narrator." Such mild criticism hardly detracts from the book's overall value, as the reviewer notes in the next line: "For the most part, however, the characters speak eloquently for themselves." Indeed, *Elbow Room*, the collection, received the Pulitzer Prize for Fiction in 1978.

Quincy Jones and Peggy Lipton on the Hollywood Walk of Fame © Bettmann/Corbis

Criticism

David Kelly

Kelly is an instructor of English literature and creative writing. In this essay, Kelly looks at the story as posing a philosophical rather than a social problem.

Anyone who has read James Alan McPherson's short story "Elbow Room" can see that it, like many of McPherson's works, is concerned with the complexities of race relations in America. At the story's center is a biracial couple, Paul and Virginia: he is white, and, as a member of the youth movement that came of age in the sixties and seventies, is ready to stand up against the racist traditions that he learned in the Midwest. She has traveled the world enough to know that the opposition to her blackness that she faces in America is not universal. Their story is related by a narrator who is black, is a friend of theirs, and is also aware of his role as narrator, communicating at times with an editor who questions the relevance of details he gives while telling Paul and Virginia's story.

It is not just the basic situation of Paul and Virginia that marks this as a story about race, however. Racial issues are all over it, in practically every paragraph. Paul's father, back in Kansas, is openly hostile to the couple's courtship and eventual marriage, refusing to attend the wedding and warming only slightly when he hears that a grandchild is on the way. Virginia's father, Mr. Daniel Valentine, attends their wedding but is only slightly less wary, threatening his wrath against Paul if he ever makes her "cry about something that ain't the fault of her womanly ways." And the narrator tests Paul's resolve at almost every step, quizzing him about his attitudes toward black people and white people and his understanding of the word "nigger."

"Paul is driven by a search for himself and Virginia is driven to defend innocence, and in this they compliment each other well. The narrator, though, is just as driven as either of them in his quest for stories."

With so much racial tension in the atmosphere, it is strange that the editor and the narrator cannot agree upon a basic story. A pattern presents itself from the start: the narrator gives details that do not seem relevant to Paul and Virginia's story; the editor calls for more clarity, more explanation; and the narrator replies that he cannot be any clearer, that what is presented on the page *is* the story. Readers share the editor's frustration, suspecting that there is either something that could be explained more clearly or that the differences in perspective that separate the editor and the narrator are the ones that will always separate whites and blacks. At the end of the story, the narrator seems resigned to being less than understood.

But the insufficiency of language to explain the twisted nuances of race in America does not mean that the story is left incomplete: it only means that the story is *not* really about race relations at all. This is a story about people trying to find themselves in a larger sense than racial identity. It is not a story about what it is to be black or white, but about what it is to be human. Each of the principle characters here is looking for something to believe in. Readers quite easily identify the motivation that drives each. What is not so easy to tell, however, is how much racial identity has to do with their various drives.

The story starts by introducing Paul Frost as a sort of legendary figure: he comes from Kansas like thousands of other men during a period referred to dreamily as "that time." At first, he seems to be an idealist, possibly too much of a rebel for his own good: after refusing to participate in the draft or to go back where he came from, he ends up, while working with mental patients, questioning his own sanity. Falling in love with Virginia is explained as "his last act as a madman." One could infer from this introduction either that true love keeps him from drifting aimlessly any longer, or that he only believes that he loves Virginia, in order to give meaning to a rebellious but unfocused life. Reading this as a story about race, it is stubbornness at least as much as love that bonds Paul to Virginia. She even calls him stubborn late in the story, when discussing Paul with the narrator. But another way to look at it would be to concentrate on the man that Paul was before meeting Virginia. He tried a few things, but he was not adrift; he stood up against the draft board, but he was not just looking to pick a fight.

The racial reading would imply that Paul is only interested in Virginia for racial reasons, leading to the explanation that he does not really love her, but merely thrives on the glares they draw when they walk down the street together. Paul, though, suffers for his love. He allows everyone from his parents to her parents to the narrator to question his motives. He delves into reading because he questions his own motives. The one trait that stays constant throughout Paul's life, even more than his willingness to stand against the status quo, is a thirst for knowledge.

This thirst is perhaps easier to see in Virginia. She is presented as a smart, confident, worldly woman, one who is strong enough to stand against the racist forces that would try to repress her spirit. She is secure enough with her own personality to travel the world alone, and to let insults go without response. Still, she does have a weakness: the narrator points out, often, that her entire demeanor seems to convey the message, "*Don't hurt my baby*!" When the story is read as a polemic about race, one could find that this soft spot in Virginia implies a tenderness found in all black women, no matter how guarded their demeanor. Perhaps the need to live life defensively is what makes her tender side stand out. Still, it seems to be a characteristic that would grow in a woman like Virginia regardless of race. She happens to be a caring woman, with "maternal" instincts ("maternal" in quotes because she spends most of the story looking out for not an actual infant, but her husband).

It makes more sense to see that Virginia is looking to fill this emptiness inside of her than to see her solely as a representative of black women everywhere. Her defining moment comes when she

What Do I Read Next?

- McPherson burst onto the national literary scene when his short story "Gold Coast" was published in the *Atlantic* while he was still in law school. It has been included in *The Best American Short Stories of the Century* (1999) and can also be found in McPherson's first short story collection, *Hue and Cry* (1968).
- McPherson tells the story of his life, wrapping it around the difficult decision to sell his childhood home and evict the elderly tenants who rented from him in *Crabcakes: A Memoir* (1999). This collection of essays is every bit as terse and intellectually wound as his fiction.
- In his essay "What America Would Be Like Without Blacks," Ralph Ellison explores themes similar to those about which McPherson writes in his story. Ellison examines the fractured nature of the American identity when it comes to race. His essay is included in *The Collected Essays of Ralph Ellison* (1995).
- McPherson is often associated with the late Leon Forrest, one of the leading African American novelists of the late twentieth century. Forrest's crowning achievement is *Divine Days* (1993). The novel is about an aspiring playwright in Chicago in the 1960s.
- Studs Turkel's *Race: How Blacks & Whites Think & Feel about the American Obsession* (1993) lets ordinary people explain their perspectives about this delicate but overreaching subject.

---

looks back at her independent life, a life that she will lose once her baby is born, and says, "I was *whiter* than white and *blacker* than black. Hell, at least I got to *see* through the fog." This could be the claim of someone who has lived her life to fight the system, but it is more likely someone who has transcended the system entirely, at least for a short while. True, race is a significant part of Virginia's identity, but she at least has known another identity beyond race. The fact that her pregnancy makes her think about racial issues again does not mean that she is only a product of the racial construct.

The story of Paul and Virginia draws attention to race because they approach it from the opposite sides, but the narrator is no more nor less a part of the same situation. Paul is driven by a search for himself and Virginia is driven to defend innocence, and in this they compliment each other well. The narrator, though, is just as driven as either of them in his quest for stories.

One thing that "Elbow Room" never actually defines is what the narrator means when he talks about "stories." He hints at it, saying what kind of stories have become stagnant in what part of the country and identifying the ways in which his quest for stories changes his relations with friends. He drifts away from Paul and Virginia when their story loses its interest and toward a convict who is taken in by the upper class. The stories that he is interested in seem to revolve around race, and the varieties of race relations America can come up with, though he admits that the combinations are limited. Though race may be the subject matter of the stories he seeks, the fact that he is driven to seek stories is even more important. It is the fact of his obsession, not the object of his obsession, that defines who he is.

This, at last, explains why the work that he submits to his editor feels incomplete. It may well be that the story of race in America is incomplete, and that his telling of this tale is only meant to reflect that: still, he should be able to turn the events surrounding Paul and Virginia into a recognizable narrative. He realizes that race is an obstacle for each of them, and that they need some "elbow room" from it, but he also realizes that there is more to each of them than race alone can account for. What he is missing, what he cannot explain to the editor, is not a final word on the complexities of race, but rather a final word on the wide scope of life.

Judging just from what the narrative says, there is nothing too devastating in the lives of the Frosts. Paul may never understand why he cannot understand his wife's experiences, Virginia may never know the freedom she thought she could attain, and their child, young Daniel, might be as burdened by his roots as every other child. They are faced with frustration, not destruction. They are frustrated by the limitations put on them because of society's racial views, but that is only part of it. Each of them, and the narrator too, has a life beyond race. The lesson of this story is not that race hinders, but that freeing oneself of the expectations of race is only the beginning.

Source: David Kelly, Critical Essay on "Elbow Room," in *Short Stories for Students*, Thomson Gale, 2006.

Laura Pryor

Pryor has a bachelor of arts from the University of Michigan and twenty years experience in professional and creative writing with special interest in fiction. In this essay, she explores the recurring metaphor of imprisonment used by James Alan McPherson in this story.

In his short story "Elbow Room," James Alan McPherson explores the attitudes and conditions that have segregated blacks and whites in the United States, not just physically but psychologically. McPherson uses the recurring metaphor of prisons and imprisonment to illustrate the boundaries that prevent true communication between races. Both blacks and whites in the story are living within their own psychological prisons, though the nature of these prisons is not exactly the same.

First readers meet Paul Frost, a white man from Kansas. The theme of confinement is presented early in his history, when Paul refuses to go to war and instead opts for "alternate service in a hospital for the insane." After spending time with the inmates, he finds that many of them are not insane; then he begins to fear that his beginning to understand them may actually means that he too is insane. (The fear that understanding another person will cause one to become that kind of person occurs again later in the story, when Paul's father accuses him of "beginning to think like a Negro.") Paul flees to California, where "Activity kept him from thinking about being crazy and going back to Kansas." It is in California that he meets and marries Virginia Valentine.

Paul's prison, as symbolized by the mental hospital, is a psychological one. Late in the story, Paul tells the narrator, "You may not think much of *me*, but my children will be great!" The narrator replies, "They will be black and blind or passing for white and self-blinded." The ingrained, often unconscious attitudes of whites form their prison, their mental boundaries, but because they are comfortable and unconscious of their own limited thinking, most are not even aware of their own confinement. They are, as the narrator says, self-blinded. Paul is aware that his thinking is limited in some way, but he spends the entire story groping for the walls of his prison, never fully discovering the perimeters of his cell. Others are completely unconscious of these structures and boundaries, accepting them as a given, such as the woman the narrator meets at a cocktail party: "This woman looked me straight in the eye while denouncing prisons with a passionate indignation. Periodically, she swung her empty martini glass in a confident arc to the right of her body. There, as always, stood a servant holding a tray at just the point where, without ever having to look, my hostess knew a perfect arc and a flat surface were supposed to intersect." It does not even occur to the woman that the servant might not be there; in her world, the unconscious assumption is the servant is always there. The narrator explains it this way (referring to Paul): "More than a million small assumptions, reaffirmed year after year, had become as routine as brushing teeth. . . . This was an unconscious process over which he had little control. It defined his self for him."

Interestingly, this description is very similar to the process of institutionalization experienced by actual prisoners. Craig Haney, a professor of psychology at the University of California at Santa Cruz in studying the psychological effects of imprisonment, writes that "The various psychological mechanisms that must be employed to adjust [to prison life] . . . become increasingly 'natural,' second nature, and, to a degree, internalized. . . . few people who have become institutionalized are aware that it has happened to them." People are not born with prejudice, but the installation of these attitudes occurs in such tiny increments, day by day, that as for institutionalized persons, people never even realize it has happened.

Obviously the blacks in the story are more aware of their prisons, as many of the limitations they face have been imposed upon them by others. Virginia fights not just psychological boundaries, but practical and political ones as well. Virginia is portrayed as a fighter, a tough customer with a tender heart. She curses liberally and wears the "type of cap popularized by movie gangsters in the forties." According to Craig Haney, this outward display of toughness is a common defense mechanism for individuals in actual prisons. He writes that "because there are people in their immediate environment poised to take advantage of weakness . . . Some prisoners learn to project a tough convict veneer that keeps all others at a distance."

Virginia is originally from Tennessee, but leaves "on the crest of that great wave of jail-breaking peasants." With the advent of the civil rights movement and legislation providing new freedoms and protections for minorities, for Virginia and other blacks "the outside world seemed absolutely clear in outline and full of sweet choices." The sixties brought new freedoms, both literally and psychologically, a willingness to abandon old ways of thinking. However, this change did not last. As McPherson writes, "But then their minds began to shift." The old prejudices returned: "It took several months before they became black and white." This phenomenon also has parallels in the experience of actual prisoners. Later in the story, the narrator becomes interested in the story of a man recently freed from prison after fifty years' incarceration. Like Virginia and her friends, "He was alive with ambition, lust, large appetites." Yet he never lifts his window blind, and in his room, he stays within a small perimeter, hesitating when he nears the door. Haney writes, "some inmates may come to depend heavily on institutional decision-makers to make choices for them and to rely on the structure and schedule of the institution to organize their daily routine. . . . in extreme cases, profoundly institutionalized persons may become extremely uncomfortable when and if their previous freedom and autonomy is returned." Initially thrilled at their new freedoms, both blacks and whites eventually returned to the familiar prison of their previous assumptions, just as some freed prisoners intentionally commit crimes to return to the familiar rhythms of prison life. The idea of having more freedom than one can handle is brought up again later in a conversation between Paul and the narrator. The narrator tells him, "I saw a picture on a calendar once of a man posed between the prairie and the sky. He seemed pressured by all that space, as if he were in a crucible."

Like the unnamed prisoner, and like Paul, Virginia is unable to find her way out of her prison—she is "black and blinded"—but she keeps fighting to keep her mind open and hold onto optimism. Though she is aware of the limitations of the mind, she tells the narrator, "But didn't I make some elbow room?" The admirable struggle she has gone

one of the key messages of the story is that there are no easy scapegoats, explanations, or answers for the failure of Americans to fully integrate as a society."

through just to make psychological "elbow room"—a term that indicates a fairly small amount of personal space—illustrates just how difficult it is to shift ingrained ways of viewing the world, even when one is willing and eager to do so. For those ambivalent to the idea of change, progress is even slower. Paul's father's first step towards change is simply to mention, in conversation with Paul, "the full name of the black janitor who swept out his office."

McPherson neither places blame nor excuses anyone from it. In fact, one of the key messages of the story is that there are no easy scapegoats, explanations, or answers for the failure of Americans to fully integrate as a society. The editor continually demands of the narrator: "Clarify the meaning of this comment," and "Explain. Explain." The narrator demurs, however, as he is aware that it is the imposition of mental structures, forms, and categories handed down from generation to generation that exacerbates the very problems he is describing. In other words, there is no clarity; there is no explanation. The walls of people's prisons are hazy and undefined, making them far more difficult to escape than walls of concrete and iron bars.

Source: Laura Pryor, Critical Essay on "Elbow Room," in *Short Stories for Students*, Thomson Gale, 2006.

Bonnie Weinreich

Freelance writer Bonnie Weinreich has a bachelor's degree in English and has worked as a reporter for a daily newspaper. In this essay, Weinreich considers the different ways the word nigger is used in James Alan McPherson's short story, "Elbow Room," and how its variety of uses

"Paul, in his effort to overcome the obstacles inherent in his marrying a black woman, is akin to the black person who is caught between saving his own identity and fitting into the dominant white American culture."

reflects the difficulty in communicating across racial lines.

How is the reader to approach James Alan McPherson's use of the word nigger in his short story "Elbow Room?" For sensitive white readers who understand the word to be a racial slur, its familiar and easy use, especially by Virginia Valentine, an African American woman, is hard to comprehend. On the other hand, black readers, viewing the word from the inside, know its use by blacks comes out of self-knowledge and an intimacy not available to white readers. However, not all African Americans view the word the same or use it in the same way. The varying uses and attitudes of the word lead to conflict when Virginia's white husband, Paul Frost, attempts to understand what is meant by the word "nigger."

McPherson's black narrator defines a "nigger" as "a descendant of Proteus, an expression of the highest form of freedom." (In Greek mythology, Proteus is a sea god who attends Poseidon and changes his own form or appearance at will.) It is in this shape shifting that the word "nigger" must be understood.

Virginia's use illustrates the favorable connotation of the word. Although a country woman by birth, she has traveled the world. She begins "calling herself 'nigger' in an affirmative and ironic way." When angry, she yells, "Don't play with me now, nigger!" but her real meaning is "*Don't come too close, I hurt easily*." She truly loves Paul, and she tries to protect him from the insults of racism she knows he will endure. Through experience, she has become comfortable in her skin, but she realizes that Paul is not.

Paul wants to understand a group to which he does not belong, but he can never entirely comprehend the black experience because it is defined in part as that culture which is not the culture of white people. In trying to find his way, he asks the narrator, "What is a nigger? . . . I mean, what does it *really* mean to you?" The narrator responds with his "Proteus" definition, which is, in fact, no definition at all. Paul is upset when children call him "nigger," but Virginia does not understand his distress. She says she "just laughed at the little crumb-snatchers." Paul says Virginia is "a bundle of contradictions. She breaks all the rules. You all do." In this story, the use of the word "nigger" may be seen as a metaphor for the inability to qualify the black experience. Virginia's contradictions make it hard for Paul to understand her, just as the shifting meaning of the black idiom (a group of words peculiar to a given language or a characteristic style) makes it impossible to define.

McPherson turns the tables on his white main character; in "Elbow Room" Paul seems to be the odd man out. His family refuses to attend the wedding, while Virginia's parents, who are not exactly ecstatic over their daughter's choice of husband, show up for the event bearing food and gifts. Paul, in his effort to overcome the obstacles inherent in his marrying a black woman, is akin to the black person who is caught between saving his own identity and fitting into the dominant white American culture. In the end, the narrator points out a variety of people, black and white, whom he considers to be "niggers." Paul, who fails to understand, thinks the narrator believes he is a racist. "I know what a *nigger* is, too. It's what you are when you begin thinking of yourself as a work of art!" Paul says, and according to the narrator, "there was no arrogance at all left in his voice." Paul's statement may be both positive and sarcastic.

After the narrator and Paul have a falling out, Virginia calls the narrator to try to smooth things over. In the course of their conversation, she says "there's a lot of us *niggers* that ain't so hot." She admonishes the narrator, saying he and "that nigger of mine" have to learn patience. Later, pregnant with Paul's child, she meets the narrator for tea. Virginia sums up her attempt to do the right thing regarding the families who have started making "gestures" upon learning of her pregnancy:

> "I'm black. I've accepted myself as that. But didn't I make some elbow room, though?" She tapped her

temple with her forefinger. "I mean up *here*!" . . . When times get tough, *anybody* can pass for white. Niggers been doing *that* for *centuries* . . . wouldn't it of been something to be a nigger that could relate to white and black and everything else in the world out of a self as big as the world is? . . . That would have been *some* nigger!"

The narrator replies that she was "some nigger," yet later he advises her "for the sake of your child, don't be black. Be more of a classic kind of nigger."

In this passage, the variety of ways the characters use the word reinforces two points and adds another dimension to it. First, since both of these characters are black, each intuitively understands the other. Second, within this brief exchange, the word "nigger" takes on several different meanings. Finally, can a white person understand without explanation what a "classic nigger" is? Could Virginia's husband, Paul, understand?

Much has been written about the use of invective language, and about the use of the word "nigger" in particular. The long history of hate entwined around the word has generated a body of written work and many legal cases. In his book *Nigger: The Strange Career of a Troublesome Word*, black Harvard Law professor Randall Kennedy calls it "the paradigmatic slur. It is the epithet that generates epithets. . . . Arabs are called sand niggers, Irish the niggers of Europe, and Palestinians the niggers of the Middle East." Theories about the word's origin vary, but Kennedy says that "nigger" is derived from *niger*, the Latin word for black. Kennedy observes that blacks have appropriated the language of their oppressors much the same as other marginalized groups do, in the way women use [b——] and gays use "queer."

Perhaps one of the most debated works in which the word "nigger" appears is Mark Twain's *The Adventures of Huckleberry Finn* (1884). The story of a boy and a runaway slave contains more than 200 instances of the word. But Kennedy and McPherson agree that Twain's use of the word was to point out the evil of racism, not support it. McPherson wrote in his essay "It Is Good to Be Shifty in a New Country": "Twain was writing about the possibility of friendships across racial lines, at a time when such emotional connections were considered radical. He was writing about the struggles of the *human* heart *confined to* the structure of white supremacy."

The debate about the use of "nigger" remains relevant. Kennedy observes the differing uses of the word by black entertainers. Comedian Richard Pryor is considered the first prominent entertainer to use the word in front of multiracial audiences, in both friendly and derogatory ways, but after a trip to Africa, he stopped the practice. Chris Rock, a popular comedian, makes a distinction in his uses of black and "nigger," using the latter in a derogatory manner. Author and comedian Bill Cosby contends all blacks are hurt when some use the word. Rappers use the word, and variations such as *nigga*, liberally, while white entertainers, such as the famous white rapper, Eminem, do not use the word for fear of being perceived as racist. Yet Kennedy contends, "There is much to be gained by allowing people of all backgrounds to yank *nigger* away from white supremacists, to subvert its ugliest denotation, and to convert the N-word from a negative into a positive appellation."

The word "nigger" is emblematic of racial division in the United States. At the time "Elbow Room" was published, McPherson defended himself against black nationalists by referring to black author Ralph Ellison (1914–1994), his friend and mentor. McPherson said Ellison believed "something called America did exist; that it had a culture; that black Americans were, by our unique history and special contributions and the quality of our struggle, heroic; that self-imposed segregation, especially of the imagination, was a mistake." Ellison told McPherson, "Never segregate yourself."

In his essay, "On Becoming an American Writer," McPherson refers to Albion W. Tourgee, who argued against segregation before the U.S. Supreme Court in 1896 in the famous case of *Plessy v. Ferguson*. (Tourgee lost when the Court ruled that segregation was legal if equal facilities were offered to both races, commonly known as the "separate but equal" ruling.) McPherson says Tourgee's model of citizenship would be a synthesis of opposite races or classes and represent the United States in its totality. McPherson said this was the model he was aiming for in the collection that includes the title story "Elbow Room."

The relationships of the interracial couple of Paul and Virginia, their families, and the narrator provides a framework in which McPherson displays his belief in the humanity of all people regardless of race, and his understanding that the complexities inherent in relationships cross racial lines. The author employs varying uses of the word "nigger" as one tool to demonstrate the dichotomy between blacks and whites. Virginia uses the word in a variety of ways, while Paul cannot achieve a clear understanding of it. The narrator offers explanations that are obtuse and says Paul must find his own definitions. Readers' understanding these usages are affected by their skin color. McPherson has said, "As a writer, I have never forgotten that the truest voices are always found at the center of tremendous storms. I have learned to listen for them." The use of the so-called protean word "nigger" spotlights the difficulties faced by the characters in "Elbow Room" as they try to bridge the racial divide.

Source: Bonnie Weinreich, Critical Essay on "Elbow Room," in *Short Stories for Students*, Thomson Gale, 2006.

Phillip M. Richards

In the following review, Richards discusses Crabcakes, McPherson's memoir, comparing themes in the work to those found in his Elbow Room collection.

Pulitzer-Prize winner James Alan McPherson has written two highly regarded collections of short fiction, and the pleasures and insights offered by *Crabcakes* are those of a well-crafted story. This memoir uses the epiphanies and dramatic resolutions of fiction to generate the religious and ethical insight of spiritual autobiography. McPherson traces the psychological path from early alienation to his personal renewal in an intimate circle of friends, a number of whom are deeply influenced by Japanese culture. Gaining entrance into Japanese forms of community and piety, McPherson experiences an acute personal conversion. However, when he makes broad social claims for his personal experience, he puts himself on problematic ground. *Crabcakes* ultimately attempts to illuminate late twentieth-century interracial American life through personal introspection.

The starting place of this plot is the helterskelter world of McPherson's hometown of Baltimore, a realm of racist police and the decay of a once vital inner-city world. We see this racism in McPherson's encounter with a state trooper who impounds his car as he drives outside the city. We see it again in the memory of McPherson's meeting with a car full of policemen in the city. In Baltimore, the narrator is alternately a victim of racism and an agent of the forces that undermine what he will eventually understand as the communitas offered by Japanese society. His involvement with this world reaches crisis proportions with the death of Channie Washington, an elderly tenant of McPherson's Baltimore property. Preparing to unburden himself of his unprofitable rental house, McPherson begins to confront the issue of community and his relationship to others. Mrs. Washington, who for years included friendly, affirming letters with her rent, is an anticipation of the organic relations that McPherson will find in Japanese culture. As McPherson makes preparations to evict the rental property's other occupant, a Mr. Butler, Washington and her life are dimly but increasingly understood as a humanizing force within an eroding inner-city world. The warmth with which she addresses McPherson in her letters evokes community as does the meal she serves him when he returns to Baltimore from Iowa (where he now teaches). Washington, who has selflessly raised an extended family, is described by McPherson as the "Fountainhead . . . that keeps the 'we,' the 'us' collected."

One of Baltimore's humanizing features is the consumption of crabcakes near the downtown harbor, where people from all over the city eat the delicacy in groups at stands. At one point McPherson speaks of the crabcake eating as a communion, and the activity as a ceremony that brings Baltimoreans of all ranks together in a regional understanding. However, Channie Washington and the crabcake eating are anticipations of a later sense of community that are not fully understood by McPherson in the early part of his narrative. These early premonitions are a point of departure for the narrator's encounter with the world through the lens of his Japanese experience.

The book's second section invokes McPherson's experience of community from the vantage of insights gained in his Japanese conversion. McPherson's decisive entrance into Japanese life takes place during his second trip to Japan when he establishes an intense friendship with Natsuko Ishii, a friendship that fully overcomes his feelings of alienation as an American black. During a train ride, her simple acts of care for him (she wipes sweat from his face) give McPherson a new, powerfully symbolic sense of selfhood and an appreciation of Japan. McPherson shows us a world of stylized social ritual and community, a world that values the union of formal and natural gestures. McPherson feels most whole as a person when he becomes part of the Japanese flow of "naturalness" in social gatherings such as a meal, a reception, or even having a few drinks in a bar. In the course of his relationships with Ishii and other Japanese, he meets a number of people involved in the worlds of literature, publishing, and business. And in the midst of a broad number of friendships he consolidates his sense of himself as an insider in the communal world of Japanese culture.

Like McPherson's short stories in *Elbow Room, Crabcakes* moves from social complications to moments of moral insight. These ethical discoveries are based on the contrast between the alienated world of the West and the organic social world of McPherson's Japan. In MePherson's view, the West represents a society of estranged selves who proffer a variety of masks to each other, avoiding true intimacy. America in particular is described by the author as a world in which a "natural" revelation of oneself is considered naive at best and foolhardy at worst. This alienation is particularly acute among blacks, who must present their own impassive mask toward whites who do not regard them as fully human. Indeed, some of McPherson's most moving and acute meditations on race concern the psychological and emotional dislocations that stem from the estrangement of blacks from the majority population of American society. America emerges in a series of James Baldwin-like reflections as a world in which the black and white populations can never truly know each other. McPherson himself participates in these dislocations in the decaying world of Baltimore, and they come into full focus during his trip to Japan.

On the other hand, the world of Japan is one in which true intimacy—the kind of intimacy that Channie Washington sought—is realized in the various forms and gestures of social life. This ritualized intimacy occurs at dinners, in visits to sacred places, in the celebration of a friend's day of death, and in the use of ceremonial gifts as tokens for greeting. The community in Japan is one of highly tuned sympathies, regulated by social rituals, and defined by well-wrought understandings. McPherson not only commits himself to this vision of organic community shared with his small circle of Japanese and American friends but presents this vision as an exemplary one for his readers.

McPherson's gradual and increasingly complicated entrance into this world—and his importation of its values to America—create the book's dramatic structure. Through a series of complications, McPherson arrives at the central moral vision of community. This literary dynamic generates the book's chief ethical insight. In contrast to the vacuity of an estranged American culture of masks, the "natural" intimacy of Japanese community makes possible a broad human vision spanning the extremes of joy and tragedy.

The book's climax takes place as McPherson portrays the contradictions of this broad Japanese vision. In the spirit of Japanese intimacy, McPherson involves himself in the familial catastrophe of a neighbor, Howard Morton, who is losing a son to cancer. Visiting with Morton in a moment of crisis,

These ethical discoveries are based on the contrast between the alienated world of the West and the organic social world of McPherson's Japan."

McPherson keeps a pair of visiting Japanese friends waiting by themselves in a restaurant for three hours in what for him is an unpardonable offense. He therefore violates the trust and intimacy of one relationship in order to sustain another. This violation raises the central question of the book's final section: how does one choose between allegiances to intimate friends?

Here, McPherson sacrifices the ceremonial gesture of the dinner for one of communal sympathy. In this case, the "natural" and "formal" social understandings of the Japanese world come into sharp, tragic conflict. And this conflict is intense because McPherson has structured his sense of his relationship between himself and others upon Japanese values of community. McPherson's entrance into the Japanese ethos involves his acceptance of a tragic element that he learns to accept as the cost of intimacy.

McPherson's book projects a self-consciously literary vision of society and of the author's status. In many ways it is an orientalist travel book to an exotic East of Asian virtues. *Crabcakes'* meditations on race echo the early essays of James Baldwin. And the nearly surreal account of the reptilian state trooper who impounds his car invokes the postmodern mode of Ralph Ellison's *Invisible Man.* The book's telling moments of self-consciousness, moreover, alert us to the special conditions that surround McPherson's entrance into Japanese society. After an arranged lecture in which McPherson expounds his views of Japanese culture, a young Japanese woman tells him that he does not understand her country. The possibility of a skewed vision is easy to understand. McPherson is introduced to Japanese society by people who already admire him and desire further contact with him. Although he is a cultural outsider, McPherson is a highly successful American author, who mingles easily with the literary and publishing elites of Japan.

McPherson maintains a strident sense of a pervasive American racism, even though he moves in a racially integrated social world. He has taught at prestigious universities and numbers distinguished members of the academy among his friends. The world or his academic Iowan neighborhood is by his own description a decidedly multicultural one. Indeed, it is hard to conceive of a person such as McPherson outside of the newly democratized and integrated world of the American university. The problematic nature of McPherson's assumptions is complicated by the sparseness of the narrative on matters of real importance in understanding the nature of McPherson's experience. There is little mention of an immediate group of American family and friends around McPherson. Aside from an extended account of his Japanese friendships, we do not learn much of the author's life itself during this period. And it is ultimately difficult to tell the extent to which his portrait of himself and his country represents the dislocation of black American life or personal idiosyncrasy.

Despite the book's emphasis on McPherson's conversion to a japanese communitas, *Crabcakes* remains a curiously self-centered work. This book is peculiarly focused upon McPherson's response to a few elements in the world around him. His encounters with his Japanese friends concern their impact upon his particular predicament as an alienated black American. His accounts of the Japanese are particularly devoid of the tensions of individual personalities, the complexities of the other selves. He seeks to read himself and his own personal transformation within the uniquely Japanese vision of community. That is, McPherson seeks the same therapeutic relationship with ritualized community that an earlier generation of Americans sought with nature. Indeed, this book is a deeply religious attempt to come to grips with a self-centered alienation.

McPherson's highly personalized version of the race problem largely ignores the larger social and historical context in which his experience takes place. This context, which is the recently opened world of elite American life, is now available to people of extraordinary talent such as McPherson. The author's crises are the natural concomitant of black mobility in this sphere of privilege. In *Hue and Cry* as well as in *Elbow Room,* McPherson acutely observed the transformation of a transitory segregated world in a set of remarkable stories. McPherson is part of a cohort of black intellectuals and professionals confronted with the white world from the peculiar vantage of integrated life, social and political realities to which he only vaguely alludes. In one sense, the book's ideal of a Japanese-influenced organic community is an exotic, romanticized therapy for a black middle-class angst.

McPherson's resolution to his angst is furthermore typically American. He presents himself in a highly idiosyncratic and individualistic way, but his very individualism makes him a recognizable phenomenon. He is an American traveler who carries what the Emerson of "Self-Reliance" calls the "giant of self" abroad. Indeed, the authority of this book's narrative voice emerges from its participation in a larger American tradition of individual self-renewal. Despite important differences between McPherson and a figure such as Walt Whitman, the author of *Crabcakes* also seeks to transcend the pressures of a culturally limited American self.

However, McPherson's focus on psychological and emotional details of personal transformation has blinders. For all of his precise introspection, this book lacks a larger sense of McPherson's place in a changing racial world where others share his plight. He cannot relate his own personal dislocations to a broader experience of dislocation. Acutely attentive to the dynamics of personal renewal, this book is somewhat oblivious to the history in which that life is to be renewed. McPherson's vision represents a deeply American optimism and naivete.

Source: Phillip M. Richards, "Ritual and Self-Renewal," in *Dissent*, Vol. 47, No. 3, Summer 2000, pp. 117–20.

Robie Macauley

In the following review, Macauley pays praise to the many virtues—including depth, control, and humanity—McPherson displays in the stories in Elbow Room.

With his first book of stories, *Hue and Cry,* James Alan McPherson established his standpoint as that of a writer and a black, but not that of a black writer. He refused to let his fiction fall into any color-code or ethnic code, remarking, "Certain of the people happen to be black and certain happen to be white; but I have tried to keep the color part of most of them far in the background, where these things should rightly be kept." Occasionally, he found this credo impossible to maintain, especially when a story demanded strong identification with strong black characters—as in the fine place. "A Solo Song: For Doc," which retraced the lifetime service of two railroad dining car waiters, a study in pride and injury.

For the most part, however, he was able to look beneath skin color and clichés of attitude into the hearts of his characters. "Margot" (a character in "Hue and Cry"), he says, "might have been white instead of black and the story would have been just as real and just as sad." This is a fairly rare ability in American fiction where even the most telling kind of perception seldom seems able to pass an invisible color line. Black writers—with the exception of Ralph Ellison—too often see white characters as some configuration of externals, and white writers, perhaps even more grossly, have done the same with blacks.

In McPherson's title story, "Elbow Room," Virginia is the wife in an interracial marriage that has proved to be a ruinous struggle for a kind of psychological synthesis. With bitter humor she says: "When times get tough, *anybody* can pass for white. Niggers been doing *that* for *centuries*. . . . But wouldn't it of been something to be a nigger that could relate to white and black and everything else in the world out of a self as big as the world is?"

Such selves, black or white, require an act of imagination that is almost never realized in the actual world; this is one of McPherson's recurrent themes. In "A Loaf of Bread," Harold Green is a white grocer in a black neighborhood; Nelson Reed is the leader of a demonstration against Green's excessively high prices.

"Such selves, black or white, require an act of imagination that is almost never realized in the actual world; this is one of McPherson's recurrent themes."

The two are curiously similar and each, in his own way, is a moral man; yet, because neither can comprehend the other's troubles, each considers the other evil. Their drama works out in a series of ironies (too complex to be summarized in a review) and, it seems to me, produces a symbolic truth magically beyond what might have been mere sociological observation.

In "The Problems of Art," a white lawyer tries with sympathetic imagination to understand his black client and her defense witness while, at the same time, they are imagining he is involved in complicity to avoid justice. The lawyer makes her innocent in his mind while, from equal warmheartedness, they make him guilty.

There are a number of good stories in *Elbow Room* devoted to solely black experiences. Among the best are "The Story of a Dead Man" (an exuberant comedy in spite of its title), "The Story of a Scar" and "The Silver Bullet." The latter is ostensibly about another common inner-city occurrence—black hoods strong-arming a black barkeeper for protection money. One of the hoods is a would-be gang member; the other is a racketeer with a marvelously parodic line of talk: "Our organization is a legitimate, relevant, grass-roots community group . . . We have the dynamic. You [the gang] have the manpower. Together, we can begin a nationalization process." But, as the crisis approaches, there is a subtle shift of feeling about the realistic scene and—as often in McPherson's fiction—we sense both reality and parable. And, of course, the parable is about terrorism and the illusions of terrorism.

A fine control of language and story, a depth in his characters, humane values, these are a few of the virtues James Alan McPherson displays in this fine collection of stories.

Source: Robie Macauley, "White and Black and Everything Else," in *New York Times*, September 25, 1977, p. 271.

Sources

Haney, Craig, "The Psychological Impact of Incarceration: Implications for Post-Prison Adjustment," December 2001, pp. 6–8.

Beattle, Ann, "The Hum Inside the Skull—A Symposium," in *New York Times Book Review*, May 13, 1984, pp. 1, 28.

Jefferson, Margo, "Black Manners," in *Newsweek*, October 17, 1977, p. 116.

Kennedy, Randall, *Nigger: The Strange Career of a Troublesome Word*, Pantheon Books, 2002, pp. 27, 50–51, 139, 175.

Macauley, Robie, "White and Black and Everything Else," in *New York Times*, September 25, 1977, p. 271.

McPherson, James Alan, "Elbow Room," in *Elbow Room*, Little, Brown, 1972, pp. 215–41.

———, "It Is Good to Be Shifty in a New Country," in *A Region Not Home: Reflections from Exile*, Touchstone Simon and Schuster, 2000, p. 184.

———, "On Becoming an American Writer," in *A Region Not Home: Reflections from Exile*, Touchstone Simone and Schuster, 2000, p. 25.

Review of *Elbow Room*, in the *New Yorker*, November 21, 1977, p. 230.

Twain, Mark, *The Adventures of Huckleberry Finn*, Bantam, 1981, p. 281.

Further Reading

Beavers, Herman, *Wrestling Angels into Song: The Fictions of Ernest J. Gaines and James Alan McPherson*, University of Pennsylvania Press, 1995.

The one book-length study of McPherson's work is really a half book, with chapters about Gaines alternating with the McPherson chapters, but Beavers gives a good overview of both authors' published fiction.

Perlmann, Joel, "Reflecting the Changing Face of America: Multiracials, Racial Classification, and American Intermarriage," in *Interracialism: Black-White Intermarriage in American History, Literature, and Law*, edited by Werner Sollors, Oxford University Press, 2000, pp. 506–34.

Perlmann discusses the ways that Americans have been forced to redefine their identities as the boundaries that defined and separated the races have broken down. This is the situation described in the story, which Perlmann examines from a sociological perspective.

Reid, Calvin, "James Alan McPherson: A Theater of Memory," in *Publishers Weekly*, December 15, 1997, pp. 36–37.

This article is based on interviews with McPherson about his aversion to the business of publishing and the long periods that have passed between publication of his fiction.

Wallace, Jon, "The Politics of Style in Three Stories by James Alan McPherson," in *Modern Fiction Studies*, Vol. 3, No. 1, Spring 1988, pp. 17–26.

Wallace's academic study of "Elbow Room" and two other stories focuses on the ways that McPherson places characters in positions where they have to defend their individual personalities against the encroachments of the world.

The Elephant Vanishes

Haruki Murakami

1991

Haruki Murakami's "The Elephant Vanishes" was first published in English in the *New Yorker* in November 1991 and is found in his short story collection *The Elephant Vanishes: Stories* published by Alfred A. Knopf in 1993. Jay Rubin translated the story from Japanese into English. The short story was also included in the anthology *The Oxford Book of Japanese Short Stories*, edited by Theodore Goossen. *The Elephant Vanishes: Stories* consists of seventeen short stories told in first-person point of view.

Like other stories in this collection, "The Elephant Vanishes" focuses on a strange incident that leaves its protagonist disoriented. An unnamed narrator tells the story of how an aged elephant and its keeper mysteriously disappear one night from his town's elephant house. The narrator, who is the protagonist of the story, recalls the events leading up to the elephant's sudden vanishing, the news coverage of the incident, and the futile efforts of the townspeople to find the elephant and the keeper. He also discusses the strange circumstances of the elephant's disappearance, which indicate that the elephant apparently vanished into thin air. After meeting a magazine editor who is a potential love interest, the narrator ends up talking about how he witnessed the elephant shrinking or the keeper becoming bigger or both on the night of their disappearance, and the story concludes with the bewildered narrator lamenting the loss of the elephant and the keeper. Like other Murakami stories, this one is imbued with a sense of things being out of order in

urban, contemporary society, which leaves its characters feeling alienated, disillusioned, and unable to make choices about their lives.

Author Biography

Haruki Murakami was born on January 12, 1949 in Ashiya City, Japan, a suburb of Kobe. The son of two high-school Japanese literature teachers, Murakami became fascinated with American pop culture as a teenager and began reading works of American literature in English as an adolescent. In 1968, he began studies at Tokyo's Waseda University, eventually graduating with bachelor's degrees in screenwriting and Greek drama in 1975. In 1971, he had married fellow Waseda student Yoko Takahashi. With Takahashi, Murakami opened a jazz bar called the Peter Cat in a Tokyo suburb in 1974, and together, they managed the club until 1981, when Murakami began devoting himself full-time to his writing.

In 1979, Murakami published his first book, a novel entitled *Hear the Wind Sing*, which he first wrote in English and then translated into Japanese. *Hear the Wind Sing* won the prestigious Gunzo Award, a first-novel prize, and the book launched Murakami's career as the leading fiction writer of Japan's post-war generation. Following this novel, Murakami published two more novels, *Pinball, 1973* (1980) and *A Wild Sheep Chase* (1982), which was the first of Murakami's works to be translated into English. In 1981, Murakami also began publishing his translations of works by modern American writers from English into Japanese, including writings by Grace Paley, Raymond Carver, Ursula K. Leguin, and F. Scott Fitzgerald. In 1985, Murakami published his fourth novel *Hard-Boiled Wonderland and the End of the World*, which garnered major critical and commercial success in Japan and won the coveted Junichiro Tanizaki Prize.

Murakami's fifth novel *Norwegian Wood* (1987) sold over two million hard-cover copies in Japan. He published his sixth novel *Dance, Dance, Dance* in 1988 and his seventh novel *South of the Border, West of the Sun* in 1992. From 1985 to 1995, Murakami lived abroad, first in Greece and Italy and then in the United States where he held positions at Princeton University, Harvard University, and Tufts University. While at Tufts, Murakami wrote his three-volume novel *The Wind-Up Bird Chronicle* (1994–1995).

Haruki Murakami Photograph by Katsumi Kasahara. AP Images

Although primarily known as a novelist, Murakami has also written several volumes of short stories, seventeen of which were published in his English-language collection *The Elephant Vanishes* (1993), in which the short story "The Elephant Vanishes" appears. Some of these short stories, translated into English by his regular translators Jay Rubin and Alfred Birnbaum, appeared originally in the *New Yorker*.

Following his return to Japan, Murakami published a two-volume non-fiction book *Underground: The Tokyo Gas Attack and the Japanese Psyche* (1997–1998) and, following that, novels *Sputnik Sweetheart* (2001) and *Kafka on the Shore* (2005), as well as another short story collection *After the Quake: Stories*, translated into English by Jay Rubin in 2002. Murakami's works have been translated into over twenty languages, and his many awards include the Noma Award for new writers in 1982, the Yomiuri Literary Prize in 1996, and the Kuwabara Takeo Award in 1999.

Plot Summary

"The Elephant Vanishes" begins with the narrator recalling how he read in the newspaper about the disappearance of an elephant from his town's elephant house. The narrator, who remains unnamed throughout the story, describes his daily routine, which includes reading the newspaper from start to finish. He then describes the article that tells about the elephant's mysterious disappearance the day before. He notes that according to the article, both the elephant and its keeper have vanished leaving authorities baffled.

The narrator interrupts his description of the newspaper article to relate how the elephant had come to be adopted by the town a year earlier. He recalls that when financial problems caused a private zoo to shut down, the zoo's other animals had been placed in various zoos throughout Japan. However, because the elephant was so old, other zoos would not take it, so the elephant remained in the abandoned zoo until an agreement was reached among various parties in the town. The parties included a high-rise condo developer who had bought the land where the old zoo had stood, the mayor of the town, and the former zoo's owners. The narrator describes the negotiations among the parties, as well as opposition to the plan by opponents of the mayor, who eventually accepted the new plan.

The narrator notes that the debate about the elephant problem concluded with the town's taking charge of the ancient elephant and relocating it to an elementary school's old gym, which was located in a clearing in a wooded area. The elephant's aged keeper from the zoo also came to live in a small, prefab house next to the elephant, so he could continue to tend to the animal's needs.

The narrator goes on to humorously recall the elephant-house dedication ceremony. He describes in detail how the elephant was secured to a concrete slab by a heavy steel chain and shackle around its right rear leg. He describes the keeper as "not an unfriendly" old man who maintained a close, mysterious bond with the elephant that the narrator futilely tried to understand.

The narrator then says that after a year of living in the new location, being visited by elementary school children and others, the elephant completely vanished without warning. Resuming his description of the newspaper article about the elephant's disappearance, the narrator says how odd he finds the article to be. He attributes the article's strangeness to the reporter's efforts to maintain a neutral, objective tone, while clearly being confused by the absurdity of the situation.

The narrator then gives three reasons why the elephant could not have escaped—in spite of the reporter's use of this wording—but instead had to have vanished. The narrator points out that the steel cuff binding the elephant had been found still locked in the house and that this improbable event had occurred in spite of the fact that the keys to the cuff were kept in locked safes in police headquarters and the firehouse. The narrator notes that both keys were found in their respective safes after the elephant's disappearance.

The narrator also points out that the elephant house had been surrounded by a massive fence consisting of heavy iron bars almost ten feet high. In addition, the only entrance to this enclosure had been found locked from the inside after the elephant's disappearance. The third strange circumstance the narrator describes is the lack of elephant tracks. He notes that a steep hill occupied the back of the elephant house, so that the only route of escape would have been a path at the front of the house, which completely lacked elephant prints in its soft earth. Following his listing of these circumstances, the narrator reiterates that the elephant could not have escaped but had to have vanished.

The narrator adds, however, that the mayor, the reporter, and the police would not openly admit that the elephant had vanished and that the police were investigating the incident. He recalls how the mayor held a news conference defending the

Media Adaptations

- *The Elephant Vanishes* was adapted as a play by Simon McBurney and performed at the Setagaya Public Theatre in June of 2003. A description of the adaptation of the book to the stage appears online at http://www.ums.org under the title "An Elephant's Long Journey," written by Jay Rubin, one of Murakami's translators.
- The publisher Random House maintains an official Murakami website at http://www.randomhouse.com/features/murakami which features ample information about the author, his books, and other online resources pertaining to Murakami.

elephant security system and denouncing the persons responsible for the elephant's disappearance. The narrator describes news coverage of the event, which called for citizens knowing anything about the incident to come forward. As he drinks his second cup of morning coffee, the narrator thinks about telling the authorities what he knows but decides against contacting the police, as he thinks they would never believe him.

The narrator then recalls how he cut out the elephant article and pasted it into a scrapbook he fastidiously keeps of all the articles about the elephant. He relates how he watched the seven-o'clock news, which showed hunters with rifles, Self-Defense troops, police, and firemen searching for the elephant in the woods and hills of the Tokyo suburb where the narrator resides. The narrator states that although the search took several days, the authorities were unable to find a single clue concerning the elephant's whereabouts. As he recalls reading and pasting all the news clippings into his scrapbook, the narrator talks about the pointlessness of the articles, which reveal nothing substantial about the incident. He states that over many months, interest in the incident waned as the elephant case fell into the category of "unsolvable mysteries." In spite of the reduction of general interest in the elephant story, the narrator says that he continued to visit the old elephant house whenever he got a chance. He describes the thick chain around the gate and "the air of doom and desolation" that hung over the empty space.

In the final part of the story, the narrator recalls meeting an editor of a magazine for young housewives several months after the elephant's disappearance. The narrator meets the editor at a party his company is throwing to launch its new line of kitchen appliances. Since the narrator is in charge of the company's publicity campaign, he shows the editor around the display, and he explains the principle of unity governing the design of the kitchen appliance line. The editor questions the importance of unity in a kitchen and asks the narrator what his personal opinion of the matter is. He declines to answer until he's off work and says how "things you can't sell don't count for much" in the pragmatic world in which they live.

After debating whether the world is indeed pragmatic, the editor and the narrator continue to flirt and talk over champagne and later over drinks in the hotel's cocktail lounge. Although the conversation flows smoothly at first and the narrator recalls being drawn to the editor, he notes that things took a turn when he brought up the topic of the elephant. He immediately regrets bringing up the subject, but the editor presses him for more details when he says he was probably not shocked by the elephant's disappearance. After balking a moment, the narrator tells the editor what he knows about the elephant.

He tells the editor that he is probably the last person to see the elephant before it disappeared, as he saw the elephant after the zoo closed that evening. The narrator explains that he had sometimes watched the elephant and the keeper through an air vent in the elephant house's roof, which was visible from a spot on a cliff behind the house. He recalls how impressed he had been by the obvious trust and affection the elephant and the keeper displayed when they were out of the public eye.

When the editor asks him whether he always liked elephants, the narrator admits that he did, although he is not sure why. The editor also asks him if there was anything unusual about the elephant or the keeper on the night of the disappearance. After hesitating, the narrator says there was and there wasn't. He goes on to explain that although the keeper and the elephant were doing the same things they always did, the balance in size between the two of them had changed. He tells the editor that either the elephant had shrunk or the keeper had gotten bigger or both simultaneously. When asked, he also admits that he did not tell the police, because he thought they would not believe him and that he would have become a suspect in the case.

When pressed further about the occurrence, the narrator states that he can only say he probably saw the change in appearances, since he does not have any proof of the change actually happening. To himself, he notes that he had the feeling that "a different, chilling kind of time was flowing through the elephant house—but nowhere else."

When the editor asks him whether he believes that the elephant either shrunk until it was small enough to escape or dissolved into nothing, the narrator again hesitates and says he does not know what happened and that it is impossible for him to imagine events beyond what he thinks he saw. Following this revelation about the elephant, the conversation between the editor and the narrator becomes awkward, and they part outside the hotel.

The narrator says that that was the last time he saw the editor. Although he considered asking her out for dinner, he ended up not doing so due to a sense of emotional paralysis that he experiences after the elephant's vanishing. The story ends with the narrator describing his unease following the incident and how in spite of succeeding more than ever in his job, he feels bewildered and permanently unsettled. He comments that the papers print almost nothing now about the elephant and that the elephant and its keeper will never return.

Characters

The Editor

An unnamed editor of a magazine for young housewives appears in the second part of the story as the narrator's potential love interest. She meets the narrator at a party to launch an advertising campaign thrown by the manufacturing company for which the narrator works. An intelligent and curious twenty-six-year-old woman, the editor talks to the narrator about the kitchen appliances his company is selling, the idea of pragmatism, and other topics at the party and afterward while they are having drinks in a hotel bar. Although they seem to enjoy an initial connection, after the narrator recounts his witnessing of the bizarre circumstances leading to the elephant's disappearance, the conversation dead ends and after leaving the lounge, the editor does not see the narrator again.

The Elephant

The unnamed elephant is a symbolic character in the story, representing an old way of life. Although its exact age is not known, the elephant arrived in the town from East Africa twenty-two years before it disappeared. The elephant is so old that it cannot be relocated to another zoo when the town's zoo closes. The elephant maintains a close bond with its keeper, and the two characters mysteriously vanish at the same time.

The Mayor

The mayor negotiates the agreement among the town, a real-estate developer, and the zoo's former owners to relocate the elephant to new surroundings after the old zoo closes down. A minor character, the mayor is a kind of stock figure of a suburban politician who holds ineffective news conferences following the elephant's disappearance.

The Narrator

An unnamed narrator tells the story of the disappearance of an old elephant and its keeper from the Tokyo suburb where he lives. A thirty-one-year-old man who works for the public relations section of a major electrical appliance manufacturer, the narrator obsessively tracks the elephant's story from the time of its relocation to an old elementary school gym through its mysterious vanishing. He meticulously keeps a scrapbook of articles on the elephant's disappearance and witnesses the strange circumstances that may account for the occurrence. Like many of Murakami's characters, the narrator is an isolated and quirky person who seems bewildered by the absurdity of his daily life. He also meets and thinks about courting a young magazine editor. However, following the elephant's disappearance, the narrator finds that he has become so unsettled by the loss of balance in the world that he cannot act, and he never bothers to ask the editor out.

Noboru Watanabe

The only named character in the story, Noboru Watanabe is the sixty-three-year-old zookeeper who has tended the elephant for over ten years. The narrator describes the keeper as a "reticent, lonely-looking old man," who faithfully takes care of all the elephant's needs and lives next to the elephant after it is relocated from the old zoo. The keeper and the elephant enjoy a special bond, which the narrator notices as he spies on them through an air vent in the elephant house. The keeper is generally kind to children who come to see the elephant, and the zoo authorities describe him as knowledgeable and dependable. However, the keeper remains a mysterious character throughout the story, and in the end, he disappears along with the elephant.

Themes

Imbalance

One of the major themes of the story is the idea of things being out of balance. This theme is introduced when the narrator tells the editor about the importance of unity in kitchen design, as he states, "Even the most beautifully designed item dies if it is out of balance with its surroundings." The narrator later emphasizes the importance of balance between a creature and its environment when he talks about witnessing the change in the elephant's size in relation to the keeper's size. He states that the balance in size between the two has become more equal, because the elephant has shrunk or the keeper has gotten bigger, or both. Following the disappearance of the elephant and the keeper, the narrator again expresses the idea that "things around

Topics For Further Study

- Read the scene in the story in which the narrator meets and talks with the editor. With a partner, re-enact this part of the story as a scene in a play. You may want to work in small groups to create scenery and adapt the dialogue.
- Imagine that it is 1985, and you are living in a major city such as Los Angeles, New York, London, or Tokyo. Write a short journal entry that describes what your life is like on a typical day. Be creative, and use details that show what daily life is like, including your daily habits. You may want to research what was going on in the city of your choice before you write.
- Pick a Japanese or American company and research the products that company sells. Then, imagine you are a public relations executive for that company and write and give a speech to persuade people to buy that company's products. Create a slogan and use supplementary photos, charts, or other graphics in your presentation.
- Take a trip to the zoo and observe the elephants and find out how the elephants are cared for, what they eat, and what their habits are. Then, write an article about the elephants. You may also want to include details about where the elephants originally came from, how they came to live in the zoo, and arguments against confining animals in zoos.
- Explore the ideas of balance and imbalance by creating a work of visual art that shows both states. Think about using color, shape, and size to heighten your effects. You may want to consult an art instructor or book to learn more about balance as a principle of art.
- Rewrite the ending of the story by telling it from the keeper's or the elephant's point of view. Tell that character's version of what happened on the night the narrator observed the elephant shrinking and explain what happened to the elephant and the keeper and where they are after they disappear from the elephant house.

me have lost their proper balance." He is no longer able to take action on his own behalf, as he is haunted by this sense that the urban world is out of balance, and he feels that a kind of natural balance has broken down inside him.

Appearances and Reality

Related to the theme of imbalance is the difference between appearances and reality. The narrator points out that the article covering the story of the elephant's disappearance is strange, because the reporter tries so hard to maintain that the elephant escaped, when the facts indicate that the elephant had to have almost magically vanished. The characters in the story try to maintain an appearance of normality in the face of an event that defies logic, leading to pointless acts that do not address the nature of the situation. The discrepancy between reality and appearances also arises in the narrator's job as he basically just goes through the motions, trying to maintain a professional, pragmatic approach although he does not personally believe that a kitchen has to have unity or any of the other maxims his company invokes to sell its products. The narrator finds that he cannot reconcile the differences between appearances and reality, and as he questions his own perceptions, he experiences a sense of disorientation and confusion.

Modern Times

Another theme of the story concerns how modern developments have supplanted old ways of life. The story takes place in an affluent Tokyo suburb during the 1980s, when Japan was experiencing an economic boom. The event that sets all the other events of the story in motion is the construction of high-rise condos, which literally take the place of the old zoo, forcing the elephant to be relocated to the new elephant house. The old elephant and its aged keeper are emblems of former times, ways of life, and longstanding intuitive relationships, which have been pushed aside by commercial ventures. Throughout the story, Murakami lightly satirizes the absurdity of modern life, particularly when the narrator describes the town's reaction to the elephant's disappearance. The reactions of various townspeople such as the mayor, a "worried-looking" mother, the police, Self-Defense Force troops, an anchorman, and the reporter show how inept and illogical conventional urban responses can be. As the narrator puts it, the newspaper articles were all "either pointless or off the mark." Police response is ridiculous and futile. In all, the absurd civic response to the bizarre situation of a misplaced elephant shows, in almost a comic way, how urban mindset fails to imagine, much less comprehend, the fantastic or intuitive.

Alienation

Throughout the story, Murakami subtly reveals how the vanishing of the old ways leaves people feeling disoriented and how the new ways of being create a sense of disconnection and unease. The narrator, for example, performs his job as a public relations executive successfully by espousing the commercial viewpoint that "things you can't sell don't count for much." Because in truth he does not necessarily believe this statement, saying it and operating from this pragmatic mode seem to confound the narrator, confusing him about his purpose in life. Like other Murakami characters, he is also a loner, a single person, living alone with no apparent ties to family or friends. The narrator watches the elephant and the keeper and marvels at their closeness, their special bond. In the wake of the elephant's disappearance, the narrator feels despondent, more isolated and alone than ever.

Style

Setting

The short story takes place in a suburb of Tokyo during the 1980s, when Japan was experiencing an economic boom. The town is affluent, and its inhabitants enjoy a relatively peaceful life, which is only occasionally disrupted by bizarre incidents such as the vanishing of the elephant. Prosperity has led to new developments such as the high-rise condos destined to replace old institutions like the zoo. The story also takes place at a time when the process of Americanization was well under way in Japan, as the narrator states that his company likes to use English words such as "*kit-chin*" to sell products.

Point of View and Conflict

The story is told from the first-person point of view, with an unnamed narrator relating the events. The primary conflict in the story is internal, with the narrator trying to make sense of the events immediately preceding the elephant's disappearance and the essentially strange but apparently normal world he inhabits. At the end of the story, the conflict remains mostly unresolved, as the mystery of the elephant's disappearance is never solved, and the narrator feels unsettled by a permanent sense of imbalance in the wake of the elephant's vanishing. The first part of the story is propelled by the narrator's recollections of the events leading up to the elephant's vanishing and his thoughts on how the case was handled by his town and in the newspapers. The last part of the story focuses on the narrator's recollections of his conversation with an editor and includes dialogue between the two characters.

Flashback

Several times in "The Elephant Vanishes," Murakami uses the device of flashback to present action that occurred before the beginning of the story. He begins the story in the past, and most of the story consists of the narrator's recollections of events in the recent past. Murakami begins the story with the narrator relating what he was doing when the elephant disappeared from the elephant house. He then uses flashback as the narrator recalls earlier events such as the elephant's relocation to the elephant house from the zoo that went out of business. This flashback gives the reader information about the town, its workings, and how the elephant and its keeper came to live in the new elephant house.

Dialogue

Murakami also employs dialogue to relate events that occurred prior to the beginning of the story. The last part of the story consists mostly of dialogue between the narrator and the editor. In this dialogue, the narrator reveals what he saw the night the elephant and its keeper vanished. The dialogue also serves to reveal the personalities of the narrator and the editor.

Motifs

Murakami uses the motif of water to reinforce readers' awareness of disappearance or a sense of dissolution. When describing how general interest in the elephant's disappearance waned after some months went by, the narrator states, "Amid the endless surge and ebb of everyday life, interest in a missing elephant could not last forever," thus likening daily life to the eroding action of ocean tides. The water motif occurs again several paragraphs later, when the narrator compares summer memories to water flowing "into the sewers and rivers, to be carried to the deep, dark ocean." Here too the water motif conveys a sense of things disappearing inevitably into a vast ocean. Since water can evaporate into air and is inherently unstable, this motif mirrors the vanishing, parallels the idea of impermanence, and suggests the narrator's sense of being unsettled by a world out of balance.

Murakami also specifically invokes the image of rain to convey a sense of sadness and gloom. Describing the empty elephant house, the narrator states that "A few short months without its elephant had given the place an air of doom and desolation that hung there like a huge, oppressive rain cloud." Later when he talks to the editor, the narrator notes several times the presence of a soundless, damp rain, again suggesting the presence of a persistent eroding and unsettling force. After their conversation takes a turn toward the weird, when the narrator starts talking about the elephant, the narrator compares ice melting in the editor's drink to a "tiny ocean current." With this image, Murakami again creates a feeling of things dissolving in some insidious, pervasive force.

Simile

Murakami uses similes or comparisons using "like" or "as" throughout the story to describe various states or situations, as when the narrator likens the atmosphere of the empty elephant house to "a huge, oppressive rain cloud." In another example, the narrator says that "a number of unremarkable months went by, like a tired army marching past a window."

Historical Context

Murakami wrote and first published "The Elephant Vanishes" in Japanese during the 1980s, and the story is set in Japan during this time. At the time of the writing, Japan was experiencing economic development, as were many countries in the world, including the United States. Following its crushing defeat in World War II, Japan had the fastest growing economy in the post-war period from 1955 to 1990. During the 1980s, Japan became the leading industrial state of East Asia, and it continued into the early 2000s to support one of the most advanced economies in the world, with only the United States out-producing it. With rapid industrialization during this time, Japan also became a thoroughly technological culture, with city dwellers using modern conveniences such as commuter trains, cars, and appliances. However, along with embracing technological advances and other aspects of modern life, Japan as of 2005 maintains traditional customs and culture, with modern and traditional values coexisting sometimes uneasily side by side.

The story reflects the affluence of middle-class Japanese society during the 1980s, with the building of high-rise condos in the narrator's town and the narrator's own success in his public relations job for an appliance manufacturer. It takes place in a wealthy suburb of Tokyo, one of the largest cities in the world. However, as in other Murakami stories, this short story could theoretically take place in any number of cities in the world, as very few details in the story mark the setting as specifically Japanese.

Murakami is widely recognized as one of the most popular novelists of his generation of writers, who grew up in post-World War II Japan and who disregarded traditional Japanese culture in favor of embracing American Pop culture. The story reflects the overall sensibility of Murakami's generation of writers, who were seemingly more interested in stylistic invention than overt political themes and who eschewed traditional Japanese modes of storytelling. However, Murakami also uses satire and humor to critique the banality of the culture he evokes, with its emphasis on selling products, materialism, and ultimate failure to value or experience the deeper, more mysterious aspects of life. As Celeste Loughman notes in her review of the collection in *World Literature Today*, Murakami has remarked that "'Something has vanished in these twenty-five years, some kind of idealism. It has vanished, and we became rich.'" She comments that "His people are part of the get-rich society of mass production. They work in law offices, in quality control for department stores, in PR for appliance manufacturers. All are dissatisfied."

Critical Overview

The Elephant Vanishes: Stories, the collection in which "The Elephant Vanishes" appears, has received much acclaim from American and Japanese critics, who have lauded Murakami's originality

An elephant and his trainer in an elephant house © Bettmann/Corbis

and cosmopolitan style. Herbert Mitgang writing in the *New York Times* notes: "There are 17 charming, humorous and frequently puzzling short stories in *The Elephant Vanishes*, some of which first appeared in *The New Yorker*. Nearly all bear the author's special imprint: a mixture of magical realism, feckless wandering and stylish writing, often ending at a blank wall." Similarly, an anonymous reviewer writing in *Publishers Weekly* praises Murakami's unique talents, concluding that "In both his playful throwaway sketches and his darkly comic masterpieces, Murakami has proven himself a virtuoso with a fertile imagination."

While acknowledging that Murakami has his detractors in Japan with some critics dismissing Murakami's writings as not serious enough to be high literature, Celeste Loughman in her review in *World Literature Today*, notes that the author remains "immensely popular in Japan." She also praises Murakami's subversive satirical techniques and his ability to critique contemporary Japanese society in fresh ways, as she notes, "Dissatisfaction with life in a depersonalized, mechanistic society is an overworked theme. Murakami's stories rise above the cliché by the inventiveness, the fantasies and dreams, with which the characters respond to their situations."

Like other reviewers, David L. Ulin writing in the *Los Angeles Times Book Review* applauds Murakami's renderings of a strange, supremely international world: "But the 17 stories here also reflect strains of literature and popular culture ranging from classical fairy tales to 'The Twilight Zone,' making "The Elephant Vanishes" one of the most consistently universal volumes of fiction you'll ever come across, a book that reflects the often dissassociating experience of living at the end of the 20th Century, even for those who've never been within 5,000 miles of Japan."

Criticism

Anna Maria Hong

Hong is a published poet and the editor of the fiction and memoir anthology Growing Up Asian American. *In the following essay, Hong discusses how Murakami humorously and empathetically portrays a modern world marked by a sense of imbalance, emptiness, and unease.*

Like many of the stories in Murakami's acclaimed collection *The Elephant Vanishes: Stories,*

What Do I Read Next?

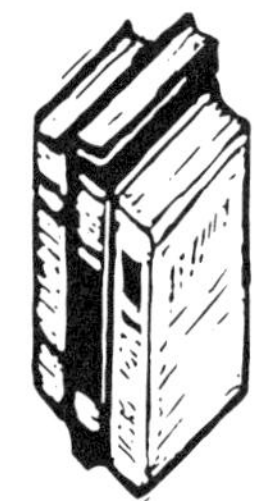

- Murakami's *The Wind-up Bird Chronicle: A Novel* (1994–1995) traces the story of Toru Okada, an ordinary Japanese man who experiences a strange, unsettling journey when his cat and his wife disappear and he goes searching for them.
- In *Underground: The Tokyo Gas Attack and the Japanese Psyche* (1997–1998), Murakami gives a riveting factual account of the tragic events that took place in Tokyo on March 20, 1995, when followers of the religious cult Aum Shinrikyo unleashed deadly sarin gas into the Tokyo subway system, killing and injuring many commuters on their way to work.
- Murakami's two-volume novel *Norwegian Wood* (1987) tells a realistic love story of a man who falls in love with two women. This book catapulted Murakami to fame, as it sold over four million copies in Japan.
- Murakami's novel *Kafka on the Shore* (2005) follows the strange paths of two characters: fifteen-year-old Kafka Tamura, who runs away from home in Tokyo to a town called Takamatsu, and Nakata, an elderly man who cannot read or write but who can speak with cats.
- Japanese American historian Ronald Takaki's *Strangers from a Different Shore: A History of Asian Americans* (1989) provides a comprehensive history of the contributions and struggles of different Asian Pacific Islander American groups, including Japanese Americans in the United States from the early 1800s through the twentieth century.
- Cynthia Kadohata's novel *The Floating World* (1989) tells the story of a Japanese American family traveling around the United States during the 1950s in search of work and home. Narrated by the twelve-year-old Olivia, the novel depicts family dynamics against a backdrop of the so-called floating world of menial jobs and shifting locales.

"The Elephant Vanishes" focuses on the life of an individual haunted by a sense of general disequilibrium. In this story, that individual is an unnamed narrator who relates how an old elephant and its keeper suddenly disappear one night from his town's elephant house. As an obsessive chronicler of the events related the elephant's disappearance, the narrator recalls news coverage of the incident, the futile attempts of the townspeople to find the elephant and the keeper, and the strange facts surrounding the case, which indicate that the elephant apparently vanished into thin air. In relating this odd, humorous, and surrealistic tale, Murakami lightly satirizes the problems of contemporary, urban society and explores the phenomena of alienation and imbalance that many people experience in the modern world.

The story opens with the narrator, a thirty-one-year-old public relations executive at a major kitchen appliance manufacturing company, telling how he read about the elephant's disappearance in the newspaper. From this initial description, Murakami draws attention to the absurdity of contemporary life by having the narrator recall the details of the article, as the narrator states, "The unusually large headline caught my eye: ELEPHANT MISSING IN TOKYO SUBURB, and, beneath that, in type one size smaller, CITIZENS' FEARS MOUNT. SOME CALL FOR PROBE." This headline seems both implausible and ridiculous, but as the narrator's recollection of events continues, the reactions of the townspeople to the missing elephant seem more and more absurd.

The first part of the story proceeds with the narrator interrupting his description of the newspaper article to tell how the elephant came to live with its keeper in a lone elephant house. He notes that the elephant's age led to its adoption by the town a year before the animal disappeared. When a private zoo had to close due to financial problems, the zoo relocated the other animals to zoos throughout Japan, but because the elephant was so old, no one would take it. The elephant then remained alone in the abandoned zoo until a deal was struck by the town's mayor, the developer who had bought the land the zoo was on, and the former zoo's owners. The narrator meticulously recounts the debates over how to deal with the elephant problem and the eventual outcome, with the town taking care of the elephant and relocating it to a new elephant house along with its longtime keeper. Throughout this section, Murakami pokes fun at modern life, again by having the narrator recall all the details with a wry, detached tone. Following his description of the new elephant house dedication ceremony, the narrator says, "The elephant endured these virtually meaningless (for the elephant, entirely meaningless) formalities with hardly a twitch, and it chomped on the bananas with a vacant stare. When it finished eating the bananas, everyone applauded."

In this part of the story, Murakami also sets up the central theme regarding how commercialism and urban developments have supplanted older ways of life. The story is set in a wealthy Tokyo suburb during the 1980s, when Japan, the United States, and other countries were experiencing an economic boom. The event that sets the other events in the story in motion is the closing of the old zoo due to financial problems and the buying of that land by a developer who plans to build high-rise condos. This act—the literal replacement of a place of recreation and enjoyment with the money-making project—forces the elephant to be relocated to the new elephant house. The old elephant and its elderly keeper represent longstanding relationships and symbolize former ways of life, which have been pushed aside by commercial ventures. The narrator emphasizes that it is the elephant's age that keeps it from being adopted elsewhere, as it is deemed too feeble to be a good investment. But the relationship between the keeper and the animal is one of familiarity, love, and trust, not financial arrangements.

As the narrator begins again to describe the newspaper article about the elephant's disappearance, he discusses the facts surrounding the case that make it highly improbable that the elephant actually escaped. Upon rereading the article, the narrator concludes that the elephant had to have miraculously vanished somehow much to the bafflement of the town's authorities, who persist in denying this possibility. As he goes on to recount the town's responses to the elephant's vanishing,

"That longing for solace accounts for the narrator's strange, obsessive interest in the elephant and the keeper, as they represent old ways of life that are being pushed to the literally invisible margins."

the narrator points out the futility of these actions, and again in having the narrator relate these details, Murakami satirizes the blind literalness and lack of imagination in modern life. Among other details, the narrator recalls how the mayor held a news conference defending the elephant house's security system and denouncing persons responsible for the elephant's disappearance and politicizing an event which defies ordinary comprehension: "'This is a dangerous and senseless anti-social act of the most malicious kind, and we cannot allow it to go unpunished.'"

The narrator also describes the reactions of a "worried-looking" mother interviewed on the news; Self-Defense Force troops, firemen, and policemen combing the woods for the elephant to no avail; and the silly commentary of a news anchorman about the incident. As he notes how interest in the story inevitably waned after several months of not finding the elephant or discovering how it disappeared, the narrator also mentions how dissatisfying all the official responses were. As he puts it, "Despite their enormous volume, the clippings contained not one fact of the kind that I was looking for." The narrator searches for answers regarding the mysterious case, which these typical contemporary actions have all failed to address, and he is left feeling increasingly bewildered. Another aspect of modern life is the often bizarre discrepancy between unanswered questions and the reductive, matter-of-fact news reporting that distorts a story in order to compress it.

As the story progresses, the narrator continues to feel confused by the elephant incident and saddened by the disappearance of the elephant and its keeper. He feels "the air of doom and desolation" hanging over the empty elephant house, which he continues to visit. His sense of disorientation following the vanishing is so strong that he finds he cannot make decisions he would like to make. His confusion becomes most apparent after meeting a magazine editor at a party thrown by his company. The narrator recalls how he and the editor flirted at the party and continued their conversation at a hotel bar afterward as two people who "were beginning to like each other." However, after telling the editor about the elephant case, which had occurred a few months earlier, the narrator finds that their conversation becomes awkward.

While talking about the case, the narrator admits to having seen the elephant and the keeper on the night of their disappearance and says he was probably the last person to have seen them. He explains that he had been in the habit of spying on the keeper and the elephant through an air vent in the elephant house, which was visible from a spot on a cliff. When the editor asks if there was anything unusual about the two on the night they disappeared, the narrator goes on to say that there was and there was not. After hesitating, he says that although the two were doing what they always did, their relative size seemed to change, as either the elephant had shrunk or the keeper had gotten bigger or both. When the editor asks if he thinks the elephant shrunk until it was small enough to escape or "simply dissolved into nothingness," the narrator concludes that he does not know and that he has a hard time imagining what happened beyond the strange sight that he thinks he saw.

The editor and the narrator part ways soon after this conversation, and the narrator says he never saw her again. In spite of wanting to ask her out for dinner, he ends up never doing that, because it does not seem to matter one way or the other. The story concludes with the narrator admitting to feeling paralyzed. He finds it difficult to take action of any kind on his own behalf. He describes a sense of external and internal imbalance, which has left him disoriented:

> I often get the feeling that things around me have lost their proper balance, though it could be that my perceptions are playing tricks on me. Some kind of balance inside me has broken down since the elephant affair, and maybe that causes external phenomena to strike my eye in a strange way. It is probably something in me.

Although the narrator blames himself for his sense of things being not quite right, Murakami conveys that the narrator alone is not to blame, as the banality of the world in which the narrator lives fails to provide the connection, continuity, and security that older ways of life offered. In the last few paragraphs of the story, the narrator notes that even as he feels things have lost their proper balance, he has become more successful than ever in his job, selling appliances by espousing a pragmatic viewpoint which he does not believe. The narrator points out that his campaign has been successful, because people crave "a kind of unity in this *kit-chin* we know as the world." In this statement, both the narrator and the author seem to emphasize that as modern society replaces traditional modes with things to buy, people will continue to long for some kind of security or sense of familiar order.

That longing for solace accounts for the narrator's strange, obsessive interest in the elephant and the keeper, as they represent old ways of life that are being pushed to the literally invisible margins. The elephant and the keeper palpably demonstrate what has been lost in the transition to modern culture, as the two of them display an unusually strong bond of affection. The narrator watches them on a regular basis, because he marvels at the empathy he perceives, as he notes, "Their affection was evident in every gesture."

This long-term closeness and warmth contrasts dramatically with the isolation the narrator experiences in his everyday life as a company man and with the empty gestures offered by the narrator's society at large, which fails to see the mystery at the heart of the vanishing much less to explain it. The pragmatic, consumerist contemporary world provides no room for the kind of intimate, intuitive bond shared by the elephant and the keeper, and Murakami seems to suggest that their vanishing is inevitable in the face of the new prosperity and materialistic values. Murakami subtly underscores the immeasurable price of this loss by his narrator's paralysis. The loss fills the last lines: "The elephant and keeper have vanished completely. They will never be coming back."

Source: Anna Maria Hong, Critical Essay on "The Elephant Vanishes," in *Short Stories for Students*, Thomson Gale, 2006.

Celeste Loughman

In the following essay, Loughman explores how the stories in The Elephant Vanishes *"offer a good overview of the patterns and variety to be found in Murakami," including a connection to early Shinto beliefs in "The Elephant Vanishes."*

The opening scene of Natsume Sōseki's 1914 novel *Kokoro* shows Sensei, the central figure, at a beach accompanied by a Westerner, alluding to his and the Japanese attraction to the West. In the end, however, following General Nogi's example after the Emperor Meiji's death in 1912, Sensei makes the traditional samurai choice of committing suicide to redeem his honor. Similarly, in Junichirō Tanizaki's 1928 novel *Tade Kuu Mushi* (Eng. *Some Prefer Nettles*) there is a scene wherein Kaname, the male protagonist, boards a ship on which, given the choice, he selects a Japanese room rather than a Western one. Nevertheless, he changes from the kimono he is wearing into a gray flannel suit. Although the novel ends ambiguously, it is very likely that Kaname's future lies not with his modern, westernized wife or with his Eurasian mistress, but with the puppetlike figure who embodies, or at least plays the role of, the passive, submissive Japanese woman. Examples such as these have been repeated innumerable times since Commodore Perry docked in Tokyo Bay in 1853. They reflect the concern, even obsession, of the Japanese with the inroads of Western culture on Japanese society, a concern that has produced contradictory responses ranging from indiscriminate borrowing of Western ways to the cry "Expel the Barbarians."

No such conflict between Japan and the West exists in the works of Haruki Murakami, arguably Japan's most popular novelist. Whereas the characters in early-twentieth-century Japanese fiction could and usually did choose traditional Japanese ways, Murakami knows that no such choice is possible now. Japan has come too far. If a conflict still exists, his characters are not engaged in or even aware of it. So enmeshed are they in the forms of Western, and particularly American, culture that they accept these forms as integral to contemporary Japanese life. Nonetheless, their essential Japaneseness is never truly lost in spite of what the works appear to say.

Reading *Anna Karenina,* the narrator of the short story "Sleep" remarks: "Like a Chinese Box, the world of the novel contained smaller worlds, and inside those were yet smaller worlds. Together, these worlds made up a single universe, and the universe waited there in the book to be discovered by the reader." No comparison of Murakami with Tolstoy is intended by the reference, but the Chinese box is an appropriate image to designate the structure of Murakami's works. The short stories collected in the volume *The Elephant Vanishes* offer a good overview of the patterns and variety to be found in Murakami.

The outer world or container of his fiction, the geographic boundary of Japan and Tokyo in particular, is indisputably Japanese. People drive to

> "When least serious, he uses parody, satire, and sometimes fantasy to show his people trying to make sense out of life in a high-tech, consumer society in which they know that 'things you can't sell don't count for much.'"

Shinjuku, Aoyama, and Roppongi; they travel the Tokyo subways and take the Yamanote Loop. The environment is stable, fixed. Within that geographic frame, however, is the far less stable world of social interaction in which traditional Japanese culture has all but disappeared and there are no fixed markers anywhere. Notably absent is the sense of group identity, a cornerstone of Japan's social structure. In the context of Murakami's fiction, Chie Nakane's excellent analysis of Japan's group consciousness, *Japanese Society,* first published a quarter of a century ago (1970), seems quaint. Nakane writes: "In group identification, a frame such as a 'company' or 'association' is of primary importance; the attribute of the individual is a secondary matter" (3). She notes the "exceedingly high degree" of emotional attachment to one's company (4) to the point of limiting social life to the members of the work group. Murakami's narrators have no such involvement. They are so-called "salarymen" who work in law offices, in quality control for department stores, in PR for appliance manufacturers. Bored and dissatisfied, some quit their jobs; others escape into dream and fantasy; all are emotionally and psychologically detached from their work group.

The family group fares no better. Whether single, married, or divorced, the narrators are disconnected, alone. Concerning kinship in Japan, Nakane cites the adage "The sibling is the beginning of the stranger" (6). Contradicting this view, the bond between the narrator and his sister in "Family Affair" is the closest family relationship to be found among the stories. Physically separated from their parents and living together in Tokyo, the two enjoy their casual, unstructured, and uncommitted lives. Tension develops between them when the sister becomes engaged to a computer engineer who is engrossed in his job, has strong family ties, and follows traditional courtship behavior. The narrator sneers at the conventionality and formality of the fiancé, the only one who is given a name in the stories. Yet, in a rare example of the force of tradition, the sister will marry the man, vaguely recognizing that the way she and her brother have been living does not have "the *feel* of what real life is all about." She is attracted to the order and stability her fiancé represents: "There's nothing wrong in having one guy like him in every family." Marriages in the stories are unhappy, dissolving, or dissolved. The women who choose to leave their husbands are those who are economically independent with careers of their own. In *A Wild Sheep Chase* the wife, reflecting the sexual freedom that some contemporary Japanese women are experiencing, leaves the narrator to live openly with his friend. The traditional Japanese housewives who stay with their husbands are invariably lonely and unable to communicate with them. In all instances the men, when they are aware at all of their marital relationships, seem bewildered by their wives' dissatisfaction and unhappiness.

The lack of group identification is only one indication of the breakdown of traditional Japanese culture in the stories. The signs are everywhere; and like those highlighted by Roland Barthes in *Empire of Signs,* they signify emptiness, but with a difference. Whereas Barthes found an empty center in signs of traditional Japanese culture, such as its food, its landscape, and its poetry, Murakami's works are almost completely emptied of Japanese signs. His characters eat pasta, McDonald's hamburgers, and sometimes vichyssoise; they listen to Willy Nelson, Three Dog Night, and Ravel; the date markers for events in their lives are not Japanese but the year Johansson and Patterson fought for the heavyweight title or when Paul McCartney was singing "The Long and Winding Road." Murakami overloads his works with Western images to make his point. For example, in a story already filled with similar references, it is gratuitous for the narrator to comment, "I was brushing my teeth to Bruce Springsteen's 'Born in the U. S. A.'" ("Family Affrair"). The characters' immersion in the pop culture of the West is not, however, treated disparagingly by Murakami. In fact, he has said, "To tell the truth, I have no interest in traditional Japanese lifestyle." At the same time, however, he is pointing out the emptiness of the signs, which signify nothing beyond their momentary, superficial function. Ignoring their traditional culture while absorbing the forms but not the substance of another culture, his people have lost their moorings and are adrift.

To a considerable degree, Murakami's characters are universal stock figures of contemporary literature, almost a cliché of the existential condition. Lonely, fragmented, unable to communicate, they live a mechanical, purposeless existence. They have become merely their functions, as Emerson warned. Vaguely they sense that something is missing in their lives. Some are shallow with little interior life; others have a deep need for meaning and self-fulfillment. Mostly they are simply bewildered by their sense of disconnection and loss. Murakami's tone is sometimes comic, sometimes sympathetic and serious. When least serious, he uses parody, satire, and sometimes fantasy to show his people trying to make sense out of life in a high-tech, consumer society in which they know that "things you can't sell don't count for much" ("The Elephant Vanishes").

"The Dancing Dwarf" is in part a parody of mass production. The narrator works in the ear department of an elephant factory, a business that is needed because people do not want to wait for elephants to give birth naturally every four or five years. Instead, one real elephant is spliced to make five elephants. Thus, four-fifths of each manufactured elephant is "reconstituted," but no one notices the distortion in an age which demands, to use Ezra Pound's description, "an image of its accelerated grimace." In "The Kangaroo Communique" Murakami satirizes the "I," who is attracted to emptiness and whose principal desire is to "exist in two places simultaneously." "I want to be a McDonald's Quarter Pounder and still be a clerk in the product-control section of the department store." In his job answering customer complaints, he is sexually aroused by a letter from a woman because she is absent from it. What excites him, he tells her in his response, "is that there's no *you* in the whole piece of writing," only the story itself.

The shallowness of the narrator is also the focus of "A Window," a more serious story about loneliness. The twenty-two-year-old college student has a part-time job critiquing letters written by students in a correspondence school. It is obvious that many of those enrolled simply need to communicate with someone, anyone, particularly the thirty-two-year-old woman who invites the narrator to lunch when he leaves his job. She is a recurring figure in the stories, the traditional Japanese wife who waits at home alone for a husband she rarely sees and with whom she cannot communicate. Her loneliness and limited choices do not touch anything deep in the narrator, whose sensitivity is limited to recognizing a good hamburger. He simply wonders why she continues to stay with her husband. Ten years later his shallowness is still intact. Passing the building where she lived, he asks himself, "Should I have slept with her? That's the central question of this piece."

One narrator could be telling many of the stories in the collection. Several have the same history and experience a similar sense of loss, mystery, and bewilderment in their lives. The narrators of "The Second Bakery Attack" and "The Wind-up Bird and Tuesday's Women" both worked part time mowing lawns, were graduated from the law department of a reputable university, failed the bar exam several times, got married, and worked for a considerable period at a low-level job in a law office. They are connected to the narrator of "The Last Lawn of the Afternoon." The three stories, which show the narrator at different stages, contain key ideas that run through the collection, particularly the concern with a lost past, a lost self. Attempting to recapture his past through memory, the thirty-four-year-old narrator of "The Last Lawn of the Afternoon" recalls being a nineteen-year-old college student on the last day of his lawn-mowing job. His work is careful, methodical, beautiful. The customer is a lonely widow who drinks all day; and when he is finished mowing, she gives him a drink and takes him to her daughter's room to show him the girl's things but really to keep him there. She engages him in a game of "signs" by asking him to tell what the daughter's things signify about the girl as a person. His answers lead away from the girl to conjectures that relate to himself: "What matters is . . . she hasn't really taken to anything. Her own body; the things she thinks about, what she's looking for, what others seek in her . . . the whole works." Uncertain of so much about himself, he is sure of one thing: "All I wanted, it came to me, was to mow a good lawn." Limited though the goal may be, it is the closest that any of Murakami's characters come to having an ideal. The point of the story is that the ideal and the self who held it have vanished, as expressed in the line "Not once since then have I mowed a lawn."

The search for a lost past or a lost self is treated more directly in the other two stories. "The Second Bakery Attack" is also told retrospectively, recounting an incident when the narrator was two weeks married and working in a law office. The couple's insatiable hunger, which pointedly developed only after the marriage, evokes the narrator's recollection of his attempt, while a college student, to rob bread from a bakery with his friend. The baker thwarted the robbery by giving the students bread in return for their listening to Wagner overtures. As the narrator sees it, the outcome was a turning point, rooting him in a life of conventionality. He went back to the university, graduated, took a job in a law firm, studied for the bar exam, married. At his wife's instigation, they now set out to rob another bakery. The wife, who inexplicably has a shotgun and masks and seems to know how to conduct a robbery, serves to illustrate the idea of the mystery we are to one another. They can find no bakery, only McDonald's—the implications are obvious—where they succeed in stealing hamburgers. For a moment he, symbolically at least, has retrieved his past, changed it, and made possible a different future. Contrived though the story is, it is part of the pattern of dissatisfaction with one's life and one's self that afflicts all the narrators.

In "The Wind-up Bird and Tuesday's Women" the narrator is thirty years old, has been married for a while, has failed the bar exam several times, and has quit his longtime job in a law office, though he doesn't know why except that he wants "to settle in a new life cycle." For the moment he is a house-husband while his wife works. He too wonders what happened to his old self, but this lost self is the one with ambition, the one voted runner-up as "Most Likely to Succeed." "So where had I screwed up?" he asks himself. The answer is in the wind-up bird of the title, a metaphor for contemporary society mentioned several times in the story and even explained for the reader: "A regular wind-up toy world this is, I think. Once a day the wind-up bird has to come and wind the springs of this world." By quitting his job and probably deliberately failing the bar exam, he is rejecting a world of mechanical rituals emptied of meaning. Paradoxically, however, to escape from his confusion, he, like the characters in other stories, takes refuge in ritual behavior and methodical attention to detail, the only stability he has: "Whenever things get in a muddle, I always iron shirts." He does so in twelve steps, never deviating from the sequence. His marriage is part of the muddle, and his day has what one senses is a routine ending: "Me drinking my beer, my wife sobbing away."

Although Murakami is not proposing a return to the traditional Japanese life-style as a remedy for the restlessness, confusion, and dissatisfaction that he portrays, he is conscious of the loss of idealism that marked Japan earlier in the century: "Something has vanished in these twenty-five years, some kind of idealism. It has vanished, and we became rich." His people live in a rich society which they find wanting. They show its insufficiency as a source of fulfillment by, for example, withdrawing from the race for success and riches or attempting to retrieve a lost self. Murakami shows that neither materialism itself nor the preference for Western popular culture is the problem. The problem is that that's all there is. The idealism which has disappeared has not been replaced with anything else as a source of meaning and self-fulfillment.

An intimate link is implied between lost or confused personal identity and the lost connection with Japan's cultural past. Occasionally someone senses that link, if only obliquely, as in "A Slow Boat to China." (The title, taken from a 1940s American song, suggests the role of America in the acceleration of that lost connection.) In the story China is less a specific place than it is a metonym for the most influential source of Japanese culture. As the narrator says, "Not any China I can read about. . . . It's a part of myself that has been cut off by the word China." As usual, the narrator is bewildered: "There are some things I don't understand at all. I can't tell what I think about things or what I'm after. I don't know what my strengths are or what I'm supposed to do about them." The story is slight, a culling from the past of the few encounters the narrator has had with Chinese in his thirty years. The first such encounter occurred twenty years earlier, when he was a student assigned to take an exam at a Chinese elementary school. He remembers the flawless order and the words of the Chinese test proctor, "And be proud." The second encounter, at nineteen, was with a female co-worker who astonished him with her diligence and commitment to perfection on the job. She is another example of flawless order and one who lived the proctor's words. Although the narrator insists that it was a mistake, he disoriented her when, after a date, he put her on a train going in the wrong direction. The values that he sensed in the Chinese from these encounters impressed and, at nineteen, disconcerted him. The most recent encounter, however, is with a high-school acquaintance who has lost connection with his cultural past. The narrator remembers the Chinese as a close-knit, self-contained group that remained apart from the rest of the students. Since then, though, his fellow student has been absorbed by the Tokyo way of life, and the Chinese have become for him simply people to whom he can sell encyclopedias. "China," the narrator concludes, "is so far away."

When it was remarked to him about one of his stories that it could have easily taken place in America, Murakami replied: "But you see, what I wanted was first to depict Japanese society through that aspect of it that could just as well take place in New York or San Francisco. You might call it the Japanese nature that remains only after you have thrown out, one after another, all those parts that are altogether too 'Japanese'" (*NYTBR,* 28). Within the world of social interaction in a materialistic society is the innermost world, or box, of Murakami's works, the interior life of his characters where imagination often roams free and where the essential Japaneseness of Murakami can sometimes be found—specifically, in the echoes of early Shinto and Buddhist thought.

In "A Slow Boat to China" images of Tokyo assail the narrator as he rides the train:

> The dirty façades, the nameless crowds, the unremitting noise, the packed rush-hour trains, the gray skies, the billboards on every square centimeter of available space, the hopes and resignation, irritation and excitement. And everywhere, infinite options, infinite possibilities. An infinity, and at the same time, zero. We try to scoop it all up in our hands, and what we get is a handful of zero. That's the city. That's when I remember what that Chinese girl said. *This was never any place I was meant to be.*

He is not aware of the ironic reference to Buddhist thought in his use of the terms *infinity* and *zero.* To him the city of Tokyo, a synecdoche for Japan, represents infinite possibilities for self-fulfillment that equal nothing, zero. Zen Buddhism, however, posits the opposite, that nothing equals everything because one becomes one's true self in nothingness, which means a state of being beyond intellection. D. T. Suzuki uses the terms *zero* and *infinity* to describe the process of self-realization: "The realm of absolute subjectivity is where the Self abides. 'To abide' is not quite correct here, because it only suggests the statical aspect of the Self. But the Self is ever moving or becoming. It is a zero which is a staticity, and at the same time an infinity, indicating that it is all the time moving" ("Lectures," 25). The nihilistic emptiness of Japanese society implied in "a handful of zero" is also an ironic contrast to the Buddhist concept of *sunyata,* "emptiness," which refers to ultimate reality or truth and is synonymous with "nothingness":

"Sunyata is the point at which we become manifest in our own suchness as concrete human beings, as individuals with both body and personality. And at the same time, it is the point at which everything around us becomes manifest in its own suchness" (Nishitani, 90).

There is another allusion to Buddhist thought in the story. After being knocked out while playing baseball as a boy, the narrator comes to and says, "*That's okay, brush off the dirt and you can still eat it.*" Though he has never understood what the words meant, a parallel comment by Suzuki clarifies the statement. When discussing the teachings of Ichiun (a philosopher of swordsmanship) and the legendary Buddha, he says: "Both want us to scratch away all the dirt our being has accumulated even before our birth and reveal Reality in its isness, or in its suchness, or in its nakedness, which corresponds to the Buddhist concept of emptiness (*sunyata*)" (*ZJC,* 179). The boy's epiphany was a recognition that beneath the accumulated "dirt" of Japanese society one could still find the source of self-fulfillment and truth in the foundations of Japanese culture. Twenty years later he knows that that time has passed and that the only "words of wisdom" he could utter now would be like those of the Chinese girl: "*This is no place for me.*" In spite of his characters' indifference to traditional Japanese culture, in the allusions to Buddhist thought Murakami is showing that at some unconscious level Japan's cultural past is not forgotten.

Murakami's characters live exterior lives that are efficient, predictable, and mechanical to create the illusion of purpose and meaning. At the same time, inside they are saying "This is no place for me" and often escape into their interior worlds of fantasy and dream, where imagination runs free. The relationship between the reader and the narrator varies among the stories. Sometimes the reader knows that what the narrator is experiencing is simply an imaginary projection from within himself. At other times the reader is asked to accept nonrational or metaphysical experiences as objectively true. And in still other instances the reader is left in doubt about what is physically experienced or what is imagined. An example of this last situation is "The Wind-up Bird and Tuesday's Women." Of the three "Tuesday's women," the reader can be sure only of the wife's physical presence. The second woman is a pornographic telephone caller who knows the narrator's personal history and, in a sequence of calls, tries to arouse him sexually through descriptions of her erotic poses and behavior. Later, as he wanders down the alley behind his house in search of his lost cat, he encounters the third woman, actually a precocious teenager who invites him to sunbathe with her. She begins talking to him about death as a concrete entity:

> I think about what it would be like to cut the thing open with a scalpel. Not the corpse. The lump of death itself. There's got to be something like that in there somewhere, I just know it. Dull like a softball—and pliable—a paralyzed tangle of nerves. I'd like to remove it from the dead body and cut it open.

The only hint that the gruesome conversation has not actually taken place is that the narrator has been dozing, and the girl speaks the words in a whisper after she awakens him. The reader is left speculating whether the encounters with the strange women were imagined, a projection in the first instance of his desire for sexual vitality, which could be viewed as an impulse to life, and in the second instance a contrary fascination with death. Viewed as a projection from within, the encounters reveal desires that he cannot express directly and openly.

No such ambiguity exists in "The Little Green Monster," one of the two stories in *The Elephant Vanishes* that have a female narrator. Here is a housewife who is left alone all day and well into the night with nothing to do but look out at the garden. Hearing a sound, she thinks at first that it comes from within herself, as pointedly it does. The ground breaks open, and out of it comes an ugly creature with claws, a long nose, and green scales that then makes its way into the house. The creature means no harm, however. It seeks only her love. Its ugly exterior "masked a heart that was as soft and vulnerable as a brand-new marshmallow." She responds to its expression of love by torturing it with cruel thoughts until it withers and dies. The images of the soft Japanese wife with the underlying desire for cruelty and the beauty of heart that lies beneath an ugly exterior link the story to others in its contradiction between interior and exterior selves.

Unlike the narrator of "The Little Green Monster," the "I" of "The Elephant Vanishes," the title story, is rooted in objective reality and questions his uncanny experience, which, however, would be accepted within the cosmic view of early Shinto. He is the conventional Japanese "salaryman," successful in his PR role promoting the sale of kitchen appliances. In his leisure time he occasionally peers into the elephant house from a cliff to watch the elephant and its trainer during their private time. When the zoo is closed to make way for a high-rise condo development, the elephant is transferred to a special house, where he is secured by a cuff and chain on his leg. As the narrator watches, he witnesses the unusual affinity between the two in which their sizes are mysteriously balanced. The narrator has the feeling "that a different, chilling kind of time was flowing through the elephant house—but nowhere else." The feeling is reinforced when, without the cuff or chain being broken or unlocked, the elephant and his trainer vanish. Although the narrator becomes more successful than ever in his job, the elephant episode has left him with the sense that the world in which he lives is somehow out of balance and that whatever he does or does not do makes little difference. He knows that the relationship he believes he witnessed is incredible, like something from a primordial time; yet it is consistent with the world view of the early Japanese, who "took it for granted that they were integrally part of the cosmos, which they saw as a 'community of living beings,' all sharing the kami (sacred) nature" (Kitagawa, 12). In such a world view the magic that the narrator witnessed would not be incredible at all.

The connection with Shinto beliefs is more direct and obvious in those works in which Murakami uses spirit possession as the fantastic element—for example, the sheep in *A Wild Sheep Chase* and the dwarf in. "The Dancing Dwarf." In Shinto, *kami* (gods or spirits, sometimes spirits of animals), good or evil, could possess human beings (Kitagawa, 14), controlling them completely. The implied reader in both works is asked to accept, along with the narrators, the reality of spirit possession. In both instances, the fantastic experiences occur at a point of extreme dissatisfaction with day-to-day life. In *A Wild Sheep Chase* the narrator's wife has divorced him; he is about to give up his partnership in an advertising business and, like other Murakami characters, does not know what he wants or what to do next. Unlike the realistic, conventional society which frames *A Wild Sheep Chase* and "The Elephant Vanishes," the fantastic elements in "The Dancing Dwarf" occur in a society already made absurd by its business of manufacturing elephants. The narrator is bored with his job making elephant ears when the dwarf comes into his dream and dances to a miscellany of music—Rolling Stones, Mitch Miller, Charlie Parker, Frank Sinatra—in a sylvan setting while the narrator watches, eating grapes. He learns the history of the dwarf, who had been given a room in the palace after the king, a lover of music, had watched the dwarf dance. The rumor was that "the dwarf used an evil power on the palace," causing a revolution that resulted in the king's death and the dwarf's escape into the forest. To get a beautiful girl to sleep with him, the narrator allows the dwarf to possess him temporarily so that he can lure the girl with his dancing, the arrangement being that if the narrator utters a sound during the experience, the dwarf will possess him permanently. Like a perverse fairy tale, as he makes love to the girl she turns into a corpse-like creature being devoured by maggots. By not uttering a sound, the narrator wins—but only temporarily. Being chased by police who have heard of his connection to the dwarf, the narrator is driven into the forest, where it is assumed the dwarf will eventually take control of him, because, as the dwarf told him, "No one has the power to change what has been decided." Human powerlessness is also an issue in *A Wild Sheep Chase,* as one of the characters commits suicide to free himself from possession by a sheep which has inhabited and left several persons at will.

Suicide is the choice also of the female narrator of "Sleep," which brings together several key ideas already presented: the emptiness of contemporary Japanese life, the search for a lost self, and especially the problem of the divided self and its echoes of Shinto and Buddhism. The narrator is a conventional Japanese housewife but with no discernible reason for complaint. Indeed, she can be regarded simply as a malcontent. She lives a comfortable middle-class life with her son and dentist husband, who doesn't drink or socialize and who is faithful, kind, and attentive but whom she doesn't like very much nevertheless. An insomniac for seventeen days, she welcomes sleeplessness. She feels no physical fatigue and performs her marital duties with detached efficiency during the day while at night her mind "floated in its own space," alive and free. A typical Murakami character, she wonders, "Where had the old me gone, the one who used to read a book as if possessed by it?" As if to reclaim that lost self, in her wakeful hours she eats chocolates and reads *Anna Karenina* with intensity, as she had done as a teenager.

Her insomnia began when she awakened from a bad dream, and in what she thinks is either a trance or a dream, a gaunt old man appears at the foot of her bed and pours water ceaselessly over her feet from a seemingly bottomless pitcher. She has no idea what the ritual means, but it may easily be seen as a purification rite that can be connected to Shinto, of which purification is a central characteristic: "What concerned the early Japanese was not moral sins but physical and mental defilements, which had to be cleansed ceremonially by exorcism and abstention" (Kitagawa, 13). The narrator has concluded that people live in the "prison cells of their own tendencies," hers being "those chores I perform day after day like an unfeeling machine." "The same physical movements over and over" are like an accumulation of dirt over her essential self, so that death becomes for her a drastic but necessary rite of purification. Her nocturnal activities take her to the waterfront, where a policeman warns her that a man had been killed there recently and his companion raped. Courting death, she dresses like a young man and returns to the waterfront, where her car is attacked.

The basic conflict in the story is the narrator's mind-body split. She refuses to sleep because she is resentful that her mind must also rest to repair her body, which is being consumed by its "tendencies": "My flesh may have to be consumed, but my mind belongs to me." Her attitude is better understood if considered in the context of the subject-object bifurcation of ego consciousness in Zen Buddhism. Ego consciousness or awareness "is expressed as affirmation of itself," which "includes itself both as affirmer and as affirmed" (DeMartino, 143)—that is, both as a subject and as an object. The ego as subject has only "conditioned subjectivity," because it "is forever bound to itself and its world as object" (DeMartino, 144). While not understanding fully the nature of her problem or her quest, the narrator of "Sleep" in her reference to "prison cells" recognizes her bondage to herself as object. Her attitude and behavior actually express her desire "to overcome the divisive inner and outer cleavage separating and removing the ego from itself—and its world—in order that it may fully be and truly know who and what it is" (DeMartino, 154).

The desire to be freed from the subject-object dichotomy is even more explicit in "The Girl from Ipanema," in which the narrator imagines that his heart is somehow linked with that of the Ipanema girl, "probably in a strange place in a far-off world" (quoted in Rubin, 496). He then conjectures about another link in his consciousness:

> Somewhere in there, I'm sure, is the link joining me with myself. Someday, too, I'm sure, I'll meet myself in a strange place in a far-off world. . . . In that place, I am myself and myself is me. Subject is object and object is subject. All gaps gone. A perfect union. There must be a strange place like this somewhere in the world.

The subject-object division in ego consciousness is everywhere in Murakami. With its dual stories and dual narrators, the novel *Hard-Boiled Wonderland and the End of the World* is in fact an allegory of the divided self and the struggle of the ego toward self-realization. Nothing other than the state of complete subjectivity, or *sunyata,* is being described when the narrator is told, "It's a peaceful world. Your own world, a world of your own makin'. You can be yourself there. You've got everythin' there. And at the same time, there is nothin'. Can you picture a world like that?" The narrator's answer is "Not really," the same one that the narrators in any of the stories could give.

Murakami's breezy tone, his hapless people with their empty centers, and especially his catalogues of Western popular culture often make his work appear trivial. However, as in a detective story (a genre of which Murakami is fond), these characteristics are a red herring leading the reader away from the author's essential Japaneseness and his serious intentions that are found in the innermost world of his stories. He has said: "I want to reconstruct a morality for this new world, this economic world. My generation, we are in a way disappointed, but we have to survive. We have to survive in this society, so we have to establish a new morality."

No doubt in part because of his popularity, critics have questioned Murakami's seriousness as a writer. One formidable detractor is the distinguished writer Kenzaburōōe. ōe does not classify Murakami's work as serious literature, *junbungaku,* which he translates in English as "sincere or polite literature." In a discussion of the decay of Japanese literature, ōe says that "any future resuscitation of *junbungaku* will be possible only if ways are found to fill in the wide gap that exists between Murakami and pre-1970 postwar literature." His standard for judgment is literature produced between 1946 and 1970 "that strived to provide a total, comprehensive contemporary age and a human model that lived it." ōe's dismissal of Murakami is unjustified, but he has a point. In spite of Murakami's expressed goal of creating a new morality for the contemporary, economic world, his works do not show what that moral ideal is, nor has he created characters who would be capable of recognizing it. The many allusions to Japan's early religions function not as an idealism envisioned by Murakami but rather as primal memory, an intimation of the longing to be fulfilled in oneself and to live in harmony with one's world. His composite narrator, however, is "caught between all that was and all that must be" and can say only, "This is no place for me." Reading Murakami's work, one senses that the best is still to come.

Japanese children and their attendants on a playground © Bohemian Nomad Picturmakers/Corbis

Source: Celeste Loughman, "No Place I Was Meant to Be: Contemporary Japan in the Short Fiction of Haruki Murakami," in *World Literature Today*, Vol. 71, No. 1-Jan, Winter 1997, pp. 87–94.

David L. Ulin

In the following review, Ulin calls The Elephant Vanishes *"one of the most consistently universal volumes of fiction you'll ever come across."*

For better or worse, we live today in an atmosphere of cultural cross-pollination, where words and images are transmitted across continents at the speed of television, and the writing of one society can influence the writers of another until the idea of boundaries becomes nearly irrelevant.

In some circles, it's fashionable to lament this process, to see it as responsible for a kind of mass homogenization that will ultimately render all of us, no matter where we live, as mostly the same. But such laments neglect the basic fact of imagination, the human race's great saving grace. After all, if, as E.M. Forster once said, the purpose of literature is to record "the buzz of implication" of a specific time in history, then perhaps we are on the threshold of some sort of global writing, one that will emphasize our commonalities rather than the differences between us, and allow us to reimagine our relationships with the world.

This intention seems to be central to the work of Haruki Murakami, whose collection of short stories, *The Elephant Vanishes,* has just been published in the United States for the first time. One of Japan's best-selling authors, Murakami grew up reading American paperbacks in the port city of Kobe and claims Raymond Chandler as his biggest influence, although his stripped-down, off-handed prose seems more akin to that of Raymond Carver—which makes sense, since he's Carver's Japanese translator.

But the 17 stories here also reflect strains of literature and popular culture ranging from classical fairy tales to *The Twilight Zone,* making *The Elephant Vanishes* one of the most consistently universal volumes of fiction you'll ever come across, a book that reflects the often disassociating experience of living at the end of the 20th Century, even for those who've never been within 5,000 miles of Japan.

Part of the way Murakami pulls this off is by ignoring the most obvious markers of his Japanese settings, minimizing the importance of place in driving his narratives along. Thus, while much of the material in *The Elephant Vanishes* takes place in the suburbs of Tokyo, it's a Tokyo that's been essentially deracinated, that, except for certain surface details of geography, could be any city in the industrialized world.

"The Wind-Up Bird and Tuesday's Women," for instance—the first story in the collection—opens with the narrator cooking, spaghetti and "whistling the prelude to Rossini's 'La Gazza Ladra' along with the FM radio." Even when he goes outside to look for his missing cat, we have no clear indiction of where it is exactly that he lives. And in "The Second Bakery Attack," a newlywed couple, looking to assuage "an unbearable hunger" in the middle of the night, ends up at McDonald's, where, "[w]earing a McDonald's hat, the girl behind the counter flashed me a McDonald's smile and said, 'Welcome to McDonald's.'"

"The Second Bakery Attack," actually, works as a signifier for the entire collection—starting off with a situation that's relatively mundane, then slowly and irrevocably getting out of hand. The couple, it turns out, are not going to McDonald's to buy anything; they are there to hold the place up, as a way of exorcising a demon from the husband's past. What's more, the whole thing is the wife's idea, and the husband goes along with it as if in a dream, at once a part of the action and slightly detached from it. Even after the fact, the only thing he can do is to wonder passively about-what's occurred. "I'm still not sure I made the right choice," he explains. "But then, it might not have been a question of right and wrong. Which is to say that wrong choices can produce right results, and vice versa. I myself have adopted the position that, in fact, we never choose anything at all. Things happen. Or not."

All in all, it's a rather amoral perspective, but, we can see the essential truth behind it, the way things do tend to happen without much conscious control. In fact, this may have a lot to do with why the work in *The Elephant Vanishes* seems so accessible, so reflective of how so many of us live our lives. For, like us, Murakami's characters inhabit a universe that is morally and socially ambiguous, and often go through the motions of their day-to-day existence at somewhat of a loss. In contrast to most Japanese literature, his narrators—all of the pieces in this collection are written in the first-person—are outsiders, if not exactly loners, then on their own, people who have jobs, not careers. And their disassociation gives Murakami's writing an ironic, quizzical edge that really hits home—because it seems like the most intelligent response to so much of what's going on.

For, like us, Murakami's characters inhabit a universe that is morally and socially ambiguous, and often go through the motions of their day-to-day existence at somewhat of a loss."

It also opens these stories up to a striking sense of playfulness, a feeling that if "Things happen. Or not," anything can happen at any time. Murakami makes the most of this, allowing reality to veer off its tracks again and again, much to the quiet amazement of his characters. There's "Sleep," in which a housewife stops sleeping for 17 days, and discovers that "[p]retty soon, reality just flows off and away." Or "TV People," in which a man's apartment is invaded by reduced-size human replicas—"slightly smaller than you or me. . . . About, say, 20 or 30 percent," who first bring him an "ordinary Sony color TV," then slowly disconnect him from his life until "the words slip away." Even the collection's title piece, with its account of an elephant that disappears from the elephant house, assumes a kind of magical realist tone when the narrator admits that he was the last person to see the animal in captivity and that it appeared to have shrunk.

Of course, not all of the writing in *The Elephant Vanishes* is so phantasmagoric. The exquisite and affecting "On Seeing the 100% Perfect Girl One Beautiful April Morning" explores the thoughts of a man in the few brief seconds that it takes him to pass his "100% perfect girl" on "a narrow side street"; "Was it really right for one's dreams to come true so easily?" he asks himself as she goes by. And "The Silence" recounts the experience of a man who was tortured with the silent treatment during his final term in high school; the whole point of this saga is to express the man's conviction that "it's impossible, in my own mind, to believe in people. . . . When I think of these things . . . I wake my wife up and I hold on to her and cry. Sometimes for a whole hour, I'm so scared."

"I want to write a Japanese novel with a different material, with a different style, but in Japanese. I think it would help change Japanese literature from inside."

Whether offbeat or down-to-earth, what all of Murakami's stories have in common is the idea that we live in a world without equilibrium, which may be the most universal thing about them at all. For who among us hasn't felt that life is somehow out of whack, that if we could just see better it might all make more sense? As the narrator of "The Elephant Vanishes" puts it, "I often get the feeling that things around me have lost their proper balance. . . . Some kind of balance inside me has broken down."

Source: David L. Ulin, "Disorder Out of Chaos," in *Los Angeles Times Book Review*, April 4, 1993, p. 3, 11.

Elizabeth Deveraux

In the following interview with Elizabeth Deveraux, Murakami expounds on how he wants "to test Japanese culture and writing from outside Japan."

Forget about cherry blossom time, the crags of Fujiyama, tea ceremonies; most especially forget about exquisitely penned haiku. Today Haruki Murakami is Japan's premier novelist, and he's earned that rank by breaking all the rules.

Hard-Boiled Wonderland and the End of the World, due this month from Kodansha (Fiction Forecast, Aug. 2), shows off this iconoclastic style. Its plot is a feat of what seems to be a double-jointed imagination. Dizzying and dazzling, it involves an intelligence agent who can "launder" and "shuffle" data in his brain, and a drama simultaneously playing out within the agent's unconscious. Like Alice, the agent embarks on a fantastic journey that begins when he travels down an impossible hole, and his adventures are conveyed with the glittering and mutable energy of kaleidoscopic images. Only gradually do broader patterns emerge, and the novel becomes a terrifyingly urgent tale of survival and surrender.

If the story is strange and startling, the setting is just as surprising: the geography is of a modern Japan, but the heritage is Western, the prose awash in references to American and European culture. From a bottomless reservoir come allusions to *The Wizard of Oz,* Bogart and Bacall, *Star Trek,* Ma Bell and Jim Morrison, discussions of Turgenev and Stendhal, Camus and Somerset Maugham. The only thing distinctly Japanese is the food.

"I might like Japanese food," says Murakami, meeting *PW* in Kodansha's New York offices, "but I like Western literature, Western music." His fusion of Japanese language and Western sensibility represents a turning point for Japanese literature.

"Most Japanese novelists," Murakami explains, "are addicted to the beauty of the language. I'd like to change that. Who knows about the beauty? Language is a kind of a tool, an instrument to communicate. I read American novels, Russian novels; I like Dickens. I feel there are different possibilities for Japanese writing.

"At first, I wanted to be an international writer. Then I changed my mind, because I'm nothing but a Japanese novelist: I was born in Japan and I speak Japanese and I write in Japanese. So I had to find my identity as a Japanese writer. That was tough.

"You have to know that the writing in Japan for Japanese people is in a particular style, very stiff. If you are a Japanese novelist you have to write that way. It's kind of a society, a small society, critics and writers, called high literature. But I am different in style, with a very American atmosphere. I guess I'm seeking a new style far Japanese readership, and I think I have gained ground. Things are changing now. There is a wider field."

Most would agree that Murakami has indeed gained ground. More than 12 million copies of his books are in print in Japan, he's received a string of prestigious awards and been translated into 14 languages. A prolific translator himself, he has introduced writers as diverse as F. Scott Fitzgerald, Truman Capote and Raymond Carver, Paul Theroux and John Irving to Japan. A self-described "wanderer," he has lived all over the world, from Greece and Italy to a current stint as a visiting fellow at Princeton University.

"I want to test Japanese culture and Japanese writing from outside of Japan. It is very hard to explain that," he says, and pauses to deliberate. "It's a kind of translation. When I translate from English to Japanese, the story is the same, but the language is different. Something has changed by translation. I like to do the same thing for my own writing. I want to write a Japanese novel with a different material, with a different style, but in Japanese. I think it would help change Japanese literature from inside."

The son of a teacher of Japanese literature, Murakami, who was born in 1949, grew up reading American fiction. He learned English in junior high and high school. "My marks in English weren't so good," he says in the first of a series of deceptively modest remarks and disclaimers, an unprepossessing style matched by his casual dress and careful, slow speech. "But I enjoyed reading in English," he continues, "it was quite a new experience." Raymond Chandler was a favorite. When he went to Waseda University, he studied drama, everything from Greek tragedy to contemporary works. "I tried to write when I was a college student, but I couldn't, because I had no experience. I gave up my writing when I was 22 or 21. I just forgot about it.

"I didn't want to, you know, get into a company." (Neither do his characters.) "I wanted to do something by myself, with myself. I started a small jazz club in Tokyo. It was fun. I owned that club for seven years.

"One day I found I wanted to write something. I was so happy that I wanted to write again, and that I *could* write this time. It's a blessing. Since then I've been happy all the time, because I can write."

Back then, he says, "I had only nighttime for writing. I would be at the club until one o'clock or two o'clock in the morning, and then I'd come back, sit down at the kitchen table and write my story."

He produced *Hear the Wind Sing,* published in Japan in 1979, which he describes as a "a young-man, things-are-changing kind of novel," set in 1970, the "age of the counterculture." The story, he says, is realistic, but the style is "not conventional, a Kurt Vonnegut style. I was strongly influenced by Vonnegut and Richard Brautigan. They are so lively and fresh."

He doesn't want to see *Hear the Wind Sing* translated, however, and labels it (and his next book, *Pinball 1973,* which appeared in 1980) "weak." Not too weak to win the Shinjin Bungaku Prize? Ah, replies Murakami, "you have to know there are many prizes in Japan."

The prize so easily dismissed was from Kodansha, which, like other Japanese houses, has an award for newcomers. Kodansha was first to see the novel ("There are no agents in Japan," the author explains), and Murakami chose the publisher because it "is the biggest, very prestigious." He has remained with Kodansha ever since, and enjoys his relationship with editor Yoko Kinoshita. "It's not the usual thing, a woman publisher," he adds. "In Japanese companies it's mainly men who get good jobs. My editor is doing well."

A *Wild Sheep Chase,* which he calls a "fantasy/adventure," was Murakami's third book, published in Japan in 1982, and shares its protagonist with the earlier two. "I feel somehow that *Wild Sheep Chase* is my first novel," he says now. "It's the first book where I could feel a kind of sensation, the joy of telling a story. When you read a good story, you just keep reading. When I write a good story, I just keep writing."

That joy propelled him to produce four collections of short stories between 1982 and 1986 (a fifth was published last year, as was a volume of travel pieces). "I like storytelling. I don't find it difficult to make a story." In 1985, *Hard-Boiled Wonderland* appeared and captured the celebrated Tanizaki Prize. Nevertheless, the suceess of his next novel took everyone by surprise. *Norwegian Wood* (1987), titled after the Beatles song, is a love story, "quite different" from his other books, "totally realistic, very straight"; it sold two million copies. In 1989 came *Dance Dance Dance,* which is a sequel to *A Wild Sheep Chase* and slated to follow *Hard-Boiled Wonderland* into English.

Kodansha decides which books to bring to the U.S. "They ask my advice," says Murakami, "but I think they're right in their decisions."

The first book to appear in English was *A Wild Sheep Chase* (published here in 1989) which drew rave reviews. Like *Hard-Boiled Worderland,* it has an unusually intricate and inventive plot. Readers may well be surprised to learn that Murakami creates the plot as he goes along. "I write one chapter and then the second chapter, and so on . . . It comes out automatically.

"I don't know what's going to happen—but it's going to happen. I have fun when I write."

The fun spills into his prose, which is so playful that the *New York Times Book Review* called Murakami "a mythmaker for the millennium, a wiseacre wise man." Murakami is quick to credit the translator of his novels, Alfred Birnbaum: "He's a good man, a good guy. His translation is so lively."

Birnbaum, for example, came up with the English title for *A Wild Sheep Chase;* the original was *The Adventure of the Sheep.* "I have another translator, Jay Rubin," Murakami continues. "He's good as well. Alfred is more free, Jay is more faithful to the original." Americans will have a chance to sample Rubin's translation in a September issue of the *New Yorker,* where a story by Murakami will appear.

Murakami describes his own translations as "very faithful." He began translating at almost the same time as he began writing fiction, and first approached stories by F. Scott Fitzgerald. How does he select a work for translation? "Sometimes a book appeals to me because I want to introduce it to Japanese readers. That's one reason. Another reason is that I want to learn something from this book, and translation is the best way. You can read every detail, every page, every word. You can learn so much. It's my teacher.

"I want to try many different styles. Translation is a kind of vehicle. One time you can write F. Scott Fitzgerald and one time Raymond Carver. It's a transformation."

These days Murakami's schedule at Princeton is flexible, and he defines his role there as a kind of "observer." He speaks contentedly of his carrel at the university library, where he has been researching material for his new book, "about politics, about history, love, everything. I've been researching the war between Japan and the Soviet Union in 1939 in Manchuria. I'm interested in prewar history in Japan, in China."

Princeton holds a number of attractions beyond the library. He originally visited the institution in the '80s, lured by his interest in Fitzgerald. It also affords him the quiet he seeks. Almost shyly, he says, "You know, I'm pretty famous in Japan. I don't like that, the social life. I like jogging. I jog, and I work six hours a day. I take a walk with my wife [Yoko Takahashi; they got married while both were students at Waseda University]. I listen to music, I read. I have no time to meet people, to go somewhere to have dinner. But they expect me to do it, because I'm famous.

"I lead a very quiet life, it's my kind of life. We lived on a Greek island [from 1986 to 1989]. It was a perfect place to be a writer."

Murakami and his wife, who have also resided in Rome and Athens and traveled extensively, like living in the U.S. "In Europe, they are stiff, and we are always foreigners. But in America they accept us. America is a very special place, very accepting of other cultures."

His sojourn at Princeton will end next June, but he and his wife would like to stay in the States for another few years, perhaps relocating to Boston. "I like moving. If you are a writer, you can live anywhere. We have no children, and we are free to go everywhere. I like to move every two years or so. I feel it's time to go, and we move. It's so simple."

At the moment, Murakami is contemplating a translation of Grace Paley's work. He also cites Tim O'Brien, whose *Nuclear Age* and *The Things They Carried* he has translated. "I like him best . . . these days," he qualifies.

He calls John Irving "a good story-teller," and has translated *Setting Free the Bears,* which, he says, Irving doesn't particularly like. Because it's an early work? "Yes," says Murakami. "He likes his latest book. That makes sense, of course. But I like *Settinq Free the Bears* because it is so young and fresh."

Does Murakami have a favorite among his own books? "My latest one, the next one! The one that I am writing now."

Source: Elizabeth Deveraux, "PW Interviews: Haruki Murakami," in *Publishers Weekly*, Vol. 228, No. 42, September 20, 1991, pp. 113–14.

Sources

Loughman, Celeste, Review of "The Elephant Vanishes," in *World Literature Today*, Vol. 68, No. 2, Spring 1994, pp. 434–35.

Mitgang, Herbert, "From Japan, Big Macs and Marlboros in Stories," in *New York Times*, May 12, 1993, p. L C17.

Murakami, Haruki, "The Elephant Vanishes," in *The Elephant Vanishes: Stories*, translated by Jay Rubin, Vintage International, 1994, pp. 308–27.

Review of *The Elephant Vanishes: Stories*, in *Publishers Weekly*, Vol. 240, No. 5, February 1, 1993, p. 74.

Ulin, David L, "Disorder Out of Chaos," in *Los Angeles Times Book Review*, April 4, 1993, pp. 3, 11.

Further Reading

Goossen, Theodore W., ed., *The Oxford Book of Japanese Short Stories*, Oxford University Press, 2002.

This anthology, which includes a version of "The Elephant Vanishes," comprises short stories from the end of the nineteenth century to the early 2000s.

Henshall, Kenneth G., *A History of Japan: From Stone Age to Superpower*, Palgrave Macmillan, 2001.

Henshall, a New Zealander professor of Japanese studies, provides a sweeping and lively account of the history of Japan, focusing on both political and cultural history.

Ikeno, Osamu, and Roger Daniels, eds., *The Japanese Mind: Understanding Contemporary Culture*, Tuttle Publishing, 2002.

The editors, a Japanese professor and a British professor living in Japan, provide a guide to some aspects of contemporary Japanese culture, including rituals, myths, and ideas about social organization.

Rubin, Jay, *Haruki Murakami and the Music of Words*, Harvill Press, 2002.

Rubin, a translator and Harvard professor of Japanese literature, combines biography and critical analysis to portray Murakami. Rubin chronicles Murakami's obsessions, such as his fascination with cats and other animals, as he analyzes Murakami's writings.

Varley, H. Paul, *Japanese Culture*, 4th edition, University of Hawaii Press, 2000.

Now in its fourth edition, Varley's book has been praised as an introductory text on Japanese history and culture.

Holiday

Katherine Anne Porter

1960

"Holiday" by Katherine Anne Porter originally appeared in the *Atlantic Monthly* in December 1960 but received more attention when it was included in *The Collected Stories of Katherine Anne Porter* in 1965. The story, however, had much earlier origins; Porter first wrote "Holiday" in the early 1920s, based on a personal experience she had had several years earlier. Unsatisfied with the story, she set it aside and did not rediscover it until 1960, when she enlisted a friend to help her organize her personal papers. As she wrote in her introduction to *The Collected Stories of Katherine Anne Porter*, "the story haunted me for years and I made three separate versions, with a certain spot in all three where the thing went off track. So I put it away . . . and I forgot it. It rose from one of my boxes of papers, after a quarter of a century, and . . . I saw at once that the first [version] was the right one." After a few minor changes, she sent it to the *Atlantic Monthly*. She won an O. Henry prize for the story in 1962.

"Holiday" tells the tale of a young woman who, seeking to escape her troubles, takes a holiday to a rural Texas farm owned by a very traditional German family. The story centers on her relationship with the family's deformed and crippled servant girl. Later she discovers the girl is actually the eldest daughter of the family, though she is virtually a slave in the household. The main character's fascination and identification with this girl allows Porter to explore themes of alienation, isolation, and the complete sacrifice of an

individual for the good of the greater community (in this case, the family). Like much of Porter's work, the story is drawn from her own experiences, and many critics believe that the main character (whose name the reader never learns) is Porter herself, describing her own alienation as a woman artist in a patriarchal society.

Author Biography

Katherine Anne Porter was born Callie Russell Porter on May 15, 1890, in Indian Creek, Texas, and lived a life that rivals any fiction. In her ninety years, she endured poverty, hardship, and severe illness; married and divorced four husbands; spent time with revolutionaries, literary giants, and powerful politicians; and traveled extensively. She witnessed two world wars, the Great Depression, and at age 82, covered the launch of the first mission to the moon for *Playboy* magazine.

Porter's life matched her flamboyant personality; she was gregarious, flirtatious, and quick to anger. Her lively social life often stalled her work, and she had many years in which she produced nothing but reams of correspondence. She lived much of her life in different countries, including Mexico, Germany, France, and Belgium.

Her mother died when Porter was just two, after which she was raised by her strict grandmother, who died when the child was eleven. Her father sank into depression after her mother's death and showed little interest in his children. Mired in poverty, she was eager to escape by marrying. At fifteen she married John Henry Koontz, the twenty-year-old son of a wealthy Texas family. But the couple was unhappy. Still, Porter remained legally married to Koontz for nine years, making this the longest of her four marriages.

Porter's first writing job was on the *Fort Worth Critic*. After a couple years in the newspaper business, she moved to New York and in 1920 published her first short stories. During the 1920s she wrote many stories that remained unfinished until much later in her life, including "Holiday." She also lived in Mexico for a time. Stories she published during this time include "Virgin Violeta," "Magic," "The Jilting of Granny Weatherall," and in 1929, "Flowering Judas," which was her most acclaimed work to date. In 1927, while in Massachusetts, Porter joined many other literary figures in protesting the execution of Nicola Sacco and Bartolomeo Vanzetti, two Italian anarchists who had been convicted of a brutal murder in Boston in 1921.

Katherine Anne Porter Photograph by Paul Porter. AP Images

Porter began the 1930s with an unproductive (though lively) two years in Mexico where she met her third husband, Eugene Pressly. (Her second, Eugene Stock, she had married in 1924 and divorced in 1926.) In 1932, Porter and Pressly sailed to Europe on the *S.S. Werra*. Porter later used many of her experiences on the ship for her one and only novel, *Ship of Fools*. The couple lived briefly in Germany then in Paris, before returning to the States. In Paris, Porter published several stories, including "The Grave," "That Tree" and "Hacienda." In 1935 the collection *Flowering Judas and Other Stories* was published. In 1937 Porter's stories "Noon Wine" and "Pale Horse, Pale Rider" were published in small literary magazines; in 1939 they were published along with "Old Mortality" in *Pale Horse, Pale Rider: Three Short Novels*, which drew great critical acclaim. Porter left Pressly and then married Albert Erskine, a young graduate student, in 1938, which quickly proved to be a mistake. In 1940 Porter and Erskine separated, and Porter took up residence at Yaddo, the artists' colony in New York, where she wrote "The Leaning Tower."

The 1940s were unproductive. Porter contracted with publishers for many projects but finished few. In 1945, she accepted a position as a screenwriter. Though she was highly paid, she found the censorship intolerable. In 1948 she taught one year at Stanford University then returned to New York.

In 1953, Porter taught at the University of Michigan, and the next year, she taught at the University of Liege, Belgium. In 1955, she returned to the States and completed her novel in the fall of 1961. *Ship of Fools* made Porter wealthy for the first time in her life. The 1963 movie further increased her fortune. In 1966, *The Collected Stories of Katherine Anne Porter*, which included "Holiday," won the National Book Award and the Pulitzer Prize.

In 1970, *The Collected Essays and Occasional Writings* was released. Her last work was "The Never-Ending Wrong," an essay on the Sacco-Vanzetti trial. On September 18, 1980, Porter died at the age of ninety.

Plot Summary

The main character of "Holiday" begins the story by telling readers that this was a time in her life when she was "too young for some of the troubles" she was having (though she never specifies exactly what the troubles are). Wanting to escape these troubles, she decides to take a holiday to the country. She confides this desire to her friend Louise, who exclaims that she has the perfect place: a Texas farm run by a traditional German family. While the narrator is skeptical of Louise's idyllic description of the farm ("Louise had . . . something near to genius for making improbable persons, places, and situations sound attractive") she agrees to the idea, and a few days later she arrives at the Müller farm.

When she arrives at the station and surveys the "desolate mud-colored, shapeless scene," she feels justified in her skepticism. A boy of about twelve arrives and drives her to the farm in a ramshackle old wagon. At the farm, she meets the busy Müller family, including Mother Müller, a sturdy, imposing woman with a face "brown as seasoned bark." The oldest daughter is Annetje, the middle daughter Gretchen, and the youngest is Hatsy. The narrator is shown to her attic room by Hatsy, and after seeing her charming room—"For once, Louise had got it straight"—her attitude towards her holiday begins to improve. She enjoys the sounds of German being spoken in the home, because she does not speak German, and no one will expect her to understand or respond.

At dinner, the men of the family—Father Müller, his two sons, and the husbands of his daughters, who all live together at the farm—sit at the table, while the women stand behind them and serve them. The narrator, being a guest, is seated at the men's side of the table. It is at dinner on her first night at the farm that she first encounters Ottilie, a badly deformed and mute servant girl who cooks and serves the meal. She is ignored by the Müllers as she serves their dinner: "no one moved aside for her, or spoke to her, or even glanced after her when she vanished into the kitchen."

It does not take long for the narrator to settle into the daily rhythm of life at the Müllers. She helps out with chores, entertains the many children of the Müller daughters, and enjoys watching the landscape come to life as spring arrives. One evening she is so enchanted by this natural beauty that she does not return to the farm until late in the evening, after the Müllers have already had their dinner. Hatsy calls for Ottilie to come and serve her dinner. As the narrator is waited on by the servant girl, for the first time she notices that Ottilie has the same slanted blue eyes and high cheekbones as the Müllers.

The family works the entire day on the farm, especially the women, who are constantly scrubbing the floors, milking the cows, and tending the children. While Father Müller is the wealthiest farmer in the community, this wealth does not translate into a life of leisure for his family. On Sundays, however, they all dress up to go dance to the music of a brass band at the Turnverein, a pavilion in a nearby clearing. Here all members of the little German community meets to socialize. One Sunday, the community comes instead to the Müller house for the wedding of Hatsy and her fiancé. After the wedding, a huge feast is served by the unfortunate Ottilie, who continues to toil while the rest of the Müllers celebrate the happy event. "[N]othing could make her seem real," the narrator observes, "or in any way connected with the life around her."

One morning shortly after the wedding, the narrator encounters Ottilie on the porch, peeling potatoes. Suddenly Ottilie jumps up, dropping the knife, and beckons to her. She grasps the narrator's sleeve and pulls her into the house, into her little bedroom, and shows the narrator an old photograph of a young child, about five years old. Ottilie pats the picture and then her own face and points out the name written on the back of the photo: Ottilie. The narrator then realizes that Ottilie is actually the eldest daughter of the Müllers. Ottilie begins to sob, and the narrator, for the first time, no longer finds her strange or distant, but feels a connection to her: "for an instant some filament lighter than cobweb spun itself out between that living center in her and in me . . . so that her life and mine were kin, even a part of each other."

Life goes on at the Müller home; Gretchen gives birth to a baby boy one rainy evening, and the next day neighbor women stop by to see the newborn and do a little socializing. An impending storm sends them home early, and soon the Müller clan is laboring to save their farm and animals from torrential rains. In the downpour Mother Müller goes out to the barn, saves a newborn calf, and milks all the cows. She returns to the house, soaked to the skin, and barks out orders to the rest of the family as though nothing unusual has happened.

The next morning, however, it becomes clear that Mother Müller is not as indestructible as she seems. She takes to her bed with a fever, and as she becomes less and less responsive, the family begins to panic. They cannot send for the doctor because of the continued rain and flooding. By the afternoon, Mother Mueller is dead.

Two days later, just after the family has left the house to bury Mother Müller, the narrator, who is in her attic room, hears a terrible howling. Thinking something has happened to the family dog, she runs downstairs and discovers Ottilie in the kitchen, moaning and howling in her grief. The narrator goes outside and hitches up the pony to the rickety wagon that brought her there to the Müller house, and begins driving Ottilie to join the funeral procession. Once riding in the wagon, however, Ottilie begins to laugh. The narrator realizes that what Ottilie really needs is "a little stolen holiday, a breath of spring air and freedom on this lovely, festive afternoon." They head off for a drive together, to return in time for Ottilie to prepare a meal for the mourners; "They need not even know she had been gone."

Characters

Louise

Louise is the narrator's friend, who recommends the Müller farm as the ideal spot for her holiday escape. Louise has a gift for describing people and places in exaggeratedly positive terms, and she describes the Müller farm as a pastoral, homespun paradise. The narrator, who is skeptical of Louise's descriptions, finds it to be considerably less appealing at first.

The Müller Family

The Müller family itself is such a cohesive unit that it functions as one character in the story. The members of the Müller family sacrifice their individual hopes and desires (assuming they have any) for the good of the family. Married couples do not go off on their own but are simply absorbed into the family; before Hatsy is even married, a new room has been added to the house for her and her husband. Every family member labors daily on the farm: "everybody worked all the time, because there was always more work waiting when they had finished what they were doing then." The only member of the family who stands out as having his own opinions and interests is Father Müller. The Müller sons and sons-in-law are mentioned only in passing, in large part because they spend their day in the fields, and the narrator spends her time either alone or with the other women.

Annetje Müller

Annetje is the eldest of the Müller daughters (next to Ottillie.) She has four children (one a newborn) and is hoping for a fifth. Annetje has a special affection for the baby animals on the farm; "The kittens, the puppies, the chicks, the lambs and calves were her special care." Of all the Müller daughters, Annetje has the gentlest nature, but even she treats Ottilie with indifference.

Father Müller

If Mother Müller is the brawn of the family, then Father Müller is the brains. While there are descriptions of Mother Müller engaged in strenuous physical activity on the farm—carrying heavy pails of milk on a yoke over her shoulders, carrying a calf on her back to safety during the storm—the readers' only indication of Father Müller's labor is in concert with the other men of the family: "The men . . . went out to harness the horses to the ploughs at sunrise." Father Müller is an atheist, who likes to sit in the parlor in the evening and read *Das Kapital* or play chess with his sons. Father Müller wields not physical but financial power: he is the wealthiest man in the German community, from whom almost all the other farmers rent land. His money allows him to overcome the community's objections to his atheism. When the townsfolk will not elect his son-in-law as sheriff because of Father Müller's beliefs, Father Müller threatens to raise their rent. Mother Müller raises some mild objections, afraid that the pastor will not christen the family's babies; Father Müller dismisses these by telling her that if he pays the pastor good money, the pastor will christen them. His faith in the power of money is tested, however, when Mother Müller is dying: "A hundert tousand tollars in the bank . . . and tell me, tell, what goot does it do?"

Gretchen Müller

Gretchen, who is pregnant at the outset of the story and then gives birth to a son, is the "pet of the family, with the sly, smiling manner of a spoiled child." The reader learns little else of Gretchen, who exists mainly in the story as another example of the Müller daughters' fecundity. In fact, the name Gretchen is a German pet form of Margaret; St. Margaret is the patron saint of expectant mothers.

Huldah Müller

Huldah, whose nickname is Hatsy, is the antithesis of Ottilie in every way. Nimble and full of energy, she is the quintessential Müller daughter, and everything that Ottilie can never be. Hatsy even earns praise from stern Mother Müller ("she's a good, quick girl.") With her wedding just around the corner, Hatsy is just beginning her life, whereas Ottilie's future is one of continued toil and suffering.

Mother Müller

Though the traditions and community of the Müllers are patriarchal, Mother Müller is the true center of the family, their "rock" (at one point she is described standing behind Father Müller "like a dark boulder.") This is not really a paradox, because Mother Müller's character is not at all feminine; she is as manly, if not more so, than Father Müller. Louise, in her initial description of Mother Müller, calls her a "matriarch in men's shoes." The narrator says she has "the stride of a man," and "[strides] about hugely, giving orders right and left." Noting that none of the children looks like Mother Müller, the narrator also states "it was plain that poor Mother Müller had never had a child of her own." Literally, of course, this is untrue, but the description serves to further de-feminize her. Mother Müller is more the foreman of the family than the mother, the engine that keeps the daily operation functioning smoothly. Even when she is on her deathbed, the rest of the Müllers futilely await her orders: "The family crowded into the room, unnerved in panic, lost unless the sick woman should come to herself and tell them what to do for her."

Ottilie Müller

Ottilie is the key figure in "Holiday," as she represents both an unfolding mystery and a symbol of the narrator's own alienation. Though at first she is presented as a crippled servant girl, the reader later learns that she is actually a member of the family, the eldest Müller daughter, deformed in childhood by an unnamed illness. Ottilie is largely ignored by the family, except when being given orders. Her need for connection and recognition surfaces when she shows the narrator her childhood portrait; she wants someone, anyone, to recognize that she is a member of this family. Because Ottilie cannot speak or bear children, the family sees her ability to work as her sole worth as a human being. The ability to bear children is key to the Müllers; all the Müller daughters are in some stage of giving birth. Annetje has a newborn, Gretchen is pregnant and gives birth during the story, and Hatsy has her wedding, which, in this community, means that babies are soon to come. It is inferred that the narrator herself is alone and without children; at the dinner table, as the family guest, she is seated with the men. Her inability to speak German makes her almost without voice in this household, just as Ottilie is. As a fellow outsider, the narrator finds herself drawn to Ottilie and finds herself both pitying her and empathizing with her.

The Narrator

The nameless narrator who tells the story of her visit to the Müller farm is a somewhat mysterious character. At the outset readers learn only that she is a young woman who is going through a difficult time in her life and is looking for an escape, a holiday from her troubles. Little other concrete information is revealed, but through her thoughts and actions she demonstrates kindness, compassion, and a love for nature. The story is told in a detached, observational way, and because the family speaks mostly German, there is very little dialogue and almost none involving the narrator herself. The reader gets the impression that the narrator herself feels detached and alienated from the world, and though she is running from the world, what she really wants and needs is connection. She offers to help Hatsy with chores, she plays with the children, and she reaches out to Ottilie, with whom she identifies as a fellow outsider.

Themes

Alienation

The most obvious example of alienation is that of Ottilie, the crippled Müller daughter. The fact that she is made to labor intensively for the rest of the family is not in itself evidence of alienation, because all of the Müllers work hard. However, by being responsible for cooking and serving all the family's meals, Ottilie is automatically prevented from taking part in the key social events of the Müller family life: the daily meals, the wedding celebration, even her own mother's funeral. Being unable to speak isolates Ottilie from the rest of the family. This alienation is intensified by the Müllers's attitude towards her: unable to deal with their feelings about her and her condition, they simply ignore her. More attention is lavished on the cows and sheep than on poor Ottilie, who is only spoken to when a meal is being requested.

The narrator is also alienated from the family; first, because she is an outsider, second, because she does not speak German. Her childless, husbandless status makes her even more of an oddity in a house fairly bursting with babies. A woman on her own in the early 1920s, when this story was originally written, was looked upon with both curiosity and suspicion. As though to emphasize this unfeminine condition, she is seated on the men's side of the table at dinner.

Because the majority of Porter's work is drawn from personal experience, this story can also be seen as a comment on the alienation Porter experienced as a woman artist on her own in the 1920s, and throughout her life. A woman devoting her life to her work, in this era, was seen as unnatural, someone who has turned her back on the kind of life embraced by the Müller women: serving a man, having his children, and caring for them. The narrator's obvious affection for the Müllers and their way of life shows her ambivalence about this choice.

Sacrifice

Whatever individual opinions, ambitions, and desires of separate family members, the Müllers have sacrificed for the collective family good. They have sacrificed so much of their individuality, in fact, that they all act as parts of one homogenous whole. As the narrator says, "I got a powerful impression that they were all, even the sons-in-law, one human being divided into several separate appearances." Even their appearance is not that separate; they all have the same high cheekbones and "slanted water-blue eyes." Ottilie, whose deformity has rendered her inescapably unique, still shares these features with the rest of the family. Even the boy whom Hatsy marries "resemble[s] her brothers enough to be her brother," maintaining the homogenous nature of the group.

No one has been forced to sacrifice more than Ottilie; she has been reduced to the state of a slave. Both literally and figuratively, she has no voice in the family. Worst of all, she has been forced to sacrifice human connection, by being banished from family gatherings and celebrations. She is completely ignored.

Parallels can be drawn between the Müller family and communist societies. One of the basic tenets of communism is the equality of all citizens, and the equal distribution of the products of labor. This equality necessitates, of course, a quashing of personal ambition and a greater dedication to the

Topics for Further Study

- How would this story have been different if the narrator could speak German? If Ottilie could speak? Write a conversation between the narrator and Ottilie.
- Research the meanings of some of the German names used in the story. Do the meanings of the names correlate to the personality or role of the characters? Explain any connections you discover.
- Research the percentage of American women in the workforce in 1920, 1960, and today. Draw a graph charting the difference. Now research the average wages of women in these three years compared to the average wages of men, and chart your findings.
- What kind of "troubles" do you think the narrator is trying to escape by going on her holiday? Write a "prequel" to this story that describes the problems she is leaving behind and how they came about.

progress of the whole than to the advancement of the individual. Father Müller is a devotee of Karl Marx's *Das Kapital*, but only to the point that it is practical. As Marx did, he rejects religion; however, he cannot resist the temptation to use his power and wealth to get what he wants. In this way, he is illustrative of one of the main weaknesses of communism: its failure to account for the self-serving desires that are a part of human nature.

Cycles of Life and Nature

In escaping to the Müller farm, the narrator has placed herself with a family and a community living in harmony with nature and the natural cycles of life. This has a restorative effect; the narrator says, "It was easier to breathe, and I might even weep, if I pleased. In a very few days I no longer felt like weeping."

In her one month at the Müllers, the narrator witnesses a birth, a death, a wedding, a violent storm, and the rebirth of the landscape that is barren when she arrives. In other words, in just one month she witnesses the complete cycle of life, both for the Müllers and for nature. Only Ottilie seems to be out of sync with these natural rhythms, with her unsteady gait and indeterminate age: "The blurred, dark face was neither young nor old, but crumpled into criss cross wrinkles, irrelevant either to age or suffering."

Gender Roles

Accepted as part of nature's way are the strict gender roles adhered to by the Müllers. The married women stand behind their husbands at the dinner table and serve them. All childcare, of course, is the women's responsibility, as is the milking of the cows. Hatsy's new husband is harshly rebuffed when he offers to help Hatsy with the heavy pails of milk that Mother Müller brings into the house after milking the cows in the storm. "The milk is not business for a man," she tells him.

The narrator, as a guest, is seated on the men's side of the table at dinner. Ottilie does not sit on the women's side of the table, because she is too busy serving the meal. Ottilie and the narrator are also the only two women in the family without children or husbands. In this household, they are almost genderless, and as such their role is uncertain. Ottilie's job is well defined, but the family seems unable to relate to her in any other way. She is not a mother, she is not a wife, she is not a child; like the narrator, she is a grown woman alone, a role for which the Müllers (and much of society in the early 1920s) have no references.

Style

Point of View

"Holiday" is told in the first person point of view. This viewpoint ordinarily gives the reader intimate insights into the main character's feelings, motivation, and character, but in "Holiday" there are only a few scenes in which this is true, mainly those scenes involving Ottilie. The rest of the story is told in a detached, objective style, describing the family and their daily life. For instance, the narrator describes the entire deathbed scene in which the panicked, bewildered Müller family watches Mother Müller die, without expressing a single emotion of her own. Indications of the narrator's state of mind are given more indirectly. For example, when she first arrives, she is disappointed with the landscape, frightened by the dog ("of the detestable German shepherd breed") and begins to write an angry letter to Louise for recommending the farm so highly. After meeting the family and seeing her room, however, she scraps her angry letter and begins a new one: "I'm going to like it here." Her descriptions of the blossoming landscape parallel her own transformation: "Almost every day I went along the edge of the naked wood, passionately occupied with looking for signs of spring. The changes were so subtle and gradual I found one day that branches of willows and sprays of blackberry vine alike were covered with fine points of green; the color had changed overnight, or so it seemed."

The first person point of view also serves to keep the story centered on the lives of the Müller women, because the Müller men leave the house to work in the fields each day, and the narrator, as a woman, would certainly not be asked to go along.

Setting

"Holiday" is set in a German farming community in rural Texas, near the Louisiana border. Though the landscape may be Texan, everything else—the language, dress, traditions—is decidedly German. As the narrator says of the Müllers, "never in any wise did they confuse nationality with habitation."

Because the Müllers's livelihood and prosperity depends on it, the land figures prominently in the story. The narrator and the family view the land in very different ways, however. The narrator comments frequently on the beauty of the land, the spring flowers, the fireflies in the orchard. The family rarely comments on or stops to appreciate the beauty of nature, but sees the land strictly in economic terms.

When the narrator first arrives, she is disappointed by the "soaked brown fields" and "scanty leafless woods" and finds the Müllers's house unwelcoming: "It stood there staring and naked, an intruding stranger." Clearly she is describing not just the house, but herself, emotionally drained and vulnerable from her troubles, and a stranger to the Müller family. Later descriptions of the house are more appealing: "we ate breakfast by yellow lamplight, with the grey damp winds blowing with spring softness through the open windows." Her attic room is described as "homely and familiar." Similarly, as the days go on, she is no longer an "intruding stranger" either, as she comes to know the family and their daily routine.

Dialogue

There is very little dialogue in "Holiday," partly due to the fact that the family speaks mainly German. After the narrator arrives at the Müller farm, she rarely speaks directly in quotation marks; what little she says, she paraphrases for the reader: "I tried to tell her that I was not hungry"; "I told her indeed I did like it so." Ironically, the only direct quotation from the narrator after she arrives at the farm is, "Thank you," which she says to Ottilie when she serves her dinner. This lack of dialogue from the narrator reminds readers of the language barrier and the fact that the narrator has come to the Müller farm for contemplation and solitude, to sort out the troubles of the life she has left behind. As she says, "I loved that silence which means freedom from the constant pressure of other minds and other opinions and other feelings, that freedom to fold up in quiet and go back to my own center." Her chosen silence contrasts dramatically with that of Ottilie, for whom silence has been imposed as a handicap.

Irony

One form of irony is the difference between what is expected and what actually happens. In this story, the narrator takes a much needed holiday by visiting the Müller farm. She gets away from her unidentified troubles and for awhile lives as a guest, not having to work or make her own way. The title of the story becomes ironic in the final paragraphs when the guest gives the handicapped daughter and servant, Ottilie, a little holiday. The family are off at the funeral of the mother. Ottilie expresses her grief for her mother, and at first the narrator assumes she wants to attend the funeral with the other family members. But then she realizes the only thing she can do for Ottilie is give her a little holiday, a ride in the countryside. Ottilie cannot escape her handicap or her place as servant in her own family, but for this brief outing she is treated as a guest and given a reprieve. Thus the word has two applications and is handled ironically.

Historical Context

Communism and the Red Scare

Though "Holiday" was first published in 1960, the influences that shaped the story come from the time at which it was written, the early 1920s. Just a few years earlier, Lenin and the Bolsheviks had overthrown the czar in Russia. The revolution fostered increasing paranoia about communism in the United States, especially for business tycoons who feared the organization of labor. This paranoia, dubbed the Red Scare, led to the enactment of some dubious laws, including the Sedition Act of 1918, which prohibited citizens from making public remarks critical of the government and its policies. Union organizer and socialist Eugene Debs was tried and convicted under this law in 1918 (he was later released when the Sedition Act was repealed in 1921.) Katherine Anne Porter claimed on more than one occasion that she herself was a communist in the early 1920s, when this story was written. Because communism in Russia was still in its early stages, many Americans—especially workers oppressed by the business giants created by the industrial revolution—were sympathetic to its ideals of equality. Later, Porter became disillusioned with communism and abandoned it.

Devaluation of the German Mark

There is some irony in the great prosperity of the Müllers, who live in a German community virtually untouched by American culture, because at the time this story was written the value of the mark in Germany was plummeting to record lows. Before World War I, one U.S. dollar was worth about four German marks; by the end of 1923 one U.S. dollar was worth four *trillion* German marks. The precarious state of the German economy set the stage for Adolf Hitler's rise to power.

New Freedoms for Women

The 1920s were years of unprecedented freedoms for women in the United States. In 1920, women finally achieved the right to vote, a cause that Katherine Anne Porter had championed for many years. Women were also entering the workforce in

Compare & Contrast

- **1920s:** Early in 1920, the Communist Party of the United States (CPUSA) has about 60,000 members. However, the "Red Scare" period, during which Woodrow Wilson's attorney general orders the arrest of some 10,000 suspected communists and anarchists, helps reduce the party's membership to 7,000 by 1929.

  1960s: The Great Depression and the alliance of Russia and the United States in World War II gave the CPUSA membership a boost in the 1930s and 1940s, but this time it is the scare tactics of Senator Joseph McCarthy and the revelation of Stalin's crimes that diminish membership. By 1960 the party has around 10,000 members, down from an estimated peak of 100,000 during the war. The prosperity of the 1960s means that few are inspired to join the party, and though radicalism has increased in the late 1960s, the Communist Party does not play a significant role, and membership remains low.

- **1920s:** During the 1920s, 21.4 percent of women over the age of sixteen are a part of the labor force. Most of these women have clerical, domestic, or factory jobs. Very few have children.

  1960s: In 1960, 37.7 percent of women over the age of sixteen are employed; by 1970 this figure will have increased to 43.3 percent. By 1965, approximately thirty-five percent of mothers with children under eighteen are employed. Women in the workforce are aided by some important legislation in the 1960s. First, in 1963, Congress passes an Equal Pay Act, which requires equal wages for men and women doing equal work. Then in 1964, the Civil Rights Act prohibits discrimination against women by any company with twenty-five or more employees.

- **1920s:** In 1920, farmers make up 27 percent of the labor force. There are close to 6.5 million farms in the United States.

  1960s: In 1960, farmers make up just 8.3 percent of the labor force, and though the population has increased by about seventy-five million, the number of farms in the United States has fallen to under four million.

greater numbers than ever before. However, the woman who worked away from home was still an anomaly, the exception rather than the rule.

Critical Overview

A common criticism of Katherine Anne Porter's work is simply that there is too little of it. In the *New York Times Book Review* in 1939, in a review of *Pale Horse, Pale Rider*, Edith H. Walton writes, "One wishes, only, that she could manage to be more productive." In a 1965 review of *The Collected Stories of Katherine Anne Porter*, a *Time* magazine critic states, "An author who in 71 years has published only 27 stories and one novel can scarcely be considered a major writer."

Though the critics were disappointed with the quantity of her work, most were very pleased with the quality. In a *New Republic* review of *The Collected Stories*, Joseph Featherstone writes, "Few writers in America or anywhere else have matched the purity of her English, her powers of deep poetic concentration, her intelligence, her responsiveness to the inner life of her characters, her sharp sense of the pressing forces of history, nationality, and social atmosphere." Walton puts it more succinctly: "There is, in short, a kind of magic about everything that Miss Porter writes." Howard Moss, in a review of *The Collected Stories* in the *New York Times Book Review*, calls Porter "a poet of the short story."

Though negative reviews of Porter's short stories were in the minority, not everyone was charmed by her often grim view of life and human

A farmhouse in the American South with Spanish moss in the foreground © E. O. Hoppe/Corbis

nature. In the *Time* magazine review of *The Collected Stories* mentioned earlier, the reviewer writes, "She sees her characters less as people who must live than as problems to be solved. There is too little warmth and softness in her art." Bitterness and cynicism crept into some of her later work, especially her novel, *Ship of Fools*. As Mary Gordon writes in a 1995 article on Porter's work in the *New York Times Book Review*, "To act with malignity would seem, in Porter's mind, to be as natural to humans as drawing breath."

However, in this same article, Gordon praises the short story "Holiday": "Lost in the bitterness and cynicism with which Porter wrote *Ship of Fools* is the joy in nature and in simple living that marks her greatest short stories. This pleasure suffused the breathtaking "Holiday" (1960), which took her more than 30 years to write." She mentions Porter's gift for detail: "Porter earns her right to speak about humanity, about life and death, because she has so firmly rooted her perceptions in the soil of the particular." Howard Moss, in the review mentioned earlier, agrees; he describes her stories as "firmly grounded in life; and the accuracy and precision of their surfaces . . . hold in tension the confused human tangle below."

"Holiday" did not receive a great deal of critical attention in its first release in 1960 and was overshadowed by some of Porter's more acclaimed stories when it was released in *The Collected Stories* in 1965. Some reviewers did make mention of it in their review of the book; Joseph Featherstone writes that in addition to her previously released work, "Miss Porter has added four uncollected stories, one of which, "Holiday," ranks with her best." Howard Moss writes in his review, "The author has added . . . a magnificent new long story, 'Holiday.' "

To summarize, many critics agree that Porter was unarguably a master of the short story, whose one outing as a novelist was admirable, but not of the same quality as her shorter works.

Criticism

Laura Pryor

Pryor has a bachelor of arts from University of Michigan and twenty years experience in professional and creative writing with special interest in fiction. In this essay, Pryor examines the ways in which Porter likens the Müller family to animals

What Do I Read Next?

- *The Collected Stories of Katherine Anne Porter* (1965) includes all the stories from Porter's three collections, *Flowering Judas and Other Stories*, *Pale Horse, Pale Rider*, and *The Leaning Tower and Other Stories*, plus four other stories not previously published in book form.
- Porter was well known as a prolific writer of letters to her friends and lovers. The book *Letters of Katherine Anne Porter* (1990) provides a selection of her correspondence dating from 1930 to 1963, including letters to Robert Penn Warren and Hart Crane.
- *Ship of Fools* (1962) is Porter's only novel. Though not as critically acclaimed as her short stories, it was extremely popular when it was released. A 1963 movie was made of the book, starring Vivien Leigh.
- Porter considered fellow southerner Eudora Welty her protégée, as well as a good friend. Porter wrote the introduction for Welty's first collection, *A Curtain of Green and Other Stories* (1941).

in nature, and the implications this comparison has for their treatment of Ottilie.

When the nameless narrator of "Holiday" comes to the Müller farm, she encounters a family living such a natural, basic existence, in harmony with the land about them, that they are almost like a group of animals. Yet they are not living like animals in the negative sense of the phrase; they simply lead their lives in an instinctual, physical manner, never questioning the hard and fast rules that govern their way of life. To emphasize this natural, animal existence, Porter weaves animal similes and metaphors throughout the story, both likening people to animals and vice versa. When Hatsy and Mother Müller milk the cows, for example, their first task is "separating the hungry children from their mothers." After Hatsy pulls the calves away from the cows, the calves bawl "like rebellious babies." Later in the story when Gretchen gives birth to a son, Porter turns the comparison around: "The baby bawled and suckled like a young calf."

The Müller daughters care for their children much like animals in nature. The babies are carried constantly; there are no mentions of playpens or cradles: "Annetje, with her fat baby slung over her shoulder, could sweep a room or make a bed with one hand, all finished before the day was well begun." When caring for their children, the Müller daughters are described as being "as devoted and caretaking as a cat with her kittens."

It is not just the Müllers's actions that are subject to these comparisons, but the Müllers themselves. The whole family shares an "enormous energy and animal force." Gretchen is described as a kind of young lioness: "the tawny Gretchen . . . wore the contented air of a lazy, healthy young animal, seeming always about to yawn." Towards the end of the story, when Ottilie begins to howl with grief, the narrator first believes it is the family dog caught in a trap. This is the only animal comparison used in describing Ottilie; though the family has excluded her from the funeral, they cannot deny her this natural connection with the rest of the family: her grief.

Even the Müllers's dinner customs have parallels in nature. In a pride of lions, for example, the males are always allowed to eat first, even though it is the lionesses that hunt for the food. Similarly, the Müller men eat first while their wives stand behind their chairs and serve them.

Following the same customs and rules they have for generations, the Müllers's life would be a harmonious, unquestioning one, if it were not for Ottilie. On the straight and narrow path that the Müllers tread, life has thrown them an unexpected curve. In nature, weak or injured animals that cannot keep up with the pack or herd are often abandoned, as they constitute a burden and a threat to the livelihood of the group. Ottilie, in her capacity as a tireless servant, has found a way to "keep up." The narrator rationalizes the Müllers's "use" of Ottilie: "they with a deep right instinct had learned to live with her disaster on its own terms, and hers; they had accepted and then made use of what was for them only one more painful event in a world full of troubles." This rationalization, however, begs the question: what would have happened if no "use" could have been made of Ottilie? Then what would the Müllers's instincts have guided them to do? Would they have followed the ways of nature and abandoned her? Or would they have been forced to "evolve," to embrace the idea that a human life could have an inherent value without achievement or contribution?

Society has answered these questions in different ways throughout history. For years the mentally and physically disabled were placed in institutions that were little more than warehouses, relieving families of the burden of their physical care but providing little emotional or intellectual stimulation (a so-called civilized form of abandonment). Gradually efforts to include the disabled in the mainstream of society increased, allowing them new freedoms and enabling them to contribute in their own ways.

The narrator of "Holiday," finding the complications of her own life burdensome, is drawn to the Müllers's simple way of living, the natural rhythms, the clearly defined roles. Yet even while attempting to escape her unnamed troubles, she is confronted with new ones. Her experience with Ottilie forces her to face the fact that no matter how simply people try to live, they will still be confronted with situations that are inherently complicated and problems that have no easy solutions or no solutions at all. She realizes this at the end of the story: "Drawing the pony to a standstill, I studied her face for a while and pondered my ironical mistake. There was nothing I could do for Ottilie, selfishly as I wished to ease my heart of her." She and Ottilie can only enjoy "a little stolen holiday" from the harsh reality of their problems.

Though this story was written in the 1920s, before the rise of Hitler, there are some parallels between the Müllers's predicament and Hitler's plan for Germany and the rest of Europe. The Müllers are all homogenously Aryan, the Hitler ideal: blond, strong, and forceful. Yet in Hitler's Germany, Ottilie would have been exterminated; Hitler had no tolerance for the weak, deformed, or mentally deficient. Hitler's "survival of the fittest" value could also be described as being "in harmony with nature." The German people's desire for a simple answer to their problems, a scapegoat, allowed a despot to rise to power and kill millions of innocent people.

"The narrator finds that a 'simple' life that emulates the ways of nature has both its attractions and limitations."

The narrator finds that a "simple" life that emulates the ways of nature has both its attractions and limitations. Still, in the end it is nature that provides her and Ottilie with solace as they drive down the lane of mulberries to the river, leaving their troubled lives behind, if only for a few moments.

Source: Laura Pryor, Critical Essay on "Holiday," in *Short Stories for Students*, Thomson Gale, 2006.

Mary Titus

In the following essay, Titus explores biographical sources in Porter's "Holiday" and Porter's depiction of "conflicts of gender and vocation" in the story.

According to Katherine Anne Porter's friend, Robert Penn Warren, the "alienation of the artist" occurs as a "basic theme," "implicit, over and over" in her fiction and "finds something close to explicit statement" in her story, "Holiday" (Warren 11). Warren's suggestion, made almost fifteen years ago, points toward a central concern of this beautiful, neglected story. In "Holiday" Katherine Anne Porter depicts the alienation of the woman artist in a culture that advocates motherhood, not authorhood, as a woman's natural and ideal achievement. The story was a painful one for Porter to write, not just because its subject was extremely important to her, but also because it was rooted in two deeply troubling personal experiences, both crucial to her thoughts on gender and vocation. She began "Holiday" in 1923, but was unable to complete the story until 1960.

"Like many women of her generation, Porter viewed motherhood and authorhood as mutually exclusive."

Raised by her grandmother, Katherine Anne Porter grew up exposed to profoundly contradictory views of a woman's proper role. The ambivalence and anxiety about gender role and vocation apparent in her fiction reflects the shifting cultural positions on women that surrounded her as she moved from childhood in 1890's rural west Texas to young womanhood in 1920's Greenwich Village. Porter's grandmother lived in and accepted the domestic sphere of nineteenth century women, but Porter grew up witnessing first the achievements of the New Woman, who often chose a career and social activism over courtship and marriage, and then the gradual discrediting of those achievements and ultimate transformation of the New Woman from self-made heroine to old maid and "invert." The women of Porter's own generation, particularly artists and professionals, experienced powerful social pressures not to make choices which could potentially separate them from the heterosexual path of marriage and childbearing. Frequently this pressure came in the form of accusations of sexual deviance. For a heterosexual and ultimately heterosexist woman like Katherine Anne Porter, suggestions that her career ambitions unsexed her were deeply disturbing. Although she rebelled against her upbringing, seeking far more expansive and varied opportunities for creative expression as well as intellectual, cultural and sexual freedom, her rebellion was characterized, in the words of her biographer Joan Givner, by "a complicated ambivalence" (Givner 67).

Porter never entirely relinquished a belief that domesticity, marriage, and most of all, childbearing denote female success; as Givner comments, it is remarkable "how closely linked her idea of femininity was with fertility" (Givner 92). Like many women of her generation, Porter viewed motherhood and authorhood as mutually exclusive. In her mind, becoming an artist required an unnatural rejection or repression of her sexuality; it meant becoming, in Porter's own words, "monstrous." Among her unpublished papers are notes on Saint Rose that clearly express her struggles with conflicts of gender and vocation. Writing of women saints and women artists she concludes:

> The body of woman is the repository of life, and when she destroys herself it is important. It is important because it is not natural, arid woman is natural or she is a failure. . . . Therefore women saints, like women artists are monstrosities. . . . You might say that if they are saints or artists they are not women.

Implicit in these notes is the assumption that a woman is defined by her biological capabilities; her body "is the repository of life," and if she denies this she "destroys herself." Overall, the influences of her family background and cultural milieu fed an "anxiety of authorship" in Porter, and her works bear the marks of struggle, often simultaneously "identifying with and revising the self-definitions patriarchal culture has imposed" on women (Gilbert and Gubar 51, 79).

In "Holiday" Katherine Anne Porter turned her attention fully toward questions of gender and vocation. The story sets an anonymous narrator down on a black-land Texas farm in very early spring. Although characterization is cryptic, everything suggests that this narrator is an artist, most likely an aspiring writer. "Holiday" traces her observations of a culture that binds women to the natural order through marriage and parturition. The story consistently exposes and resists patriarchal authority; however, on other issues it is more ambivalent. As the natural world unfolds into spring, the narrator must come to terms with painful feelings of alienation and sterility. In particular, she must face her fear that, in choosing another path, she may have "destroyed" herself, become like her narrative double, Ottilie, the handicapped Mueller daughter. What is remarkable about "Holiday" are the times when the story expresses joyous acceptance of the maimed, alienated self. In a sequence of epiphanic moments, the narrator realizes that although her life choice may separate her from traditional womanhood, she yet remains a part of nature, one more marvelous creation. At the story's close, Porter's narrator goes on a second holiday, taking a brief but free and festive journey away from the alienation and anxiety of being a woman and an artist in a patriarchal culture.

Porter began "Holiday," in 1923, but was unable to complete the story until 1960. According to her introduction to her 1965 *Collected Stories,* "The story haunted me for years and I made three separate versions, with a certain spot in all three where the thing went off track." Typescript evidence reveals that the "certain spot" that stumped Porter was her opening. She struggled with setting up a context for the narrative, in particular describing the "troubles" that brought her narrator to the Mueller farm. Her decision in 1960 was to sidestep the entire problem, and she does this by choosing silence. The published story begins with a cryptic allusion to "troubles" and then a refusal to tell: "It no longer can matter what kind of troubles they were, or what finally became of them." The voice here originates in the Katherine Anne Porter of 1960, approximately thirty-seven years after she first started "Holiday" At the age of seventy she could truthfully say of her troubles when she was 23 and 24 (her age when some of the story's source events occurred) or 33 and 34 (her age when she wrote the story): "It can no longer matter what kind of troubles they were, or what finally became of them." That Porter did have troubles at both times in her life, and both times have bearing on "Holiday" is very clear from biographical evidence. Both moments, a decade apart, probably underlie the narrative's opening silence, and both illuminate Porter's final text.

The first biographical source for "Holiday" is an event Porter rarely mentioned and seems to have hoped would disappear from the record: her nine-year-long early marriage, begun at age 16, to John Koontz, a young Texan from a wealthy Swiss family (which she consistently identified as German) (Givner 88). John Koontz proved an unhappy choice for Porter, and the marriage was full of disagreements. Looking at photographs from these nine years and reading the biographical record of 1906 to 1915, one discovers a young woman full of romantic notions, engaging, flirtatious, eager to dress well and show herself off to advantage. She also longed to begin a family and romanticized her relationship to her sister Gay's first child, Mary Alice, dreaming that she would become the child's "Tante," and pretending "to herself that she and not Gay was the child's mother" (Givner 96). Unhappily, the marriage met few of her expectations. John Koontz seems to have been a steady but conservative husband, and his family on the whole disapproved of Porter's flirtatious personality and spendthrift pleasures. Furthermore there were no children. The marriage to Koontz likely provided some of the setting and family characterization of "Holiday," from the Koontz ranch, which Porter enjoyed visiting, to the death of the family patriarch, Henry Koontz, after exposure in a winter storm while tending his cattle (Givner 88–95).

According to Joan Givner, the opening of "Holiday" reflects Porter's final response to her marriage—flight. Givner draws language from that opening to describe Porter's personal decision: "Once she faced the fact that her marriage was 'trouble that did not belong to her' she hardened her resolve to run from it 'like a deer'" (Givner 98). Certainly all of Porter's "tradition, background, and training"—to continue quoting from "Holiday"—had taught her otherwise; her flight from John Koontz when she was in her early twenties was a dramatic and devastating flight away from the expectations surrounding the life of a young woman from her family background. Porter's decision not only shocked the Koontz's but also incited her father's intense disapproval, which did not diminish for years to come (Givner 99). However, for Porter's vocational aspirations escape was crucial, the first step toward an independent, creative career.

"Holiday" also rises out of another biographical moment, one of the more mysterious in Porter's life. Her letters indicate that she wrote most of the story during 1924, while she was involved with Francisco Aguilera, a romantic Chilean studying for a Ph.D. at Yale. According to Porter many years later, Aguilera was the source for naming her fictional alter-ego, Miranda. The relationship was brief; by the end of the summer Porter and Aguilera were no longer involved; however, Porter's letters to Genevieve Taggard that fall state that she is pregnant. Joan Givner thinks that this pregnancy never actually occurred; in fact Givner speculates that Porter could not bear children (Givner 92). None of Porter's friends from the time ever noticed any physical changes, and none of Porter's extant letters, except those to Taggard, mention the pregnancy. What is intriguing is the convergence of three incidents in the letters to Taggard: the pregnancy, the appearance of Miranda, and the creation of "Holiday." To excerpt from the letters:

> October 31, 1924: "I am completing two stories, both far too long in germinating."
>
> November 14, 1924: "I have finished my story 'Holiday' in a bath of bloody sweat, and am resting . . . dear darling', had you heard, out of the air, maybe, that I am going to have a baby about the middle of January? Now I've passed the danger period of losing it I can't keep silent any longer. Write and tell me how mad I am."
>
> November 28, 1924: "jedsie, darling—you're not to trouble about me. I'm doing well enough, I have been a madwoman, and I know it, but I can't possibly come out of my trance to establish any mood of regret. So far as the child is concerned, it is all more

> than well—but everything else in my personal life has been a blank failure—in all, I mean, that touches my love. But, I will see you afterward. I will bring Miranda. (Her name and sex have been definitely chosen for seven months at least) and we will talk about everything for days."
>
> Thursday, undated: "On December second my child was born prematurely and dead, and though I have never been in danger, still it is better in every way to be quiet. . . . My baby was a boy. It was dead for half a day before it was born. There seems to be nothing to say about it."

Certainly there is much here that we can never know; the letters are cryptic, and they form the only known record of these events in Porter's life. Yet after acknowledging that supposition can only partially unravel this mystery, speculation is invited, tracing the few threads that seem to form a pattern.

The letters first break silence and then reinvoke it. There is "nothing to say"; "it is better in every way to be quiet." They twice confess madness: "tell me how mad I am"; "I have been a madwoman and I know it." They suggest that Porter was in a heightened mental state—a "trance." She views the child, whom she knows will be female and named Miranda, as "more than well," a mark of success in a "personal life [that] has been a blank failure." All the positive birth imagery in the letters, however, belongs to her writing, not her pregnancy. Two stories are "germinating" and "Holiday" comes to birth, "in a bath of bloody sweat," a labor so great that afterwards Porter is "resting." The arrival of "Holiday" coincides with the end of the "danger period"of losing the baby, each is at least a viable rough draft.

Overall, the letters as much as describe the potential birth of the fictional alter-ego, Miranda, as they do an actual pregnancy. Conflating childbirth and creative literary production, they suggest that Porter was seeking a way to resolve the conflicts between gender and vocation that she found so painful and so fundamental. Rather than producing a child, and so fulfilling biological potential, she will produce Miranda, an equally marvelous being. She will be no less a mother because she is an artist, for the creative labors are akin, the outcomes equal.

That Porter's labor to resolve her conflicts of gender and vocation feels both deeply personal and dangerous is apparent in both the repeated invocations of silence and repeated fears that she has become a madwoman. And in the end all her hoped for achievements come to nothing. "Holiday" lay unfinished for thirty-six years; the child, a boy, was stillborn. Dead and male, the child is a bitter conclusion to Porter's hopes. The brave new world, the many wonders, which would accompany Miranda, whether she be a viable alter-ego for Porter's fiction, or an actual child, are lost—she can be neither mother, nor author. As she writes Taggard, "it is better in every way to be quiet. . . . There seems to be nothing to say."

In "Holiday," the story that emerged in "a bath of bloody sweat" but then lay incomplete for over thirty years, Porter also pursued a healing vision, seeking an image of the woman writer as a part of fertile nature, neither unnatural, nor monstrous. Like Porter fleeing her first marriage, the narrator of "Holiday" is a refugee from love. Her disillusionment, underlying the story's opening silence, emerges when she first sees the warm light of the farm house kitchen and finds her "feelings changed again toward warmth and tenderness, or perhaps just an apprehension that I could feel so, maybe, again." The hesitancies of her phrasing suggest the extent of her learned caution. That she was once steeped in love's romantic promises is evident in her confession that all the German she knows is "five small deadly sentimental songs of Heine's learned by heart." German represents the patriarchal language in "Holiday"; it was also the language of the Koontz's. In "Holiday" the narrator's knowledge of German is limited to sentimental cliches; wise now, she is aware that such knowledge, taken to heart, is "deadly." Most likely through her youthful marriage to John Koontz, Porter first confronted the disjunction between romantic language and actual experience.

To live at the Mueller farm is to live in the heart of a patriarchal order, as Porter makes entirely evident. The narrator's friend Louise identifies the Mueller's as "a household in real patriarchal style—the kind of thing you'd hate to live with." Old Testament figures, the Muellers seem larger than life, solid, physical, bound to the natural cycles of the earth and body. Obedient to these cycles, the family women follow lives devoted to marriage, childbirth, the care of men and of children. The story is unabashed about the narrator's entrance into this ultimate patriarchal order, ruled by "Old father, God almighty himself, with whiskers and all." Choosing to stay with such a family, this alienated, solitary woman chooses to set herself against a culture where gender relations are traditional in structure and unquestioned. In such an environment, her own choices and struggles stand out clearly for self-examination, and in the course of "Holiday" she explores her feelings about women's roles under patriarchy and her relationship to them, at times seriously opening up these roles to question at other times describing them with longing or reverence. On the surface, the fecundity of the farm world suggests that the family's patriarchal order is not just natural, but even blessed. Yet throughout, "Holiday" troubles this smooth surface, providing glimpses of the limitations for women of life under patriarchal rule.

"Holiday" satirizes its ruling patriarch, Father Mueller. A highly successful capitalist who reads *Das Kapital* reverently, Father Mueller continually buys more land, extending his authority outward from the family holdings, and then uses his economic power to control local politics. At home he maintains a similar economic control over his children, keeping them and their offspring within the family house, refusing to understand why marriage should "take a son or daughter from him." In this way, too, Father Mueller builds his wealth. The labors of his offspring, their spouses and their children, contribute to his profits, for it is assumed natural in a patriarchal, capitalist organization like this family that all the labor of family members should be unpaid. Why then would Father Mueller want to let any children leave his house? "He always could provide work and a place in the household for his daughters' husbands." Resting in the parlor evenings, reading *Das Kapital,* travelling to town to make purchases, or seated in "his patriarch's place at the head of the table," Father Mueller heads up a hierarchical organization in which all other men and women are ranged, each in their place, beneath him, obedient to his word.

Besides Father Mueller, the men in "Holiday" receive little attention; they are not the interest of the narrative. Throughout "Holiday" is laden with imagery of maternity: women marry, give birth, care for human and animal offspring, milk cows and feed men in a landscape moving from winter to spring, where the fields lie "ploughed and ready for the seed." As DeMouy rightly points out, "Maternity is the mark of this tale, made in so many places it astounds. Imagery, symbolism, setting, time, character, even gesture communicate maternity in 'Holiday'" (167).

The Mueller women's lives, devoted to the domestic and nurturant labors, represents women's lives within patriarchal tradition. The narrator, overly self-conscious about her own choices, is drawn to them, finding "the almost mystical inertia" of the Mueller's minds relaxing, for it releases her from her own intense mental activity. Their "muscular life" provides a "repose" for her intellectual one. Yet it is not a life she would choose. In the course of the narrative, she notes how repetitive and unreflecting this family's day may be and recognizes that they lack the intellectual and aesthetic awareness that is so central to her own consciousness. Even the play of the Mueller children repeats the laborious demands of constant nurturing. In silence they move their toys through a day's tasks: "They fed them, put them to bed; they got them up and fed them again." For variation, the children "would harness themselves to their carts," an image that confirms what the text everywhere else suggests, that the Mueller's life is little different from animal life. It is physical, instinctive. The women in particular exist in a state of mental sleep, or half-waking. For example, Gretchen, the family's favorite daughter, "wore the contented air of a lazy, healthy young animal, seeming always about to yawn." Raising their children, the women "were as devoted and caretaking as a cat with her kitten."

In the portrayal of Mother Mueller, the matriarch, "Holiday" suggests most powerfully the negative side of traditional womanhood. If Father Mueller as capitalist and patriarch controls the labor of his family, Mother Mueller works to sustain the gender roles which order and perpetuate the family structure. Called "the old mother," by the narrator, she emerges from the descriptive language surrounding her as a powerful, dark, somewhat fearsome woman, whose voice is a raucous shout. Her colors, amidst the pale blues and greens which characterize the family and the landscape, are elemental blacks and browns. With her "seamed dry face . . . brown as seasoned bark" and her teeth "blackened," she looms behind her husband "like a dark boulder," suggesting the forces of nature which underpin and sustain the patriarchal order. The old mother's power is most evident in the milking scenes that dominate her characterization. That she is fully bound to this labor is suggested by the description of her daily passage to the barn wearing a "wooden yoke, with the milking pails covered and closed with iron hasps." Her unmarried daughter Hatsy does not yet carry the full maternal burden—the "milk yoke"; thus she is described as running beside her mother, lightfooted, swinging two tin pails. When later Hatsy's new husband tries to carry the full pails of milk, the old mother stops him, shouting "No! . . . not you. The milk is not business for a man." Milk is women's business, and money is men's in this story.

Both Father and Mother Mueller work to maintain these distinctions around which gender has historically been structured. When she dies and at her deathbed he momentarily loses his faith in money; the family is thrown into disorder, unbound from its necessary verities. As Father Mueller cries out over Mother Mueller's body, "hundert thousand dollars . . . tell me, tell, what goot does it do?" the children break into a "tumult utterly beyond control." However the mother's death only briefly shatters the family order. Because that order is structured around natural cycles, the entire farm confirms its continuance: "they would hurry back from the burial to milk the cows."

When the narrator of "Holiday" arrives she feels she has no part in the natural cycles that structure the Mueller world. She is a winter figure who comes to this fecund patriarchal order seeking healing and renewal. She rides to the farm on the felicitously named spring wagon, whose mysterious harnesses suggest her own interest in finding a way to attach herself to the positive, forward movement of the season. Yet she is in every way separate from the Mueller family, particularly in the intellectual vocation most evident in her fascination with language. Although she longs for freedom from hearing and speaking, the narrator is obsessed with interpretation of signs of all sorts. When we first meet her, seated on her trunk at the station, she is thinking about writing, mentally composing, a letter to her friend Louise, and "beginning to enjoy" the task just as it is interrupted by the Mueller boy. Louise is clearly a discriminating reader, and the narrator is much concerned with her audience. She is also mindful of the differences between fact and fantasy, as well as the requisite talents for a literary career. She has decided that "unless [Louise] was to be a novelist, there was no excuse for her having so much imagination." One might note as well that for this narrator a career as novelist can certainly be a woman's goal. The contents of Louise's beloved attic further confirm this awareness.

As she rides toward the farm, the narrator continues to ponder language and composition. She admires the formal qualities of "a river shaped and contained by its banks, or a field stripped down to its true meaning." The harness of the spring wagon, "a real mystery," takes up much of her thinking, as she attempts to find meaningful order in its structure: "It met and clung in all sorts of unexpected places; it parted company in what appeared to be strategic seats of jointure . . . Other seemingly unimportant parts were bound together irrevocably with wire." Later in the narrative, after she finds herself bound to Ottilie, the Mueller's handicapped daughter, with "a filament lighter than cobweb," the narrator will demonstrate her own ability to handle the mysterious connections of the harness, when she takes Ottilie out for a second holiday journey in the spring wagon. With her curiosity about language, the narrator also puzzles over the name "spring wagon," unable to see why it should belong to this "exhausted specimen." It is a testimony to the intricacy of this story's symbolic layering that the wagon's progress, "with a drunken, hilarious swagger," also describes Ottilie's movements: "Her head wagged. . . . Her shaking hand seemed to flap . . . in a roguish humor." Both the wagon and Ottilie are "exhausted specimens," and both are also, as we shall see, the unexpected vehicles of the narrator's rejuvenation.

The narrator's interest in language and meaning exists simultaneously with a longing to escape from language, to descend into a preverbal internal world from which she can be reborn. As she settles into her attic room, and hears the murmur of German beneath her, she finds pleasure in listening to the "muted unknown language which was silence with music in it." Once relieved of the possibility of communication, she imagines she can travel toward her essential self:

> I loved that silence which means freedom from the constant pressure of other minds and other opinions and other feelings, that freedom to fold up in quiet and go back to my own center, to find out again, for it is always a rediscovery, what kind of creature it is that rules me finally.

The narrator's journey from her troubles is also a journey toward freedom, and that freedom entails not only discovering her own authority, what "rules [her] finally," but also her own "opinions" and "feelings." She must escape her own life and learned expectations, and she must free herself from the expectations inscribed in language itself. Anne Goodwyn Jones has commented on the movement away from language in "Holiday," suggesting that "it is precisely the experience of moments of prelinguistic experience, of unintelligible sound, that [allows] the narrator to begin to work through her own suffering." From her descent into a state free of language's structures and ingrained, controlling meanings, the narrator can emerge essentially linguistically newborn. She can "re-enter the symbolic so that eventually she can tell us this story."

It is important to keep in mind here that the language the narrator cannot understand, German, is the language of patriarchy in the story. To find herself as a woman artist, she must first escape this language, and thus escape the expectations for women which it inscribes. Finding a location outside patriarchal texts is a necessary act for the narrator early in "Holiday"; it is a stage in her personal revision and healing. As Jones argues, the break from language in "Holiday" represents a break "from the stable and coercive representational structures, relational possibilities, and dichotomous subject constructions of the patriarchal . . . household." It is just such a break that the narrator desires: she is looking for a new way to define herself as a woman, outside of those structures. She seeks to construct her own language, first by finding silence.

Looking for guidance on her journey, the narrator follows the advice of her friend and mentor, Louise. Louise is an interesting figure, most notably as a storyteller, who possesses "something near to genius for making improbable persons, places, and situations sound attractive. She told amusing stories that did not turn grim on you until a little while later." Louise sends the narrator to a place rich in symbolic potential for an aspiring woman writer—the attic of a patriarchal household. Although the narrator could sleep downstairs with the family, in what womanly Hatsy clearly thinks is a "better place," both the narrator and Louise love the attic—"My attic," as Louise fondly calls it. High in the rafters of the Mueller house, the attic is a small sloped-ceiling bedroom that has sheltered at least one other literary women in the past. Piled in a corner are the writings of nineteenth century women: *"The Duchess,* Ouida, Mrs. E.D.E.N. Southworth, Ella Wheeler Wilcox's poems." The inhabitant before Louise was "a great reader," who passed on these women's texts to her successors.

The description of the attic room in Porter's "Holiday," with its shingled ceiling, "stained in beautiful streaks, all black and grey and mossy green," recalls the inscribed walls of Charlotte Perkins Gilman's "The Yellow Wallpaper." In fact the room as a whole, tucked up at the top of the patriarchal household, is a familiar location in women's writing: the place of retreat and creativity. Porter's manuscripts indicate that she worked at length on her description of the attic; in fact it was the location of most of her revisionary labor. Not only does she place it atop an especially patriarchal household, but she also describes the house itself in a way that recalls the Gothic manor houses in which fictional women guilty of too much imagination so often have languished. In the final version of "Holiday," the house is "staring and naked, an intruding stranger" in the landscape; "The narrow windows and steeply sloping room oppressed me," the narrator confesses, "I wished to turn away and go back." In contrast to the house, the attic room is far from alien—it is "homely and familiar." The attic comforts the narrator, for it confirms Louise's description, but even more is suggested. Although it is a place the narrator has never been physically, yet it is a place she knows, and has visited before. Perhaps entering this space so familiar to creative women within the patriarchal household, she feels she has come to her own right location. Joan Givner succinctly points to this possibility, noting: "In short, the situation [of the attic bedroom] is that of the woman writer's anomalous position under patriarchy." It is interesting that in her drafts of "Holiday," Porter's description of the attic contained images of both the sexual renunciation and the deathliness she feared accompanied her vocation. In both the second and third draft; she elaborates on the room's bed. To draw from the third draft, "The puffy big bed suggested goosefeather under the white knitted counterpane, the flat white pillows stood up like small marble tombstones."

"Holiday's," exploration of a woman writer's anxiety about vocation and patriarchal expectations coalesces in the narrator's relationship with Ottilie, the Mueller's handicapped daughter. The narrator powerfully identifies with Ottilie, feeling that she and this mute woman are "even a part of each other." The text invites a reading of Ottilie as the narrator's double, a doubling that Jane Krause DeMouy extends further when she reads the unnamed narrator as Miranda, Porter's fictional counterpart. Certainly all three women—Porter, the narrator, and Ottilie—are linked by their estrangement from women's traditional lives in "Holiday," the narrator and Ottilie are both alienated from the patriarchal household, from its visual affiliations, its language, and its cycles of marriage and parturition. Like Ottilie, this self-conscious, literary narrator is "a stranger and hopeless outsider."

Because she simultaneously believes in and rejects the definition of female identity everywhere expressed by the Mueller women's labors, the narrator is both drawn to Ottilie, and horrified by her. She sees a woman free from sexual and emotional attachments, mute and unknowable, and she sees a woman who is unsexed and disfigured, barred from participating in the traditional life patterns of the other Mueller women. In the narrator's mind, Ottilie is both the most complete and the most damaged human being in that household; in short, her feelings toward "the servant" are deeply ambivalent. In an extended passage, she meditates on the consequences of Ottilie's isolation:

> I got a powerful impression that [the Muellers] were all, even the sons-in-law, one human being divided into several separate appearances. The crippled servant girl . . . seemed to me the only individual in the house. Even I felt divided into many fragments. . . . But the servant girl, she was whole, and belonged nowhere.

To be bound or to have been bound to others is to lose one's wholeness and individuality. Yet in the common mass there is comfort, familiar rituals, shared love. Ottilie represents a location outside patriarchy; she " belonged nowhere." Like the intellectual or rebellious woman in the 19th century attic, this mute, painfully crippled woman in the Mueller kitchen and her counterpart, the solitary, observant narrator with her secret wound, inhabit "the marginal life of the household."

The narrator's anxiety about her pursuit of an alternative language is also apparent in her descriptions of Ottilie with her uncontrollable body, "formless mouth," and eyes "strained with anxiety." Outside of language, Ottilie appears outside of meaning, incomprehensible, unreal: "Her muteness seemed nearly absolute; she had no coherent language of signs;" "nothing could make her seem real, or in any way connected with the life around her." Ottilie's alienation disturbs the narrator, for it suggests the risks of her own quest to escape patriarchal inscription and limitation. Rejecting the verities of language and tradition, she risks losing all order and meaning, risks incoherence, silence, or insanity.

Throughout "Holiday," the narrator suffers painful, contradictory emotions through her identification with Ottilie. At times it seems to her that Ottilie is whole and unplaced, "neither young nor old, living her own secret existence." At other times she sees Ottilie as a victim, her face broken in "blackened seams as if the perishable flesh had been wrung in a hard cruel fist." In her identification with Ottilie, the narrator draws up waters from her own well of unhappiness. She watches the kitchen door through which Ottilie enters with "wincing eyes, as if I might see something unendurable enter through it." What is unendurable to confront is her own projected suffering, and in her wish for Ottilie's death—"Let it be now, let it be *now*"—the narrator expresses a desire to escape the profound suffering that accompanies her own sense of isolation and difference.

Ottilie and the narrator are the women in the Mueller house who do not marry and bear children; they are outside, unsexed, "mutilated, almost destroyed." Ottilie's illness, which the narrator describes as " congenital"—or from the womb—bespeaks her own womb-sickness, or unnatural female condition. In this sense of being unnatural, even monstrous, the two women express Porter's own fears. Jane Krause DeMouy makes this connection well, noting that the narrator—like Porter—"cannot change her ingrained view of femininity and its fulfillment; neither can she live that way. Thus in her mind she is like Ottilie, an arrested and crippled figure of a woman who will never bear life." Yet "Holiday" manages to work through this terrible confrontation with the mutilated female self to some reconciliation. Ottilie is as much the narrator's double—in whom she confronts the dangers potential in her vocational choice—as she is the vehicle of the narrator's joyous realization that this choice may bring not only losses, but also positive, compensating rewards. Bound by their difference, both women are excluded from traditional womanhood, but in "Holiday" this does not mean, finally, that they are entirely "not natural" or "monstrosities"—Porter's words for women artists and saints.

To counter such anxieties, Porter turns to the natural world, and shows how her narrator lives in and is even blessed by its beauty. Although her culture may view her as unnatural, she yet participates in the essential life impulse that flows through everything and finds a joyous freedom in the marginality and difference that sets her outside of patriarchal expectation. "Holiday" achieves its affirmative vision in a series of epiphanic moments. In each the narrator finds that both she and her double—the figure of her most extreme sense of alienation—belong to nature and participate in its festive beauty.

Porter establishes the narrator and Ottilie's distinct difference from the Mueller household in a single, sweeping perspective. Out for her morning walk, the narrator looks back toward the farm and sees that "The women were deep in the house, the men were away to the fields, the animals were turned down into the pastures, and only Ottilie was visible." The two women literally stand out from the mass life of the family and the animals. This moment of recognition leads to a complex and intimate moment with Ottilie. Obeying the mute woman's gestures, the narrator follows her into her cloistered bedroom. In contrast to the attic, which suggested the intellectual inheritance of literary sisterhood, Ottilie's room suggests the prison of silent, unwanted women's lives. It is "bitter-smelling and windowless," with a "blistered looking-glass"—an image suggesting Ottilie's distorted reflection of the narrator. Here the narrator learns that Ottilie is not only the eldest of the Mueller sisters, but also bound to her with ties equally intimate. Looking at a photograph of Ottilie as a sturdy child, the narrator realizes that "the bit of cardboard connected her at once somehow to the world of human beings . . . for an instant some filament lighter then cobweb spun itself out between that living center in her and in me, a filament from some center that held us all bound to our unescapable common source, so that her life and mine were kin, even a part of each other." This recognition is powerful and fearsome; Ottilie flees and the narrator is left gazing at "the photograph face downward on the chest." If she glanced up at this moment, one wonders, would she see her own face in the "blistered mirror" "mutilated, almost destroyed," like Ottilie's face?

The moment is brief. Yet in her epiphanic recognition that she and Ottilie are not only kin to each other, but bound with all life to an "unescapable common source," the narrator realizes that no matter how much she may be alienated from what the story figures as the natural cycles of human life, yet she is no less a part of life itself. In their source, she and Ottilie are joined to humanity. This healing knowledge, which the narrator reaches through her bond with a woman who is as much or more Other to patriarchy than she is herself, builds on an earlier moment in the narrative when the narrator found that although her freedom from domestic duties separated her from traditional women's lives, it also freed her for aesthetic appreciation. In fact her freedom brings her into a relation with the natural world that may be equally if not more enriching. Rather than being a laboring participant, she can become an appreciative observer.

Often spending her days following a narrow lane down to the river, "passionately occupied with looking for signs of spring," the narrator seeks renewal and vocational confirmation from the natural world, and she receives both in one glorious gust of beauty. Returning late to the house, she finds the orchard "abloom with fireflies"; she had never seen "anything that was more beautiful":

> The flower clusters shivered in a soundless dance of delicately woven light, whirling as airily as leaves in a breeze, as rhythmically as water in a fountain. Every tree was budded out with this living, pulsing fire as fragile and cool as bubbles.

The soundless, intricate movement of the fireflies evokes thoughts of art as much as nature in the narrator. She is touched both literally and figuratively in their transforming light: "When I opened the gate, their light shone on my hands like foxfire. When I looked back, the shimmer of golden light was there, it was no dream." Entering the house, she immediately meets Hatsy "on her knees in the dining room, washing the floor with heavy dark rags," doing her labor at night so that "the men with their heavy boots would not be tracking it up again." The juxtaposition is vivid and intentional. Bound to her domestic labors, particularly her service to men in the household, Hatsy may be part of the cycles of parturition, but she is also alienated from nature as a source of aesthetic beauty, and from the blessing it can lay on the hands of the woman artist. Her hands are full of "heavy dark rags," not of visionary light that is yet "no dream."

It is the death of Mother Mueller that brings the narrator to a final sequence of confrontations with her own life choices, her underlying fears, and her recognition of the viability of laughter and the possibility of joy. While the funeral procession gathers outside the house, the narrator, up in her attic, undergoes a vicarious experience of dying. Porter rewrote this moment several times in her drafts, it was important to her, yet its meaning remains elusive. The published narrative tells us that the narrator realized, on the funeral day, "for the first time, not death, but the terror of dying." And overcome by that terror she lay in her room and felt that she too was passing away—"it was as if my blood fainted and receded with fright, while my mind stayed wide awake to receive the awful impress." In her first draft Porter was even more explicit about the death experience:

> I went to my room and lay down, an awful foreboding certainty closed over me like a vast impersonal hand. Life was squeezed away drop by drop, a cell at a time I was dying as I lay there.

In both versions, when the funeral procession moves off, she is relieved; "As the sounds receded, I lay there not thinking, not feeling, in a mere drowse of relief and weariness." The vicarious experience seems in part a passing away of all the mother stood for in the story. Lying on her white bed, with its pillows like "small marble tombstones," the narrator may be letting go of her own motherhood. With the passing of the matriarch's body, she is set free from the rigidity of Mother Mueller's view—milk is the business for a woman. Relinquishing once essential, self-defining beliefs, she experiences a sort of death and release. Her drowse is broken by a howl, not from a trapped dog, as she first imagines, figuring still her own entrapment, but instead from Ottilie crying out in the kitchen below. Ottilie's grief is her own, but at the same time it is the narrator's Both women are experiencing—as internal and external fact—the loss of the mother. It is interesting that women who have become mothers cannot hear this grief. As she heads toward the kitchen, the narrator sees Gretchen peacefully asleep, "curled up around her baby."

When the narrator enters the kitchen, Ottilie lays her "head on [her] breast," as if she is the narrator's child, the grieving, crippled self birthed with her aspirations. Gathering Ottilie in her arms, the narrator helps her into the spring wagon, which she can now harness herself. Her journey seems ironic at first, for initially she imagines that Ottilie wishes to be a part of the funeral procession, to belong to and be governed by the family rituals, and thus she hurries to join the others, "a bumbling train of black beetles," "going inch-meal up the road." Her haste suggests she will attempt to bring her crippled and anomalous self back into the old order, pursuing a mindless, insect-like uniformity. But as the narrator guides the wild, swaggering spring wagon toward the dark procession, she touches Ottilie and confronts fully and irrevocably the fact of this other woman's—and her own—difference:

> my fingers slipped between her clothes and bare flesh, ribbed and gaunt and dry against my knuckles. My sense of her realness, her humanity, this shattered being that was a woman, was so shocking to me that a howl as doglike and despairing as her own rose in me unuttered and died again, to be a perpetual ghost.

In an intriguing discussion of "Holiday," Joan Givner reads this moment in a biographical light. Touching Ottilie's bare flesh, she argues, the narrator touches the possibility of love between women, particularly women artists, a love that frees them to take paths other than those laid out for traditional womanhood. For this reader, it is more likely that touching Ottilie, the narrator experiences not potential physical relations but rather pure anguish, touching once again her own crippled womanhood, as she viewed it. The howl that rises in her is again grief at the loss of the mother within herself, echoing Ottilie's earlier howl at the mother's death without. The narrator's "unuttered" yet "despairing" howl expresses a never completely comforted grief that belonged to her creator as well as to herself. As Porter's fiction again and again confirms, the loss—the giving up of traditional womanhood—remained in her mind like a "perpetual ghost" that continued to haunt her for most of her life.

What is marvelous in "Holiday" is the recognition of joyous compensations for the loss of traditional womanhood. As the narrator reverberates with shock and despair, Ottilie breaks into laughter and "clap[s] her hands for joy. . . . The feel of the hot sun on her back, the bright air, the jolly senseless staggering of the wheels, the peacock green of the heavens: something of these had reached her." Ottilie's joy springs from the natural world around her and thus repeats again for the narrator the lesson of her epiphany in the blooming orchard. Although she may not lead the life considered natural for a woman, she is yet a part of nature, in no way alienated from its beauty and blessings, and thus neither is her counterpart Ottilie. Together the two women share a celebratory moment that is rebirth and liberation. Like a baby, Ottilie "gurgled and rocked in her seat." She leans on the narrators and marvels Miranda-like, "waving loosely around her as if to show me what wonders she saw." The narrator joins her celebration, recognizing that both she and Ottilie are "equally the fools of life." This is a healing realization, full of the laughter that accompanies the rollicking wagon and Ottilie's wagging head.

Yet Ottilie and her companion are also "fellow fugitives from death," as the narrator goes on to realize; they have escaped the mother's funeral, and they are momentarily beyond the patterns of life and death which governed the matriarch. In its final paragraph, "Holiday" echoes Frost's poem, "The Road Not Taken." The narrator turns the spring wagon away from the "main travelled" road to one less taken, her narrow lane to the river where she first sought the signs of spring. Now with her new healing knowledge, she can take that different path, with Ottilie close beside her. "We had escaped one more day at least," the narrator exults, "We would have a little stolen holiday." With these words "Holiday's" narrative repeats itself, but with a difference. Whereas the narrator's first holiday from her troubles took her only to the margins and attics of the patriarchal household, this second springtime holiday takes her completely away from the household toward new, less charted possibilities.

"Holiday" represents Porter's most positive fictional resolution of the conflicts between being a woman and being an artist. The story does show the alienated narrator inhabiting the symbolic space of her nineteenth century predecessors; like them she risks social condemnation—"madness"—by her choices, risks always being a "hopeless outsider" to traditional women's lives.

Yet for this narrator, brought into existence in 1924, the attic of her literary foremothers is a "homely and familiar place." In the same way, she can come to terms with her dark double, expression of her fears of alienation and unwomanliness—her monstrous, unsexing vocational choice. Ottilie is the reflection in a blistered mirror of the narrator, yet this narrator comes to realize that neither she nor Ottilie are unnatural. Both are bound to each other and to a common life source. Ottilie is part of the patriarchal family, wrung by its hard fist into her mutilated form. The product of that system, she yet escapes it by her difference. With the narrator she goes on a holiday, celebrating a joyous relation with nature that is free from nature's demands. The road less travelled takes these two women, shoulder to shoulder, wagging and clapping in joyous irreverence, away from the rituals of motherhood. Ottilie and the narrator are an odd, absurd, even grotesque couple. Although a holiday from patriarchy begins in alienation and ends with a suppressed howl of anguish, it also provides epiphanic moments of joy and freedom. Outside of language and thus free from its constraining definitions, inhabiting the very margins of the father's household, the lives of these two women are not inscribed in the narrative of patriarchy, and they simply ride, laughing together, out of the whole story—enjoying a "stolen holiday . . . on this lovely, festive afternoon."

Source: Mary Titus, "'A Little Stolen Holiday': Katherine Anne Porter's Narrative of the Woman Artist," in *Women's Studies*, Vol. 25. No. 1, November 1995, pp. 73–93.

Sources

Featherstone, Joseph, Review of *The Collected Stories of Katherine Anne Porter*, in *New Republic*, Vol. 153, September 4, 1965, pp. 23–26.

Gordon, Mary, "The Angel of Malignity: The Cold Beauty of Katherine Anne Porter," in *New York Times Book Review*, April 16, 1995, pp.17–19.

Moss, Howard, Review of *The Collected Stories of Katherine Anne Porter*, in *New York Times Book Review*, September 12, 1965, pp.1, 26.

Porter, Katherine Anne, "Holiday," in *The Collected Stories of Katherine Anne Porter*, Harcourt Brace, 1972, pp. 407–35.

———, Introduction, in *The Collected Stories of Katherine Anne Porter*, Harcourt Brace, 1972, pp. v–vi.

Walton, Edith H., Review of *Pale Horse, Pale Rider*, in *New York Times Book Review*, April 2, 1939, p. 5.

Review of *The Collected Stories of Katherine Anne Porter*, in *Time*, Vol. 86, November 5, 1965, pp. 122, 125.

Further Reading

Brown, Julie, ed., *American Women Short Story Writers: A Collection of Critical Essays*, Garland Publishing, 2000.

This collection of original and classic essays examines the contributions that female authors have made to the short story.

Goldberg, David J., *Discontented America: The United States in the 1920s*, Johns Hopkins University Press, 1998.

Goldberg examines how the major issues of the decade—women's suffrage, Prohibition, immigration restriction, and racial intolerance—were symptomatic of the postwar generation's discomfort with diversity.

Jordan, Terry G., *German Seed in Texas Soil: Immigrant Farmers in Nineteenth-Century Texas*, University of Texas Press, 1994.

Jordan explores how German immigrants in the nineteenth century influenced and were influenced by the agricultural life in the areas of Texas where they settled.

McLellan, David, ed., *Karl Marx: Selected Writings* Oxford University Press, 2000.

This collection of Marx's writings includes selections from the *Communist Manifesto* and *Das Kapital*, the latter being Father Müller's "bible" for all his business dealings.

Hot Ice

Stuart Dybek

1984

Stuart Dybek's story "Hot Ice" takes place in a changing working-class neighborhood of Chicago during the 1970s. As is typical of much of his work, Dybek mixes realism with fantasy to create a specific sense of place. At the center of the story is an urban legend about a girl who was drowned in a lake in the nearby park decades earlier and then frozen in the local ice house and the miracles that people around the neighborhood attribute to her. Her story affects the lives of three young men: Pancho, who is fanatically religious to the point of mental instability; his brother Manny, the cynic; and Eddie, who feels both the weight of tradition and the struggle to live a good life in a harsh environment. As they move through their days, Dybek renders with precise clarity the details of a city in transition, mixing memories of ice delivery and sharpening carts and streetcars and riding boxcars with the oppressive, looming presence of the county jail and the boarded windows of a neighborhood that is slipping away from memory.

The story was published in *Antaeus* in 1984, and the following year it was chosen for the O. Henry Award for short fiction. It is one of four Dybek stories that have won O. Henrys, three of them coming from the collection in which "Hot Ice" appears, *The Coast of Chicago*. In 2004, *The Coast of Chicago* was chosen for the city's "One Book, One Chicago" program, which encouraged not just students but all citizens to participate in a city-wide discussion club about the book.

Stuart Dybek © Doug McGoldrick. Reproduced by permission

Author Biography

Stuart Dybek was born on April 10, 1942 into a Polish family, in a Chicago neighborhood similar to the one in this story. He attended Catholic grammar and high schools and then enrolled at Loyola University, on the other side of the city where a more urbane culture prevailed. He was the first person in his family to go to college. His original major was pre-medicine, but he switched to English after a year. Still, he did not think of becoming a writer. After earning a bachelor's degree from Loyola in 1964, he was a case worker for the Cook County Department of Public Aid, a job that he pursued out of a drive to work for social justice. At the same time, he worked on his master's degree from Loyola, which he earned in 1967. He married his wife Caryn in 1966.

After earning his first master's degree, Dybek went into teaching, first at a Catholic high school in the Chicago suburb of Morton Grove and then for two years at Wayne Aspinal School in St. Thomas, Virgin Islands—a lush tropic environment that was about as far from his upbringing as he could get. In 1968 he entered the prestigious Writers' Workshop program at the University of Iowa, earning a master of fine arts degree in 1973. He then went to Western Michigan University in Kalamazoo, where he was still teaching as of 2005.

In 1979, Dybek published his first book of poetry, *Brass Knuckles*. His first book of short stories, *Childhood and Other Neighborhoods*, came out the following year and earned him much critical praise. *The Coast of Chicago*, the collection from which this story comes, was published a decade later, in 1990. By the time of its publication, Dybek had been honored with numerous writing awards, including a Whiting Writers' Award, a Guggenheim, an NEA fellowship, a Nelson Algren Award, four O. Henry Awards, a PEN/Malamud Award, and a lifetime achievement award from the American Academy of Arts and Letters. In 2003, he published the story collection *I Sailed with Magellan*.

Plot Summary

Saints

"Hot Ice" is divided into sections with a topic title for each. It begins with the story of girl who had been molested then drowned in the park lagoon about thirty years earlier, during World War II. According to the story, her father found her body and traveled with it on a streetcar to an icehouse across the street from the Cook County Jail, at 26th and California, in Chicago. Her body is rumored to still be frozen there and to have special, magical powers: Big Antek, an old neighborhood alcoholic, claims that he once locked himself in the meat locker of a butcher shop where he worked and the girl's frozen body, temporarily stored there, kept him alive throughout the weekend. The nun at the local school believes the girl should be canonized as a saint.

This story is discussed by the three main characters of "Hot Ice": Pancho Santora, his brother Manny, and their friend Eddie Kapusta. Pancho, who has always been deeply religious, believes that she does hold magical powers, though the other two doubt the story, especially the part about her father riding on the streetcar with a dripping corpse from the lagoon. Pancho asserts his belief in modern saints, referring to Roberto Clemente, a baseball player who died in a plane crash while on his way to help earthquake victims in 1971.

Amnesia

The second section begins with Pancho already gone from the neighborhood and in jail. Eddie and Manny walk through the neighborhood, as they do on most nights, to go to the Cook County Jail, where Pancho is being held for a crime that is not clearly identified in the story. At his sentencing, the judge offered Pancho the chance to go into the military instead of going to jail, but Pancho, who has been fixated with religion since he was a little boy, laughed and sang to himself and claimed that his one goal in life was to pose for the pictures on holy cards. Manny visited him every week for three weeks, but Pancho eventually asked him to quit coming because he did not want to be reminded of the world outside.

Passing through the neighborhood, Manny and Eddie reflect on the signs of desolation: empty storefronts, wrecking balls, and railroad tracks that have been paved over. When they reach the jail, they walk around it, shouting Pancho's name. Inside, prisoners call back to them, mocking. They ask if anyone knows Pancho Santora but are told that the name is not familiar.

Grief

At the start of this segment, Dybek reveals that Pancho has disappeared while in jail, with no definitive explanation of where he has gone. There are dozens of theories, ranging from his having committed suicide or been murdered to his having escaped and gone to Mexico or just to the North Side of the city. Some people claim to have seen him walking the streets or in church. He has become a legendary figure.

When the chapter opens it is Easter Week. In the months since the last chapter, Eddie Kapusta has only seen Manny Santora once, at Christmas time. They ran into each other at a bar, then walked over to the jail, where they threw snowballs at the wall. Now, on Tuesday before Easter, Eddie goes to Manny's house, where they fall into a casual conversation, as if they had not been separated for months.

They go back to the jail, where they once had hollered up at the building when they believed that Pancho was inside. There, they shout again, but instead of joking with the inmates, Manny taunts them, calling them racial and ethnic names and reminding them that they are trapped without freedom. When Eddie tries to stop him, he shouts louder, with worse insults, until the people inside take up a chant for him to shut up and the guards in the tower turn their searchlights on. Eddie finally persuades him to flee, and as they stand behind the icehouse across the street Manny talks about his anger toward everyone inside the jail, from the prisoners to the guards to the wall itself. He says he is going back the next night, and Eddie goes along, afraid to let him go alone.

The next night Manny again shouts obscenities at the jail until searchlights and sirens drive them away. Hiding by the railroad tracks, Manny recalls a time when he was young, when he and some friends rode the freight train that ran on those tracks east to the lake shore. Eddie says he is not going to the jail with him again, and Manny agrees to do something else the following night.

Nostalgia

On Thursday night, they take drugs and carouse the city, passing a bottle of wine between them. Eddie leads the way to a nightclub with a neon window display that he admires and explains that his hobby has always been looking at window decorations.

When they pass by an open fire hydrant, Manny says that he can smell the water of Lake Michigan coming out of it. It reminds him of when his family used to go to the lakefront at night to fish for smelt, a small silvery fish that is captured in nets by the thousands. Since Eddie does not know about smelt, they take a bus to the lake. On the way Manny tells a story about one time when he was young and swam out away from the shore, how he wanted to keep swimming away but returned when he heard his frantic uncle calling for him.

After taking amphetamines all night, they take quaaludes as the sun comes up. They sit talking at Manny's kitchen table for a long time and then remember that it is Good Friday. Manny wants to follow a ritual that Pancho made up—going to services at seven churches on Good Friday. Eddie goes along with him, though he can hardly keep awake. While Manny goes to the front of each church to observe the service, Eddie sits in the back. At the last one, before falling asleep, he realizes that the emptiness he has always felt is a sense of grief for the living.

Legends

The final section of the story starts with the perspective of Big Antek, the neighborhood alcoholic who claims to once have been saved from freezing by the girl in ice. He has recently returned to the neighborhood after having been in the Veterans Administration hospital, and he feels that the neighborhood has changed in the weeks while he was gone.

Eddie and Manny approach him, laughing and drinking and in a good mood, and offer to buy him a drink, which Antek refuses. When they start mocking the story of the frozen girl he becomes angry. Eddie tells him that the icehouse where she is supposedly stored is slated for demolition. Antek goes with them to the icehouse and stands outside while Manny and Eddie climb up the wrecker's crane to enter the building through the roof.

From outside the building, Antek imagines them working their way around in the dark, lighting a road flare that they stole, passing huge blocks of thawing ice until, in the building's basement, they find what they are looking for: a beautiful blonde girl encased in a block of crystal clear ice.

Having found her, Eddie and Manny decide that they cannot just leave her there. They ease the block onto an old railroad handcar that is on the track that backs up into the building and start the car in motion. The tracks, as Manny observed earlier, go to the lakefront, and they decide to take her to the lake and set her in the water, where she will finally be released from the ice.

Characters

Big Antek

Big Antek is a local character known throughout the neighborhood. He is an alcoholic who has worked at numerous butcher shops, cutting off fingers out of clumsiness and drunkenness until he only has a few left. Young people like Eddie and the Santora brothers go to Antek because they know that he will buy liquor for them.

During World War II, Big Antek served in the navy, ending up in a hospital in Manila. When he returned home to his neighborhood he found his name included on a plaque commemorating those who had died in battle. Some time later, when he was already solidly within his cycle of being fired for on-the-job drunkenness at butcher shops, he locked himself in the freezer of one on a Friday night and claims that he would have died if it had not been for the legendary girl drowned in the lagoon, whose body, frozen in a block of ice, was in the freezer, radiating energy that magically kept Antek alive until Monday morning.

At the end of the story, Eddie and Manny, who have been out all night, come to Antek to ask him to buy them some more alcohol. They tell him that the old icehouse, where the girl's frozen body is allegedly stored, is marked for demolition. Antek convinces them to go there and try to retrieve the body. He waits outside while the younger men go in and imagines their movements inside, seeing in his mind's eye the hallways that they would go down and blocks of ice melting in front of them until they actually find the girl.

Eduardo

See Eddie Kapusta

Eddie Kapusta

Eddie is one of the main characters in this story. It is through his perspective that readers are first told the story of the girl frozen in ice, with the details that Eddie remembers hearing ever since his childhood. He is a young man of Polish descent in a neighborhood that is increasingly becoming Mexican. He is close friends with Pancho and Manny Santora.

Eddie, whose last name is the Polish word for "cabbage," is characterized as an observer. While Pancho is a religious fanatic and Manny is a realist, Eddie does not have any such clear-cut perspective. Instead, he is noted for his devotion to his friends. For a long time during the period covered by the story, he loses contact with Manny because he has to quit high school and work a night job to pay his bills, but then, one spring day months after they have seen each other, he goes to Manny's apartment, and they resume their friendship just as it had been before. When Manny turns angry about losing Pancho and goes to the county jail to shout obscenities at those inside, Eddie would like to stay away, but he feels obliged to go along rather than letting Manny get into trouble alone.

While they are out on the street drinking, Eddie takes Manny to see one of his favorite window displays, the neon palm tree at the Coconut Club. He explains that his hobby ever since he was young has been looking at the decorations in windows, indicating that he is more of an observer in life than a participant. While Manny attends Good Friday mass, Eddie sits in the back of the church. It is there that he realizes that his life has been full of mourning for the living, which would account for his affection for the way the neighborhood once was but will not be any more.

In the end, though, Eddie shakes off his moroseness and becomes an active participant, presumably helping Manny steal the frozen girl from the icehouse and take her to the lake, where she is set loose from the suspended animation that has held her for decades.

Padrecito

See Pancho Santora

Manny Santora

In the story, Eddie describes Manny as a realist. He is one only by contrast to his older brother

Pancho, who spends his childhood fantasizing about being a religious figure. In grammar school, Manny found it difficult to deal with the nuns who considered him a disappointment after his pious brother, and so he transferred from the Catholic school to the public school, which he seldom bothered to attend.

When Pancho is in jail, Manny is devoted to him, visiting him regularly until Pancho asks him to stop; after that, Manny still goes to the jail with Eddie, walking around the walls at night, shouting out Pancho's name. After Pancho disappears, Manny becomes angry and abusive when he goes to the wall of the jail, shouting offensive comments that make the prisoners inside angry enough to chant in unison against him. He continues to go back, taking a chance that the guards will arrest him, until Eddie refuses to go with him, at which point he loses his anger almost immediately and gamely offers to do something else, as if he had not been full of rage just moments before.

Manny's devotion to the memory of Pancho drives him to follow a ritual that Pancho made up of going to seven churches on Good Friday, even though he and Eddie have been out all night drinking and taking drugs and are beyond the point of exhaustion. While Eddie finds it difficult to keep up, Manny follows the ceremonies with the interest Pancho would have shown.

Manny's true personality is shown in a childhood memory that he shares with Eddie. He recalls being at the lakefront once in the middle of the night while his family was fishing for smelt. He swam away from shore, relishing his freedom and the touch of the water, only coming back because he thinks of his uncle on the pier, desperately calling for him. His dream of escape is mirrored in the end when they leave to release the girl in ice at about the same place in the lake, giving the freedom that Manny once desired.

Pancho Santora

Pancho is the oldest of the three friends who prowl around together at the beginning of this story, the older brother of Manny. He is devoutly religious and always has been, though his fascination with religion manifests itself in unique ways. As a child, he pretended to be a priest when he was playing in the back yard with the other children, which led to his nickname, Padrecito, or Little Priest. He served as an altar boy and spent money on different colored shoes so that they would match the different colored vestments that priests wore on various feast days. He believes in the miraculous powers of the girl in ice because he believes in miracles in general. The nuns at his grammar school love Pancho, and later in his life, after he has fallen into trouble with the law, Eddie notes that Pancho would have been fine being an altar boy all his life, that it was his vocation.

In high school Pancho is a member of a street gang called the Saints. He is arrested on a charge that Dybek does not explain in the story, and at his trial laughs at the judge who tries offering him the option of going into the military instead of going to jail. In jail, Pancho's spirit deteriorates. After a few months he tells his brother to stop visiting, because he does not want to be reminded of the outside world until he can go into it again.

Pancho's eventual fate is not explicitly given: everyone in the neighborhood knows that he is gone from the county jail, but there are dozens of rumors about what happened to him. Some people say that he hanged himself or was killed by another inmate; others say that he became a trustee and escaped; others say that he was transferred to another jail for the mentally ill; and others say they have seen him walking the streets of the neighborhood or lighting a candle in church or riding by on an elevated train. In the end, he has become as much of a neighborhood legend as the girl frozen in ice.

Themes

Religion

One of the most prevalent themes in this story is religion, in particular how Pancho Santora relates to Catholicism. Pancho is described from the start as believing in "everything—ghosts, astrology, legends." In particular, he focuses his willingness to believe on the religion in which he is raised. As a small boy he dresses up like a priest and pretends to hold Mass in his back yard. When he is old enough, he becomes an altar boy, whose job it is to assist the priest in serving the Mass.

The nuns at the Catholic school admire Pancho because he is so devoted to his duties as an altar boy. He believes that he has a guardian angel, which is a specifically Catholic concept. He also does penance during Lent, inflicting pain on himself and offering up his suffering for the souls in purgatory. By the time he is an adolescent and in trouble with the law, he ruins his chance to avoid jail time by being glib with the judge, wearing his necktie like a headband and telling the judge that he plans to grow up to pose for holy cards.

Topics For Further Study

- The story explains that Big Antek came home from World War II to find himself listed on a plaque of people who had died in the war. Research the story of someone who was erroneously listed as dead in war, in the terrorist attacks of September 11, 2001, or in Hurricane Katrina, and write a short story about how their family dealt with finding out they were alive.
- Read about the lives of Catholic saints and prepare a chart explaining which ones you think would be Pancho's favorites and why.
- Find a modern myth in your area that is similar to the story of the girl frozen in the ice, and report to your class on what is known about how this myth began.
- Diagnose Pancho's psychological state, from the beginning of the story until the people of the neighborhood lose track of him. Explain which psychological conditions best describe his actions.
- At the end, Eddie and Manny ride off on a railroad handcar. Create a model of a handcar and prepare an explanation of how one works.

Pancho's fixation with Catholicism is easy to understand: he lives in a predominantly Catholic neighborhood. The neighborhood is changing from Polish to Hispanic, and both populations have strong ties to the Catholic Church. One sign of the Catholic influence on the neighborhood is the very fact that Manny and Eddie can find seven churches within walking distance on Good Friday. Another is the hymn, "Tantum Ergo," which they hear even as they are walking up the street. Dybek reinforces the reader's awareness of religion by marking time in terms of the Christian calendar, with scenes set at Christmas, Lent, Holy Week, Easter, etc.

Community

"Hot Ice" often relates events from a communal perspective, giving readers facts as they are understood by everyone who lives in the neighborhood. The first case of this is the initial story of the girl in ice. The details given are identified as being the ones Eddie Kapusta heard, but it is also clear that the story is known by all. Everyone knows Big Antek's story, too: how he once was saved by the girl in ice and how he has lost his fingers working at a succession of butcher shops. The communal perspective is made even clearer when Pancho disappears from the county jail: stories come in from all over the neighborhood, with rumors of sightings and speculation, but no one, not even Pancho's own brother, knows for sure what happened to him. All of these theories suggest a community of people who struggle to answer the same question, who know each other, talk to each other, and are aware of significant events in one another's life.

Post-War Society

This story could not have taken place before 1971 because the death of Roberto Clemente, is mentioned, which occurred that year. Still, there is much about the environment surrounding Eddie, Manny, and Pancho that hearkens back to a more distant past, particularly to the period just after World War II. The most direct connection to this time is Big Antek, with whom they interact regularly, if only to have him buy liquor for them. The war and the injuries he sustained in it changed Antek's life and are probably the cause of his drinking problem, which has given him a skewed outlook, making him believe he was saved by the frozen girl. Big Antek lives in the past, in his memories of ice delivery trucks and rag carts and Bing Crosby playing on tavern jukeboxes, and he tries to make the young people see that history and care about it.

The neighborhood's link to the past is not only tied to the views of one man, though. This story depicts a working-class neighborhood that is past its prime, decaying from neglect. During the war and the years immediately following the neighborhood was in its prime. During World War II, U.S. industrial cities such as Chicago ran at full tilt, churning out products for the war effort, and after the war, with bombed-out European cities trying to rebuild, the booming U.S. economy kept these cities productive. The streets now are deserted, with no thriving businesses mentioned beside taverns where people while away their lives. But the city features that were functioning around the time of the war—icehouses, streetcars, freight trains, and the regular rhythm of a fully functioning economy—haunt the memories of older neighborhood men.

Coming of Age

The three main characters in "Hot Ice" are in their teens, even though their socioeconomic situation has caused them to take on adult behaviors early. The events of the story cause each of them, in his own way, to cross over from childhood to adulthood.

At the beginning of the story, Pancho is poised between two sets of beliefs. He is a devout Catholic, but he also is a gang member and engages in life on the streets. When he is arrested and brought before a judge, he claims both identities: he says that he wants to be a holy card model (which Dybek foreshadows earlier in the story by saying that the nuns thought Pancho looked like a saint, such as St. Sebastian or Juan de la Cruz), but he also points out that he is a captain, which is a street gang title. On the streets, this dual personality has served Pancho well, but in jail he faces tougher conditions than he has ever known, and he snaps. When Manny visits, he finds that Pancho's buoyant spirit is gone and that he has lost his faith in his guardian angel.

Eddie approaches life as a bystander at the beginning of the story. He recalls stories, but not stories in which he participated. His favorite hobby is looking in storefront windows, not engaging with the people inside. At the end of the story, though, he becomes involved, helping Manny free the girl's body from the ice that has held it frozen for decades. Like her, he is shaking off inertia.

Manny describes himself as a loner, and throughout the story, when faced with adversity, he tries to reinforce that self-image by driving people away. When he thinks Pancho is in jail, he jokes with the people inside, but once Pancho has disappeared he turns angry. He disappears from Eddie's life for months. He mocks Big Antek for believing in the girl in ice. In finding the girl at the end, and in deciding to facilitate a rescue of her by letting her drift off into the lake (a dream of freedom he once had for himself), Manny is no longer a loner: he has matured into a man who understand responsibility.

Style

Point of View

This story is told in third-person limited omniscient point of view, which means the author limits what he reveals to certain characters, all of which is told in third person. For the most part, the narrative focuses on Eddie Kapusta's thoughts, but at various times it drifts into the minds of other characters or into the perspective of the community as a whole. For instance, the opening paragraphs, relating the background information about the girl in ice, contain a broad perspective, explaining what a variety of people knew or thought of the story, but this information is then planted into Eddie's mind, with the narrative mentioning several times that the details being relayed are just the version that Eddie had heard or had imagined.

As the story progresses, the focus stays with Eddie, making this predominantly his story. When Manny acts erratically, for instance, the narrative does not explain what he is thinking, but it does give Eddie's thoughts about his behavior. When Eddie and Manny do not see each other for a few months, the narrative explains what Eddie has been up to, while Manny's actions are left unexplained.

One notable shift in the point of view occurs when the narrative dips into the mind of Big Antek, which occurs in two significant places. In the "Saints" section, the description of Antek's night in the freezer is begun as something that he told to Pancho: as the paragraph progresses, however, Dybek gives finer and finer details about that night, things that Antek would not have related in a story, about physical sensations and brand names. It is clear after a while that the story has temporarily shifted to Antek's point of view. The "Legends" section is mostly from Antek's point of view, giving his thoughts as he stands outside Buddy's bar and sees Eddie and Manny approach. When they are separated from him, having gone into the icehouse, the narrative reveals their actions as Big Antek imagines them. The very last section is then told from Manny's point of view, with his observations and thoughts.

Myth

Myths are usually handed down from generation to generation, with no direct evidence of their source. Often myths incorporate supernatural elements. In "Hot Ice," Dybek uses the emotional power of myths to charge modern life with a sense of religious awe.

He starts the story with the mysterious tale of the girl who was drowned and then frozen in ice by her grieving father. The tale includes several elements, such as the fact that the girl was young and innocent and her father carried her to the icehouse on a trolley car, that sound exaggerated. The fact that the basic story has grown to mythological importance can be seen in Big Antek's description of her great beauty and of her shining hair and in the way he and others attribute miracles to her.

The disappearance of Pancho represents a myth in the making. Readers can see the members of the community trying to fill in the gap in their knowledge about his fate by grasping at rumors. While some of the rumors, such as the ones that have him die in jail or run away to another country, might seem plausible, it is more likely that the ones that have him remain a part of the community as a ghost or phantom are the ones that will survive to be told to future generations.

Historical Context

Rust Belt

Chicago is one of the large northern U.S. cities that fell from prominence in the 1970s, losing its place as an important manufacturing center as economic conditions changed. These cities, dotting the map from Illinois to New York, came to be referred to collectively as the Rust Belt.

Historically, the United States has been a world-class economic power, in part because of its huge crop lands in the South and its manufacturing base in the North. Cities such as Chicago, Detroit, Pittsburgh, Cincinnati, and Buffalo, which had good methods of transportation (rivers, lakes, or railroads), developed as centers for industry, with factories that pumped out the manufactured goods, from cars to paper to buttons, that powered U.S. economic growth. Particularly after World War II (1939–45), which had itself brought an end to the previous decade of economic depression, the industrial cities in the North produced the durable goods that made the United States one of the world's economic superpowers.

In the 1960s and 1970s, though, U.S. manufacturing lost its dominant position in the world market. Innovations in transportation and shipping, new trade agreements, and continuing struggles between organized labor and corporate owners led to conditions that made it less expensive for U.S. companies to import goods made overseas than to buy American-made products. Manufacturing became less and less important as a part of the economy, taken over by service jobs and jobs dealing with information processing in the new computer age. Factories closed and jobs left the cities. Areas such as the one described in "Hot Ice" that had once been bustling with factories and with well-paid factory workers became depressed and empty. Populations in the Rust Belt cities dropped throughout the seventies, eighties, and nineties, but as of the early 2000s are on the rise again.

The Transformed Catholic Church

In this story, the main characters, particularly Pancho, retreat from the harshness of their blighted urban surroundings into the colorful mysteries of the Catholic Church. At the time, however, the Catholic Church was actively trying to be more open and less mysterious. In the early 1960s, under the auspices of Pope John XXIII, the church convened the Second Vatican Council (commonly referred to as Vatican II) to initiate changes that would make the Church more open to its followers and the people more familiar with their clergy and liturgy. Over the course of four annual meetings, from 1962 to 1965, the council discussed such matters as the church's relationship to other faiths, the role of the clergy in the lives of their followers, and the reform of the liturgy used during Mass. The form of the council was open debate, so that conservative and progressive movements within the church were able to express their concerns equally.

In the end, Vatican II led to the most significant changes in the Church since the Reformation. Mass was changed from the traditional Latin to the language of parishioners. Music was given a more prominent role. Lay people—those not fully ordained by the Church—became participants in the Mass. Priests and bishops became more accessible to the people they serve, instead of being insulated in the church bureaucracy.

Traditionalists regretted the changes that had made the Catholic Church more accessible, feeling that the religious experience should be based in mystery not familiarity. By the time this story was published, the tide had turned against the changes

Compare & Contrast

- **1984:** Many veterans who returned in the 1960s and 1970s from Vietnam continue to suffer from post-traumatic stress disorder. The assumption is that Vietnam vets are like Big Antek, struggling with the fracture that military service has made of their lives.

  Today: Because of experiences with returning Vietnam veterans, the U.S. government increases its efforts to care for veterans' mental health, although such programs are not always properly funded.

- **1984:** High school students dropping out of school can find well-paying, hard labor jobs.

  Today: Many manual labor jobs go overseas. High school education is necessary for even basic employment in the post-computer age economy.

- **1984:** Stories about ice houses and trolley cars contain enough familiar elements to be romanticized by those telling neighborhood legends.

  Today: Legends still pop up about modern ideas such as cell phones and chat rooms. Some websites specifically report on urban legends.

- **1984:** The traditional Polish population of Chicago's Little Village/Pilsen neighborhood, where this story takes place, is becoming mixed with Mexican immigrants.

  Today: Little Village/Pilsen boasts the largest Mexican community in the Midwest and is second only to East Los Angeles in the country.

- **1984:** A judge might offer a young man who has been arrested the option of joining the military instead of going to jail.

  Today: Many communities adapt mandatory sentencing guidelines that strip judges of the power to offer such an option.

- **1984:** Fishing off-shore near Chicago for rainbow smelt in Lake Michigan is popular, mostly among people from working-class families, as it has been for generations.

  Today: Most of the smelt in the lake are gone, their population having been decimated in the late 1980s by a loss of mysis shrimp, their primary food source.

made by Vatican II. Pope John Paul II, who began his reign in 1978, was one of history's most popular popes, traveling widely to encourage participation in the Church by those who had traditionally been left out, but he was also strongly conservative, opposing the progressives who wished to bring changes to the church, such as acceptance of homosexuals or ordination of women.

Critical Overview

After "Hot Ice" was published in *Antaeus* in 1994, it was chosen for the prestigious O. Henry Award for short fiction. It is one of four Dybek stories given this award; this story and two of the other award winners are included in the 1990 collection *The Coast of Chicago*.

The 1990 *Antioch Review* refers to *The Coast of Chicago*, Dybek's second collection, as "paradoxically vivid and realistic," calling his portrait of growing up in Chicago "richly remembered." Don Lee, writing in *Ploughshares*, focuses on Dybek's propensity for shifting from what he calls "a gritty realism befitting Chicago's South Side to metafictional techniques which transform images into reverie, the tangible into the mythic." He finds that, given the diversity of the subjects Dybek writes about, such shifts are entirely pertinent, noting, "Nothing could be more appropriate."

In Michiko Kakutani's review of *The Coast of Chicago* for *New York Times Book Review*, she compares the book to Sherwood Anderson's classic short story collection *Winesburg, Ohio* (1919). While Kakutani finds that the Dybek's book lacks Anderson's cumulative effect, mostly due to the lack of a common character carrying over from story to story, she thinks that the individual stories in *The Coast of Chicago*, including "Hot Ice," "possess an emotional forcefulness: they introduce us to characters who want to take up permanent residence in our minds, and in doing so, they persuasively conjure up a fictional world that is both ordinary and amazing."

In March of 2004, the mayor of Chicago announced that *The Coast of Chicago* had been chosen as that year's entry in the city's "One Book, One Chicago" series. This honor includes having the book read at high schools and colleges throughout the city in hopes of creating a massive book club spreading across one of the country's largest metropolitan centers. In addition, the city arranged public reading from the book by actors from the world-renown Steppenwolf Theatre Company; discussion groups; and tours of the neighborhoods discussed in the stories.

Criticism

David Kelly

Kelly is an instructor of creative writing and literature. In this essay, Kelly explains how the story does not divert from conventional reality as much as it first appears to do so.

Stuart Dybek's story "Hot Ice" ends with the memorable scene of two neighborhood friends, who have been estranged, united in a combined effort: they ride off on, of all things, a railroad handcar, a device hearkening back to the Civil War period, transporting a corpse frozen in a block of ice. The corpse signifies a local legend, in which a young woman was rumored to have been killed some thirty years earlier and carried to the local ice house by the deceased girl's grieving father. In the ensuing years the girl's fame has grown: she has been nominated for sainthood by the parish nun and Big Antek, the local drunk whom everyone knows, swears that her body, in its ice block, was in a freezer he managed to lock himself in over a weekend and that her presence kept him from freezing. Dybek renders Chicago's Pilsen neighborhood, as he does in other stories, in harsh, unforgiving scenes of urban decay. In this story the residents want to believe that this miraculous corpse is among them, protecting them with its magical powers, but wanting and getting are in no way connected in the cold reality of "Hot Ice."

"'Rumors were becoming legends,' Dybek tells his readers, 'and no one knew how to mourn a person who had just disappeared.' The element of the unknown and the discomfort about unknowing are the main ingredients needed for an instant urban legend."

The late appearance of the actual girl in ice and the way that Manny Santora and Eddie Kapusta deal with finding such a mythic figure appear to come from a reality that is different than the one set up in the preceding pages. They are certainly welcome developments, providing relief from the grueling existence and empty dreams that fill up this long story: readers cannot help but feel, maybe for the first time, that things will turn out well for these characters. Nonetheless, these events represent a different reality than the one that has been established. At least, they seem to. However, the fact that the corpse in an ice block exists and that two characters ride off on a handcar to release it into the lake are clearly prepared for throughout the story.

This is a story about urban reality, but within that reality, this is a story about myths. It establishes two categories of myths, religious and secular, and examines the circumstances in life that lead people to repeat them, build on them, and eventually start creating new myths of their own. The story of the frozen girl is just one of numerous myths told in the Pilsen neighborhood, creating an environment of heightened expectation. Dybek contrasts the oppressiveness of city life, consisting of crumbling buildings, police and jailers, drugs and alcohol, and unemployment, with the characters' own beliefs in

What Do I Read Next?

- Tony Fitzpatrick, a Chicago poet and artist, covers roughly the same territory that Dybek does in his poetry collection *Bum Town* (2001).
- Many critics point out that Dybek's writing comes out of a Chicago tradition of gritty realism that started with James T. Farrell, the author of the *Studs Lonigan* trilogy in the early 1900s. The three Lonigan books—*Young Lonigan*, *The Young Manhood of Studs Lonigan*, and *Judgment Day*—have been collected in one edition as *James T. Farrell: Studs Lonigan* (2004).
- The lyricism of Dybek's fiction becomes solidified in his poetry. His *Streets in Their Own Ink* (2004) are drawn from his own life, taking a closer look at his upbringing and the Chicago that he once knew.
- For thumbnail sketches of stories that have circulated in Chicago neighborhoods for years, readers may enjoy *Chicago Sketches: Urban Tales, Stories, and Legends from Chicago History*, published in 1996 by June Skinner Sawyers. Her explanations of the local lore are quick summaries, but they capture the sketchy, mischievous nature of such stories.

---

powers from beyond their experiences, like those of their myths, can save them.

The setting Dybek uses for "Hot Ice" is based on a real place: the Pilsen neighborhood exists as of 2005 with the streets, intersections, and landmarks mentioned in the story, including the Douglas Park lagoon where the girl was rumored to have drowned and the Cook County Jail where Manny and Eddie meet at night, and the shoreline of Lake Michigan. The sounds, smells, and sights of this neighborhood are meticulously rendered. The story is not limited to recording empirical reality, however. It stretches current reality backwards, rendering for readers a neighborhood that contains vestiges or memories of its own past. Streetcars, ragmen, knife sharpening carts, icemen, taverns with Bing Crosby on the jukebox, and butcher shops that would hire the crazy old neighborhood alcoholic who has already cut off several fingers at other butcher shops, all these elements convey the neighborhood as it once was.

Just like the two levels of everyday life—the old, which is a dim and quickly fading memory, and the new, which does not have anything appealing to offer the story's young men—there are also two levels of myths. The old ones are the Catholic myths, the stories of martyrs and saints that have inspired the faithful for generations. These are the ones that are taught to the neighborhood children, with unpredictable results. In this story, Pancho is fanatically devoted, Eddie is guardedly reverent, and Manny is flat-out skeptical (at least until he follows in his brother's footsteps by attending Good Friday services, but even then his is a secular, not sacred, devotion). Regardless of one's level of commitment, one cannot live in the neighborhood Dybek describes without being aware of its Catholic tradition.

The newest level of myth is represented here by the stories surrounding Pancho Santora and his disappearance. This mythology is so new that readers can see it developing throughout the course of the story. Pancho's experience is established from the beginning of the story as the perfect fertile ground from which a myth can grow. He has spent his life surrounding himself with mystery, associating himself with not only the Catholic traditions but with ghosts and astrology as well, which shows his religious devotion to be part of his general inclination toward the supernatural. But Pancho is more than just a head-in-the-clouds idealist: he is a man of the people, a gang member, a product of his tough urban environment, and he ends up in one of the least idealistic environments imaginable, the county jail.

In jail, Pancho becomes the inspiration for a new urban myth, one that springs from within the neighborhood and stars a local boy: the story of the man who disappeared from custody. Like all myths, this one has something familiar in it. Jail break stories often entail the basic premise of a person managing to get lost within a system that exists manifestly to keep tabs on people. Moreover, as is common with myths, Pancho's story exists in various versions. Some of the theories about his fate (such as that he might have killed himself or had his throat slashed or even that he was allowed to take the judge's offer retroactively and choose military service over jail) seem plausible. Others (such as people's reports that he walked out unnoticed, that he fled to Mexico, or is now haunting the El) may seem less likely, but that imaginative element makes them suitable for gossip. "Rumors were becoming legends," Dybek tells his readers, "and no one knew how to mourn a person who had just disappeared." The element of the unknown and the discomfort about unknowing are the main ingredients needed for an instant urban legend.

The story of the girl in ice is the bridge between the sacred myths of the church and the newly-forming secular one about Pancho. As the ancient nun, Sister Joachim, calls attention to in the story, the legend of the girl is certainly similar to church-sanctioned stories about martyrs: notable similarities are that the girl who dies defending her virginity is enshrined immediately by her father and is credited with miracles and cures. The links to the Pilsen neighborhood of a generation or two back, just real enough and yet fanciful enough, are established with the details about the streetcar and the icehouse. In telling this tale, carrying it forward, Eddie and Manny and the young men of the day open their imaginations to miraculous occurrences in their own times.

This story would be complete if it left things at this point, showing how Christian tradition affects myths developed two generations back, which spawn new myths. But at the end Dybek changes this story from one about imagination to one about reality, with the girl in ice as more than just a legend: she actually shows up. Before her appearance, all of the fantastic elements of the story are in the minds of the neighborhood people, stewing under the oppression of unyielding reality, aching for a miracle. Having her actually appear in the story changes the tone, giving the story in a more playful and imaginative guise.

At least, it would, if she actually did appear. The scene in which the girl in ice is found is itself shrouded in mystery, in unreality. For one thing, Dybek tells the events through the point of view of Big Antek. Antek is the one person in the story who claims to have actually seen the girl in ice, but the circumstances in which he claims to have seen her are dubious. The widely accepted narrative has her body taken to the icehouse immediately after she drowns, and it is in the icehouse that she is found three decades later: Antek's report that he encountered her in a butcher's freezer may be a figment of his liquor-soaked mind, a convenient fiction for someone desperate to believe. Antek's reliability as a witness is questionable at best, and the happenings in the ice house at the end are told from his perspective. Dybek paints the whole scene of the girl's eventual discovery with lurid, surreal descriptions, from the break-in through the roof to the screwy sense of order that takes over any abandoned building (in this one, it is the odd sight of ice machines stacked floor-to-ceiling) to the slanted, melting ice blocks to the unnatural light of the road flare that illumines Manny and Eddie's way.

Perhaps the most obscure detail, though, is the one that immediately precedes the discovery of the girl. Eddie and Manny, straining to see into the blocks of ice, find their vision confounded by the thousands of cracks forming inside of the massive blocks: "They could only see shadows and had to guess at the forms: fish, birds, shanks of meat, a dog, a cat, a chair, what appeared to be a bicycle."

Was the girl from the lagoon actually frozen in the icehouse? The idea seems unlikely from the start, as the three protagonists point out in arguing its probability in the opening scene. It seems more likely at the end, when Manny and Eddie think they have found her and decide to free her; the narrative relates her discovery as a matter of fact, not delusion. But their having found her is only as likely as their actually having seen a dog or a cat or a bicycle frozen in a block of ice.

In the end, they probably do ride off toward the lake with a block of ice: though the act of commandeering a railroad handcar and taking off down the tracks with it is unlikely, it is just the sort of remnant from a bygone era that the neighborhood Dybek describes here could support. They probably do not, however, actually find the girl in ice, but only fantasize that they do. There is plenty of evidence throughout the story for believing that readers are not meant to believe that the block of ice actually contains human remains. Manny and Eddie have been up all night, drinking and taking drugs; the ice factory is dim, abandoned, and shadowy, with strange lights suggesting bizarre phantasms; and they have heard legends about the girl's existence all their lives.

The story works just as well without having to believe that Dybek is claiming an actual miracle. Taking the characters at their word, believing what they believe, would make the world of the work a magical place where supernatural things can occur. Being skeptical, though, makes it even more magical: Dybek's neighborhood is a place where two people can look into the lurid obscurity of a block of ice and hallucinate the same thing, bringing the myth to life with their imaginations.

Source: David Kelly, Critical Essay on "Hot Ice," in *Short Stories for Students*, Thomson Gale, 2006.

Claire Kirch

In the following interview conducted in October 2003, Dybek discusses with Claire Kirch his youth in the ethnically mixed South Side of Chicago, and his discovery of and approach to writing.

You can take the man out of Chicago, but you can't take Chicago out of the man—especially if you are talking about Western Michigan University English professor Stuart Dybek. Though Dybek has lived in Kalamazoo for almost 30 years, his gritty yet magical short stories are set almost exclusively in the Southwest Side of Chicago (overlapping neighborhoods known as Pilsen and Little Village, and later called El Barrio). Dybek's elegiac stories, with their strong sense of place in memory and interlinked characters, have been compared to Joyce's *Dubliners* and Anderson's *Winesburg, Ohio.* A regular contributor to literary, magazines and anthologies, he's regarded with an almost cultlike reverence by his fans for his stories and poems.

Ten years after the publication of his last collection, readers are going to be surfeited with Dybek's prose and poetry, this fall and next year. *Childhood and Other Neighborhoods,* originally published in 1980 by Viking and reissued in 1990 by Ecco was released one more time by the University of Chicago Press last month. *Coast of Chicago,* first published in 1990 by Knopf, will be reissued this month by Picador. And a new collection of short stories, *I Sailed with Magellan,* will be published by FSG this month. Dybek's first collection of poems, *Brass Knuckles,* originally published in 1979 by the University of Pittsburgh Press, will be reissued by Carnegie Mellon Press in the spring. And in a not-too-common circumstance of one press publishing both an author's prose and poetry, FSG will simultaneously publish Dybek's second collection of poems, *Streets in Their Own Ink.*

PW and Dybek arranged to meet one rainy Friday afternoon in October at Shaman Drum Books, in the heart of Ann Arbor. It must have been football weekend: the streets were clogged with students and townies. Clutching a dogeared galley of *I Sailed with Magellan, PW* walked through Shaman Drum inquiring of every, middle-aged man in the store if he was Stuart Dybek. He was nowhere to be found—until *PW* spied a slightly built male figure outside, leaning casually against the front of the store, wearing a battered green suede jacket. He looked exactly like one of the street-savvy, tough-guy, weather-beaten characters in a Dybek short story. And it was Dybek.

Like his *I Sailed with Magellan* alter ego, Polish-American teen Perry Katzek, Dybek grew up in a close-knit, working class ethnic neighborhood on the South Side of Chicago in the 1950s and early '60s. Dybek's parents were immigrants. While the neighborhood now is populated mostly by Mexican-Americans, during Dybek's youth it was a neighborhood in transition. It had long been populated by Poles and Czechs, with Latinos newly added to the ethnic mix—disparate groups whose cultural differences were bridged by the Roman Catholic Church. "The South Side of Chicago has always been a quintessential neighborhood, the target of migrations. In writing about this little ethnic enclave, I am writing about America," he pronounces, as we sit in the kind of trendy, pseudo-hippie cafe that one finds only in American college towns like Ann Arbor, Ithaca or Chapel Hill.

Dybek's father, Stanley, was a foreman a the International Harvester plant, which manufactured thinks and farm implements. His mother, Adeline, worked as a truck dispatcher. Dybek recalls his youth as a "benevolent time." He describes the neighborhood as one with a "working-class ambiance, rather than a middle-class sensibility." He explains, "Because of the church, there was a strong sense of community. We all shared the same religion, though there otherwise was not a lot of assimilation in this so-called melting pot. There were also a lot of kids—so there was this huge tribal sense that transcended ethnic lines. We had huge amounts of unsupervised time. Our parents did not schedule after-school activities for us—they had other things to do. We created a world of our own, side by side with the adult world. They ignored us, and we ignored them. It was a 'might makes right' world that we created, straight out of *Lord of the Flies*. There was enormous joy and vitality, though mixed with fear, having so much freedom. This exhilaration provided a great counterbalance to the economic stresses and tensions that were such a part of our lives."

Dybek can pinpoint the exact moment when he realized the importance of language and imagination in his universe. "I remember the year, the day, the very moment that my life as a writer began," he declares with relish about an experience in the fourth grade. "One morning my mother was sick with the flu. My father had woken me up that morning and left a bowl of this awful stuff—they called it Ralston; on the table for me. I had not done my homework yet and had to write a one-page essay on Africa 'the Dark Continent' for school. So I pushed the Ralston away, and decided to do my homework instead. I tried to describe the trees in Africa. But 1 was a city kid—the highest things I'd ever seen in my life were the skyscrapers in Chicago. I wrote the phrase 'the tree-scraped skies.' It was as if a bolt shot through me. Literally, it was a moment of epiphany. I had discovered metaphor. It was the first time I felt this enormous connection to language. For me, writing no longer was just something that had to do with school."

Dybek obviously feels strongly about honing his writing to perfection as he leans forward, warming to the subject. "I try to make my prose tactile and sensuous. My writing contains a lot of images, a lot of smells. I try to make the rhythm of the language musical in my stories." Dybek compares his efforts to the poems of Eugenic Montale: "Montale describes a lemon grove in such a way . . . by god, you read that poem, you are there, you are there in that lemon grove in Italy. I want the reader to be there. I want the reader to feel sensually scenes I create oil the page. I want life on the page. I want nay writing to be like music, tactile and emotive. I want the reader to feel this stuff."

"Write what you know and the rest will follow" might be a time-worn cliche, but in Dybek's case, it's the truth. Dybek recalls not using his childhood memories as a springboard or Chicago as a backdrop in his early work. Instead, he tried to create conventional short stories with generic American characters. "I wanted to imitate my models—like F. Scott Fitzgerald," he admits. "My early stories did not have a particular place. They were more about . . ." Dybek pauses, embarrassed at the thought of his early efforts. "I can't remember. None were published."

"'I try to make my prose tactile and sensuous. My writing contains a lot of images, a lot of smells. I try to make the rhythm of the language musical in my stories.'"

Searching for his narrative voice, Dybek looked to his literary forebears for inspiration. "Funny thing about Chicago writers is how many come from the South Side," he declares. "James Farrell, Theodore Dreiser, Saul Bellow, Gwendolyn Brooks. . . . The South Side of Chicago is a microcosm of America. All these big themes are available to you—they rise out naturally front the material. Themes like poverty, faith, prejudice, immigration, assimilation, race, class. . . . Instead of imposing my own biases or some kind of aesthetic agenda, I want them to come naturally out of the material—like Eudora Welty writing about the South or Joyce about Dublin."

Although Dybek recognizes that his work is greatly, influenced by the Chicago style of realistic writing, his work goes be yond into a realm all his own that can only be called "Chicago magical realism." Certainly, Dybek's Chicago is a real place of garbage-strewn alleys, street vendors hawking their wares and rundown apartment buildings rocked by the rumblings of a passing El train. But there's also magic and joy in Dybek's Chicago, perhaps springing from that heady, combination of ethnic folkways and Roman Catholic rituals that colored Iris childhood and now infuses his tales. Statues of saints may wink at school-children, tulips bloom on an inner-city street, dead girls frozen in ice perform miracles and spontaneous parades of people wind through the streets. Dybek's tales are a seamless mixture of the real and the fantastic, the tangible and the mythic, the sacred and the profane.

Though his working-class characters live hardscrabble lives in the inner city, they never lose hope. They constantly look for and find beauty around them—even though the orchids two characters pick turn out to be irises, the dawn turns out to be the lights of Gary, Ind., and the ship's lights on Lake Michigan are those of a pumping station. While discussing the characters inhabiting his stories, Dybek says, "I really wanted there to be—even in the midst of the grittier side of life—humor, vitality, a full palate of human emotion. I don't think you can demonstrate humor or vitality except by testing it. Imagination allows people to survive. It's not just escape: imagination allows you to reject definitions imposed on you by redefining the world through the power of the imagination."

Dybek's entire life might be said to imitate his art. The story of how Dybek got his first collection of short stories, *Childhood and Other Neighborhoods,* published by a major New York publishing house could be a story straight out of Stuart Dybek's metafictional world. It's a modern fairy tale—complete with fairy godmother editors and magical manuscripts—in a realistic and hard-boiled New York publishing house setting. "Back in those days, here were such things as junior editors and slush piles that these assistants actually combed through. My manuscript literally came over the transom at Viking. The story is that an editor's assistant at Viking was laughing hysterically while reading one of my short stories. The editor came out of her office and wanted to know what was going on. She then read the manuscript and laughed hysterically. My phone rang, and a voice said, 'Hey, we like your manuscript.'" Dybek pauses for emphasis: "I had no agent or anything. I was shocked, and remember thinking, 'How could this happen to me?'"

But like the Chicago of his youth that may or may not have ever existed, Dybek mourns the demise of publishing as it used to be. "I bridged that change in the publishing world. I came in when publishing was the way it was. Books were art, not 'product.' I've been around, and have seen the enormous changes in publishing that have occurred in the last two decades. What happened to me at Viking 25 years ago could never happen today. Now you send your manuscript to an agent, you don't just send it unsolicited to a publisher."

Dybek's recollections of his entree into book publishing continue with yet more larger-than-life characters added into the mix. Dybek describes his longtime editor, Elisabeth Sifton, in reverential tones. "She was not that first editor at Viking who discovered me, but she became my editor at Viking. She is a kind of iconic figure in publishing, a real old-style editor. We started out at Viking. I followed her to Knopf, and then followed her to Farrar, Straus & Giroux. She's a delight to work with, and it's a privilege to work with her. Almost any book she does I like. We have similar tastes. She is a great, great editor."

Asking about FSG publishing his newest collection of stories this fall as well as his new collection of poems, *PW* can see where Dybek's fantastic stories come from. Dybek's entire life and career seem to be based on cosmic coincidences. "Montale is one of my favorite poets. His primary translator in the United States is none other than Jonathan Galassi, the publisher at FSG, who is absolutely wonderful in his own right. This is absolutely amazing to me—to work with the same people who work with Montale." There is wonder in Dybek's voice as he says, "I am so lucky." Perhaps. Or maybe Stuart Dybek is just one hell of a raconteur, who can't help seeing the magic in the everyday world around him.

Source: Claire Kirch, "Windy City Oracle: Stuart Dybek," in *Publishers Weekly*, Vol. 250, No. 44, November 3, 2003, pp. 49–50.

Thomas S. Gladsky

In the following essay, Gladsky explores Dybek's rendering of ethnicity and cultural and spiritual heritage in his stories.

The new world culture and old country heritage of approximately fifteen million Americans of Polish descent are among multicultural America's best kept secrets. Historically a quiet minority, they have been eager to acculturate, assimilate, and melt into the mainstream.

One of the consequences of this has been a failure to acquaint other Americans with Polish culture—its history and literature—or to establish a recognized ethnic literary tradition. This is not to say that there is not a Polish presence in American letters. From the 1830s and the arrival of the first significant body of Polish emigres, primarily officers exiled after the 1831 uprising against the tzar, American writers have created Polish literary selves in plays, fiction, poems, and in prose works numbering perhaps as many as two hundred. Many of these contain abbreviated characterizations, predictably simplistic portraits, or, in some cases, merely composite Slavic cultural representations. At the same time, a few writers of classic ethnic and immigrant fiction, such as Karl Harriman (*The Homebuilders* 1903), Edith Miniter (*Our Natupski Neighbors* 1916), and Joseph Vogel (*Man's Courage* 1938), have sensitively explored the culture of Americans of Polish descent. Despite their efforts, what has emerged, as Thomas Napierkowski, Caroline Golab, and others have argued, is a set of stereotypes that have in certain ways attempted to transform a culture into a caricature.

Beginning in the 1930s, descent writers themselves began to examine the Polish self in a multiplicity of ways when Monica Krawczyk, Victoria Janda, and Helen Bristol turned to the immigrant generation as the subject of their poetry and fiction. Two decades later Richard Bankowsky produced a remarkable tetralogy about the arrival and dispersal of a turn of the century immigrant family. Bankowsky's *A Glass Rose* is perhaps the best novel about Slavic immigration in all of American literature. Wanda Kubiak (*Polonaise Nevermore*) and Matt Babinski (*By Raz* 1937) have described Poles in Wisconsin and Connecticut. In a series of novels in the 1970s, Darryl Poniscan followed the fortunes of the Buddusky clan in eastern Pennsylvania and elsewhere. In fiction for children, Anne Pellowski lovingly describes growing up ethnic in the Latsch Valley of Wisconsin. In numerous poems, *The Warsaw Sparks,* and his soon to be published memoir, *Szostak,* Gary Gildner explores both old and new world selves in sensitive ways. Most recently, Anthony Bukoski looks back to a rapidly vanishing Duluth community in *Children of Strangers.* In short, when one also considers the "Solidarity generation" of Czeslaw Milosz, Eva Hoffman, Stanislaus Baranczak, Janusz Glowacki, W. S. Kuniczak, and others, the Polish experience in American literature becomes demonstrable if not exceptional.

Even so, contemporary writers of Polish descent face complex problems, some of which are, of course, shared to some degree by all those who write about ethnicity. An ever-narrowing definition of multiculturalism that virtually excludes Eastern Europeans is one. Competing waves of Polish immigrants, dividing the ethnic community into descendants of the largely peasant immigration of 1880–1914, a post-war influx of "displaced persons," and a newer, more highly educated, urban Solidarity generation, is another. Added to these are America's general unfamiliarity with Polish culture, originating during the period of great immigration when nativists tended to lump all Slavic peoples together and to promote caricatures and stereotypes of Poles in particular.

Stuart Dybek is a case in point. The author of numerous poems and short stories, including a collection of verse (*Brass Knuckles* 1976) and

"Dybek makes it clear that the pull of Catholicism is both spiritual and cultural and that it is rooted in the immigrant experience itself."

two collections of fiction (*Childhood and Other Neighborhoods* 1986 and *The Coast of Chicago* 1990), Dybek is among the first writers of Polish descent (who write about the ethnic self) to receive national recognition. Reviewers have praised him as a regional writer (Chicago) and as a social critic who sides with those on the margin. They have compared him with Bellow and Dreiser and pointed to his city landscapes and spare, terse dialogue while, unfortunately, ignoring the ethnic dimension in his work. To be sure, Dybek does indeed write about the human condition. He gives us primarily initiation stories of urban adolescent males stretching into adulthood, expressing their sexuality, bravado and intellectual independence and realigning their social identity. Chicago with its particularized ethnic neighborhoods is a marked presence in their lives.

For Dybek, who grew up in southside Chicago, ethnicity is itself a natural and integral part of the human condition. The population in his neighborhood was mainly Eastern European and Hispanic. As he describes it: "The Eastern Europeans—Poles and Czechs—were migrating out; the Hispanics were migrating in. Each group had its own bars; they shared the same churches" ("You Can't Step Into the Same Street Twice"). Ethnicity, moreover, is also a condition of the contemporary literary experience. If not itself the central thrust of Dybek's work, it is one of those doorways, as he prefers to describe it, that leads to "some other dimension of experience and perception that forever changes the way one sees life." It is no surprise therefore that ethnicity is everywhere in his works. In "The River," a Ukrainian kid fiddles a nocturne. The girl in "Laughter" is Greek. The upstairs neighbors in "Chopin in Winter" speak Czech. The eccentric teacher in "Farewell" comes from Odessa. Hispanics appear in a number of stories; but Polish ethnicity is the tie that binds Dybek's protagonists together and supplies the cultural temperament in his fiction. Young men are named Swantek, Marzek, Vukovich, Kozak, and Gowumpe. Grandmothers called Busha worship in churches named St. Stanislaus. Relatives refer to soup as zupa; the neighbors listen to the Frankie Yankovitch Polka Hour; passersby speak Polish. Here and there we hear about mazurkas, Paderewski, Our Lady of Czestochowa, babushkas, and DPs, a recurring reference to non-native born Americans of Polish descent.

But what kind of ethnicity is Dybek portraying and how does he, a third generation American at some distance from his cultural roots, choose to represent his own cultural heritage? What, in effect, is Polish about these stories and what is the relationship between old and new expressions of ethnicity inside and outside Polonia? To some, Dybek's fiction may appear to be anachronistic, in that his frame of reference excludes the post-war and more recent Solidarity immigration that has transformed the Polish community in the United States, especially in Chicago, the setting for much of his work. Dybek, it could be argued, understands ethnicity almost exclusively from the point of view of the peasant generation and its descendants. In truth, the period of immigration and old world ties has long ago ended for his ethnic Poles. Consequently, he does not focus on assimilation and acculturation; nor are his characters busily collecting and preserving bits and pieces of their old world heritage. To the contrary, his protagonists are young, streetsmart, third generation Americans who know little, if anything, about Poland's past or present or the cultural nuances of the immigrant generation from which they are descended.

If anything, Dybek shows this generation resisting its ethnic impulses even as it rushes toward them. His young protagonists are updated modernists who, like Stephen Daedalus or Alfred Prufrock, wander city streets content with their own alienation and superior to the urban blight and social chaos that surround them. They are loners, eccentrics, budding intellectuals. They have no conscious sense of themselves as Polish-American or as ethnic in the usual sense of descending from a common history, religion, geography, and set of traditions. They are consumed instead with adolescence, environment, friends—with life in deteriorating and changing southside Chicago. They prefer Kerouac, the White Sox, Edward Hopper and rock music. Dybek's young Chicagoans thrive on melancholy, feast on loneliness, inhabit the "hourless times of night." They are refugees from Edward Hopper's "Nighthawks," which Dybek features prominently in his work. At the same time, they are acutely aware that they ache for something they cannot name "but knew was missing," as the narrator of "The River" phrases it; and that "things are gone they couldn't remember, but missed; and things were gone they weren't sure ever were there." Primarily, their narratives are remembrances of youthful things past.

For them, ethnicity and memory are interwoven naturally and succinctly. Consequently ethnicity in these stories is everywhere and yet almost beyond reach. Polish culture, for example, often enters through the back door. Dybek never identifies his characters as Poles, nor do they refer to themselves as Polish or as Polish-American. Polishness is rather cumulative, dependent partly on recurring signifiers and partly on the interconnectedness of the stories themselves. In "typical" fashion, he draws attention to the presence of cultural differences in the first few lines and then proceeds to develop a generic ethnic cultural landscape which seems to have few particular Polish markers. This approach is evident even in the first story in *Childhood and Other Neighborhoods.* The title, "The Palatski Man," itself calls attention to otherness, although only midway in the story does Dybek explain that palatski, apparently a regional American corruption of plocki, the Polish word for potato pancake, was a food once sold by vendors in southside Chicago. In the first page the reader also encounters the Slavic-sounding name Leon Sisca and the Catholic mysteries of Palm Sunday. The children attend St. Roman's grammar school, have friends named Zmiga and another named Raymond Cruz, "part Mexican" and perhaps part Polish. In addition, the children define their surroundings in terms of their parish church, which distinguishes their neighborhood from the adjoining one where "more Mexicans lived." Apart from the fact that the palatski man stammers in "foreign English," no other overt references to ethnicity in general or to Polishness in particular occur.

This approach is repeated elsewhere. In "The Wake," Dybek looks at one evening in the life of Jill, a southside Chicago teenager whose surname and particular cultural heritage remain anonymous. Dybek, however, establishes Till's parameters, physical and psychological, within an ethnic landscape. On her way to the wake, she hears the bells of St. Kasimir's church and walks along the street that serves as a boundary between her neighborhood and St. Anne's, "an old Slavic neighborhood that had become Spanish." She heads toward Zeijek's Funeral home, "a three-story building domed with its fake Russian onion." Reminiscent of Joyce Carol Oates's "Where Are You Going, Where Have You Been?" Jill eventually drives off with an intrusive Hispanic whose ethnicity poses no threat to her. We learn that the culture of Jill's neighborhood is Slavic-Hispanic. She drives by the hot tamale man with his striped umbrella; she hears radios turned to Latin stations; and she refers to the young man's car as "Pancho." There is no dominant ethnic "theme" in "The Wake," no social or generational problems, no hint of cultural oppression or collision. Ethnicity is muted, understood, and natural—an integral part of the contemporary urban experience and cultural context—but not exclusively tied to national boundaries, even though one suspects that Jill might be of Polish descent.

In other stories in *Childhood and Other Neighborhoods*, *The Coast of Chicago*, and elsewhere, Dybek constructs a more specifically Polish ethnic identity for his characters, their neighborhood, and their frame of mind. In "The Cat Woman" and "Blood Soup," the two stories that immediately succeed "The Palatski Man," Dybek repeats the pattern of the opening story, relying primarily on names, words, and surface features to establish an ethnic landscape. At the outset, the reader learns that buzka and busha are what some people call their grandmothers. The reader also meets characters with Slavic-sounding names such as Swantek and Stefush (a Polish diminutive for Stephen). The cat woman, Swantek's grandmother, fingers her rosary and tunes her radio to the polka station. She also shares cabbage soup with her neighbor, Mrs. Panova. In stories like "The Cat Woman," the ethnic markers suggest a composite Slavic cultural landscape although discerning readers might interpret the markers as the outlines of Polish-American culture.

A distinctly Polish frame of reference becomes evident only in "Blood Soup," the third story in *Childhood*, where, in addition to Busha "clutching the crucifix" and references to such old world Catholic practices as the kissing of holy pictures, Dybek includes more compelling evidence of Polish ethnicity. On occasion, he uses Polish words (usiadz, dziekuje, dupa, czarina, rozumiesz) without translation. His young hero remembers the traditional Polish custom of blessing the Easter breakfast food: colored eggs, ham, bread, kraut, horseradish, and kielbasa. More importantly, in this story Dybek moves beyond ceremonies and the surface features of ethnicity when he tries to capture something of the old world temperament that differentiates Eastern Europeans from Americans and first generation ethnics from their descendants. At one point, Stefush recognizes that his grandmother is different in more substantive ways that merely her taste for czarnina, a peasant soup made from duck's blood. He senses in her "a kind of love he thought must have come from the old country—instinctive, unquestioning like her strength, something foreign that he couldn't find in himself, that hadn't even been transmitted to his mother."

Ethnicity, particularly the culture of Americans of Polish descent, is cumulative in Dybek's writing. Often one story clarifies and extends an ethnic dimension introduced in another. For example, in order to understand fully what Dybek means in "Blood Soup" by "a kind of love" that "must have come from the old country," we must turn to "A Minor Mood," published some seven years later. This is a familiar tale of immigrants and their descendants. Joey, a young third generation American, remembers attacks of bronchitis and his granny swooping down upon him, bathing his neck with a glob of Vicks and wrapping it in her babushka, applying camphor to his chest, filling the rooms with steam, mixing honey, lemon, Jim Beam, and boiling water for him to drink (and for herself too). These were mornings, he concludes, "to be tucked away at the heart of life, so that later, whenever one needed to draw upon the recollection of joy in order to get through troubled times it would be there." All of "A Minor Mood," in effect, develops and expands the ethnic temperament alluded to in "Blood Soup," although a few ethnic signifiers can be noticed.

Only once does Dybek turn to what might be called a paradigmatic ethnic tale in order to define the contemporary Polish-American self. In "Chopin in Winter," a story about the conflicting claims of descent and consent, the aging Dzia Dzia tells his own story to his grandson—his trek from Krakow to Gdansk to avoid being drafted into the tzarist army, his immigration to the coal mines of Pennsylvania and the barges of the Great Lakes. At one point, Dzia Dzia's story melts into that of another Polish immigrant and national icon, Frederick Chopin. "Chopin, he'd whisper hoarsely to Michael, pointing to the ceiling with the reverence of nuns pointing to heaven." More than telling his story, the old man provides a cultural frame for the third generation, creating an image of what it means to be ethnic.

Dybek does not mean to stop here, however, with romantic and sentimental notions of heritage;

he is more interested in cultural fusion, in that uniquely American acculturating process described by Werner Sollors in *Beyond Ethnicity* as the tension between "our hereditary qualities" and our position as "architects of our fate." Grandfather, for instance, mentions in "Chopin in Winter" that Paderewski dearly loved Chopin; but Michael does not know Paderewski, a sign of his distance from his cultural heritage. Instinctively, Grandfather connects their American and Polish heritages in a comic but revealing and shrewd fashion, by asking, "Do you know who's George Washington, who's Joe Dimaggio, who's Walt Disney? . . . Paderewski was like them, except he played Chopin. . . . See, deep down inside, Lefty, you know more than you think." Even in this, one of Dybek's most "Polish" stories, cultural transmission gives way to a new cultural pattern of consent and descent. For Americans of Polish descent, ethnicity means knowing about Joe Dimaggio and Paderewski, Washington and Chopin, Disneyland and Krakow.

Ethnicity also means Catholicism; in fact, Catholicism in the form of childhood experiences with the church, the parochial school, or the religious practices and attitudes of the immigrant generation permeates these stories and poems and often is the singular definer of Polish culture. Even here Dybek concentrates not on Polish but on ethnic expressions of and responses to Catholicism. In a recently published chapbook, *The Story of Mist,* Dybek begins by wondering what it is "about the belly button that connected it to the Old Country?" To explain, he immediately turns to religious metaphors, noting that "outside, night billowed like the habits of nuns through vigil lights of snow," while Busha's "rosary-pinched fingers" promised to lead inward. But it is the tolling of the bells from the steeple of St. Kasimir's that serves as the umbilical cord between old and new world culture. When he hears them, he knows that "Krakow is only blocks away, just past Goldblatt's darkened sign."

The parish church is thus the center of vision in a significant number of stories. In "The Wake," Jill uses the church steeple to locate her whereabouts in the neighborhood. Ladies murmur the rosary in front of the icon of Our Lady of Czestochowa in "Neighborhood Drunk." In a fit of madness Budhardin destroys the inside of the parish church in "Visions of Budhardin." Old women walk "on their knees up the marble aisle to kiss the relics" and Eddy and Manny try to visit all the neighborbood churches in "Hot Ice." "The Woman Who Fainted" does so at the 11:15 mass. Stanley's girlfriend lives across from the Assumption Church, leading him to call her "the Unadulterated one." To the young protagonists in these stories, the church represents the mystery of old world culture—of Polishness itself.

Consequently, Dybek frequently turns to childhood experiences with the clergy, the parochial school, and the rituals and mysteries of Eastern European Catholicism in order to develop plot and theme. There is little that is peaceful, consoling, or even attractive in these memories and experiences, however. We read about the cruelty of Father O'Donnel. We meet Sister Monica who loses her teaching assignment because she becomes hysterical in front of her fifth grade class. We listen to the narrator of "The Dead in Korea," remembering how he was made to kneel on three-cornered drafting rulers in parochial school. At the same time, Dybek writes about the mystical attractions of Catholicism that draw his young people toward familiar ritual and ceremony despite their growing skepticism. This is perhaps best expressed in "Hot Ice," where Manny and Eddie reenact a childhood ritual of visiting seven churches on Good Friday afternoon. They walk from St. Roman's to St. Michael's, from St. Kasimir's to St. Anne's, from St. Pius's to St. Adalbert's, then finally to the church of St. Procopius. At first, they merely peek in and leave, "as if touching base." But soon their "familiarity with small rituals quickly returned: dipping their fingers in the holy water font by the door, making the automatic sign of the cross as they passed the life-sized crucified Christs that hung in the vestibules where old women and school kids clustered to kiss the spikes in the bronze or bloody plaster feet."

Dybek makes it clear that the pull of Catholicism is both spiritual and cultural and that it is rooted in the immigrant experience itself. He makes this connection through the recurring presence of old people, the last of the immigrant generation. Usually these characters are grandparents engaged in helping third generation youngsters understand their cultural identity. Dzia Dzia in "Chopin in Winter," Busha in "Blood Soup," the old man in "The Apprentice," and Gran in "A Minor Mood" all help to introduce their grandchildren to Polish history, tradition, and temperament.

At other times Dybek integrates the immigrant generation into the mystique of Polish Catholicism. He does this primarily through repeated references to older women involved in one form of worship or another. The narrator of "The Woman Who Fainted," intrigued by the ritualistic fainting that often occurs at the 11:15 mass, observes the hand of an "old woman in a babushka" that darts out to correct the dress hem of the fainting lady. In "Chopin in Winter," Mrs. Kubiak joins the regulars at morning mass, "wearing babushkas and dressed in black like a sodality of widows droning endless mournful litanies." And in "Good Friday" a two-page story published in *Gulf Coast*, the young narrator, entranced with the church organ, the statues, Sister Monica, the incense and the holy water, focuses ultimately on the "old women, babushkaed in black, weeping as they walk on their knees up the marble aisle to the altar in order to kiss the relic." These people, Dybek implies, are nothing less than old world culture transfigured into the new world. In this sense Dybek captures both the attraction and rejection of whatever it is that Polish culture has come to mean in post-war America.

In fact, rejection and denial and the subsequent reshaping of cultural identify are essential ingredients of the ethnicization that occurs in these stories. In a very real sense all of Dybek's fiction is about social disorganization and reorganization in the classic sense of these principles outlined by Thomas and Znaniecki in *The Polish Peasant in Europe and America.* The alienation that exists in Dybek's younger characters results as much from cultural tensions, however, as it does from socioeconomics and shifting philosophical perspectives. Typically, Dybek contrasts the immigrant generation with its third generation descendants with an eye toward showing cultural transformation, or he describes the simultaneous act of acquiring and rejecting a cultural past. While "ethnicity" is still the norm by which his protagonists view the world, Dybek insists that contemporary urban ethnicity must be defined differently from that of preceding time periods. Thus he attempts to differentiate between old and new ethnicity even in his ethnically Polish characters.

For example, while Dybek on the one hand offers sympathetic portraits of grandparents and other first generation Americans of Polish descent and sensitively explores the essentials of Polish culture, he on the other hand frequently presents these cultural representatives as eccentric grotesques out of touch with the times and their adopted culture. Typically he portrays the immigrant generation as the cultural "other" rather than as the cultural norm. In fact, the more Polish the characters are, the more eccentric and grotesque they and their cultural practices tend to look to the reader. The "Palatski Man," the opening story in *Childhood and Other Neighborhoods,* sets this tone and outlines this direction. The palatski man, not dignified with any other name, is a rather frightening and threatening figure (at least to the two youngsters in the story). He is an exotic street vendor who appears to live with the peddlers, ragpickers, and other cultural outsiders in makeshift housing near an urban dumping ground. The food he sells is culturally unrecognizable although Slavic sounding. His white clothing and white cart, while ordinary enough, are undercut by his foreign-sounding English (although we never hear him talk) and his involvement in Palm Sunday Eucharistic rituals with other ragmen. Although we do not learn the palatski man's cultural heritage, his characterization, his ragged associates, and their surreal surroundings create an atmosphere of strangeness and alienation toward the culture represented by the word palatski.

This point of view permeates those stories involving Americans of Polish descent. In "The Cat Woman," Dybek almost rushes to associate ethnicity with strangeness when he calls the woman buzka, introduces her "crazy grandson as Swantek," and then proceeds to explain that Buzka drowned the excess neighborhood kittens in her washing machine. With this introduction, the ethnicity of the immigrant generation (buzka) and those (Swantek) who remain most closely associated with their old world habits is enough to divorce it from the cultural norm. "No one," Dybek succinctly comments, "brought laundry anymore to the old woman." The story ends with grotesque images of despair and degeneration. Swantek sleeps on old drapes beside the furnace, "vomiting up cabbage in the corners and covering it with newspapers," and Buzka and her old friend Mrs. Panova blow on their spoonfuls of soup "with nothing more to say," their radio turned to the polka hour. In other stories, we meet Big Antek, the local drunk; the uncle of Tadeusz, who spends his nights picking up the debris of a culture on the move; and Slavic workers missing parts of hands and arms that have been "chewed off while trying to clean machines" ("Sauerkraut Soup"). Such is the price of the old ethnicity, which in this case is represented as servile labor, alcoholism, a meanness toward animals, a taste for cabbage soup, and, most importantly, as descent from an inferior national culture.

In these rather traditional interpretations of second and third generation behavior, the usual signifiers of ethnicity—language, religion, history, customs and other conventional cultural markers—lose their privileged position even though they remain as a frame of reference. Nowhere is this better illustrated than in his adolescent protagonists' ambivalent relationship with Catholicism, which in Polish terms is inextricably and historically tied to nationalism. In other words a rejection of Catholicism is tantamount in these cases to a rejection of national, that is to say Polish, identity. "Visions of Budhardin," "The Long Thoughts," "The Woman Who Fainted," and "Sauerkraut Soup" all dramatize the act of coming to terms with the religion of descent. One narrator, remembering his parochial education, explains what he regarded as the fear underlying religion, and reveals that the summer "after my sophomore year in high school was the last summer I went to church." Those who continue to at tend do so from habit and custom. In "Hot Ice," Eddie admits that "he had given up, and the ache left behind couldn't be called grief." In "Visions of Budhardin," the protagonist, in a rage of pent up resentment, ravages the church which so callously ignored his childhood needs. But Marzek in "Sauerkraut Soup" speaks for all Dybek's disillusioned Polish Catholics when he says: "I had already developed my basic principle of Catholic education—the Double Reverse: (1) suspect what they teach you; (2) study what they condemn." The words and deeds of these characters document their hostility to the culture of their ancestors and their inability to any longer understand or sympathize with this kind of ethnicity.

In effect, Dybek shows the transformation from immigrant to ethnic and beyond. Throughout, a sense of loss is coupled with an acceptance of change as his spokespersons lament the disappearance of the Polish southside. The narrator in "Blight" returns to his old neighborhood after a few years and confesses that he "was back in my neighborhood, but lost, everything at once familiar and strange, and I knew if I tried to run, my feet would be like lead, and if I stepped off a curb, I'd drop through space." Dybek thus points to a condition of ethnicity that characterizes the American Polish community as the recently published stories of Anthony Bukoski (*Children of Strangers*) also makes clear. In Dybek's stories, as in Bukoski's, the core of old world Polish culture is almost lost. Neighborhood demographics and Parish churches have changed, and only a few Polish-born Americans are left to transmit and interpret Polish traditions and customs. In "Blood Soup," Uncle Joe's meat market is full of Mexican kids and Big Antek explains to Stefush that, in regard to his efforts to help his grandma make her beloved old world soup, "we don't sell fresh blood no more." Mrs. Gowumpe (pigeon, in Polish) tells Stefush how things were: "I used to work in the yards," he explains. "All those DPs working there . . . Polacks, Lugans, Bohunks. People who knew how to be happy." Now Mr. Gowumpe, grandma Busha, the palatski man, and the other first generation Poles are poor, isolated, lonely, and few in number. Nonetheless, they are the voice of cultural memory.

Dybek's fiction is not elegiac, however. Ethnicity is positive, pervasive, and dynamic in these stories; and the movement is toward a new understanding of ethnicity that is based not on national origins but on a shared sense of ethnicity as a condition of Americanness. Dybek's protagonists aren't Poles; they're not even Polish- American by traditional definition. They have, paradoxically, reinvented and reinterpreted themselves (Fischer 1950). For this generation ethnicity is a sociopolitical reality, a sensitivity to pluralism, and, as James Clifford phrases it, "a conjunctural not essential" state of mind. More than that, ethnicity is not even a necessary condition of descent because for Stuart Dybek cultural pluralism has supplanted nationality and a new level of multicultural awareness has replaced ethnocentricity. Dybek himself calls attention to this in an essay entitled "You Can't Step Into the Same Street Twice": "Besides the ethnic tribes of Slavs and Hispanics whose language and music and food smells permeated the streets, there was another tribe, one that in a way transcended nationality, a tribe of youth, of kids born to replenish the species recently depleted by WW II."

In his stories, Dybek replicates the tribal and cultural landscape of Chicago. Those who live in the older ethnic neighborhoods have experienced a change from a basically Eastern European population to a mixed neighborhood of Americans of Hispanic and Slavic descent, primarily Mexican and Polish. More importantly, Dybek's third generation fellow Polish ethnics are just as frequently paired with Hispanic friends as with fellow "Poles": Ziggy Zilinski and Pepper Rosado in "Blight," Eddy Kapusta and Manny and Pancho Santoro in "Hot Ice," Ray Cruz and John in "The Palatski Man." There are few instances of ethnic rivalry in this landscape. Quite the contrary, the commingling of Latino and Slav is economic, sociological, and cultural-a product of shifting demographics and resulting neighborhood changes, the result of shared environment and social class. They both identify with and like "the other." From this a new sense of ethnicity—an emblem of contemporary America—arises.

On the surface, the new ethnicity appears to be nothing more than the camaraderie of friends thrown together by demographics. In reality, the union of Pole and Chicano represents the changing face of America and of Polish Americanness. Stanley Rosado is Pepper to some and Stashu to others, reflecting his Mexican father and Polish mother. When David, the descendent of Poles, goes to a bar with friend, he drinks a Coca-Nana rather than vodka or piwo. The Mexican music on the jukebox sounds "suspiciously like polkas." David now listens to "CuCuRuCuCu Paloma" on the radio, and Eddie Kapusta sings in Spanish.

Tellingly, Eddie identifies more with Spanish than he does with the Polish language. He is struck with the word juilota (pigeon). It seems the perfect word because in it "he could hear both their cooing and the whistling rush of their wings." Equally telling, Eddie cannot remember "any words like that in Polish, which his grandma had spoken to him when he was little." Eddie's relatives may likely turn out to be Hispanic in the sense that Richard Rodriguez, in Hunger of Memory, believes that he may become Asian. In the words of Rosalie Murphy Baum, "multicultural contact has defeated the ethnic norm."

When all is said and done, Dybek's ethnic characters seem to say that "what they are" doesn't really matter in terms of history, language, geography. The new urban ethnic accepts ethnicity while rejecting nationality. Traditional ethnic borders give way to a heightened social and moral sense that replaces geographic maps and national origins. In "Hot Ice," Eddie Kapusta arrives at this insight: "Most everything from that world had changed or disappeared, but the old women had endured—Polish, Bohemian, Spanish, he knew it didn't matter; they were the same . . . a common pain of loss seemed to burn at the core of their lives." Grandma in "Pet Milk" is illustrative. She knows about the old country and the new, where "all the incompatible states of Europe were pressed together down at the staticky right end" of the radio dial. Grandma also seems to know that ethnicity in America means something more than national origin. Consequently she is happy to listen to the Greek station or the Ukrainian or the Spanish although, of course, she would prefer listening to polkas. And in "Hot Ice," Eddie elaborates on the changing face of ethnicity when he admits to himself, "Manny could be talking Spanish; I could be talking Polish. . . . It didn't matter. What meant something was sitting at the table together."

What also matters is that in Dybek's hands the Polish ethnic self assumes what some may regard as a new identity. And Dybek emerges as a writer who offers examples of the way experience, history, and ethnicity crossbreed. To be sure, Dybek does indeed try to present the preciousness of America's Polish heritage and the exceptionalism of the ethnically Polish American. He is, at the same time, eager to resist parochialism and exclusivity. His characterization of his young heroes and heroines as romantic rebels and urbanized American versions of Keats, Proust, Dostoevsky and others whom they have read, leads him beyond mere ethnicity even though his fiction is rooted in the cultural neighborhoods of southside Chicago. While attempting to capture the unique flavor of a particular ethnic group, Dybek has created a multi-layered and multi-dimensional ethnic self. This self reflects the image of a trans-ethnic urban America, a diorama of a diverse cultural landscape where ethnicity transcends national origins but remains vital and where the ethnic and the modern self are not only compatible but are the essence of postmodernism and, as Andrew Greeley puts it, "a way of being American."

Source: Thomas S. Gladsky, "From Ethnicity to Multiculturalism: The Fiction of Stuart Dybek," in *MELUS*, Vol. 20, No. 2, Summer 1995, pp. 105–18.

Sources

Kakutani, Michiko, "Lyrical Loss and Desolation of Misfits in Chicago, in *New York Times Book Review*, April 20, 1990, p. C31.

Lee, Don, Review of *The Coast of Chicago*, in *Ploughshares*, Vol. 17, No. 1, Spring 1991, pp. 228–29.

"Noted by the Editors," in *Antioch Review*, Vol. 48, No. 4, Fall 1990, pp. 545–46.

Further Reading

Casey, Maud, "Chicago Stories: A Profile of Stuart Dybek," in *Poets & Writers*, Vol. 31, No. 6, November/December 2003, pp. 34–40.

This cover story, published just as Dybek's book *I Sailed with Magellan* was about to come out, contains background information about his life in the location where the story is set, as well as information about his career and influences.

Gladsky, Thomas S., "From Ethnicity to Multiculturalism: The Fiction of Stuart Dybek," in *Melus*, Vol. 20, No. 2, Summer 1995, pp. 105–18.

This thorough examination of Dybek's stories includes background information about the Polish American literary tradition.

Kantowicz, Edward, "Polish Chicago: Survival Through Solidarity," in *Ethnic Chicago: A Multicultural Portrait*, edited by Melvin G. Holli and Peter d'A. Jones, William B. Eerdmans Publishing, 1977, pp. 173–98.

Kantowicz looks at the history of Chicago's Polish community, one of the city's dominant ethnic groups, based in the neighborhood that Dybek discusses in the story.

Kirch, Claire, "Windy City Oracle: Stuart Dybek," in *Publishers Weekly*, Vol. 250, No. 44, November 3, 2003, pp. 49–51.

This article, based on an interview with Dybek, outlines his thoughts about writing and about the ways the publishing business changed over the years he has been a writer.

Nickel, Mike, and Adrian Smith, "An Interview with Stuart Dybek," in *Chicago Review*, Vol. 43, No. 1, Winter 1997, pp. 87–102.

In addition to other issues, Dybek talks about being labeled a "Chicago writer," despite the fact that he has not lived in Chicago in years.

In the Middle of the Fields

Mary Lavin

1998

Mary Lavin's "In the Middle of the Fields" is often referred to as one of thc author's "widow stories," a group of stories that Lavin wrote in the late 1960s that reflect her own struggles with widowhood. Patricia K. Meszaros, in her article on Lavin for *Critique*, writes that her widowhood "informs" this work "in her searching and compassionate portrayals of loneliness." "In the Middle of the Fields" is one of the most gripping stories in this group in its focus on the efforts of a recently widowed woman to resist the pull of the past in order to function in the present.

The unnamed woman is determined to run the farm herself after her husband dies. During the day, she demonstrates an independent spirit that suggests she will ultimately succeed in her attempt to establish a new life and identity for herself. Yet in the evening, her fear of being alone makes her more vulnerable to her memories. An encounter one night with Bartley Crossen, a neighboring farmer whom she employs to cut her grass, highlights the tenuous balance she has struck between past and present and the sometimes overwhelming sense of loss she experiences. In this intimate and sensitive story, Lavin reveals the painful consequences of death on those left behind.

Author Biography

Mary Lavin was born in East Walpole, Massachusetts in 1912 to Thomas and Nora Lavin, who were both Irish immigrants. The family moved back to

Mary Lavin Reproduced by Kennys Galway on behalf of the Estate of Mary Lavin

Ireland in 1922, living first in Athenry, County Galway, and later in Dublin.

In Dublin, Mary attended the Loreto Convent School, and in 1934 she graduated from University College, where she received honors in English. In 1936 she completed a thesis on Jane Austen that earned her a master of arts. She was working toward a Ph.D. and teaching French at the Loreto Convent School when she wrote her first short story, "Miss Holland." After many rejections, "Miss Holland" was finally published by *Dublin* magazine in 1938.

Lavin married William Walsh, an Irish barrister, in 1942 and a year later they had a daughter whom they named Valentine. Also in 1942, Lavin had a collection of her short stories published entitled *Tales from Bective Bridge*. The collection received acclaim in Ireland as well as in the United States and won the James Tait Black Memorial Prize.

In 1944, Lavin's first novel, *Gabriel Galloway* was originally published in the *Atlantic Monthly* in seven consecutive issues. In 1945, the novel was published in its entirety under the title, *The House in Clewe Street*. The following year, after the birth of her second daughter as well as the death of her father, Lavin published her second book, *The Becker Wives and Other Stories*. Although at this point in her career, Lavin realized that the novella was her preferred form, she completed the novel *Mary O'Grady*, published in 1950.

Her husband, William, died soon after the birth of their third child in 1954, forcing Lavin to raise her three daughters and manage their farm by herself. She handled these responsibilities and at the same time earned two Guggenheim Foundation fellowships. In 1961 she was also awarded the Katherine Mansfield Prize and in 1968 the University of Ireland awarded her a Doctor of Letters degree.

In 1967, Lavin published another collection of stories, *In the Middle of the Fields*. Stories she published in the late 1960s are often referred to as her "widow stories." Patricia K. Meszarus, in her article on Lavin for *Critique*, writes that Lavin's widowhood "informs most of her middle and later work . . . in her searching and compassionate portrayals of loneliness and sometimes willful isolation."

Mary Lavin continued writing short stories for magazines such as the *New Yorker* up until the mid-1980s. She died in Dublin in March 1996.

Plot Summary

Part 1

"In the Middle of the Fields" begins with a description of a recently widowed, unnamed woman in her house in Ireland. Surrounded by fields, she feels her house is like an island but admits that she is less lonely on the land where she and her husband had lived together. Nonetheless, she often experiences anxiety during the day, and she is always fearful at night. The townspeople have talked about how she must be feeling about her loss, but she insists that they do not know. When they tried to talk to her about their own memories of her husband, she became annoyed since their reminiscences triggered her own.

When the story opens, the widow is concerned about the grass in the fields that needs topping (trimming), and she worries about how much it will cost. Ned, the old farm hand, suggests that Bartley Crossen, a neighboring farmer, could do the job, noting that her husband "knew him well." Initially, she cannot recall who Crossen is, but then she declares that she has seen him but never met him. When Ned tells her that he will set up a meeting, she insists he come before dark because she does not like to be downstairs at night. She locks herself and her children in their rooms after dark, dreading a knock at the door. Ned tries to reassure her that no one would pay her a visit at night and insists that she is safe. He makes sure that whenever he needs to come at night to tend to something on her farm, he announces himself as he comes up the walk so that she will not be afraid. When he does come, she is grateful to have someone in the house.

Crossen arrives at the house with Ned before dark while his wife waits outside in the car. As they discuss the job, Crossen looks out over the fields to the riverbank that he claims he knows well. He tells them that when he was young, he courted a girl there, who the woman later discovers became his first wife. Crossen tells her that he can do the job in the morning and that he will be fair with the price. As Crossen leaves, Ned whispers to her, "he's a man you can trust."

After Crossen departs, Ned tells her about Crossen's first wife, Bridie Logan, who, he claims, was "as wild as a hare" and "mad with love." The two married young, and soon after Bridie got pregnant. Too soon after the baby was born, Bridie decided to help Crossen milk the cows. When he told her that it would be too far for her to walk, she jumped on her bike and pedaled out of the gate. As she got to the bottom of the hill, she turned the bike around and started "pedaling madly up the hill again." Half way up the hill, she started to bleed internally, and later that day she died.

Ned notes that the baby was strong and that Crossen's second wife, who had more sons with Crossen, did a fine job of raising it. When the woman asks Ned whether Crossen has forgotten about Bridie, Ned tells her that he has and that it will be the same with her. But she shakes her head "doubtfully."

At night in her room, the widow wonders if Crossen has really forgotten Bridie. As she brushes her hair, Crossen knocks on the door, which fills her with fear. When Crossen calls out, she recognizes his voice and comes down the stairs to let him in. He apologizes for disturbing her so late when he sees her with her hair down and in her dressing gown. He tells her he has never seen such "a fine head of hair" and that it makes her look like a young girl. When she smiles with pleasure at his compliment but sharply exclaims that she does not feel like one, he responds that he can see she is a sensible woman.

They begin to discuss cutting the grass, and Crossen tells her that cutting the tops off costs him as much as cutting hay. He admits that she does not get an immediate return from cutting the grass, but she will in the long run as it will be better for her cows to eat. When she angrily disagrees, he insists that he made "a special price" for her, especially because she does not now have a man to take care of the farm for her. She declares that she can take care of the farm herself to which he responds, "that's what all women like to think!"

When he tells her that he would like to do the job later in the week rather than the next day, she gets angry, insisting that by the time he gets around to it, her fields will be ruined. He admires her authoritative stance but tries to maintain his position, insisting it will be only a few days. When she stands firm, he gives in. As he prepares to leave, he tells her that he hopes that she does not think he was trying to take advantage of her and that no one in the community thought that she would stay there after her husband died.

He then asks her if she gets lonely at night. When she corrects him with "you mean frightened?" he says yes, but assures her that she is safe there. She admits that she is "scared to death sometimes," which makes her go up to her room so early in the evening. When he responds sympathetically, she asks him to wait until she goes upstairs and then turn off the light as he leaves. He is genuinely troubled about her fears and asks whether anyone could stay with her but then realizes that that would not work out.

As she "somewhat reluctantly" starts up the stairs, he calls to her, asking how to put out a light. She comes down again saying she will do it. While he blocks the doorway, Crossen grabs her arm and inquires "are you ever lonely—at all?" and then asks for a kiss. He tries to get a better hold of her, but she wrenches her arm free and escapes out into the lighted hall. As she begins to laugh, he appears "pathetic in his sheepishness," which she is surprised to admit touches her. She tells him that he should not feel badly, that she really did not mind, but he is miserable, claiming "I don't know what came over me." She tries to make him feel better, but he remains dejected. After an awkward silence, she tells him that she will see him in the morning, but he does not immediately go. He feels the need to talk about the incident, insisting that he did not mean any disrespect. He cannot understand why he did it and wonders what his wife would say if she knew. She tells him not to tell her.

Crossen muses about how good his wife Mona has been, how she took care of his and Bridie's son from the time he was a week old. He admits that he is grateful to her as he remembers Mona taking the baby all day, each day to her house next door, bringing him back for a while in the evening, and then taking him back to sleep with her. She helped him become "a living man" again. Eventually he decided that he should marry her, which would make things more convenient. When Crossen insists that he has shamed Mona, the widow argues that what happened has nothing to do with her, adding that it has nothing to do with any of them except Bridie. She demands that he blame her, and with a note of hysteria claims, "you thought you could forget her" but he could not. After her outburst, Crossen leaves without looking back while exclaiming, "God rest her soul." Lavin does not make it clear whether he was referring to Bridie or the widow.

Characters

Bartley Crossen

When the main character first meets Bartley Crossen, a neighboring farmer, she observes "something kindly in his look and in his words." Ned, the farmhand, insists that Crossen is decent and "a man you can trust." He often is solicitous in his dealings with her, mentioning his wife waiting for him at home, which she understands as "meant to put her at *her* ease." When he comes to her house at night, he tries to allay any fear of his motives when he says, "I'm long gone beyond taking any account of what a woman has on her. I'm gone beyond taking notice of women at all." This claim proves false, however.

Crossen's relationship with his first wife Bridie suggests that he is a passionate man. Ned notes that he had the same passion for her as she for him. They were both "mad with love . . . she only wanting to draw him on, and he only too willing!" He tries to suppress his memories and feelings for Bridie, perhaps out of respect for his second wife and also to avoid the pain of the past. The only comment he makes about Bridie is that he "courted a girl" down by the riverbank. His passionate nature remerges when he visits the main character at night. He reveals his obvious attraction to her when he notices her hair and later when he asks for a kiss.

Before his passion causes him to shame himself, he displays confidence in his business dealings with her, standing "stoutly" in her hallway. This easy confidence allows him to accept her harsh words. When, after he compliments her, she sharply insists that she does not feel young, her words seem "to delight him and put him wonderfully at ease." He responds that she is a sensible woman and tells her to stay the way she is.

Bridie Crossen

Bridie, Crossen's first wife, gets so caught up in her passion for her husband that it clouds her vision and ultimately leads to her death. Ned calls her "wild as a hare" and "strong as a kid goat." She was "mad with love" for Bartley and did everything she could to please him. Her passion grew after they were married to the point where, Ned claims, "it was . . . as if she was driven on by some kind of a fever." Her desire for his praise caused her to scrub the house until there was little left to scrub. Her lack of common sense in her relationship with him became evident when she got on the bike too soon after the birth of their child, an impulsive act triggered by her desire to be with him.

Mona Crossen

Mona, Crossen's second wife, always comes with him when he works on other farms. She stays in the car, sitting rigidly, "the way people sat up in the well of little tub traps long ago, their knees pressed together, allowing no slump." She is a good woman according to Ned and Bartley, who describe how she cared for his child with Bridie. Both insist that she raised the child as if he were her own.

Ned

Ned, the main character's loyal farmhand, initiates the action of the story when he brings Crossen to cut the grass. Ned likes to chat and to gossip about his neighbors, but not in a malicious way. In this sense, he serves as a narrative voice, filling in all the relevant details about the characters. He shows considerable kindness and concern for the main character. Noting her night fears, he tries to assure her that she is safe, that no one would come to the house at night. He always takes care to call out to her when he comes in the evening to tend to the farm. When he realizes that the past is weighing heavily on her, he tries to assure her that "everything passes in time and is forgotten."

The Woman

The first line shows the duality of the main character, her vulnerability and her strength. She is isolated, "islanded by fields" but also "like a rock in the sea." She feels nameless anxieties and fears as she struggles to take care of the farm after the death of her husband, dreading in particular, a knock after dark, which can paralyze her with fright.

Her practical side emerges as she tries to control her thoughts of her husband, insisting that they are only "dry love and barren longing." She recognizes the danger in living in the past and determines to make a new life for herself. Thus, she gets impatient with neighbors who want to reminisce about him, which inevitably triggers her own painful memories. Her common sense and her survival instincts emerge in her dealings with Crossen. She realizes what must be done on the farm to keep it successful. When she feels as sluggish and heavy as her hair, she immediately brushes it so that it and she become energized.

She refuses to allow Crossen to put her in a vulnerable position. Although at first, she appreciates his compliment about her hair, she immediately adopts a stern tone with him, letting him know that he must treat her as an equal. Each time he tries to insist that she is a woman and therefore needs the help of a man, she reasserts her independence and strength. However, her thoughts about Bridie's influence over Crossen remind her of her own fears about the power of the past and her vulnerability emerges. By the end of the story, the main character has made progress toward establishing an independent identity and a new life without her husband, but she remains vulnerable to her fear of being alone and her memories of the past.

Themes

Passion

Passion is clearly evident in Crossen's relationship with Bridie and only suggested in the main character's with her husband, but both appear to share the same intensity and the same difficult consequences. Bridie was "mad with love" for Crossen, which only strengthened after their marriage. Ned notes that "it was like as if she was driven on by some kind of a fever." She did everything she could around the house and the farm to make him proud of her. Immediately after she had her baby, her love for him prompted her to get out of bed and join him in milking. She jumped on her bike and pedaled madly down the road, trying to encourage him to chase her. Yet her passion ended up destroying her when the vigorous exercise caused internal bleeding. Crossen, Ned insists, was mad with love for her as well, which becomes evident when Crossen notes that after she died, he was no longer "a living man."

Topics for Further Study

- Read two other short stories by Mary Lavin and write an essay comparing and contrasting the main themes.
- So much of the emotion in this story remains beneath the surface. How would you film this story, allowing for the suppressed emotions while conveying them? Write a screenplay for the final scenes in the story, beginning with Crossen's arrival at night.
- Investigate the emotional stages that one goes through when a loved one dies. Chart these stages in a PowerPoint presentation.
- Write a short story about the main character twenty years from the time in which the story is set.

Although we never get a glimpse of the relationship that the main character had with her husband, she hints at the intensity of their love for each other when she tries to suppress her memories, which she claims are only "another name for dry love and barren longing." She and Crossen have both suffered from the loss of a dearly loved partner; she insists that his grief over Bridie is to blame for Crossen's attempted kiss. By declaring that Bridie still has such a powerful influence on Crossen, the widow suggests that her husband has a similar hold on her.

Sexism

Although Crossen is often sympathetic and solicitous toward the main character, he also displays sexist attitudes in his encounters with her, which ironically helps reinforce her independent spirit. When, for example, as they are haggling over the grass cutting, Crossen insists, "I'm not a man to break my word—above all, to a woman," she immediately questions his motives and gets on her guard. This stance helps her remain firm in her insistence that he do the job the next morning.

Crossen's quick change of heart concerning the job suggests his need to gain control over her.

He had originally agreed to come the following morning to complete the job, but he immediately changes him mind, insisting that he needs more time. When he comes at night to speak to her about it, he appears much more forceful than he had that morning, arguing with her about the value of topping grass. In an effort to gain the upper hand, he tries to assert his superiority as well as placate her, insisting, "I'm glad to do what I can for you, Ma'am, the more so seeing you have no man to attend to these things for you." His suggestion of her weakness only reinforces her strength, though, and she rejoins, "Oh, I'm well able to look after myself!"

Style

Landscape as Symbol

Lavin's evocative descriptions of the landscape reflect the woman's character and situation. At the beginning of the story, Lavin uses natural figures to describe the woman: she appears "like a rock in the sea," suggesting both her strength and isolation. Lavin turns the word "island" into a verb to reinforce this sense of separation when she claims that the woman is "islanded by fields." The grass, with its "ugly tufts of tow and scutch," give the farm "the look of a sea in storm," symbolizing her own struggles with memories of her married life and fears of her lonely future. Maurice Harmon, in his article on Mary Lavin in *Gaéliana*, finds that these descriptions provide a "clear analysis of her own state of mind" and determines that the detail is "compact, flexible and capable, adjusted to her character."

Narrative Silence

Lavin conveys a pervasive silence in the story, which sometimes suppresses intense emotions. Her depiction of the characters' silent surface with feelings roiling immediately below it suggests the possibility of an impending explosion. Dialogue between the characters is kept at a minimum, especially when it veers too closely to the unhealed grief and anxiety about present problems. When, for example, Crossen speaks about his first wife, whose memory still haunts and influences him, he provides only a few understated details: "I courted a girl down there when I was a lad." He hints, though, at the devastation he experienced after her death when he admits that his second wife, helped "knit" him back into "a living man," but he is unable to express his deep love for Bridie. The main character never gives voice to her "vague, nameless fears" that could destroy her efforts at establishing a strong sense of self. These suppressed emotions come out unexpectedly when Crossen asks the main character for a kiss, and later when she "hysterically" insists that Bridie was "the one did it!"

Historical Context

Realism

In last half of the nineteenth century, writers turned away from the earlier romantic style, which idealized nature and rural life. Writers in the late 1800s, who were later called realists, focused more on the actual difficulties of common life and the natural and social forces that determined people's lives. They rejected the celebration of the imagination typical of Romantic literature and instead took a practical look at what shapes personality and what kinds of problems confront people, both in society and in nature. Realists focused on the hardships in the commonplace and how people often succumbed to them. Their depiction of the human condition was not embellished by happy coincidences and providential help, which are central parts of romanticized literature.

Writers who embrace realism use settings and plots that reflect their characters' daily lives and realistic dialogue that replicates natural speech patterns. Literary movements such as naturalism and modernism came in vogue during the early part of the twentieth century, but realist fiction regained popularity during the 1930s and continued to be enjoyed into the early 2000s, especially in the genre of the short story. Doris Lessing, Elizabeth Bowen, and Mary Lavin from the United Kingdom and Eudora Welty, Willa Cather, and Flannery O'Connor from the United States have been recognized as twentieth-century masters of the form.

Changing Roles for Women

During the first few decades of the twentieth century, feminist thinkers on both sides of the Atlantic engaged in a rigorous investigation of female identity as it related to all aspects of a woman's life. Some declared the institution of marriage to be a form of slavery and thus recommended its abolition. Others derided the ideal of the maternal instinct, rejecting the notion that motherhood should be the ultimate goal of all women. The more

Compare & Contrast

- **1960s:** Abortion is legalized in the mid-sixties in Britain and the United States, yet it is still severely limited in Ireland, a predominantly Catholic country.

  Today: Federal and state governments chip away at abortion rights in the United States as anti-abortion groups gain strength. Women in Ireland, led by the Irish Family Planning Association, continue to petition the government there for easier access to abortions, which still remain illegal except in cases in which the mother's health is threatened.

- **1960s:** In 1963, Soviet cosmonaut Valentina Tershkova becomes the first woman in space.

  Today: Women continue to travel in space as well as run large corporations. Media mogul Oprah Winfrey is one of the most powerful and wealthiest people in the world.

- **1960s:** In 1963, *The Feminine Mystique* by Betty Friedan is published. The book chronicles the growing sense of dissatisfaction women feel about the unequal treatment they receive in the home, the workplace, and in other institutions.

  Today: Women make major gains in their fight for equality. While the Equal Rights Amendment is approved by Congress in 1972 but never ratified, women successfully fight discrimination in the United States. The Equal Opportunities Commission in the United Kingdom enables women there to gain equal treatment and opportunities in the workforce.

conservative feminists of this age considered marriage and motherhood acceptable roles only if guidelines were set in order to prevent a woman from assuming an inferior position to her husband in any area of their life together. A woman granted equality in marriage would serve as an exemplary role model for her children by encouraging the development of an independent spirit.

The early feminists in England and the United States, such as Eleanor Rathbone who became a leading figure in England's National Union of Women's Suffrage Societies, were able to gain certain rights for women, including the right to vote. They were not able, however, to change the widely held view that a woman's place is in the home. During World War II, American and British women were encouraged to enter the workplace where they enjoyed a measure of independence and responsibility. After the war, however, many were forced to give up their jobs to make room for returning troops.

Roles for women began to change during the 1960s and 1970s. During the decades following World War II, women continued to join and stay in the workforce. They also began to demand reproductive rights. The availability of birth control and the legalization of abortion had the greatest impact on these changing roles. Women now had greater control over their pregnancies and the responsibilities that came with them. Some women started work while raising their children, and many began after. After they became financial contributors to the household, British and American women began to demand childcare and equal pay. During the 1960s, women's groups began to appear throughout Great Britain and the United States that helped raise their participants' awareness of women's issues.

Critical Overview

The critical response to Mary Lavin's short fiction has been overwhelmingly positive. A group of her stories, including "In the Middle of the Fields," published in the late 1960s and gathered together in the third volume of *The Stories of Mary Lavin*, has been singled out as among her finest. In his

An isolated farmhouse in County Down, Northern Ireland Michael St. Maur Sheil/Corbis

review of this volume, Richard F. Peterson notes that these stories are most often referred to as her "widow stories." He writes that they "represent a major phase in Mary Lavin's career in which she added new power and control to her fiction by occasionally dramatizing her painful adjustment to widowhood." Peterson cites the "powerful influence of memory on the emotions of Mary Lavin's widows, especially in preserving the pleasure of married life and the pain of loss."

Reva Brown, in her review of the same volume of Lavin's stories, considers the author to be a "superb storyteller" who has "the capacity to take an apparently ordinary, even banal, situation and to compress within the few pages of her short story an entirely credible small world." Brown praises Lavin's "sensitive insight into the human condition" in these stories, noting "nothing extraordinary happens to [her characters], but their lives and feelings are portrayed with a clear vision and empathy that transforms these 'ordinary' people into something special." She concludes that Lavin's characters are "fully rounded and believable, depicted with a subtle wit and humour that sets up echoes of irony, pathos or recognition in the reader."

Commenting on the widow stories, Maurice Harmon in his article on Mary Lavin in *Gaéliana* writes that they have "a kind of all-round decency, compassion and common-sense." Harmon praises the unity of the stories where "all the elements—characterisation, theme, imagery, structure, style—are brought together in the service of the larger over-view" and concludes that "the pace of the narrative matches the sense of wisdom and experience embodied in the main character."

Harmon singles out "In the Middle of the Fields" for its "narrative ease," especially in the opening paragraphs that, he argues, provides important character details. Richard F. Peterson also praises the story in his review, commenting that in it, Lavin "reveals the intense loneliness of the widow immediately after the death of her husband."

Criticism

Wendy Perkins

Perkins is a professor of American and English literature and film. In this essay, Perkins explores the interplay of past and present in the story.

Mary Lavin published several stories in the 1960s that explore the often devastating sense of loss experienced by women after the death of their husbands. The recently widowed, unnamed main character of "In the Middle of the Fields," one of the most compelling of these "widow stories," struggles to survive the loss of her husband as she takes over the operation of their farm. While she determines to live in the present and establish a sense of continuity for herself," she is forced to recognize the strong pull of a past that interferes with her attempts to create an independent, secure sense of self.

Richard F. Peterson notes, in his article on Mary Lavin in *Modern Fiction Studies*, that her widow stories mark "a phase in a long and difficult struggle to understand the relationship between past memories and the emotional pain of the present in finding a new life and identity." This struggle appears immediately in the first paragraph of "In the Middle of the Fields." The main character's present strength of spirit is suggested by Lavin's likening her to "a rock in the sea," yet the sense of loss is pervasive for her, even that of the cattle's "gentle stirrings" as they move to the woods in the evening. The loss of her husband has created "anxieties by day, and cares, and at night vague, nameless fears." Harmon notes that these feelings are "preventing her release, threatening to bury her as well as her husband." They spring from the woman's recognition that death is not absolute, that her husband is never fully absent. Her anxieties arise from her fear that her memory of him will pull her into the grave, preventing her from establishing herself in the present.

The main character experiences what Patricia K. Meszaros, in her article on Lavin for *Critique*, calls a sense of "willful isolation." She tries to maintain continuity by staying on the farm by herself since "she was less lonely for him here in Meath than elsewhere." Her neighbors appear foolish to her when they believe that she "hugged tight every memory she had of him." She fights the urge to live in the past, understanding that memories are "but another name for dry love and barren longing." And so she becomes annoyed when they visit her farm and talk of her husband, which triggers her own thoughts of him.

In his article on Lavin in *Gaéliana*, Maurice Harmon concludes that the main character in the widow stories "knows what she is doing, has known love and passion, feels a keen sense of loss, but is determined to 'take hold of life.'" The widow in "In the Middle of the Fields" forces herself to focus on the present and the upkeep of her farm. "It wasn't him *she* saw when she looked out at the fields"; she saw that the grass needed topping so that the fields would not be ruined. Yet, at night, she cannot avoid the impact of change—the absence of her husband. Her fear of being alone threatens to undermine her emerging independence. This fear causes her to lock herself and her children upstairs every night and to dread a knock after dark. She becomes grateful when Ned, the farmhand, comes on an errand at night, "relaxed by the thought that there was someone in the house."

Her vulnerability returns when she tells Crossen that she is 'scared to death sometimes.'"

Her sense of self becomes stronger during the day, as when she discusses topping the grass with Bartley Crosson. Harmon argues that she is "practical and capable in dealing with [him] about farming matters, is equally able to deal with him when he tries to kiss her and does so with understanding and sympathy." Yet her response to Crossen reveals both her strength and her weakness as she struggles to resist the pull of the past and her fear of the present.

During her first meeting with Crossen, she brings up the issue of price immediately, suggesting that she will not be taken advantage of. Yet, she appears vulnerable after Ned tells her about the death of Crossen's first wife Bridie. When she asks him if he thinks Crossen has forgotten about her, Ned answers in the affirmative and insists, "it will be the same with you, too. . . . Everything passes in time and is forgotten." She, however, remains doubtful.

Lavin illustrates the conflict between the past and the present as the main character sits in her room later that night. Initially, as she thinks about Crossen and Bridie, her hair appears "sluggish and hung heavily down" "like everything else about her lately." Yet, it jumps with electricity when she brushes it, and her spirits begin to lift with her hair. Immediately, though, the new life that stirs within her is counteracted by the terror she feels when she hears a knock at the door.

What Do I Read Next?

- *Death in the Family* (1957), by James Agee, is the tragic tale of the effect of a man's death on his family.
- Edna O'Brien's novel *House of Splendid Isolation* (1994) focuses on the relationship between an Irish widow and an escaped Irish Republican Army gunman who has taken refuge in her home.
- Lavin's *The House in Clewe Street* (1945) chronicles the coming of age of a young man in Ireland.
- "The Demon Lover," (1955) one of the most popular stories by the Irish writer Elizabeth Bowen, focuses on a woman whose lover is killed in the war.

Her responses to Crossen after he enters her home reflect this same duality. At first, still shaken by her response to the knock, she runs downstairs, still in her nightclothes, which makes her appear vulnerable. She regains her composure when she sharply rebuffs Crossen's compliment about her hair, which she had not stopped to pin up. However, she is forced to admit her anxieties about her lights short circuiting.

When the two begin to discuss cutting the grass, she is able to regain her composure and sense of purpose. Crossen tries to persuade her to delay the job by playing on her assumed weakness when he declares, "I'm not a man to break my word—above all, to a woman." This places her immediately on her guard as she insists he do the job in the morning. She stands her ground, even when he reminds her that she has "no man to attend to these things" for her. Angered by his attempts to take advantage of her situation, she speaks to him authoritatively until be throws up his hands and agrees to come in the morning, admitting that he has been "bested."

Her vulnerability returns when she tells Crossen that she is "scared to death sometimes." When he sympathizes with her, she feels divided, part of her wanting to accept his kindness and the other wanting to reject it. Ultimately, she gives in to her fears and asks him to turn off the lights for her after she goes up stairs. Yet his sympathetic response has touched her and makes her hesitate on the stairs.

When Crossen grabs her and asks for a kiss, her strength returns and she rebuffs him. At this point she is able to deal with him practically, touched by his humiliation yet maintaining a "matter-of-fact" tone when she insists that nothing serious has occurred. She patiently listens to his story about how his second wife Mona helped raise his and Bridie's child, revealing the depth of his suffering when he admits that Mona helped knit him back "into a living man."

Perhaps it is this note of suffering that stirs the woman, making her impatient for him to leave. When Crossen insists that he has shamed Mona, she becomes increasingly agitated and declares that what happened had nothing to do with any of them except Bridie. Reaching the point of hysteria, she exclaims, "you thought you could forget her . . . but see what she did to you when she got the chance!"

The woman has concluded that Crossen's momentary passion for her, which threatens the continuity of his present life, was caused by his inability to forget the love he felt for Bridie. Her outburst suggests that she fears that she will never be free from her own memories, that the past will continue to cause problems in the present. When Crossen exclaims, "God rest her soul," he is most likely referring to the woman, whom he now knows suffers as much as he has from the pull of the past.

Lavin refuses to resolve the tension between the past and the present in the story, suggesting that the woman will have a difficult time as she searches for a new and satisfying life for herself. Harmon concludes that Lavin clearly has "important things to tell us about ourselves and does so with sophistication, warmth and intelligence." Her compassionate study of one woman's struggle with the power of the past in "In the Middle of the Fields" reveals the painful consequences of loss.

Source: Wendy Perkins, Critical Essay on "In the Middle of the Fields," in *Short Stories for Students*, Thomson Gale, 2006.

Patricia K. Meszaros

In the following essay, Meszaros explores Lavin's "treatment of the relationship between femininity and creativity" in her writing, however "oblique and ambiguous" it is.

Although Mary Lavin's portrayal of the Irish middle-class character has been compared with some justice to the portraits in *Dubliners,* only a few of her many fine short stories are quintessentially Irish in setting or plot, and little of her work is known except among specialists in Irish literature. She herself has said, "I did not read the Irish writers until I had already dedicated myself to the short story," and she claims to have been influenced most by "Edith Wharton, the pastoral works of George Sand, and especially Sarah Orne Jewett." Before she thought of becoming a writer, she had prepared herself at University College Dublin for an academic career, completing a master's thesis on Jane Austen and beginning a doctoral dissertation on Virginia Woolf. A recent study of her work estimates that sixty percent of her stories have a female protagonist or narrator, and a number of her later stories form a quasi-autobiographical cycle exploring widowhood and the attainment of self-sufficiency in a solitary, middle-aged woman writer. That Mary Lavin's work has continued to suffer neglect is surprising, while both the women writers she most admires and those (like Doris Lessing and Jean Rhys) who are her near-contemporaries are receiving a great deal of critical attention. The growing interest in books by and about women no doubt prompted New American Library to bring out in 1971 a paperback reprint of Lavin's novella, *The Becker Wives* (1946), yet even that work does not seem to have found an audience. None of the recent major critical works on women writers so much as mentions Mary Lavin.

Part of the reason, perhaps, is hinted at in the title of the critical study by Angeline Kelly cited above: Lavin is not a feminist in the contemporary sense; she is a "quiet rebel" who prefers to take an ironic stance, like Jane Austen, directing her detached gaze upon the foibles of men and women alike. Her vision has little in common with that of Doris Lessing, or of Sylvia Plath, or even Virginia Woolf, whose work and life inspired her own first attempt at writing fiction. Yet the treatment of women in Lavin's stories, particularly her treatment of the woman as artist, is at least as central to an understanding of her work as her treatment of the Irish character. One should remember, however, that "there is no such thing as *the* female genius, or *the* female sensibility." If Lavin's treatment of the relationship between femininity and creativity differs in important ways from the treatment of similar themes in the work of more fashionable writers, that is all the more reason to enrich our understanding of "the female sensibility" by paying close attention to her work.

"The group of 'widow stories' focus on the widow's struggle to live independently but they evoke at the same time a strong sense of the emotional and sensual deprivation of the widow's life."

The biographical fact most often advanced as essential to an understanding of Lavin's later fiction is that she was widowed when she was forty-two, after twelve years of marriage, left with a farm to run and three young daughters to rear. Her experience of widowhood, indeed, informs most of her middle and later work, both indirectly, in her searching and compassionate portrayals of loneliness and sometimes willful isolation, and directly, in her stories about widows, including her writer figure, Vera Traske. Oddly, however, these stories reveal very little about the feminine creative sensibility. Vera is a woman, a widow, who just happens (like the author) to be a writer. One of Lavin's earliest published works, "A Story with a Pattern" (1945), and one of her most recent, "Eterna" (1976), allude to the tensions in the lives of creative women more explicitly, as does her richly resonant and complex but unsettling novella, *The Becker Wives.* Even though Lavin's interest in the woman as artist spans her whole career as a writer, her treatment of the creative woman is always oblique and ambiguous. Creative women are never narrators or centers of consciousness in the stories in which they appear, and evidence of their talent is either unreliable or unavailable. The focus of these stories is instead upon the effects such women have upon those around them, and the pervasive irony makes the author's attitude toward her female artist-figures difficult to assess.

On the other hand, Lavin's attitude toward her own work is not ambiguous. Very early in her career she recognized that the short story was to be her *métier,* and she has repeatedly spoken slightingly and apologetically of her two novels, *The House in Clewe Street* (1945) and *Mary O'Grady* (1950). In her frequent comments about the craft of the short story, she has made fascinating suggestions of a direct relationship between her life as a *woman* writer and her esthetic as a writer of *short stories.* The experience, the temperament, and the talent that fashioned this esthetic, as I hope to show, also account for the author's ambivalence toward her female artist characters. Such ambivalence is most evident in *The Becker Wives,* the most extended treatment in Lavin's fiction of the woman-as-artist theme. The meaning of this novella (or long short story) itself can also be illuminated by placing it in the context of other stories making direct or indirect use of the theme and of the author's own statements on her work. *The Becker Wives* is thus the centerpiece, the primary exhibit, in my argument, but the purpose of the whole is to demonstrate that Mary Lavin's vision of the woman as artist is both highly individual and one that finds its perfect embodiment in the short story form.

The very early work, "A Story with a Pattern," addresses explicitly the question of the nature of the short story and implicitly the situation of a young woman writer. The protagonist encounters at a party a middle-aged man who criticizes her published stories for their lack of plot and conclusive endings, saying that her work will never appeal to a wide audience because "a man wants something with a bit more substance to it." Pressed by the writer to give an example, the critic tells a "true" story with a neat, O. Henry-like twist at the end, but the writer offends the critic by objecting that life "isn't rounded off like that at the edges." The story's title obviously refers to the patterned tale told by the critic but may also refer to the larger pattern of the frame story, one that Lavin may already have begun to observe in her own development as a writer. Concerned to practice her craft in a way that would not falsify her experience and—like all young writers—to establish her identity, she had to confront traditional notions about the proper form and content of the short story. By placing the confrontation in "A Story with a Pattern" between a female author and a male critic in a social context, she demonstrates her awareness of the difficulties faced by the woman writer in the search for her own authentic voice in her fiction. At the time she wrote this story Lavin was receiving advice and encouragement from Lord Dunsany, one of her earliest admirers, who praised her in his preface to her *Tales from Bective Bridge* (1943) but who recommended to her in private correspondence that she place more emphasis on plot and that she take O. Henry as a model.

However, to claim that a specifically "feminist" consciousness is revealed in this story, or indeed in any of Lavin's other works, would be a distortion. The group of "widow stories" is a case in point. Some of them, like "Happiness," "The Cuckoo-spit," and "In the Middle of the Fields," focus on the widow's struggle to live independently in the present rather than in memories of the past, but they evoke at the same time a strong sense of the emotional and sensual deprivation of the widow's life. Even more *à propos,* the stories which portray the widowed Vera Traske specifically as a writer—"Villa Violetta" (1972) and "Trastevere" (1971)—clearly make the point that both personal happiness and a secure environment conducive to work are to be found in male protection and companionship. These two stories, however, have less to tell us about the author's sense of the place of art and creativity in a woman's life than does another of the "widow stories" whose protagonist is *not* presented as a writer, even though Lavin has admitted that the "Mary" of "In a Café" is herself. This story, indeed, may represent a transition between the earlier stories that (despite the wariness of the protagonist of "A Story with a Pattern") were sometimes marred by pat conclusions and the more searching, complex, and equivocal later work. As Lavin said in a recent interview, "For years I wrote for fun," but in the years immediately following her husband's death she became increasingly serious and self-critical.

"In a Café" (1960) links the motifs of a widow's new-found independence and the preservation of her husband's memory to esthetic vision in a significant way. Two women, one young and recently bereaved after a brief marriage, the other (the story's center of consciousness) older and two years widowed after a long and happy marriage, meet in a café frequented by students and artists. By chance they exchange a few pleasantries with a young man at the next table, a painter, some of whose work hangs for sale on the café's walls. Later, alone, the older woman seeks out the artist in his studio, telling herself that she will look at the rest of his paintings and perhaps purchase one of them. Receiving no answer to her knock at his door, she impulsively bends to peer through the slot of the letter-box, gaining only a partial view of the interior which is yet enough to tell her much about its inhabitant's poor and solitary existence: "an unfinished canvas up against the splattered white wainscot, a bicycle-pump flat on the floor, the leg of a table, black iron bed-legs and, to her amusement, dangling down by the leg of the table, dripping their moisture in a pool on the floor, a pair of elongated, grey, wool socks." The scene is at once comic and pathetic. A door from an inner room opens, and the young painter appears to her as two "large feet, shoved into unlaced shoes, and . . . bare to the white ankles. For, of course, she thought wildly, focusing her thoughts, his socks are washed!" She springs to her feet and runs away.

This grotesque experience both frees the widow from her past and enables her to reclaim it. Earlier in the story, we had been told of her inability, since his death, to recall her husband's face. Now as she walks back to her parked car, his image comes to her vividly. The story ends:

> Not till she had taken out the key of the car, and gone straight around to the driver's side, not stupidly, as so often, to the passenger seat—not till then did she realize what she had achieved. Yet she had no more than got back her rights. No more. It was not a subject for amazement. By what means exactly had she got them back though—in that little café? That was the wonder.

Clearly, the widow's regaining of "her rights" is closely connected in the story with esthetic experience. When she first sees the paintings in the café, we are told, "She knew what Richard would have said about them. But she and Richard were no longer one. So what would *she* say about them?" When she peers through the hole in the letter-box into the painter's bare little flat, she has herself become a sort of artist, focusing, as does Lavin herself as the writer of short stories, on limited and selective but vivid and telling details, deriving from them a compassioniate vision of human isolation. The articulation and acceptance of this vision enable the character to accept her own circumstances and thus to live her own life in the present while having her past restored to her as memory.

Some support of the view that this story expresses something of the author's faith in the restorative and even redemptive power of her craft comes from Lavin's only published piece of criticism, the "Preface" to her *Selected Stories* (1959), in which she recounts a childhood experience, when she was taken by her father to see about having her "small gold watch" mended. With dismay the child notices that the watchmaker's hands are palsied, shaken by "some kind of ague," and that "all down the front of his waistcoat and jacket, stains and slops of food showed how badly he was disabled." But then the old man takes the watch in his hands, bracing his wrists against the side of the table, and the little girl marvels at "the fixity, the sureness of those fingers when once they had entered the intricate world of their craft." The moral Lavin attaches to this anecdote is that "like that old man, I . . . had applied myself so singly to the art of fiction that I had maimed, and all but lost, the power to express myself in any other form." The reader, however, may perceive a larger meaning. Obviously, the image of the watchmaker is appropriate, for like the writer of short stories he must have a delicate, precise touch. But the other parallel, not made explicit by the author herself, is with his apparent handicap. Later in the essay she speaks of the necessity of writing "in snatches of time filched from other duties, and particularly of late years when I have had to run the farm from which we get our livelihood." Even before her husband's death, soon after the publication of her first book, she had spoken in an interview of looking forward to "having the morning hours to herself in the autumn when the baby would be in her crib and the older girls in school." Lavin seems consciously to have developed her technique as a writer to accommodate her personal situation, and she even maintains that her work is the better for the demands placed on her time by her domestic responsibilities: "I believe that the things that took up my time, and even used up creative energy that might have gone into writing, have served me well. They imposed a selectivity that I might not otherwise have been strong enough to impose upon my often feverish, overfertile imagination. So if my life has set limits to my writing I am glad of it. I do not get a chance to write more stories than I ought; or put more into them than ought to be there." She seems to believe not just that her craft enables her to overcome what might be viewed as the handicap of her personal circumstances, but also that those circumstances in themselves have forced her to refine and develop her craft.

Clearly, Lavin's view of the particular conditions affecting the woman as artist, as presented both in her stories and in her remarks on her own work, is a highly personal and perhaps even unique one among twentieth-century women writers. Despite her early interest in and admiration for Woolf, she seems to have no inclination to yearn for a room of her own, and she seems almost entirely lacking in that sense of confinement within the social and esthetic conventions of a male-dominated world that feminist critics find to be so pervasive in writing by women. Although her later works, particularly the Vera Traske stories, must be seen at least partly as personal responses to a devastating personal loss, it is nevertheless significant that even in the early novella, *The Becker Wives,* where we find Lavin's most sustained treatment of the woman as artist, traditional concerns of women writers are handled in untraditional ways.

The novella explores the venerable theme of the disruptive influence of the artist on an ordered society. From Plato through Shakespeare to Goethe and Coleridge the motif has been sounded, but here it is modulated into a new key because the artist is a woman and therefore doubly mysterious, potentially more disruptive. An archetypal figure older than that of the artist with "flashing eye" and "floating hair" is the *fatal woman,* and Lavin has vested the power of both figures in the character of her woman-artist. Flora, the poet, the actress, is also *la belle dame sans merci.* At the same time, *The Becker Wives* resonates with questions that have filled the diaries, letters, and published works of talented women for at least two hundred years. Do the woman's traditional roles in society inevitably stifle her creativity? Is the creative impulse in women perhaps an unnatural deviance of the maternal instinct; or, to put it differently, is motherhood the natural end, the apotheosis indeed, of female creativity? Much of the richness and subtlety of this work derives from the way in which the author has brought to a single focus in her central character the romantic myth of the artist, the myth of the fatal woman who has been seen both as the artist's muse and as his nemesis, and the new myth of the destructive conflict between femininity and creativity endured by the woman-artist.

The mystery surrounding the woman-artist is enhanced in two ways by the narrative technique of *The Becker Wives.* First, Flora is presented only from the outside, as the Beckers see and imagine her, so that we gain no direct insight into her consciousness. Second, the work is unique for Lavin in that it introduces into the solid, closely observed domestic world of middle-class Dublin not only a mythic dimension but also an element of almost gothic mystery, as if Ligeia had come to live among the Forsytes. Marianne Moore's definition of poetry describes the world of *The Becker Wives* almost exactly: an imaginary garden with real toads.

The toads are the Beckers themselves, a family of wealthy corn merchants—four brothers and a sister—who, like Galsworthy's Forstyes, are long on family solidarity and earnest materialism but short on grace, wit, and imagination. All the Becker children take spouses as like themselves as they in turn are like their parents; all, that is, except the youngest brother Theobald, who wants a wife with more to recommend her than "suitability for marriage and child-bearing." Theobald is actually no more enlightened than the rest of his family; he is merely more snobbish. Nevertheless, he manages to marry the beautiful, talented Flora, who paints, plays the piano, and writes poetry, but whose real talent seems to be for acting. From the beginning the Beckers are charmed by Flora's piquantly histrionic behavior: she brings "into all their homes, as into their lives, more air . . . more colour, more light," and with Theobald's brother Samuel as her ally, she improves their taste in furniture and art. Best of all, she entertains them with her pantomimes and impersonations, most frequently of one of the other Becker wives. As Flora's acting proves to be an obsession, Theobald's pride turns to irritation. Samuel, in contrast, begins to watch Flora almost compulsively, and as his pregnant wife Honoria takes to staying at home, he seeks Flora's company in the evenings.

The Becker wives are prolific; at any given time two or three of them are to be found in various stages of pregnancy. But Flora remains slim and ethereal, and though her sisters-in-law privately pity her, she seems unconcerned. Eventually, however, the other wives notice that the object of Flora's impersonations has become almost exclusively Honoria. Finally one day Flora sits in a corner sewing a small white garment, refusing to answer to her name. Begging the family not to tease her, she points toward Honoria, basking in the sun outside: "As for that one, . . . that wretched creature out there: if someone doesn't stop her from driving me mad, I won't answer for what will become of her." This is no impersonation; Flora has exchanged places in her own mind with Samuel's wife. To Samuel, Flora confides her secret, speaking in Honoria's voice:

> You're the only one I trust. You won't let her drive me mad, will you, like she's been driven mad herself? That's it, you see. No one knows but me and I didn't tell anyone before now. But I knew it all the time. She's mad. Mad! She was really always mad. Her family was mad—all of them. Her father died in a madhouse.

Just before Samuel closes the door on his appalled family, they see him put his arm around Flora's shoulders, saying tenderly, "Hush, Honoria. Hush, hush."

The Becker Wives can be most readily interpreted in terms of the most universal of the myths to which it alludes, as a fable about a fragile poetic sensibility which temporarily disturbs but is ultimately quelled by an uncongenial environment. One version of this classic story locates the seeds of destruction in the artistic sensibility itself; thus Peterson says that Lavin's novella "concludes with a troubling vision of the artist who goes too far," that it tells of "a young woman whose gift of insight becomes a maddening curse, preventing her from entering the comfortable, commonsense Becker world." At the same time, that world itself, the narrative makes clear, is not one in which the poetic temperament can thrive. At the end, Samuel reflects that Flora was "a flitting spirit never meant to mix with the likes of them."

Largely because of the presence of Samuel, the romantic myth of the artist proves to be inadequate to a full interpretation of the narrative, for while Flora is the story's central character, Samuel's expanding consciousness focuses our vision, his quickening imagination stirring our sympathy. To the extent that it is Samuel's story, *The Becker Wives* follows the classic pattern of a youth's encounter with seductive pleasures and his resulting loss of innocence. As the seductress, however, Flora represents not sensual gratification but the lure of a world of imagination from which the Beckers are insulated by their complacent materialism. When the two worlds are brought into conflict, the Beckers' dimension is rendered in specific physical detail, but Flora's dimension is rendered in archetypal images. Similarly, we can explore Samuel's responses and trace the development of his imaginative awareness because he clearly belongs, like the great majority of Lavin's characters, to a world in which the human psyche *can* be explored. Flora we can only know—because what she represents *can* only be known—in a series of avatars. The realm of myth is made to impinge upon the realm of literally represented reality in this narrative in a way that is directly related to its fullest meaning.

The first pages of the novella establish the Beckers as dull people, so lacking in interest even to themselves that, having dinner in a fashionable restaurant, they evince only a bovine placidity, sitting "stolid and silent, their mouths moving as they chewed their food, but their eyes immobile as they stared at someone or other who had caught their fancy at another table." In the following pages, however, the narrative expands in connotative richness as a shift in focus records for the first time Samuel's perceptions: "Like limelight the moon shone greenly down making the lighted windows of the houses appear artificial, as if they were squares of celluloid, illuminated only for the sake of illusion. He hoped Theobald wouldn't insist on dragging him back to reality." Samuel is evidently the one Becker susceptible to esthetic emotion, the only one who will be in any way prepared to understand Flora.

Before she herself appears, Flora is presented in images refracted from other imaginations, first in Theobald's casual remark to his sister Henrietta that "Flora doesn't eat as much as a bird," so that "Henrietta's imagination rose with a beat of wings, and before her mind's eye flew gaudy images of brightly plumed creatures of the air." Caught up in the image, Theobald then makes a quite uncharacteristic slip of the tongue when, speaking of his intention of surprising his sisters-in-law by introducing Flora at a family party, he says, "I'm not going to miss an opportunity like this for killing two stones with the one—I mean two *birds* with the one *stone*."

The slip is not lost on Henrietta, and when that evening Theobald arrives with his bride-to-be as the family is finishing dinner, it occurs to her that "all the seated Beckers, and all their seated guests, seemed to have been turned to stone." Yet the woman who has produced this Medusa-like effect does not seem to Henrietta to be at all forbidding in appearance:

> Flora was small. She was exceedingly small. She was fine-boned as well, so that, as with a bird, you felt if you pressed her too hard she would be crushed. But in spite of her smallness, like a bird she was exquisitely proportioned, and her clothes, that were an assortment of light colours, seemed to cling to her like feathers, a part of her being. . . . She accepted her clothes as the birds their feathers: an inevitable raiment.

Henrietta's impressions seem to be highly subjective, however, for they are not corroborated by the other observers: Flora seems to have the power of exciting and confusing the imaginations of those who meet her for the first time. In James's mind she evokes "gaudy and tinsel images" of the dancers from the operettas of his youth, while to Samuel she appears as the goddess Flora, in "a vision . . . of a nymph in a misty white dress, with bare feet and cloudy yellow hair, who in a flowering meadow skipped about, gathering flower heads and entwining them in a garland," even though he notices that she is dressed not in the "assortment of light colours" that had seemed to Henrietta like feathers but in "a trim black suit."

More perceptive than the others, Samuel soon realizes that indeed the "real" Flora is protean, that she actually *becomes* what she imagines herself to be, even when she is alone, and fascinated, he becomes "more and more dependent" upon her friendship. Flora's influence on Samuel refines his sensibilities and heightens his awareness of character. He no longer attempts to impress Theobald or boasts that his wife is a heiress. His ability to recognize in Flora's secret transformations the "naive and childish" expression of his wife Honoria or the "cold and shallow" stare of Theobald implies a new clarity of judgment, and toward Flora he now exhibits exquisite tact:

> It was becoming Samuel's biggest pleasure to watch his new sister-in-law in the act of departing from her own body and entering that of someone else. But he was careful to guard her secret for her, and even when he saw the transformation coming, he'd bend one part of himself to the task of diverting the attention of the family, while the other part of him he'd give over to furtively watching her and sharing in her adventure.

The images in which Flora herself is described progress from the conventional and natural to the strange and hieratic. Initially seen by the Beckers as a bird-like creature, a dancer, a flower-goddess, Flora presents herself as a maker of images (a pretend photographer), as a flame "withering the life" out of people, as the keeper of an imagined "little green dragon" over which her fingers move "delicately, guardedly, as if her pet had some prohibitive quality, such as a scaly skin," and as a woman capable of "departing from her own body and entering that of someone else." So, although we see her through Samuel's eyes as a powerfully attractive woman, we know so little of her real nature that we can not feel her to be a sympathetic character.

The scene marking the highest point in the development of Samuel's awareness also most poignantly reveals Flora's essential mysteriousness. One evening Samuel calls to find Flora alone in an unlighted room, pressed against the side of a window, staring upward at "the thin spikes of the first stars." She seems "like the bowsprit of an ancient ship, . . . and as sightless." Samuel whispers, "Who is it? . . . Who are you now?" and although she answers in her normal voice, "Why Samuel! What a strange thing to ask! I'm Flora, of course, who else?" for Samuel the moment has been an epiphany:

> Yes, it was Flora: but if ever a person was caught in the act of self-impersonation, that person was Theobald's wife, for in that tense, motionless figure which a moment before had been unaware of his presence, he realized that Flora had concentrated her whole personality. And the essence of that personality was so salt-bitter that a salt-sadness came into his heart too.

He is prepared for the end, and when Flora retreats permanently into her fantasy world, Samuel knows "that the terrible terrible sadness that had settled on his heart would lie upon it forever." In the last scene, despair settles on him as he looks out the window at the fat, stodgy children of his other sisters-in-law, knowing that the child "his wife Honoria was carrying would be like them, as like as peas in a pea-pod."

Samuel is a victim of *la belle dame sans merci*; having lost his beloved "flitting spirit," he has been abandoned like Keats's knight, where "no birds sing." Flora is presented in such a way as to suggest many of the avatars of the *femme fatale.* Like Poe's Ligeia, her family origins and circumstances are obscure, and like her she attempts to usurp the identity—if not the body—of another woman. Like Lamia or Lilith, she might be regarded as the seducer of young men and the barren, envious stealer of other women's children. An allusion may even be made to the Celtic analogue of Lilith, Blodeuwedd or Blathnat, whose name means literally "flower-face," and who was turned into a bird—an owl, like Lilith—after she betrayed her husband. The Medusa is suggested in the way Flora seems to turn the Beckers to stone when they first meet her, and Samuel's apprehension of her agelessness and inscrutability ("like the bowsprit of an ancient ship, . . . and as sightless") is reminiscent of Pater's description of *La Gioconda:* "She is older than the rocks among which she sits; like the vampire, she has been dead many times," and learned the secrets of the grave. "The important difference between these versions of the *femme fatale* and Lavin's version is that Flora is not evil," certainly not sexually destructive. Her implied threatening of Samuel's wife and unborn child is pathetic rather than sinister, because she speaks as a passive and ineffectual "Honoria," directing her words toward a "Flora" who no longer exists.

If Lilith in her various incarnations expresses fear of the independent, dominant woman, seen as a sexually and socially destructive being, in this remaking of the myth by a female writer her emasculating, murderous aspect is suppressed while her exciting, disturbing aspect is retained and expanded by combination with the myth of the socially disruptive artist. Whatever danger this fatal woman represents is due not to her being a woman alone but to her also being an artist—she is something less and something more than the legendary *femme fatale.* Moreover, the "fatal" woman herself is ultimately destroyed; the woman-artist becomes her own victim. Here both the myth of the romantic artist at odds with society and the myth of the fatal woman merge with the myth of the conflict between femininity and creativity. In the light of this myth, we can see Flora as doomed not only by the frustratingly conventional environment into which she has married, but also by the role set for her as a woman in that society.

As *la belle dame* is traditonally sterile, so also the female artist is traditionally childless; at least in the popular imagination, there has been "an eternal opposition of biological and aesthetic creativity." It is probably no coincidence that Samuel's wife, the woman whose identity Flora tries to usurp, the woman who is almost indistinguishable from the other wives and whose child will be as like theirs "as peas in a pea-pod," bears the somewhat unusual name, "Honoria." *The Becker Wives* was first published in 1946. Given Lavin's interest in Woolf, she would likely have read the posthumous collection, *The Death of the Moth and Other Essay,* published in 1942. That collection contains the text of Woolf's talk on "Professions for Women," and the talk itself contains the now famous passage in which the author describes how, in order to find her own identity as a writer, she first had to kill the spectral "Angel in the House," that "ideal" woman who was sympathetic and self-sacrificing, who "excelled in the difficult arts of family life." The reference to the "Angel in the House" is of course an allusion to a popular Victorian poem by Coventry Patmore; the name of the heroine of that poem is "Honoria."

Flora may in this light be seen as a martyr to the untenable position imposed by her society upon the woman-artist. As Stewart describes the dilemma of the female writer, "To be a heroine, she must nurture, help, inspire; by defining her independence as an artist, she turns into a gorgon. . . . She must die as this mythic 'feminine' woman in order to give birth to herself as an artist." The fragile Flora, unable, under the pressures of Becker family life, to sustain her lonely artistic selfhood, succumbs to what for her can only be a spurious, borrowed identity. As one of the commentators on the work has said, "Her schizophrenia really represents for her an embrace of comfortable, sane, solid middle-class values: pregnancy and propriety." Ironically Flora, whose name is that of a classical fertility goddess, is "fertile" only in her imagination. She can give birth neither to a real child nor to herself as an independent artist.

That the work is rich and complex should be apparent, but the mythic patterns which delineate both its universality and originality, imposed on the narrative like templates, leave some ends and pieces uncovered. In the last analysis, Flora remains a highly ambiguous character, and although she is certainly pathetic, she is not tragic. The "salt-sadness" which appears to Samuel to be the essence of Flora's being may be interpreted by the romantic reader as the terrible isolation of the artist, but it may be only an early manifestation of the illness soon to overtake her. If we are to believe the final revelation spoken by Flora in Honoria's voice, we must relinquish the notion that the woman-artist has been "driven mad" by her impossible circumstances, for her madness is hereditary: "Her father died in a madhouse." Even what the Beckers take to be Flora's extraordinary acting ability may be a manifestation of schizophrenia rather than talent. Indeed, looking back over the narrative, we can find no clear evidence that Flora has attained more than a "ladylike" level of accomplishment in any of the arts, or that she is anything more than a lovely dilletante and follower of fashions.

The reader may have been taken in by the power of the myths invoked by the narrative, myths which express the fears of society about women and about artists—that the beautiful, independent woman is a dangerous seducer of innocent youth, that the artist is akin to the madman and just as dangerous to society, that the creative impulse in woman is a substitute for the maternal instinct and that the female artist is likely to be barren. *The Becker Wives* seems to explore the frightening possibility that all these myths may be true, but the narrative as a whole suggests that such myths at worst cause us to accept stereotypes as truths and at best obscure life's complexities and ambiguities.

In creating Flora, Lavin has admitted that the sources of creative energy are dark and potentially dangerous, and she has faced some of our worst fears (and perhaps her own) by portraying a dichotomous situation in which, on the one hand, the charismatic female artistic personality ends by destroying itself while, on the other, female domestic animals go on placidly reproducing their kind in a world devoid of beauty. At the same time, however, the ironic authorial voice seems to suggest that the dichotomy is false. Whether Flora is to be seen as a scapegoat or as a demon exorcised, her flaw is a too-vivid imagination that allows fantasy to over-balance reality and finally to obliterate it. That she remains a mystery is a clue to her significance for the author, who once deplored her own "feverish, overfertile imagination" and proposed to control it within the limits of the short-story form, even while she felt constrained by her domestic responsibilities and yearned for more time to follow her creative bent.

That same ambivalence appears once more, in some of the same ways, in one of Lavin's most recent stories. In "Eterna" she again portrays a creative woman who apparently goes mad. Once again we see the woman only from the outside, through the eyes of a rather ordinary character. Once again we cannot know for sure whether the woman is genuinely talented, whether she is driven mad by her restrictive environment or has carried the seeds of madness within her from the beginning.

The story's center of consciousness is a mediocre provincial doctor, complacently married to a very ordinary woman. One day in the National Gallery of Dublin, where he has gone while waiting for his wife, he encounters a madwoman whom he recognizes as a figure from his past and is thus forced to remember an incident he would rather forget. Not long out of medical school, he had been called to a convent to treat a young nun, Sister Eterna, injured in a fall from a scaffold while she had been painting a mural. Several visits later, when she impulsively showed him her treasure, a battered catalog from the National Gallery, he had committed a breach of propriety and professional ethics by speaking too familiarly to her, saying he would love to show her the paintings there. Much later he had heard that she had left the convent. Upset at first to see the once haughty young nun in her present condition, he regains his equilibrium as his wife approaches: "People had to learn to clip their wings if they wanted to survive in this world. They had to keep their feet on the ground. That was what Annie had taught him to do—God bless her." Annie, with her bundles of children's clothing bought on sale, is one of the Honorias of the world, and the doctor, with his smug hypocrisy, is one of the Theobalds.

Consistently, unmistakably ironic toward the doctor and his wife, the narrative voice of "Eterna" is entirely silent about the nun, who does not appear as a character except in the reminiscences of the doctor. Eterna is even more of a mystery than Flora. Thus, still apparently fascinated by the relationship between female creativity and madness, still apparently moved by the restrictions and insults suffered by the artistic temperament, Lavin is yet unable or unwilling to present the woman as artist in other than an oblique and ambiguous way.

The world from which her mysterious women-artists retreat, on the other hand, is a real world, and its flawed actuality is reported with zest by a witty, ironic voice, the instrument of a shaping and controlling imagination. Like the widow of the story, "In a Café," the artist as writer of short fiction organizes her experience by scrutinizing the world outside herself closely and compassionately but from an ironic distance. To conquer loneliness and isolation, she confronts them directly but keeps them contained within a small frame. The mysteries of creativity she refuses to look at directly, except through the veil of myth. Faced with conflicting demands upon her time and energy, the woman-artist steadies her wrists, as it were, like the old watchmaker, and concentrates all her craft upon the small but complex object before her. Perhaps the work most revelatory of Lavin's attitude toward her own life and art is the fine story, "Happiness." It tells of the death of Vera Traske, who suffers a stroke while cultivating her garden, from the point of view of her daughter, who recognizes that her mother's belief in and pursuit of "happiness" has been a conscious commitment requiring great courage and control. That control, manifested as craftsmanship, is the essence of Mary Lavin's image of the artist.

Source: Patricia K. Meszaros, "Woman as Artist: The Fiction of Mary Lavin," in *Critique*, Vol. 24, No. 1, 1982, pp. 39–54.

Sources

Brown, Reva, Review of *The Stories of Mary Lavin*, Vol. 3, in *British Book News*, February 1986, pp. 110–11.

Harmon, Maurice, "Mary Lavin: Moralist of the Heart," in *Gaéliana*, Vol. 5, 1983, pp. 113–26.

Lavin, Mary, "In the Middle of the Fields," in *A Green and Mortal Sound*, edited by Louise DeSalvo, Kathleen Walsh D'Arcy, and Katherine Hogan, Beacon Press, 1999.

Peterson, Richard F., "The Circle of Truth: The Stories of Katherine Mansfield and Mary Lavin," in *Modern Fiction Studies*, Vol. 24, No. 3, Autumn 1978, pp. 383–94.

———, Review of *The Stories of Mary Lavin*, Vol. 3, in *Studies in Short Fiction*, Vol. 24, No. 2, Spring 1987, pp. 170–71.

Further Reading

Church, Margaret, "Social Consciousness in the Works of Elizabeth Bowen, Iris Murdoch, and Mary Lavin," in *College Literature*, Vol. 7, No. 2, Spring 1980, pp. 158–63.

In this comparative study, Church examines Lavin's attacks on habit and social rigidity in her stories. She studies how Lavin's characters rethink social roles in their efforts to forge better relationships with each other.

Dunleavy, Janet Egleson, "Mary Lavin, Elizabeth Bowen, and a New Generation: The Irish Short Story at Midcentury," in *The Irish Short Story: A Critical History*, edited by James Kilroy, Twayne, 1984, pp. 145–68.

Dunleavy explores the Irish context of Lavin's work in political and social terms and compares it to that of other Irish writers.

Gibbons, Luke, *Transformations in Irish Culture*, University of Notre Dame Press, 1996.

In this collection of essays, Gibbons examines the political and cultural influences on Irish life and the tensions that ultimately arise between the establishment of a national and an individual identity.

Shumaker, Jeanette Roberts, "Sacrificial Women in Short Stories by Mary Lavin and Edna O'Brien," in *Studies in Short Fiction*, Vol. 32, No. 2, Spring 1995, pp. 185–97.

This study looks at different forms of female martyrdom and their relationship to sexuality in short stories by Lavin and by O'Brien.

Marry the One Who Gets There First

Heidi Julavits

1998

"Marry the One Who Gets There First" subtitled, "Outtakes from the Sheidegger-Krupnik Wedding Album," by Heidi Julavits, was first published in *Esquire*, in 1998. It was also published in *The Best American Stories, 1999.* The story is set in Stanley, Idaho, at a mountain lodge where a wedding is about to take place. It is a darkly comic tale about love and betrayal structured around the descriptions of thirty-six photographs. Julavits got the idea for this photo-based structure from a photo essay which featured pictures that were not included in people's final wedding albums. At the time, Julavits was also preparing for her own wedding and was all too aware of how wedding albums capture the unwavering cheer of the day. The less glamorous, at times irreverent, photos that were not considered worthy of inclusion in the albums gave Julavits the idea for her satirical story, which takes aim at the myths associated with romantic love and exposes some of the darker secrets of the not-so-happy couple.

Author Biography

Heidi Julavits was born in 1968, in Portland, Maine. Her mother taught English and her father was an attorney. As a child, Julavits excelled at mathematics but decided in ninth grade to concentrate instead on books and reading. She attended Deering High School in Portland and then

Dartmouth College. After graduation from Dartmouth, she traveled in Asia, and on her return to the United States she settled in San Francisco, where she worked as a copywriter. During her twenties she worked at many jobs, including waitress, movie extra, fashion copywriter, and English teacher.

When Julavits entered Columbia University's graduate writing program, she began writing short stories in earnest. She found it was a real challenge and that her first stories were thirty-five to forty pages long. She gradually learned how to cut them down to more manageable length, and she honed her craft by attending the annual Bread Loaf Writers Conference for several summers.

Some of Julavits stories were published in periodicals such as *McSweeney's* and *Story*. "Marry the One Who Gets There First" appeared in *Esquire* in April 1998 and was selected for the anthology, *The Best American Short Stories, 1999*. Julavits was also in that year named a Writer on the Verge by *Village Voice Literary Supplement*.

In 1998, on her thirtieth birthday, Julavits achieved sudden success when the publisher Putnam offered her a two-book deal for an advance that was reported to be in six figures. This money enabled her to give up working as a waitress and concentrate on her writing.

Julavits's first novel, *The Mineral Palace*, took her several years to write. It was published in 2000 to critical acclaim. Set in Pueblo, Colorado, in the Depression Era of the 1930s, the novel focuses on the troubles of a young wife and mother who must come to terms with her future.

Julavits's second novel, *The Effect of Living Backwards* (2003) tells the story of sisters Alice and Edith, whose plane is hijacked as they travel to Edith's wedding in Morocco. The novel had its origins in an incident that affected Julavits's family. In 1973, one of her father's cousins was killed on a plane that was blown up by Palestinian terrorists as it sat on a runway in Rome.

With her husband, Ben Marcus, who is a writer, editor, and professor, Julavits co-founded in 2000 *The Believer*, a literary magazine. She created a stir in the literary world by writing an essay in the magazine in which she criticized book reviewers for being too ready to write negative reviews and make attacks on authors.

As of 2005, Julavits and her husband live in Brooklyn, New York. They have one child.

Plot Summary

The story told in "Marry the One Who Gets There First" is organized by means of a series of thirty-six snapshots, the descriptions of which act as cues for the details that accompany them, which tell of present and past events. The occasion is a wedding at the Rocky Mountain Lodge that overlooks the Sawtooth Mountain Range in Stanley, Idaho.

Photos 1–6

In Photo 1, June Sheidegger, who is the younger sister of the bride, Violet, leans on the porch railing of the lodge in her revealing bridesmaid's dress. In Photo 2, Violet, half-dressed, sits as her Grandma Rose pins hot rollers in her hair. She has been poring over maps during the week, hoping to find that the Lower Stanley Municipal Building where she is to be married is in fact part of an adjacent township called Diamond Heights. She does not like the idea of getting married in a place called Lower Stanley. However, Louis Krupnik, her fiancé, likes the name, seeing in it suggestions of building great things from humble beginnings. He looks through a manila file and comes across a wedding photo taken at the same lodge in 1953. On the back of the photo is an inscription, written by Stan, the groom, saying that he knew he would marry his bride Rhoda the first minute he saw her. Louis takes this as a sign relevant to his own situation.

In Photo 3, June sorts through a shoebox of letters in front of the fireplace at the lodge. She cuts the letters into strips and puts them back in the box. Photo 4 shows Violet flipping through a fashion magazine while receiving a pedicure. It transpires that Louis has a drawerful of T-shirts emblazoned with the names of women's fashion magazines. Violet has learned that Louis has slept with women from each of the magazines, a fact which bothers her only when she and Louis have sex.

In Photo 5, Louis' brother and June's brother Bart toss a football on the front lawn of the lodge. The text tells of Violet and Louis's first date, at a restaurant, which got off to a bad start but ended with the two kissing frantically in a park near the Hudson River in Manhattan, New York.

In Photo 6, a badly thrown football spooks a horse. Norton Black, the stable hand, is tossed from his horse. He dislikes the stupidity of the lodge guests, who are usually from the city.

Photos 7–14

In Photo 7, Grandma Rose knocks a glass vase to the floor. Grandma Rose believes in omens and has structured her life around them. She knew as soon as she met Joe Sheidegger that she would marry him. She is certain because after she knocked a flute to the floor, Joe quoted a Chinese proverb which her grandfather used to repeat. She saw this as an omen.

Photo 8 shows Louis, fresh from the shower and wrapped in a towel, snapping a self-portrait. The narrator tells of how Louis used to help his late father's photography business during summer vacations when he was at high school. He would look at all the customers' photos before slipping them into the yellow envelopes. His attention is arrested by a photograph of a girl in a red dress in front of a Ferris wheel. He immediately falls for her, declaring her to be the girl of his dreams.

In Photo 9, Grandma Rose and Grandpa Joe's live-in caretaker, Margie Adams, licks the buttercream frosting off the feet of a plastic bride and groom. June has asked Margie to bake into the wedding cake a boxful of shredded blue paper.

Photo 10 shows Violet dancing in her panties holding a salad bowl over her bare breasts. She later reflects on unwanted wedding gifts received by her parents, such as a salad bowl and serving platters, which she regards as relics of her childhood.

Photo 11 shows Louis walking to his minivan and seeing June on the porch. He recalls when they first met. He was visiting San Francisco and was in a bookstore, when he saw her looking in the window. He thought she was looking at him, but in fact she was observing her own reflection in the window. He followed her, thinking she was the girl of his dreams. They did not waste any time in beginning to have sex, apparently during their first encounter.

The next photo, number 12, shows Violet and her brother Bart playfully flogging their mother with napkins. After his own marriage, Bart makes a habit of visiting a dominatrix service (where women flog men, for a fee), and his wife discovers the charges on his credit card.

Photo 13 returns to Grandma Rose, who is crying at the prenuptial luncheon because her husband always makes her leave such occasions before she is ready. She complains to Margie that she married the wrong man.

In Photo 14, Louis cuts himself shaving as he notices June outside. When he started seeing June he did not at know that she was Violet's sister. He had only just begun dating Violet. He found out the truth when he went to the Sheideggers' summer house on Lake Sunapee for the Fourth of July weekend, and both June and Violet were in attendance.

Photos 15–21

Photo 15 shows June looking at a photograph of her and Louis, taken by themselves on a self-timer, at the guest shack in Lake Sunapee. They are naked under a blanket on a bunk bed. Violet was out at a party and had asked June to keep Louis entertained.

In Photo 16, Grandpa Joe starts the car, leaving his weeping wife behind. He is driving to a nearby Indian reservation, where he intends to gamble at the casino.

In Photo 17, Violet, in her bathrobe, makes a call from an outside pay phone. She can smell and hear the preparations for the wedding feast and considers buying the young staff some beer. But then she stops and reminds herself that her life is not about being generous but about knowing others' secrets and desires.

Photo 18 shows Louis pulling out an envelope from his backpack. Inside it are photos of his father's mistress, which Louis discovered after his father died. His father's mistress looks very like, and probably is, the girl in the red dress that Louis had decided, in his teens, was the girl of his dreams. He reflects on how his father's situation resembled his own.

June, in the lodge kitchen in Photo 19, contemplates a cockroach on the wall. Louis wrote to her asking her to get rid of all the letters he had written to her. June then looks at the wedding cake and smiles, knowing she has done what he asked her to do.

In Photo 20, Louis looks at his reflection in a mirror and fingers an antique watch which was given to his father by his mother, Ida, on their wedding day. But the watch gave his father a rash, so Ida wore it instead. Louis went to visit her as she was dying in hospital; she thought he was her dead husband and yelled at him. It appears that his parents, both now dead, were unhappily married.

In Photo 21, June talks to Susan Minturn, another bridesmaid. Susan lives in Atlanta and is to marry Bart. After their marriage, Susan uses Bart's sexual inadequacy as a reason to feel superior to him.

Photos 22–28

Photo 22 shows Violet at a payphone, wearing her wedding dress. It is revealed that Violet discovered

June and Louis together and took revenge by taking a lover of her own named Shane. She would lie to Louis that she was taking tuition, and Shane would duly pay her to offset suspicions. Violet did not feel guilty. On the contrary, she was proud of the fact that she was now developing secrets and deceptions of her own.

In Photo 23, Louis and June are shown arguing behind the horse stables before the ceremony. It appears that Violet has discovered the photo of Louis and June in bed together. Louis rips the photo to pieces.

Photo 24 shows Violet again at the payphone. She is calling Shane, but he is not at home. She feels claustrophobic at the knowledge that her life is narrowing in possibilities as a result of her marriage to Louis.

A crying June, in Photo 25, digs a hole with the heel of her shoe and buries the pieces of the photo. She sees Louis leaning against the side wall of the stable, and they both watch through a hole in the wall as a man, probably Norton Black, is about to make love to a naked woman who is lying on a horse blanket. Louis starts to cry.

In Photo 26, Louis, hearing the strains of Mendelssohn's "Wedding March," stuffs the envelope containing photos of his father's mistress inside June's handbag by the fireplace.

In Photo 27, Violet enters the chapel. She sees Louis and she is immediately aware that he knows she has found out about his affair with June.

Photo 28 shows Hope, the young woman whom Norton Black has made love to, walking up from the stables. She is no longer a virgin and alternates between feeling lost and victorious.

Photos 29–36

In a scene that takes place after the wedding, Photo 29 shows the newlyweds being driven around the property in a chuck wagon. Violet's veil and fake blond braid lie on the road, having been snagged on a piece of fencing.

Photo 30 shows June in the wagon after Louis and Violet have left. She is undoing Violet's braid and weeping. But then she becomes aware of the ridiculous nature of her situation and laughs at herself.

In Photo 31, Grandma Rose is fast asleep at the reception while her husband thinks about what he will do when they get home. Perhaps he will read, play cribbage alone, or watch television while his wife sleeps.

In the next photo, Number 32, Louis and Violet cut the cake.

In Photo 33, June runs into the hills behind the lodge. She finds in her purse three photos that Louis placed there. Two of them are of Louis's father's mistress, and one is of the 1953 wedding at the lodge. They mean nothing to her, and she throws them away.

In Photo 34, Louis and Violet chew on the cake. Louis retrieves from his mouth a strip of paper, which contains a fragment of a letter he wrote to June, telling her that that she is the only one for him.

As Louis plunges his hand into the cake and comes up with little bits of blue paper (Photo 35), he realizes what has happened and wants to throttle June. He and Violet avoid each other's eyes. Then she pulls his hand to her mouth and eats madly—cake, frosting, and scraps of blue paper. At first he is horrified, but then he responds by doing the same. He feels he hardly knows the woman who is now his wife but believes he was fated to marry her.

In Photo 36, it is nearly dark, and June accepts a ride from Norton Black in a pickup truck. He is going to buy some beer. The narrator speculates that maybe, like the other lovers in the story, June and Norton will seize on some detail that seems significant to them and convince themselves they are made for each other and marry. Maybe they will tell the story of how they first met to their children and grandchildren and claim that they were simply destined to be together.

Characters

Margie Adams

Margie Adams is Grandma Rose and Grandpa Joe's live-in caretaker. She is also a pastry chef. At June's request, Margie bakes a boxful of shredded letters into the wedding cake.

Norton Black

Norton Black is the stable hand at the Rocky Mountain Lodge. He is unhappy in his job, but he is known by the summer lodge staff for his sexual prowess. At the end of the story he meets June for the first time and takes her for a beer.

Hope

Hope is a young woman who works at the lodge. The lodge staff calls her "Hope the Slut" because they think she sleeps with Norton Black so that he will buy her a beer. But they also envy and admire her.

Louis Krupnik

Louis Krupnik marries Violet Sheidigger. Both of Louis's parents are dead, and he runs the family business, Krupnik Bros. Photographic Supplies and Development, in Manhattan, New York City. Louis is a badly flawed character. He is described as "Orphan, Pessimist, Voyeur, Liar." He is also shallow, manipulative, and a womanizer. Soon after he begins dating Violet he begins an affair with June, Violet's sister, and writes letters to her saying that they are meant for each other. There is a streak of romanticism in his nature, and he tends to think of each woman he goes with as the embodiment of all his dreams.

Susan Minturn

Susan Minturn is a friend of Violet, and a bridesmaid at the wedding. She lives in Atlanta, Georgia, where she works as a buyer for a department-store chain. Later she marries Bart Sheidigger, whom she both loves and pities.

Shane

Shane is Violet's secret lover. Violet started to see him when she discovered that Louis was having an affair with June. Shane intrigues her because he possesses a "certain saintly quality . . . an excessive goodness always verging on perversity."

Bart Sheidigger

Bart is the brother of Violet and June. He later marries Susan Minturn. Bart is sexually inadequate and deviant, spending thousands of dollars on a dominatrix service. Susan is aware of this, but she is tolerant of his behavior.

Grandpa Joe Sheidigger

Grandpa Joe Sheidigger is the grandfather of Violet and June. His wife is unhappy with his inconsiderate behavior, but in his own way he tries to be protective of her, even though he starts their quarrels intentionally. He seems happy in his solitary way.

June Sheidigger

June Sheidigger, Violet's younger sister, is rather manipulative and cunning, and she is quite happy to continue her affair with Louis behind her sister's back. When he breaks off with her she gets her revenge on him by putting the shredded letters he wrote to her in the wedding cake.

Grandma Rose Sheidigger

Grandma Rose Sheidigger is unhappily married to Joe. She married him because she believed that their union was fated, but she later came to regret her decision.

Violet Sheidigger

Violet Sheidigger marries Louis Krupnik. Violet is a student of psychology and has just written a paper entitled "Alleviate Chronic Depression Through Positive Word Usage." She tries always to be upbeat and is naïvely optimistic. Her character has a dark side, however. She has made a life out of knowing others' secrets and desires, and she is not known for her generosity. She likes to think that she can see through the hypocrisy and shallowness of others. When she discovers that Louis is having an affair with June, she gets her revenge by taking a lover, Shane. Through this choice, she learns the thrill of deception, and she feels no guilt in lying to Louis. Violet has no illusions about Louis's womanizing, and although she has doubts about the wisdom of her course; she tries to convince herself that she is doing the right thing in marrying him.

Themes

Betrayal, Deception, and the Foolishness of Love

Although the occasion of the story is a wedding and thus a time of love and celebration, underlying it lie darker truths of deception, betrayal, lust, and folly. The deceptions practiced by Louis on Violet, and by Violet on Louis (not to mention June's deception of her sister) are gross and obvious, and knowing this, bride and groom do not exactly rush to the altar, aflame with love.

But perhaps more important than deceptions of others are the self-deceptions that are practiced in the name of love. Characters in this story choose their spouses for the wrong reasons, based on unrealistic, naïve ideas of romantic love as well as other superstitious ideas that they have inherited from their culture. For example, when she was a young woman, Grandma Rose believed in omens. She thought that because Joe, a young man she had only just met, happened to quote a Chinese proverb that her grandfather also used to quote, he must be the one for her. Thus, she ignored signs to the contrary ("he smelled foreign and always would"). It is later divulged that Joe had been coached

Topics For Further Study

- What qualities should a person look for in a spouse? Do men and women seek different qualities in their partner? What makes for a happy, long-lasting marriage? In answering these questions, interview several couples (they can be neighbors, older relatives, or friends of the family) who have been married for many years, and then make a class presentation in which you discuss your findings.
- Why is the divorce rate so high in the United States? Why has the divorce rate increased since thirty or forty years ago? What are the effects of divorce on children? Write an essay that lays out the results of your research.
- Form groups containing four students each. Each person writes a description of another photo to add to the story, and a paragraph of text to go with it. Try to write in a way that fits the themes of the story. These photo descriptions can be inserted at appropriate points in the story. Make a class presentation, entitled "Outtakes from the Outtakes from the Sheidegger-Krupnik Wedding Album," describing each photo, where it goes in the story, and why it was left out of both the album and the original outtakes.
- Write a series of fictional diary entries, spread out over several weeks or months, describing the course of a romantic relationship that started in a blaze of glory and ended in heartbreak. Try to describe exactly how the diary writer feels on first falling in love, and have him/her pinpoint the moments of disillusionment and what he/she has learned (if anything) from the experience.

---

regarding this proverb by Jimmy Wong, the Chinese boss of the mah-jongg parlor that he visited before he took Rose on their first date. Jimmy Wong had assured Joe that the proverb worked like a charm on the ladies—and he was right. Misled by her belief that she was fated to be with Joe, Grandma Rose set herself up for a lifetime of regret.

As a result of this belief in fate and destiny as the determining factors in love and marriage, characters in the story get carried away by their romantic desires and read into coincidences more than the situation really warrants. They adopt a kind of optimistic fatalism. Naïvely, they accept the idea that there is only one special person with whom they are destined to share their lives. This is what happened to Louis's mother. When Louis visits her on her dying day in hospital, she mistakes him for her dead husband and reproaches him with scorn: "The one, the one, you were *the one*. Bah!" Like Grandma Rose, it appears that she made a hasty decision and has spent many years regretting it, indeed until her dying day.

Louis himself falls into the same trap of illusions. He holds a romantic idea about meeting the "Girl of his Dreams," just as his mother thought that her husband Saul was "THE ONE OF MY DREAMS." Louis has held this idea since he was a teenager, when he thought that the girl in the red dress in the photograph was the girl. He has carried the photo around with him ever since. Later, he convinces himself that June is the only one in the world who is meant for him (at least that is what he tells June). Then when he finally gets to the altar with Violet, he convinces himself that he is fated to marry her, even though he feels he does not know her very well. He sees in the idea of fate an explanation of the mystery of why his parents, grandparents, and great-grandparents married as they did, "their loves as fated as they are accidental."

The theme of the story is brought home finally in the narrator's speculations about how Norton Black and June, who have just met, will probably seize on some irrelevant coincidence that will convince them—blinded as people are by their longings for true love and union with another person—that the other is the special one marked out by destiny to be their beloved: "Maybe Norton will see in June a strange resemblance to his dead sister and June will admire the way he wears a pocket watch in his jeans like her Grandpa Joe." But, the narrator warns, they are as likely as not to end up in a lonely marriage, even though—the human capacity for self-deceit being so great—they may believe all their lives that a special fate united them and that there was nothing they could do to alter or question it.

Style

Cinematic Technique

The unusual structure of the story, based on descriptions of thirty-six photographs, enables the author to switch scenes rapidly, alternating between present and past, and introduce a large number of characters and situations in a relatively brief story. The technique is as much cinematic as it is literary, with strong visual images and rapid changes of scene. The story's subtitle, "Outtakes from the Sheidegger-Krupnik Wedding Album," provides a hint about what the author is trying to accomplish. These are photos that did not make it into the happy couple's album, no doubt considered unsuitable for such a dignified celebratory occasion. Like the story as a whole, the photos effectively deconstruct the familiar wedding photos, with everyone all smiles and dressed to the nines, that adorn a million mantels in homes the world over. They are candid, irreverent, risqué, not for the public eye. The very first photo sets the tone: June in her bridesmaid's dress, wearing no underwear that might impede the view of "the unfettered swell of [her] behind." The photos reveal characters in undignified, unglamorous moments: Louis falling backward into a bramble bush; June and Susan applying lipstick in the washroom; June hiking her dress up to her thighs; Margie Adams licking the buttercream frosting off the cake. The bride and groom are sometimes shown semi-dressed, their physical nakedness a kind of visual metaphor of the stripping away of the masks through which they hide their real selves that occurs in the text. Louis, for example, is shown just out of the shower with only a towel around him and cutting himself shaving; Violet appears in nothing but her panties and also half-dressed with her hair in rollers. She is also shown in other unguarded and unflattering snaps: receiving a pedicure; in her bathrobe, hair wet, making a phone call; adjusting her garter just before she enters the chapel. It is as if the photos take the reader backstage at a theater. The characters are about to go onstage and play certain roles, but the reality of who they are outside the show is very different. The photos reveal life more as it really is, behind the staged glamour of the big wedding.

Historical Context

Sexual Morality and American Culture

"Marry the One Who Gets There First" depicts sex (including casual sex), infidelity in a committed relationship, sexual betrayal, lust, voyeurism, and sexual deviance. The sexual elements are presented explicitly, as in Violet's thoughts about the sex she engages in with Louis. In this uninhibited approach to her themes, Julavits was reflecting American popular culture of the late-1990s, in which such issues were presented in the media with an explicitness that would have been unthinkable to earlier generations, even during the period of sexual freedom in the 1960s. A typical example was *Sex and the City*, a cable television program which originally began broadcasting on the HBO network in 1998 and quickly attracted a large audience. Based on the 1997 book of the same title by the journalist Candace Bushnell, the show ran for six successful seasons until 2004. It focused on the sex lives of four women in their thirties and forties in New York City, and it was notable for the women's graphic language and ribald humor. The sexual topics that came up during the show included extramarital affairs, "threesomes," lesbianism, condoms, oral sex, and, repeatedly, the size of the male sexual organ.

During the same period of the late-1990s, television talk shows flourished in which invited guests would divulge the most intimate details of their personal lives. These confessional shows ranged from the sedate but extremely popular afternoon *Oprah Winfrey Show* to more raucous and tasteless productions such as *The Jerry Springer Show*. Springer would invite guests to talk about the problems in their lives, often concerning sex and sexual relationships, and ensure that they were confronted on camera by romantic rivals, cheating spouses, and anyone else whose presence could be guaranteed to arouse passions and lead to an unpleasant scene—unpleasant, that is, for everyone except the audience, both in the studio and in living rooms across the nation, for whom the most angry confrontations, sometimes involving fistfights and hair-pulling, made up the most entertaining shows. When in 1998 and again in 1999, Springer was ordered by Studio USA, who produced the show, to reduce the amount of foul language and the number of physical confrontations on the show, ratings fell dramatically.

While TV talk shows pushed the limits of what was acceptable on the air, the same trend occurred in radio. So-called shock jock Howard Stern, addressing a huge audience of commuters in the morning, brought new levels of obscenity to the airwaves, with jokes and stories about everything from bodily functions to sexual perversions. The more outrageous Stern became, the more his ratings soared, although many protested that he was bigoted and a racist and a misogynist. In the early 1990s, several stations were fined by the Federal Communications Commission (FCC) for airing a Stern show that was deemed especially obscene. In 1995, the radio station operator Infinity Broadcasting Corporation was fined $1.7 million for Stern's excesses, but none of these measures put a dent in the shock jock's position as a cultural icon of 1990s America.

Discussions of sex also became more explicit in the news media during the 1990s, in part, due to a desire to report on and to stem the AIDS/HIV epidemic, which involved explaining how the virus could and could not be communicated.

In 1998, sexual morality in public life became the subject of national attention due to the scandal involving President Bill Clinton's relationship with Monica Lewinsky, a young single woman who had worked as an intern at the White House. Clinton at first denied under oath that he had had an improper relationship with Lewinsky but later admitted the truth of the allegations. He was impeached by the U.S. House of Representatives for perjury and obstruction of justice, and the case was sent to the Senate for trial. In February, 1999, Clinton was acquitted on both charges, and he remained in office until the end of his term.

For months as the scandal unfolded, the news media focused on explicit details of the president's sexual behavior with Lewinsky. Many parents were shocked at how talk about sexual terms and sexual acts were taking place on the evening news when their children were watching. However, the public as a whole was unwilling to condemn Clinton for what many saw as a private matter. In fact, Clinton's approval ratings, as measured by opinion polls, soared during the scandal and impeachment. Years of exposure through television and radio talk shows, as well as movies, to explicit discussions of sex, as well as stories of sexual infidelity, helped to create a cultural climate in which such acts were not considered especially shocking or reprehensible by the majority of Americans. Conservatives, however, took the Clinton scandal as an example of the moral decline of the country, and this was a factor in the victory of the Republican candidate, George W. Bush, in the presidential election of 2000.

Critical Overview

Short story writers usually only capture the attention of literary critics when they publish their first collection of stories in book form. Since Julavits has yet to publish a short-story collection, "Marry the One Who Comes First" has so far not received any attention from reviewers or critics, although it did receive the distinction, after publication in *Esquire* magazine, of being included in *The Best American Short Stories, 1999.*

Julavits has expressed her preference for writing novels rather than short stories, and her two novels, *The Mineral Palace* (2000) and *The Effect of Living Backwards* (2003), are the works on which her growing literary reputation is based.

Criticism

Bryan Aubrey

Aubrey holds a Ph.D. in English and has published many articles on literature. In this essay, he discusses how Julavits uses her characters, particularly Louis Krupnik, to satirize the idea of romantic love.

On the evidence of "Marry the One Who Gets There First," Julavits is a writer with a rich gift for satirizing deeply ingrained cultural beliefs about love and marriage. Against the background of an elaborate, traditional wedding in a splendid western setting, Julavits savagely scythes away at the shallow, one might even say half-baked, ideas that people employ to explain why they chose that particular person to be their spouse and torpedoes the "happy-ever-after" cliché that supposedly describes married life with the person of one's dreams. Louis Krupnik and Violet Sheidegger are not even happy *before*, so their chances of being happy *after* seem unlikely, to say the least. Julavits's world as depicted in this story is shallow,

A bungalow in the mountains surrounded by pine trees © Gunter Marx Photography/Corbis

sly, deceitful, and full of anguish, both potential and actual. It is not the world depicted in a million pulp romance novels or in umpteen Hollywood romantic comedies, in which true love always triumphs over all obstacles and setbacks. Such starry-eyed escapism is not for Julavits; in its satirical thrust "Marry the One Who Gets There First" has more in common with *Seinfeld*, the mordantly funny 1990s television situation comedy in which love between the sexes, whilst earnestly sought, is always superficial, brittle, and short-lived.

The notion of romantic love has had a grip on the Western imagination since the phenomenon of courtly love emerged in the twelfth century. In courtly love, a knight would worship and idealize an aristocratic lady in whom he saw the highest beauty and perfection. Erotic passion was felt but not acted upon. In contrast, worship of the lady became the means by which the knight proved himself to be both noble and selfless. Such love was not seen as being the basis for a marriage. The lady who was the object of the knight's devotion was usually married herself, and upper-class marriage in medieval times was not a matter of romantic love, but was usually arranged for purposes of familial or political advantage.

The belief that romantic love should be the basis of marriage did not appear until comparatively recently, in the Victorian age, and as of the early 2000s its grip has not relaxed. Nowadays, romantic love carries an astonishing burden of expectation for those who fall under its sway. It is not uncommon for men and women alike to invest all their hopes in meeting Mr. or Ms. Right, who will be the embodiment of all their dreams and the answer to all their prayers. When a suitable partner comes along and people "fall in love," they feel excited and elevated, as if they are more fully alive than ever before. They believe, often without question, that they have met the person who will somehow complete them and make them happy. It is a heady, exhilarating feeling, erotic and passionate yet somehow seeming spiritual and transcendental as well. For many people, cultivating this love of their lives then takes priority over everything else. As Robert A. Johnson puts it in *We: Understanding the Psychology of Romantic Love*, his illuminating study of romantic love in the context of the Tristan and Iseult myth, "Romantic love is the single greatest energy system in the Western psyche. In our culture it has supplanted religion as the arena in which men and women seek meaning, transcendence, wholeness, and ecstasy."

In "Marry the One Who Gets There First," the primary carrier of this cultural myth about romantic love is Louis Krupnik. Louis may be a liar and a cheat, but he is also a romantic and a dreamer. His romantic ideals revealed themselves early in his life. When he was still at high school he was captivated by a photograph of a girl in a red dress that he found while working in his father's photography business. Convincing himself that she was the culmination of a "divine search," he promptly installed her as "the Girl of His Dreams." The capitalization well conveys the transcendental importance he ascribed to this mysterious, alluring female whom he had never met and whose identity he did not know. The cultural obsession with romantic love had already reached out and grabbed Louis and made him its prisoner. In that sense, he was unconscious of what he was doing; his thoughts and feelings about the opposite sex were prescribed for him before he was even born. He was preprogrammed to invent a Girl of His Dreams. As Robert Johnson explains:

> Romantic love is not just a form of 'love,' it is a whole psychological package—a combination of beliefs, ideals, attitudes, and expectations. These often contradictory ideas coexist in our unconscious minds and dominate our reactions and behavior, without our being aware of them. We have automatic assumptions about what a relationship with another person is, what we should feel, and what we should 'get out of it.'

When Louis puts the photo "the Girl of His Dreams" in his wallet and carries it around with him for many years, he is carrying a visual symbol of his psychological condition, his dependence on an invented, projected, unrealistic ideal. "The Girl of His Dreams," Louis no doubt imagines, will be the salve for all his pain, the precious One who will transmute his misery—for surely Louis, the son of unhappily married parents, did not have an enjoyable childhood—into the purest bliss.

Had Louis been content to live a quiet life and keep "the Girl of His Dreams" only in his pocket, he might have avoided causing too much suffering for others, but when he meets June, who unlike the girl in the red dress is a real, flesh-and-blood woman, he immediately bestows on her the same exalted, dangerous title. He does not seem to know that dream girls appear only in dreams and can do no otherwise. Significantly, his very first sight of June is based on a misinterpretation and an illusion. Louis is in a bookstore in San Francisco and June is outside, examining her own reflection in the window. But instead of grasping this clue to June's vanity and self-absorption, Louis mistakenly thinks

> "The cultural obsession with romantic love had already reached out and grabbed Louis and made him its prisoner. In that sense, he was unconscious of what he was doing; his thoughts and feelings about the opposite sex were prescribed for him before he was even born."

she is gazing directly at him. The relationship therefore begins with an illusion and continues with one, since no woman can long bear the burden of being the Girl of Louis's Dreams, or of any man's dreams, come to that. Louis simply projects onto June his ideal, which is unrelated to who she in reality is—the flirtatious, deceitful, cunning June would not seem to be the dream of any man in his right mind—and wildly overestimates what she is able to bring to him in the relationship. Since romantic love, as T.S. Eliot said of humanity, cannot bear too much reality, the course of the relationship between Louis and June is wholly predictable. Louis spends some time telling her that she is the only woman in the world for him, but all too soon things end in bitterness and recrimination—and also June's revenge, as Louis's own words literally come back to haunt him in the wedding cake.

Having chosen, if that is the right word, Violet over June, Louis ends up believing that the marriage he has just that minute solemnized, to a woman—he suddenly realizes—he barely knows, is the result of a destiny that cannot be countermanded. The idea that there is an immutable destiny that leads two people to unite in love and marriage is often part of the "psychological package" mentioned by Johnson that accompanies romantic love. Such beliefs go back a long way in the Western cultural tradition. In Shakespeare's play *The Merchant of Venice*, one of the characters

What Do I Read Next?

- The Lighthouse Inkwell website contains an interview with Julavits. It can be found at http://www.lighthousewriters.com/newslett/gems.htm and in it Julavits talks about her writing process, mainly in connection with her first novel, *The Mineral Palace*.
- In an interview with Ron Hogan that can be found online at http://www.beatrice.com/interviews/julavits/ Julavits talks to the online literary magazine *Beatrice* about her first novel.
- When asked in an interview by the publisher Virago to name her favorite book by a female author, Julavits selected *Middlemarch* (1872–73) and *Daniel Deronda* (1876), both by George Eliot. She admired both novels because they "deal with issues of marriage and the constraints of both genders in way that feels uncannily contemporary."
- *The Mineral Palace* (2000), Julavits's first novel, is set in Depression-Era Colorado, where Bena Jonssen moves because her physician husband is to take up a new job there. Much of the story focuses on Bena's difficulties, including her husband's alcoholism. Bena falls in love with a rancher and eventually faces up to the traumas she has suffered in her life. Reviewers praised Julavits's brilliance with language.
- *Sex in America* (1995), by Gina Kolata, presents in popular format the results of an authoritative study, involving interviews with over three thousand Americans, of sexual behavior in the United States. The book covers information such as how people find sexual partners, how often they engage in sex, how common certain sexual practices are, what people think of erotica and how often they read it or look at it, and the extent of homosexual behavior and of sexually transmitted diseases.

---

approvingly quotes an old proverb, "The ancient saying is no heresy / Hanging and wiving goes by destiny." This is of course a proposition that cannot be empirically tested. It might be argued that if two people married and spent their lives together, they were de facto destined to do so, but that says nothing about what might have happened had they made different choices earlier in their lives.

Curiously, Violet, the other main participant in this dark comedy, seems to believe in the power of choice. Unlike Louis, she appears not to labor so much under the illusions of romantic love. She knows Louis for who he is and even permits herself some doubts about her chosen course of action. Violet subscribes to, one might say, an alternative reality, in which people shape their own lives by the kind of language they choose to describe their experiences. It is a belief system Julavits treats satirically, describing Violet as a student of "language therapy" and presenting her poring over a map, trying to establish that she is getting married not in a place with the negative-sounding name Lower Stanley but in the adjacent township that is happily named Diamond Heights. Julavits's target here may be the kind of popular psychology that appears in countless self-help books and magazines designed to empower people and allow them to take charge of their lives by positive thinking, the underlying premise being that reality is a result of the thoughts humans think and the words they use to express them.

Unfortunately, this approach does not appear to be working very well for Violet. If the best that her vaunted power over language can manifest is a Louis Krupnik and a wedding cake full of shredded love letters addressed to her sister by her groom, she might perhaps be advised to return to the drawing board and start blaming fate instead.

Source: Bryan Aubrey, Critical Essay on "Marry the One Who Gets There First," in *Short Stories for Students*, Thomson Gale, 2006.

Laura Pryor

Pryor has a bachelor of arts from University of Michigan and twenty years experience in professional and creative writing with special interest in fiction. In this essay, she examines how Heidi Julavits incorporates the theme of photography into the story of the Sheidegger-Krupnik wedding.

"The camera never lies," the old saying goes. In Heidi Julavits's "Marry the One Who Gets There First," the camera may not lie, but everyone else does. The wedding of June Sheidegger and Louis Krupnik is so framed in deceit on all sides that there are no innocent parties, only fellow liars. What many of the characters fail to realize, however, is that they have been lied to not only by their lovers, but also by their own misperceptions and distorted vision.

Julavits structures the story as a series of "outtakes" from the Sheidegger-Krupnik wedding album, but it doesn't take long for the reader to realize that these are no ordinary wedding photographs. These are not the posed, smiling portraits people are accustomed to finding in wedding albums. In Julavits's "outtakes," the camera truly does not lie; what's more, the camera is everywhere. It's highly unlikely, for instance, that a photographer would be on hand to take a picture of Violet, the bride, calling her lover Shane from a pay phone or one of the lodge staff workers fastening her belt after a tryst with the stable hand, yet this photographer is omniscient, giving us brief instants of truth amidst the tangle of lies the characters tell each other and themselves.

The photography theme is woven throughout the story in both obvious and subtle ways. Louis the groom, who is cheating on his fiancé with her own sister June, runs the family business, Krupnik Bros. Photographic Supplies and Development, where he voyeuristically examines the photos of strangers. He and June take a self-timed photograph of themselves in bed together. When he finds a photograph of his father and another woman, he realizes his father cheated on his mother.

The characters view each other distortedly through the prisms of their own desires and prejudices, never truly seeing each other clearly. Louis, for instance, believes June to be the "Girl of his Dreams," because she resembles a photograph of a girl he saw while working at his father's business. Throughout the story, when Louis sees June, he sees her through various lenses; when he first meets her she is gazing at her own reflection in a bookstore window, and Louis sees her through the glass.

> "Ironically, while the characters focus on these tiny coincidences and omens, they ignore many far more obvious pieces of information about their relationships."

He sees her again later, examining her reflection in the window of the lodge. When he is shaving in preparation for his wedding, he sees her reflection in the mirror, through the bathroom window—two more lenses. Only near the end of the story do the characters have moments of clarity in which they see themselves and others clearly. Here there are no mirrors or windows: "Suddenly, without the aid of any reflective surface, [June] catches a perfect and absurd image of herself—weeping in the back of a chuck wagon, clinging to a piece of fake hair with nails painted a deep, sad red because of its appropriate name (Other Woman)—and for the first time in a long time, she laughs at herself." When Louis cuts the cake with June, he looks around and discovers "he doesn't recognize a single one of the guests . . . nor does he recognize the woman beside him with whom he grasps a knife handle." For the first time, he is seeing clearly.

Reflective surfaces, prisms—these surface again in the story of Violet's Grandma Rose and Grandpa Joe. Grandma Rose believes they are fated to be together because on their first date, when she nervously broke a champagne flute and Joe recited a poetic Chinese saying Rose's grandfather was fond of. Later, when arranging flowers, Grandma Rose shatters a glass vase. Then at the prenuptial luncheon, after a spat with Joe, Rose knocks her juice glass to the floor and breaks it. "I married the wrong man," she says and then grinds the broken glass to dust with her heel. This image brings to mind the Jewish wedding tradition in which the groom breaks a glass with his foot, which symbolizes (among many other things) the bride's loss of innocence. Rose has apparently abandoned the naive illusions she carried into her marriage, illusions based largely on a Chinese saying Joe picked up from the proprietor of a mah-jongg parlor who assured him it "Works ladies like charm." Similarly, Louis recalls a scene from his past in which his mother, near death, hurls his father's watch at him, believing in her delirium that Louis is actually her deceased husband. The watch's crystal breaks and his mother says, "The one, the one, you were *the one*. Bah!" Like Grandma Rose, her illusions about her husband have finally been shattered.

Like a photographer, Julavits uses light and dark symbolically to tell her story. The bride and her sister are like negatives of each other; "Violet was as blond and stupid as June was dark and wise." Violet tries to use words to shed a positive light on situations, calling Louis's ordinary blue shirt "refreshingly insouciant" and the cheap wine they drink with dinner "spirited" and "tumescent." Later, however, after readers learn that she framed Louis and June and then had an affair with a man who paid her "to offset suspicions," it is clear that Violet is not as snow-white as she appears. "Rather, she reasoned she was developing her own secrets, her own desires, her own darknesses, that she was no longer the obvious blond optimist . . . the girl too stupid to know the thrill one can get from deception." As the story closes, June leaves behind Louis and the bride in white and walks barefoot along the road, where she meets Norton Black, and it is implied that this is the beginning of a new and lasting relationship. Despite the use of black and white, light and dark, one of the messages Julavits communicates is that in romantic relationships, there are no heroes and villains, and no relationship is without its flaws. At the outset of the story, Louis appears to be an irredeemable pervert and Violet sweet and trusting; by the conclusion, they have both moved from black and white to shades of grey.

Julavits's view on the long-term relationships in the story is often cynical. Most notably she pokes fun at the "signs" and "omens" that individuals cling to as evidence that their union is fated. When Louis finds an old photograph of a married couple at the municipal building, "he believed that this photograph . . . was meant as a sign to him." Grandma Rose believes that because Grandpa Joe uses the same Chinese saying as her grandfather, they are destined to be together. When Violet calls her lover Shane just before the wedding and he is not home, "a part of her believes she must find some meaning in the fact that Shane is not home to comfort her, that she has been pushed to do the right thing." Louis is initially attracted to June because she looks like the "Girl of his Dreams," a stranger in a photograph he sees while working in his father's photo shop. Just as people attach sentimental importance to photographs, believing them to represent entire periods of their lives rather than the single, often staged, instant that they actually capture, they also attach meaning to minor incidents that may actually mean nothing. As Julavits writes about Grandma Rose and the Chinese proverb, "In a world full of empty coincidences and accidents, she read this as an omen of their fated union." Louis observes this in another way while working at the photo shop and peeking at the customers' pictures: "he became entranced by the odd pieces of the world people found worth preserving—a door with a brass street number, a tin of muffins, the mole on a woman's forearm." Ironically, while the characters focus on these tiny coincidences and omens, they ignore many far more obvious pieces of information about their relationships. For instance, Violet is well aware that Louis is a womanizer and a voyeur, but this information does not prevent her from becoming his wife.

Julavits's cynicism is lightened by some tender moments. Grandpa Joe goes to sleep with "one protective hand on the upturned hip of his sleeping wife"; Louis realizes that Violet "knows and loves him for all the ways that he has always been unknowable." The very fact that these flawed characters choose to marry at all, despite obvious arguments against it, is in itself an act of great optimism. Just as the wedding camera captures the posed, smiling faces of the bride and groom—and none of their anxieties—the mind romances reality into something a little easier to swallow. In the final analysis, the need for a partner is so great that we decide it is better to believe our romantic version of a relationship and stay together than to see it clearly and end up alone. Julavits ends the story with a scene from Norton and June's future relationship: "And maybe on certain evenings—when they're looking at their carefully posed wedding photographs, and the sun is setting, and the air is like it was the night Norton found June barefoot by the road—they'll believe their own tales about how love is a fixed, unquestionable thing, written in stars and in stones."

Source: Laura Pryor, Critical Essay on "Marry the One Who Gets There First," in *Short Stories for Students*, Thomson Gale, 2006.

Bonnie Weinreich

Bonnie Weinreich has a B.A. in English and is a freelance writer and former reporter for a daily newspaper. In this essay on Heidi Julavits's short story "Marry the One Who Gets Their First" Weinreich observes the way the author uses photographs as a vehicle to tell a story of love and betrayal.

Why do people choose the spouses they do? Is it fate, preordained by a cupid no one sees until some set of circumstances coalesce into a wedding in which everyone wonders what on earth they are doing? Or is it a well-considered decision, coupled with love and lust, in which two people realize they are really meeting each other for the first time as the bride walks down the aisle toward the groom? According to Heidi Julavits's short story, "Marry the One Who Gets There First," it is both and more. Julavits uses the camera lens as a magnifying glass to expose the frailties and failures of the members of the wedding.

Julavits polishes into a shiny gem the time-honored process of using pictures as inspiration for writing. She both frames the story in photographs and uses pictures within the narrative to move the action forward. While she designates the sections as a series of photos numbered 1 through 36, they might be considered the pauses in a videotape to capture the actions of her characters. In addition, she casts the captions to these pictures in the active voice and present tense, giving these freeze frames a "real time" feeling. These captions also guide the reader through shifts of point of view by showing the reader a picture first. (Point of view is the angle of vision from which the author tells the story.) The subtitle, "Outtakes from the Sheidegger-Krupnik wedding album," further substantiates the notion that these segments are a chronicle of the real story, the one left on the cutting room floor.

Although it is a cliché to say a picture is worth a thousand words, this story is remarkable in its ability to carry several subplots in the short story form, which typically confines itself to one tightly-woven plot line, but here the author juggles the stories of the bride, groom, sister, friend, and parents with agility and style, all expertly written in fifteen pages. Her ability to fit so much in her story is facilitated by the framework and the use of photographs as pegs to hang the action on. Pictures of the wedding party, parents, and strangers take readers on a sight-seeing tour that is sometimes confusing and often brutally honest.

The 1990s witnessed changes in visual media. Indeed, over the second half of the twentieth century, the television evolved from a small, moon-shaped screen peering out of large wooden cabinet into the so-called big screen and back again into a miniature screen that can be worn on the wrist. By the early 2000s people own digital cameras, throw-away cameras, and cell phones with cameras. Cars have visual displays. Music is visual, thanks to videos and television stations that play them. Julavits is attuned to contemporary readers' conditioning to the visual, and the form of the story and her diction create vivid pictures in the mind's eye, the most visual of all appliances.

"Photo by photo, scene by scene, the author melds humor with betrayal, creating of satire of modern-day relationships."

With economy of language, the bride, Violet, and the bride's sister, June, are introduced in the first sentence, and conflict immediately is conveyed by the fact June refuses to wear a slip under her sheer bridesmaid's dress. In addition, the sexual overtones in June's description hint at the trouble to come. In the space of one two-sentence paragraph, the author gives readers two main characters—the sisters, the personality and attitude of June, and the setting, the Sawtooth Mountains, and she does it with sass and clarity: "The startling views of the Sawtooth Mountain Range serve as only a momentary distraction from the unfettered swell of June's behind inside the peach fabric, indicating June also decided to forgo underwear." Clearly, June is mooning her sister and the wedding, and as the story unfolds readers come to understand why: she has been having an affair with the groom.

The groom, Louis, runs the family photography business, and in his voyeuristic snooping through his customers' photos he has discovered a picture of a woman he considers to be his Dream Girl. When he meets June, her resemblance to his picture hits him like a thunderbolt, but he is already involved with her sister. He embarks on an affair with June, convinced Violet is in the dark. However, Violet is on to them and sets a trap into which they fall, while she carries on with a man who pays her for her favors. In addition, Louis has discovered a picture that reveals his father had a mistress. In the course of all these assignations, readers must wonder if a sympathetic character can be found. Presented with fathers who have cheated on their mothers, to the friend whose love "is inextricably linked with pity, as well as a heady feeling of superiority" for her fiancé, the bride's brother, to the groom and the bride and her sister who are betraying each other in a number of ways, readers have to stretch to find sympathy for any of the them. In addition, one wonders why these characters have come to a lodge in the Sawtooth Mountains of Idaho from Manhattan for their wedding. Perhaps it is the jagged-edged backdrop which accentuates the raggedness of their relationships.

None of these characters seems too much in love, although June might have been with Louis before he dumped her and decided to stick with her sister, who got to him first. In fact, these relationships appear to be exercises in one-upmanship, particularly from the point of view of the main female characters, who believe they have beaten their lovers at their own game. The author seems to be saying that no one wins in the midst of all this double dealing.

For a bit of comic relief, the author reveals that June has foregone wearing underwear to impress the cook, whom she believes to be a lesbian. (Comic relief is a humorous scene or incident in the course of serious drama to provide relief from the emotional intensity and, by contrast, heighten the seriousness of the story.) June wants the cook to bake Louis's love letters into the wedding cake since Louis demanded that June get rid of this incriminating evidence. Regardless of the cook's sexual proclivities, which the author leaves undetermined, she does cook the shredded letters into the cake because June tells her they are fortunes and a spin on the cliché, "eat your own words," ensues as the bride and groom find strips of Louis's love letters to June in their mouths as they eat their wedding cake. The scene is serious and amusing at the same time, and it is representative of the simultaneously funny and heartbreaking tenor of the story as a whole. Photo by photo, scene by scene, the author melds humor with betrayal, creating of satire (a literary work in which vices, follies, stupidities, abuses, etc., are held up to ridicule and contempt) of modern-day relationships.

Louis's perspective shifts from a feeling that "he has arrived to be married at the wrong wedding," to an inexplicable sensation that "he is suddenly the man on the inside, slightly less bewildered, looking out." These feelings contrast with Violet's earlier resignation that "she has been pushed to do the right thing, despite the secret lives she and Louis lead."

The introduction of Norton Black in Photo 6 seems peripheral, but in Photo 25, which suggests that Black has sex with one of the college women who works in the kitchen, Julavits foreshadows the ending in which he picks June up on the side of the road leading from the lodge. (Foreshadowing is the presentation of material to prepare the reader for action to come.) In addition, the author uses omens and signs seen by various characters to foreshadow coming events. For example, Rose Sheidegger believes she was fated to marry her husband when he used a quotation her grandfather used, although her husband received the saying from a mah-jongg parlor owner who told him it "works ladies like charm." Later in the story, Rose laments that she "married the wrong man."

In the final frame the author summarizes the quandary of the members of the wedding, and concludes that "they'll believe their own tales about how love is a fixed, unquestionable thing, written in stars and in stones." In "they" the author refers to the wedding party as well as Norton and June.

On the face of it, the author has spun a tale of superficial people trying to get the best of each other. But every family puts up a façade in an effort to disguise its flaws, hide the black sheep, obscure its scandals. Although the members of the wedding are trying desperately to pose their pictures, they are fooling neither themselves nor each other. Upon close observation, the reader "sees" the many layers woven into the story: the eternal question of what is love, how one picks a mate, and what part fate plays in the process, and whether one person can truly know another.

The author leaves it to readers to decide, and the beautifully written ending confirms what readers sense all along—nobody knows the answers.

Source: Bonnie Weinreich, Critical Essay on "Marry the One Who Gets There First," in *Short Stories for Students*, Thomson Gale, 2006.

Sources

Johnson, Robert A., *We: Understanding the Psychology of Romantic Love*, Harper, San Francisco, 1983, p. xi.

Julavits, Heidi, "Marry the One Who Gets There First," in *Esquire*, April 1998, pp. 106–12, 143.

Shakespeare, William, *The Merchant of Venice*, Act 2, scene 9, lines 82–83, The Arden Shakespeare, Methuen, 1979, p. 68.

Virago, "Heidi Julavits, Interview," www.virago.co.uk

Further Reading

Jankowiak, William, ed., *Romantic Passion: A Universal Experience?,* Columbia University Press, 1995.

This book presents anthropological research that examines whether romantic love is a universal experience or, as some have argued, only a Western phenomenon. The research across 166 cultures shows that romantic love is known in at least 147, or 89 percent, of these cultures.

Singer, Irving, *The Nature of Love: The Modern World*, University of Chicago Press, 1987.

The third and final volume in Singer's study of the history of Western thought is about the nature of love. It covers twentieth-century psychologists, writers, and philosophers of love such as Sigmund Freud, Marcel Proust, D. H. Lawrence, Bernard Shaw, and Jean-Paul Sartre, whose tendency was to question or deny the possibility of successful erotic love relationships between men and women.

Tennov, Dorothy, *Love and Limerence: The Experience of Being in Love*, second edition, Scarborough House, 1999.

Based on research conducted on college students, Tennov provides an engaging account of the psychology of romantic love. Tennov also discusses the different ways in which men and women experience romantic love and the biological basis of the phenomenon. She gives some advice about how to deal with it.

Welwood, John, ed., *Challenge of the Heart: Love, Sex, and Intimacy in Changing Times*, Shambhala, 1985.

This excellent anthology contains thirty-six essays on all aspects of love, culled from a wide variety of writers, including D. H. Lawrence, Robert Bly, Rainer Maria Rilke, Wendell Berry, and Alan Watts. The essays address the questions and difficulties that arise for people in intimate relationships.

Proper Library

Carolyn Ferrell

1993

"Proper Library" by Carolyn Ferrell was first published in the literary journal *Ploughshares* in 1993. It was selected for the collection *Best American Short Stories 1994* by editor Tobias Wolff, which brought Ferrell's work to the attention of Houghton Mifflin editor Janet Silver, who offered her a book contract. In 1997, the book *Don't Erase Me* was released, a collection of eight first-person stories featuring mostly poor black girls and women. "Proper Library," however, tells the story of a young black boy, a gay teenager living in the housing projects of the South Bronx in New York. Ferrell's experiences directing a family literacy project in the South Bronx helped her to render a disturbingly accurate and poignant portrait of the challenges faced by Lorrie and his family and the attitudes and prejudices that govern their lives. Despite the difficulties Lorrie faces, however, the story is not entirely bleak; his own confidence, compassion, and optimism leave the reader feeling that he may someday succeed in fulfilling his dreams.

Author Biography

Carolyn Ferrell was born in Brooklyn, New York, on April 29, 1962, and was raised on Long Island. She began writing at the age of six, beginning with poetry she describes as "often terrible," then moving on to stories.

In 1980, Ferrell began her studies in creative writing at Sarah Lawrence College in New York. During her four years at Sarah Lawrence, she studied with such accomplished authors as Grace Paley and Allan Gurganus. After graduating in 1984, she lived in Germany for four years, studying German literature and also working as a high school teaching assistant on a Fulbright scholarship. Ferrell is a skilled violinist, and during her years in Germany she was a member of both the Berlin Sibelius Orchestra and the Brandenburgisches Kammerorchester.

After her years in Germany, Ferrell returned to New York, teaching adult literacy first in Manhattan then in the South Bronx (where "Proper Library" takes place). She also directed a family literacy project in the South Bronx.

Ferrell then began studying for her master's degree in creative writing at City College of New York. It was during this time that she began submitting her stories to literary journals. Soon her stories were published in *Callaloo*, *Literary Review*, and *Fiction*. The story "Proper Library" was published in the journal *Ploughshares* in 1993 and was selected for *The Best American Short Stories 1994*. Two years later, in 1996, Ferrell returned to Sarah Lawrence College as a teacher of creative writing.

The following year (1997) was an eventful one. Ferrell got married to Linwood Lewis, a psychologist also teaching at Sarah Lawrence, and the couple had their first child, Benjamin. This was also the year that her first book, a collection of short stories entitled *Don't Erase Me*, was released. It was an impressive debut; the book won the Art Seidenbaum Award for First Fiction from the *Los Angeles Times* and the Zacharis First Book Prize from *Ploughshares*. Stories from the collection have been anthologized in *Giant Steps: The New Generation of African American Writers*, *Children of the Night: Best Short Stories by Black Writers, 1967 to the Present*, and *Streetlights: Illuminating Tales of the Urban Black Experience*. *Streetlights* was edited by Doris Jean Austin, whom Ferrell credits as being a mentor and major influence on her writing.

As of 2005 Ferrell continued to teach creative writing at Sarah Lawrence College and was working on a novel to be published by Houghton-Mifflin. She lives with her husband Linwood Lewis and their two children (daughter Karina was born in 2002) in New York.

Carolyn Ferell © Photo by Lorin Klaris

Plot Summary

"Proper Library" tells the story of one day in the life of Lorrie Adams, a fourteen-year-old gay black boy living in the housing projects of the South Bronx. Lorrie lives with his mother, his morose Aunt Estine, and a wide assortment of sisters, cousins, nieces, and nephews. Lorrie loves to take care of "the kids," braiding their hair, ironing their clothes, and teaching them math and vocabulary words. There are nine little kids in all, but Lorrie points out, "when my other aunt, Samantha, comes over I got three more."

Lorrie's day begins with his mother's reminder that when he returns home from school, they will "practice the words." Lorrie learns new vocabulary words each week with his mother, who sees his potential and wants him to pass his City-Wide tests. Despite his obvious intelligence, Lorrie repeatedly fails the tests and is held back. His acerbic cousin Cee Cee has the answer: "If you wasn't so stupid you would realize the fact of them holding you back till you is normal."

After a warning from his mother, "Don't let them boys bother you now," Lorrie heads to school. He is met at the front door by Tommy, the husband of his sister Lula Jean, who "has a lady tucked under his arm and it ain't Lula Jean." Another sister, Anita, slips him a letter knife and, in a reference to Lorrie's former lover Rakeem, says, "If that boy puts his thing on you, cut it off. I love you, baby."

On his way to the bus stop, Lorrie is approached by Layla Jackson with her baby whom she calls Tee Tee. She begs Lorrie to take the baby, because her mother will not and Layla needs a sitter. Lorrie tells her he cannot take Tee Tee now, but if she brings him by the school later he will take the baby home with him. Layla agrees, and before she leaves she tells Lorrie that her cousin Rakeem wants to see him.

At this point, Lorrie tells the story of his six-month affair with Rakeem. He met Rakeem under the Bruckner Expressway, where one day they had sex. Rakeem told him, "This is where your real world begins, man." Lorrie stopped going to school and instead met Rakeem under the expressway every day. Finally, Lorrie told Rakeem he wanted to go back to school. He tried to tell him about "the words" and to encourage Rakeem to go back to school too.

Now, Lorrie gets on the bus for school. On the bus he sees his friend Joe Smalls, the only heterosexual boy in school who treats Lorrie kindly. He also sees Laura, "the only white girl in these projects that I know of." He says, "I feel sorry for her," even though when Lorrie gets on the bus she immediately calls him a "faggot". Another girl joins in with more insults. Lorrie says nothing but keeps walking to the back of the bus: "It's the way I learned: keep moving." He sits next to Joe, who tells him how his baby's mother, Tareen, did his math homework for him the night before, even though she is no longer in school. Lorrie listens to Joe's story but all the while, "I feel all of the ears on us." "Keep moving," Lorrie repeatedly tells himself. Finally, the bus arrives at school.

When he gets off the bus, Rakeem is waiting for him. Rakeem is back in school now, thanks to Lorrie's encouragement, and tells Lorrie the news that he made it into Math 3. Lorrie congratulates him and says, "See what I told you before, Rakeem? You really got it in you to move on. You doing all right, man." Rakeem asks Lorrie to meet him later that night behind Rocky's Pizza. Lorrie is tempted, because he misses Rakeem, but tells himself, "The kids are enough. The words are important. They are all enough."

In first period, Lorrie has science with Mr. D'Angelo. Lorrie has a crush on Mr. D'Angelo and smiles adoringly at him. A classmate notices and says, "Sometimes when a man's been married long he needs to experience a new kind of loving, ain't that what you think, Lorrie?" This gets her thrown out of class by Mr. D'Angelo, who is perspiring, unnerved by Lorrie's attentions. Lorrie thinks to himself, "Mr. D'Angelo, I am in silent love in a loud body. So don't turn away. *Sweat.*"

In third period, Lorrie has Woodworking for You. He daydreams about "the kids" while waiting to use the power saw. His friend Joe Smalls talks to him about how Tareen got half his math problems wrong. "Be glad you don't have to deal with no dumb-ass Tareen b——," Joe says. Lorrie knows the other boys are listening to their conversation. Soon they all chime in: "Why you talking that s——, Joe, man? Lorrie don't ever worry about b——es!" After several more comments, the teacher, Mr. Samuels, turns off the power saw and begins to laugh. Then he actually joins in: "Class, don't mess with the only *girl* we got in here!" Encouraged, the boys pile on more insults, telling Lorrie to get out. Lorrie picks up his school bag and leaves the classroom. "Inside me there is really nothing except for Ma's voice: *Don't let them boys.*"

Layla Jackson comes to the school to drop off Tee Tee and see her boyfriend Tyrone (Tee Tee's father). Lorrie holds Tee Tee while Layla and Tyrone kiss each other. They are both HIV positive, and "Everyone says that they gave themselves AIDS and now have to kiss each other because there ain't no one else." Holding Tee Tee and watching Tyrone and Layla sends Lorrie into a reverie about his affair with Rakeem. He tells himself, "It will never be more."

Lorrie arrives home with Tee Tee to find his mother upset; she needs Lorrie to watch Tommy and the kids while she goes out to bring Lula Jean home from the movies, "which is where she goes when she plans on leaving Tommy." Lorrie makes Tommy some tea and talks to him. Then he starts to get out his dictionary to learn his vocabulary words, but the kids want a bath and baby Tee Tee is sick. Lorrie realizes that he will know the words without studying; "The words are in my heart."

Lorrie's mother comes home and sets things right: she gives Tommy a tongue-lashing, tells Layla to get her sick baby out of her house, and tells Lorrie she has not forgotten the special dinner she promised him, for learning his new words. Lorrie tells her they will practice the words later, "but I got to go meet Rakeem first." Lorrie's mother looks shocked but does not stop him. Lorrie is eager to see Rakeem, but he has learned from his earlier experience. "I am coming back home. And I am going to school tomorrow. . . . I will be me for a few minutes behind Rocky's Pizza and I don't care if it's just a few minutes."

Characters

Anita Adams

Anita is the only one of Lorrie's sisters who thinks he is beautiful. She is also protective of him; before he leaves for school she gives him a letter knife and tells him to use it on Rakeem if "that boy puts his thing on you."

Lorrie Adams

Fourteen-year-old Lorrie Adams, whose full name is Lawrence Lincoln Jefferson Adams, is the main character of "Proper Library," and he narrates the story of his day. He is his mother's only son, and as she tells him, "the only real man I got." Lorrie is extremely bright, compassionate, and empathetic; he describes the plight of the only white girl on the bus, Laura, with great sympathy, even though the first thing she says when he boards the bus is "faggot." Lorrie's primary struggles as a gay teen are withstanding the persecution of his schoolmates and reconciling his ambition to make something of his life with his desire for Rakeem, his former lover. Lorrie describes the different loves of his life as "flavors of the pie," and his favorite flavor is the love he has for the children in the household. He channels all of his love and affection into caring for them, teaching them, entertaining them, even ironing their clothes. In fact, he has taken on the role of parent. It is never specified which children belong to which of Lorrie's sisters or cousins; he just calls them "the kids."

Mrs. Cabrini

Mrs. Cabrini is the only teacher that encourages Lorrie; she tells him, "Put your mind to your dreams, my dear boy, and you will achieve them. You are your own universe, your own shooting star."

Cousin Cee Cee

Cee Cee is Lorrie's critical, hostile cousin who delights in telling him how stupid he is to think he can make something of his life: "Practicing words like that! Is you a complete a—hole?" When Lorrie tries to teach new words to her kids, Cee Cee tells him, "it will hurt their eyes to be doing all that reading and besides they are only eight and nine."

Mr. D'Angelo

Mr. D'Angelo is Lorrie's science teacher, on whom he has a crush. Lorrie's obvious infatuation unnerves the teacher.

Layla Jackson

Layla Jackson is Rakeem's cousin who "might have AIDS." She and her boyfriend Tyrone have a baby they call Tee Tee. Like most of the women in the story, Layla's self-esteem hinges on her ability to keep Tyrone with her; at one point she falls apart because she suspects Tyrone (who is also HIV-positive) is going to a support group to meet other HIV-positive girls. Lorrie loves to hold baby Tee Tee, but Layla displays a lack of tenderness towards him; when Lorrie says he cannot take the baby until after fifth period, she says, "That means I got to take this brat to Introduction to Humanities with me. . . . He's gonna cry and I won't pass the test on Spanish Discoverers." She is the only girl in the story, however, who expresses any concern over her grades or schoolwork.

The Kids

Lorrie refers to the large brood of small children living with him and his mother as "the kids." Lasheema, Shawn, Sheniqua, Tonya, Tata, Willis, Byron, and Elizabeth are the names mentioned, but there are nine all together, and twelve if Lorrie's sister Samantha brings her children to the house.

Laura

Laura is the only white girl in the Bronx projects whom Lorrie knows. When some of the black girls at school threatened to beat her up, she cried and told them that her real parents were black. This made the other girls laugh, and they decided to make her their friend. Laura calls Lorrie a "faggot" when he gets on the bus in the morning, and for the rest of the bus ride, "I can feel Laura's eyes like they are a silent machine gun."

Lula Jean

Though Lula Jean, Lorrie's married sister, is mentioned frequently throughout the story, she is never actually at home until near the conclusion when Lorrie's mother brings her home from the movies, "where she goes when she plans on leaving Tommy." Even then she says nothing, but readers get an inkling of her character when Lorrie tells us, "They got four kids here and if Lula Jean leaves,

I might have to drop out of school again because she doesn't want to be tied to anything that has Tommy's stamp on it." Clearly Lorrie feels a greater sense of responsibility towards "the kids" than Lula Jean does.

Ma

Lorrie's mother is described as having "the same face as the maid in the movies." Whatever hopes or expectations she may have once had for her children now rest squarely on Lorrie's shoulders. She is very affectionate with him; she has "big brown hands like careful shovels, and she loves to touch and pat and warm you up with them." After they have a good session practicing vocabulary words, she touches Lorrie's face with her hands and calls him, "Lawrence, My Fine Boy." She seems resigned to the irresponsible behavior of her other children and Tommy, Lula Jean's husband, even though caring for all of their children certainly places a burden on her and Lorrie.

Rakeem

Rakeem, the cousin of Lorrie's friend Layla Jackson, is Lorrie's former lover. Lorrie met Rakeem everyday under the Bruckner Expressway to have sex, instead of going to school. After six months' absence from school, Lorrie told Rakeem he wanted to go back. He has not been with Rakeem since, but he misses him. Lorrie tells himself again and again that he can do without Rakeem, that the love he has for his family will sustain him. Rakeem feels differently. He says to Lorrie, "you think I'm a look at my cousin Layla and her bastard and love them and that will be enough. But it will never be enough." Rakeem goes back to school, thanks to Lorrie's encouragement, and makes it into Math 3. He says, "Man, I don't got nothing in me except my brain that tells me: Nigger, first thing get your ass up in school. Make them know you can do it."

Mr. Samuels

Mr. Samuels is Lorrie's teacher in Woodworking for You; according to Lorrie, "He doesn't fail me even though I don't do any cutting or measuring or shellacking. He wants me the hell out of there." When the other boys in class begin harassing Lorrie, Mr. Samuels joins in, calling Lorrie a "girl".

Joe Smalls

Joe Smalls is the only heterosexual male friend that Lorrie has at school. He chats with Lorrie on the bus and in woodworking class about his girlfriend, Tareen. Though he does risk the disapproval of his friends in being kind to Lorrie, he is only willing to stick his neck out so far; when the other boys in Woodworking for You begin to hurl insults at Lorrie, "Joe Smalls is quiet and looking out the window."

Aunt Estine Smith

Lorrie's Aunt Estine Smith, who lives with the family, insists that the children call her by both her first and last names. She is a bitter woman who "can't get out of her past"; her husband, David Saul Smith, was lynched from a tree in 1986, which Lorrie says is "her favorite time to make us all go back to." The only thing Lorrie admires about Aunt Estine is her backless blue organza dress. According to Lorrie, "Estine Smith is not someone but a walking hainted house." However, Estine does make one of the more astute observations of the story when she grumbles about Tommy, "Why do we women feel we always need to teach them? They ain't going to learn the right way. They ain't going to learn s——. That's why we always so alone." With the exception of Lorrie, this seems to be a fairly accurate summation of men's behavior in their world.

Tommy

Tommy, Lula Jean's husband, expresses the typical attitudes men have towards women in the story. Overall, Tommy does not seem to be a bad sort; before he arrives at the house with a different woman under his arm, Lorrie describes him with admiration. Tommy tells Lorrie what a "hidden genius" he is, tests him on his math, and tells him jokes and stories from the Bible. When he kisses Lula Jean, Lorrie says, "he searches into Lula Jean's face for whole minutes." While the members of the household are angry with him for bringing home this strange woman, the fact that Lula Jean will stay with Tommy seems to be a foregone conclusion. When she does return, he berates her for threatening to leave him: "You keep going that way and you won't ever know how to keep a man, b——."

Themes

Gender Roles and Stereotypes

Gender roles in Lorrie's world are very narrowly defined, and the penalties for violating their

Topics For Further Study

- Research the spread of AIDS in the black community. What percentage of AIDS cases among African Americans is spread by male-to-male sexual contact? Heterosexual contact? Intravenous drug use? Now compare these percentages to those in the overall population. Make a chart showing the results. What conclusion about the spread of this disease does your chart suggest?
- Define the vocabulary words that Lorrie studies in the story: independence, chagrin, symbolism, nomenclature, filament, apocrypha, soliloquy, disenfranchise, catechism. Which of these words might have special significance to Lorrie, given the challenges he faces day to day? After each definition, write what that word might mean to Lorrie.
- Think about a sequel to this story, showing Lorrie in the future. What do you think will happen to Lorrie as an adult? Will he make it to college? If yes, what career do you think he might pursue? Write a day in the life of Lorrie, ten years after this story occurs.
- Research the struggle for gay and lesbian rights in the United States. How is this similar to the civil rights movement? Make a timeline of both movements, including important events and legislation, and write a paragraph pointing out differences and similarities between the two.

boundaries are harsh. Men are not allowed to express tender emotions or vulnerability, and they regard women, at least outwardly, as second-class citizens valuable mainly for sex and childrearing. This dynamic is illustrated most vividly in the relationship between Lorrie's sister Lula Jean and her husband Tommy. Tommy clearly loves Lula Jean; when he kisses her "he searches into Lula Jean's face for whole minutes," and he tells Lorrie, "This is what love should be." Still, this attachment does not stop him from bringing home a strange woman and then lamenting later that "b——es out here nowadays" do not appreciate the things he does for them. Similarly, Joe Smalls' girlfriend Tareen stays up late doing his homework (even though she no longer goes to school because she is caring for their child) and then Joe complains bitterly when she gets some of the problems wrong, telling Lorrie that "that . . . Tareen b——h . . . nearly got [me] an F in Math 3." For the men, portraying this image of machismo is crucial. These attitudes explain why only women in the story encourage or express affection for Lorrie. Of his two male teachers, one avoids him, and the other openly ridicules him; only Mrs. Cabrini has words of encouragement. The men are too threatened by the idea of being seen as possibly homosexual to treat Lorrie with common respect or kindness.

For the women, keeping a man is all-important, even if the men treat them poorly. For Layla Jackson, who is HIV positive, the main concern is not that she may fall ill and die, but that no boy will sleep with her for fear of contracting the virus. Her condition makes it doubly crucial that she hang onto Tyrone, who is also HIV positive. Many of the teenage girls in the story have babies, whom they seem to regard as an unfortunate by-product of keeping their man. The message given to these girls is clear: a woman without a man is nothing. Tommy makes this clear when Lula Jean returns home after threatening to leave him: "You keep going that way and you won't ever know how to keep a man, b——h."

The Importance of Words and Language

Lorrie's mother consistently impresses upon him the importance of proper language, the power of words. "Let's practice the words this afternoon when you get home, baby," is the first line in the story that she says to him. The title of the story is taken from his mother's insistence on "proper words with proper meanings," and Lorrie's difficulty with the word "library". As he explains, "All my life I been saying that 'Liberry.' And even though I knew it was a place to read and do your studying, I still couldn't call it right. . . . I'm about doing things, you see, *finally* doing things right." Ironically, in the paragraph immediately following, his hostile Cousin Cee Cee attacks him with these words: "What you learning all that s——for? . . . Is you a complete a——hole?" Cee Cee passes her attitude onto her children, discouraging them from reading and learning new words with Lorrie.

The damaging and self-defeating attitudes that plague the characters in "Proper Library" reveal themselves in the language they use. The word "b——h" is used, not as a profanity or insult, but as a matter-of-fact synonym for "girl" or "woman." The dialogue of nearly every character in the story is liberally laced with profanity. In fact, as with the word "b——h," the profanity has become so commonplace that it is no longer even recognized as profanity; it is the standard. Lorrie is the only character who does not use profanity in the story; even his mother says to Layla Jackson, "Layla, you can get . . . out of here . . . do your 'ho'ing somewhere out on the street where you belong." The most important words, however, the ones that sustain Lorrie and give him the ability to cope with his situation, also come from his mother. His mother calls him "Lawrence, My Fine Boy." She tells him, "You are on your way to good things." Even the name she has given him reflects her high expectations: Lawrence Lincoln Jefferson Adams.

Love and Sex as Nourishment

A recurring theme of "Proper Library" is the idea that love and sex are nourishment, as critical and as life-sustaining as food. This theme is introduced in the first two paragraphs of the story. "Boys, men, girls, children, mothers, babies. . . . You always got to keep them fed. Winter summer. They always have to feel satisfied." The second paragraph lists sources of nourishment: "Formula, pancakes, syrup, milk, roast turkey with cornbread stuffing. Popsicles, love, candy, tongue kisses, hugs, kisses behind backs, hands on faces, warmth, tenderness, Boston cream pie, f——ing in the butt." Lorrie calls the many different kinds of love in his life "flavors of the pie." It is this love that gives him the strength to remain optimistic despite the persecution he faces every day at school. "Love is a pie and I am lucky enough to have almost every flavor in mine," he says. He says "almost" all the flavors, because he is no longer seeing Rakeem. Though the teen mothers in the story seem to feel little tenderness towards their children, Lorrie's love for the kids is his "favorite flavor of the pie."

Often when Lorrie feels or experiences love in the story, food is nearby. His love affair with Rakeem occurs under the expressway "where the Spanish women sometimes go to buy oranges and apples and watermelons cheap." Rakeem tells him not to go back to school, and Lorrie agrees: "A part of me was saying that his ear was more delicious than Math 4." When Rakeem asks Lorrie to meet him later, the location for the meeting is behind "Rocky's Pizza."

The love he gets from his mother represents another "flavor of the pie." When he leaves for school, his mother is making pancakes, and she promises him a special dinner if he studies his vocabulary words. They practice Lorrie's vocabulary words in the kitchen.

The withholding of food and of love are described similarly. Aunt Estine, who rarely has a kind or optimistic word for anyone, tells the household, "Lazy . . . Negroes you better not be specting me to cook y'all breakfast when you do get up!" When Layla gives baby Tee Tee a rare kiss on the forehead, Lorrie says, "he glows with what I know is drinking up an oasis when you are in the desert for so long."

Style

Point of View

The story is told in the first-person point of view by Lorrie. Readers are privy to Lorrie's thoughts and emotions. This is important, because it is Lorrie's compassionate, kind, and optimistic thoughts that keep the story from being a bleak portrayal of inner-city life. Also, because few characters in the story have taken the time to really get to know Lorrie, any other point of view would give the reader an incomplete portrait of him. Rakeem does not fully understand his love for the kids; his mother and family do not want to hear about his desires for Rakeem. This is a taboo subject; when Lorrie says he is going to meet Rakeem, "Ma has got what will be tears on her face because she can't say no and she can't ask any questions."

Flashbacks, Punctuation, and Repeated Phrases

Though "Proper Library" tells the story of just one day in Lorrie's life, readers learn much more about him and his family through flashbacks that are separated from the current-day story by blank space. The current-day story is written in the present tense, while the flashbacks are written in the past tense. Quotation marks are not used when characters talk; combined with the shifting from present to past tense, the absence of quotation marks gives the story a fluid, stream-of-consciousness quality, as if the story is being thought on the page, rather than written. Often commas and other punctuation are omitted. For instance, when Layla Jackson approaches Lorrie to ask him to baby sit Tee Tee, she says, "Thanks Lorrie man I got a favor to ask you please don't tell me no please man." After which Lorrie tells the reader, "Layla always makes her words into a worry sandwich."

One phrase Lorrie repeats throughout the story is "keep moving." Whenever schoolmates are harassing him, he repeats the phrase in his head. In these emotional situations the language keeps moving, also, through the omission of commas or the repeated use of "and" to connect thoughts in a stream. When he is forced to leave woodworking class, he tells the reader, "My bones and my brain and my heart would just crumble if it wasn't for that swirling wind of nothing in me that keeps me moving and moving." When Laura calls him a "faggot" on the bus and then continues to stare at him, he thinks, "Keep moving. The bus keeps rolling and you always have to keep moving. Like water like air like outer space." The phrase has a positive meaning as well; Lorrie teaches the kids math, because he believes, "It's these numbers that keep them moving and that will keep them moving when I am gone." Other phrases that are repeated throughout the story include Lorrie's "flavors of the pie" metaphor, the "click, click" of Aunt Estine's impatient heels, and "I feel all of the ears on us," which he says both times he talks to Joe Smalls during the story.

Setting

Outside his home, Lorrie's world is hard, both literally and figuratively. His love affair with Rakeem is conducted not in the comfort of a bed or even the back seat of a car, but underneath the concrete bridge supports of the expressway, in a broken shopping cart. When Lorrie tells the story of how Rakeem escaped some gang members by telling them he had AIDS, he describes how the boys ran off, "rubbing their hands on the sides of the buildings on the Grand Concourse." In woodworking class, the teacher's face "is like a piece of lumber. Mr. Samuels is never soft." Images and threats of violence follow Lorrie throughout the day. Before he steps out the door, his sister gives him a letter knife to carry with him to school. The boys threatening him in woodworking class are using a power saw; one of them tells Lorrie to "take your sissy ass out of here 'less you want me to cut it into four pieces." And when Laura stares him down on the bus, her eyes are "a silent machine gun."

At home, the images are soft, full of the warmth of human contact. His mother strokes his face with her hands; some of the kids, wanting their hair done, come to Lorrie and "sit around my feet like shoes"; all the kids pile on the bed with Tommy and Lula Jean as they are kissing. As Lorrie says, "I know I am taken care of."

Historical Context

Acquired Immune Deficiency Syndrome (AIDS)

When acquired immune deficiency syndrome (AIDS) was first recognized in the 1980s it was looked upon by many as a "gay plague," a disease only affecting homosexual men. By the time this story was written in 1993, however, thousands of heterosexuals had died of AIDS, and low income African Americans in the inner city were especially at risk, for several reasons. First, intravenous drug use is more prevalent in inner-city neighborhoods, and the sharing of contaminated drug paraphernalia is one of the most common methods of contracting the human immunodeficiency virus (HIV). In addition, drug use also impairs judgment and increases the likelihood that the user will engage in unprotected sexual intercourse. As a result, it is estimated that as many as 30 percent of all AIDS cases are caused directly or indirectly by intravenous drug use. Second, teens in the inner city are more sexually active and more likely to have unprotected sex (as is demonstrated by the high rate of teen pregnancy). Lorrie, as a gay teen having unprotected sex in the inner city, is at extremely high risk of getting the HIV virus.

In 1991, two years before this story was published, basketball great Magic Johnson announced that he had HIV, and in the same year this story was released, tennis star Arthur Ashe died of AIDS, which he had contracted through a contaminated blood transfusion. These two high-profile cases made many more African Americans aware of the dangers AIDS posed to everyone, not just to gay men. The number of known deaths from AIDS in

Compare & Contrast

- **Early 1990s:** In 1990, there are 223 pregnancies for every 1000 black teenage girls between the ages of fifteen and nineteen. This is nearly twice the rate for the overall population; the overall teen pregnancy rate is 116 pregnancies for every 1000 teenage girls.

  2000s: By 2000, teen pregnancies have declined significantly both in the African American and overall populations. The teen pregnancy rate for black teens, however, continues to be significantly higher. In 2000, there are 153 pregnancies for every 1000 teenage black girls aged fifteen to nineteen; the rate for the overall population of teen girls is 83 pregnancies per 1000.

- **Early 1990s:** Both the number of new cases of AIDS diagnosed and the number of deaths from AIDS peak in the United States in 1993, the year this story is first published. There are nearly 80,000 new cases of AIDS reported in 1993, and over 40,000 deaths.

  2000s: Greater awareness of the precautions necessary to prevent AIDS significantly reduces the number of new diagnoses. After about 1998, the number of new cases reported remains at around 40,000. After 2000, the number of reported deaths remains at around 18,000 per year. Unfortunately, in the black community, there is not as much improvement. In 2003 half of all the people diagnosed with new cases of HIV or AIDS are black.

- **Early 1990s:** In 1994, some 25 percent of white households with children are single-parent households. In the black community, 65 percent of households with children are single-parent households.

  2000s: The percentage of black children living with married parents makes a significant increase between 1995 and 2000, from 35 to 39 percent. This rate is the highest percentage in decades, which some experts attribute to resurgence in the popularity of marriage in the black community.

- **Early 1990s:** In 1992, among whites aged sixteen to twenty-four, some 7.9 percent are high school dropouts. Among blacks in the same age group, about 13.6 percent drop out of school. Hispanics have the highest rate at 27.5 percent. Over one third of the black female dropouts cite pregnancy as their reason for dropping out (about one fourth of white female respondents cite pregnancy as the reason for leaving school).

  2000s: In 2001, the dropout rate for whites aged sixteen to twenty-four drops slightly to 7.3 percent; black students make a more significant improvement, reducing their dropout rate to 10.9 percent. Hispanics make the least improvement; the dropout rate among Hispanics aged sixteen to twenty-four in 2001 is 27 percent, attributable in part to difficulties with the English language. Part of the reduction in dropout rates may be due to the drop in the teen pregnancy rate.

---

the United States reached a peak in 1993, with 41,920 Americans dying of the disease, up from 23,411 in 1992.

Racial Unrest: The Rodney King Case

On March 3, 1991, Los Angeles police stopped black motorist Rodney King on a drunken driving charge; King resisted arrest and was brutally beaten by the officers. A bystander videotaped the incident, and the four police officers were charged with assault. On April 29, 1992, the officers were acquitted, triggering six days of massive rioting in Los Angeles. Fifty-four people were killed and hundreds of buildings were damaged or destroyed. In a federal trial in 1993, two of the officers were found guilty of violating King's civil rights and were sentenced to thirty months in prison. To many in the African American community and elsewhere, the case was a frustrating example of discrimination in the justice system. This sentiment was

A long view of an urban development project AP Images

further intensified when the venue of the original case was moved from Los Angeles, where the incident had occurred, to Simi Valley, a suburb with a much smaller African American population and a disproportionately large number of law-enforcement officers.

Critical Overview

At the time that "Proper Library" was first published, Carolyn Ferrell was just beginning her career as a published author. Tobias Wolff selected the story for *Best American Short Stories, 1994*, which brought Ferrell's work to the attention of Janet Silver, an editor at Houghton Mifflin. Silver asked Ferrell if she had a book manuscript, but Ferrell had just three stories to show her at the time. Those three stories were enough to earn a first book contract.

The book, *Don't Erase Me*, which was released in 1997, earned Ferrell both critical acclaim and awards. The journal *Ploughshares*, in which "Proper Library" was originally published, gave *Don't Erase Me* the John C. Zacharis First Book Award; the *Los Angeles Times* awarded it the Art Seidenbaum Award for First Fiction. In their praise of the collection, critics often mention Ferrell's talent for authentic dialogue. A reviewer from the *Washington Post Book World* writes, "Carolyn Ferrell has a gift for the authentic spoken voice—male and female, black and biracial, gay and straight.'' In a review of the book in *Ploughshares*, Elizabeth Searle agrees: "To create such fully realized voices, Ferrell capitalizes on her keen ear and her playful sense of speech rhythms. Her characters come to life in dead-on dialogue."

Critics also note how many of her characters (such as Lorrie) maintain a spark of hope despite their grim situations, giving the stories an uplifting quality. The reviewer from the *Washington Post Book World* writes that Ferrell's characters "never stop hoping for a better life, doggedly pursuing their goals and struggling to maintain their integrity rather than succumb to despair." Other reviewers feel that Ferrell's poetic and compassionate use of language also helps to soften the harsh reality of the world she describes. A review in *Publishers Weekly* states, "While hope is in short supply for many of Ferrell's characters, her poignant and often poetic language shines brightly, illuminating a harsh world." Katharine Whittemore, in the *New York Times Book Review*, also praises the poetic quality of Ferrell's writing: "You're tempted to cull a glossary of phrases from DON'T ERASE ME . . . but her book is much more than poetic plums."

Though *Don't Erase Me* is the only book Ferrell had published as of 2005, her stories have been anthologized in numerous collections, and she was as of that year at work on her first novel.

Criticism

Laura Pryor

Pryor has a bachelor of arts from University of Michigan and twenty years experience in professional and creative writing with special interest in fiction. In this essay, Pryor examine how Lorrie's homosexuality actually benefits him in his inner-city neighborhood.

Millions of gay and lesbian teens have found that their sexual orientation makes them the subject of ridicule, cruelty, and persecution. This is certainly the case for Lorrie Adams in Carolyn Ferrell's "Proper Library." From the minute he steps onto the bus in the morning until he returns home in the afternoon, Lorrie is constantly on his guard, reminding himself to "keep moving." He can feel the hostility of his schoolmates, and he knows they are watching his every move; he can even "feel the ears" on him when he engages in innocent conversation with his friend Joe. Even before his woodworking classmates begin to harass him, he knows what is coming: "I'm feeling the rest of the ears on us, latching, readying. I pause to heaven. I am thinking I wish Ma had taught me how to pray."

Because Lorrie is a black teen living in the inner city, however, his homosexuality is a source not just of persecution, but also protection. For instance, Rakeem escapes some gang members by telling them he has AIDS; because Rakeem is gay, they believe him and run away. Clearly in Lorrie's neighborhood the image of AIDS as a "gay disease" still persists (though, in fact, the two people in the story who actually are HIV positive are heterosexual).

Lorrie's homosexuality gives him an advantage greater than just protection from physical violence; the greatest benefit Lorrie gains from being gay is freedom from the strict code of behavior adhered to by the heterosexual men in his world. The other men and boys in "Proper Library" have been taught to deny any tenderness, vulnerability, or need; in their relationships with women the goal is to avoid any commitment or dependence. Lorrie's father, in his complete absence from the story, is an example by omission: he is never mentioned. Women are seen primarily as potential sexual conquests, and sex is the primary preoccupation of Lorrie's classmates. A boy named Franklin in Lorrie's shop class sums it up this way: "Hey, Lorrie, man, tell me what you think about, then? What can be better than thinking about how you going to get to that hole, man?"

For Lorrie, the sheer impossibility of conforming to the neighborhood standard of machismo frees him from those limiting gender boundaries. Because the men in his community would prefer to deny the existence of homosexual black men, no comparable code of behavior or social role exists for them, and Lorrie is free to invent himself as he goes along, feeling connected to the children and caring about others. Many critics cite this denial of homosexuality in the black community as a reason for the neglect of AIDS issues by black leaders and politicians (especially male black leaders).

Homosexuality seems to be a greater advantage for Lorrie than it is for Rakeem, perhaps because Lorrie is more effeminate. There are some cues that this is the case. For instance, Aunt Estine, speaking of her past in the South, tells Lorrie that if he had "twitched [his] ass down there like [he does] here, they woulda hung [him] up just by [his] black balls." Rakeem, being less effeminate, still feels it is possible for him to fit in. As he tells Lorrie, "I got to get people to like me and to stop seeing me. . . . So I got to hide *me* for a while. Then you watch, Lorrie, man: much people will be on my side!" Unlike Rakeem, Lorrie has accepted the fact that fitting in at school is not possible for him; he is satisfied to fit in at home, with his mother and the kids. Rakeem also seems to attach greater importance to sex than Lorrie does. When they have sex under the expressway, Rakeem tells Lorrie, "This is where your real world begins, man." Lorrie, however, considers his desire for Rakeem only another "flavor of the pie."

Being gay, Lorrie avoids not just the expectations and stereotypes for men in his community, but also the roles adhered to by the women. Ironically, Lorrie has more of the positive qualities one normally associates with femininity than the girls in the story do. He is more maternal, nurturing, and protective towards the children in the story than their own mothers. Yet because Lorrie is a boy, he escapes the low expectations his community has for women. For instance, Lorrie's mother takes the time to coach him on his vocabulary

"For Lorrie, the sheer impossibility of conforming to the neighborhood standard of machismo frees him from those limiting gender boundaries."

words, make sure he has all his books in order before he goes to school, and exhorts him to do things "the proper way." There is no indication that she has ever done any of this for her daughters, and the fact that her house is full of their children on a daily basis implies that doing things "the proper way" was not made a high priority for the girls in the house. Their choice of men is another example of these low expectations; of the two husbands mentioned in the story, one is unfaithful, and the other is physically abusive. With the exception of Layla Jackson, who struggles to continue her education with Tee Tee in tow and the specter of AIDS following her, none of the girls in the story appears to have goals greater than getting a man and hanging onto him (the latter being something all the men have been taught to avoid). Given the men they choose, these goals are not very high.

Another reason Lorrie is less affected by the expectations and stereotypes of his community is that few of the people who ascribe to these rules of behavior are willing to spend time with Lorrie. Lorrie's companions are either too young to have internalized these attitudes (the kids) or are compassionate enough to ignore them (Joe Smalls, Layla Jackson). His own kind and compassionate nature is supported by their friendship.

Though most teens would not volunteer for the persecution Lorrie endures each day, his inability to conform to his peers' standards of behavior may well be his means for one day rising above them. Without being coerced into living within the dominant code, Lorrie is able to think and feel for himself, which in the long run is the ultimate freedom.

Source: Laura Pryor, Critical Essay on "Proper Library," in *Short Stories for Students*, Thomson Gale, 2006.

Sheldon Goldfarb

Goldfarb has a Ph.D. in English and has published two books on the Victorian author William Makepeace Thackeray. In the following essay, he discusses the way the protagonist copes with adversity in "Proper Library" and compares the story to modernist works such as Ulysses *and* The Great Gatsby.

Towards the end of Carolyn Ferrell's "Proper Library," the schoolboy protagonist, Lorrie, decides to learn three new words to impress his mother. The words themselves are interesting, in that they seem to relate to Lorrie's situation as described in the story. The first is "soliloquy," a word that implies being alone and unheard, among the most famous soliloquies being the sad solitary speeches made by Hamlet in William Shakespeare's famous play of that name. The word "soliloquy" means talking to oneself, and the whole story is one in which the reader enters Lorrie's thoughts and in effect overhears him talking to himself about his lonely, unhappy life.

The second word is "disenfranchise," meaning to deprive someone of rights and power, which certainly seems to be Lorrie's situation: he seems trapped in a world full of responsibility without rights. He is responsible for taking care of numerous children and must endure all sorts of abuse from schoolmates, and also from at least one teacher, because he is gay. At times he feels totally isolated and alone, and his only recourse is to "keep moving," a refrain of his, which means not just physical moving, though he does that to escape some unpleasant situations, but also psychological or metaphorical moving, to escape in his head by remembering something pleasant while nasty things are happening.

The third word is "catechism," perhaps the most interesting one of all. Narrowly the word means an instructional book about the principles of religion. Lorrie, however, has no religion, something he regrets when he is caught in a difficult situation and wishes he could pray. At least, he has no orthodox religion; he does have some mystical moments concerning words and numbers which seem almost religious, and so the word is relevant not just in pointing out the lack of religion in Lorrie's life but also in reminding the reader that Lorrie does have a form of religion of an unorthodox kind, something he perhaps needs to sustain him.

The word "catechism" can also be taken in a more general sense, simply to mean any book of instruction in principles and rules. In this sense it

"The story seems to recommend trying, not complaining and brooding, in the manner of Aunt Estine, who at the end of story hits her head on the doorframe, as if the author is punishing her for her negative attitude. The story seems to suggest trying to accomplish things, trying to fulfill one's desires."

makes an ironic contrast with Lorrie's approach to life, because Lorrie is the antithesis of rule-following. Even setting out to learn three words at this moment is in a way breaking a rule. He goes on to say that his mother had promised him a big turkey dinner if he learned four new words. Four words, not three, but Lorrie decides to learn three. It is as if he cannot do what is expected of him; he cannot bring himself to follow the rules. He follows his own path, most notably in his sexuality. So while his schoolfellows are all talking about pursuing girls, he has no interest in that, being gay, and he suffers because they mock him and call him names as a result.

Lorrie's inability to follow the rules can be seen as well in his approach to math. He seems to love math. He teaches math to the other children, and yet he keeps failing the math tests and is held back as a result. The problem is that his love of math seems to be a love of the feel of the numbers. At least, when he teaches math to the others, they "like the feel of the numbers and seeing them on a piece of paper." This response is an example of the religious feeling Lorrie seems to bring to the world or at least an example of how he is more interested in feeling than in reasoning and abstraction. However, reasoning and abstraction and getting the right answer are needed to pass the math tests and that is why he keeps failing. He seems to be almost mystically in tune with numbers; he can give "real live explanations" of them, but on the tests he is not given a chance to provide these explanations: "the people don't ask any questions: they just hold me back." He fails and as a result is in danger of not fulfilling his dream of going to college.

The mystical approach to numbers can also be seen in Lorrie's approach to words. It turns out that there is no time for him to sit down with the dictionary to study his three chosen words, because "the kids come in and want me to give them a bath and baby Tee Tee has a fever and is throwing up all over the place." His responsibilities intervene; with his mother at work, he is the one who is constantly looking after the children, and at least in this instance that means he cannot take the time to study his dictionary. But not doing so does not seem to matter. "I look at the words," he says, "and suddenly I know I will know them without studying." Now, perhaps the reader is supposed to find this foolish, to see it as a feeble excuse for not studying, but it does seem that Lorrie has an intuitive side that allows him to connect to things such as his words in an unorthodox way. But this intuitiveness or mysticism or emphasis on feelings over rationality often seems to put him at odds with the society around him.

Another problem for Lorrie could be referred to as a clash of desires. He really enjoys taking care of the children. When he is being called names on the bus, he consoles himself by remembering his four-year-old sister, Lasheema, whose hair he braids. He remembers enjoying the feel of her hair and remembers feeling ecstatic when he and Lasheema look at themselves in the mirror. When one of his schoolmates hands him her baby to take care of, he enjoys that too. He says, "Tee Tee likes to be in my arms. I like for him to be there." But as already mentioned, fulfilling his desire to take care of children can interfere with his desire to learn words, with his desire for education. The opening paragraph of the story indicates that the responsibility of taking care of others is not all fun; it seems rather to be an unbearable burden: "it's never-ending, never-stopping," he says.

Another clash of desires involves Lorrie's relationship with his boyfriend, Rakeem. Lorrie feels good around Rakeem, so good that at one point in the past he stayed out of school for six months to be with Rakeem beneath the Bruckner Expressway, sitting in a broken shopping cart while Rakeem comforted him and made love to him. Clearly, the desire for Rakeem interfered with his desire for education. As the story begins Lorrie has sworn off seeing his old boyfriend, and yet just as clearly he misses him. Only with Rakeem, he thinks, can he "be me," and so he decides to see him again behind Rocky's Pizza. He somehow hopes that he can combine his sexual love and his desire for education. Before he gave up seeing Rakeem, he had thought he could bring Rakeem into the world of words, saying, "Hey, wasn't there enough room for him and me and the words?" At the time Rakeem had said, in a very rude way, No. Now Lorrie is hoping that somehow Rakeem may be ready.

It may be a foolish hope, but it is somehow contagious; it infects the reader. Here is a young boy, fourteen years old, who is shunned by almost everyone because he is gay, who is weighed down by almost impossible family responsibilities, who at times feels very depressed and alone, but who somehow by the end of the story is full of positive feeling, making the story itself feel positive. In this way it is somewhat reminiscent of the novel *Ulysses* by James Joyce, in which the struggles of Leopold and Molly Bloom are somehow overcome in the characters' minds so that the book ends with an affirmation (Molly Bloom's "Yes") rather than anything depressing. Another similarity between Ferrell's story and Joyce's novel is that both use the technique of "stream of consciousness"; that is, the story is narrated through the characters' unedited, free-flowing thoughts.

The ending of "Proper Library" is, it is true, a bit different from the "Yes" at the end of *Ulysses*. Just before the end of Ferrell's story, there is the uplifting moment in which Lorrie goes off to see Rakeem with the hope that somehow he can integrate his love life and his desire for education. But at the very end of the story, as Lorrie goes out the door, a description is given of his sister, Lula Jean, being angrily berated by her cheating husband. It is a reminder that things are not always pleasant and do not always work out.

It seems unlikely that Lorrie can integrate all his desires and get everything he wants. Here is a gay youth who loves children, who wants to be able to nurture children. "Me, I love me some kids," he says. "I need me some kids." One does wonder how he will get some, being gay. There are also the obstacles of race and class. Lorrie is an African American youth living in a very poor neighborhood. Without explicitly saying so, the story seems to suggest that this background will make life difficult for Lorrie too. Lorrie is a poor, black, gay youth who wants education, love, and family; one can see the problems.

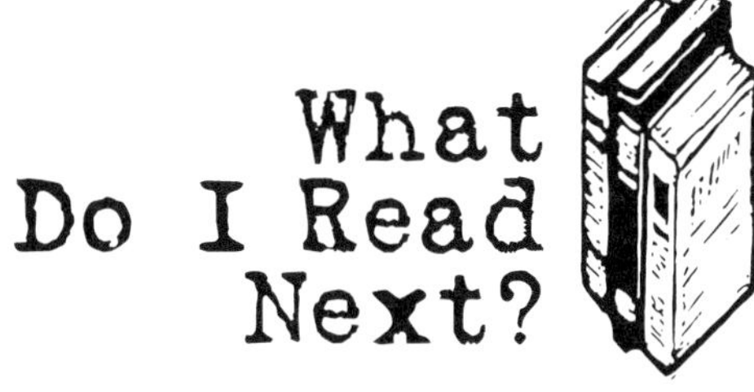

- "Proper Library" appears in Ferrell's award-winning collection of short stories entitled *Don't Erase Me* (1997). Most of the stories in the collection portray the lives of poor back girls and women; the title story tells of a young woman whose stepfather has infected her with the HIV virus.
- *Streetlights: Illuminating Tales of the Urban Black Experience* (1996) is a short story collection that includes both a story from Carolyn Ferrell and one from her late mentor, journalist Doris Jean Austin.
- Doris Jean Austin's *After the Garden* (1988) follows the lives of a black family living in New Jersey in the 1940s and 1950s. Austin was known primarily as a journalist, and this novel was her fiction debut.
- *Giant Steps: The New Generation of African American Writers* (2000) includes Ferrell's story "Can You Say My Name?" as well as stories by noted authors Edwidge Danticat, Danzy Senna, and Randall Kenan.

Yet the story has an upbeat feel to it. There is the stark reminder at the very end of the problems in relationships. There are moments earlier on when Lorrie seems quite depressed, most notably in his first class of the day, when a schoolmate mocks his sexual orientation right in class and he thinks: "why does every day start out one way hopeful but then point to the fact that ain't nothing ever going to happen?" Later in that same class, when the teacher springs a surprise quiz on them, Lorrie says that all the students are unhappy as a result, "but no one is more than me, knowing that nothing will ever happen the way I'd like it to."

But this pessimism does not sum up Lorrie's general attitude. Shortly after this low point halfway through the story the pendulum begins to swing the other way. First, there is a low point in shop class when even the teacher joins in the mockery, calling Lorrie a girl; next Lorrie remembers being with Rakeem. In an almost defiant moment, he holds onto his love even though he is mocked for it, and this moment is mixed in with Lorrie's watching two HIV-positive people kiss; in the midst of their disease they can love, just as in the midst of being humiliated, Lorrie can love.

It is instructive in this context to consider Lorrie's attitude to his aunt Estine. Aunt Estine is constantly talking about the past and being depressed about it. Lorrie cannot stand this attitude. He thinks she would be better off escaping by putting on a fancy dress and dancing around rather than dwelling on a horrible moment which occurred years before. "I never want to be like her, ever," he says, and he is not like her, not usually. He keeps looking ahead, not back, and except for occasional moments keeps a positive attitude.

Early in the story, Lorrie, in what seems like a repetition of things his mother has told him, says, "Things got be in place. There has to be order." Later his mother is insistent that he learn "proper words with proper meanings" and that he learn to "say them right." In trying to go along with what his mother wants, he looks up the word "library" and discovers that it is not pronounced "liberry" as he had always thought. Now he is dedicated to saying that word, and other words, correctly.

This dedication sounds admirable, but the reader may have doubts about Lorrie as the devotee of order and doing things right. Lorrie is not someone who follows orders well, and he is not someone who does things right; at least, he is not someone who does things according to social norms. He is gay in a straight world. He approaches numbers through his feelings and words through his intuitions. His cousin Cee Cee tells him he is not "normal," and according to social standards perhaps he is not. He does have talents, though. One of the teachers at school, Mrs. Cabrini, tells him his intelligence will take him far, adding, "Put your mind to your dreams, my dear boy, and you will achieve them."

Indeed maybe he will. Though he wants family and education while at the same time pursuing a homosexual relationship with someone who distrusts learning, though he keeps failing math because he feels the numbers instead of getting the right answers, though he learns only three words when he is supposed to learn four, though his family responsibilities interfere with his studying, maybe somehow it will all work out. After all, his lover Rakeem does go back to school too, suggesting that perhaps Lorrie can bring him into his world of words after all. When his mother comes home at the end of the story, she says she remembers she promised him "that special dinner," as if he will get the dinner without having learned the fourth word. Maybe a person can succeed after all the story seems to be saying. Maybe despite obstacles and adversity there is still hope. Maybe even a person who does not fit in can find his place or at least try.

The story seems to recommend trying, not complaining and brooding, in the manner of Aunt Estine, who at the end of story hits her head on the doorframe, as if the author is punishing her for her negative attitude. The story seems to suggest trying to accomplish things, trying to fulfill one's desires. It is an attitude again reminiscent of Joyce's *Ulysses* and of one stream of the early twentieth-century modernist movement: though the universe may be hostile or incomprehensible, though it may be impossible to succeed, the point is to try anyway, to "beat on . . . against the current," as F. Scott Fitzgerald puts it at the end of *The Great Gatsby*. There seems to be a strong current running against Lorrie, but he is beating on against it in a positive way that makes the reader hope he will succeed, whatever doubts there may be.

Source: Sheldon Goldfarb, Critical Essay on "Proper Library," in *Short Stories for Students*, Thomson Gale, 2006.

David Remy

Remy is a freelance writer in Warrington, Florida. In the following essay, he examines the ways in which Ferrell's characters struggle against social norms as they pursue their individual dreams and desires.

In "Proper Library," Ferrell offers the reader a gritty urban landscape populated by characters who struggle to be free. However, as a result of the social mores that shape the community in which they live, all of the story's characters but one are governed by what they believe they *should* do, whether it is choosing a particular group of friends, making good grades at school, being faithful to a partner or spouse, or, as in Lorrie's case, upholding the idea of what it is to be a man. Thus, by exploring conventional beliefs about education, relationships, and identity, Ferrell reveals her characters' innermost conflicts and desires, all the while instilling her fictional world with a renewed sense of hope.

An important social pressure the story addresses is the need to belong to a group, especially if a character has been marginalized because of race or sexual orientation. For example, Laura, a white girl whose "blue eyes and red hair" and "thin flippy hair in cornrows" stand out among a bus full of dark African American girls, remains unaware that she is often an object of ridicule by the very group she wishes to join. Nevertheless, she tries to earn her place within it, even though her physical appearance, let alone her personality and temperament, are clearly different from those of the B-Crew Girls. The need to belong to a group that will protect her from isolation is so strong that Laura invents a new identity for herself: she tells her classmates that she is "really a Negro" of southern heritage. Furthermore, in an attempt to prove herself worthy of the group, Laura attacks Lorrie (the similarity in their names may be intentional, as both characters exist in society's margins) by calling him, "Faggot." At best, however, Laura is merely tolerated. She is a "mascot" rather than a member. In the end, her attempts to win favor go unrewarded, for the B-Crew Girls do not bother to wake her when the bus reaches her stop.

Similarly, Lorrie and Rakeem emulate the girls' counterparts, the B-Crew Boys, but only to a point. When meeting for the first time after a few weeks, if not months, Lorrie and Rakeem greet each other with the B-Crew Boy handshake—but that's as far as the association goes, a fact Lorrie acknowledges when he says, "Only we are not B-Crew members, we get run over by the B-Crew." Lorrie is well aware that he is an outsider, a pariah, who, because he is homosexual, will never belong to the neighborhood's main social group of boys. Furthermore, the B-Crew Boys have already threatened Rakeem with physical violence in an attempt to steal his sneakers, yet he was able to scare them away by telling them that he has contracted AIDS from his cousin, a lie that, ironically enough, may have saved him from injury but which confirms his status as an outsider. Unlike Laura, who abandons her identity to belong to a group, Lorrie and Rakeem merely appropriate the B-Crew Boys' rituals to form a brotherhood of two.

Another social norm that exerts itself upon the characters in "Proper Library" is the belief that one can improve one's chances for a better future through education. This value is reinforced, even by those who do not necessarily subscribe to it, as Lorrie teaches his younger brothers and sisters Math 4 concepts with the hope that they will be able to succeed later in life. "It's these numbers that keep them moving and that will keep them moving when I am gone," he observes. In Ferrell's fictional world, there is always hope. For example,

> "Lorrie remains true to himself, refusing to let the cruelty of his classmates deter him from becoming his own person, and in order to do this he must make others' expectations secondary to his own."

Layla, a teenage mother with a chaotic life, becomes upset at the thought of missing her Spanish Discovers test because she cannot find a babysitter. Layla focuses intently on the present so that her past mistake will not interfere with her future. Other students in her situation might have abandoned their studies without making half the effort. Even Rakeem, a streetwise character who once disparaged Lorrie for going to school, wants to make good grades, but only so that he will become popular. "I got to get people to like me and to stop seeing me," he says. Perhaps, if he makes good grades and is thus able to blend in with the majority of students, no one will notice that he is gay. "You really got it in you to move on," Lorrie tells Rakeem. Lorrie does not pass judgment on Rakeem's need to conform; rather, he generously offers his support because he wants his beloved to succeed.

Lorrie, the story's protagonist and narrator, feels more strongly than other characters the need to improve his life through education because, thus far, he has shown the most promise academically. However, at times this promise almost becomes a burden for him. He is smart enough to teach Math 4 to the kids, yet he remains enrolled in a Math 1 class. More important, he fails the city exams every year and is held back. "I know it's no real fault of mine," Lorrie says, but one wonders if he is not purposefully defying his family's and his teachers' expectations of him. "Put your mind to your dreams, my dear boy, and you will achieve them. You are your own universe, you are your own shooting star," one teacher reminds him. Lorrie takes this advice to heart, his narrative voice often shifting from first to second person, as though he is giving himself instructions. Lorrie strives for a better life, yet he knows that his dreams and desires do not necessarily coincide with those of his community.

The expectations Lorrie feels most strongly, however, are those expressed at home. Lorrie's mother appreciates his efforts to become a better student, yet she believes that his success depends upon his meeting an acknowledged standard rather than on his fulfilling his individual promise by virtue of his own means. "Lawrence, My Fine Boy," Lorrie recalls his mother saying, "[y]ou are on your way to good things. You just got to do things the proper way." Lorrie concentrates on learning his vocabulary words not to please his mother but because he knows that words, not numbers, are instruments of persuasion, for it is through words that he will eventually communicate his heart's desire. Words represent the future, in as much as they can express the unknown, yet they also express hope and fulfillment, especially with regard to the search for love. "I'm about doing things, you see, *finally* doing things right," Lorrie says. Defying expectation, Lorrie vows to become the person he wants to be, according to his own criteria and in his own time.

Cultural ideas and traditions are often so imbedded within a society that they dictate how relationships should be conducted in both life and death. For instance, Aunt Estine never mentions the good times she shared with her husband, David, who was lynched by a mob; instead, she keeps her husband's memory alive by evoking his death. In the end, nothing remains but a grim reminder that death is stronger than love. (Layla and Tyrone, the couple purported to have AIDS, also echo this theme, though they openly demonstrate their love for each other as if time has stood still.) Estine keeps herself alive by constantly reminding everyone that she is alone. She wears her widowhood like a badge of honor, yet the memory of her marriage does not provide her with solace.

Lorrie observes that Aunt Estine has turned her back on life and embraced death, an existential perspective symbolized by the blue evening gown that hangs in the closet. The dress represents what Estine once was—a vivacious young woman who enjoyed parties, dances, the nightlife—and not the bitter crone she has become. Lorrie sees Aunt Estine as living in the past. For him, her words represent her inability to escape the past. "If you can escape, why don't you all the time?" he wonders. "You could dance and fling your arms and maybe even feel love from some direction. You would not perish. *You* could be free." He concludes that "Estine Smith is not someone but a walking hainted house." Her identity has become synonymous with the past, a past which she inhabits like a ghost.

Tommy and Lula, by contrast, struggle with mores concerning fidelity and the responsibilities a man should fulfill for his family. Though Tommy expresses his love for Lula like a dreamy newlywed, saying, "This is what love should be," whenever he gazes into her eyes, he also sees other women on the side. When Lorrie catches Tommy with another woman, Lorrie, usually an understanding and forgiving person, immediately hates him for betraying Lula. Tommy justifies his philandering by telling Lorrie, "Man, you don't know these [b——]es out here nowadays. You want to show them love, a good time, and a real deep part of yourself and all they do is not appreciate it and try to make your life miserable." Lorrie knows that Tommy's words cannot justify his infidelity, especially when Tommy espouses his love for Lula: "Well, at least I got Lula," he says. "Now that's some woman." Does the search for true love extend beyond society's moral boundaries? In Tommy's case, definitely not, but Ferrell allows the reader to decide if Lorrie's quest for love and identity does not transcend what would otherwise be obstacles to his happiness.

In the community, fidelity is not only a man's chief responsibility to his wife and family but also a measure of his worth. When Lula finds out about Tommy's latest peccadillo, Lorrie's mother tells her son-in-law, "You are a stupid heel. Learn how to be a man." In her eyes, a "man" is steadfast and faithful. A "man" does not take his wife for granted and run around with other women—in broad daylight, no less! Aunt Estine expresses the frustration the women in the community feel when their men refuse to abide by the social code: "Why do we women feel we always need to teach them? They ain't going to learn the right way. They ain't going to learn s——t. That's why we always so alone." Tommy's hypocritical words and actions have a positive effect on Lorrie, however. He sees the possessive side of love and decides that his love must be given freely to Rakeem, without expecting anything in return.

Lorrie also feels pressure to be a "man," someone who will provide for his family. He routinely prepares meals when Aunt Estine or his mother is too busy, and he makes sure the kids know their math lessons before he undertakes his own studies. Without Lorrie, the house would no longer be a refuge for his immediate family and even for members of the community. However, his homosexuality threatens the family's home life, as transitory as it is, because he is often the target of aggression. His absence, for whatever reason, would endanger the family's security because he takes on so many of the responsibilities that the "man of the house" traditionally would perform. "Lorrie," his mother reminds him, "you are my only son, the only real man I got. I don't want them boys to get you from me." Aunt Estine issues a more stern warning, telling Lorrie that, if he behaved in the South the way he does here, he would be hung by his "black balls" from a tree. His sister Anita is also aware of the violent responses Lorrie's sexuality arouses in other people. "You are my best man, remember that," she tells Lorrie, giving him a letter opener with which he can defend himself.

Outside the home, Lorrie must prove that he is a man by withstanding the taunts and jeers of his classmates, many of whom are cruel and merciless in making fun of his homosexuality. On the bus, his classmates call "[f]aggot," and "tight-ass homo" while in woodworking class, the most masculine subject offered at school, Lorrie's classmates tease him because he does not have a girlfriend. Even the instructor joins in, saying, "Class, don't mess with the only *girl* we got in here!" Whenever these assaults occur, Lorrie steels himself by reminding himself to "Keep moving, keep moving." He proves that he is a man by refusing to fight back. Lorrie remains true to himself, refusing to let the cruelty of his classmates deter him from becoming his own person, and in order to do this he must make others' expectations secondary to his own.

Lorrie refers to his struggle for identity when he says that his mother named him "for someone else," not the person he has become. He confers the name Lorrie upon himself because it best suits his personality, his idea of himself. His given name, "Lawrence Lincoln Jefferson Adams," recalls two of the greatest U.S. emancipators, and Ferrell establishes the association to remind readers that Lorrie yearns to be free. He wants to find love and express the love he feels within himself, even though that love contradicts dominant social mores. Lorrie's growing sense of who he is remains tied to movement, though this concept is not expressed consciously or in clear terms, for Lorrie often finds himself in survival mode. "Keep moving" suffices. Lorrie prods himself to move forward, if ever so slowly, for stasis, such as that embodied by Aunt Estine, means psychic death. Always a moving target, Lorrie knows that both his sense of self and his ability to love will die if he ceases moving toward his ideals of what both can be.

For Lorrie, conforming to social expectations by acting macho or by dating girls is never a question. Rather, his problem is whether he should indulge his desire to be with Rakeem. In Lorrie's view, his love for Rakeem can coexist with his other dreams and desires. "I could welcome him into my world if he wanted me to," Lorrie thinks. "Hey, wasn't there enough room for him and me and the words?" Words from his vocabulary list such as "independence" and "soliloquy," which he learns at his mother's bidding, encapsulate Lorrie's attempt to become an individual in spite of his family's and his community's assumptions about him. Before long, Lorrie no longer needs to remind himself of his goal, for he has already decided his fate: "I look at the words and suddenly I know I will know them without studying," he says. The words exist within him. He embodies their meaning; therefore, he is able to act upon his desires, yet he knows that he will also return home. He will not repudiate his family or the values his mother has instilled in him, all of which have brought him to this profound moment of realization—this epiphany—that makes him announce, clearly and unequivocally, his intention to see Rakeem.

Ferrell's "Proper Library" reveals the ways in which social expectations mold the members of a community through established ideas regarding education, relationships, and identity. However, Lorrie, the story's hero, defies these expectations to create his own destiny and, with it, a proper life.

Source: David Remy, Critical Essay on "Proper Library," in *Short Stories for Students*, Thomson Gale, 2006.

Sources

Ferrell, Carolyn, "Proper Library," in *Don't Erase Me*, Houghton Mifflin, 1997, pp. 1–20.

Fitzgerald, F. Scott, *The Great Gatsby*, Scribner, 1925, p. 182.

Joyce, James, *Ulysses*, Penguin, 1986, p. 644.

Lee, Don, "Carolyn Ferrell, Zacharis Award," in *Ploughshares*, Winter 1997–98, pp. 222–24.

Review of *Don't Erase Me*, in *Publishers Weekly*, April 21, 1997, p. 59.

Review of *Don't Erase Me*, in *Washington Post Book World*, September 14, 1997, p. 8.

Searle, Elizabeth, Review of *Don't Erase Me*, in *Ploughshares*, Fall 1997, Vol. 23, No. 2–3, pp. 226–27.

Whittemore, Katharine, Review of *Don't Erase Me*, in *New York Times Book Review*, September 14, 1997, p. 26.

Further Reading

Anderson, Elijah, *Code of the Street: Decency, Violence, and the Moral Life of the Inner City*, Norton, 2000.

Sociologist Elijah Anderson details how crime in the inner city stems from a complex set of social mores or codes, which are ultimately self-defeating for the individuals who live by them.

Boykin, Keith, *One More River to Cross: Black and Gay in America*, Doubleday, 1996.

Boykin, a gay black man who served as a special media assistant to President Clinton from 1993 to 1994 and as a liaison with both the homosexual and African American communities, examines the interactions between the black gay community and the white gay and black straight communities. He examines issues such as the black community's failure to address AIDS-related problems and discrimination within the gay community.

Cohen, Cathy, *The Boundaries of Blackness: AIDS and the Breakdown of Black Politics*, University of Chicago Press, 1999.

Cohen explores why AIDS has been a neglected issue in the black community and why traditional black leaders have remained silent about the disease.

Williams, Rhonda Y., *The Politics of Public Housing: Black Women's Struggles against Urban Inequality*, Oxford University Press, 2004.

Through dozens of interviews, Williams creates an intimate portrait of poor black women in urban America, challenging the stereotypes and labels with these women's real life experiences.

The Pugilist at Rest

Thom Jones

1993

"The Pugilist at Rest," by Thom Jones, was first published in the *New Yorker* in 1992 and then reprinted as the title story in Jones's first collection of short stories in 1993. The collection was widely praised by reviewers, who regarded Jones as an exciting new voice in American fiction.

The story is told by a first-person narrator who is a decorated Vietnam veteran and former Marine boxing champion. He now suffers from debilitating depression, for which he takes heavy doses of medication, and from epilepsy. At the end of the story, he agrees to undergo psychosurgery that may cure his condition but could also, he fears, ensure that he spends the rest of his life in an institution.

"The Pugilist at Rest," which takes its title from a famous Roman sculpture of a boxer, draws on the author's own experience. Jones trained as a Force Recon Marine, although he did not serve in Vietnam, and was also a boxer. Like the narrator of the story, he suffers from epilepsy. He told an interviewer for the *Austin Chronicle* that his best friend was killed in Vietnam, and for a while he was reluctant to write about the war because he did not feel he had the right to do so. But then he realized he was angry that his friend had been cheated of his life, so he started writing about Vietnam for his friend.

Author Biography

Thomas Douglas Jones was born in Aurora, Illinois, on January 26, 1945, the son of Joseph Thomas Jones

Thom Jones Rex Rystedt/Time Life Pictures/Getty Images

and Marilyn Faye (Carpenter) Graham. His father was a boxer, and Jones took up the sport as a teenager. He said in a 1995 interview in *Poets & Writers Magazine* that he had conflicts with his father and later his stepfather and did not take kindly to people pushing him around, and this fact contributed to his interest in boxing. He also reported that he had been fired from various jobs because he refused to take orders.

Jones joined the U.S. Marine Corps and trained as a Recon Marine. But in 1963, before he was sent overseas, he was honorably discharged after sustaining an injury in a boxing match, which led to his developing epilepsy. He was hospitalized on various occasions with epilepsy and even spent some time in a mental ward.

Only one of the twenty Marines Jones trained with survived the Vietnam War. In 1968, Jones married Sally Laverne Williams, the former girlfriend of one of Jones's friends who had been killed in Vietnam.

Jones had resumed his education, and he graduated from the University of Washington with a bachelor of arts in 1970. He then enrolled in the prestigious writing program at the University of Iowa. In the interview mentioned above, he said all he had ever wanted to do was write. At the University of Iowa, Jones's teachers suggested that he take a mentally undemanding job while he was writing. Jones took their advice and for eleven years worked as a janitor at North Thurston High School. He graduated with a master of arts degree in creative writing in 1973.

However, it was not until 1991 that his work was published. The breakthrough came when the *New Yorker* published his story "The Pugilist at Rest" in 1991. The story won the O. Henry Award in 1993. More published stories soon followed, in magazines such as *Esquire*, *Harpers*, the *New Yorker*, *Playboy*, and the *Paris Review*. "The Pugilist at Rest" then became the title story of Jones's collection of stories published in 1993, which received a National Book Award nomination. Many of these stories contain characters who are shaped by their experiences in Vietnam.

Jones received the Best American Short Stories Award from Houghton Mifflin, for four successive years, from 1992 to 1995, and he was a Guggenheim Fellow, 1994–1995. In 1995, he published his second collection of stories, *Cold Snap: Stories*; a third collection, *Sonny Liston Was a Friend of Mine*, appeared in 1999. Both collections were lavishly praised by critics.

As of 2005, Jones lives in Olympia, Washington. He teaches writing and gives readings throughout the United States.

Plot Summary

"The Pugilist at Rest" begins as the first-person narrator recalls, many years after the event, an incident that took place in August 1966 at a twelve-week boot camp he attended at the Marine Corps Recruit Depot in San Diego, California. One recruit got caught writing a letter to his girlfriend when he should have been taking notes on the specs of the M-14 rifle. His letter began "Hey Baby," and that became the name by which he was subsequently known by the other recruits. The narrator goes on to explain that Hey Baby was not in the Marine Corps for long. He had a habit of harassing the narrator's buddy, a small and unassuming recruit named Jorgeson. One day, only two weeks from the end of boot camp, the narrator sees Hey Baby give Jorgeson a nasty shove with his M-14, which almost knocks Jorgeson over. The narrator, who is a big man, intervenes, striking Hey Baby hard in the temple with the butt of his M-14. Hey Baby is badly injured, sustaining a fractured skull. There is an investigation into the incident, but the narrator is not caught. Even though three other recruits saw him strike Hey Baby, they do not betray him to the authorities. They are silent because they do not like Hey Baby; by contrast, the narrator is popular with the other recruits.

The story then returns to the present, as the narrator explains that he had been cleaning the attic when he came across his old Marine dress-blue uniform. He also took out the various medals he won in the Vietnam War, including the one that gives him most pride, the Airborne wings. This signifies that he was a Force Recon Marine, a member of a reconnaissance unit.

He then recalls what happened to him and his buddies in Vietnam. Only three days after they arrived, they were parachuted in on a routine reconnaissance patrol near the DMZ (the demilitarized zone that marked the border between South Vietnam and North Vietnam). His team moves across a clear field while he is sent to investigate a small mound of loose red dirt in the jungle nearby. The mound turns out to be an anthill, but as he approaches it, the Marines are attacked by North Vietnamese troops. The narrator is blown into the air by the impact of a mortar round. He suffers concussion but is mostly unhurt, although his M-16 rifle is jammed. Several of the other Marines are killed by the mortar round, but the narrator sees Jorgeson firing back at the enemy as they advance. He also sees Second Lieutenant Milton firing his .45 pistol and assumes that his M-16 has also jammed. Milton has his arm shot off by a rocket but continues to fire his gun. Jorgeson is alone in the open, firing his M-16 as the North Vietnamese fire at him. He then runs to a dead Marine and takes his M-60 machine gun and fires, killing more North Vietnamese Army (NVA) troops. The surviving North Vietnamese either take cover or turn back and head for the trees. Jorgeson keeps firing and also looks across at the narrator and smiles. Moments later, he is hit by a rocket grenade.

The enemy converge on the dead Marines, and it appears they have forgotten about the presence of the narrator. But then one North Vietnamese soldier remembers him and moves in his direction, only to turn back when Jorgeson gives a huge shriek. The NVA soldier bayonets Jorgeson in the heart.

The deadly incident ends with an air strike by American planes, called in by the narrator. They drop bombs and napalm. (Napalm is a highly flammable explosive used by the United States in Vietnam to burn an area and incinerate the enemy.) The narrator escapes by running as fast as he can.

The narrator completes three tours of Vietnam but he is badly scarred by his experiences. Wanting revenge for the death of Jorgeson, he possesses what he calls a reservoir of malice and sadism in his soul and says that he committed unspeakable crimes and was awarded medals for his acts.

When he returns to the United States, he becomes a heavy smoker and a borderline alcoholic. He remains in the Marines, garrisoned at Camp Pendleton in California. In the mid-1970s, at the age of twenty-seven, he participates in a boxing match with a light-heavyweight boxer from Marine artillery. The narrator is a former Marine boxing champion, and he wins the vicious fight on points. But he takes a bad beating and suffers serious consequences. Over the next two weeks, he has constant headaches and double vision.

As his health gradually deteriorates, he becomes introspective, wondering why he enjoys getting into fistfights and inflicting pain on others. The only thing that gives him relief is the pessimistic writings of the nineteenth-century German philosopher Arthur Schopenhauer (1788–1860).

About a year after the boxing match, the narrator begins having seizures, a form of epilepsy sometimes called Dostoyevski's epilepsy, after the nineteenth-century Russian writer who suffered from the same condition. Like Dostoyevski, the narrator experiences a kind of ecstasy a split second before the fit starts that makes him feel he is experiencing the supreme, divine reality. But then the feeling goes and he doubts the existence of God.

As he continues to suffer from epilepsy, he rarely leaves the house. To avoid falling injuries, he wears headgear, and he also carries his mouthpiece, which he slips into his mouth just prior to an attack, to stop himself from biting his tongue. The seizures get more frequent, and he takes many prescribed drugs to treat the condition. He acquires two dogs that are trained to watch him as he sleeps and ensure that if he has a seizure he does not suffocate himself face down in his bedding. He also suffers from serious psychological problems, as indicated by the fact that he takes amitriptyline, an anti-depressant, and thorazine (a drug used to treat disorganized and psychotic thinking).

A neurosurgeon visits him and says he can treat his depression through a surgical procedure called cingulotomy. The doctor says that this procedure cauterizes a small area of the brain, and the narrator will no longer have to rely on drugs to treat his mental problems. Cingulotomy is a controversial treatment that destroys bundles of nerve connections in the brain. It is used as a last resort to treat mental illness in patients for whom other treatments have been ineffective.

The narrator is not convinced that the cingulotomy will work, but his condition is so bad that he believes he cannot go on the way he is, so he agrees to the procedure. He believes that it could go wrong and he may end up as a "vegetable."

He thinks of his friend Jorgeson, knowing that Jorgeson was a hero, and wishing he were alive. He also reveals that he claimed the credit for killing the enemy soldiers who in fact had been killed by Jorgeson. He was almost awarded the Medal of Honor, but there was no one to corroborate his story.

He wonders also about the vision of supreme reality that he gets before his seizures. Perhaps, he thinks, it is merely a neurochemical phenomenon, nothing to do with God.

The story ends with the narrator hoping that if the operation goes wrong, he will at least be allowed to keep his dogs. He fears being sent to an asylum.

Characters

Lance Corporal Hanes

Lance Corporal Hanes is an experienced Marine with two Purple Hearts who has only twelve days left on his tour of duty in Vietnam. He is killed when the platoon comes under fire from the North Vietnamese. The narrator is angry that Hanes, since he had such a short time left, was not sent to the rear, out of harm's way.

Hey Baby

Hey Baby is the nickname of one of the Marine recruits at boot camp. He is large and fairly tough, but he is a bully and is not liked by the other recruits. He takes to picking on Jorgeson, the narrator's buddy. But when he shoves Jorgeson hard with his rifle, the narrator responds by striking him in the temple with the butt of his rifle. Hey Baby suffers a fractured skull.

Jorgeson

Jorgeson is a friend of the narrator since they were both training to be Marines at boot camp in San Diego. At boot camp, Jorgeson is an unconventional character. Drawn to being an artist rather than a Marine, he wants to live a Bohemian lifestyle, drinking, playing jazz, hanging out with Jack Kerouac and other beatniks, studying Zen Buddhism and astrology. The narrator thinks Jorgeson has a skeptical attitude regarding his Marine training, but he changes his mind when he runs into Jorgeson again at Camp Pendleton, where Jorgeson is working as a clerk. He has gained fifteen pounds through weight training, and his training routine includes running seven miles in full combat gear. It is Jorgeson who persuades the narrator to join him and train as a Force Recon Marine. He no longer talks about becoming an artist. When he is sent to Vietnam with the narrator and their team is attacked in the field, Jorgeson puts out steady fire against the enemy before he is felled by a rocket grenade. As he is dying, it may be that he saves the narrator's life by distracting the attention of a North Vietnamese soldier.

Second Lieutenant Milton

Second Lieutenant Milton is fairly new to the Marines. When the Marines come under fire in Vietnam, Milton is the only one other than Jorgeson who returns fire. But he can only use his .45, which is not much use in this situation. He is soon killed by a rocket.

The Narrator

The unnamed narrator is a Vietnam veteran who suffers from epilepsy and depression. As he looks back on the major events of his life, he recalls being at boot camp, where he first met his friend Jorgeson. At boot camp he first revealed the aggressive behavior that has characterized his life ever since; he fractured the skull of another recruit with the butt of his rifle. The narrator is more emotional than Jorgeson; Sergeant Wright's speeches about how a Marine would do anything to save the life of another Marine brings tears to his eyes. After boot camp he attends communication school in San Diego, which he deliberately flunks. Then Jorgeson talks him into becoming a Force Recon Marine. He is the only one in his platoon who escapes the carnage of the attack by the North Vietnamese, which takes place when he has been in Vietnam for only three days.

The narrator's experiences in battle scar him for life. On his three tours of Vietnam, he does things of which he would not have thought he was capable. Filled with the desire to avenge the death of Jorgeson, he perpetrates what he knows are war crimes, for which he is not reprimanded but awarded medals. His medals include the Navy Cross, but this is only because he claims the dead Jorgeson's deeds as his own. He does not feel remorseful about the lies he told.

After returning to the United States, he remains in the Marines, at Camp Pendleton, but he is a troubled man. He drinks too much and gets into fights. While boxing, he suffers a head injury in a fight, which results in epilepsy. He also suffers from serious long-term depression, for which he is heavily medicated. The drugs make him feel languid and unable to do anything.

Despite his rough exterior and disturbed mind, the narrator is also a reflective man with an interest in philosophy. He derives comfort from absorbing the pessimistic philosophy of Schopenhauer, and he also reads the Russian novelist Dostoyevski. Stimulated by mystical insight that occurs in the split second before his seizures begin, he speculates about the existence of God. His hero is Theogenes, the ancient Greek boxer who reportedly won all of his 1,425 fights to the death. The narrator keeps on his wall a black and white picture of the Roman statue copied from the Greek and known as "The Pugilist at Rest," which may be of Theogenes. He studies it and reflects on the expression of resignation on the battered but noble face of the boxer.

Sergeant Wright

Sergeant Wright is in charge of the Marine recruits at Marine Corps Recruit Depot in San Diego. He is a tough Marine and is admired by the men, who regard him as "the real thing, the genuine article."

Themes

The Masculine Code

The story presents an ideal of manhood in terms of toughness and aggression. In the narrator's world, real men put their masculinity to the test in extreme conditions, whether on the battlefield or in the boxing ring. Courage, fearlessness, and endurance are the qualities to be cultivated. Men must show other men what they are made of. In the boxing match, for example, the narrator makes a decision to stay in the fight because his buddies are watching, and he cannot let them down. The fact that he does not get knocked out is as much due to will power as brute strength. He believes when men act with aggression, they are being true to their own nature, which explains why the narrator feels exhilarated during the fight, as he did on the battlefields of Vietnam. There is no fear in such situations. Even though he takes a beating in the boxing match, he is sorry when the fight is over. The assertion of manhood is one of life's main thrills.

The macho ideal is emphasized in Marine training, as the raw recruits are transformed into tough warriors who will think nothing of charging

Topics for Further Study

- Research the types of brain injury caused by boxing. How many boxers have died over the last decade directly as a result of injuries sustained in the ring? Should there be more regulations to make boxing safer? Should boxing be banned altogether?
- The narrator in the story was probably in Vietnam during the Tet offensive in 1968. What was the Tet offensive? In what sense did it mark a turning point in the war?
- What are the symptoms of depression? How is depression treated? How does depression alter the way a person feels and the way the person perceives the world? Write two separate paragraphs describing a significant incident in your life. Write the first paragraph from the perspective of an emotionally level state of mind. Then write the second paragraph about the same incident from the perspective of a depressed mood. Note how different the same incident can sound when told from two radically different psychological perspectives.
- Select a piece of visual art—a painting, photograph or sculpture. Describe it and also describe its significance for you. What does it tell you about life that is so appealing? What questions does it pose for you, and what questions does it answer? For inspiration, re-read the passage in the story where the narrator describes the sculpture, "The Pugilist at Rest."

an enemy machine-gun nest to save their buddies. Those who cannot be toughened up simply drop out. From the outset, the narrator is out to prove his toughness, as shown in his assault of Hey Baby, his declaration to the Marine colonel that he wants to be in the infantry because he did not join the Marines to sit at a desk all day, and his final decision, influenced by Jorgeson, to become an elite Recon Marine. Jorgeson also embodies the masculine ideal, as shown by the fact that he quickly gives up his original desire to be a beatnik and an artist and gets absorbed by the masculine world.

Heroism

Although the story presents a pessimistic view of human nature, it also contains a glimpse of the traditional heroic ideal. This is seen in Jorgeson's actions when the Marines are ambushed by North Vietnamese troops. Although Jorgeson has never before been exposed to enemy fire, he stays cool and returns fire on the enemy. His situation is desperate, but he keeps his head, firing his M-16 in "short, controlled bursts," killing a lot of enemy soldiers. Even when he is mortally wounded, his shriek distracts the attention of a North Vietnamese soldier who is heading in the narrator's direction. The narrator believes that Jorgeson screamed on purpose in order to save his, the narrator's, life. Jorgeson, therefore, lives up to the highest ideals of the Marine Corps.

The minor character Second Lieutenant Milton is also presented in a heroic light. Even though his M-16 is not working, he fires at the enemy with his .45 pistol and still tries to reload even when his entire arm is severed by a rocket.

Pessimism

Pessimism about human nature and human life pervades the story. The narrator knows that human life is difficult at best and often made worse by the actions of other humans. "The world is replete with badness," he says, and he regards it as a kind of hell. Sickness and suffering are all around. He points out that in the United States of the twentieth century, in spite of great material abundance, personal and social problems abound. There are still prisons and nursing homes, homelessness and alcoholism. Wherever one looks, the narrator seems to suggest, one finds evidence of cruelty and hopelessness. Nor does he hold out any hope for improvement because that is the nature of things. He has arrived at this view of life not only from his own experience but also through his reading of the philosopher Schopenhauer, who believed, like the Buddhists, that life is suffering, the perpetual restless striving of desire. Every desire that is satisfied only gives rise to another desire, and so the cycle goes on forever. The narrator believes there is never any final rest or fulfillment, only discontentment and misery. Pleasure is always fleeting, an illusion that veils the reality of life. According to this philosophy, which the narrator embraces with relief, the only attitude worth cultivating is that of stoic resignation to the way things are.

Style

Imagery and Symbolism

The narrator frequently brings attention to one image: the blue eyes of his friend Jorgeson. There is nothing remarkable about Jorgeson's appearance other than his "very clear cobalt-blue eyes": "They were so remarkable that they caused you to notice Jorgeson in a crowd. There was unusual beauty in these eyes, and there was an extraordinary power in them." While Jorgeson is firing at the enemy, he turns and looks at the narrator "with those blue eyes," and just as Jorgeson is about to die, the narrator sees in his eyes "a final flash of glorious azure before they faded into the unfocused and glazed gray of death." Later, the narrator is reminded of Jorgeson's eyes by the color of his Marine uniform, not because they were the same but because each color was so startling.

Jorgeson's eyes suggest some courageous quality he possessed that enabled him to rise above the horror of battle and the strife of life. Jorgeson's eyes may also symbolize the friendship between him and the narrator, the bond they shared. The blue eyes also represent perhaps a kind of beauty that transcends this world, the sort of beauty known to artists. Jorgeson's original desire, after all, was to become an artist. However, the image of Jorgeson's eyes might also be intended to show what happens to beauty in this cruel world, since Jorgeson's exposure to combat lasts a mere twelve minutes, in contrast to the narrator, a far less heroic figure, who survives three tours of Vietnam without serious injury.

The story's central symbol is the Roman sculpture known as "The Pugilist at Rest." The narrator studies it and is inspired by the figure depicted in the sculpture, who he believes may be the boxer, Theogenes. The sculpture is a symbol of the brutality of male competition. The boxer bears on his muscular body the signs of many battles. But in spite of the brutality of his occupation, the boxer's face, in the eyes of the narrator, has nobility. His character had been tested in combat, and he has passed the test. There is also calm in the boxer's facial expression. He is a symbol of philosophical resignation to the reality that life is suffering, which is the philosophy that the narrator has learned from Schopenhauer.

Historical Context

Vietnam War

In the summer of 1966, when the narrator in "The Pugilist at Rest" was attending boot camp in San Diego, the war in Vietnam was steadily escalating as the United States sought to prevent communist North Vietnam from taking over South Vietnam, which had a non-communist government. American planes began bombing Hanoi, the capital of North Vietnam, in late June, 1966, and by the end of the year the number of U.S. troops stationed in South Vietnam had risen to 385,300. This figure rose to 475,000 by the end of 1967 and peaked at 543,000 troops by 1969.

However, the war was becoming intensely unpopular at home. Nightly television news broadcasts from the battlefields brought the reality of the conflict home to the American public. American casualties were high, the United States seemed increasingly likely to lose the war, and to many Americans the war was morally unjustifiable. In April, 1967, an estimated 400,000 protesters marched against the war in New York City. In October of the same year in Washington, D.C., 100,000 people demonstrated outside the Pentagon. Also in 1967, Martin Luther King Jr. exercised his moral authority by publicly speaking out against the war.

In 1968, the North Vietnamese launched surprise attacks on a number of South Vietnamese towns, including the capital city, Saigon. Known as the Tet offensive, the attacks showed the American public that the United States, despite the presence of its huge military forces, was not winning the war. Later that year, peace talks began in Paris and the bombing of North Vietnam was halted. There were continued massive protests against the war in Washington D.C. and other cities.

The war dragged on for another four years before a cease-fire was signed in Paris in January 1973. North Vietnam released 590 American prisoners of war, and the last U.S. troops left the country.

U.S. War Crimes in Vietnam

The narrator in "The Pugilist at Rest" commits "unspeakable crimes" in Vietnam, yet he is not court-martialed but given medals. This point touches on the issue of American war crimes in Vietnam and their cover-up, which was a controversial and divisive issue in the United States during the late-1960s and early 1970s. One notorious incident took place on March 16, 1968, at the village of My Lai, in which between 347 and 504 civilians were killed by American soldiers. The victims were mainly old men, women, children, and babies. Two initial Army investigations in 1968 concluded that the massacre did not take place. However, irrefutable details, including photographs, emerged in 1969. In 1971, Lieutenant William Calley, the leader of a platoon of soldiers who carried out the massacre, was convicted of the premeditated murder of twenty-two civilians. He was initially sentenced to life in prison but instead served only three and a half years of house arrest in his Army quarters at Fort Benning, Georgia. Calley claimed that he was following orders from his captain, Ernest Medina, who denied ordering any killings. Medina was tried and acquitted.

Several other investigations were conducted into alleged war crimes in Vietnam. A group known as the Vietnam Veterans Against the War organized the Winter Soldier Investigation in 1971, seeking to show that My Lai was not an isolated incident and that such crimes were the inevitable result of U.S. war policies in Vietnam. During the Winter Soldier Investigation, over one hundred Vietnam veterans gave testimony about war crimes they had committed or witnessed in Vietnam. However, no further war crimes trials were held.

Post-Traumatic Stress Disorder

Post-traumatic stress disorder (PTSD) can result from a traumatic experience such as combat in war or from any highly stressful experience, such as natural disasters (fire, flood, earthquake); torture or rape; an automobile or airplane accident; or childhood physical abuse. The traumatic event may retain its power, years later, to evoke the same emotions, such as panic or terror, which the person felt at the time. Any stimulus that the person perceives as being related to the trauma can trigger memories of the original event along with the accompanying psychological reactions. The emotions may also return as nightmares or what are called PTSD flashbacks, in which the person finds himself re-experiencing the traumatic experience.

Compare & Contrast

- **1960s:** In 1963, the drug sodium valproate (VPA) is found to be effective in controlling epileptic seizures. In 1968, the Epilepsy Foundation of America is formed, dedicated to promoting the welfare of people with epilepsy.

  1990s: Congress passes the Americans with Disabilities Act in 1990, preventing discrimination against anyone with a disability, including epilepsy.

  Today: In 2000, the Epilepsy Foundation of America holds a conference, "Curing Epilepsy: The Promise and the Challenge," in which it sets goals, including the prevention and cure of epilepsy. Epilepsy is effectively treated with medication that prevents seizures from occurring. A new procedure called vagus nerve stimulation (VNS) uses a device to prevent seizures by sending a small pulse of electricity to the vagus nerve, a large nerve in the neck.

- **1960s:** In spite of its huge manpower and technological superiority, the United States cannot defeat the enemy in Vietnam. The war is a divisive issue among Americans and saps American self-confidence.

  1990s: The United States and its allies are victorious in the Gulf War in 1991, in which Saddam Hussein's Iraq is evicted from Kuwait following the Iraqi invasion. The victory is hailed by many as laying to rest the ghost of Vietnam and restoring America's belief in itself and its armed forces.

  Today: The continuing conflict in Iraq, in which the United States has 135,000 troops but is failing to quell a growing insurgency, is compared by some to the quagmire of Vietnam. Supporters of the war, however, argue that the United States must continue the quest to bring democracy to Iraq and not abandon it to probable civil war.

- **1960s:** After two well-publicized deaths from injuries received in the boxing ring, there are calls for boxing to be banned. In 1962, Cuban boxer Benny Paret dies ten days after being badly beaten in the twelfth round of a fight with Emile Griffith at Madison Square Garden in New York City. The following year, featherweight boxer Davey Moore dies after a fight with Cuban boxer ltiminio (Sugar) Ramos at Dodger Stadium. As a result, California's governor Pat Brown asks the State legislature to ban boxing, and bills to outlaw the sport are introduced in several states, although no bills are passed.

  1990s: Boxing becomes safer as a result of changes made in the 1980s. Title bouts are limited to a maximum of twelve rather than fifteen rounds, and referees are quicker to end bouts in which one boxer is being exposed to dangerous punishment.

  Today: There are fewer deaths from boxing than in previous decades. Boxing ranks eighth in fatality rates for all sports, with 1.3 deaths per 100,000 participants, according to the Johns Hopkins Medical Institute. However, the risk of incurring brain damage as a result of repeated blows to the head remains high, and there are still boxing fatalities. In 2005, Becky Zerlentes becomes the first female boxer to die in a sanctioned boxing match in the United States. She dies twenty-four hours after being knocked out in the third round of an amateur bout in Denver.

(In the story, the narrator says he can still feel and smell the heat waves of napalm that he experienced in Vietnam.) PTSD is classified as an anxiety disorder; it may include symptoms such as depression or anti-social behavior (such as the aggressive behavior of the Vietnam veteran in "The Pugilist at Rest").

The incidence of PTSD is higher among Vietnam veterans than in the general population. According to the National Vietnam Veterans

Two young men in a boxing match The Library of Congress

Readjustment Survey (NVVRS), conducted from 1986 to 1988, 31 percent of male veterans and 27 percent of female veterans had experienced PTSD at some point in their lives. (In the general population the figures are 5 percent and 10 percent, respectively.) Although the survey found that the majority of Vietnam veterans had successfully reintegrated into society, a substantial minority had difficulties. Forty percent of male veterans had been divorced at least once; almost half of the men suffering from PTSD at the time of the survey had been arrested or in jail at least once, and 11.5 percent had been convicted of a felony. Thirty-three percent of male veterans had at some point experienced alcohol abuse or dependence.

Some problems experienced by Vietnam veterans may have been exacerbated by the fact that the war was unpopular in the United States, and the veterans returned to a bitterly divided country. Rather than being welcomed as victorious heroes, as the veterans of World War II had been, these veterans were sometimes mistrusted and subjected to abuse by fellow citizens angry at the war and its outcome.

Critical Overview

Jones's collection of stories *The Pugilist at Rest* was received enthusiastically by reviewers, who hailed the author as a strong new voice in American short fiction. According to *Publishers Weekly*, "Jones's voice . . . is irresistible—sharp, angry, poetic. His characters . . . are scarred, spirited survivors of drug abuse, war and life's cruel tricks." Most reviewers noted the similarities between the title story and many of the other stories. According to John Skow, in *Time*, the book "is a sheaf of extraordinary short stories, most of them about scarred, damaged men on the far side of violence. The viewpoint does not vary much: a straight-on, wondering stare back through the wreckage." Skow admired the strength and clarity of the voice in the stories and commented that "it is hard to imagine the author finding another as effective." Like Skow, Mary Hawthorne, in the *Times Literary Supplement* noted that that the pugilist in the stories is always the same figure presented in different ways. But this figure "rarely achieves the grace of his ancient prototype . . . he is by turns swaggering, intolerant, self-righteous, aggressive, deluded—desperate to prove his manly 'realness.'" Hawthorne also noted that Jones is "a man's kind of writer" who "reveals much about the condition of the American male psyche."

Criticism

Bryan Aubrey

Aubrey holds a Ph.D. in English and has published many articles on twentieth century literature. In this essay, Aubrey discusses the narrator's attempts to escape his suffering through the philosophy of Schopenhauer, as well as the significance of his epilepsy.

The depressed, epileptic Vietnam veteran who narrates "The Pugilist at Rest" and whose life is a toxic cocktail of pain, cruelty, aggression, and suffering is not an isolated figure in Jones's short fiction. The same basic character appears in "Break on Through" and "The Black Lights," the two stories that immediately follow "The Pugilist at Rest" in Jones's first collection of stories. All three stories are told in the first person by a Force Recon Marine who has been on several tours of Vietnam and has won medals for his courage in combat. His is a violent, masculine world in which the tougher and more ruthless a man is, the more respect he is accorded by his peers. It is a world awash in drugs of all kinds that are used to assuage pain, whether physical or mental. Life in these stories is lived in the raw, on the edge. It is also lit up from time to time with the strange exhilaration that men feel in the heat of combat. The narrator in "The Pugilist at Rest" says that he felt completely alive in the war zones of Vietnam, even in the midst of mayhem and death, and he reports the same experience in the boxing ring, during the fight that results in his brain injury. Similarly, the unnamed narrator in "The Black Lights" says, as he and a fellow Marine ignore an order to pull over and drive through a checkpoint as they leave a psychiatric military hospital in California:

> For a moment I felt like I was back in the jungle again, a savage in greasepaint, or back in the boxing ring, a primal man—kill or be killed. It was the best feeling. It was ecstasy.

Surprisingly also, the protagonists in these stories, despite the macho world in which they live and the fact that they have only a high school education, are also reflective, philosophically inclined men who read philosophers such as Arthur Schopenhauer and Friedrich Nietzsche, and writers such as Marcel Proust and Franz Kafka, none of whom would be considered exactly staple reading for the average Marine. These readings help them to grapple with the craziness and cruelty of their lives as tortured souls, bound, like Shakespeare's King Lear, on "a wheel of fire." As that wheel turns and turns from day to day, they occasionally glimpse moments of escape into some higher realm of understanding. In "The Black Lights," for example, the patients in the psychiatric ward are provided with entertainment at Christmas. As the narrator watches the square dancers perform, he reports:

> I saw myself as if from on high, saw the pattern of my whole life with a kind of geometrical precision, like the pattern the dancers were making, and it seemed there was a perfect rightness to it all.

In "The Pugilist at Rest," the narrator glimpses two avenues of escape, neither of which can give him lasting relief. First, he manages to find some "peace and self-renewal" in the pessimistic philosophy of Schopenhauer. The book he reads is Schopenhauer's *The World as Will and Representation*, first published in 1819 and revised and expanded in 1844. This book was later regarded as one of the most important philosophical works of the nineteenth century, although it made very little impact at the time of publication. Schopenhauer's philosophy has much in common with Buddhism and Hinduism, the latter as found in texts such as the Upanishads. According to Schopenhauer, the constant elements in human life are want, care, lack, and pain. Suffering cannot be avoided. Genuine, lasting happiness is not possible because humans are driven by the constant, restless need to satisfy some desire or craving. As soon as one desire is satisfied, another takes its place. All pleasures are fleeting and also illusory, in the sense that they mask or hide the reality of life, which is suffering. The world is simply not designed to support human happiness. Misery is not an accident that can somehow be rectified; it is the natural condition of man. In Schopenhauer's view, the only attitude worth cultivating is one of resignation, a calm acceptance of the way things are. This alone can free a person from the endless wheel of desire and enable him to view life objectively, beyond the striving for small satisfactions that are only temporary diversions and distractions from the truth about the human condition.

The narrator sees this kind of Schopenhauerean resignation in the ancient sculpture known as "The Pugilist at Rest." The boxer's face bears the marks of pain and suffering. Like every human being in his or her own way, he has endured many blows. Yet the narrator sees something more than suffering in the man's face: "There is also the suggestion of world weariness and philosophical resignation." It may be that the pugilist is about to face another fight to the death, but he has no fear. He accepts life for what it is and has no false expectations. He will take what is to come, whether good or bad, with equanimity. As such, the ancient pugilist serves as an inspiration to the narrator, who keeps a photograph of the sculpture in his room and studies it. A tough man, much battered by life, he seeks consolation through philosophy and art, and there is something very moving about his contemplation of this grainy black and white photograph. A poorer reproduction of this Roman statue, which is itself a copy of a Greek original, could hardly be imagined. But through it all he senses its grandeur.

"It may be that the pugilist is about to face another fight to the death, but he has no fear. He accepts life for what it is and has no false expectations."

The narrator's second avenue of escape from the grim daily reality of his life is scarcely an ideal one, since it is associated with the epilepsy that causes him so much distress. In the split second before the epileptic seizure begins, he experiences an indescribable feeling of ecstasy in which he knows beyond any shadow of doubt that God exists. He calls it "my vision of the Supreme Reality," but he cannot explain it any further, and he does not pretend to understand it. It is "slippery and elusive" when he tries to recall it after it has gone, and later he comes to doubt the truth of what he experiences in those moments.

Such are the narrator's occasional consolations—Schopenhauer and the "aura" that precedes an epileptic seizure—for his life of "tedious, unrelenting depression." But they are not enough; they do not make the same imprint on his life that his afflictions do. The reader senses this not only from the overall tone of the narrator's story and the pessimism he expresses at the end, as he awaits a risky form of psychosurgery that may do as much harm as good, but also from the style in which the narrator writes. When he writes about suffering and violence, his prose is vivid and conveys a palpable, in-the-moment sensation. Recalling his Vietnam experience, for example, he describes in clinical detail the fatal wound sustained by Milton:

> I could see the white bone and ligaments of his shoulder, and then red flesh of muscle tissue, looking very much like fresh prime beef, well marbled and encased in a thin layer of yellowish-white adipose tissue that quickly became saturated with dark-red blood.

Of the boxing match in which he takes a beating, he writes, "It felt like he was hitting me in the face with a ball-peen hammer. It felt like he was busting light bulbs in my face."

The similes and metaphors here are striking and apt; the voice renders direct, real experience that cuts to the quick. As the narrator himself admits, he feels fully alive in such moments of violence and danger. But when he writes about the aura that precedes his epileptic seizure, his gift for language seems to desert him. Instead of describing his own experience, he discusses that of others, giving the reader a short tour of some notable figures in history who suffered from the same form of temporal lobe epilepsy. It is as if he has switched from recording the raw experience of suffering in the present to the more objective mode of the historian. He seems particularly fascinated by the case of Dostoyevski, who, apparently, "experienced a sense of felicity, of ecstatic well-being unlike anything an ordinary mortal could hope to imagine." The narrator goes on to report that Dostoyevski "said that he wouldn't trade ten years of life for this feeling, and I, who have had it, too, would have to agree."

There is an oddly detached, derivative quality to this description, quite unlike the narrator's vivid description of injury and violence. In contrast to his first-hand accounts of violence and mayhem, he relies on someone else to describe the epileptic experience and then tamely says that he agrees with it. Later, he says that in this moment, the "murky veil of illusion which is spread over all things" is lifted, but he makes no attempt to explain what the illusion is. The impression left on the reader by this change in the narrator's style is that the so-called illusion is in fact more real, more stubborn, and

What Do I Read Next?

- Jones's *Sonny Liston Was a Friend of Mine: Stories* (1999) is his third collection of stories. Like *The Pugilist at Rest*, the collection includes stories about damaged boxers and Vietnam veterans, desperately trying to keep their lives afloat, but also some very different voices, such as a high school vice-principal and a ninety-two-year-old woman.
- In *Home to War: A History of the Vietnam Veterans' Movement* (2002), Gerald Nicosia reports on interviews with six hundred Vietnam veterans who became active in the antiwar movement or worked as veterans' advocates. Nicosia, whose sympathies lie with the antiwar movement, focuses on the leaders of Vietnam Veterans Against the War. He also covers such topics as the Veterans Administration's record on Agent Orange (a toxic chemical defoliant used by U.S. forces in Vietnam that led to health problems for those exposed to it and contaminated the land) and on post-traumatic stress disorder (PTSD).
- *Vietnam: A History* (2nd edition, 1997), by Stanley Karnow, is a highly acclaimed political and military history of Vietnam from its origins at the end of World War II to the collapse of South Vietnam in 1975. Karnow is former Southeast Asian correspondent for *Time* and *The Washington Post*, and his account has been widely admired for its depth of understanding and lack of bias.

---

more persistent than the fleeting illumination that supposedly shatters it, which is never conjured up with the same force as the violence and suffering endured (and dished out) by the narrator. In the end, it appears that the moments of apparent escape, far from being revelations of truth, are themselves the illusion; the reality is the revolving wheel of fire on which the narrator is bound and from which there is no escape.

Source: Bryan Aubrey, Critical Essay on "The Pugilist at Rest," in *Short Stories for Students*, Thomson Gale, 2006.

Sanford Pinsker

In the following review, Pinsker marvels at Jones's technique and promise in The Pugilist at Rest.

Given the sheer number of stories in *The Pugilist at Rest* that focus on boxers (either punch-drunk visionaries or battle-scared survivors) and the fact that Jones himself has more than 150 fights to his credit, one is tempted to describe the fiction in terms of feints and counterpunches, left hooks and right jabs. But I think the most telling lines from this impressive debut collection come from "Mosquitoes," one of the rare stories set among the groves of academe. At issue are not only the conventional trappings that make Middlebury College so predictable and depressing (Volvos with dogooder bumper stickers, wives simultaneously beautiful and b——y, and the requisite folksingers), but also the stories that Clendon, the protagonist's brother, reads and tries to write:

> Clendon had given me a number of literary magazines to read including stories of his own. I'm a reader, I read them but it was always some boring crap about a forty-five-year-old upper-level executive in boat shoes driving around Cape Cod in a Volvo. I mean you actually do finish some of them and admit that "technically" they were pretty good but I'd rather go to back-to-back operas than read another story like that. It was with relief that I returned to the medical journals.

Jones, one hardly need add, does not write those kinds of stories. Like the protagonist of "Mosquitoes"—an ER specialist with a two-pack-a-day habit and an attitude—he hankers for redder meat. The results are stones set in Marine Corps training camps and the jungles of Vietnam, amid the clutter of Bombay or the seedy places where down-and-out fighters rehash their old bouts. What each of the 11 stories features, however, is a vision of life as fierce as it is uncompromising, and a technique so skillful, so unobtrusive, that readers nearly forget that they are in the presence of Art.

Consider, for example, the opening lines from "Wipeout": "I believe in the philosophy of rock 'n' roll. Like, 'If you want to be happy for the rest of your life, don't make a pretty woman your wife.' I mean, who can refute that? Can Immanuel Kant refute that?" Or these from the collection's title story:

> Theogenes was the greatest of gladiators. He was a boxer who served under the patronage of a cruel nobleman, a prince who took great delight in bloody spectacles. Although this was several hundred years before the times of those most enlightened of men Socrates, Plato, and Aristotle, and well after the Minoans of Crete, it still remains a high point in the history of Western civilization and culture. It was the approximate time of Homer, the greatest poet who ever lived. Then, as now, violence, suffering, and the cheapness of life were the rule.

Jones's protagonists live in a zone beyond the niceties of illusion, much less the conventions of decorum. Small wonder, then, that they gravitate toward philosophers like Nietzsche or Schopenhauer, at the same time they keep their eyes wide open and their fists cocked:

Has man become any better since the time of Theogenes? The world is replete with badness. I'm not talking about that old routine where you drag out the Spanish Inquisition, the Holocaust, Joseph Stalin, the Khmer Rouge, etc. It happens in our own backyard. Twentieth-century America is one of the most materially prosperous nations in history. But take a walk through an American prison, a nursing home, the slums where the homeless live in cardboard boxes, a cancer ward. Go to a Vietnam vets' meeting, or an A.A. meeting, or an Overeaters Anonymous meeting. How hollow and unreal a thing is life, bow deceitful are its pleasure, what horrible aspects it possesses. Is the world not rather like a hell, as Schopenhauer, that clearheaded seer—who has helped me transform my suffering into an object of understanding—was so quick to point out? They called him a pessimist and dismissed him with a word, but it is peace and self-renewal that I have found in his pages.

My hunch is that the paragraph says much about Jones's artistic aims and explains why his stories are filled with the flesh and blood that technically accomplished tales about middle-aged executives with boat shoes usually lack. Indeed, not since Raymond Carver burst onto the literary scene with *Will You Please Be Quiet, Please?* (1976) has there been a short story collection, or a writer, with so much sheer promise.

"Jones's protagonists live in a zone beyond the niceties of illusion, much less the conventions of decorum."

Source: Sanford Pinsker, "A review of *The Pugilist at Rest*," in *Studies in Short Fiction*, Vol. 31, No. 3, Summer 1994, pp. 499–500.

Kevin Miller

In the following review, Miller praises Jones's characterization in The Pugilist at Rest, *and the "urgency and restlessness" with which he writes.*

Already commercially successful, with half the entries previously in the *New Yorker, Harper's,* and *Esquire,* Thorn Jones's debut collection is best described as utterly uncompromising. From his gallery of hard-assed, hard-headed, hard-luck, or simply hard cases, to the way these stories are written and sequenced, Jones demands much of the reader—and more often than not gives much in return. *The Pugilist at Rest* isn't quite the "knockout" suggested by some of the advance notice, but like the "brain lightning" experienced by several of his epileptic characters, there are flashes here of memorable and auspicious brilliance.

Three stories narrated by Vietnam vets open the collection; indeed, the first seven of the eleven entries are all told in the first person. Although such sequencing almost invites objection on the grounds of monotony, for the speakers sound very much alike, the voice that does emerge here is singularly compelling. The narrator of the title story is typical. Middle-aged, epileptic from one too many head blows in a Marine Corps boxing ring, and now facing brain surgery, he recalls the battlefield death of his lieutenant in a voice that's direct, ironic, and almost preter-naturally focused on the scene's absurd horror: "It [a rocket] took off his whole arm, and for an instant I could see the white bone and ligaments of his shoulder, and then red flesh of muscle tissue, looking very much like fresh prime beef, well-marbled and encased in a thin layer of yellowish-white adipose tissue . . . he stayed up on

> "*The Pugilist at Rest* isn't quite the 'knockout' suggested by some of the advance notice, but there are flashes here of memorable and auspicious brilliance."

one knee with his remaining arm extended out to the enemy, palm upward in the soulful, heartrending gesture of Al Jolson doing a rendition of 'Mammy.'" By the next page, the same narrator is quoting Schopenhauer—philosophy being a favorite compass for Jones's tough guys as they try to reason their way through such unreasonable lives.

"Sometimes a bad beating could do a fellow a world of good," opines another of Jones's narrators. And with "philosophy" like that, there's plenty of machismo at play in *The Pugilist at Rest*—machismo that, in the words of several of his narrators, occasionally crosses over into misogyny. The library lizard narrator of "Wipeout" for example, is also conversant with the great thinkers, although he appears to find the likes of Kant chiefly useful in seducing and exploiting women ("The scorpion stings, it can't help itself"). Similarly, in "Unchain My Heart," the collection's sole female narrator sounds as though she could be Mr. Wipeout's dream girl. Speaking of her lover, this New York City magazine editor pleads, "I need him to f—— my brains out."

Irritating as that is, you've got to admire Jones's courage in dishing up first-person story after story featuring characters who are sometimes downright repugnant. He doesn't moralize. He doesn't stack the deck. He simply lets his people talk. Make of them what you will.

At the same time, any suspicions about the author's character will surely be allayed by the appearance, near the end of the book, of "I Want to Live" an engrossing and sensitive piece—in the third person, though stream-of-consciousness in effect—about a middle-aged woman dying of cancer. Two more third-person keepers make for a strong finish: "A White Horse" and "Rocket Man." In the former, the most memorable story in the collection, an American advertising man, on a kind of epileptic bender, rescues a diseased horse from a Bombay beach, while the latter approaches a Richard Yates-like pathos in its depiction of a boxer and his alcoholic trainer.

That Jones's stories are apparently drawn from his life isn't especially newsworthy. What is, is the urgency and relentlessness, perhaps because of Jones's life, with which *The Pugilist at Rest* is written. That in itself sets this collection head and shoulders above most recent American debuts. Jones's characters may give out and they may give you trouble, but what redeems them all is that they never give in.

Source: Kevin Miller, "A review of *The Pugilist at Rest,*" in *Ploughshares*, Vol. 19, No. 2, Fall 1993, pp. 241–42.

Brooke Horvath

In the following review, Horvath praises the raw power of the stories in The Pugilist at Rest, *noting the extreme and often bleak nature of their characters and situations.*

The eleven stories comprising this debut collection have an impressive history: within the space of a year, eight of them appeared in the *New Yorker, Esquire, Harper's, Story,* and elsewhere, and the volume's title selection deservedly took first place in the 1993 0. Henry Awards and was also reprinted in *Best American Stories 1992.* The dust jacket boosts are equally deserved, John Barth dubbing Jones "a remarkable new American writer" and Michael Herr praising the book's exploration of "the codes and rituals of what we call American manhood." Herr's comment targets one of the collection's thematic centers; another can be found in the remark of one of Jones's narrators: "human behavior, ninety-eight percent of it, is an abomination." Indeed, these two thematic points of reference often come together as the "codes and rituals" of American manhood prove responsible for many of life's abominable moments.

Organized into sections, the first three stories deal with Vietnam and conjure a "funny universe where God couldn't keep the faithful alive but the Devil could." A boxer and member of a Marine recon team, Jones's narrator—and many of the collection's stories feature essentially the same protagonist—finds in war as in boxing "the science of controlling fear" and a test of manhood

> "If these stories are more than vaguely autobiographical, as I suspect them to be, they spring from a life I would not have wished on anyone, but it is one mark of Jones's power that he has been able to face up to and stare down that life and to connect with these eleven body blows."

that involves both taking and dishing out pain through the commission of "unspeakable crimes." Part two—which many readers will find hopelessly misogynistic—presents three stories of men (one from the woman's point of view) whose code of masculinity defines women as b——es to be seduced and left, often with their compliance. The three stories of part three are a more diverse group, turning to look through a son's eyes at his mother's rocky love life, a special-ed student whose limited life as a school janitor almost disappears when he falls for and marries the town slut, and a widow dying of cancer (this last almost too horrific in its details and bleak in its vision to bear). The two stories concluding *The Pugilist at Rest* tell of an ad man suffering, like the narrator of the Vietnam stories, from left-temporal-lobe epileptic seizures and a prizefighter's friendship with his washed-up trainer.

These are bleak, violent, crazed, butt-kicking stories of men and women—but mostly men—seeking psychic/spiritual balance in extreme, character-testing experiences. They are stories whose trying-to-get-straight vision of life comes out of Schopenhauer and Nietzsche, whose work is quoted several times. Through it all, Jones's characters pay heavy prices to learn hard lessons: that, in or out of the jungle, in Vietnam or back in the World, the "best feeling" is that heady rush of the "primal man" who knows that it all boils down to "kill or be killed," that the best one can hope for is a tenacious hold on one's will to live despite the odds, despite the lack of good reasons to do so. If these stories are more than vaguely autobiographical, as I suspect them to be, they spring from a life I would not have wished on anyone, but it is one mark of Jones's power that he has been able to face up to and stare down that life and to connect with these eleven body blows. In *The Pugilist at Rest* readers will learn what Melville meant about shouting "No! in thunder" and what Leonard Cohen means when he talks about something that "looks like freedom but feels like death."

Source: Brooke Horvath, "A review of *The Pugilist at Rest*," in *Review of Contemporary Fiction*, Vol. 13, No. 3, Fall 1993, pp. 224–25.

Ted Solotaroff

In the following review, Solotaroff examines the conflicted psychology of Jones's characters and the social relevance of the stories in The Pugilist at Rest.

The hangups of the life load the opportunities of the writer. Load as with guns, and load as with dice. There are several interactive furies in the writing persona of Thom Jones, the much-vaunted new fiction writer; propelled by his talent for dramatizing them, they make this collection of stories seem like a three-car collision in the Indy 500. Lots of power and lots of wreckage pile up as each situation races along its violent or otherwise "wired" premise to its baleful destination.

Jackknifed at the front is the Vietnam experience. As told in three stories, in his own words and reflections, they center on the training, recon operations and postcombat crackup of a Marine hero, champion boxer and romantic philosopher: i.e., a deep brute. A victim of his own bravado, he expresses, often inadvertently, the special destructiveness that hovered over the war itself and that lives on in a half-life of psychological and moral radiation. A recent article in *Rolling Stone* estimated that at least a tenth of the men who fought in Vietnam are now homeless and that half suffer from chronic seizures of violence and despair known euphemistically as post-traumatic stress disorder. Along with the walking wounded is the righteous brutality, the Ramboism that the Vietnam War, both in our conduct and defeat, continues to reinforce. (This point is lost upon the idiot moralist at the *Wall Street Journal* who blamed the civil disobedience of the antiwar movement for the

> "A victim of his own bravado, he expresses, often inadvertently, the special destructiveness that hovered over the war itself and that lives on in a half-life of psychological and moral radiation."

murder of David Gunn, the Florida obstetrician who performed abortions, by a member of Operation Rescue. Yet whose legacy is Operation Rescue if not that of the Moral Majority and the other cultural warriors of the right? Weren't any of the managers of The *Wall Street Journal* listening to Patrick Buchanan and his shock troops at the Republican Convention?)

Which is not to say that Thom Jones is a fictionist of the radical right. Though at times he comes close. As another of his protagonists, a surgeon, explains himself: "We are diluting and degrading the species by letting the weaklings live. I am guilty of this more than anyone. I took the Hippocratic oath and vowed to patch up junkies, prostitutes, and violent criminals and send them back out on the streets to wreak more havoc and mayhem on themselves and on others." Even in his less truculent stories, Jones's recurrent narrator shows pretty much the same macho elitism, though sensitized by a heroic wound, a Jake Barnes who still has his balls but suffers from epileptic seizures—as well as an ambiguous moral lesion. The title story is emblematic of the "attitude" of the others.

Jones's self-hero is not given a name in "The Pugilist at Rest," but in the following story about combat experience he is called "Hollywood," which I'll use here for convenience and, to some extent, for appropriateness. Hollywood preps for fighting in a people's war—perhaps the main reason the war was so anomalous and so morally destructive for Americans—by fracturing the skull of a fellow recruit in boot camp. The event is more chilling in its matter-of-factness than in its performance. His platoon is running to the drill field, rifles held at port arms:

> I saw Hey Baby give Jorgeson a nasty shove with his M-14. Hey Baby was a large and fairly tough young man who liked to displace his aggressive impulses on Jorgeson, but he wasn't as big or as tough as I. . . . I set my body so that I could put everything into it, and with one deft stroke I hammered him in the temple with the sharp edge of the steel butt plate of my M-14. . . . I was a skilled boxer, and I knew the temple was a vulnerable spot; the human skull is otherwise hard and durable, except at its base. There was a sickening crunch, and Hey Baby dropped into the ice plants along the side of the company street. . . . To tell you the truth, I wouldn't have cared in the least if I had killed him. . . . Jorgeson was my buddy, and I wasn't going to stand still and let someone f—— him over.

Behind the all-but-lethal excess of the payback lurks a suggestive conflict. Jorgeson's unusually beautiful and powerful "cobalt-blue eyes" as well as his beatnik ways both attract and bug Hollywood, who is drilling himself in the Semper Fi attitude, and he resolves this ambivalence by an act of violence whose magnitude affirms both his protectiveness and his toughness. "Hey Baby was a large and fairly tough young man who liked to displace his aggressive impulses on Jorgeson, but he wasn't as big or as tough as I." The style is the man. In this assertion of butch psychology, complete with the clinical jargon and fussy grammar, lies much room for narcissistic havoc.

Jones is not unsubtle. "The Pugilist at Rest" begins with Hey Baby being humiliated after he is caught writing a letter to his girlfriend in the midst of a lecture on the muzzle velocity of the M-14. So there is a kind of chain reaction of conflict between the male self as "hard-core" and human that continues to explode throughout the story. For reasons left unexplained, Jorgeson becomes even more combative than Hollywood and they both end up in an elite recon unit, where Jorgeson dies heroically, surrounded by enemy dead, his eyes in "a final flash of glorious azure." From there on the way is open to equivocally remembered mayhem. "Hey Baby proved only my warm-up act. There was a reservoir of malice, poison, and vicious sadism in my soul, and it flowed forth freely in the jungles and rice paddies of Vietnam. . . . I wanted some payback for Jorgeson. I grieved for myself and what I had lost. I committed unspeakable crimes and got medals for it."

What's he saying? A novelist of steadier moral vision kept his Kurtz distinct from his Marlow in dealing with "the horror, the horror" of colonialism, which the United States entered belatedly in a big way to ring down its curtain. As perpetrator, explainer and judge, Thom Jones has his hands full, and the right sometimes seems to knoweth not what the left is doing. Even so, this conflict between self-images of sensitivity and virility provides much of the tone and narrative rhythm that lift his Vietnam stories off the ground of banality and also reflects the moral dilemma of the Vietnam vet caught between the pride of having fought in and survived the Green Hell and the guilt over what it took to do so. Since his fellow citizens provide little reinforcement for the first and much for the second, the Vietnam veteran is thrown back on comradeship with the fallen and with the Corps or the Army, just as he was during the fighting itself, to lift his conduct off his conscience. This is why the Vietnam Memorial, unlike those of previous wars, remains so emotionally active, and why the most effective rehab facilities for Vietnam vets are ones run by themselves with the discipline of boot camp.

"It's only fair," as Hollywood remarks, that his own payback should be a head injury delivered by a fellow Marine at a boxing smoker after the war. Medical opinion is unclear about the consequent damage-and-treatment, but Hollywood prefers to regard it as "Dostoyevsky's epilepsy," which puts him in the company of St. Paul, Muhammad, Black Elk and Joan of Arc. "Each of these in a terrible flash of brain lightning was able to pierce the murky veil of illusion which is spread over all things. Just so did the scales fall from my eyes."

For Hollywood there are two sets of scales: one that blocks the transcendent, another that prevents us from seeing that all of us mostly live in a "world of s——," as the expression went in Vietnam. For this, Hollywood draws his authority from Schopenhauer, who has taught him about the will to power and its grievous consequences as well as "how hollow and unreal a thing is life, how deceitful are its pleasures, what horrible aspects it possesses."

All of this—the machismo, the suffering, the terminal resignation—coalesces for Hollywood into the figure of "The Pugilist at Rest"—a Roman statue copied from the early Greek, perhaps of the famous Theogenes, who, 1,400 fights to the death behind him, waits for the next with a world-weary perspicacity in his eyes beneath the scar tissue.

The statue is the only figure, pugilist or otherwise, at rest in these stories: the sight of the shore for a man struggling in an undertow. In "Break on Through" the tutelary figure is Satan himself, who visits Hollywood one night in the jungle and leads him into "the purple field"—the zone of the sixth sense that separates the killer from the killed, whose most memorable inhabitants are an elegant Indian who specializes in torture and a Navy Seal who has already fragged an officer and is more scary to his unit than are the Vietcong. "The Black Lights" shifts the devastation to a Marine psycho ward where Hollywood is under the care of Eagle Hawkins, a manic psychiatrist with a prosthetic nose, his own having been bitten off by a recovering catatonic. It is Hawkins who gets the narrator to keep a journal in whose entries one can see the premises of the striking persona that dominates this collection ("I am a boxer dog of championship lineage. . . . Once my jaws are clamped on something it cannot escape. . . . I do not have that liquid, soft expression you see in spaniels, but rather assertive eyes that can create a menacing and baleful effect. . . . Before my accident . . . I had been a great hero of the circus—the dog shot from cannons"). Striking in its being as over-bearing as it is tormented: Ayn Rand meets Dostoyevsky.

In civilian life, the Thom Jones narrator is no less hard-core. In "Wipeout" he still keeps a body count, though now it is female. During the course of an affair with a superior woman, "a Zen chick," he comes down with a serious flu: "I was suddenly vulnerable, a tenderhearted sentimentalist. I was on the verge of turning human and having feelings and so on." But luckily for both of them, she gets pregnant and he throws her out. "I couldn't believe the cruel words that spat from my vicious filthy mouth. There was this sense of unreality." But again, it's hard to know where contrition ends and boasting begins. First he is plagued with longing and self-loathing. Then he realizes, "But you have to be true to yourself. The scorpion stings, it can't help itself. There are no choices. Besides, the action gets even better when the word gets around."

Several of the other stories are similar documents of a licensed id and a fragile ego taking comfort from reading Nietzsche. In "Rocket Man" the former is embodied in a rising light heavyweight and the latter in an alcoholic corner man who instructs him in the positive side of "the will to power." In "Mosquitoes," they come together again in a trauma surgeon who intervenes in his brother's pretentious marriage by getting it on with his cheating but beautifully breasted wife. Or the persona shifts genders in "Unchain My Heart," the story of an affair with a dominating and singularly priapic scuba diver, formerly a bank robber, as told by an extraordinarily macha, so to speak, New York editor.

That Thom Jones has been so quickly bumped up the line of new writers makes, I guess, a point that corroborates Christopher Lasch's view of a culture of narcissism. It should be said, though, that Jones is more than just another talented young writer who is a pushover for himself and muscular male values. What he understands deeply as well as clinically is pain and mortality, the validating elements of his balefulness. The only other stories as intense as the military ones are a close account of a woman's struggle with a particularly rapid form of cancer, a kind of Tet offensive within the body, and of an American advertising man undergoing an "epileptic fugue" of amnesia on a fetid beach in Bombay, whose "loathing for everything on the face of the earth, including himself," is lifted by a local physician whom he gets to save a dying horse.

It will be interesting to see what happens to Jones. Most serious matters are closed to the hard-boiled, as Saul Bellow once remarked, and unless you're a Jonathan Swift it's hard to sustain interest in a point of view that prefers pedigreed boxers and horses to humans. There's a lot of tangled family distress aching at the back of these stories about angry people and their power trips, which begins to be addressed in a recent *New Yorker* story, where Jones's sentiment flows to a psychotic sister rather than to the familiar, enraged narrator. If I were his editor, I'd suggest he keep going in that direction. As a Vietnam veteran, he needs Nietzsche like a hole in the head.

Source: Ted Solotaroff, "A review of *The Pugilist at Rest*," in *Nation*, Vol. 257, No. 7, September 6, 1993, pp. 254–57.

Sources

Hawthorne, Mary, "With Attitude," in *Times Literary Supplement*, March 4, 1994, p. 21.

Johnson, Tyler D., "In Person," in *Austin Chronicle*, Vol. 18, No. 29, http://www.austinchronicle.com/issues/vol18/issue29/books.inperson.html.

Jones, Thom, *The Pugilist at Rest: Stories*, Little, Brown, 1993, pp. 3–27, 82, 85.

Review of *The Pugilist at Rest*, in *Publishers Weekly*, Vol. 240, No. 15, April 12, 1993, p. 47.

Shakespeare, William, *King Lear*, edited by Kenneth Muir, Methuen, 1972, act 4, scene 7, p. 178.

Skow, John, Review of *The Pugilist at Rest*, in *Time*, June 28, 1993, Vol. 141, No. 26, p. 72.

Further Reading

Kelleher, Ray, "The New Machoism: An Interview with Thom Jones," in *Poets & Writers Magazine*, Vol. 23, No. 3, May/June 1995, pp. 28–37.

This is a wide-ranging article in which Jones talks about boxing, mysticism, and epilepsy, and how they fuel his imagination as a writer.

LaPlante, Eve, *Seized*, HarperCollins, 1993.

LaPlante chronicles the lives of three ordinary people who suffer from temporal lobe epilepsy (TLE), as well as discussing prominent figures from the past, including Saint Paul, Dostoyevski, Gustave Flaubert, and Lewis Carroll, who also suffered from TLE. She analyzes the connection between TLE and creativity.

Pinsker, Sanford, "Review of *The Pugilist at Rest*," in *Studies in Short Fiction*, Vol. 31, No. 3, Summer 1994, pp. 499–500.

Pinsker admires the stories for their "vision of life as fierce as it is uncompromising," as well as Jones's skillful technique. He also comments that not since Raymond Carver's first collection of short stories has a writer of so much promise appeared.

Schumock, Jim, *Story Story Story: Conversations with American Authors*, Black Heron Press, 1999, pp. 248–67.

This book contains interviews conducted by Schumock on his radio program with nineteen American authors. The interviews focus on the connections between the writers' lives and their work.

Solotaroff, Ted, "Review of *The Pugilist at Rest*," in the *Nation*, Vol. 257, No. 7, Sept 6, 1993, pp. 254–57.

Solotaroff notes the ambivalent psychological dynamic operating in the narrator who is both fascinated and repelled by his buddy Jorgeson's artistic side, which is at odds with his own ostensibly macho attitude. The narrator balances both sides by a ferocious act of violence against Hey Baby which is also protective of his friend.

The Scarlet Ibis

James Hurst

1960

"The Scarlet Ibis," by James Hurst, was first published in the July 1960 issue of the *Atlantic Monthly* magazine. The story is also available in *Elements of Literature: Third Course* (published by Holt, Rinehart, and Winston, 1997). The story focuses on the troubled relationship between two young boys: the narrator and his mentally and physically disabled brother, Doodle. It explores the conflicts between love and pride and draws attention to the effects of familial and societal expectations on those who are handicapped. The narrative unfolds against the background of the carnage of World War I, with its associated themes of the dangers of attempting to make others over in one?s own image, the brotherhood of all mankind, and the waste of life resulting from a lack of love and compassion. In the course of the story, Doodle becomes symbolically identified with a rare and beautiful scarlet ibis which, finding itself in a hostile environment, dies. The ibis's story resonates not only with Doodle's own fate but with the fate of those from the United States and other countries who died in the war.

"The Scarlet Ibis" was the first and only work of Hurst's to achieve widespread recognition. It quickly achieved the status of a classic, being reprinted in many high-school and college literature text books. Its value to students of literature lies in its rich use of such devices as foreshadowing and symbolism, its sensitive use of setting to comment on the action, and its compassionate treatment of universal human values and limitations, as

James Hurst Courtesy of James Hurst

well as its compelling, character-driven plot. In an interview with this reviewer, Hurst said that he wrote the story as part of a process of coming to terms with the failure of his early singing career, but that the work has no direct autobiographical relevance and is a "work of imagination."

Author Biography

James Robert Hurst was born in 1922 on a farm by the sea near Jacksonville, North Carolina, the youngest of three children of Andrew and Kate Hurst. He attended North Carolina State College and served in the United States Army for three years during World War II. Though he had studied to become a chemical engineer, he realized that he preferred music and became a student at the Juilliard School of Music in New York. Aiming for a career as an opera singer, he traveled to Rome, Italy, for further study, living there for four years. On his return to the United States, he soon decided that he lacked operatic talent and abandoned his musical ambitions. In 1951 he began a career in the international department of Chase Manhattan Bank, New York, where he continued to work until he retired in 1984.

During his first ten years at the bank, Hurst wrote in his spare time. He published short stories and a play, mostly in small literary magazines. "The Scarlet Ibis" was his first story to appear in a national magazine. It was first published in *The Atlantic Monthly* in July 1960 and won the magazine's Atlantic First Award for fiction that year. The story, as Hurst said in a telephone interview with this reviewer, "took on a life of its own." It was quickly granted the status of a classic and has been published in many high-school and college literature textbooks since the late 1960s. None of Hurst's other stories achieved similar recognition.

Plot Summary

"The Scarlet Ibis" opens with the narrator, Brother, reminiscing about a remarkable event that took place when he was a young boy at his family home at the end of the summer of 1918. A scarlet ibis, an exotic bird that does not belong in the narrator's region, landed in a tree in the family garden. This memory sparks off another in Brother's mind: the birth of his mentally and physically disabled brother, Doodle, when Brother was six years old. Nobody expected Doodle to live except Aunt Nicey, who delivered him. Doodle is a disappointment to everyone, particularly to Brother, who had wanted a brother who could run, jump, and race with him. A sobbing Mama believed he would never do these things and warned that he may not be mentally "'all there.'" Brother, appalled by the prospect of having a mentally retarded brother, plans to kill him. But one day, Doodle grins at Brother, and Brother decides that he is "'all there.'"

By the time he is two, Doodle can only lie in bed or crawl backwards like a doodle-bug (hence Brother's choice of nickname, which sticks). Daddy builds a go-cart for him, and Doodle and the rest of the family press Brother into pulling him along with him everywhere he goes. Brother takes Doodle to Old Woman Swamp, where they pick flowers and make garlands for themselves. Doodle cries at the beauty of the place.

However, Brother is sometimes cruel to Doodle. He shows him the coffin that Daddy ordered after Doodle's birth and stored in the barn loft and makes him touch it, threatening to leave him there if he does not. Doodle calmly declares that the coffin is not his but reacts with terror to the threat of being left alone, crying, "'Don't leave me.'"

When Doodle is five, Brother feels embarrassed at having a brother who cannot walk and decides to teach him in secret. Doodle believes that he cannot walk and, indeed, does not see the need to. But Brother takes Doodle to Old Woman Swamp and laboriously works with him until he succeeds in learning to walk. On Doodle's sixth birthday, the boys reveal Doodle's new ability to the family. They all delightedly embrace Doodle, and when Doodle tells them that Brother taught him, they hug Brother too. Brother cries with unspoken shame, in the knowledge that his real motive was not love, but pride. Doodle's go-cart joins the coffin in the loft.

Not content with his success in teaching Doodle to walk, Brother begins to teach him to run, swim, climb trees, and fight. In May and June 1918, the cotton and corn crops fail due to drought and a hurricane. People begin to talk of places in France where their men have been killed in the war. Brother worries that school will be starting soon and that Doodle is not ready. He pushes him harder. Doodle begins to decline in health, but Brother ignores the warning signs.

One day, the family is eating lunch when a strange croaking noise is heard in the garden. Doodle is the first outside to investigate; the rest of the family follows. They find a large red bird sitting in the bleeding tree. It flutters and falls from the tree, landing dead at their feet. Daddy identifies it as a scarlet ibis, a native of the tropics. He believes a storm must have blown it off course. Doodle wants to bury the bird, but Mama forbids him to touch it as it may carry disease. While the rest of the family goes back inside to continue eating, Doodle finds a way to bury the bird without directly touching it. When he comes back into the house, he looks pale and says he is not hungry.

After lunch, Brother takes Doodle to Horsehead Landing to continue his rowing lessons. Storm clouds gather. Doodle is tired and frightened. When he gets out of the boat, he collapses in the mud. He has failed and both boys know it. They start for home, with Brother walking faster and faster to try to outpace the storm. A tree is shattered by a bolt of lightning. Doodle, who has fallen behind, cries out, "'Brother, Brother, don't leave me! Don't leave me!'" Brother, feeling bitter at Doodle's failure, cruelly runs as fast as he can until he can no longer hear Doodle's voice. Finally, Brother grows tired and waits for Doodle, but he does not appear. Brother goes back and finds Doodle dead. He has been bleeding from the mouth, and his neck and the front of his shirt are red with blood. The position of his body is reminiscent of that of the scarlet ibis. Brother recognizes the link between the ibis's fate and Doodle's. He weeps, sheltering Doodle's body from the rain with his own.

Characters

Brother

Brother is the lead protagonist of the story and also the narrator. He is not given a name but is referred to by Doodle, his brother, only as "Brother." He is six years old when Doodle is born. Brother has a high opinion of his own ability to run, jump, and climb, and wants a brother with whom he can share these activities. When it becomes clear that Doodle is capable of little more than lying on a rubber sheet and crawling backwards, Brother grows ashamed of Doodle's limitations and regularly taunts him. Though Brother loves Doodle, the love is tainted with cruelty and embarrassment.

At the urging of Doodle and his parents, Brother reluctantly allows Doodle to accompany him on all his expeditions, pulling him along in his go-cart. Driven by shame at having a crippled sibling, Brother forms a plan to secretly teach Doodle to walk. Eventually, he succeeds. This initial success is not, however, enough for Brother, who is determined that Doodle will not shame him by being seen as different when he starts school. Brother pushes Doodle to do more and more strenuous activities until one day, he breaks into a run, leaving Doodle trailing. Doodle overstrains himself trying to keep up and dies of a heart attack. Brother weeps over his fallen brother and recognizes the symbolic link between Doodle and the beautiful and rare scarlet ibis that had fallen dead from a tree in the family garden earlier that day.

Daddy

Daddy, the father of Brother's family, has a coffin built for Doodle soon after his birth, in the belief that he will die. When Doodle survives, Daddy builds a go-cart for Doodle so that Brother can pull him around.

Doodle

Doodle is the mentally and physically retarded younger brother of the narrator, Brother. His family initially calls him by his given name, William Armstrong, but Brother nicknames him Doodle (after a doodle-bug, because of his habit of crawling backwards) and the name sticks. From the first,

Doodle is a disappointment to his family, especially to Brother, because Doodle can only lie on a rubber sheet and crawl backwards. Everyone expects Doodle to die, but he defies them all and survives, becoming a loving boy with a strong attachment to Brother. Doodle is pulled around in a go-cart by Brother until Brother teaches Doodle to walk. This achievement, however, seems more important to Brother than it does to Doodle.

Doodle's real strengths lie not on the level of his physical prowess, but on a more subtle inward level, to which Brother seems blind at the time the action takes place. From the beginning of his life, Doodle defies death and refuses to recognize the coffin that Daddy builds for him as his own. He shows a sense of wonder and respect for the natural world, crying with wonder at the wild beauty of Old Woman Swamp. He is the first to notice the visiting ibis and honors the bird by giving it a careful burial while finding a way of respecting his mother's orders not to touch it. The fact that Doodle is the only member of the family to care for the scarlet ibis enough to bury it shows his compassionate heart and emphasizes a symbolic link between boy and bird. This symbolic link is confirmed when Doodle dies on the same day as the bird and in a way that mirrors its fate.

Doodle's greatest fear is of being left behind by the impatient Brother on their expeditions together. When this happens one day, he dies of a heart attack while trying to keep up with Brother.

Mama

Mama, the mother in Brother's family, despairs of Doodle's future from the beginning. She tearfully predicts that Doodle will never run or climb with Brother and believes that he might not be mentally normal. When the scarlet ibis drops dead from the tree, Mama forbids Doodle to touch the bird in case it is diseased. Mama's attitude to Doodle is reflected in her attitude to the bird: in both cases, she fails to see the beautiful and miraculous and expresses only fear and anxiety.

Aunt Nicey

Aunt Nicey is aunt to Brother and Doodle. She delivers Doodle and is the only person who believes that he will live. She has a religious nature, giving thanks to God when Doodle shows everyone that he can walk. Because Doodle is born with a caul, traditionally believed to be "Jesus' nightgown," Aunt Nicey warns that he should be treated with special respect since he may turn out to be a saint. Though prompted by superstitious belief, the comment shows an appreciation of Doodle's spiritual qualities and foreshadows a suggested symbolic link between Doodle, the ibis, and Christ.

Themes

Conflict between Love and Pride

"The Scarlet Ibis" explores the conflict between love and pride in Brother's relationship with his physically and mentally disabled brother, Doodle. Brother loves and appreciates Doodle, as can be seen in the incident when the brothers fantasize about living in Old Woman Swamp, when Brother is overwhelmed by the beauty of the images that Doodle conjures up.

Love is accepting and compassionate in its nature. But Brother's love for Doodle is challenged by two very human failings: pride, and the cruelty that results from it. Brother feels embarrassed and ashamed of Doodle's limitations and obvious differences from other people. They threaten his sense of pride. He decides to make Doodle do all the things that other people do in spite of the fact that Doodle himself sees no need to conform. Teaching Doodle to walk is Brother's first success. When Brother's family congratulates him on his success, he cries with shame, because he knows that he acted not out of love but out of pride, "whose slave [he] was." Brother's pride again triumphs over love when he continues to push Doodle to harder physical feats in spite of Doodle's obviously declining health. In the end, Doodle's heart fails under the strain, a victim of Brother's insistence. Well might Brother reflect, "I did not know then that pride is a wonderful, terrible thing, a seed that bears two vines, life and death." In this case, the "life" aspect is the undoubted progress that Doodle makes under Brother's demanding tutelage, and the "death" aspect refers to the fate of the fragile boy.

The Desire to Make over Others in One's Own Image

All of the family, except Brother, accepts Doodle as he is. However, their acceptance is not portrayed as entirely positive, as it comes with a heavy dose of resignation and hopelessness about Doodle's prospects. Mama and Daddy are so convinced that he will die soon after birth that Daddy orders a coffin for him. When Doodle does not die, Daddy makes the go-cart, accepting that Doodle will never

Topics For Further Study

- In "The Scarlet Ibis," Hurst uses natural elements of the setting to comment on the action or the characters. These include plants, birds, insects, and weather phenomena. Make a list of some of these natural elements and write a paragraph on each, explaining how they comment on the action or the characters. Where appropriate, research the habits, habitat, behavior, appearance, symbolic value or other aspects of each natural element and use your findings to elucidate your answers.
- Research the lives of two disabled people: one who is alive today, and one from history (born at any time before 1920). Write an essay on the lives and achievements of each. Include in your composition the following: the problems they faced and how they responded; society's and their family's attitudes to, and treatment of, them; and how the life and achievements of each may have been affected if they had been born in the other's time period.
- Write a short story in which the main character has a disability, or imagine that you have a particular disability and write a "day-in-the-life" diary entry. If you have a disability in real life, choose a different disability for this exercise. Take into account in your story or diary entry how your disability will affect your feelings, actions, perceptions, relationships and choices.
- Research the history of eugenics from its scientific beginnings in the nineteenth century to the present day, considering aspects such as selective breeding, enforced sterilization, human genetic engineering, and the use of eugenics to justify genocide. Write a report giving some arguments that have been made for and against each of these aspects of eugenics. Bear in mind that different sectors of society, such as disabled people, scientists, doctors, the non-disabled population and governments may well have different views, so try to gather your arguments from a variety of sources to reflect the full range of opinion. In each section, give your own view based on what you have learned.
- Research the experiences of a person who participated in World War I. This could be a person in active military service, or a nurse, journalist, ambulance driver, etc. Imagining that you are that person, write a letter to your family at home telling them about some of your recent experiences and your reflections on them.

walk. The consignment of coffin and go-cart to the loft are signs of the progress that Doodle makes in being like his older brother.

Brother's impatience with Doodle's limitations is as ambiguous as the rest of the family's acceptance of them. But Brother's attitude is the more dangerous because it forces change on a body that is not equipped to deal with it and on a mind that does not desire it. Brother's success in re-making Doodle in his own image is greeted as wonderful progress by everyone except Doodle. When Brother tells him that he must learn to walk, Doodle asks, "'Why?'" Neither does Doodle understand why he should struggle to avoid being different from everybody else at school. Because the story is told from the point of view of Brother and not Doodle, it is not clear how much Doodle's life is improved by his new skills. But it is certain that after the initial success of the walking project, Brother's attempts to push Doodle further are destructive to Doodle's health and eventually contribute to his death.

Brother tells us several times that his efforts with Doodle are motivated by pride: he is ashamed of having a disabled brother. There is a suggested parallel here with the background theme of World War I (1914–18), and many readers see an implied critique of the war in the story of Doodle and Brother. Significant numbers of American troops were sent to fight in Europe in the summer of 1918, when "The Scarlet Ibis" is set. Anti-war movements, like those gaining ground in 1960 when the story was written, point out that wars fought against other nations necessarily involve attempts to make over other nations in the aggressor's image. Prerequisites to such attempts, say these movements, are pride and arrogance: the aggressor nation has a conviction that it is in some way better than the victim nation and has a right to re-make the victim nation in its own image. This is generally as destructive and pointless in the long term as Brother's attempts to remake Doodle. World War I, far from being the "war to end all wars," as was claimed at the time, was soon followed by World War II (1939–45). Though leaders claimed at the time that war was the only option, many modern scholars question this view. Hurst does not shy away from emphasizing that the war's main legacy in the United States was the deaths of many men, a fact that he drives home in his references to American war graves and deaths.

People who are Different

Both Doodle and the scarlet ibis stand out as different; indeed, they are unique in the environment in which they find themselves. "The Scarlet Ibis" dramatizes the ways in which people respond to those who are different or disabled. At one end of the spectrum, Doodle's family believes that any meaningful quality of life is impossible and expects the boy to die. At the other end, Brother is determined to re-make Doodle so that he conforms to the norm and no longer embarrasses Brother. Doodle fails to identify with either expectation, refusing to die or admit that the coffin made for him is his, and remaining oblivious to Brother's insistence that he should not be different from the other children at school. In a sense, Doodle floats above the expectations of others like the winged beings of his fantasies. But finally, he succumbs in the face of the pressure of Brother to try to become the same as everyone else.

Brotherhood

It is significant that the lead protagonist of the story is known only by his relationship to Doodle: "Brother." This detail alerts readers to the fact that brotherhood is a major theme. Brother's love for Doodle is bound up with cruelty and shame. Doodle, for his part, is strongly attached to, and reliant upon, Brother and his main fear is of being left alone by him. He is terrified at Brother's threat to leave him in the barn loft if he does not touch the coffin, and cries, "'Don't leave me.'" He echoes these words with greater intensity on the day he dies, as Brother, bitter at Doodle's failure to perform the physical feats he has set for him, runs ahead of him in the rain. This time, Doodle cries, "Brother, Brother, don't leave me! Don't leave me!" Brother does leave him, if only temporarily, and the result is Doodle's death.

Because the story takes place against the background of World War I, Doodle's words and the theme of brotherhood suggest a wider resonance. Brotherhood among soldiers fighting in appalling conditions in mud-filled trenches was a frequent theme in war literature and even on war memorials. Loyalty to one's fellow soldiers was seen as vital; if a soldier was injured, the loyalty or betrayal of his colleagues could mean the difference between his living or dying. There are many stories of heroism involving men risking their own lives to save a fallen colleague and equally stories of horror involving wounded men being left to die. In a more universal sense, the carnage of the war brought home the need to embrace the ideal of the brotherhood of all mankind regardless of differences in nation of origin, race, or religion.

Style

Setting

"The Scarlet Ibis" is set in and around Brother's family home in the American South. The story is laden with rich descriptions of the natural environment, in the family garden and the nearby countryside. Hurst never describes the setting for its own sake; it always comments on the action. For example, the description of the "blighted" summer, with the hurricane bringing down trees and ruining crops, is introduced immediately after Brother recounts his intensification of Doodle's learning program. These images of devastation emphasize the destructive effects of Brother's pushing Doodle beyond his limits.

Moreover, the nearby Old Woman Swamp embodies nature's abundance and beauty. For Brother and Doodle, it seems to signify a world of infinite possibilities and the glory of life. Doodle cries with wonder when he first sees it, and the boys gather wild flowers and make garlands and crowns with which to bedeck themselves. The suggestion is that this is a place where they feel royal, beautiful, and wealthy (the flowers are referred to as "jewels"). Old Woman Swamp is also where Brother teaches Doodle to walk, which, in spite of its disastrous outcome, represents a widening of Doodle's horizons. Doodle fantasizes about living a blissful existence in Old Woman Swamp.

Foreshadowing

Hurst frequently uses foreshadowing to suggest an upcoming event. This technique creates suspense as the reader waits for the resolution of a certain narrative thread. The first paragraph is an example: "It was in the clove of seasons, when summer was dead but autumn had not yet been born." This image of death is reinforced by the reference to the "untenanted" oriole nest that rocks "like an empty cradle." Cradles usually contain babies, a sign of new life, but this one is empty, suggestive of a dead child. Next follows a reference to "the last graveyard flowers," which speak "the names of our dead," evoking the image of men who have died in the war. These images combine with other elements, like the doctor's warning about Doodle's weak heart, to foreshadow the death of Doodle.

Symbolism

The scarlet ibis is a carefully chosen symbol. To understand why, it helps to know a little about the bird. A native of the South American tropics, the scarlet ibis is vivid red. Its color derives from the shrimps that form the bulk of its diet; if there are no shrimps, it loses its color. It needs a particular habitat in order to thrive as it only feeds in shallow waters along the coast, in mud flats and lagoons. The scarlet ibis is an endangered species which has not bred successfully in its natural habitat since the 1960s. Reasons for this include development of coastal areas, water pollution, and depletion of food sources. Scarlet ibises are colonial nesters, meaning that they nest in large flocks; they rely on the presence of other birds of their own species.

The ibis in "The Scarlet Ibis" is symbolically linked with Doodle from the beginning of the plot, as the memory of the ibis's arrival triggers in Brother's mind the memory of Doodle, and Doodle immediately feels a bond with the bird. Like the ibis, Doodle is a being alone, different, singled out, with no flock, out of his natural environment. Like the ibis, he does not thrive in the environment in which he finds himself: he is delicate, sickly, and fragile. But while the ibis's beauty is obvious to Doodle, Doodle's beauty of spirit is hidden inside an unattractive exterior; thus, the bird externalizes Doodle's inner nature. Doodle is associated with winged and divine beings, just as the bird is literally a winged creature. Both boy and bird are characterized by sacred imagery. It could be argued that both are symbolically linked with Christ.

Narrative Technique

The story is told as a first-person reminiscence by Brother, who looks back from some time in his maturity to events that took place in his childhood. Thus he is able to imbue the raw events with his reflections on the lessons he learned from them. For example, Brother as a boy would not be able to explain that the reason he cried after his family congratulated him for teaching Doodle to walk was his shame at having acted from pride, "whose slave [he] was." This is the reflective adult speaking. The narrative technique of reminiscence also enables Brother to foreshadow events before they are described in the narrative, as in "I did not know then that pride is a wonderful, terrible thing, a seed that bears two vines, life and death." This statement suggests that Brother will at some point realize this truth, apparently through some catastrophic event, as indeed happens.

That readers only observe the other characters through Brother's eyes might suggest that their sympathies lie with him. However, many readers will sympathize more with Doodle because of the emotional honesty of the adult Brother. He has had time to reflect on events and he lays bare the less admirable aspects of his character and of his feelings for Doodle, showing us the "knot of cruelty borne by the stream of love." If Doodle has a harsh side to his character, it is not presented; he comes through as an innocent.

The adult Brother remains closely in touch with the negative emotions that many children feel for their close relatives. Children tend to be more open than adults about having mixed emotions for those close to them. They will declare that they hate their mother, brother, or best friend, only to show minutes later the love and devotion that they also feel. Adults tend to suppress such negative emotions because they are more able to see the consequences of expressing them. The adult Brother, however, does not gloss over his negative feelings for Doodle, and this candor increases readers' sympathy for the younger boy, the target of those feelings.

Historical Context

World War I and the Growth of the Anti-war Movement

By July 1918, the United States was sending over 3,000 troops every month to Europe to fight in World War I (1914–18). By the end of the war in November 1918, total U.S. combat deaths numbered 51,000; U.S. non-combat but war-related deaths numbered 62,000.

Though the horrors of World War I led to its being dubbed "the war to end all wars," this hopeful prediction did not become fact. World War II began in 1939 and continued until 1945. Virtually all countries that participated in World War I were involved in World War II. Over 405,000 Americans were among the approximately 50 million people who died as a result of the war. This 50 million includes those who died in the Holocaust, the name given to the Nazis' program of extermination of peoples they deemed genetically inferior, and the United States' atomic bombings of civilians in the cities of Hiroshima and Nagasaki in Japan.

Though the United Nations was set up in 1945 to prevent the outbreak of another world war, peace proved elusive. By 1961, the year after the publication of "The Scarlet Ibis," in response to a perceived Communist threat, the United States had deployed 4,000 troops in South Vietnam. The cold war was reaching its height, with tensions between the United States and the Soviet Union running high. In February 1960, France tested its first atomic bomb; the Soviet government had determined by 1959 that any future war would be nuclear and worldwide. In October 1960, U.S. presidential candidate John F. Kennedy first suggested the idea of the Peace Corps, which would promote understanding between the United States and the rest of the world. U.S. involvement in Vietnam and the cold war marked a significant rise in the peace movement, which first become organized after World War II. The peace movement advocated the withdrawal of U.S. troops from Vietnam on the grounds that this would lessen tensions in the region and result in less bloodshed and that other nations should be allowed to work out their problems without foreign military intervention. Though by April 1970, approximately 115,000 U.S. troops had been withdrawn from Vietnam, complete withdrawal only took place in 1973.

Eugenics

It is difficult to read "The Scarlet Ibis" without a consideration of the history of the philosophy of eugenics. Eugenics (from the Greek for "good breeding") aimed to improve human hereditary traits through social interventions: for example, selective breeding; enforced sterilization of people seen as genetically inferior; and genetic engineering. Selective breeding was suggested by the Greek philosopher Plato (c. B.C. 427–c. B.C. 347), but the modern eugenics ideology, which developed from the growing discipline of genetics, was formulated in 1869 by Sir Francis Galton (1822–1911), a British anthropologist and cousin of the founder of evolutionary theory, Charles Darwin (1809–1882).

Eugenicists of a religious frame of mind fused Galton's scientific arguments with the biblical injunction: "I the Lord thy God am a jealous God, visiting the iniquity of the fathers upon the children unto the third and fourth generation of them that hate me" (Deut. 5:9). In this light, enforced sterilization of those considered to be degenerate was seen as a moral duty. The Supreme Court upheld eugenic sterilization in 1927, with the pronouncement of Judge Oliver Wendell Holmes (1841–1945), as quoted in Trent's book *Inventing the Feeble Mind*, that "three generations of imbeciles are enough."

Eugenics was supported in the early twentieth century by many prominent thinkers but became discredited after World War II, when it was seen to be the key idea justifying genocide by the Nazis (it was still practiced, however, by many national and regional governments into the 1970s and has as of 2005 been taken up by proponents of human genetic engineering). The Nazis had decided that anyone who did not conform to the so-called Aryan ideal (tall, blond, of Nordic appearance, and intelligent) should be eradicated. This objectionable group included people who were different from the norm, such as gypsies, homosexuals, intellectuals, dissidents, and the disabled, as well as all of European Jewry.

While the vocal proponents of eugenics have traditionally been drawn from the educated elite, an unofficial form of genocide of disabled people was practiced by ordinary families well into modern times. Acting from the standpoint that a disabled child was a financial burden and that such a child was likely to have a poor quality of life and would be better off dead, families would simply allow such a child to decline and die. This neglect happened in hospitals as well as private homes, showing that at least some of the medical community shared this view.

In "The Scarlet Ibis," the family loves Doodle and would never countenance deliberately allowing

Compare & Contrast

- **1910s:** By July 1918, the United States has sent one million troops to Europe to fight in World War I (1914–1918), a force augmented by an average of 200,000 men per month until the armistice is signed on November 11, 1918. After the war ends, certain works of literature and people in wider society ask whether the war was necessary.

  1960s: In 1961, in response to a perceived Communist threat, the United States deploys 4,000 troops in South Vietnam. By July 1965, some 75,000 U.S. troops are in Vietnam. The figure continues to climb to more than 510,000 early in 1968. Opposition to U.S. involvement in the war begins in 1964 on college campuses. Protests against the draft begin in 1965, when the student-run National Coordinating Committee to End the War in Vietnam stages the first public burning of a draft card in the United States.

  Today: Between 2003 and 2005, many global protests are held worldwide against the U.S./British-led invasion of Iraq. These protests include several said to be the biggest peace protests before a invasion actually began.

- **1910s:** Many prominent thinkers support eugenics, which aims to improve human hereditary traits through social interventions such as selective breeding and enforced sterilization of mentally or physically disabled people. In the United States, the Eugenics Record Office (ERO) opens in 1910. In years to come, the ERO collects many family pedigrees and concludes that those who are mentally and physically unfit come from poor backgrounds.

  1960s: Eugenics is widely discredited after it becomes clear that during the 1930s and 1940s the Nazis forcibly sterilized hundreds of thousands of people whom they viewed as mentally and physically unfit and killed thousands of disabled people through compulsory euthanasia programs. However, enthusiasm for eugenics quietly continues in some parts of the scientific community and within some national and regional governments, which pursue enforced sterilization of disabled people.

  Today: Human genetic engineering to bring about higher intelligence and fitness and to eradicate disability is advocated by some scientists. The Human Genome Project, which aims to map the human genetic makeup, makes modification of the human species seem possible again. The legalization of the patenting of genetic discoveries means that in theory, profits can be made from human genetic engineering, and corporations become involved in eugenics.

- **1910s:** Unofficial euthanasia, in which disabled children are allowed to die, is practiced within families and sanctioned by members of the medical profession. In the event that the child is kept alive, institutionalization for life, funded by the state, is the favored approach.

  1960s: The civil rights and women's rights movements add momentum to an activist movement for disability rights that begins after World War II ends in 1945. For disabled persons to remain within the family as children and to have independent lives as adults instead of being institutionalized are major goals of this movement.

  Today: The Americans with Disabilities Act is signed into law in 1990 by George H. W. Bush. It is a wide-ranging civil rights law that prohibits discrimination based on disability. It includes a section obliging public services to embrace service for people with disabilities.

him to die. Nevertheless, they fully expect him to die and are even receptive to this outcome by providing him with a coffin before the event. Brother, on the other hand, favors a more aggressive course of forcing Doodle to fit into his preconceived notion of what a brother should be. While Doodle's family expects him to become invisible through death, Brother expects him to become invisible by conforming. When Brother fails, he runs off and leaves Doodle, which leads to his death. Both the family's and Brother's attitudes toward Doodle raise uncomfortable questions about society's attitudes toward disability.

Disabled Persons' Rights

Before the middle of the nineteenth century, it was common in American and European societies for mentally or physically disabled people to live within their families and to be integrated into society to whatever extent possible. However, in the 1870s, there arose an attitude that a disabled child posed a serious financial burden on members of the laboring class and should be placed for life in an institution funded by the state. Families often did not object, since there was a great social stigma attached to having a disabled child, perhaps due to the widespread belief that such an event was God's judgment for bad behavior on the part of the parents or their ancestors or even evidence of immoral inbreeding between relatives. Frequently, families who institutionalized their children did not visit them or talk about them to other people.

Institutionalization remained the favored approach to disability in many countries as recently as the 1970s. Conditions in the institutions varied from good to appalling. With the growing prosperity after World War II, however, activism grew among parents on behalf of their disabled children. This activism was partly inspired by a return to belief in human rights after the Nazi genocide. A desire grew for disabled children to remain within their families and receive the same care and services, including education, as so-called normal children. Deinstitutionalization followed, and in 1975 Congress in passing the Education for All Handicapped Children Act guaranteed free public education to children with disabilities.

Critical Overview

"The Scarlet Ibis" was the first story by James Hurst to appear in a national magazine. It was first published in the *Atlantic Monthly* in July 1960 and won the magazine's Atlantic First Award for fiction that year. The magazine's introduction describes "The Scarlet Ibis" as a "touching story of a boy and his crippled brother."

Soon after its publication, the story, as Hurst said in a telephone interview with this reviewer, "took on a life of its own." It was quickly granted the status of a classic and has been published in many high-school and college literature textbooks since the late 1960s.

Beginning in 1951, Hurst wrote other short stories and a play over a ten-year period, some of which were published in small literary reviews. None achieved the recognition accorded to "The Scarlet Ibis." Despite the story's undoubted quality, the fact that it was not followed by any work of comparable stature means that neither the story nor Hurst attracted the attention of reviewers or critics. Thus this reviewer was unable to find any reviews or academic criticism relating to the story or its author. However, one textbook in which "The Scarlet Ibis" is reprinted, *Elements of Literature: Third Course* (1997), and the Internet give many examples of classroom assignments on the story, testifying to its popularity within school and college literature courses.

Criticism

Claire Robinson

Robinson is a writer and editor. In the following essay, Robinson analyzes how the story of the life and death of a disabled child is explored by Hurst's use of symbolism.

In James Hurst's "The Scarlet Ibis," the arrival of the scarlet ibis is mentioned in the first sentence, suggesting that it has major significance. The memory of the ibis's visit triggers the memory in Brother's mind of his brother Doodle. The bird's red color, combined with the fact that it alights in the bleeding tree, combines to create an image of blood, foreshadowing later events in both the ibis's and Doodle's lives. The link between the ibis and Doodle is further developed later in the story, when the ibis's arrival is described in detail. Doodle is the first to notice the bird and the first outside to investigate further. He is wonder-struck by the sight. At that point, the bird falls dead out of the tree. Daddy goes to get the bird book and establishes that it is a scarlet ibis, a native of the

A peacock with its tail spread Photograph by Robert J. Huffman. Field Mark Publications. Reproduced by permission

tropics that must have been separated from its flock and blown in by a storm. Readers understand that the bird is out of its natural environment, alone, weakened, and fragile. Doodle, too, is a creature out of his natural environment, too weak to do the things Brother expects of him, with a skin too sensitive even to bear the sun's rays, and expected not to survive at the beginning of his life. In "The Scarlet Ibis," James Hurst establishes a symbolic link between the bird and the disabled boy that illuminates the significance of the boy's life and death.

The bird's arrival on the wings of a freak storm raises the questions: What is Doodle's natural environment? Where is his flock? The answers are not given explicitly but are suggested symbolically. Doodle is frequently characterized by images of winged beings. There is the ibis itself, to which Doodle is symbolically linked; there are the people who inhabit his fantasies who have wings and fly wherever they want to go; and there is Brother's comment that giving Doodle the name William Armstrong is "like tying a big tail on a small kite." Finally, there is Doodle's favorite fantasy of a boy with a golden robe and a pet peacock who spreads his magnificent tail. This boy's robe is so bright that the sunflowers turn away from the sun to face him. The only light that could be brighter than the earth's brightest source of light, the sun, would have to be of divine origin. Winged beings include earthly birds but also heavenly angels.

Other images in the story link Doodle with a divine level of existence. Aunt Nicey, the spiritual conscience of the family, remarks that Doodle was born in a caul and explains that "cauls were made from Jesus' nightgown" and that caul babies must be treated with respect because they might be saints. She also compares his learning to walk with the Resurrection. Aunt Nicey's reverent and deeply spiritual appreciation of Doodle reflects his own attitude toward the ibis, particularly when he solemnly conducts a burial service for the bird.

Aunt Nicey's view of Doodle and Doodle's view of the ibis show readers there is another way of responding to beings who are different, other than expecting them to die (Doodle's family) or forcing them to become the same as everyone else (Brother). It is possible to love, honor, and respect a being for its uniqueness. This possibility is suggested in Doodle's vision of the boy with the golden robe and the peacock. The vision is a wish-fulfillment for Doodle's own life: that instead of being singled out for his perceived inadequacies, he is singled out and adored even by the flowers for his glorious and shining appearance. However,

> "There is a sense in the story that the rough, ordinary world is not ready to receive and nurture such rare beings as Doodle or the blown-in ibis."

it is significant that saints, the scarlet ibis, and boys with peacocks do not live in the everyday world: a saint only becomes a saint after his or her death; the ibis lives in the far away tropics and when taken out of its natural environment, dies; and the boy with the peacock is only a fantasy. There is a sense in the story that the rough, ordinary world is not ready to receive and nurture such rare beings as Doodle or the blown-in ibis.

The story shows readers that the response of the world to special beings is sadly, all too often, to cut off their wings, to remain oblivious to their uniqueness and to confine them in a prison of limited expectations. Two symbols of the limited expectations that the family have for Doodle are the coffin and the go-cart. Daddy has the coffin made when he believes that Doodle will die soon after birth. When it is clear that Doodle will not die, Daddy has the go-cart made so that Brother can pull the otherwise immobile Doodle around. Daddy acts out of love, but the symbolism tells an uncomfortable truth. Both items that he makes for Doodle are small wooden boxes. The family's expectations of him fit into a small wooden box. What would a beautiful bird or a winged person, or a boy with a golden robe and a peacock, do in a small wooden box? On one hand, Daddy's actions can be seen as acceptance of his condition, but on the other hand, they shut out the possibility of change. Doodle is serenely certain that the coffin is not his—he intends to live. Both coffin and go-cart are consigned to the barn loft when it becomes evident that Doodle has grown beyond the family's limited expectations.

Brother, too, in spite of his obsession with having a sibling who will not limit him or hold him back in his activities, also puts Doodle into a box of sorts. He claims that "Renaming my brother was perhaps the kindest thing I ever did for him, because nobody expects much from someone called Doodle." Until then, Doodle had been called by the grand-sounding name of William Armstrong. Brother renames him after a lowly bug. The word "doodle" also means a hastily done, unfinished drawing, so the nickname may carry a suggestion of Doodle's disability. Brother's act in renaming his brother seems anything but kind. It is as limiting and dismissive as the family's determination that Doodle will die soon after birth. Readers are alerted to this point by Aunt Nicey's disapproval of the renaming, on the grounds that it would not befit a saint.

The ibis, like Doodle, carries the touch of the divine, its death being suggestive of that of Christ. The ibis alights in a bleeding tree, and Christ is said to have bled from his wounds on the cross. The tree may be a symbol of the cross, for Christ is said to have been crucified on a tree. The ibis dies and falls from the tree, as Christ died on the cross. The colors of the dead ibis (scarlet plumage and white veil over the eyes) are those seen in many churches at Easter. They are the symbolic colors of the Passion of Christ, evoking respectively earthly suffering and spiritual serenity, humankind and the Godhead. Doodle's kneeling before the dead ibis and reverent burial of the bird while other members of his family continue their lunch is reminiscent of those loyal disciples of Jesus who cared for his body after his death, while, presumably, the sinners and unbelievers were preoccupied with their grosser needs.

Doodle has a spiritual awareness of the course of his life. After burying the ibis, Doodle returns to the house pale, quiet, and not interested in finishing his lunch. Just as he knows that the coffin his father made for him is not his, he now seems to know that the death of the scarlet ibis foreshadows his own death. He is proved right the same day.

That Doodle, through the ibis, is symbolically linked with Christ implies that he has a transformative function in others' lives. This point is borne out in the story. Doodle creates visions of beauty and oneness with nature in Brother's mind, such as his picture of their living together in Old Woman Swamp in a house built from whispering leaves and his vision of the golden-robed boy with the peacock. This vision moves Brother to an ecstasy beyond words, so that all he can do is whisper, "Yes, yes." More importantly, Doodle provides an opportunity for Brother to learn and exercise the Christ-like virtues of unconditional love and compassion.

What Do I Read Next?

- The novel of German author Erich Maria Remarque *All Quiet on the Western Front* (1929) is a grimly realistic portrayal of experiences of ordinary German soldiers during World War I. Remarque's stance is staunchly anti-war. This novel has become the major classic fiction text relating to World War I for high-school and college students.
- In 1915, during World War I, the French Red Cross asked American novelist Edith Wharton to make a tour of military hospitals near the frontline to publicize the need for medical supplies. Wharton's articles about these visits to the frontline were collected and published in her book *Fighting France from Dunkirk to Belforte* (1915; reprinted by Greenwood Press in 1975).
- *Mental Retardation in America: A Historical Reader (The History of Disability)* (2004), edited by Steven Noll and James W. Trent, features essays by a range of authors who approach disability from differing points of view. It covers topics ranging from representations of the mentally disabled as social burdens and threats; the relationship between community care and institutional treatment; historical events such as the legalization of eugenic sterilization; the evolution of the disability rights movement; and the passage of the Americans with Disabilities Act in 1990.
- Joseph P. Shapiro's book *No Pity: People with Disabilities Forging a New Civil Rights Movement* (1994) reviews how society's relations to disabled people has been affected by the passage of the Americans with Disabilities Act. He draws on the stories of disabled people, including polio-afflicted activists, athletes, armed services veterans, and elderly people who owe their survival to medical and technological advances. While the author cites encouraging progress in disabled rights, he notes that disabled people still struggle to be accepted on equal, independent terms.

Though Brother fails to absorb this lesson while Doodle is alive, his penitent tears over Doodle's dead body and his reflections elsewhere in the story on the dangers of pride show that he has learned at last, albeit at the cost of Doodle's life. This is another suggested link between Doodle and Christ: both had to die so that those left alive could learn the gospel of love and compassion. In sheltering Doodle's body with his own from the "heresy of rain" (another Christian reference), Brother finally gives Doodle the selfless love and protection that proved so elusive while he was alive.

Source: Claire Robinson, Critical Essay on "The Scarlet Ibis," in *Short Stories for Students*, Thomson Gale, 2006.

Sheldon Goldfarb

Goldfarb has a Ph.D. in English and has published two books on the Victorian author William Makepeace Thackeray. In the following essay, Goldfarb discusses religion and duality in "The Scarlet Ibis."

"The Scarlet Ibis" is a deceptively straightforward story, apparently about the guilt the narrator feels over the death years ago of his little brother, Doodle. On the surface, the story is about not forcing people to do things beyond their abilities, about recognizing people for their own individual talents and not forcing them to fit a common mold. The unnamed narrator, known only as Brother, seems to suggest that he should not have pushed Doodle to do the normal, everyday things other little boys do: running, swimming, climbing trees, rowing a boat. Doodle, delicate and physically handicapped from birth, was not able to do these things, and pushing him to do them killed him.

> "Perhaps both the ibis and Doodle are meant to be Christ figures, dying for others' sins and somehow bringing them grace."

Yet there seems to be so much more in the story. For one thing it bristles with imagery, allusions, and symbols. There is the symbol of the scarlet ibis, the dead red bird to which Doodle is compared at the end. There are all the references to flowering and dying plants, especially in the opening paragraph, in which the narrator talks of "rotting brown magnolia petals" and "graveyard flowers" and a "bleeding tree." Moreover, there is the strange reference at the very end of the story to "the heresy of rain."

What might "the heresy of rain" mean? A heresy is a belief opposed to orthodoxy, especially orthodox religion. In the story, Brother tries to shelter Doodle's body from "the heresy of rain," though Doodle is dead and one would think beyond need of sheltering. The sheltering is clearly an action of guilt, and perhaps of belated love, and it also seems to be an attempt to preserve Doodle's similarity to the scarlet ibis. In death, Doodle is covered with blood, creating a resemblance to the scarlet bird which died earlier that day. Perhaps "the heresy of the rain" stems from the fear that the rain may wash away the blood and destroy the resemblance.

But if rain is the heresy, is the orthodoxy the notion that Doodle in some way is like the scarlet ibis? The ibis, as the children's father determines, is native to the tropics, far south of the family's home, which appears to be somewhere in rural North Carolina near Raleigh (given the reference in the story to Dix Hill, a mental institution in Raleigh). In North Carolina, the ibis is exotic and out of place. It is also full of "grace," a term which may simply mean charm but which is also a Christian term for the divine love through which human beings may obtain salvation. When the ibis arrives, it lands in a "bleeding tree," which literally means a tree oozing sap but which also suggests an allusion to the Cross on which Christ died.

Perhaps both the ibis and Doodle are meant to be Christ figures, dying for others' sins and somehow bringing them grace. Or if that is reading too much into this sad little story, then perhaps it is just about a brother's remorse. Yet the odd use of the word "heresy" at the end, along with several other references to religion, implies more meaning.

In the most triumphant part of the story, when Brother manages to teach Doodle to walk, Aunt Nicey comments that the big surprise the two boys keep promising had better be as "tremendous . . . [as] the Resurrection," and it is in a way. Raising Doodle to his feet, getting him to stand and then walk when everyone had said it was impossible seems almost akin to raising someone from the dead. Interestingly, the person who performs this resurrection is not Doodle, but Brother. It is Doodle in a way, of course, for he is the one who stands and walks, but really the work was Brother's. Brother pushes Doodle to do it, putting Doodle on his feet at least a hundred times a day and picking him up when he falls. In a telling remark, Brother says that the enterprise seemed so hopeless that "it's a miracle [he] didn't give up." This comment about working a miracle makes Brother seem like a Christ figure, having the power to work miracles and perform a resurrection.

Proud of his achievement, Brother begins to believe in "[his] own infallibility," another Christian term especially associated with the Catholic Church, which holds the pope in his exercise of his office to be infallible. Of course, in the story Brother turns out to be seriously fallible, so perhaps his association with miracles and resurrection should not be taken to mean that he is God-like, or perhaps he is some sort of false god; after all it is Doodle who is compared to the magical or sacred scarlet ibis. Aunt Nicey suggests that Doodle might turn out to be a saint, and certainly Doodle has some saint-like attributes. He is the compassionate one who goes out to bury the dead ibis while the others laugh at his awkwardness; the one who seems most inspired by nature, crying with wonder because the swamp is so pretty; and the one with a mystical imagination, conjuring stories about boys in golden robes, people with wings, and magnificent peacocks with ten-foot tails.

Perhaps Hurst is pointing out the duality of religion, especially the duality in Christian religion. Jesus, after all, can be thought of as the crucified meek and mild martyr, but also as the powerful worker of miracles who raised others and himself from the dead. Certainly, the dualities in this story suggest religious duality. On the one hand, Brother, a fairly conventional boy, is "pretty smart" at things like "holding [his] breath, running, jumping, or climbing the vines." On the other hand, Doodle can hardly do any of those things, but he has a gift for storytelling, loves to talk, and is compassionate and full of wonder at natural beauty.

Unfortunately, even years later Brother does not seem to recognize Doodle's talents. Doodle's storytelling Brother calls "lying"; his talk is ignored by the rest of the family; and his compassion for the dead ibis is scorned by them. Only by comparing Doodle to the ibis does Brother seem to suggest that Doodle was at all special. More typically, Brother refers to Doodle as crazy, though he does say Doodle was not "a crazy crazy," just "a nice crazy, like someone you meet in your dreams." This last comment indicates that there may have been something magical about Doodle, but mostly what Brother seems to express is his guilt over forcing Doodle to do things that were beyond him. Brother seems unaware that there was something that Doodle could do that was beyond the others.

The story itself, though, does seem to bring this message home, as if to say that, in a world of dualities, dualities are needed. There is a need for the active side of life, the running and the jumping and the climbing, and also for the more contemplative and mystical side, the Brother side and the Doodle side. Moreover, it is important that everyone has at least a little of each: even Doodle wants to be able to move around a little; on his own he strives to crawl, not content to remain motionless on his stomach on the bed in the front room. When he learns to walk, he is happy; the whole story is happy, with "Hope no longer hid . . . but . . . brilliantly visible" and Doodle and Brother crying for joy while they lie on the soft grass smelling the sweetness of the swamp.

Of course, that the sweetness is in a swamp may give readers pause; with every positive there comes a negative, it seems. The very opening of the story is about bright flowers which seem full of life but which are also dying. Life and death exist together, and in Brother's feelings for Doodle both affection and cruelty exist, as he says himself when explaining why he forced Doodle to touch the little coffin.

It would be easy to interpret the story as a condemnation of Brother and his ordinary way of life, with praise for Doodle's contrasting mystical qualities. The story does seem to suggest that special qualities such as Doodle has should be respected and that someone like Doodle, who has talents of a certain type, should not be forced to ignore those talents in favor of running and climbing and jumping. But the story does not reject these activities outright. When Doodle expresses reluctance about learning to walk and says he just "can't do it," when he says that instead of practicing they should just make honeysuckle wreaths, the story does not seem to agree with him. It turns out that he can learn to walk and is happy to do so. If there is magic and godliness in the spiritual life, so there is some too in the life of physical activity. The world needs both, the story seems to say.

The danger comes when one side of life crushes out the other: when Brother pushes Doodle to become just like an ordinary boy, he pushes too hard. He does not allow for differences. To Brother it is a horrible thing to be "different from everybody else," and he is especially worried that his little brother will leave him open to shame if he is still different when he starts school. At some level Brother has thought that it would be better to have no brother at all than a brother who might shame him. When Doodle was first born and it seemed that he might be mentally as well as physically handicapped, Brother even thought of smothering him. When it becomes clear that Doodle is "all there," Brother gives up his overt plan to kill him, but in some sense he kills him still, all because Doodle is different.

The effect is sadness, not only at the end of the story, when Brother cradles his dead brother, but at the very beginning when Brother describes his life years later. Instead of a garden of riotous flowers, some rotting and rank but others blooming, instead of a wild, living land, Brother now has a "prim" garden, a house that is gleaming white, and a "pale fence" standing "straight and spruce." It sounds clean and neat, but also sterile, and instead of the bleeding tree there is a grindstone, something mechanical instead of natural, something lifeless, something that never had life in it.

Ultimately a question remains about "the heresy of rain." For Brother, the rain attempts to kill the magical ibis quality of his little brother, Doodle. If having the grace of true religion in this story means being scarlet like the ibis, then the rain that washes away the scarlet blood is the enemy. But it was Brother's own shame that killed Doodle, and the true heresy seems to be the fear of difference, the fear of dualities, the fear of accepting contrasting aspects. True religion, this story seems to say, consists in acknowledging and accepting both sides of life, the active and the spiritual. When one side destroys the other, the result is death or worse than death, a lifeless existence of grindstones, prim gardens, and pale fences instead of the joyous experience of death-in-life in the swamp.

Source: Sheldon Goldfarb, Critical Essay on "The Scarlet Ibis," in *Short Stories for Students*, Thomson Gale, 2006.

David Remy

Remy is a freelance writer in Warrington, Florida. In the following essay, Remy examines the ways in which Hurst's narrative strategies control time and influence the story's interpretation.

Though laden with symbolism, "The Scarlet Ibis" is a story that combines elements of biblical fable, romance, and mystery to capture the reader's interest. It is the way in which the story is told, rather than its symbolic content, however, that makes the "The Scarlet Ibis" linger in the reader's imagination. Part of this attraction derives from Hurst's creating a narrative structure that is as anomalous as the bird itself, for he incorporates narrative techniques that are not traditionally found in the short story. Nevertheless, the narrative moves at a pace that makes the reader want to know what happens and why, the reader's sense of time and causality influenced by the narrative point of view. Through narrative techniques that illuminate the brothers' relationship as the story moves from present to past, the narrator, Brother, manipulates time to create an air of mystery, arousing the reader's suspicion that, indeed, Doodle's death, unlike that of the scarlet ibis, may have been the result of design rather than accident.

By using a first-person narrator to tell the story, Hurst immediately establishes rapport between the reader and the narrator, whose voice remains personal and convincing from beginning to end. Moreover, the narrator, Brother, is always at the center of the story's action. It is through his eyes that the reader understands Doodle's character and the sequence of events that leads to the story's melodramatic climax. However, one of the limitations of the first-person narrator is that he or she can only express his or her thoughts and perceptions. Despite having a strong even domineering character, Brother lacks omniscience.

The benefits of using a first-person narrator far outweigh the detriments, however, for Brother elicits the reader's sympathy from the outset, shaping causality and structuring time to enhance his account of events. As the narrator, Brother determines *when* the reader receives information. The story's chronology, which moves from the present to the past, with compressed periods of time omitted in between, influences the reader's understanding of how the story unfolds. The order of events is structured so that it supports Brother's beliefs and perceptions, his way of viewing the world. Therefore, Brother establishes an emotional and temporal distance as he looks upon his younger self, a narrative stance that invites the reader to identify with the wiser, more mature adult he has become.

Although not commonly found in the short story form, a circular narrative allows Brother to record the movement of time and evoke a bygone era. The seasons and the school year serve as guideposts for the trials and tribulations, the successes and failures that mark a boy's coming of age. There is a cyclical movement of time associated with these traditional beginnings and endings, a rhythm closely tied to nature and to the expectations Brother places upon himself and Doodle. Now, many years after the "clove of seasons," the present meets the past to close the circle, raising the reader's curiosity about why Brother chooses this particular time and place to tell his story.

Another narrative technique not traditionally found in the short story is the flashback, which, because the short story form usually emphasizes a particular moment in time rather than several periods extended over a longer period, is better suited for narrating events that occur within a novel. Nonetheless, Hurst uses flashback to great effect in "The Scarlet Ibis" because of the story's focus on the sweep of personal history and the transformation that has apparently occurred within the narrator. Brother evokes the past to help the reader understand the present, especially as it relates to the narrator's sense of loss. The opening paragraphs are suffused with images of death and decay, and, in this respect, the use of flashback establishes a vivid contrast between the present and Brother's vision of his childhood life in and around Old Woman Swamp.

The image of the revolving grindstone signals the beginning of the flashback, transporting the reader to a more innocent time that Brother remembers with a mixture of fondness and regret. Here the reader pauses to wonder if, perhaps, Brother is embarking on a type of confession story, one that will account for the narrative's melancholic tone. Regardless, that tone soon dissipates as Brother tells the reader about his success in giving his baby brother a name that is not only appropriate given his handicaps but which is actually preferred by the family. The tone becomes proud and almost defiant when Brother tells of how he, through sheer will and perseverance, was able to work a miracle in making Doodle walk. The flashback records Brother's triumphs as he dominates his younger brother. Each test that Doodle passes leads to yet another, more difficult test of his loyalty. Normally, a flashback ends when the present intrudes upon the past, thus bringing the narrative full circle, yet Brother never returns the story to the present moment. Instead, he remains focused on the past, making the reader wonder why.

Hurst introduces a different kind of time by introducing parallels to the archetypal brothers in conflict, the biblical story of Cain and Abel. This parallel Hurst helps the reader identify the roles his characters play. Brother and Doodle's relationship to each other becomes clearer against the backdrop of history or fable. Thus, this parallel functions like a narrative "shortcut," a way of establishing for the author a mythopoetic context in which the story's action occurs. In "The Scarlet Ibis," the archetypes of the good, obedient brother and the proud, covetous one stand outside time, for the essential qualities of each character have remained intact through the ages. The relationship between the brothers represents a moral flaw inherent to human nature—namely, that even the best of intentions can lead to deadly rivalry when pride becomes too strong.

Since Brother is the story's narrator, he becomes the author's obvious choice for bearing the weight of the biblical parallel. From the very beginning of the flashback sequence, Brother tells the reader that he wants a brother, someone "to race [with] to Horsehead Landing, someone to box with, and someone to perch with in the top fork of the great pine behind the barn, where across the fields and swamps you could see the sea." Brother desires a companion against whom he may measure himself and with whom he may share nature's beauty. Yet, instead of having a brother who is his equal, someone who could push him to greater heights of achievement, Brother finds himself having to care for Doodle, whom he refers to as a "disappointment" and a "burden." Like Cain, Brother *is* his brother's keeper; hence, his name resonates with biblical—and moral—significance.

Hurst extends the similarity in sibling rivalry by bestowing upon Brother traits that are associated with Cain, whom the Bible records as the first person to commit murder. Rather than focusing on this aspect of Cain's biography, however, Hurst establishes other parallels. Like Cain, who was a farmer, a man who tilled the soil and harvested its yield, Brother possesses an extensive knowledge of plant life, especially that found in the swamp. Indeed, Brother's childhood knowledge of botany is

"Brother establishes an emotional and temporal distance as he looks upon his younger self, a narrative stance that invites the reader to identify with the wiser, more mature adult he has become."

extraordinary. But Cain's dominion over the earth does not last forever, for the soil becomes cursed once he spills Abel's blood upon the ground. Similarly, Brother views nature as dead and decaying years after the "clove of seasons":

> The flower garden was stained with rotting brown magnolia petals and ironweeds grew rank amid the purple phlox. The five o'clocks by the chimney still marked time, but the oriole nest in the elm was untenanted and rocked back and forth like an empty cradle. The last graveyard flowers were blooming, and their smell drifted across the cotton field and through every room of our house, speaking softly the names of our dead.

Brother's sense is that time has been suspended, separated from nature's recurrent nurturing elements, though the reader does not yet understand why.

Another character trait that clarifies and develops the correspondence between Brother and Cain is pride. When asked by God where Abel is, Cain, who has recently murdered his brother in a field, is proud enough—and defiant enough—to respond to God's question with one of his own: "Am I my brother's keeper?" Cain's pride and defiance fuel his capacity for violence. When God learns of Abel's murder, he places a mark on Cain so that no one may seek vengeance, and thus Cain wanders the earth forever like a vagabond. Though his whereabouts for the past several years remain unknown, Brother also possesses the potential for violence, which is the biblical legacy that has been handed down to him. Brother's violent tendencies are perhaps more shocking when the reader realizes that he regards life and death matter-of-factly, as though his being inconvenienced is of paramount importance: "It was bad enough having an invalid brother, but having one who possibly was not all there was unbearable, so I began to make plans to kill him by smothering him with a pillow." Whether Brother tries later to act out this impulse remains unclear.

Brother's cruelty toward Doodle, however, is not impulsive, erupting in brief flashes of anger that dissipate quickly and are soon forgotten; rather, Brother's cruelty is sustained like an undercurrent of malice, for the tests he makes Doodle endure are both a product and a measure of Brother's self-aggrandizement. Brother is able to control his cruelty only because his pride—and the adulation that he seeks from adults—needs reinforcement. This need for reinforcement and a narcissistic love temper Brother's actions, though his penchant for understatement reveals that he never fully comprehends the extent of suffering he causes his brother: "There is within me . . . a knot of cruelty borne by the stream of love, much as our blood sometimes bears the seed of our destruction, and at times I was mean to Doodle." This cruelty first appears when Brother takes Doodle up to the loft to touch his coffin, a scene in which Doodle's cry—"Don't leave me. Don't leave me."—foreshadows the story's ending. When Brother finally expresses his sincere remorse, it is from a moral and emotional viewpoint tempered by the passage of time: "I did not know then that pride is a wonderful, terrible thing, a seed that bears two vines, life and death." Unfortunately for Doodle, Brother's realization arrives too late.

Hurst combines narrative elements to create an air of mystery and suspense in the story, revealing an outcome that is far from certain. The use of a circular structure and the tone of the story's narration inform the reader that Brother has survived some traumatic and life-altering event, for he cannot look at nature in the same way he did before. The paradise he enjoyed as a boy is gone forever. Obviously, this loss is connected to Doodle, but Hurst leaves the reader to decide the extent of that association. Furthermore, the story's first-person narration makes the reader question whether Brother is an unreliable narrator. This is a conceit that Hurst develops later in the story, though from the outset Brother's narrative style causes the reader to wonder what information, if any, he may conceal. Parallels to Cain and Abel compound a sense of impending violence, one that is satisfied rather anticlimactically at the story's end.

Hurst, however, carries the Cain and Abel parallel only so far, forcing the reader to adjust his or her expectations. Although the reader knows that Brother will not accept Doodle's failure to attain the desired skills and level of fitness before the school year begins, the question remains about how cruel Brother will be when he confronts his disappointment, for he takes Doodle's failure personally. Brother has already shown, in the scenes involving Doodle's casket and his various tests of physical endurance, that he can be merciless in making his younger brother conform to his ideal of normal health and physical agility. Doodle is aware that he will bear the brunt of his brother's anger and disappointment. Brother acknowledges as much when he says, "I knew he was watching me, watching for a sign of mercy."

However, just as Hurst builds the story's suspense to an almost unbearable level, Brother casts doubt in the reader's mind about the sequence of events that have transpired and which are to follow. The story builds to a climax, yet not all of the pieces of the story lead to a satisfactory conclusion. With first-person narration, the reader knows only the version of events that the narrator chooses to tell, and it is important to remember here one aspect of the story that, until now, seems out of place, not only with regard to the narrative but also with regard to Brother's character.

By Brother's own admission, the only thing Doodle was good at was "lying," which is, the way Brother describes it, merely the exercise of a child's imagination. Doodle's "lies," which are never uttered by him directly but are told from Brother's point of view, are fanciful tales, not malicious acts of gossip. However, in telling the reader that Doodle was a good liar, thus indicating, by implied comparison, that he, the narrator, is a bad one, is Brother himself engaged in the act of lying? Given his pride and his competitive nature, it seems improbable that Brother would be willing to make such a concession if it did not suit his purposes somehow. Thus, Hurst creates suspense by making the reader question the veracity of Brother's story. The unreliable narrator is one of the most popular characters in fiction because, during the course of reading the story, the reader acquires a wider range of knowledge than does the narrator. There is an element of surprise when contradictions reveal themselves. Because the narrator is unreliable, events described within a story may lead to moments of dramatic irony, which appears to be Hurst's authorial intent.

As the story nears its end, it seems ironic that Brother, who has kept Doodle within his sight almost from the moment he was born, should not be present during his brother's moment of greatest need. This contradiction indicates more than just a lapse in character; it indicates a narrative gap which raises a question about how Doodle actually died. Was it death by misadventure, suicide, or murder? Did Doodle possess enough knowledge of plant life to choose the deadly nightshade as his instrument of release? The only character who could possibly answer these questions is Brother, who, as both character and narrator, has proven himself to be less than trustworthy.

Throughout the story, Hurst employs a combination of narrative techniques that imbue "The Scarlet Ibis" with an air of intrigue and mystery. The story's open-ended conclusion ensures that the characters and events retain a timeless quality long after Brother finishes telling his sad tale of loss and regret.

Source: David Remy, Critical Essay on "The Scarlet Ibis," in *Short Stories for Students*, Thomson Gale, 2006.

Sources

Ebor, Donald, ed., *The New English Bible with Apocrypha*, New York: Oxford University Press, 1972, pp. 4–5.

Hurst, James, Telephone conversations with author, July and September 2005.

———, "The Scarlet Ibis," in the *Atlantic Monthly*, July 1960, pp. 48–53.

King James Bible, Deuteronomy 5:9.

Trent, James W., Jr., *Inventing the Feeble Mind: A History of Mental Retardation in the United States*, University of California Press, 1994, p. 199.

Further Reading

Keegan, John, *The First World War*, Vintage, 2000.
This book is a vivid account of the causes and progress of World War I, drawing on diaries, letters, and action reports of the time. Keegan concludes that the war was unnecessary.

Keller, Helen, *The Story of My Life*, Bantam Classics, 1990.
Born deaf and blind, Keller refused to be crushed by her disabilities and went on to become an effective suffragist, pacifist, social reformer, and author. She helped start several foundations that in the early 2000s continue to help the deaf and blind. This joyful, perceptive, and beautifully written autobiography is credited with helping to change social attitudes toward the disabled.

Nies, Betsy L., *Eugenic Fantasies: Racial Ideology in the Literature and Popular Culture of the 1920s*, Routledge, 2001.
Nies draws on psychoanalytic theory, anthropology, and literary theory to argue that the rise of eugenics served as a palliative for anxieties over war-torn bodies and a means of repairing the loss of belief in the white male as defender of the nation.

Trent, James W., *Inventing the Feeble Mind: A History of Mental Retardation in the United States*, University of California Press, 1995.
Trent traces the U.S. history of treatment of disabled people, including institutionalization, neglect, sterilization, medical abuse, and mistreatment. The book is illustrated with disturbing photographs.

A Small, Good Thing

Raymond Carver

1983

"A Small, Good Thing," an award-winning story by American short story writer and poet, Raymond Carver, was published in Carver's third major collection of stories, *Cathedral*, in 1983. In his first two collections, Carver had established himself as a new and compelling voice in American literature and a master of the short story form. In *Cathedral*, he took his craft to new levels of insight into the human condition. "A Small, Good Thing" is generally regarded as one of Carver's finest stories, in which he goes beyond the spare narratives and unrelieved bleakness of some of his earlier work. The story is about Scotty, an eight-year-old boy who dies three days after being hit by a car as he walks to school. In language that is simple on the surface but reveals a host of telling details, Carver depicts the grief of the parents and their quarrel and final reconciliation with a baker who was baking a birthday cake for Scotty. Although tragic and disturbing, "A Small, Good Thing" conveys a message of forgiveness, kindness, and the healing power of human community.

Author Biography

Raymond Carver was born on May 25, 1938, in Clatskanie, Oregon, the son of Clevie Raymond, a laborer, and Ella Beatrice Raymond, a homemaker. In 1941, the family moved to Yakima, Washington.

Carver's father was a great storyteller and also read aloud to his son. Carver later attributed his desire to become a writer to his father. During adolescence Carver enjoyed fishing, hunting, and baseball, but his main goal was to write. He graduated from Yakima High School in 1956 and the following year married Maryann Burk, who was sixteen years old. By 1958, they had a daughter and a son and had moved to Paradise, California, where Carver entered Chico State College. At Chico, Carver studied under the novelist John Gardner.

For the next decade or so, Carver worked at a series of low-wage jobs, including gas station attendant and hospital cleaner, in order to support his family while he also continued his education. He received a degree from Humboldt State College in 1963, after which he moved to Iowa and enrolled in the Iowa Writers' Workshop. But due to lack of money he was unable to finish the two-year program. He returned to California in 1964 and lived in Sacramento, where he continued to work at odd jobs for several years. In 1967, he filed for bankruptcy and also had a drinking problem, but he was beginning to make his mark as a writer. His story "Will You Please Be Quiet, Please?" was included in *The Best American Short Stories, 1967*. In 1968, his first book of poems, *Near Klamath*, was published, followed in 1970 by a second collection, *Winter Insomnia*.

In the early 1970s, Carver took on a series of temporary teaching positions, at the University of California at Santa Cruz, then University of California at Berkeley, and the Iowa Writers' Workshop. However, teaching seemed to exacerbate Carver's alcohol abuse, and in 1974, he was fired from the University of California at Santa Barbara for failure to meet with his classes. He filed for bankruptcy again.

In 1976, Carver's first collection of stories, *Will You Please Be Quiet, Please?*, was published by McGraw-Hill to critical acclaim. However, Carver was still plagued by alcoholism and was hospitalized several times for treatment. He finally gave up alcohol in June 1977, and his life took a more positive turn. In that year, his second collection of stories, *Furious Seasons*, was published by Capra Press.

In 1981, Carver's third collection of stories, *What We Talk About When We Talk About Love*, was published by Knopf. Critical praise was unanimous, and Carver was regarded as a master of the short story genre. In 1983, another collection of stories appeared, again published by Knopf. This was *Cathedral*, which contained the story "A Small, Good Thing." The book was nominated for a National Book Critics Circle Award and the Pulitzer Prize. "A Small, Good Thing" won an O. Henry Award and appeared in the Pushcart Prize annual.

Raymond Carver © Sophie Bassouls/Corbis Sygma

In 1984, Carver, who had by this time divorced his first wife and was living with the poet Tess Gallagher, moved to Port Angeles, Washington. His collection of poetry, *Where Water Comes Together with Water*, was published by Random House in 1985, and another poetry collection, *Ultramarine*, appeared in 1986.

In 1987, Carver, who was a heavy smoker, was diagnosed with lung cancer. Two-thirds of his left lung was removed, but the cancer reappeared the following year. In June 1988, Carver married Tess Gallagher. He died of lung cancer on August 2 at his home in Port Washington.

Plot Summary

"A Small, Good Thing" begins on a Saturday afternoon in an unnamed American city. Ann Weiss, a young mother, drives to the shopping center and orders a chocolate cake for her son Scotty's eighth birthday, which will be on Monday. The baker is a taciturn man, and Ann does not take to him.

He promises the cake will be ready on Monday morning.

On Monday morning, Scotty is walking to school with another boy when he steps off the curb at an intersection and is knocked down by a car. The car stops but when Scotty gets to his feet and looks as if he is all right, the car leaves the scene. Scotty walks home but then collapses on the sofa and loses consciousness. He is taken to the hospital, where he is diagnosed with mild concussion and shock. He is in a deep sleep, but Dr. Francis, his doctor, says this is not a coma. Ann and her husband, Howard, wait anxiously at the bedside.

That evening, Howard returns home to bathe and change clothes. As he walks in the door, the phone rings. A voice on the other end of the line says there is a cake that was not picked up. Howard does not know what the man is talking about and hangs up. While Howard is bathing, the phone rings again, but the caller hangs up without saying a word.

Howard returns to the hospital after midnight. Scotty has still not awakened, but Dr. Francis insists there is nothing to worry about and that he will wake up soon. A nurse comes in and checks on Scotty. She tells the parents he is stable. The parents are worried but try to reassure themselves. Dr. Francis examines Scotty and again says he is all right other than a hairline fracture of the skull. He is not, according to the doctor, in a coma; his sleeping is the restorative measure the body is taking in response to shock, and he should wake up soon.

The parents try to comfort each other. Both of them have been praying. An hour later, another doctor, Dr. Parsons, enters the room and tells the parents that they want to take more x-rays of Scotty, and they also want to do a brain scan. He explains that this is normal medical procedure. Scotty is wheeled out on a gurney. His parents accompany him to the x-ray department and then return with him to his hospital room.

They wait all day, but Scotty still does not wake up. Dr. Francis continues to assure them that the boy will wake soon, but Ann and Howard become increasingly anxious. On his next visit, Dr. Francis confesses that there is no reason why Scotty has not awakened yet, but he still insists the boy is in no danger. Pressed by Ann, he admits that Scotty is in a coma, but that all the signs are good.

Ann goes home to take a bath and feed the dog. On her way out of the hospital, she cannot find the elevator and enters a small waiting room in which a black man and his wife and teenage daughter are waiting for news of their son, Franklin. The man explains to Ann that Franklin was stabbed in a fight, even though he was not directly involved in it.

Ann returns home. At five o'clock in the morning, after she has just fed the dog, the phone rings. The man says a few words, mentioning a problem to do with Scotty, and then hangs up. Ann calls the hospital, but there has been no change in Scotty's condition. Howard thinks the caller may have been the same person who called him earlier. He wonders whether it might be the driver of the car who knocked Scotty down. Maybe the man is a psychopath and has somehow got hold of their telephone number, he suggests.

Just before seven in the morning, Ann returns to the hospital, where she inquires at a nurses' station about the condition of Franklin. A nurse informs her that Franklin died. When Ann enters Scotty's room, Howard tells her that the doctors have decided to run more tests on the boy. They are going to operate on him, since they do not know why he is not waking up. Just then Scotty opens his eyes and stares straight ahead, then at his parents. The parents are relieved and talk to him, but he does not respond. He opens his mouth and howls, then seems to relax, but stops breathing.

The doctors say that his death is caused by a hidden occlusion, and that it was a one-in-a-million chance. Dr. Francis is shaken and commiserates with Ann and Howard. He says there will be an autopsy.

At about eleven o'clock, the Weisses drive home and try to deal with their shock and grief. Ann calls her relatives; Howard goes outside to the garage, where he sits down and holds Scotty's bicycle. Then the phone rings, and it is once more the mystery caller, talking about Scotty. Ann swears at him and hangs up. She collapses over the table and weeps.

Much later, just before midnight, the phone rings. Howard answers, but the line goes dead. They both know that it is the same caller. Ann says she would like to kill him. Then she suddenly remembers the birthday cake and realizes that it has been the baker calling her to harass her for not collecting the cake.

Ann and Howard drive to the shopping center to confront the baker, even though it is about midnight. Ann knocks twice on the back door of the bakery. The baker comes to the door and recognizes Ann but says he is busy. He says he still has the three-day old cake and she can collect it if she wants to, for half-price. He repeats that he is busy and has to get back to work. Ann angrily tells him that Scotty is dead. She feels dizzy and begins to cry.

The baker's manner softens. He fetches two chairs and asks Ann and Howard to sit down. He sits down also and tells them how sorry he is about Scotty's death and sorry for his behavior, too. He asks them to forgive him. He makes them some coffee and offers them some fresh-baked cinnamon rolls. He says it is good to eat something in a time like this. Ann eats three rolls, and she and Howard listen as the baker tells them about his loneliness and what it feels like to be childless. He speaks of his repetitive, empty work as a baker, preparing for other people's celebrations. They talk until daylight, and neither Ann nor Howard thinks about leaving.

Characters

The Baker

The baker is a somber, taciturn man with an abrupt manner. He is probably in his fifties. When Ann orders the birthday cake from him, he will not chat or be friendly with her, and his behavior makes her uncomfortable. When Ann does not collect the birthday cake, the baker makes harassing phone calls to her home. But later he asks for forgiveness, acknowledging that he was in the wrong. It transpires that he is lonely and childless. In spite of the fact that he is constantly busy as a baker, he feels his life is empty. He has forgotten whatever dreams he may once have had for his life, but he shows some kindness and compassion for Ann and Howard.

The Black Man

The middle-aged black man waits at the hospital with his wife and daughter as his son Franklin undergoes an operation.

Dr. Francis

Dr. Francis is in charge of Scotty's treatment at the hospital. He is handsome, tanned, and wears a three-piece suit. His manner is reassuring and kind.

Dr. Parsons

Dr. Parsons works in the radiology department at the hospital.

Ann Weiss

Thirty-three year old, Ann Weiss is the wife of Howard and mother of Scotty. She lives a comfortable middle-class life and is devoted to raising her young son. Grief-stricken by his death, she is aroused to fierce anger by the behavior of the baker and goes to confront him. But she calms down as the baker talks, offers her something to eat and tells her of his life.

Howard Weiss

Howard Weiss, husband of Ann and father of Scotty, is well educated, with a graduate degree in business, and is junior partner in an investment firm. He is happy with his successful life. Nothing bad has happened to him until the accident involving Scotty.

Scotty Weiss

Scotty Weiss is the son of Howard and Ann Weiss. On the morning of his eighth birthday, he is walking to school when he steps off the curb at an intersection and is hit by a car. He walks home but collapses on the sofa. In the hospital he slips into a coma. After seeming to regain consciousness for a moment, he dies.

Themes

Compassion, Forgiveness, and Community

The death of Scotty is a heart-wrenching tragedy, but out of it, from the most unlikely of sources, comes compassion, the opportunity for forgiveness, and the creation of a sense of human community in the face of the suffering that is common to all.

The situation at the beginning of the story seems perfect. A loving mother orders a birthday cake for her young son's birthday party. What could be more representative in microcosm of the joys of human community than a birthday party for a child? Then comes the tragic accident, and the precariousness of human happiness is revealed.

Before her world is shattered, Ann Weiss shows herself to be a person who likes to make connections with others; she likes to communicate and be friendly. When she first encounters the baker, she tries to engage him in conversation, but he will not be drawn out of his gruff, taciturn manner. He makes no comment at all about the child and his birthday party. As Ann thinks about him,

Topics For Further Study

- Do some Internet research on the medical condition known as coma and make a class presentation about it. What is a coma? What causes people to fall into a coma? Do people recover from comas? What treatment is given to people in a coma?
- Research the role played by food and the eating of food in religious rituals. What is the connection between food and spirituality? Why do many religions have dietary laws or restrictions? What purpose do they serve? You may use examples from any religious tradition. Write an essay that describes your findings.
- Write a poem based on "A Small, Good Thing." Try to convey the story and its theme in no more than 20-25 lines. Your poem can be in any form and told from any point of view. As an alternative, you could write the story as a song of maybe 5-6 verses. Remember that in either poem or song, you will not be able to include all the details that are found in the story. You need to pick out the most important elements and find ways of expressing them in the new form.
- Read the story "The Cathedral," by Carver, and write a short essay comparing it to "A Small, Good Thing." In what ways are the two stories similar? Which story do you prefer, and why?

she seems subconsciously to search for some way in which she might connect with him. She seeks the common, human element, and thinks that because he is an older man, he must have children somewhere who must have had their cakes and birthday parties: "There must be that between them, she thought." But she is still unable to befriend him because he insists on keeping a mental wall between them.

A similar incident occurs later in the story, when Ann is in the midst of her family crisis. She still seeks connection with others, a bridge between separate, private worlds. When she meets the parents who are waiting for news of their son, Franklin, she wants to talk more with them, since they are in a situation similar to hers: "She was afraid, and they were afraid. They had that in common." She wants to tell them more about the accident to Scotty, but she does not know how to begin: "She stood looking at them without saying anything more." Again, even though she senses the connections between very different people—the family is black, the baker is much older than she—she is unable to articulate it or get others to feel it.

The emerging dynamic of the story is therefore between community and isolation, or between distance (separation) and communication and closeness. Ann and Howard are examples of closeness; they are a loving couple who had a warm family life with their young son. The sympathetic and kind Dr. Francis is also able to share in this sense of fellowship between humans. After Scotty's death, as Dr. Francis consoles Ann, "He seemed full of some goodness she didn't understand."

But the baker places himself outside that circle of community. He does not permit himself to reach out to others. This is clear from his interaction with Ann at the beginning, but it becomes more pronounced in the phone calls he makes to the Weisses' home. At first, he is merely unlucky. It is quite reasonable for him to call and point out that the cake has not been collected; he just happens to catch Howard at the wrong time, and Howard knows no more about a birthday cake than the baker does of Scotty's accident. It is an unfortunate incident, ripe with misunderstanding, and demonstrates how easily in this story things can go wrong. But after this incident, the baker is more culpable. He allows his resentment that the cake has not been collected to fester, and he makes harassing calls. Unwittingly, he is completely at odds with what the situation demands; where empathy and compassion are called for, he offers only malice.

Only at the end of the story does this situation change. In the most unlikely of circumstances, the three people in the bakery manage to reach out to one another. This happens only after they reach an extreme of hostility and lack of understanding. It is the baker who makes the first move by apologizing, asking for forgiveness, and talking about his own frustrations and disappointments. They all learn that what they have in common is suffering. This is the bond that, when acknowledged, leads to compassion and understanding. The baker in his loneliness, and Ann and Howard in their grief, in the darkness of the night and the warmth of the bakery, create for themselves a renewal of the bonds of community through the simple ritual of sharing food.

Style

Setting

Other than the fact that the story appears to be set in the United States, there is a lack of specificity in the setting. The town is unnamed and could be anywhere. Also, there are few clues as to when the story takes place. It was published in 1983 but could as easily be set in 1963 or 2003. It seems to take place within a kind of bubble, without reference to anything larger than itself. The only clue comes when Ann refers to the black man and woman as Negroes, a term not much used to describe black people after the 1960s.

The lack of extraneous detail has the effect of making the stark drama and tragedy of the story stand out in sharper relief. As Carver once said in an interview with David Applefield: "My stories take place on a personal level as opposed to a larger political or social arena."

Symbolism

There is a suggestion of religious ritual in the way that the baker breaks the dark bread and shares it with Ann and Howard at the end of the story. It recalls the Catholic ritual of the Eucharist, in which the bread offered by the priest is believed to be the body of Christ. The incident is emphasized by the descriptions of the smell and taste of the bread and the physical action of eating ("They swallowed the dark bread"). The religious symbolism adds solidity and depth to this unexpected moment of communion between the three people, in which they are able to ease their troubles by sharing them. It is perhaps no coincidence that immediately afterwards, imagery of light appears twice: "It was like daylight under the fluorescent trays of light," and the three of them stay talking until the early morning, when "the high, pale cast of light in the windows" appears. The imagery of light suggests that even in the darkest tragedy, some hope is possible.

Historical Context

Minimalism

Carver's work is in the tradition of realism. When he began to publish his short stories in the 1970s, the dominant mode of literary fiction was not realism but what was sometimes called metafiction, a complex, experimental form that was as much about writing itself as about telling a story. This kind of postmodernist writing was practiced by writers such as Robert Coover, Thomas Pynchon, and Kurt Vonnegut.

Carver was not attracted to this form, and he returned to the earlier literary tradition of realism, in which the writer is more interested in presenting mundane, everyday life as it is experienced by the ordinary person. However, Carver's realism was markedly different from its nineteenth-century form, in which the elements of fiction such as character and setting were described at length and in great detail.

In contrast, Carver's work is associated with the literary movement known as minimalism, which came to dominate American short story writing in the late 1970s and 1980s. The term is a problematic one and applies more to Carver's earlier stories, up to and including the collection, *What We Talk about When We Talk about Love* (1981), than to the more filled-out stories in *Cathedral* (1983).

Minimalism is a pared down form of realism that is often distinguished more by what it leaves out than what it puts in. Novelist and short story writer, John Barth, who is known as a maximalist rather than a minimalist, described it in the *New York Times Book Review* in 1986 as "terse, oblique, realistic or hyperrealistic, slightly plotted, extrospective, cool-surfaced fiction" (quoted in Randolph Paul Runyon's *Reading Raymond Carver*). In *Understanding Raymond Carver*, Arthur M. Saltzman defines minimalism as short fiction that features "flatness of narrative tone, extreme sparseness of story, an obsession with the drab and the quotidian, a general avoidance of extensive rumination on the page, and, in sum, a striking restraint in prose style."

Compare & Contrast

- **1980s:** Carver writes mainly about people at the lower end of the socio-economic scale, and during the 1980s, the gap between the rich and the poor in the United States increases. Homelessness becomes a large social problem. It is caused by the lack of affordable housing, higher rates of joblessness, and reductions in public welfare programs that take place during the administration of President Ronald Reagan (1981–89).

  Today: Homelessness remains a social problem that successive governments fail to tackle. Housing prices continue to rise, and people working in minimum-wage jobs are increasingly unable to afford them. There are no accurate national figures on the number of homeless people in the United States. However, by way of example, in Los Angeles in 2005, an estimated 85,000 people experience homelessness every day, according to the Institute for the Study of Homelessness and Poverty at the Weingart Center, Los Angeles. In New York, an estimated 37,000 people are in shelters every night, according to the Coalition for the Homeless, New York. This figure is the highest number of homeless in New York since the Great Depression.

- **1980s:** The plot of "A Small, Good Thing" turns on telephone calls received by the husband and wife. In the 1980s, not everyone has answering machines, and there are no features such as Caller ID. Cordless phones first appear around 1980. However, they have limited range and poor sound quality and can easily be intercepted by another cordless phone. In 1986, the Federal Communications Commission grants cordless phones a different frequency, but there are still problems with range and sound quality.

  Today: With features such as voice mail and call waiting, people have many ways of receiving telephone calls and messages. Cellular or wireless telephones are nearly as common as traditional wired telephones. Millions of people use them. They have an array of functions, enabling the user to store information, make to-do lists, keep track of appointments, send or receive email, get news and other information, and play simple games. According to a study commissioned by Motorola, cell phones are changing the way people live and work. The study finds that cell phones give people a sense of personal power. Young people in particular use cell phones to send text messages, often using what has been called "generation text," which incorporates abbreviations that young people all over the world recognize.

- **1980s:** The number of deaths from motor vehicle accidents is lower than in the 1970s. The death rate falls further during the early years of the decade before rising again in every year from 1985 to 1988. In 1988, there are 48,900 deaths from motor vehicle crashes.

  Today: Deaths and injuries resulting from motor vehicle crashes are the leading cause of death for persons of every age from two through thirty-three years of age (based on 2000 data). However, traffic fatalities are falling. In 2003, the fatality rate per 100 million vehicle miles of travel falls to a historic low of 1.48, with 42,643 people killed. Much of the decrease is attributable to increased use of seat belts and a reduction in the number of people who drive while over the legal limit for alcohol.

Minimalism has been used to describe a wide variety of writers, including, in addition to Carver, Frederick Barthelme, Ann Beattie, Bobbie Ann Mason, James Robison, Mary Robison, Tobias Wolff, and others. But no writer labeled a minimalist has welcomed the term as a description of his or her work, and most writers would deny the existence of a single "minimalist school." Carver himself, although often regarded as a leader of the minimalists, rejected the term as applied to

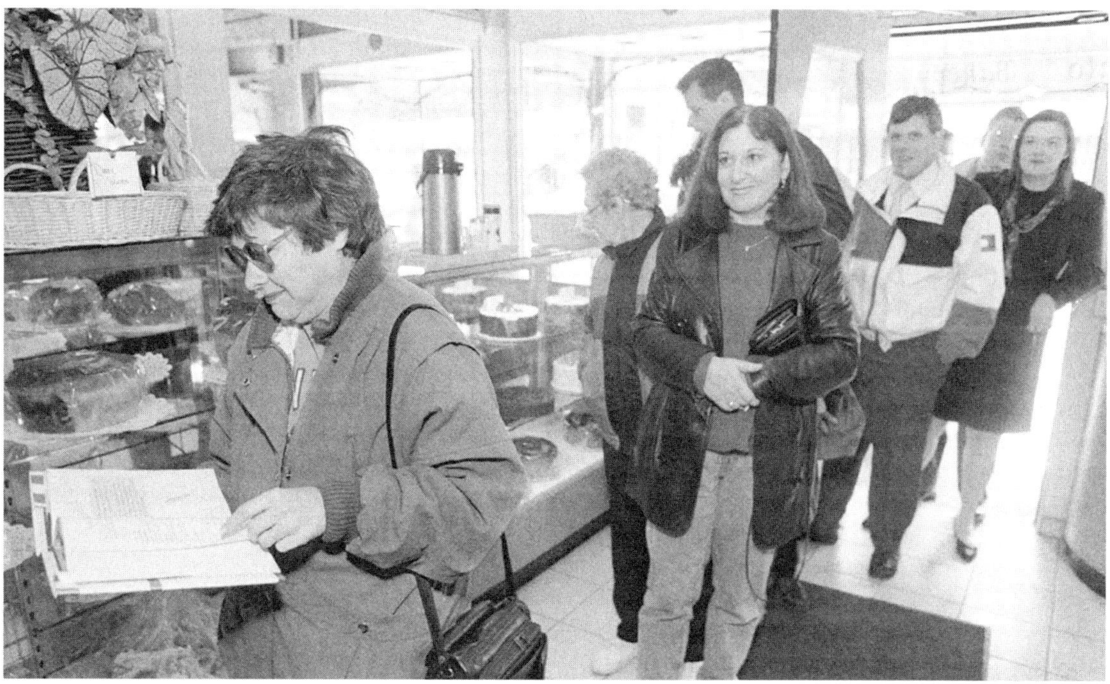

People in line at a bakery Rapose, Ann, photograph by Paul Connors. AP Images

his work. In an interview (reprinted in *Reading Raymond Carver*), he told William L. Stull:

> I'll be glad to see the appellation [minimalism] fade so that writers can be talked about as writers and not lumped together in groups where they usually don't belong. It's a label, and labels are unattractive to the people attached to the labels.

Carver also pointed out in the same interview that writers labeled as minimalists were very different from one another, a fact that tended to undermine the validity of the term.

By the late 1980s, the term minimalist was on the wane in critical discourse and there was even a backlash against it. Much of this was in reaction to writers of lesser talent than Carver who tended to imitate the form of his work without producing the same effect. Some critics argued that stories that adhered too closely to a minimalist style were deficient in terms of the range of emotions expressed and in depth of characterization.

Critical Overview

From its first publication in *Cathedral* in 1983, "A Small, Good Thing" was recognized by reviewers and critics as one of Carver's outstanding stories. In the *New York Times Book Review*, Irving Howe compares it to the earlier version of the story entitled "The Bath." He feels that teachers of creative writing who consider the earlier version superior, because of its tautness, cryptic nature, and symbolism, are wrong: "The second version, though less tidy and glittering, reaches more deeply into a human situation and transforms the baker from an abstract 'evil force' into a flawed human creature."

In the *New Republic*, Dorothy Wickenden singled out "A Small, Good Thing" as one of the best stories in the collection. She coupled it with the story "Cathedral," describing them both as "astute, even complex, psychological dramas." But she also criticized both stories for showing signs of sentimentality, and she ventured an opinion as to why this might be:

> Perhaps because he doesn't quite trust the sense of hope with which he leaves his characters, the writing at the end becomes self-consciously simple and the scenes of resolution contrived. In "A Small, Good Thing" the stark realism of earlier scenes is replaced by rather pat symbolism about communion through suffering.

In the twenty years following its publication, "A Small, Good Thing" continued to attract attention from critics, who see it as an example of Carver's stylistic development from the sparse minimalism of the earlier stories to what Kathleen Westfall Shute in *Hollins Critic* has called "richer, more emotionally and artistically complex" work.

Criticism

Bryan Aubrey

Aubrey holds a Ph.D. in English and has published many articles on twentieth century literature. In this essay, Aubrey compares "A Small, Good Thing" to Carver's "The Bath," an earlier version of the story.

Literary critics have often agreed that the stories in Carver's collection, *Cathedral*, are less bleak, more hopeful, than the stories he published earlier in his career. Some critics have seen in "A Small, Good Thing" a tale of spiritual redemption. According to this view, Scotty is an innocent, suffering, Christ-like figure, and the final scene is a symbolic echo of the Last Supper in the Christian gospel. According to William Stull, in "Beyond Hopelessville: Another Side of Raymond Carver," this scene presents "a final vision of forgiveness and community rooted in religious faith." Those who read the story in this positive light sometimes suggest that Carver invests the number three with spiritual significance: Ann is thirty-three years old; Scotty dies on the third floor of the hospital, on the third day after his injury, just as Christ was crucified (possibly, according to scholars, at about the age of thirty-three), and rose from the dead on the third day. In the story, Ann and Howard Weiss both go home for brief periods to take baths, which could symbolize some kind of spiritual cleansing and rebirth (although it might also be pointed out that this would also be a perfectly natural thing to do under the circumstances).

Some readers may find these parallels with elements of the Christian tradition rather strained and point out that the universe depicted in "A Small, Good Thing" is hardly a comforting or just one. It might best be described as random. Scotty, for example, dies in what the doctor calls a "one-in-a-million" chance event; there is no merciful Father in heaven to save him, in spite of the fact that both his parents pray for their son's life. In the world depicted in the story, prayers are not answered, and bad things are likely to happen to anyone, even the innocent. Under the smooth surface of life, some unseen menace, some dark destiny, lurks. Howard, the father, is well aware of this possibility. After Scotty is injured, Howard reflects about his own life, which up to this point has been blessed with only good things, including a good education and a good job, a loving wife, and a son: "So far, he had kept away from any real harm, from those forces he knew existed and that could cripple or bring down a man if the luck went bad, if things suddenly turned." Howard thinks not in religious terms but in terms of "forces" and "luck." After the tragedy occurs, the Weisses, as would be expected, do everything they can to convince themselves that Scotty will recover; after all, that is what the doctor keeps telling them. But the doctor's frequent reassurances tend to have the opposite effect; the fear of the parents increases, and the reader senses that there will be no good outcome of this sad little tale. Indeed, when Scotty does die, it is a doubly cruel event, because in the few moments before his death he appears to wake up, giving his stricken parents some false hope that is quickly dashed. In this bleak and cruel world, all people can do is reach out to one another, comfort one another, and try to endure, as the baker and the Weisses do in the end. It is hard to see in what sense this might be considered a story which culminates in an expression of "religious faith," since there appears to be no God and nothing in which to have faith.

Interestingly, "A Small, Good Thing" was a revised version of "The Bath," a story that appeared in Carver's earlier collection, *What We Talk About When We Talk About Love* (1981). An examination of this story and the changes Carver made for the later version sheds light on Carver's developing craft and the effect he may have intended to create in "A Small, Good Thing."

"The Bath" is an excellent example of what is meant by minimalism. It is less than one-third of the length of "A Small, Good Thing," and although it has basically the same plot as the later story, the narrative is far more sparse and is stripped of all detail. Scotty does not die, but his fate remains unknown as he lies in the hospital; Ann does not have her angry confrontation with the baker, and there is no final scene of reconciliation.

In "The Bath," Ann Weiss is not named until late in the story. At first she is merely described as the mother, and at various other times, she is the wife and the woman. Her age is not stated. The husband, Howard in the later story, is not named at all. He is simply called the father, the man, or the husband. The details of his personal life that appear in the later story (that he is a partner in an investment firm, that his parents are alive, and his brothers and his sister are all doing well) are only very briefly mentioned in "The Bath." Neither of the two doctors is named either. The second doctor is presented in this way: "A doctor came in and said what his name was. This doctor was wearing loafers." In the later story, the doctor is given a name, Parsons, and described in a little more detail: "He had a bushy mustache. He was wearing loafers, a Western shirt, and a pair of jeans." In "The Bath" the family that Ann sees in the waiting room at the hospital mentions only the name Nelson. They do not tell her, as in the later story, that Franklin, as he is now named, is their son and he was stabbed during a fight in which he was an innocent bystander. The story thus has a more impersonal quality than the later version. It is told by a narrator who seems very distant from the characters he observes, and the characters themselves display a limited range of emotions. They do not connect emotionally with others.

In an interview with Larry McCaffery and Sinda Gregory, Carver explained that in "The Bath," he wanted to emphasize the quality of menace, and this was why the story was so compressed and condensed. Menace is conveyed, for example, in the description of the husband as he returns home to take a bath after being at Scotty's bedside for hours: "The man had been lucky and happy. But fear made him want to take a bath." It is as if fear is something that clings to the skin and can be washed away, or so the man mistakenly hopes. The story ends on another note of menace. Ann answers the telephone and hears the voice of the baker, although she does not know who it is: "'Scotty,' the voice said, 'It is about Scotty,' the voice said. 'It has to do with Scotty, yes.'" The repetitions, with no further explanation given, create a menacing effect, sounding for Ann perhaps like a disembodied voice of doom for her son.

Carver liked to give his stories this quality of menace because he believed that many people feel insecure about their own lives, fearing that something could come along at any moment and destroy whatever they have.

However, after publication of "The Bath," Carver felt that the story needed to be "enhanced, redrawn, reimagined" (interview with McCaffery and Gregory). He ended up revising it so thoroughly that he considered "The Bath" and "A Small, Good Thing" to be entirely different stories, and he said that he liked the revised story much better than the original.

What Carver did in the revision was not so much create a religious framework for the story as humanize it. The quality of menace, the sense that something bad is going to happen, remains. In one respect, this feeling has been increased, since there are now two innocent victims rather than one. In addition to Scotty, there is Franklin, who, the later story explains, was at a party minding his own business when he was attacked: "Not bothering nobody. But that don't mean nothing these days," says his father. A world in which minding one's own business does not spare him from the aggression of others is a menacing one indeed.

"In the world depicted in the story, prayers are not answered, and bad things are likely to happen to anyone, even the innocent. Under the smooth surface of life, some unseen menace, some dark destiny, lurks."

Given that Carver had no wish to remove the sense of menace that hovers over the story, almost every change and addition he made to the original story resulted in a more complex and sympathetic portrayal of human emotions. In "The Bath," the characters seem to live in their own small, circumscribed worlds, like orbiting planets that make no contact with each other. But in "A Small, Good Thing" they are more willing, and often able, to reach out to others to alleviate the pain of the common human condition.

This ability to connect is apparent, for example, in Ann's greater awareness of her husband's fear and grief. After Howard tells her that he has been praying, just as she has, she reflects:

> For the first time, she felt they were together in it, this trouble. She realized with a start that, until now, it had only been happening to her and to Scotty. She hadn't let Howard into it, though he was there and needed all along. She felt glad to be his wife.

To be together, not alone, in trouble sums up the essence of "A Small, Good Thing." It is revealed in the climactic scene of reconciliation at the end

What Do I Read Next?

- *Will You Please Be Quiet, Please?* (1976) was Carver's first major collection of short stories. The stories feature blue collar characters struggling to deal with problems such as alcoholism, adultery, and despair. Many of the themes that recur in Carver's later collections appear here for the first time: the failure of people to communicate with each other, how people contrive to mismanage their lives, how people survive what happens to them and come to terms with their limitations.
- Carver admired the work of Bobbie Ann Mason. *Midnight Magic: Selected Stories of Bobbie Ann Mason* (1998) is a collection of seventeen stories from two previous collections by Mason, who like Carver has been labeled a minimalist by critics. Like Carver, Mason focuses on working-class life. Her characters live on the edge of poverty, often unemployed or in insecure employment, in rural and small-town Kentucky. Dubbed Kmart realism, Mason's is a world of chain stores, shopping malls, and cable television. Her characters have to deal as best they can with social changes and dislocations such as those caused by factory lay-offs and higher divorce rates.
- Readers may enjoy Ann Beattie's *Park City: New and Selected Stories* (1999). Beattie made her reputation in the 1970s as a writer of minimalist short stories that were published in the *New Yorker*. Some critics see her, with Carver, as being responsible for the renaissance of the short story form in the 1970s and 1980s. This is her fifth collection of stories, although all but eight of them had been previously published in book form. Unlike the settings in stories by Carver and Mason, Beattie's terrain is the urban (usually New York), educated middle class. Her characters often seem to have no real purpose or sense of destiny; small details about their lives accumulate, but the larger meaning is up to the reader to discover, if it exists.
- Tobias Wolff has sometimes been linked to Carver as a so-called minimalist, and Carver, who was generous in his praise of other writers, named Wolff as a writer he greatly admired. Wolff also admired Carver's work, and they were for a while colleagues in Syracuse University's Creative Writing Program. Wolff's collection of stories *The Night In Question: Stories* (1997) has been praised for its presentation of moral ambiguities, for it tension building, and for descriptions of how people respond to what fate brings them.

---

and also in other small details that appear in the later story but not in "The Bath." Dr. Francis, for example, who is presented in "The Bath" as a handsome man and a snappy dresser—a man seen from the outside only—retains those qualities but adds an inner dimension of warmth, empathy, and compassion. He embraces Ann and tries to console her, and he puts his arm around Howard's shoulders. These gestures too, are small, good things; they are the most the doctor can do in this tragic situation. Of course, these gestures, and the "small, good thing" of eating in the company of others, are not enough, for there is nothing that can remove the grief that results from the death of a child. Nonetheless, such gestures are not in vain. They are like candles lit in the darkness, and in grief as in despair, even the tiniest ray of light can help to dispel the gloom.

Source: Bryan Aubrey, Critical Essay on "A Small, Good Thing," in *Short Stories for Students*, Thomson Gale, 2006.

Arthur M. Saltzman

In the following essay excerpt, Saltzman explores the "reformulation" and evolution of Carver's earlier story, "The Bath," as "A Small, Good Thing" in the Cathedral *collection.*

The stories discussed above follow the general tone established in Carver's three previous collections. The absence of recourse and the unnourished hopes shrunken to a grudge; the misfired social synapses and the implied ellipses like breadcrumb trails leading from breakdown to breakdown; the "preseismic" endings that "are inflected rather than inflicted upon us"; the speechless gaps where intimacies are supposed to go—these characteristics persist. On the other hand, some of the stories in *Cathedral* do suggest an opening out that indicates, however subtly, an ongoing evolution in Carver's art.

The reformulation of "The Bath" in *What We Talk About When We Talk About Love* as "A Small, Good Thing" in *Cathedral* is an obvious place to begin to examine this contrast. Carver himself has indicated that the enhancement of the original story's "unfinished business" is so fundamental that they now seem to him to be two entirely different stories. Certainly the structure of his sentences has been changed in several instances to be less fragmentary, less constrained. For example, while she is waiting for the arrival of the doctor in "The Bath," the mother's dread is nearly wordless, and absolutely privatized: "She was talking to herself like this. We're into something now, something hard." In "A Small, Good Thing," however, Ann (she has been granted a name and a fuller identity, as have the other characters in the story) is presented as having a more extensively characterized consciousness, which is thus more sympathetic and accessible:

> She stood at the window with her hands gripping the sill, and knew in her heart that they were into something now, something hard. She was afraid, and her teeth began to chatter until she tightened her jaws. She saw a big car stop in front of the hospital and someone, a woman in a long coat, get into the car. She wished she were that woman and somebody, anybody, was driving her away from here to somewhere else, a place where she would find Scotty waiting for her when she stepped out of the car, ready to say *Mom* and let her gather him in her arms.
>
> In a little while, Howard woke up. He looked at the boy again. Then he got up from the chair, stretched, and went over to stand beside her at the window. They both stared at the parking lot. They didn't say anything. *But they seemed to feel each other's insides now, as though the worry had made them transparent in a perfectly natural way* (my italics).

With the expansion of the original version comes a development of the spiritual cost of the crisis. The result of every extension of detail in "A Small, Good Thing"—from the increased dimension of the baker when he is first introduced, to the transcendence of merely symbolic function of the black family at the hospital—is to decrease the distances

> "Unlike 'The Bath,' whose focus is the title's solitary baptism, 'A Small, Good Thing' affirms the consolations of mutual acceptance."

that separate Carver's characters from one another and Carver's narrator from the story he relates. For one critic the expansion represents a movement away from "existential realism" toward a comparatively coherent, more dramatic, and more personal "humanistic realism."

Carver's most profound revision is to carry the plot beyond the state of abeyance of Scotty's coma. ("The Bath" concludes in the middle of the phone call, just before the "death sentence" is actually pronounced.) In "A Small, Good Thing," Scotty's death spasm occurs even as the doctor is discussing with the parents the surgery that he will perform to save the boy. Having been assured only the previous day that Scotty would recover, Ann and Howard are absolutely overwhelmed, and they dazedly prepare to withstand the autopsy, to call relatives. Under these more developed circumstances the baker's call is no longer just the ironic plot gimmickry it had been in "The Bath"; instead, his interruption of and ultimate participation in the family's loss in "A Small, Good Thing" precipitates the cycle of "dramatic recognition, reversal, confrontation, and catharsis" that finally gives the story the finished contours of tragedy—the "low-rent" tragic pattern fleshed out to classic dimensions. Replacing the blank, dazed reaction of the anxious mother in the former version is her wild anger at the "evil bastard" who has blundered into their grief; when translated to the context of their open wound, his message about the birthday cake sounds ominous and malicious: "'Your Scotty, I got him ready for you,' the man's voice said. 'Did you forget him?'"

He hangs up, and only after a second call and hang-up does Ann realize that it must have been the baker. Blazing with outrage, desperate to strike out against their defeat, Ann and Howard drive to the shopping center bakery for a showdown. The baker, menacingly tapping a rolling pin against his palm, is prepared for trouble, but Ann breaks down as she tells him of the death of her son. Her debasement is complete, but Carver rescues her from the isolated defeat in which so many of his previous protagonists have been immured. The baker apologizes, and in that instant's compassion is moved to confess his misgivings and his loneliness, and the cold remove he has kept to: "I'm not an evil man, I don't think. Not evil, like you said on the phone. You got to understand what it comes down to is I don't know how to act anymore, it would seem." Their shared bond is inadequacy in the face of loss, joined by a need to be forgiven for that inadequacy. Consequently, whereas in previous stories people clutched themselves in isolated corners against their respective devastations, here they manage to come together in the communal ceremony of eating warm rolls and drinking coffee: "You have to eat and keep going. Eating is a small, good thing in a time like this."

The availability of nourishment discloses their common "hunger." Ann, Howard, and the baker begin a quiet convalescence, eating what they can, talking until morning. Unlike "The Bath," whose focus is the title's solitary baptism, a purgative reflex meant to ward off catastrophe, "A Small, Good Thing" affirms the consolations of mutual acceptance. Ann and Howard had refused food throughout the story, which suggested their desperate denial. The closing scene "exteriorizes" their misery so as to make available to them the healing impulses of the baker and the small, but significant, brand of grace that human sympathy can provide.

Source: Arthur M. Saltzman, "Cathedral," in *Understanding Raymond Carver*, University of South Carolina Press, 1988, pp. 143–47.

Mark A.R. Facknitz

In the following essay, Facknitz explores the unexpected and redemptive understanding that comes upon the protagonists of Carver's "A Small, Good Thing," "The Calm," and "Cathedral."

Raymond Carver is as successful as a short story writer in America can be. The signs of his success are many: prestigious and ample grants, publication in the best literary quarterlies and national magazines, and, from all appearances, an unperturbed ability to write the kind of stories he wishes to write. By contrast, the causes of his success are ambiguous. Carver's writing is often facile, and one might argue that he has chanced upon a voice that matches a jaded audience's lust for irony and superficial realism. Whatever the proclivities of his readers, Carver knows their passions and perversions well. In story after story, in language that babbles from wise lunatics, Carver's penetration of characters is honest and fast. But they compose a diminished race—alcoholics, obsessives, drifters, and other losers who are thoroughly thrashed by life in the first round. Only recently have his characters begun to achieve a measure of roundness, and as they have, the message of his work has shifted considerably. Once all one could draw from Carver's work was the moral that when life wasn't cruel it was silly. In several key stories since 1980, he has revealed to readers and characters alike that though they have long suffered the conviction that life is irredeemably trivial, in truth it is as profound as their wounds, and their substance is as large as the loss they suffer.

In their essay on *Will You Please Be Quiet, Please?* (1977), Carver's first major collection of stories, David Boxer and Cassandra Phillips call Carver's world one of "unarticulated longing, a world verging on silence" in which people speak with the "directionless quality, the silliness, the halting rhythm among people under the influence of marijuana," (80–81) and they rightly call such speech "realistic language of a different sort—a probe stuck beneath the skin of disassociation itself" (81). Indeed, it is hard for Carver's characters to say what they mean under any circumstances. Often they try to rephrase their ideas for inattentive listeners, who are as likely as they to be dulled by drugs, alcohol, and over-eating. Thus speech is stuporous and communication far from perfect. However, for Boxer and Phillips "passivity is the strength of this language: little seems to be said, yet much is conveyed" (81) and they compare the simplicity of Carver's dialogue to Pinter's and write of "emotional violence lurking beneath the neutral surfaces." One could go further and assert that in his early stories Carver's obsessive subject is the failure of human dialogue, for talking fails in all but the title story of *Will You Please Be Quiet, Please?*, and that story's message is that sometimes the best thing we can say is nothing.

The theme of failed speech is only slightly less domineering in *What We Talk About When We Talk About Love* (1981). An important exception is "The Calm." In the story, the narrator watches and listens from a barber chair while a drama unfolds. Its cast is composed of two pairs. In the first pair is Charles, a bank guard, who tells the men in the shop of having wounded a buck the day before, and old Albert, dying of emphysema, who is offended by Charles's brutality. Opposite them is a pair of men without names, the barber and the man with the newspaper. As the owner of the shop, the barber represents order and tranquility, while the other man is a nervous type who exacerbates the tension that develops between Charles and Albert. In allegorical terms the story combines Cruelty (Charles) and Disruption (the man with the newspaper) and makes them the antagonists of Humanity (Albert) and Order (the barber). The plot, then, is very simple: Disruption meddles in the inevitable conflict between Cruelty and Humanity and then step by step Order re-asserts itself. Thus calm is bestowed upon Order's client, the narrator in the barber chair, the witness or internal audience who has played no part in the drama but for whom the moral comes clear.

This primary narrator at moments gives way to a secondary narrator, the guard Charles, as he tells the story of the hunt which he undertook with his hungover son, a young man with a weak stomach and a worse aim. Scarcely a nimrod, Charles is defined by his doltishness and vulgarity. He tells of wounding the buck:

> It was a gut shot. It just like stuns him. So he drops his head and begins this trembling. He trembles all over. The kid's still shooting. Me, I felt like I was back in Korea. So I shot again but missed. Then old Mr. Buck moves back into the bush. But now, by God, he doesn't have any oomph left in him. The kid has emptied his g——d—— gun all to no purpose. But I hit solid. I rammed one right in his guts. That's what I meant by stunned him.

In fact, the hemorrhaging animal has plenty of oomph left in him. Though father and vomiting son follow a gory track, by nightfall they haven't caught up with the wounded deer and abandon him to slow death and scavengers. Inept and immoral, the two renounce an obligation, one that a man of Albert's fiber would likely call sacred. Charles confuses hunting with war, and in doing so he travesties the deepest symbolism of the hunt and idiotically confuses the archetypes of violence and necessity. Yet one sees a measure of perverse respect in his assumption that a bullet in the intestines amounts to nothing more than stunning. This offends Albert, and he tells Charles "You ought to be out there right now looking for that deer instead of in here getting a haircut." In other words, Albert asserts a principle that ought to be self-evident to an American man: hunting is not war; the animal is not an enemy to be loathed and tortured. Albert reminds him of his duty to administer a *coup de grace* and then, by butchering and eating the animal, justify the creature's fear and death.

Carver's characters rarely achieve a transcendent acceptance of their condition as does Ann Weiss. Indeed, more commonly they resign themselves without struggle or thought."

That such a message is implied by Albert's straightforward statement is clear from Charles's retort: "You can't talk like that. You old fart. I've seen you someplace." In a way his indignation is appropriate. Albert breaks a cultural rule as surely as the guard did in letting the wounded buck wander off. Moreover, in an American barbershop an egalitarian law inheres, and on entering one accepts a kind of truce similar to the set of restraints entering a church entails as one puts aside particulars of class and values. American males in their unspoken codes have reserved parking lots, alleys, bars, committee rooms, and the margins of athletic fields for physical and verbal violence, and they are likely to find arguments in barbershops as unsociable as spitting in a funeral parlor. Thus, the greatest deviant is the stranger with the newspaper, for his motive is malicious delight in causing trouble, in particular the disruption of the conventions of order. He is an "outside agitator" who brings out the worst in Charles and Albert, makes them breech the truce implied by the setting, and finally is more culpable than they for theirs are crimes of passion rather than malice. Albert is overpowered by righteous indignation, and Charles by the humiliation of being accused of breaking the masculine code of the hunt. The stranger defends nothing; rather, he seeks pleasure by provoking others.

The argument ends very soon, for once the barber asserts himself he easily vanquishes the man with the newspaper. First Charles leaves, complaining of the company, and then Albert goes, tossing off the comment that his hair can go without cutting for a few more days. Left with no one on whom to work his irascibility, the man with the newspaper fidgets. He gets up and looks around the shop, finds nothing to hold his attention, and then announces that he is going and disappears out the door. What has happened is not clear but the barber is nonplussed. Although he sides with Albert, allowing that after all Albert had provocation, the barber was forced to keep the peace and has lost a line-up of clients. Temporarily in a bad humor, he says to the narrator, who has said and done nothing all along, "Well, do you want me to finish this barbering or not?" in a tone that suggests to the narrator that the barber blames him for what has occurred.

The ill-feeling does not last. The barber holds the narrator's head and bends close and looks at him in the mirror while the narrator looks at himself. Then the barber stands and begins to rub his fingers through his hair, "slowly, as if thinking about something else," and "tenderly, as a lover would." The story is close to its end, and suddenly the reader has material before him that in no manner impinges on the events of the story and which, at first glance, appears irrelevant:

> That was in Crescent City, California, up near the Oregon border. I left soon after. But today I was thinking of that place, of Crescent City, and of how I was trying out a new life there with my wife, and how, in the barber's chair that morning, I had made up my mind to go. I was thinking today about the calm I felt when I closed my eyes and let the barber's fingers move through my hair, the sweetness of those fingers, and the hair already starting to grow.

Much was transpiring in the heart and mind of the narrator—who is also the internal audience—but in the long run only the general fact that he was coming to an important decision matters. Revealing the particulars of his life that bear upon the decision would shift the focus of "The Calm" from how we receive blessings from others to the use such blessings are to us. This would trivialize and demystify the story, for Carver means to imply that while important gifts can only be given to those ready to take them, we cannot give them to ourselves. They come from outside of us from barbers whose names we never learn, or, as "A Small, Good Thing" and "Cathedral" will show, from bakers and blind men whom coincidence brings into our lives. Once we read the final paragraph of "The Calm," we assume that the narrator was in a turbulent state of mind while making an ostensibly objective record, and though we see nothing of the process except the external sequence, we guess that what he witnesses makes him better able to bring order into his life. Hair grows out, and calm does not last, but the barber proves to the narrator that he cannot create order by himself, though, like Albert, who has developed a sour temper and has trouble breathing in old age, he can always let the matter go a few more days.

Procrastination is occasionally impossible. In "A Small, Good Thing," one of the best stories in the most recent collection, *Cathedral* (1984), Ann and Howard Weiss confront the destruction of well-being. Because they dare to confront the catastrophe of their son's death, they are rescued, in this case by their principal malefactor.

One Saturday Ann orders a birthday cake for a party for her son which will take place Monday afternoon. Monday morning the boy is struck by a car while walking to school. At first he appears little hurt, and walks home, but suddenly he loses consciousness and over several days his condition worsens as sleep subsides into coma and at last he dies. Meanwhile doctors, nurses, and technicians come and go, offering encouragement to the parents and looking for clues to why the boy won't wake. Each time the doctor revises his opinion of the boy's condition, Ann guesses the truth, and the discrepancy between what she is told and what actually happens broadens as the story advances. Yet the doctors are not lying. Their reason and their tests are deceiving them, and all the hypotheses, diagnoses, X-rays, and scans fail to reveal "a hidden occlusion," a "one-in-a-million circumstance," that kills the child. Thus, while all the rational and objective ways of making sense are defeated, the truth persists in the mother's worst intuitions. When the boy dies, the doctors need an autopsy because things need explaining, and they must satisfy the need to know why their minds and machines failed. The parents must make sense in another way. They must voice an unspeakable grief, and they accomplish this by listening to someone else's suffering.

Early in the story Ann goes to the baker, a man who will torment her more than he can guess. Carver develops the scene:

> She gave the baker her name, Ann Weiss, and her telephone number. The cake would be ready on Monday morning, just out of the oven, in plenty of time for the child's party that afternoon. The baker was not jolly. There were no pleasantries between them, just the minimum exchange of words, the necessary information. He made her feel uncomfortable, and she didn't like that. While he was bent over the counter with the pencil in his hand, she studied his coarse features and wondered if he'd ever done anything else with his life besides be a baker.

Much later in the story, while Ann sits by the phone after having called relatives to tell them of the boy's death, the baker phones. He has made several calls in the last few days—it was impossible to say precisely how many—and Howard and Ann have taken the calls as perverse jokes on the part of the hit-and-run driver. Through misapprehension, the cake and the boy come to have the same name, and the baker speaks in malicious metaphor when he says to the desperate woman, "Your Scotty, I got him ready for you. Did you forget him?" This is language of an extraordinary kind. No longer "minimum exchange, or the necessary information," such an utterance is a linguistic perversion for it means most when misunderstood.

When it occurs to Ann that the baker is her tormentor, she and her husband rush down to the shopping center and beat on the back door in the middle of the night until the baker lets them in. There she lights into him:

> "My son's dead," she said with a cold, even finality. "He was hit by a car Monday morning. We've been waiting with him until he died. But, of course, you couldn't be expected to know that, could you? Bakers can't know everything can they, Mr. Baker? But he's dead. He's dead, you bastard!" Just as suddenly as it had welled in her, the anger dwindled, gave way to something else, a dizzy feeling of nausea. She leaned against the wooden table that was sprinkled with flour, put her hands over her face, and began to cry, her shoulders rocking back and forth. "It isn't fair," she said.

Nothing here can be misunderstood. The facts are plain, and the steps in her understanding of what bakers can and cannot know are clear and logical. Her anger is pure, and purifying: it is as physical and overpowering as the nausea that succeeds it, and the emotion and the sensation are as honest and undeniable as her recognition that her son's death was not fair.

Her speech abolishes the social conventions, suspicions, and errors that brought them to the point of confrontation. Ann, Howard, and the baker are tangled in a subtle set of causes, and Carver suggests again, as he has in many stories (e.g. "The Train," "Feathers"), that through imperceptible and trivial dishonesties we create large lies that can only be removed by superhuman acts of self-assertion. In response to Ann's overwhelming honesty, the menaced baker puts down his rolling pin, clears places for them at the table, and makes them sit. He tells them that he is sorry, but they have little to say about their loss. Instead they take the coffee and rolls he serves them and listen while he tells them about his loneliness and doubt, and about the ovens, "endlessly empty and endlessly full." They accept his life story as consolation, and while eating and listening achieve communion. Carver ends the story at dawn, with hope, and pushes forward symbols of sanctified space and the eucharist:

> "Smell this," the baker said, breaking open a dark loaf. "It's a heavy bread, but rich." They smelled it, then he had them taste it. It had the taste of molasses and coarse grains. They listened to him. They ate what they could. They swallowed the dark bread. It was like daylight under the fluorescent trays of lights. They talked on into the early morning, the high, pale cast of light in the windows, and they did not think of leaving.

Carver's characters rarely achieve a transcendent acceptance of their condition as does Ann Weiss. Indeed, more commonly they resign themselves without struggle or thought. They are rarely attractive people, and often readers must work against a narrator's tendency to sound cretinous or Carver's propensity to reveal characters as bigots and dunces. As the story opens, the first-person narrator of "Cathedral" appears to be another in this series of unattractive types. He worries about the approaching visit of a friend of his wife, a blind man named Robert who was once the wife's employer. He has little experience with the blind and faces the visit anxiously. His summary of the wife's association with Robert is derisive, its syntax blunt and its humor fatiguing:

> She'd worked with this blind man all summer. She read stuff to him, case studies, reports, that sort of thing. She helped him organize his little office in the county social service department. They'd become good friends, my wife and the blind man. How do I know these things? She told me. And she told me something else. On her last day in the office, the blind man asked if he could touch her face. She agreed to this. She told me he ran his fingers over every part of her face, her nose—even her neck! She never forgot it. She even tried to write a poem about it. She was always writing a poem. She wrote a poem or two every year, usually after something really important happened to her.

Clearly he is jealous, and so emphasizes the eroticism of the blind man's touch. But she was leaving the blind man's office to marry her childhood sweetheart, an officer in the Air Force whom the narrator refers to as "this man who'd first enjoyed her favors," and much of his jealousy toward the first husband transfers to the blind man Robert. Thus Robert sexually threatens the narrator, with his blindness, and by virtue of being a representative of a past that is meaningful to the wife. The narrator is selfish and callous; however, he is one of Carver's heavy drinkers and no reader could be drawn through "Catheral" because he cares for him, and perhaps what pushes one into the story is a fear of the harm he may do to his wife and her blind friend. Yet Carver redeems the narrator by releasing him from the figurative blindness that results in a lack of insight into his own condition and which leads him to trivialize human feelings and needs. Indeed, so complete is his misperception that the blind man gives him a faculty of sight that he is not even aware that he lacks.

The wife and blind man have kept in touch over the years, a period of change and grief for each, by sending tape recordings back and forth. The life of a military wife depressed the young woman and led to her divorce from her first husband, but the narrator's view of her suffering is flat and without compassion:

> She told the blind man she'd written a poem and he was in it. She told him that she was writing a poem about what it was like to be an Air Force officer's wife in the Deep South. The poem wasn't finished yet. She was still writing it. The blind man made a tape. He sent her the tape. She made a tape. This went on for years. My wife's officer was posted to one base and then another. She sent tapes from Moody AFB, McGuire, McConnell, and finally Travis, near Sacramento, where one night she got to feeling lonely and cut off from people she kept losing in that moving-around life. She balked, couldn't go it another step. She went in and swallowed all the pills and capsules in the medicine cabinet and washed them down with a bottle of gin. Then she got in a hot bath and passed out.
>
> But instead of dying she got sick. She threw up.

Suicide is mundane, for him merely a question of balking at life, and dying is roughly the equivalent to throwing up, something one might do *instead,* much as the narrator stays up nights drunk and stoned in front of the television as an antidote to the "crazy" dreams that trouble his sleep. To his credit, he does not claim moral superiority to his wife, and sees the waste of his drinking and the cowardice of stayng in a job he can neither leave nor enjoy. He is numb and isolated, a modern man for whom integration with the human race would be so difficult that it is futile. Consequently he hides by failing to try, anesthetizes himself with booze, and explains away the world with sarcasm. He does nothing to better his lot. Rather he invents strategies for keeping things as they are and will back off from even the most important issues. When he wisecracks that he might take the blind man bowling, his wife rebukes him: "If you love me, you can do this for me. If you don't love me, okay. But if you had a friend, any friend, and the friend came to visit, I'd make him feel comfortable." Each ignores that she says *him,* not her, and the emotional blackmail of "if you don't love me, okay" appears not to register. He responds that he hasn't any blind friends, and when she reminds him that he hasn't any friends at all, much less blind ones, he becomes sullen and withdraws from the conversation. What she has said is aggressive and true and to respond to it would imply recognition of the many and large insufficiencies of his life. Instead, he works away at a drink and listens while she tells him about Beulah, the blind man's wife who has recently died of cancer. There's no facing this subject. He listens for a while as she talks about Beulah:

> "Was his wife a Negro?" I asked.
>
> "Are you crazy?" my wife said. "Have you just flipped or something?"
>
> She picked up a potato. I saw it hit the floor, then roll under the stove.
>
> "What's wrong with you?" she said. "Are you drunk?"
>
> "I'm just asking," I said.
>
> Right then my wife filled me in with more detail than I cared to know. I made a drink and sat at the kitchen table to listen. Pieces of the story began to fall into place.

Death is a subject they touch on often but never pursue, and they go on as married couples do in Carver's stories, never forcing a point because each hurt touches on another hurt. Thus, because each serious effort risks the destruction of a stuporous status quo that he maintains by various strategies of denial, they never touch each other.

The narrator inadvertently makes a friend of the blind man. At the end of an evening of whiskey and conversation that bewilder him and leave him sitting alone in his resentment, he is left with Robert when his wife goes upstairs to change into her robe. Together they sit, the narrator watching the late news, Robert listening, his ear turned toward the television, his unseeing eyes turned disconcertingly on the narrator. After the news there is a program about cathedral architecture and the narrator tries to explain to Robert what a cathedral looks like. They smoke some marijuana and he blunders on, failing to express the visual effect of a cathedral's soaring space to a man who, as far as the narrator can tell, has no analogues for spatial dimension. When Robert asks what a fresco is, the narrator is at a complete loss. The blind man proposes a solution, and on a heavy paper bag the narrator draws a cathedral while Robert's hand rides his. He begins with a box and pointed roof that could be his own house, and adds spires, buttresses, windows, and doors, and at last he has elaborated a gothic cathedral in lines pressed hard into the paper. When

Robert takes his hand and makes him close his eyes to touch the cathedral, he "sees." Even when he is told that he can open his eyes, he chooses not to, for he is learning what he has long been incapable of perceiving and even now can not articulate:

> I thought I'd keep them that way a little longer. I thought it was something I ought not to forget.
>
> "Well?" he said. "Are you looking?"
>
> My eyes were still closed. I was in my house and I knew that. But I didn't feel inside anything.
>
> "It's really something," I said.

The cathedral, of course, is the space that does not limit, and his perception of *something*—objective, substantial, meaningful—that cannot be seen with ordinary sight depends on his having to perceive as another perceives. In fictional terms, he learns to shift point of view. In emotional terms, he learns to feel empathy. In the moment when the blind man and the narrator share an identical perception of spiritual space, the narrator's sense of enclosure—of being confined by his own house and circumstances—vanishes as if by an act of grace, or a very large spiritual reward for a virtually insignificant gesture. Following the metaphor of the story, the narrator learns to see with eyes other than that insufficient set that keeps him a friendless drunk and a meager husband.

In a reminiscence on John Gardner, his late teacher, Carver pauses to reflect that at some point in late youth or early middle age we all face the inevitability of our failure and we suffer "the suspicion that we're taking on water, and that things are not working out in our lives the way we'd planned." For a time there is nothing anyone can do against the debilitating effect of such a recognition. But in "The Calm," "A Small, Good Thing," and "Cathedral," protagonists are taken from behind by understanding. When it occurs, understanding comes as the result of an unearned and unexpected gift, a kind of grace constituted in human contact that a fortunate few experience. Of course, Carver does not imply a visitation of the Holy Ghost, nor does he argue that salvation is apt to fall on the lowliest of creatures in the moment of their greatest need as it does, say, in Flannery O'Connor, whose benighted Ruby Turpin in "Revelation" is saved in spite of herself when shown the equality of all souls in the sight of God. Grace, Carver says, is bestowed upon us by other mortals, and it comes suddenly, arising in circumstances as mundane as a visit to the barber shop, and in the midst of feelings as ignoble or quotidian as jealousy, anger, loneliness, and grief. It can be represented in incidental physical contact, and the deliverer is not necessarily aware of his role. Not Grace in the Christian sense at all, it is what grace becomes in a godless world—a deep and creative connection between humans that reveals to Carver's alienated and diminished creatures that there can be contact in a world they supposed was empty of sense or love. Calm is given in a touch, a small, good thing is the food we get from others, and in the cathedrals we draw together, we create large spaces for the spirit.

Source: Mark A.R. Facknitz, "'The Calm,' 'A Small, Good Thing,' and 'Cathedral': Raymond Carver and the Rediscovery of Human Worth," in *Studies in Short Fiction*, Vol. 23, No. 3, Summer 1986, pp. 287–296.

Sources

Applefield, David, "Fiction and America: Raymond Carver," in *Conversations with Raymond Carver*, edited by Marshall Bruce Gentry and William L. Stull, University Press of Mississippi, 1990, p. 207, originally published in *Frank: An International Journal of Contemporary Writing & Art*, No. 8–9, Winter 1987–1988.

Carver, Raymond, "The Bath," in *What We Talk About When We Talk About Love*, Knopf, 1981, pp. 47–56.

———, "A Small, Good Thing," in *Cathedral*, Knopf, 1983, pp. 59–89.

Howe, Irving, "Stories of Our Loneliness," in *New York Times Book Review*, September 11, 1983, p. 43.

McCaffery, Larry, and Sinda Gregory, "An Interview with Raymond Carver," in *Conversations with Raymond Carver*, edited by Marshall Bruce Gentry and William L. Stull, University Press of Mississippi, 1990, p. 102, originally published in *Alive and Writing: Interviews with American Authors of the 1980s*, University of Illinois Press, 1987.

Runyon, Randolph Paul, *Reading Raymond Carver*, Syracuse University Press, 1992, p. 3.

Saltzman, Arthur M., *Understanding Raymond Carver*, University of South Carolina Press, 1988, p. 4.

Shute, Kathleen WestFall, "Finding the Words: The Struggle for Salvation in the Fiction of Raymond Carver," in *Hollins Critic*, Vol. 24, No. 5, December 1987, pp. 1–10.

Stull, William, "Beyond Hopelessville: Another Side of Raymond Carver," in *Philological Quarterly*, Vol. 64, 1985, p. 11.

———, "Matters of Life and Death," in *Conversations with Raymond Carver*, edited by Marshall Bruce Gentry and William L. Stull, University Press of Mississippi, 1990, p. 185, originally published in *The Bloomsbury Review*, January/February 1988.

Wickenden, Dorothy. "Old Darkness, New Light, in *New Republic*, Vol. 189, November 14, 1983, p. 38.

Further Reading

Leypoldt, Gunter, "Raymond Carver's 'Epiphanic Moments,'" in *Style*, Vol. 35, No. 3, Fall 2001, pp. 531–49.

Leypoldt discusses four different types of epiphanic moments in Carver's fiction: moments of sudden illumination; arrested epiphanies in which characters realize they are on the brink of a discovery but do not grasp what it is; ironized epiphanies in which the reader transcends the character's limited viewpoint; and comic epiphanies that are irrelevant to the overall plot closure.

Meyer, Adam, *Raymond Carver*, Twayne's United States Authors Series, No. 633, Twayne Publishers, 1995.

Meyer analyzes Carver's life and career and most of his fictional output. He traces the arc of Carver's artistic development, arguing that the term minimalist applies only to a portion of his work. In his analysis of "A Small, Good Thing," Meyer accepts the critical consensus that the work is one of the most effective of all Carver's stories.

Nesset, Kirk, *The Stories of Raymond Carver: A Critical Study*, Ohio University Press, 1995, pp. 61–66.

Nesset credits "A Small, Good Thing" with presenting a fullness and optimism unequalled in any other story by Carver. The psychological and spiritual expansion is due to the fact that the characters learn how to listen and communicate with one another.

Peden, William, *The American Short Story: Continuity and Change, 1940–1975*, 2nd edition, revised and enlarged, Houghton Mifflin, 1975.

Peden analyzes the significant trends and movements associated with the American short story in the thirty-five years up to the time immediately preceding the work of Carver. He discusses the work of the most outstanding recent short fiction writers, including John Updike, John Cheever, Donald Bartholme, Bernard Malamud, and Joyce Carol Oates.

The Smoothest Way Is Full of Stones

Julie Orringer

2003

"The Smoothest Way Is Full of Stones" by Julie Orringer was first published in the literary magazine, *Zoetrope: All Story*, in 2003. It was reprinted in Orringer's first collection of short stories, *How to Breathe Underwater* (2003). Orringer has been widely praised for her ability to convey the trials and tribulations of adolescent girls, as well as their ability to emerge successfully from the challenges they face. In "The Smoothest Way Is Full of Stones" a young Jewish girl from New York named Rebecca goes to stay for the summer with Esty, her cousin. Esty and her family are members of a Hasidic sect that has strict religious beliefs and practices which are quite new to Rebecca, who has been raised in a secular environment. As the summer wears on, Rebecca has to deal with her developing awareness of religion and God, as well as her emerging sexuality. These issues come together one hot July Shabbos and are connected with a forbidden book and the disturbing presence of an attractive young man.

Author Biography

Julie Orringer was born on June 12, 1973, in Miami, Florida. Both her parents were third-year medical students at the University of Miami. When Orringer was four, the family lived in Boston. When she was six, they moved to New Orleans, where she lived until she was twelve. She attended

Julie Orringer © Robert Birnbaum. Reproduced by permission

a private school, and being one of the few Jewish children in the class, she felt like an outsider. She loved reading and writing and thought she might like to write novels someday.

In 1986, the family moved to Ann Arbor, Michigan, where Orringer attended a public school from eighth grade. The book that most influenced her at the time was Charlotte Brontë's *Jane Eyre*, which she read in high school. During Orringer's school years, her mother was fighting a long battle with breast cancer, the disease that eventually killed her. Orringer says this experience gave her an early awareness that she might lose her mother, and this feeling of insecurity, loss, and the possibility of death has colored her stories.

Orringer attended Cornell University, where some of her professors began to encourage her to pursue a career as a writer. During her junior year, she started reading all the contemporary fiction she could find, including Raymond Carver, Charles Baxter, Mona Simpson, Tobias Wolff, Lorrie Moore, and Alice Munro.

Orringer graduated with a bachelor of arts degree from Cornell in 1994. She decided to continue her study of writing at Iowa Writers' Workshop at the University of Iowa and graduated with a master of fine arts degree in 1996.

After graduation, Orringer moved to San Francisco where she undertook a variety of non-writing-related jobs in order to make money while reserving her creative energies for her fiction. In 1999, Orringer received a Stegner Fellowship in the Creative Writing Program at Stanford University. By this time, her stories were being published in literary magazines and books, including the *Barcelona Review*, *Ploughshares*, *The Yale Review*, *The Paris Review*, *The Pushcart Prize Anthology*, *Best New American Voices 2001*, and *New Stories from the South: The Year's Best, 2002*. "The Smoothest Way Is Full of Stones" was first published in *Zoetrope: All Story*. Nine of Orringer's stories, including "The Smoothest Way Is Full of Stones," were published in the collection, *How to Breathe Underwater*, by Knopf in 2003. After graduating from the Stegner Program, Orringer held a three-year lectureship in fiction writing at Stanford.

As of 2006, Orringer is the Distinguished Visiting Writer at St. Mary's College of California. She lives with her husband, the writer Ryan Harty, in San Francisco.

Plot Summary

"The Smoothest Way Is Full of Stones" begins on a hot Friday afternoon in the middle of July in upstate New York. Rebecca, the narrator, a girl of about twelve or thirteen, is staying at the home of her uncle and aunt, the Adelsteins. Rebecca has been sent away while her mother recovers from the death of her infant son. That was six weeks ago, but she is still in hospital suffering from an infection and depression.

Rebecca's relatives are Hasidic Jews, whereas Rebecca's parents, who live three hundred miles away in Manhattan, New York City, are secular Jews. Rebecca's older cousin Esty, who is about thirteen, is very pious and tries to persuade Rebecca to be more observant of Jewish religious rituals and other customs.

Even though they are not supposed to be doing so, Rebecca and Esty wade into a lake and swim fully clothed out to a raft. They watch as a teenage boy comes along the lake road. He hides something under the porch steps of a house owned by the Perelmans, who are away until August. Esty recognizes the boy as Dovid Frankel and tells Rebecca that he and his family will be coming to Shabbos (Sabbath, the day of rest at the end of the week) dinner that evening at the Adelsteins.

After Dovid leaves, the girls swim ashore and investigate. Under the porch they find a paper bag and inside it is a book titled, *Essence of Persimmon: Eastern Sexual Secrets for Western Lives.* They read some of it but do not really understand it, and Esty says it is a sin to read it. But they agree to take the book home and hide it in the top shelf of their closet. Esty says they will not look at it, because that would be a sin.

They ride their bicycles home, hide the book, and help Rebecca's Aunt Malka with the preparations for Shabbos dinner. Rebecca makes a brief call to her mother in the hospital, but her mother sounds depressed, and their conversation ends before Rebecca has a chance to feel much connection with her.

At six-thirty, the female guests start arriving for Shabbos, bringing food and drink. The men are still at shul (a Yiddish word for synagogue). When Dovid arrives, Rebecca studies him carefully.

Everyone gathers around the table and the men sing "Shalom Aleichem." As they serve the food, the two girls keep their eyes on Dovid, although sometimes Rebecca looks at Mrs. Handelman, Dovid's older sister, who is pregnant. Rebecca's five little step-cousins scream as they run around and underneath the table. It is all very disorderly, quite different from the quiet dinners Rebecca is used to at home. At the end of the meal they all sing in Hebrew the Birkat Hamazon (a grace after meals), which again is something that does not happen at Rebecca's home.

Uncle Shimon then tells a story about a Jewish family thirty miles away whose house burned down in June. The only thing that was not destroyed was the mezuzah (scriptural passages in a box placed on doorposts). It was later discovered that there was an imperfection in the mezuzah; some of the letters of one of the words were smudged and misshapen. Uncle Shimon suggests that is why the house burned. Dovid expresses skepticism about this idea, and Uncle Shimon does not respond directly to his question, simply replying that he makes sure he has their mezuzah checked every year.

After dinner, Dovid steps outside, and after a while Rebecca follows him. For a few minutes they make desultory conversation about whether a smudged mezuzah causes a house to burn, and whether they believe in God at all. After Rebecca says that sometimes she hopes there is not a God because he would know all her secret thoughts, Dovid lets on that the Adelsteins are scared of her. They think that she may lead their children away from the orthodox religious path. This revelation surprises Rebecca, since she assumed the influence would be the other way round. Dovid then says that he is not scared of her, and he touches her arm. She knows that as an Orthodox Jew, he is not supposed to touch any woman who is not his mother or sister. For a moment she thinks he is going to kiss her, but then he walks back toward the house.

That night, Esty will not talk to Rebecca. She is angry and jealous because Rebecca was outside with Dovid. At night, Rebecca lies awake. She knows that Dovid was doing something against the rules, and she wonders whether she is really becoming the kind of orthodox religious girl she has been pretending to be during her stay at the Adelsteins.

In the middle of the night, Rebecca wakes and finds that Esty has gone from her bed and is in the closet, reading the forbidden book. Realizing that Esty is in love with Dovid, she tries to reassure her that nothing happened between her and Dovid. They agree to read the book for a little while and look at the drawings. They read descriptions of orgasm, masturbation, and body parts including the clitoris, but they have little idea of what it all means. Esty refuses to believe that Dovid has read it all. They close the book and hide it away again, promising to repent in the morning. During the night, Rebecca thinks about the judgment of God.

In the morning, Rebecca wakes before her cousin and steps out on the porch where she finds her uncle. She asks him whether, when a person dies, the family is supposed to have the mezuzah checked. Uncle Shimon replies that he was told by his rebbe (rabbi) that sometimes bad things just happen; people do not always know why Hashem (God) acts as he does.

Rebecca keeps the Shabbos all day, doing no work, not even turning on a light or sewing. She is not allowed to call her mother. Esty spends most of the day alone and prays a lot and studies the Torah (the first five books of the Bible, the books of Moses).

Aunt Malka tells Rebecca that her mother sounds better and that Rebecca will be going home soon. She tells Rebecca about mikveh, a spiritually cleansing ritual bath. According to Aunt Malka, the mikveh is especially important after a woman gives birth, even if the baby dies. She says it is a commandment for adult females to perform this bath every month unless a woman is pregnant for it is a ritual purification after menstruation and childbirth. Aunt Malka instructs Rebecca to tell her mother how important the mikveh is. Rebecca goes off alone and lies in the grass. She wants to know what God wants her to do, and she wants to do it.

At night, the family gathers for Havdalah, the blessings recited at the conclusion of Shabbos, separating the holy day from the other days of the week. They stand in a circle outside and sing to God, smell spices, and drink wine. Finally they sing about Eliyahu Hanavi (known to Christians as Elijah), the prophet who will arrive someday and bring the Messiah.

Rebecca calls her mother. Her father answers the phone and tells her that she can probably come home in a couple of weeks. Rebecca mentions Aunt Malka's instruction about the ritual bath. There is silence at the end of the line for a moment, before Rebecca's father asks to speak to her aunt. Although Aunt Malka is close by, Rebecca has an uneasy feeling about what might ensue, and she says her aunt has gone out for milk. Her father requests that Aunt Malka call him.

That evening, Esty leaves the dinner table without touching her food and goes to her room, where Rebecca finds her reading the erotic book. Esty tells her to explain to her mother that she has a headache and is laying down.

After dinner, as Rebecca washes the dishes, she is angry and worried about her cousin, and she also feels fear and guilt for not doing what God wants her to do. Seeing Esty leave the house and run down the yard and into the road, Rebecca runs after her. Esty has an envelope in her hand. She tells Rebecca that she has written a note to Dovid, telling him that if he wants his book back, he must meet her at the Perelmans' house the following night. Rebecca tells Esty that is forbidden, but Esty will not listen. She tells Rebecca to go back to the house and pretend Esty is in bed. Back in her bedroom, Rebecca tries to pray. After a while Esty returns, having delivered the letter.

The following day the entire family goes blueberry-picking. Esty is in a good mood and acts as if nothing unusual has happened between her and Rebecca. At home that night, Rebecca's father Alan calls Aunt Malka, who talks to him in private. When she returns, she looks as if she has had an argument or been reproached by Alan over the matter of the ritual bath. But she insists to the girls that people have to do what is right, even when others are doing otherwise. Esty takes this as a sign that she is right in her actions regarding Dovid.

At twelve-thirty that night, Esty takes the book and is about to slip out of the quiet house when Rebecca insists on going with her. Esty agrees on one condition, that if they are caught, Rebecca must take the blame. Rebecca agrees. They reach the Perelmans' backyard and wait for Dovid, who arrives at one o'clock and asks for his book. Esty shows him the package but does not hand it over. She tells him that looking at such pictures is a sin, that there are many rules for when people can have sex. Then she kisses him, and the book falls from her hand. Rebecca picks it up. She takes it to the lake and wades in. She takes off her clothes, wades in deeper and floats on her back. She lets the book fall into the water and drop to the bottom.

Characters

Esty Adelstein

Esty Adelstein, who is about thirteen or fourteen years old, is Rebecca's older cousin. Her name was formerly Erica, but after her mother became an Orthodox Jew, Erica's name was changed to Esther, a change that seemed to affect her personality. As Erica, she was a mischievous girl, talking back to her mother and doing naughty things such as throwing bits of paper at old ladies in the synagogue. But when her mother took her to Israel, Esther repented her former ways and became pious. She spends a lot of her time praying and studying the Torah and telling her cousin Rebecca that she and her mother should be more observant of Jewish religious rituals and customs. But ironically, it is Esty, in her willingness to read the book *Essence of Persimmon: Eastern Sexual Secrets for Western Lives* and in her boldness in making a nocturnal appointment with Dovid and daring to kiss him, who shows herself to be more reckless, less concerned with following the precepts of her religion than her supposedly more secular cousin Rebecca. Although she may not realize it, Esty is somewhat hypocritical in her attitudes, doing exactly what she wants while presenting a pious exterior.

Alan

Alan, Rebecca's father, does not appear directly in the story, but he speaks to his daughter and to Aunt Malka on the telephone. His conversation with Rebecca shows that he has an easy, comfortable relationship with her. But he is angry with Malka for telling Rebecca to inform her mother about the importance of the mikveh, the ritual bath. It appears that Alan has strong views about how he wishes his daughter to be raised and does not take kindly to what he regards as interference.

Dovid Frankel

Dovid Frankel, a teenage boy who attends the Shabbos dinner at the home of the Adelsteins, is tall and tanned, and both Rebecca and Esty are fascinated by him. Esty believes she is in love with him. Although Dovid comes from an Orthodox family, he shows signs of rejecting his religion. He does not believe that smudged letters in a mezuzah could be the cause of a family's house fire, and he expresses his frustration at such beliefs by going outside and kicking at the metal clothesline frame. Dovid also secretly possesses a book about eastern sexual techniques, and he deliberately touches Rebecca on the arm, even though as an Orthodox Jew he is not supposed to touch a woman who is not his mother or sister.

Lev Handelman

Lev Handelman is Mrs. Handelman's husband.

Mrs. Handelman

Mrs. Handelman is Dovid Frankel's older sister. She is eighteen years old and is pregnant.

Aunt Malka

Aunt Malka, Rebecca's aunt, was formerly Marla Vincent, a set dresser for the Canadian Opera Company in Toronto. Then she got divorced from her husband, and she and her daughter, then called Erica, went to live in Israel for a year. In Jerusalem, she met Shimon and became an Orthodox rather than secular Jew. She married Shimon and returned to the United States, changing her name from Marla to Malka. She credits her new religion with helping her to recover from her divorce. Aunt Malka now raises her large family (Shimon had five children by his former wife) according to Orthodox principles. She busies herself preparing the Shabbos dinner and organizing a family trip to pick blackberries.

Rebecca

Rebecca is a young girl of about twelve or thirteen, and is the narrator of the story. She lives in Manhattan, New York City, and her parents are secular Jews. When her mother's baby dies in infancy, Rebecca is sent to live with her aunt and uncle in upstate New York. Her relatives are Orthodox Jews, and while she stays with them Rebecca feels pressure from her cousin Esty, and from within herself, to be more observant of the Jewish religion. At home in Manhattan, Rebecca was a mischievous and adventurous girl, admitting to stealing naked-lady playing cards from a street vendor and kissing a boy from the swim team behind the bleachers. But her life changes during the summer. She and Esty spend much time praying, studying the Torah, and observing dietary laws and other Orthodox rituals and customs. These customs are quite unfamiliar to Rebecca, since in the more informal atmosphere at home she is more used to going to movies or eating a Chinese dinner. Over the summer Rebecca begins to think seriously about moral and religious questions. She wonders about the nature of God's justice, and at some moments she feels a sense of God's presence, although she is not sure what this might signify. She develops a desire to do God's will. At the end of the story she shows she has the maturity to make a moral decision of her own, as she lets the forbidden book about sexuality fall to the bottom of the lake.

Uncle Shimon

Uncle Shimon, Rebecca's uncle, is an Orthodox Jew and has lived in Israel. His first wife, with whom he had five children, died, and after meeting Malka in Jerusalem, he quickly remarried. Shimon appears to be a contented man who takes his religion seriously. He believes that each person is responsible for his relationship with God, and although his beliefs might be considered narrow, he also possesses a kind of spiritual humility. He does not believe, for example, that it is always possible to know the ways of God or why God allows certain things, even bad things, to happen.

Themes

Secular versus Religious Beliefs and Lifestyles

The story presents the tensions between two different ways of life within the Jewish communities in New York state. Rebecca, although she is Jewish, has been raised in a secular environment, without religious observance. She is not used to observing Jewish customs and rituals. The relatives with whom she stays are the opposite. They are part of a Hasidic Jewish community which rigorously observes all aspects of its faith and is suspicious of outsiders. This wariness of the world beyond the borders of their community is apparent when Dovid Frankel tells Rebecca that some of the people in the area are scared of her, believing that since she comes from worldly Manhattan, she may show her young cousins a fashion magazine—the orthodox community has a strict

Topics For Further Study

- Based on the story, do you have a negative or a positive impression of the type of Judaism it presents? Is the author, who is herself Jewish, supportive or critical of Judaism and the way it is interpreted by the Hasids? Write a short essay in which you respond to these questions, citing passages or incidents in the story to support your argument.
- Consider Aunt Malka's statement to Rebecca, "You have to do what you think is right . . . even when the people around you are doing otherwise." How do Rebecca and Esty interpret her words? When private morality conflicts with the dictates of religion, which voice should one follow? Write an essay discussing this issue, giving examples of situations in which this conflict might occur and how one might respond in dealing with them.
- What type of sex education should be taught in public schools? Should abstinence be emphasized or should the emphasis be on teaching students to make responsible decisions? Should students be informed about homosexuality? At what age? Should teens be allowed to obtain birth control pills from family planning clinics and doctors without permission from a parent? Prepare a class presentation in which you discuss these issues.
- Write a short story in which the main character experiences his or her first crush or first love and behaves in a reckless way in response to it. Try to capture the way it feels to have these feelings, and also indicate ways in which the person is changed by his or her experience. What does the character learn through falling in love?

---

dress code that involves long-sleeved blouses and long skirts for women even in hot weather—or give them the wrong foods or tell them something they should not hear. It was the same, Dovid says, when the Adelsteins first moved there. Since they were newcomers, their orthodox neighbors did not trust them. The picture that emerges is of a rather closed community that distrusts outsiders and is protective of its own religious traditions and way of life. But this works the other way, too. Rebecca's father, a secular Jew, reacts negatively when he thinks that Aunt Malka has been trying to talk Rebecca into adopting orthodox practices. It appears there is a gap between Orthodox and secular Jewish worlds that is hard to bridge.

Rebecca in a sense is that bridge. The longer she stays at the Adelsteins, the more she is influenced by her religious environment. Esty nags her about the virtues of observing of Orthodox Jewish customs, and she joins with her cousin in studying the Torah and praying. At first Rebecca just goes through the motions, pretending to be pious as she knows doing so is expected of her. When she listens to Uncle Shimon explain his belief that there is a connection between a house fire and a smudged mezuzah, she expresses her thoughts about it in an open-minded way, beginning, "If there is a God who can see inside mezuzahs." The key word is "if." Her tone suggests she neither believes the idea nor disbelieves it, and she is also sufficiently free of the constraints of religious faith to admit to Dovid that sometimes she hopes that God does not exist.

However, Uncle Shimon's words do set her wondering, late at night, about weighty concepts such as the judgment of God. In this way, gradually, Rebecca begins to develop genuine religious feelings, although she does not believe that she fully understands them or their implications: "I know I've felt a kind of holy swelling in my chest, a connection to something larger than myself. I wonder if this is proof of something, if this is God marking me somehow."

Rebecca's developing religious awareness is a personal one, based more on her own thoughts, feelings, and experiences than on the teachings of an external authority. Her most powerful experience of God comes when she is alone in nature, and she senses that it is God who is the controlling force behind all natural phenomena—the scent of clover, the bees that fly past her ears, the sun that burns her skin. It is then that she decides for herself that she wants to know more about the will of God, and she wants to follow that will in her own life. She wants to do what God wants her to do.

There is irony in this theme of emerging spirituality. Rebecca, who was feared because she might bring a secular influence into the Orthodox world, is the one who quietly becomes religious, whereas Esty, who likes to give the impression of being very pious, is in fact the one who breaks religious rules. Esty is glib. She regards it as quite all right to sin, if one repents the next day. She is the one who suggests taking the forbidden book home, not Rebecca. Rebecca has a conscience about it. When Esty says no one will know the book is there, Rebecca replies, "But *we'll* know," as if that should be enough to deter them. Esty assures Rebecca that they will not look at the book, but she is the first one who does. It is also Esty who follows her desires and arranges a nocturnal encounter with Dovid that would horrify and alarm her parents if they were to find out. It is ironic that the girl who most insists on following a religious code of conduct is the one who breaks it most flagrantly.

Emerging Sexuality

The theme of the girls' emerging awareness of sexuality is linked to moral and religious considerations. It is clear from the start that the girls are at an age where they are curious about boys and about sex, although their knowledge of both is slight. They are both drawn to the tall, tanned Dovid Frankel and are fascinated by the book *Essence of Persimmon*, even though their lack of physical maturity ensures that they do not understand much of what it describes. A book about sex is bound up in Esty's mind with sin. She says the book is "*tiuv*, abomination," although this does not stop her from reading it. Rebecca is as intrigued as Esty by the book, but not as shocked by it. It appears that she has not been taught to regard such matters as sinful. Earlier that year, before she went to stay with her relatives, she kissed a boy behind the bleachers and appeared not to experience feelings of guilt. However, her summer at the Adelsteins has changed her in some way. Her feelings after Dovid touches her arm are more complex. As she reflects on it later, she feels a "strange rolling feeling in [her] stomach." This feeling arises in part because she is becoming aware for the first time of what it feels like to have a boy touch her bare arm, but also because she knows that Dovid is doing something against the rules of his religion. Sexual morality and religion are becoming linked in her mind.

In the end, while Esty, without showing any signs of a moral struggle, reads the book and kisses Dovid, Rebecca shows a practical moral wisdom of her own. In letting the forbidden book sink to the bottom of the lake, she is acting according to her developing moral sense and also perhaps according to a feeling that the book has the potential at this stage of her life to cause more trouble than it is worth. Her action in letting the book go is not the result of a decision she has pondered with much thought, however; it seems to happen spontaneously as she plunges into the water.

Style

Point of View and Tense

The story is told in the first person by Rebecca. This angle means that all the characters are viewed through Rebecca's eyes and through her thoughts and feelings. There is no independent, objective narrator who could explain, for example, what Esty, or Aunt Malka is thinking. They are revealed only through their words and actions and how Rebecca perceives them. An example of how this focus works occurs when Rebecca asks Esty to explain why she is looking at the forbidden book. Esty "glances down and her eyes widen, as if she's surprised to find she's been holding the book all this time." The reader is not told for certain that Esty is surprised; the qualifying phrase "as if" is necessary to maintain the established point of view, which is that of Rebecca. The point of view helps to put the emphasis on the theme of Rebecca's growth toward a deeper spiritual awareness.

The other noticeable element in the construction of the story is that it is told in the present tense, which means that the action is going on as the narrator speaks rather than having happened in the past which the narrator now is recalling. Present-tense narration is unusual, since much fiction is told in the past tense, although present-tense narration is a technique Orringer uses in a number of her stories. Writers sometimes believe that using the present tense gives a story an immediacy that it might otherwise not have, although what it may gain in immediacy is offset by a lack of perspective. The narrator of a present-tense narrative has no opportunity to look back on the events he or she is describing and assess their significance.

Setting

The story is set at the time of the Jewish celebration of Shabbos (sometimes written as Shabbat). This timing helps to ground the story in the Jewish faith and provide much of the context in which Rebecca's engagement with her religion takes place. In Jewish tradition, Shabbos, the day on which no work is done, is a reminder of the fact that God rested on the seventh day of creation. It is also a celebration of how God delivered the Jewish people from slavery in Egypt. Shabbos begins at sunset on Friday and continues until sunset on Saturday. It is marked with a special dinner on Friday night at which people greet one another with the words "*good Shabbos.*" As in the story, Shabbos dinner often incorporates rituals such as candlelighting and the singing of traditional songs such as "Shalom Aleichem," which means "Peace Be with You" and is a way of giving a blessing. Aunt Malka's baking of challah is also a Shabbos tradition. Challah is braided egg bread which symbolizes the manna, the food God provided the Israelites during their years of wandering in the desert. Traditionally, food served at Shabbos includes, as in the story, gefilte fish (a ball or cake of chopped up fish) and kugel (baked pudding made of potatoes or noodles), and also chicken soup.

Historical Context

Hasidic Judaism

In the story, the Adelsteins appear to be Hasidic Jews. The Hebrew word "hasid" (or "chasid") means "pious." Hasidism is a subdivision of Orthodox Judaism and was founded by Rabbi Israel ben Eliezer, known as Bal Shem Tov (1700–60) in Ukraine. The epithet Bal Shem Tov means "master of the good name." Rabbi Israel wrote no books but promoted the ideal of simple piety by the use of parables and stories told to the uneducated masses. He believed that sincere devotion to God was preferable to scholarly knowledge of the Talmud (the authoritative body of Jewish teachings on civil and religious law, dating from in the early centuries of the Christian era).

Hasidism quickly spread throughout Eastern Europe, and its leaders developed the doctrine of the *zaddik* (the Righteous One), who was believed to be the intermediary between God and man. Rebbe Nachman of Bratslav (1772–1810), mentioned as an authority by Uncle Shimon in the story, was the great-grandson of Israel Bal Shem Tov, and was a revered but controversial *zaddik.* He is remembered in the early 2000s for his allegorical folk tales about princes and princesses, beggars and kings, demons and saints, which reveal spiritual truths. Rebbe Nachman saw himself as a messianic figure who would redeem the Jewish people. Some of his followers revered him so much that on his death they refused to acknowledge any successor. This branch of Hasidism is still in existence as of 2005 and is known as the Bratslav Hasidim.

In "The Smoothest Way Is Full of Stones," the Adelstein family appears to belong to the branch of Hasidism known as the Chabad-Lubavitch movement. There are strong Lubavitcher communities in Brooklyn, New York (numbering at least fifteen thousand people), and in upstate New York towns such as Kiryas Joel and New Square.

The Chabad-Lubavitch movement was founded in Russia by Rabbi Shneur Zalman of Liady (1745–1812) in the mid-eighteenth century. His son established the sect in Lubavitch, a small town in what subsequently became the independent state of Belarus. In Russian, the word Lubavitch means "city of brotherly love." The word "chabad" is a Hebrew acronym for the three faculties of *chachmah* (wisdom), *binah* (knowledge), and *da'at* (understanding).

The Chabad-Lubavitch movement rapidly spread throughout Russia and the wider Jewish world, becoming especially strong, in modern times, in Israel and the United States. The movement was led by a succession of leaders known as rebbes, each descended from the previous leader. The sixth rebbe, Joseph Isaac Schneersohn, was living in Poland when World War II broke out. He escaped the Nazis and arrived in New York in 1940. His son-in-law, Rabbi Menachem Mendel Schneerson, arrived in New York from Paris the following year, and on the death of his father-in-law in 1950, became the seventh Lubavitcher rebbe. It is this rebbe whose photograph hangs on the wall of Esty and Rebecca's bedroom in the story. Rebecca notices his "long steely beard and his eyes like flecks of black glass." She notices the photograph again when she is about to accompany Esty to meet Dovid ("The dread eyes of the Lubavitcher Rebbe stare down at me from the wall"). Between the death of Rabbi Schneerson in 1994 and 2005, no other rebbe had been appointed.

The Hasidim are distinctive in their dress. Men wear black coats, white shirts, a black hat, and a long beard with peyos (sidecurls). Sometimes the peyos are worn in front of the ear, or they can be

An Orthodox Jewish family at the dinner table © Bojan Brecelj/Corbis

tucked back behind the ear. In the story, Dovid Frankel has prominent peyos, "luxuriously curled, shoulder-length." Hasidic women, like Esty and Rebecca in "The Smoothest Way Is Full of Stones," dress modestly, wearing long skirts with long-sleeved shirts. In some Hasidic groups, married women sometimes shave their heads, and many wear wigs.

Relations between Hasidic men and women are more formal than in mainstream American culture. Hasidic men and women do not shake hands or touch each other in any other way unless they are married, and then only in private.

Critical Overview

Orringer's collection of stories, *How to Breathe Underwater*, was well received by reviewers. Few singled out "The Smoothest Way Is Full of Stones" for special attention, although the comment of the reviewer for *Publishers Weekly* might well apply to Rebecca in that story: "Trapped in awkward, painful situations, the young protagonists of Orringer's debut collection discover surprising reserves of wisdom in themselves."

Similarly, Lisa Dierbeck's general comment about the collection, in the *New York Times Book Review*, applies to "The Smoothest Way Is Full of Stones": "children and adults operate in a secret world of their own. They seem to exist in an underground, beyond the scope of adults' radar." This is certainly true of Rebecca and Esty; their parents have no suspicion of their secret reading of the forbidden book or their nocturnal excursion to meet Dovid.

Dierbeck also points out that "The shadow of mortality hovers over Orringer's book. More than one mother in the collection has battled cancer." Rebecca's mother, of course, has lost her infant son, and this has had an impact on Rebecca as well as her mother.

Dierbeck concludes with ringing praise of Orringer's skill as a writer: "The harsh landscape in which Orringer's characters dwell corresponds to the fierce beauty of her writing. Even the grimmest of these stories conveys, along with anguish, a child's spark of mystery and wonder."

This praise is echoed by other reviewers. In England's *The Guardian*, Emily Perkins offers the opinion that "Orringer allows her girls both self-doubt and great spirit; she gives them generous hearts, word-perfect dialogue and a fictional context that insists on harsh truths but is never bleak." In *People Weekly*, Ting Yu comments that Orringer's stories "uncover the dark, electric world of young girls on the cusp of womanhood." She adds that "Growing up is hard to do, but under Orringer's masterful care, these young girls—imperfect, broken and searching—find ways to thrive."

Criticism

Bryan Aubrey

Bryan Aubrey holds a Ph.D. in English and has published many articles on literature. In this essay, he discusses the contrast between Esty and Rebecca and Rebecca's growing spiritual awareness.

In an interview with Robert Birnbaum, Orringer said of her stories: "They tend to be about young women who are in between childhood and adulthood. They are about people who are at a moment of an incredibly difficult transition in their lives." This statement certainly applies to Rebecca in "The Smoothest Way Is Full of Stones," a story which captures with great immediacy and perceptiveness the world of adolescence in all its turmoil and uncertainty. In one summer away from home, new experiences, new ideas, and new feelings crowd in on the growing girl, and she must quickly develop ways of understanding and integrating them into her awareness of what life is and how she is going to approach it. The other young characters in the story, Esty Adelstein and Dovid Frankel, are also going through similar transitions.

The themes of the story are revealed through the relationship between Rebecca and Esty. Esty is older than Rebecca by a year or so, and initially it is she who appears to take the lead in their relationship. It is Esty who wades first into the lake, unconcerned that her parents do not allow the girls to swim. Esty has a ready-made excuse; if they are challenged on why their clothes are wet, they will tell her parents that they fell in. Deviousness seems to come naturally to Esty; behind her pious exterior she does whatever she wants to do, regardless of whether it breaks the rules. Although the reader only sees Esty through Rebecca's eyes and therefore does not have the same insight into her motivations, Esty does not seem to be conscious of the dichotomy between what she professes and what she actually does. She may have studied her religion with zeal, but she has not yet absorbed in a sincere and mature way the implications it may have for her conduct. It is Esty, for example, who suggests taking the book *Essence of Persimmon* home with them, and it is Esty, despite her assurance to Rebecca that they will not look at it, who is the first to take the book down from the top shelf in the closet and begin reading it.

Esty, however, does have an excuse. She is suffering from that most overwhelming of experiences, first love, a shattering event that has not yet, it appears, happened for Rebecca. It is because Esty is upset with Rebecca over Dovid Frankel that she heads for the closet and reads the forbidden book. Rebecca's sin was to go outside and spend a few moments alone with Dovid, an experience for which Esty apparently longs. Her subsequent jealousy may explain some of her spiteful and manipulative behavior toward Rebecca.

Esty's deviousness does not come so naturally to Rebecca, who is in the process of slowly assimilating what Esty, for all her piety, seems to have missed. Rebecca has been raised in a secular household but in the highly religious environment in which she now finds herself, she gradually develops a quiet awareness of God and some insight into the demands of a life lived in accordance with God's will. Unlike Esty, Rebecca shows no signs of adopting an excessively pious exterior, but she does indicate that she is developing an ability to listen to her religious feelings and let them guide her in honest but unostentatious way.

Rebecca's religious feelings come from many sources. Sometimes at Shabbos she feels the presence of something larger than herself, and she is also quite affected by Uncle Shimon's story about the flaw in the mezuzah that was responsible—so Uncle Shimon believes—for a house fire. His making this connection sets her thinking about the judgment of God, and the image she forms in her mind of God and religion seems to be a stern one, suggested by the forbidding face of the Lubavitcher Rebbe, whose piercing eyes stare down at her from the portrait on the bedroom wall. Rebecca even convinces herself that the death of her infant brother is God's punishment of her because she once, for a moment, wished that the baby would die. (Her wish sprang from her awareness that if the baby survived he would need constant care, and she feared as a result she might be neglected by her parents.) Religion as it comes to her in its official form is full of prohibitions, a long list of things one is supposed not to do, especially on Shabbos. There is an especially long list pertaining to when it is and is not permissible to have sex, as Esty informs her with all the confidence of one who knows: "You can't do it outside. You can't do it drunk. You can't do it during the day or with the lights on. You're supposed to think about subjects of Torah while you do it."

One of her most powerful religious experiences, however, is not mediated, at least not directly, by anything she has read or heard about God and religion. It comes directly from nature and has the stamp of personal experience, not just something someone has told her about what Judaism teaches. It comes when she is alone outside, as Shabbos nears its end. As she lies in the tall grass, experiencing nature through all her senses, she feels a presence gathering around her which culminates in a tremendous moment of new spiritual awareness:

> It is God who makes the shadows dissolve around me. He sharpens the scent of clover. He pushes the bees past my ears, directs the sun onto my back until my skin burns through the cotton of my Shabbos dress. I want to know what He wants and do what He wants, and I let my mind fall blank, waiting to be told.

By letting her mind "fall blank" Rebecca shows that she is ready to learn a more mature understanding of how to discern the will of God. She waits, passively, for God to make his will known to her rather than thinking that all she must do is slavishly follow an external code of law. By making her own individual mind blank, she allows a space for God to step in. The God that speaks directly to the mind and heart in quiet moments is quite different from the deity who harshly judges those who make one small mistake.

However, in spite of this moment of revelation, Rebecca is not yet able to free herself of the shadow of guilt and judgment, since later that night she reproaches herself, and everyone else, for not being more mindful of the demands of God as they go about their day-to-day lives.

Toward the end of the story, Rebecca's emerging religious awareness bears fruit. As Esty prepares for her reckless encounter with Dovid at night, the relationship between the cousins has been quietly reversed from what it was at the beginning. Now Rebecca, the younger of the two, is the one for whom the dictates of religion influence her attitude and conduct. Rebecca also feels a sense of responsibility to protect her cousin, even though, being so young, she is not sure what she is protecting her from.

Esty in this situation certainly needs some help. She is so much in the grip of her infatuation with Dovid that she will do whatever she feels she must in order to get what she wants. By insisting that if she and Rebecca are caught, Rebecca must take all the blame, she shows her immaturity, her failure to accept that she is responsible for her own actions. It must be said also that Rebecca is not above using unscrupulous tactics of her own, as when Esty is writing a note to Dovid, and Rebecca says she will scream for Esty's mother unless Esty tells her what she is doing.

"By making her own individual mind blank, she allows a space for God to step in. The God that speaks directly to the mind and heart in quiet moments is quite different from the deity who harshly judges those who make one small mistake."

When Esty does meet up with Dovid, she is quite brazen in her attempt to manipulate him. Faced with this aggressive and cunning girl, the previously self-assured Dovid, the same boy who confidently touched Rebecca's arm the previous evening, does not have a clue how to behave. "What do you want me to do?" he says feebly. "What am I supposed to do?" As Esty reaches up to him and kisses him, Rebecca goes about some action of her own. On their way to meet Dovid, she has been acutely aware of the moral and religious implications of what they are about to do; even the natural environment reminds her of it: "Tree frogs call in the dark, the rubber-band twang of their throats sounding to me like *God, God, God.*" Rebecca seems to have a quiet awareness that the book *Essence of Persimmon* has brought them nothing but quarrels and danger. They are too young, not ready for such a book, and she knows it. As she wades into the water and floats on her back, gazing up at the Milky Way, the water acts like a mikvah for her—the ritual bath of purification that

What Do I Read Next?

- Renowned Canadian writer Alice Munro is one of Orringer's favorite writers. Orringer singled out Munro's short story collection, *The Love of a Good Woman* (1999) for particular praise, admiring the stories "The Children Stay," "Before the Change," and "My Mother's Dream," as well as the title story. Orringer admires the way Munro describes the inner lives of her characters.
- In an interview available on the Barnes and Noble website, Orringer named George Saunders's *Pastoralia* (2001) as one of her favorite books. It is Saunders's second collection, consisting of five stories as well as the title novella. Saunders sets his stories in a disturbing near future in which capitalism and the free market rule the world, resulting in grotesque inequities. The stories feature many wretched characters in appallingly bad situations, but there are many moments of grace and humor, and in spite of the squalor, the human spirit seems to triumph. Orringer commented that the stories always hit the right emotional notes.
- Sue Fishkoff's *The Rebbe's Army: Inside the World of Chabad-Lubavitch* (2003) explores how young Lubavitchers carry their message of spiritual renewal to the wider Jewish world throughout the United States. Fishkoff, who admires and respects the Lubavitch movement, draws on many interviews she conducted, as well as her experiences in traveling with Lubavitchers to Shabbos dinners, mikvah demonstrations, and fundraising events.
- *The Chosen* (1967), by Chaim Potok, is a coming-of-age story that focuses on the friendship between two Jewish boys in Brooklyn, New York, in the 1940s. Reuven is from an Orthodox Jewish family. Danny is a member of a Hasidic sect, and his father is a respected rebbe and *zaddik*. The unlikely friendship between the boys grows against a background of World War II, Zionism, and the founding of the state of Israel.
- In Alice McDermott's *Child of My Heart* (2002), Theresa, a middle-aged woman, looks back on a summer spent working among the rich residents of East Hampton, on Long Island, New York, in the 1960s, when she was fifteen. Theresa also has to look after her visiting eight-year-old cousin. Together they weave a fantasy world, which for Theresa includes emerging sexual awareness.

Aunt Malka explained to her; it is spiritually cleansing, and she has no difficulty in letting go of the fascinating but forbidden book. She has chosen the sensible, moral choice, but done it quietly, with no great fanfare of piety.

And yet, even while Rebecca takes a mature action of which her religious, conservative relatives would approve, there is another element in this scene that suggests Rebecca is also cultivating an independent spirit and is not bound solely by the prescriptions of her religion. At the beginning of the story she pointed out that she and Esty were forbidden to swim because, they were told, it was immodest to show their bodies. Instead, they had waded fully clothed into the lake. But this time Rebecca does not hesitate to remove her shirt and skirt, and she notes how she feels the night air against her bare skin. Equivalent of a mikvah this may be, but it is one that is closely connected to the natural world in all its sensuality. The nearly naked young girl who floats serenely on the water at night is a very different person from the one who returned home with the Shabbos groceries only a few days earlier. Quietly doing what she feels is the right thing (as Aunt Malka told Esty that she must), she also shows she is growing in independence, calmly ignoring a rule for which she sees no justification.

Source: Bryan Aubrey, Critical Essay on "The Smoothest Way Is Full of Stones," in *Short Stories for Students*, Thomson Gale, 2006.

Julie Orringer with Robert Birnbaum

In the following interview, Orringer discusses with Robert Birnbaum her childhood, her ties to the South, and the short story.

Julie Orringer, with her nine excellent stories in *How to Breathe Underwater,* can be added to the list of young writers who are sustaining the viability of short form fiction. The conversation below will tell you something about her thoughts on writing and her stories and some things about her life that may illuminate her less obvious thoughts and ideas. What you won't learn is that Orringer went to Cornell as an undergraduate and then to the Writers Workshop in Iowa City followed by a Stegner Fellowship in the Creative Writing Program at Stanford. Her stories have been published in the *Barcelona Review, Ploughshares,* and *Zoetrope.*

Orringer lives in San Francisco with her husband writer Ryan Harry and she is, of course, working on her first novel.

[*Robert Birnbaum*]: *If someone were an orthodox and literal person they might look at your book and say, 'Where is that story 'How to Breathe Under Water'?' Usually the title of the collection is also a story in the book. Why does the title represent these stories?*

[Julie Oringer]: The title came to me rather late in the process. I didn't know when I was putting the stories together that this was going to be the thematic umbrella. And I was working on that story ['Isabel Fish'] and I came to that moment when the narrator is trying to imagine what's ahead as she begins scuba lessons. She is coming off a rather awful incident with a car accident and a drowning and it seemed to me this phrase, this idea of trying to breathe under water was something that maybe had some larger resonance for the other stories as well. They tend to be about young women who are in between childhood and adulthood. They are about people who are at a moment of an incredibly difficult transition in their lives. It's not just a coming-of-age transition—in fact, I am resistant to that idea of coming of age. It suggests two different states—one that you pass out of and one that you strictly enter. I feel like the title has something to do with how hard it is to redefine yourself after a loss or trauma or as you

One of the things that I resist in fiction is the idea that a terrible experience will lead to some kind of epiphany or positive change in a character."

are entering this new period of your life. And yet we somehow do it anyway.

Was that an unconscious theme? Or just what you cared about when you were writing these stories?

I think so. It's something I didn't really know that I cared about when I was younger, as I was growing up, until I had the distance from those experiences that was necessary to actually be able to write about them.

How was your childhood?

[*laughs*] How is anybody's childhood?

[*both laugh*] *That's a fair response but I'm the one asking the questions here.*

[*laughs*] That's fair, too. My childhood was great in most respects and awful in certain respects. I was very lucky. I was lucky to be born in this country, at the time that I was born, into the family that I was born into, with loving parents and a brother and sister that I was close to. But my family moved a lot because my parents were [both] physicians and they were early on in their training when I was born. In fact, they were in their third year of medical school when I was born. And that made it hard for me in certain ways—as an elementary school kid because I was the new kid and it took me a long time to dig in. That was hard enough to begin with and I was this awkward, gangly, bookish kid who would rather sit in the library and read chapters in books than trade stickers on the playground. I think things were made a lot more difficult by the fact that my mother was diagnosed with breast cancer when I was 10. And so from very early on I had to begin contemplating the idea that I would lose her and experiencing the uncertainty that that threw into our lives . . . she was sick for 10 years before she died.

[*pause*] *I ssuppose it's natural to look for biographical clues in stories. Other than a couple of stories that take place in the South I don't see any clues of a connection to the South for you. How is it that one of your stories ended up in* New Stories from the South?

I actually did spend seven years living in the South when I was growing up. I lived in New Orleans, between the ages of five and 12. It was a time when I was developing a sense of what I liked to read. When I was in elementary school—because I went to a really wonderful school, I spent a lot of time learning about the architecture of New Orleans and its history and I felt pretty at home in that place despite the problems I was having in school.

Isn't New Orleans atypical of the rest of the South, a thing unto itself?

Yes, it's probably atypical of the rest of anything in the world. New Orleans people are atypical of the South and we were atypical of most residents because we were a young Jewish family. We didn't have any old ties there. We came there because of my father's work. That was part of the strangeness of it for me. What did it mean to be a Jewish kid growing up in this place in which the biggest festival of the year was Mardi Gras—an essentially Christian festival? So I think that was an element that contributed to my sense of being somewhat on the outside of things.

Why did Shannon Ravenel consider you a Southern writer?

[*laughs*] Because that particular story took place in New Orleans and she knew that I had lived there as a child.

That was very ecumenical of her. I look at your pedigree on the dust jacket of your book and the pedigree is not at all unusual: Iowa, Stanford. If I said to you as a publisher, 'I think you are a really incredible talent Julie, I would publish anything that you want. But I would really like not to identify you. I would just like to present your work and other people that I publish in plain undecorated boards, numbered titles, and designate some anonymous names for the authors,' how would you feel about that?

How would I feel about losing the—

The personal identification with your work—

I think that would be fine.

And thereby lose an opportunity to be celebrated and acknowledged?

The work would be presented without any connection to me, the writer, at all?

Right.

I'd think that would be fine. I didn't write the stories in order to be celebrated or even to be a writer, as it were. I wrote the stories because I wanted—I had these things that I wanted to say. That I wanted to get out there for other people to understand and maybe feel some connection with. So everything else that goes along with it in terms of receiving recognition is really not even secondary—it's tertiary or something further on down the line. It's a very distant corollary to what's really important, which is that these stories are now making themselves out into the world and maybe there is a chance that someone will meet them with understanding and with common feeling.

And then what happens, what are your expectations?

After that I would like to crawl back into my hole and write my novel. [*laughs*] One of the things that I resist in fiction is the idea that a terrible experience will lead to some kind of epiphany or positive change in a character.

What happens to the reader after they have made a connection with your stories? What should they be getting that would be satisfying to you—a better understanding of the world and perhaps making the world better?

It's really hard to boil it down to one thing that I would like for them to be getting out of it. One thing that I would want [is for] them to look at these characters. This is what experience can be like for women between the ages of nine and 27. Or this is how difficult it is for other people and I don't have to feel I am alone in experiencing this profound difficulty. Or maybe something like, 'Everything doesn't have to come up roses or seem as if it is a making me heroic when it is really awful.' One of the things that I resist in fiction is the idea that a terrible experience will lead to some kind of epiphany or positive change in a character.

There is the notion that there is some nobility in suffering . . .

Yes, when some of these stories are about the most difficult things that could happen to you—being a young kid and losing your mother, for example. I don't feel ultimately strengthened by that experience. I feel like I have experienced this incredible loss. I don't want anyone to have to go through that. It doesn't mean that it won't make you think in more interesting or complicated ways about life and death but people go through hideous things in the world and to suggest that those things somehow make you a better person—

Or that they recover—

Or that they recover or that they somehow are necessary, that would be a mistake.

Tell me what it feels like to write and what it feels like when it is going well and when it is not. Your description in 'Isabel Fish' of the young girl as she recalls the actual car crash, sinking in the pond, was incredibly vivid. Or the druggie aunt in 'Care' who is taking care of her six-year-old niece and her own struggle with the decision to take the drugs she has in her pocket. And the sixth-grader who is being taunted and teased relentlessly—these were very clearly powerfully expressed. So can we focus your descriptive skills on what it is, when you are writing, that you are feeling?

In the stories that you mentioned those were moments when I had really gotten inside this character's head and I was really feeling what it meant to be her. And those are moments that come quite a ways into the story and they had taken a good deal of warming up and a good many drafts in order to get to that point where I could write inside the person that way.

Is it like taking drugs, that the first high leaves you forever trying to recreate that first feeling or buzz? Sometimes you do and sometimes . . .

Yeah. There are certainly times when there is no buzz at all, where there is nothing at all. I just feel like I am clacking out the words on a keyboard and they are just dead on the page. There are other times when I feel I have entered this fugue state where everything seems to drop away and I am almost channeling the story through the character. I don't want to sound New Agey or mystical about that but it does feel like it is something that is not entirely under my control and that is an exhilarating feeling. It is exciting.

Exciting? As being on a merry-go-round? Or a roller coaster? Or exciting as a watching something totally new?

In the sense of something totally new. If I am creating those characters and the characters have begun to attain some kind of reality—then it becomes all the more unpredictable. I have no idea what's going to happen next. Unlike a roller coaster, which picks you up and drops you down and rattles you around a little bit, this character could do an infinite number of things. I have no way of knowing what those things may be. If I understand the character then I know that at least those things are within a scope of which this person is. Or what I am trying to drive towards or work towards in subsequent drafts. Some writers are being castigated for taking big chances in their work. That's highly objectionable. Writers should be encouraged to take chances.

Is writing stories a warm up for writing the grander thing, the novel?

When I started out writing short stories I imagined that this was a kind of practice for a novel that was going to come later. As I got farther along in my studies and in the development of my writing I became so excited about the short story as a form I ceased thinking of it as anything I wanted to do as preparation. So many of the short story writers that I profoundly admire like Alice Munro or Charles Baxter or Richard Ford—I could go on and on—I saw them making something of this form that felt entirely new to me. And that was extremely engaging in itself and something that I felt I wanted to devote a long time to. I thought I might never write a novel and I didn't have a problem with that. I was happy to think that I would always work in the short story form. And the fact that I am working on a novel right now comes more out of the fact that there came along a story that I really wanted to tell that seems like it was to be too large for the scope of the short story. And so that was also a pleasure too. Now I am getting into this different form that provide its own challenges. I hope that I don't have to write as many novels as I have written short stories before I come up with one that is not terrible.

I am tempted to ask you to self-critique yourself—but I won't. Charles Baxter said something quite acute about you in the dust jacket blurb, talking about 'a headlong narrative energy.' That's exactly what I felt in your writing. But now I have forgotten what I wanted to ask.

You were going to ask me to criticize myself.

No, I don't want to do that, unless you want to. Do you know the Randy Newman song, 'God's Song'?

I don't know it.

God explains why he loves human beings even though they show foolish judgment in believing in him when he does all these bad things to man . . . I was listening to that song as I was driving into Boston today and I thought about how in three minutes and 12 seconds, Newman has encapsulated a big story so perfectly in a truly short form. I got to thinking about whether people thought about songs as stories and narratives. But I digress . . . who is reading short stories?

More and more people are reading short stories.

Are those people co-equivalent with those who are learning how to write them?

In some cases yes. But people have always read short stories in magazines. In recent years there have been some short story collections that have emerged as real favorites among readers. Like Nathan Englander's *For the Relief of Unbearable Urges* and Jhumpa Lahiri's *Interpreter of Maladies* and Adam Haslett's *Stranger Here . . .*

Richard Ford's Multitude of Sins, *ZZ Packer's* Drinking Coffee Elsewhere . . .

Yeah. I was speaking to my dad about this recently. My father is a cardiologist and he doesn't have a lot of time for reading. But he loves reading short stories because he can sit down and pick up the book and be in somebody's world for 20 minutes or an hour and follow the course of a narrative to it's completion. Or at least in the sense that short stories can be said to finish.

Sure, that was the reason magazines published short fiction—it was quick and easy—readers could take fiction in small doses. Mark Winegardner takes the position that a writer's most serious work is short form—if you really want to know a writer look at their short stories. He suggested that novels can be sloppy and allow for mistakes but writers aren't allowed to make mistakes in short fiction.

There is no room for them in the short story. And also the short story is a much more revisable form. It's awfully hard and it takes a very long time to revise a novel. It takes a long time to revise short stories certainly but it's easier to put a short story through nine or 10 drafts than to do the same thing with a novel. Maybe there is an expectation that the short story has been more carefully examined, more times, by the time it hits the page. [Tobias Wolff] finished reading and a neurosurgeon approached him and said, 'Boy I really loved the reading. I've been thinking that I'd love to do some writing.' And Toby said, 'That's funny, I was thinking I'd like to do some brain surgery.'

So as not to make the digression totally irrelevant, do you listen to music and perhaps with the thought of hearing stories?

Sometimes I really love and retain songs that are very narrative and then other times the songs I love are for their sonic quality.

'Louie Louie'?

[*laughs*] The song that I was thinking about was that great Tom Waits song 'Step Right Up' where he is compiling a variety of ad slogans, jingles, and tag-lines into this hilarious song. Selling everything from gardening services to sexual favors to new shirts to what have you. I like it when musicians are taking chances and I am pretty catholic in my musical tastes. I love jazz—Charles Mingus . . .

Did you ever hear Chuck D do a Mingus composition called 'Gun Slinging Bird?' It was on a Mingus compilation disc by Hal Wilner called Weird Nightmare. *It's a two-minute song about a fire in a nightclub and how he (Mingus) escapes by breaking out through a wall—like he had seen a man do who was being chased by a woman he had threatened with a knife. Talk about a compact story —you've never heard it?*

I'll have to check it out. I love songs that will suggest stories. I find that Nina Simone's songs are very suggestive and Cole Porter also tends to be suggestive in that way. And I tend to like fairly narrative poetry for obvious reasons. Though it's out of fashion. I am not ashamed to like it.

You're not ashamed?

No.

You have cast yourself as an odd person. Not that you are stereotypical but there is a kind of person who when there was recess in elementary school is the person who was not playing kickball but is sitting off to the side on the playground, reading a book.

I played kickball.

[*laughs*]

I would get my keister kicked instead of the ball. I did love to play outside and do all the normal things too. I was bi-polar in that sense. Maybe as a child . . . what I didn't like was the way a lot of the kids in private school that I went to in New Orleans were overly concerned with the outward trappings of wealth. It's amazing to think that in second grade everybody knows what kind of car everybody else's parent's drove, what job everybody's parents had. Even the addresses, they knew what area of town you lived in.

I ran into my son's pediatrician on the subway once. I love this guy—he's an excellent doctor but it says something that he is taking public transportation. Anyway, he told me how disturbing he found it that his patients—pre-teens—knew the income ranges of many professions and they have this acute sense of what things cost . . . sadly, that is what has been created.

It's kind of scary. For a long time, gradually, to a greater and greater extent we have been concentrating on the wrong things in our schools and in our higher education. It used to be when you went to college, we were meant to learn something about the vast array of knowledge in the world. Now what I see fairly often, particularly at Stanford, students will come in to their university education thinking, 'This is what I have to do in order to prepare myself for the job.' And sometimes student will, wonderfully, stray into other things. Many of my creative writing students have been pre-med majors or even people in the business school or engineers who have discovered there is this other thing that they really love and want to learn more about. I am glad they are doing it.

Jamaica Kincaid mentioned to me that in her teaching experience she felt as if writing students were lacking in a lot of general knowledge about the world. They just didn't know what caused a hurricane or things that one would expect people to know. It seems like you are supposed to declare your major and career path in the first grade.

I think so. If I had to declare my major in first grade I would have been a pre-med.

Were your parents both happy to have chosen medicine?

They were free choices although my father and mother were both artistically talented. My father is an incredible writer. He studied journalism before he studied medicine. He's always been extremely eloquent both on the page and in person. My mother was a violinist and a dancer and gymnast. She had to choose whether to pursue her gymnastic training under the Olympic coach Vela Karly or go to college and to medical school. She chose medical school. Even though I saw my parents making that decision for their lives I was always conscious of the fact that there were other ways that you could go. And that my parents hadn't necessarily followed a straight path to their chosen professions. I didn't write the stories in order to be celebrated or even to be a writer, as it were. I wrote the stories because I wanted, I had these things that I wanted to say. That I wanted to get out there for other people to understand and maybe feel some connection with.

So what are you going to do in your life?

Oh. [*pause*] What am I going to do with my life?

Is your life defined by whether you can write or not? If tomorrow you were unable to write something satisfactory and the day after also and so on, what would happen to you?

I would keep trying for an awfully, awfully long time. But if part of the question is what else is there in my life that's of great importance to me? I'd have to say my relationship with my husband is extremely important. He is also a writer. His short story collection is called *Bring Me Your Saddest Arizona.* His name is Ryan Hardy.

You mention him in the acknowledgments along with everyone else in the world except for me. [*laughs*]

Next time, Robert. Absolutely.

[*laughs*]

I feel like our relationship is one of the most important things that I can devote my energy and time to. As is my relationship with my brother and sister, who are five and eight years younger respectively. Today is my brother's birthday. Every time you say September 15, I get a little excited and then I remember why.

Where is he?

He's in medical school at Ohio State University in Columbus. And my sister is teaching middle school English through Teach for America in LA. We have retained this incredible bond of closeness as we have all moved into our adult years. And so, apart from writing, those relationships are incredibly important to me. And also if I couldn't write for one reason, then I would try to see what I could do actively to make the world better—through teaching or through social action. That's one of the things that we as writers better be conscious of. I am lucky enough to live in San Francisco where Vendela Vida and Dave Eggers have 826 Valencia and it's an incredible program where kids are receiving one-on-one tutoring that they would in no way have access to. It's been a pleasure to go in and work with some of the students. It makes me feel even if my writing sucks I am doing something useful.

Here you are, whatever it has taken to get you here as a young and now published writer, now you enter the fray—for lack of a better word . . .

It's a good word.

. . . you are touring to support your book and talking to total strangers. And in front of total strangers, for a period of time, and subjecting yourself to the commentary and observations and judgments and occasionally ridicule of others. How much do you pay attention to the literary press? And what do you make of the dialectic emerging on snarking? Can you talk about that? Have you gotten any bad reviews?

I have gotten some reviews that are not as positive as I would have liked. I have been thinking about this a lot simply because it is a significant change in my writing life—not my writing life but my life as this person that writes. I've been very fortunate in the way things have worked out for me in publishing. Sometimes reviewers can react against that. Reviewers sometimes like to get behind a person who is engaged in a real struggle to get their voice heard or is being under-published. Sometimes they will react against someone who has a first book coming out from a terrific publisher. Especially someone who is young.

Currently that would include Nell Freudenberger.

She has received some wonderful reviews. I think her work is terrific. But some people have also reacted against the hype around her book and it's unfair but inevitable. That's something we have to deal with and it has nothing to do with who we are as writers and what we are doing when we sit down and work on the next thing. In a baseball game you either win or lose. It's not binary in a piece of fiction.

It has nothing to do with who you are as a writer?

Not with who we are when we are sitting down and communicating with our work on the page or with the ideas that we are trying to bring to the page. If it does then that's a problem and we have to do whatever we can to get away from that. It's inevitable that it will be on our minds. That it will affect us to a certain extent. We have to do our best to minimize that.

I suppose the most important thing in writing is the text but I can't dismiss the notion that the person counts for something in this scheme. David Thomson recently reviewed a new biography of Robert Capa and discussed the question about the famous shot he took of a dying Spanish soldier—was it staged? If it was staged does it devalue the picture, the most important thing being the image on the page? But it does matter.

It does. Can I ask you a question?

O.K..

To what extent do you think about where the review is coming from when you read the review? To what extent are you thinking, 'Well, here's what this person is saying. Here's what's maybe motivating them?'

For the few reviews I read, I suppose that I do question the negative criticism. I dislike the disrespect for the effort—which is not to say that one ought to be reverential or get a pass because of the work done.

There is a story that I love that Toby Wolff tells—an experience he had after a reading. He had finished reading and a neurosurgeon approached him and said, 'Boy I really loved the reading. I've been thinking that I'd love to do some writing.' And Toby said, 'That's funny, I was thinking I'd like to do some brain surgery.'

[*laughs*] Except the difference is that writing is more accessible than brain surgery.

It can be but my brother is training to be a neurosurgeon and . . .

He can't write?

Actually, he can write. One of the reasons that people are so drawn to writing is that they see somebody stepping up and telling their stories and people think, 'Ah, yes I have stories to tell.' Or, 'I want to tell my story.' That became something that was important to me along the way. 'Ah, it's not just something that you read in a book. You can put it down on a page yourself.'

After I got done with James Wolcott's pummeling of Jonathan Lethem's new novel in the Wall Street Journal, *I did question what he was doing and I did see it as an act of bravado since Wolcott also has a book coming out. Also I thought that he might have been physically ill when he wrote the review since he was so totally unsympathetic. He started off quoting Thomas Wolfe, 'Only the dead know Brooklyn,' and then he ends the review, 'Only the dead know Lethem's Brooklyn. And they are not talking.'*

That's entirely unfair.

It is clever.

Yeah, it is but cleverness will get you a review and a cup of tea.

Did you see Clive James's piece in the Op-Ed section of the NYT *which seemed to cap off the snarkery debate?*

I did and I thought it was an excellent synopsis of the argument. It talked about the necessity of the instructive review. And that a bad review can be a plea on the part of the reviewer to make the writer see some truth about his work or the world. That's extremely important. That's one of the things, that when I was going to embark on this process of putting the work out there, I was speaking to a friend of mine, ZZ Packer, about her experience and whether or not she read reviews. Her book was beautifully reviewed but there were a couple of reviews that she found very instructive that were not unmitigatingly positive. So she said, 'Absolutely, I read the review, I might learn something about who I am as a writer and the book.' My editor's feeling was the same. I got one review that wasn't what I hoped it would be. So after that I said, 'Boy I am not going to read another review.' But my editor reminded me, 'Sometimes a review can help your work.'

Sometimes. But the issue is not the less-than-positive review, it's the hatchet job or the ad hominem snide and vicious one. Maybe the thing is also a matter of quantity. There seem to be so many critical decapitations.

The worst review is the snarky, dismissive review. If somebody really takes fierce issue with something in a book then that can be an homage in itself. The dismissive review is the one that really disrespects the time and the effort of the writing itself and that's a horrible thing to see done to someone. It would be interesting to see a compendium of reviews and see if we could trace the history of bile in reviews. [*laughs*]

I was going over the few dependable literary critics and I find that they are not prone to this slash-and-burn review. Eder is not sarcastic and b——y.

No . . .

Caldwell can be tart but she's clearly an enthusiast. James Wood can be fierce but still he seems to be respectful. Yardley, Dirda, Daniel Mendelsohn aren't hatchet carriers.

And I think that it comes out of loving to read and loving what they are seeing on the page. Not just from the standpoint of whether this writer is doing what they are trying to do to the greatest extent they can do it but also a joy at the variance of what is out there. And at the chances that people are taking. One thing that is slightly disturbing that I have seen recently in reviews is that some writers are being castigated for taking big chances in their work. That's highly objectionable. Writers should be encouraged to take chances and if they fail it should be seen within the context of what they attempted rather than as a kind of flaw of judgment in even having tried in the first place.

That would be having a greater expectation of human nature than we have any right to. Look in Boston, we have one of the great pitchers in baseball history, Pedro Martinez. If he has a bad outing at Fenway Park he is booed. They don't say, 'Oh, a bad day. Better luck next time Pete.' No, they boo him.

In a baseball game you either win or lose. It's not binary in a piece of fiction.

Right. Though I think that in a 162-game season no one game is more important. Can we go back to the song discussion? I am fascinated with the notion of creating a list—a popular contemporary pastime—of meaningful narrative story songs. I was thinking about it a lot because of Warren Zevon's death. I spent a few days listening to a collection of his songs and I found that he was really good at pulling you into the middle of his dreams and thoughts. Sometimes with the most obvious words. Like a song called 'Life'll Kill Ya.' Or, 'Gorilla, You're a Desperado,'

Big gorilla at the L.A. Zoo
Snatched the glasses right off my face
Took the keys to my BMW
Left me here to take his place

Anyway, you mentioned that you loved Cole Porter. Can you think of some songs that you might say had the same narrative force as a good piece of fiction?

Can you give me a minute on that one? [*pause*] There is a Nina Simone song I believe is called 'Four Women.' She is singing about four different characters, all black women, all beautifully distinct.

Besides the narrative force of the works by themselves the reason I am dwelling on those is because the notion of hypertextuality was a big thing for a while. We saw the manufacture of these complex CD-Roms that had all these multimedia links. And I was thinking about whether anyone had created any fiction that had musical links or visual links.

A lot of that is coming out of the MFA program at Brown.

Oh yes, Robert Coover . . .

It's not something I have found necessary to explore in my own work. I kind of love the object of the book and reading the words on a physical page. In this physical object. I love the substance and the weight of it. But I think there is a great deal of possibility for developing new forms. It's exciting that some people are doing it.

Because when I talked with them a number of younger writers have been unabashed about their shorter attention spans and the culture they grew up in which included TV and that sampling in music has something to do with it. Perhaps the cultural watering holes include more diverse kinds of information that flow into textual narratives.

It's interesting about shortened attention spans. We hear a lot about that. It's almost a commonplace in what people will say when they are talking about the x and y generation. But if we accept the idea that attention span has necessarily been shortened then it's a kind of giving up. It's saying we are not going to try to present the kind of movies or books or songs or art to these people that would require a long attention span.

Much is produced that isn't going to try . . .

That's a crime. That's a mistake.

It's just like what happens with computers. They will make you bend to their limitations. I remember reading a review of some new doo-dad and the writer pointed out that because the utensil couldn't do some particular operation the user was unlikely to challenge the limitation. Anyway Franzen writes a long book and it sells well . . .

Jeffery Eugenides wrote a 700-page book. And some short story writers are writing longer stories. Andrea Barrett wrote an incredibly long story. Alice Munro writes very long stories.

Neal Stephenson has published a 1300-page book that is the first in a trilogy, William Vollman's new book is 3000 pages. Tobias Wolff, known for short stories, has published a novel . . .

I am very excited to read it. I read the part that was excerpted in the *New Yorker.* It seemed like some of the best work that I have seen him do.

Is your world a world whose boundaries are set by being a writer or do you have any boundaries? Do you have friends who are not writers?

Oh yes.

Interests outside of who has written what?

In fact it is awful when you go out with other writers and you realize you have done nothing for four hours but talk about writing.

[*laughs*]

Writing is this thing that is supposed to be a part of the larger world. It's not supposed to be about the worlds of writers.

That is a complaint that people frequently lodge against contempory fiction.

Yes. It should be about the larger world and it is extremely important to hang out with non-writers and be interested in things that have nothing to do with writing.

Source: Julie Orringer with Robert Birnbaum, "Personalities: Birnbaum v. Julie Orringer," in *The Morning News*, http://www.themorningnews.org/archives/personalities/birnbaum_v_julie_orringer.php, October 22, 2003.

Sources

Birnbaum, Robert, "Birnbaum v. Julie Orringer," in *The Morning News*, October 22, 2003. Available online at http://www.themorningnews.org/archives/personalities/birnbaum_v_julie_orringer.php.

Dierbeck, Lisa, "Survival of the Meanest," in the *New York Times Book Review*, October 19, 2003, p. 18.

Orringer, Julie, "The Smoothest Way Is Full of Stones," in *How to Breathe Underwater*, Knopf, 2003, pp. 91–121.

Perkins, Emily, Review of *How to Breathe Underwater*, in the *Guardian*, April 3, 2004. Available online at http://books.guardian.co.uk/review/story/0,,1183507,00.html

Review of *How to Breathe Underwater*, in *Publishers Weekly*, Vol. 250, No. 34, August 25, 2003, p. 38.

Yu, Ting, Review of *How to Breathe Underwater*, in *People Weekly*, Vol. 60, No. 15, October 13, 2003, p. 50.

Further Reading

Isaacs, Ron, *Ask the Rabbi: The Who, What, When, Where, Why, & How of Being Jewish*, John Wiley & Sons, 2003.

Rabbi Ron Isaacs's book is an informative guide to all matters Jewish, aimed at teenage readers. It includes answers to serious questions about the nature of God, prayer, and death, and responds to more lighthearted questions, such as why there are so many Jewish comedians and doctors. It includes sections on "classic Jewish books," including the Talmud and the Kabbalist text, the Zohar. The author is a rabbi of a New Jersey congregation and co-director of its Hebrew high school.

Levine, Stephanie Wellen, *Mystics, Mavericks, and Merrymakers: An Intimate Journey among Hasidic Girls*, New York University Press, 2004.

Stephanie Wellen Levine spent a year living as a participant observer in the Lubavitcher Hasidic community in Crown Heights, Brooklyn, New York. Her book answers the question of whether adolescent girls raised in a religious environment such as Hasidism are able to develop an individual voice of their own or whether they are restricted to conformist, submissive roles. Levine found that the girls displayed a rich individuality within the confines of a patriarchal world. The book tells the story, through interviews, of seven Lubavitch girls.

Morris, Bonnie J., *Lubavitcher Women in America: Identity and Activism in the Postwar Era*, State University of New York Press, 1998.

This is a study of Hasidic women in the Lubavitcher sect. The emphasis is on the contribution made by women to their community since 1950, when outreach programs supported by the Lubavitcher Rebbe Menachem M. Schneerson began to empower Lubavitcher women.

Review of *How to Breathe Underwater*, in *Kirkus Reviews*, Vol. 71, No. 15, August 1, 2003, p. 986.

The reviewer offers cautious praise of Orringer's collection, but suggests that too many of the stories show little narrative progression and tend to peter out.

Glossary of Literary Terms

A

Allegory: A narrative technique in which characters representing things or abstract ideas are used to convey a message or teach a lesson. Allegory is typically used to teach moral, ethical, or religious lessons but is sometimes used for satiric or political purposes. Many fairy tales are allegories.

Allusion: A reference to a familiar literary or historical person or event, used to make an idea more easily understood. Joyce Carol Oates's story "Where Are You Going, Where Have You Been?" exhibits several allusions to popular music.

Analogy: A comparison of two things made to explain something unfamiliar through its similarities to something familiar, or to prove one point based on the acceptance of another. Similes and metaphors are types of analogies.

Antagonist: The major character in a narrative or drama who works against the hero or protagonist. The Misfit in Flannery O'Connor's story "A Good Man Is Hard to Find" serves as the antagonist for the Grandmother.

Anthology: A collection of similar works of literature, art, or music. Zora Neale Hurston's "The Eatonville Anthology" is a collection of stories that take place in the same town.

Anthropomorphism: The presentation of animals or objects in human shape or with human characteristics. The term is derived from the Greek word for "human form." The fur necklet in Katherine Mansfield's story "Miss Brill" has anthropomorphic characteristics.

Anti-hero: A central character in a work of literature who lacks traditional heroic qualities such as courage, physical prowess, and fortitude. Anti-heroes typically distrust conventional values and are unable to commit themselves to any ideals. They generally feel helpless in a world over which they have no control. Anti-heroes usually accept, and often celebrate, their positions as social outcasts. A well-known anti-hero is Walter Mitty in James Thurber's story "The Secret Life of Walter Mitty."

Archetype: The word archetype is commonly used to describe an original pattern or model from which all other things of the same kind are made. Archetypes are the literary images that grow out of the "collective unconscious," a theory proposed by psychologist Carl Jung. They appear in literature as incidents and plots that repeat basic patterns of life. They may also appear as stereotyped characters. The "schlemiel" of Yiddish literature is an archetype.

Autobiography: A narrative in which an individual tells his or her life story. Examples include Benjamin Franklin's *Autobiography* and Amy Hempel's story "In the Cemetery Where Al Jolson Is Buried," which has autobiographical characteristics even though it is a work of fiction.

Avant-garde A literary term that describes new writing that rejects traditional approaches to literature in favor of innovations in style or content. Twentieth-century examples of the literary avant-garde include the modernists and the minimalists.

B

Belles-lettres: A French term meaning "fine letters" or" beautiful writing." It is often used as a synonym for literature, typically referring to imaginative and artistic rather than scientific or expository writing. Current usage sometimes restricts the meaning to light or humorous writing and appreciative essays about literature. Lewis Carroll's *Alice in Wonderland* epitomizes the realm of belles-lettres.

***Bildungsroman*:** A German word meaning "novel of development." The *bildungsroman* is a study of the maturation of a youthful character, typically brought about through a series of social or sexual encounters that lead to self-awareness. J. D. Salinger's *Catcher in the Rye* is a *bildungsroman*, and Doris Lessing's story "Through the Tunnel" exhibits characteristics of a *bildungsroman* as well.

Black Aesthetic Movement: A period of artistic and literary development among African Americans in the 1960s and early 1970s. This was the first major African-American artistic movement since the Harlem Renaissance and was closely paralleled by the civil rights and black power movements. The black aesthetic writers attempted to produce works of art that would be meaningful to the black masses. Key figures in black aesthetics included one of its founders, poet and playwright Amiri Baraka, formerly known as Le Roi Jones; poet and essayist Haki R. Madhubuti, formerly Don L. Lee; poet and playwright Sonia Sanchez; and dramatist Ed Bullins. Works representative of the Black Aesthetic Movement include Amiri Baraka's play *Dutchman,* a 1964 Obie award-winner.

Black Humor: Writing that places grotesque elements side by side with humorous ones in an attempt to shock the reader, forcing him or her to laugh at the horrifying reality of a disordered world. "Lamb to the Slaughter," by Roald Dahl, in which a placid housewife murders her husband and serves the murder weapon to the investigating policemen, is an example of black humor.

C

Catharsis: The release or purging of unwanted emotions—specifically fear and pity—brought about by exposure to art. The term was first used by the Greek philosopher Aristotle in his *Poetics* to refer to the desired effect of tragedy on spectators.

Character: Broadly speaking, a person in a literary work. The actions of characters are what constitute the plot of a story, novel, or poem. There are numerous types of characters, ranging from simple, stereotypical figures to intricate, multifaceted ones. "Characterization" is the process by which an author creates vivid, believable characters in a work of art. This may be done in a variety of ways, including (1) direct description of the character by the narrator; (2) the direct presentation of the speech, thoughts, or actions of the character; and (3) the responses of other characters to the character. The term "character" also refers to a form originated by the ancient Greek writer Theophrastus that later became popular in the seventeenth and eighteenth centuries. It is a short essay or sketch of a person who prominently displays a specific attribute or quality, such as miserliness or ambition. "Miss Brill," a story by Katherine Mansfield, is an example of a character sketch.

Classical: In its strictest definition in literary criticism, classicism refers to works of ancient Greek or Roman literature. The term may also be used to describe a literary work of recognized importance (a "classic") from any time period or literature that exhibits the traits of classicism. Examples of later works and authors now described as classical include French literature of the seventeenth century, Western novels of the nineteenth century, and American fiction of the mid-nineteenth century such as that written by James Fenimore Cooper and Mark Twain.

Climax: The turning point in a narrative, the moment when the conflict is at its most intense. Typically, the structure of stories, novels, and plays is one of rising action, in which tension builds to the climax, followed by falling action, in which tension lessens as the story moves to its conclusion.

Comedy: One of two major types of drama, the other being tragedy. Its aim is to amuse, and it typically ends happily. Comedy assumes many forms, such as farce and burlesque, and uses a variety of techniques, from parody to satire. In a restricted sense the term comedy refers only to dramatic presentations, but in general usage it is commonly applied to nondramatic works as well.

Comic Relief: The use of humor to lighten the mood of a serious or tragic story, especially in plays. The technique is very common in Elizabethan works, and can be an integral part of the plot or simply a brief event designed to break the tension of the scene.

Conflict: The conflict in a work of fiction is the issue to be resolved in the story. It usually occurs between two characters, the protagonist and the antagonist, or between the protagonist and society or the protagonist and himself or herself. The conflict in Washington Irving's story "The Devil and Tom Walker" is that the Devil wants Tom Walker's soul but Tom does not want to go to hell.

Criticism: The systematic study and evaluation of literary works, usually based on a specific method or set of principles. An important part of literary studies since ancient times, the practice of criticism has given rise to numerous theories, methods, and "schools," sometimes producing conflicting, even contradictory, interpretations of literature in general as well as of individual works. Even such basic issues as what constitutes a poem or a novel have been the subject of much criticism over the centuries. Seminal texts of literary criticism include Plato's *Republic,* Aristotle's *Poetics*, Sir Philip Sidney's *The Defence of Poesie,* and John Dryden's *Of Dramatic Poesie.* Contemporary schools of criticism include deconstruction, feminist, psychoanalytic, poststructuralist, new historicist, postcolonialist, and reader-response.

D

Deconstruction: A method of literary criticism characterized by multiple conflicting interpretations of a given work. Deconstructionists consider the impact of the language of a work and suggest that the true meaning of the work is not necessarily the meaning that the author intended.

Deduction: The process of reaching a conclusion through reasoning from general premises to a specific premise. Arthur Conan Doyle's character Sherlock Holmes often used deductive reasoning to solve mysteries.

Denotation: The definition of a word, apart from the impressions or feelings it creates in the reader. The word "apartheid" denotes a political and economic policy of segregation by race, but its connotations—oppression, slavery, inequality—are numerous.

***Denouement*:** A French word meaning "the unknotting." In literature, it denotes the resolution of conflict in fiction or drama. The *denouement* follows the climax and provides an outcome to the primary plot situation as well as an explanation of secondary plot complications. A well-known example of *denouement* is the last scene of the play *As You Like It* by William Shakespeare, in which couples are married, an evildoer repents, the identities of two disguised characters are revealed, and a ruler is restored to power. Also known as "falling action."

Detective Story: A narrative about the solution of a mystery or the identification of a criminal. The conventions of the detective story include the detective's scrupulous use of logic in solving the mystery; incompetent or ineffectual police; a suspect who appears guilty at first but is later proved innocent; and the detective's friend or confidant—often the narrator—whose slowness in interpreting clues emphasizes by contrast the detective's brilliance. Edgar Allan Poe's "Murders in the Rue Morgue" is commonly regarded as the earliest example of this type of story. Other practitioners are Arthur Conan Doyle, Dashiell Hammett, and Agatha Christie.

Dialogue: Dialogue is conversation between people in a literary work. In its most restricted sense, it refers specifically to the speech of characters in a drama. As a specific literary genre, a "dialogue" is a composition in which characters debate an issue or idea.

Didactic: A term used to describe works of literature that aim to teach a moral, religious, political, or practical lesson. Although didactic elements are often found inartistically pleasing works, the term "didactic" usually refers to literature in which the message is more important than the form. The term may also be used to criticize a work that the critic finds "overly didactic," that is, heavy-handed in its delivery of a lesson. An example of didactic literature is John Bunyan's *Pilgrim's Progress.*

Dramatic Irony: Occurs when the reader of a work of literature knows something that a character in the work itself does not know. The irony is in the contrast between the intended meaning of the statements or actions of a character and the additional information understood by the audience.

Dystopia: An imaginary place in a work of fiction where the characters lead dehumanized, fearful lives. George Orwell's *Nineteen Eighty-four,* and Margaret Atwood's *Handmaid's Tale* portray versions of dystopia.

E

Edwardian: Describes cultural conventions identified with the period of the reign of Edward VII of England (1901–1910). Writers of the Edwardian Age typically displayed a strong reaction against the propriety and conservatism of the Victorian Age. Their work often exhibits distrust of authority in religion, politics, and art and expresses strong doubts about the soundness of conventional values. Writers of this era include E. M. Forster, H. G. Wells, and Joseph Conrad.

Empathy: A sense of shared experience, including emotional and physical feelings, with someone or something other than oneself. Empathy is often used to describe the response of a reader to a literary character.

Epilogue: A concluding statement or section of a literary work. In dramas, particularly those of the seventeenth and eighteenth centuries, the epilogue is a closing speech, often in verse, delivered by an actor at the end of a play and spoken directly to the audience.

Epiphany: A sudden revelation of truth inspired by a seemingly trivial incident. The term was widely used by James Joyce in his critical writings, and the stories in Joyce's *Dubliners* are commonly called "epiphanies."

Epistolary Novel: A novel in the form of letters. The form was particularly popular in the eighteenth century. The form can also be applied to short stories, as in Edwidge Danticat's "Children of the Sea."

Epithet: A word or phrase, often disparaging or abusive, that expresses a character trait of someone or something. "The Napoleon of crime" is an epithet applied to Professor Moriarty, archrival of Sherlock Holmes in Arthur Conan Doyle's series of detective stories.

Existentialism: A predominantly twentieth-century philosophy concerned with the nature and perception of human existence. There are two major strains of existentialist thought: atheistic and Christian. Followers of atheistic existentialism believe that the individual is alone in a godless universe and that the basic human condition is one of suffering and loneliness. Nevertheless, because there are no fixed values, individuals can create their own characters—indeed, they can shape themselves—through the exercise of free will. The atheistic strain culminates in and is popularly associated with the works of Jean-Paul Sartre. The Christian existentialists, on the other hand, believe that only in God may people find freedom from life's anguish. The two strains hold certain beliefs in common: that existence cannot be fully understood or described through empirical effort; that anguish is a universal element of life; that individuals must bear responsibility for their actions; and that there is no common standard of behavior or perception for religious and ethical matters. Existentialist thought figures prominently in the works of such authors as Franz Kafka, Fyodor Dostoyevsky, and Albert Camus.

Expatriatism: The practice of leaving one's country to live for an extended period in another country. Literary expatriates include Irish author James Joyce who moved to Italy and France, American writers James Baldwin, Ernest Hemingway, Gertrude Stein, and F. Scott Fitzgerald who lived and wrote in Paris, and Polish novelist Joseph Conrad in England.

Exposition: Writing intended to explain the nature of an idea, thing, or theme. Expository writing is often combined with description, narration, or argument.

Expressionism: An indistinct literary term, originally used to describe an early twentieth-century school of German painting. The term applies to almost any mode of unconventional, highly subjective writing that distorts reality in some way. Advocates of Expressionism include Federico Garcia Lorca, Eugene O'Neill, Franz Kafka, and James Joyce.

F

Fable: A prose or verse narrative intended to convey a moral. Animals or inanimate objects with human characteristics often serve as characters in fables. A famous fable is Aesop's "The Tortoise and the Hare."

Fantasy: A literary form related to mythology and folklore. Fantasy literature is typically set in nonexistent realms and features supernatural beings. Notable examples of literature with elements of fantasy are Gabriel Gárcia Márquez's story "The Handsomest Drowned Man in the World" and Ursula K. Le Guin's "The Ones Who Walk Away from Omelas."

Farce: A type of comedy characterized by broad humor, outlandish incidents, and often vulgar subject matter. Much of the comedy in film and television could more accurately be described as farce.

Fiction: Any story that is the product of imagination rather than a documentation of fact. Characters and events in such narratives may be based in real life but their ultimate form and configuration is a creation of the author.

Figurative Language: A technique in which an author uses figures of speech such as hyperbole, irony, metaphor, or simile for a particular effect. Figurative language is the opposite of literal language, in which every word is truthful, accurate, and free of exaggeration or embellishment.

Flashback: A device used in literature to present action that occurred before the beginning of the story. Flashbacks are often introduced as the dreams or recollections of one or more characters.

Foil: A character in a work of literature whose physical or psychological qualities contrast strongly with, and therefore highlight, the corresponding qualities of another character. In his Sherlock Holmes stories, Arthur Conan Doyle portrayed Dr. Watson as a man of normal habits and intelligence, making him a foil for the eccentric and unusually perceptive Sherlock Holmes.

Folklore: Traditions and myths preserved in a culture or group of people. Typically, these are passed on by word of mouth in various forms—such as legends, songs, and proverbs—or preserved in customs and ceremonies. Washington Irving, in "The Devil and Tom Walker" and many of his other stories, incorporates many elements of the folklore of New England and Germany.

Folktale: A story originating in oral tradition. Folk tales fall into a variety of categories, including legends, ghost stories, fairy tales, fables, and anecdotes based on historical figures and events.

Foreshadowing: A device used in literature to create expectation or to set up an explanation of later developments. Edgar Allan Poe uses foreshadowing to create suspense in "The Fall of the House of Usher" when the narrator comments on the crumbling state of disrepair in which he finds the house.

G

Genre: A category of literary work. Genre may refer to both the content of a given work—tragedy, comedy, horror, science fiction—and to its form, such as poetry, novel, or drama.

Gilded Age: A period in American history during the 1870s and after characterized by political corruption and materialism. A number of important novels of social and political criticism were written during this time. Henry James and Kate Chopin are two writers who were prominent during the Gilded Age.

Gothicism: In literature, works characterized by a taste for medieval or morbid characters and situations. A gothic novel prominently features elements of horror, the supernatural, gloom, and violence: clanking chains, terror, ghosts, medieval castles, and unexplained phenomena. The term "gothic novel" is also applied to novels that lack elements of the traditional Gothic setting but that create a similar atmosphere of terror or dread. The term can also be applied to stories, plays, and poems. Mary Shelley's *Frankenstein* and Joyce Carol Oates's *Belle fleur* are both gothic novels.

Grotesque: In literature, a work that is characterized by exaggeration, deformity, freakishness, and disorder. The grotesque often includes an element of comic absurdity. Examples of the grotesque can be found in the works of Edgar Allan Poe, Flannery O'Connor, Joseph Heller, and Shirley Jackson.

H

Harlem Renaissance: The Harlem Renaissance of the 1920s is generally considered the first significant movement of black writers and artists in the United States. During this period, new and established black writers, many of whom lived in the region of New York City known as Harlem, published more fiction and poetry than ever before, the first influential black literary journals were established, and black authors and artists received their first widespread recognition and serious critical appraisal. Among the major writers associated with this period are Countee Cullen, Langston Hughes, Arna Bontemps, and Zora Neale Hurston.

Hero/Heroine: The principal sympathetic character in a literary work. Heroes and heroines typically exhibit admirable traits: idealism, courage, and integrity, for example. Famous heroes and heroines of literature include Charles Dickens's Oliver Twist, Margaret Mitchell's Scarlett O'Hara, and the anonymous narrator in Ralph Ellison's *Invisible Man.*

Hyperbole: Deliberate exaggeration used to achieve an effect. In William Shakespeare's *Macbeth,* Lady Macbeth hyperbolizes when she says, "All the perfumes of Arabia could not sweeten this little hand."

I

Image: A concrete representation of an object or sensory experience. Typically, such a representation helps evoke the feelings associated with the object or experience itself. Images are either "literal" or "figurative." Literal images are especially concrete and involve little or no extension of the obvious meaning of the words used to express them. Figurative images do not follow the literal meaning of the words exactly. Images in literature are usually visual, but the term "image" can also refer to the representation of any sensory experience.

Imagery: The array of images in a literary work. Also used to convey the author's overall use of figurative language in a work.

***In medias res*:** A Latin term meaning "in the middle of things." It refers to the technique of beginning a story at its midpoint and then using various flashback devices to reveal previous action. This technique originated in such epics as Virgil's *Aeneid.*

Interior Monologue: A narrative technique in which characters' thoughts are revealed in a way that appears to be uncontrolled by the author. The interior monologue typically aims to reveal the inner self of a character. It portrays emotional experiences as they occur at both a conscious and unconscious level. One of the best-known interior monologues in English is the Molly Bloom section at the close of James Joyce's *Ulysses.* Katherine Anne Porter's "The Jilting of Granny Weatherall" is also told in the form of an interior monologue.

Irony: In literary criticism, the effect of language in which the intended meaning is the opposite of what is stated. The title of Jonathan Swift's "A Modest Proposal" is ironic because what Swift proposes in this essay is cannibalism—hardly "modest."

J

Jargon: Language that is used or understood only by a select group of people. Jargon may refer to terminology used in a certain profession, such as computer jargon, or it may refer to any nonsensical language that is not understood by most people. Anthony Burgess's *A Clockwork Orange* and James Thurber's "The Secret Life of Walter Mitty" both use jargon.

K

Knickerbocker Group: An indistinct group of New York writers of the first half of the nineteenth century. Members of the group were linked only by location and a common theme: New York life. Two famous members of the Knickerbocker Group were Washington Irving and William Cullen Bryant. The group's name derives from Irving's *Knickerbocker's History of New York.*

L

Literal Language: An author uses literal language when he or she writes without exaggerating or embellishing the subject matter and without any tools of figurative language. To say "He ran very quickly down the street" is to use literal language, whereas to say "He ran like a hare down the street" would be using figurative language.

Literature: Literature is broadly defined as any written or spoken material, but the term most often refers to creative works. Literature includes poetry, drama, fiction, and many kinds of nonfiction writing, as well as oral, dramatic, and broadcast compositions not necessarily preserved in a written format, such as films and television programs.

Lost Generation: A term first used by Gertrude Stein to describe the post-World War I generation of American writers: men and women haunted by a sense of betrayal and emptiness brought about by the destructiveness of the war. The term is commonly applied to Hart Crane, Ernest Hemingway, F. Scott Fitzgerald, and others.

M

Magic Realism: A form of literature that incorporates fantasy elements or supernatural occurrences into the narrative and accepts them as truth. Gabriel Gárcia Márquez and Laura Esquivel are two writers known for their works of magic realism.

Metaphor: A figure of speech that expresses an idea through the image of another object. Metaphors suggest the essence of the first object by identifying it with certain qualities of the second object. An example is "But soft, what light through yonder window breaks? / It is the east, and Juliet is the sun" in William Shakespeare's *Romeo and Juliet.* Here, Juliet, the first object, is identified with qualities of the second object, the sun.

Minimalism: A literary style characterized by spare, simple prose with few elaborations. In minimalism, the main theme of the work is often never discussed directly. Amy Hempel and Ernest Hemingway are two writers known for their works of minimalism.

Modernism: Modern literary practices. Also, the principles of a literary school that lasted from roughly the beginning of the twentieth century until the end of World War II. Modernism is defined by its rejection of the literary conventions of the nineteenth century and by its opposition to conventional morality, taste, traditions, and economic values. Many writers are associated with the concepts of modernism, including Albert Camus, D. H. Lawrence, Ernest Hemingway, William Faulkner, Eugene O'Neill, and James Joyce.

Monologue: A composition, written or oral, by a single individual. More specifically, a speech given by a single individual in a drama or other public entertainment. It has no set length, although it is usually several or more lines long. "I Stand Here Ironing" by Tillie Olsen is an example of a story written in the form of a monologue.

Mood: The prevailing emotions of a work or of the author in his or her creation of the work. The mood of a work is not always what might be expected based on its subject matter.

***Motif*:** A theme, character type, image, metaphor, or other verbal element that recurs throughout a single work of literature or occurs in a number of different works over a period of time. For example, the color white in Herman Melville's *Moby Dick* is a "specific" motif, while the trials of star-crossed lovers is a "conventional" motif from the literature of all periods.

N

Narration: The telling of a series of events, real or invented. A narration may be either a simple narrative, in which the events are recounted chronologically, or a narrative with a plot, in which the account is given in a style reflecting the author's artistic concept of the story. Narration is sometimes used as a synonym for "storyline."

Narrative: A verse or prose accounting of an event or sequence of events, real or invented. The term is also used as an adjective in the sense "method of narration." For example, in literary criticism, the expression "narrative technique" usually refers to the way the author structures and presents his or her story. Different narrative forms include diaries, travelogues, novels, ballads, epics, short stories, and other fictional forms.

Narrator: The teller of a story. The narrator may be the author or a character in the story through whom the author speaks. Huckleberry Finn is the narrator of Mark Twain's *The Adventures of Huckleberry Finn.*

Novella: An Italian term meaning "story." This term has been especially used to describe fourteenth-century Italian tales, but it also refers to modern short novels. Modern novellas include Leo Tolstoy's *The Death of Ivan Ilich,* Fyodor Dostoyevsky's *Notes from the Underground,* and Joseph Conrad's *Heart of Darkness.*

O

Oedipus Complex: A son's romantic obsession with his mother. The phrase is derived from the story of the ancient Theban hero Oedipus, who unknowingly killed his father and married his mother, and was popularized by Sigmund Freud's theory of psychoanalysis. Literary occurrences of the Oedipus complex include Sophocles' *Oedipus Rex* and D. H. Lawrence's "The Rocking-Horse Winner."

Onomatopoeia: The use of words whose sounds express or suggest their meaning. In its simplest sense, onomatopoeia may be represented by words that mimic the sounds they denote such as "hiss" or "meow." At a more subtle level, the pattern and rhythm of sounds and rhymes of a line or poem may be onomatopoeic.

Oral Tradition: A process by which songs, ballads, folklore, and other material are transmitted by word of mouth. The tradition of oral transmission predates the written record systems of literate society. Oral transmission preserves material sometimes over generations, although often with variations. Memory plays a large part in the recitation and preservation of orally transmitted material. Native American myths and legends, and African folktales told by plantation slaves are examples of orally transmitted literature.

P

Parable: A story intended to teach a moral lesson or answer an ethical question. Examples of parables are the stories told by Jesus Christ in the New Testament, notably "The Prodigal Son," but parables also are used in Sufism, rabbinic literature, Hasidism, and Zen Buddhism. Isaac Bashevis Singer's story "Gimpel the Fool" exhibits characteristics of a parable.

Paradox: A statement that appears illogical or contradictory at first, but may actually point to an underlying truth. A literary example of a paradox is George Orwell's statement "All animals are equal, but some animals are more equal than others" in *Animal Farm.*

Parody: In literature, this term refers to an imitation of a serious literary work or the signature style of a particular author in a ridiculous manner. A typical parody adopts the style of the original and applies it to an inappropriate subject for humorous effect. Parody is a form of satire and could be considered the literary equivalent of a caricature or cartoon. Henry Fielding's *Shamela* is a parody of Samuel Richardson's *Pamela.*

Persona: A Latin term meaning "mask." Personae are the characters in a fictional work of literature. The persona generally functions as a mask through which the author tells a story in a voice other than his or her own. A persona is usually either a character in a story who acts as a narrator or an "implied author," a voice created by the author to act as the narrator for himself or herself. The persona in Charlotte Perkins Gilman's story "The Yellow Wallpaper" is the unnamed young mother experiencing a mental breakdown.

Personification: A figure of speech that gives human qualities to abstract ideas, animals, and inanimate objects. To say that "the sun is smiling" is to personify the sun.

Plot: The pattern of events in a narrative or drama. In its simplest sense, the plot guides the author in composing the work and helps the reader follow the work. Typically, plots exhibit causality and unity and have a beginning, a middle, and an end. Sometimes, however, a plot may consist of a series of disconnected events, in which case it is known as an "episodic plot."

Poetic Justice: An outcome in a literary work, not necessarily a poem, in which the good are rewarded and the evil are punished, especially in ways that particularly fit their virtues or crimes. For example, a murderer may himself be murdered, or a thief will find himself penniless.

Poetic License: Distortions of fact and literary convention made by a writer—not always a poet—for the sake of the effect gained. Poetic license is closely related to the concept of "artistic freedom." An author exercises poetic license by saying that a pile of money "reaches as high as a mountain" when the pile is actually only a foot or two high.

Point of View: The narrative perspective from which a literary work is presented to the reader. There are four traditional points of view. The "third person omniscient" gives the reader a "godlike" perspective, unrestricted by time or place, from which to see actions and look into the minds of characters. This allows the author to comment openly on characters and events in the work. The "third person" point of view presents the events of the story from outside of any single character's perception, much like the omniscient point of view, but the reader must understand the action as it takes place and without any special insight into characters' minds or motivations. The "first person" or "personal" point of view relates events as they are perceived by a single character. The main character "tells" the story and may offer opinions about the action and characters which differ from those of the author. Much less common than omniscient, third person, and first person is the "second person" point of view, wherein the author tells the story as if it is happening to the reader. James Thurber employs the omniscient point of view in his short story "The Secret Life of Walter Mitty." Ernest Hemingway's "A Clean, Well-Lighted Place" is a short story told from the third person point of view. Mark Twain's novel *Huckleberry Finn* is presented from the first person viewpoint. Jay McInerney's *Bright Lights, Big City* is an example of a novel which uses the second person point of view.

Pornography: Writing intended to provoke feelings of lust in the reader. Such works are often condemned by critics and teachers, but those which can be shown to have literary value are viewed less harshly. Literary works that have been described as pornographic include D. H. Lawrence's *Lady Chatterley's Lover* and James Joyce's *Ulysses.*

Post-Aesthetic Movement: An artistic response made by African Americans to the black aesthetic movement of the 1960s and early 1970s. Writers since that time have adopted a somewhat different tone in their work, with less emphasis placed on the disparity between black and white in the United States. In the words of post-aesthetic authors such as Toni Morrison, John Edgar Wideman, and Kristin Hunter, African Americans are portrayed as looking inward for answers to their own questions, rather than always looking to the outside world. Two well-known examples of works produced as part of the post-aesthetic movement are the Pulitzer Prize–winning novels *The Color Purple* by Alice Walker and *Beloved* by Toni Morrison.

Postmodernism: Writing from the 1960s forward characterized by experimentation and application of modernist elements, which include existentialism and alienation. Postmodernists have gone a step further in the rejection of tradition begun with the modernists by also rejecting traditional forms, preferring the anti-novel over the novel and the anti-hero over the hero. Postmodern writers include Thomas Pynchon, Margaret Drabble, and Gabriel Gárcia Márquez.

Prologue: An introductory section of a literary work. It often contains information establishing the situation of the characters or presents information about the setting, time period, or action. In drama, the prologue is spoken by a chorus or by one of the principal characters.

Prose: A literary medium that attempts to mirror the language of everyday speech. It is distinguished from poetry by its use of unmetered, unrhymed language consisting of logically related sentences. Prose is usually grouped into paragraphs that form a cohesive whole such as an essay or a novel. The term is sometimes used to mean an author's general writing.

Protagonist: The central character of a story who serves as a focus for its themes and incidents and as the principal rationale for its development. The protagonist is sometimes referred to in discussions of modern literature as the hero or anti-hero. Well-known protagonists are Hamlet in William Shakespeare's *Hamlet* and Jay Gatsby in F. Scott Fitzgerald's *The Great Gatsby.*

R

Realism: A nineteenth-century European literary movement that sought to portray familiar characters, situations, and settings in a realistic manner. This was done primarily by using an objective narrative point of view and through the buildup of accurate detail. The standard for success of any realistic work depends on how faithfully it transfers common experience into fictional forms. The realistic method may be altered or extended, as in stream of consciousness writing, to record highly subjective experience. Contemporary authors who often write in a realistic way include Nadine Gordimer and Grace Paley.

Resolution: The portion of a story following the climax, in which the conflict is resolved. The resolution of Jane Austen's *Northanger Abbey* is neatly summed up in the following sentence: "Henry and Catherine were married, the bells rang and every body smiled."

Rising Action: The part of a drama where the plot becomes increasingly complicated. Rising action leads up to the climax, or turning point, of a drama. The final "chase scene" of an action film is generally the rising action which culminates in the film's climax.

***Roman a clef*:** A French phrase meaning "novel with a key." It refers to a narrative in which real persons are portrayed under fictitious names. Jack Kerouac, for example, portrayed various friends under fictitious names in the novel *On the Road.* D. H. Lawrence based "The Rocking-Horse Winner" on a family he knew.

Romanticism: This term has two widely accepted meanings. In historical criticism, it refers to a European intellectual and artistic movement of the late eighteenth and early nineteenth centuries that sought greater freedom of personal expression than that allowed by the strict rules of literary form and logic of the eighteenth-century neoclassicists. The Romantics preferred emotional and imaginative expression to rational analysis. They considered the individual to be at the center of all experience and so placed him or her at the center of their art. The Romantics believed that the creative imagination reveals nobler truths—unique feelings and attitudes—than those that could be discovered by logic or by scientific examination. "Romanticism" is also used as a general term to refer to a type of sensibility found in all periods of literary history and usually considered to be in opposition to the principles of classicism. In this sense, Romanticism signifies any work or philosophy in which the exotic or dreamlike figure strongly, or that is devoted to individualistic expression, self-analysis, or a pursuit of a higher realm of knowledge than can be discovered by human reason. Prominent Romantics include Jean-Jacques Rousseau, William Wordsworth, John Keats, Lord Byron, and Johann Wolfgang von Goethe.

S

Satire: A work that uses ridicule, humor, and wit to criticize and provoke change in human nature and institutions. Voltaire's novella *Candide* and Jonathan Swift's essay "A Modest Proposal" are both satires. Flannery O'Connor's portrayal of the family in "A Good Man Is Hard to Find" is a satire of a modern, Southern, American family.

Science Fiction: A type of narrative based upon real or imagined scientific theories and technology. Science fiction is often peopled with alien creatures and set on other planets or in different dimensions. Popular writers of science fiction are Isaac Asimov, Karel Capek, Ray Bradbury, and Ursula K. Le Guin.

Setting: The time, place, and culture in which the action of a narrative takes place. The elements of setting may include geographic location, characters's physical and mental environments, prevailing cultural attitudes, or the historical time in which the action takes place.

Short Story: A fictional prose narrative shorter and more focused than a novella. The short story usually deals with a single episode and often a single character. The "tone," the author's attitude toward his or her subject and audience, is uniform throughout. The short story frequently also lacks *denouement*, ending instead at its climax.

Signifying Monkey: A popular trickster figure in black folklore, with hundreds of tales about this character documented since the 19th century. Henry Louis Gates Jr. examines the history of the signifying monkey in *The Signifying Monkey: Towards a Theory of Afro-American Literary Criticism,* published in 1988.

Simile: A comparison, usually using "like" or "as," of two essentially dissimilar things, as in "coffee as cold as ice" or "He sounded like a broken record." The title of Ernest Hemingway's "Hills Like White Elephants" contains a simile.

Socialist Realism: The Socialist Realism school of literary theory was proposed by Maxim Gorky and established as a dogma by the first Soviet Congress of Writers. It demanded adherence to a communist worldview in works of literature. Its doctrines required an objective viewpoint comprehensible to the working classes and themes of social struggle featuring strong proletarian heroes. Gabriel Gárcia Márquez's stories exhibit some characteristics of Socialist Realism.

Stereotype: A stereotype was originally the name for a duplication made during the printing process; this led to its modern definition as a person or thing that is (or is assumed to be) the same as all others of its type. Common stereotypical characters include the absent-minded professor, the nagging wife, the troublemaking teenager, and the kind-hearted grandmother.

Stream of Consciousness: A narrative technique for rendering the inward experience of a character. This technique is designed to give the impression of an ever-changing series of thoughts, emotions, images, and memories in the spontaneous and seemingly illogical order that they occur in life. The textbook example of stream of consciousness is the last section of James Joyce's *Ulysses.*

Structure: The form taken by a piece of literature. The structure may be made obvious for ease of understanding, as in nonfiction works, or may be obscured for artistic purposes, as in some poetry or seemingly "unstructured" prose.

Style: A writer's distinctive manner of arranging words to suit his or her ideas and purpose in writing. The unique imprint of the author's personality upon his or her writing, style is the product of an author's way of arranging ideas and his or her use of diction, different sentence structures, rhythm, figures of speech, rhetorical principles, and other elements of composition.

Suspense: A literary device in which the author maintains the audience's attention through the buildup of events, the outcome of which will soon be revealed. Suspense in William Shakespeare's *Hamlet* is sustained throughout by the question of whether or not the Prince will achieve what he has been instructed to do and of what he intends to do.

Symbol: Something that suggests or stands for something else without losing its original identity. In literature, symbols combine their literal meaning with the suggestion of an abstract concept. Literary symbols are of two types: those that carry complex associations of meaning no matter what their contexts, and those that derive their suggestive meaning from their functions in specific literary works. Examples of symbols are sunshine suggesting happiness, rain suggesting sorrow, and storm clouds suggesting despair.

T

Tale: A story told by a narrator with a simple plot and little character development. Tales are usually relatively short and often carry a simple message. Examples of tales can be found in the works of Saki, Anton Chekhov, Guy de Maupassant, and O. Henry.

Tall Tale: A humorous tale told in a straightforward, credible tone but relating absolutely impossible events or feats of the characters. Such tales were commonly told of frontier adventures during the settlement of the west in the United States. Literary use of tall tales can be found in Washington Irving's *History of New York,* Mark Twain's *Life on the Mississippi,* and in the German R. F. Raspe's *Baron Munchausen's Narratives of His Marvellous Travels and Campaigns in Russia.*

Theme: The main point of a work of literature. The term is used interchangeably with thesis. Many works have multiple themes. One of the themes of Nathaniel Hawthorne's "Young Goodman Brown" is loss of faith.

Tone: The author's attitude toward his or her audience may be deduced from the tone of the work. A formal tone may create distance or convey politeness, while an informal tone may encourage a friendly, intimate, or intrusive feeling in the reader. The author's attitude toward his or her subject matter may also be deduced from the tone of the words he or she uses in discussing it. The tone of John F. Kennedy's speech which included the appeal to "ask not what your country can do for you" was intended to instill feelings of camaraderie and national pride in listeners.

Tragedy: A drama in prose or poetry about a noble, courageous hero of excellent character who, because of some tragic character flaw, brings ruin upon him- or herself. Tragedy treats its subjects in a dignified and serious manner, using poetic language to help evoke pity and fear and bring about catharsis, a purging of these emotions. The tragic form was practiced extensively by the ancient Greeks. The classical form of tragedy was revived in the sixteenth century; it flourished especially on the Elizabethan stage. In modern times, dramatists have attempted to adapt the form to the needs of modern society by drawing their heroes from the ranks of ordinary men and women and defining the nobility of these heroes in terms of spirit rather than exalted social standing. Some contemporary works that are thought of as tragedies include *The Great Gatsby* by F. Scott Fitzgerald, and *The Sound and the Fury* by William Faulkner.

Tragic Flaw: In a tragedy, the quality within the hero or heroine which leads to his or her downfall. Examples of the tragic flaw include Othello's jealousy and Hamlet's indecisiveness, although most great tragedies defy such simple interpretation.

U

Utopia: A fictional perfect place, such as "paradise" or "heaven." An early literary utopia was described in Plato's *Republic,* and in modern literature, Ursula K. Le Guin depicts a utopia in "The Ones Who Walk Away from Omelas."

V

Victorian: Refers broadly to the reign of Queen Victoria of England (1837–1901) and to anything with qualities typical of that era. For example, the qualities of smug narrow-mindedness, bourgeois materialism, faith in social progress, and priggish morality are often considered Victorian. In literature, the Victorian Period was the great age of the English novel, and the latter part of the era saw the rise of movements such as decadence and symbolism.

Cumulative Author/Title Index

C

D

I

J

K

L

T

U

V

W

Y

Cumulative Nationality/Ethnicity Index

Antiguan

Argentinian

Asian American

Austrian

Bosnian

Canadian

Chilean

Chinese

Colombian

Cuban

Czech

Danish

Dominican

Egyptian

English

Eurasian

French

German

Subject/Theme Index

A

B

C

Subject/Theme Index